THE FORGOTTEN
FAITHFUL

- UNDERVERSE -

Book 2

2ND EDITION

JEZ CAJIAO

TABLE OF CONTENTS

THANKS...AND AN EXPLANATION

Hi everyone! Okay, so for those of you that actually read these bits, thank you! For those who don't...well. We can all pretend I called them names, they'll never know after all!

So, first of all, the thanks! When I first released 'Brightblade', currently just a little over two years ago, I did it with the absolute expectation it'd tank. It'd never go anywhere, and 'being an author' would join the list of jobs I'd love to have been able to do, but never managed. (Interviewing strippers was always high on that list, but that's life!)

Instead, after two years, and thanks to all of your support, I'm now a full-time author! I get to sit here, and write, all day every day. I can pay my bills, put my kids through school and have a good life with my family. THANK YOU.

I couldn't have done it without your support. *Literally*. You buy these books, you give your time up, escaping into the worlds of madness I spin out, and you spread the word about them to others. Its massively appreciated and I wanted to thank you all first of all.

Next, I need to thank my wife, Chrissy. She looks after our hellspawn—I mean *children*—I totally mean that. She picks them up, runs around after them, wipes their tears and bandages their scuffed knees. She feeds them, and keeps them more or less sane, while I sit here, wondering if that joke is a step too far, and if anyone will spot that 'Easter Egg'.

Thank you Chrissy, you make the sun shine, and the flowers bloom. I love you Glitterbum.

To Max and Xander, my little madmen, you'll probably never read this, but if you do? Know that even now, when I'm at work, I'm thinking of you both, I love you, and I'm proud of you every day.

To my family, especially my mother, who spent so much time encouraging me to read, and never giving up on me, despite my abysmal school reports and results. I love you all, and who I am today, is thanks to you all.

To my second family, those here, and those who have gone ahead across the bridge already, thank you. You always support me, and always believe I can do it, even when I'm damn well sure I can't!

I love you all.

Lastly, I need to thank my team!

Firstly, Geneva and Kristen, my assistant and her assistant, who keep me more or less rolling, pick up the discarded madness and pat me on the head, straighten the wheels and push me back on the road. Thank you ladies, you're wonderful!

To my editing team, Jenny, Jack, Evan, Michelle, and now Sean! We're getting there, and thank you all for your help!

To my Beta and ARC readers, You have the most thankless job, you read the 'finished' article, you find all the typos and ask me if I really meant 'that'. I massively appreciate you all!

Lastly, lastly; an explanation!

The omnibus editions came about because I've always felt that as my 'first' Brightblade deserved a polish, a second pass and more to 'fix' little issues, and when I'd finished the first season? Well it seemed the perfect time to do it, especially as I'm now slightly more experienced.

I didn't want to change the story, not at all, but I wanted to tighten up the prose, cut the repeated notifications and more, and basically just improve on it.

Then it occurred to me, why stop there?

So, the Omnibus edition—*or 2nd Edition, if you're reading the books individually*—was born. The entire first season, lightly polished, tweaked, and with new art included!

Hope you enjoy it!

-Jez

UNDERVERSE SYNOPSIS

BOOK ONE:

Jax is working a dead end job, in a semi-stable relationship, and searching for his missing brother, while plagued by dreams of the UnderVerse. This terrible alternate reality is where he, and his brother Tommy, are pulled against their will on occasion. When in the dream they inhabit artificial bodies and fight to protect abandoned villages and more, standing between the inhabitants of the Old Empire and the creatures of the night.

They awaken back on earth once the threat has passed, or they've been killed, with their injuries following them. While they heal at a tremendously accelerated rate, it still requires days to recover, and in that time, they hide their injuries, lest they be locked away for self-mutilation.

After one such session, Jax decides to come clean to his GF and explain everything. Badly injured and bleeding heavily, he arrives at her home, only to find her in bed with another man. He loses control, half beating the man to death, and having his skull shattered in turn by her, using the baseball bat he'd bought her for self-defense.

Jax comes to in the hospital, chained to the bed, and is interviewed by the police and warned he faces a significant jail term. While alone and contemplating this, an unknown doctor slips in and assures him it has all been taken care of, before drugging him.

When Jax wakes up this time, it's to find himself restrained, again, but on an airplane heading to meet 'the Baron Sanguis'. A lawyer assures him that should he carry out the reasonable requests of his new employer, then not only will all legal concerns be a thing of the past, but he will find his brother as well. Jax accepts, warned that refusal means death, and meets the Baron, an inhuman monster who admits to being an interplanar traveler, and a member of the original nobility of the UnderVerse, the Realm that Jax and his brother dream of.

To be free and to find his brother Jax must travel to that shattered Realm, and open a stable portal back to this Realm, as the mana here is simply too low in concentration for the portal to be held open for more than bare seconds. Alternatively, a portal from that side, to here, would be secure and enable the nobility to return with servants and forces intact, ready to reconquer their home.

Over the next several months, as Jax is trained for the 'little task', he discovers more about the past of that Realm, including that the voice of madness that occasionally speaks to him, and that he'd written off as himself being mad to some degree, is actually the voice of the Eternal Emperor Amon, a fragment of His soul being all that's left, clinging to the genetic line.

Amon was murdered, by the Baron, His son, and others of the nobility, with the aid of the God of Death, Nimon. In the process, and as his price for this, the followers of the other nine greater gods were purged and their temples cast down. Leaving the God of Death, who dragged one of the moons down to impact the Realm, with a powerful enough surge of His 'aspect' (death) that He managed to banish the other Greater Gods.

Jax grows to hate the Baron, but has nothing left in his life beyond his missing brother, and so takes the opportunity, training heavily, before facing eleven other nobles' choices in the arena to 'earn' the right to go to the UnderVerse. He wins, barely, and trades the remains of his opponents and their personal items to their sponsors, in exchange for several magical artifacts, before passing through the great portal.

Once on the other side, and having made a deal with an opposing noble 'house' for access, he finds himself in a ruined tower. The Great Towers were bastions of the old Empire, powerfully magical, self-sustaining and intended as entire self-contained cities. At half a mile wide at the base, two to three miles high, and sustained by their own mana collectors they acted as garrisons and secure imperial bastions in places of danger.

The Tower that Jax finds himself in, however, was never inhabited fully. It was finished, intended as a research and security station, but had only a skeleton crew when it was assaulted by a SporeMother. The SporeMother, a multi-limbed monstrosity of legend, flooded the defenders with undead and possessed creatures, birthing DarkSpore creatures, parasitical clouds that could puppet flesh, turning the unprepared defenders into attackers, claiming the Tower. The few remaining survivors, beleaguered on all sides, ordered the Tower's controller Wisps to shut the entire structure down, sealing the Wisps themselves away, and preventing the creature from being able to feed on the mana of the Tower to grow stronger, expecting that the Tower would be assaulted and retaken shortly by the Imperial Legion.

Then, before reinforcements could take the Tower back, the Cataclysm came. Seas and mountains rose, islands vanished and the creatures of the deep and of nightmare were set loose to roam. When Jax arrives at the Tower he finds it dark and silent, populated by the ancient dead, with only occasional more recently killed adventurers scattered here and there. He also encounters Sporelings, immature SporeMothers, hidden in the portal chamber, fighting them and locking himself away in a side room.

Jax uses one of the spells he gained, resurrecting one of the Sporelings he killed to form a companion to fight alongside him. Using his new companion, Bob, and his weapon of choice, a bastardized naginata, Jax proceeds to clear the Tower partially, discovering the 'Hall of Memories' and its sleeping Wisp, Oracle. He is gravely injured, and alone, Bob having perished in the fight to enter the room, and when he awakens the Wisp takes the chance it unthinkingly offers, to use some of the stored knowledge of the Hall of Memories, in the form of spellbooks, to enable him to defeat the undead outside the room.

Unfortunately, all magic he has accessed so far has been through books such as this, impressing outside knowledge across his brain and damaging it each time. This final spellbook is one too many, and results in scarring, internal bleeding and more. Jax is dying and Oracle, the newly awakened Wisp, bonds herself to him in an attempt to save him, gaining access to his manapool and enabling herself to cast the needed healing spells to save his life.

Over time Jax recovers, and with Oracle's guidance, reawakens and names Seneschal, the Wisp that controlled the tower, reactivating the mana collectors and beginning the basic repairs the Tower requires, as well as awakening the Goddess of Fire, Jenae. This awakens the SporeMother, now ancient and decrepit, but still powerful. In the fight that follows between Jax, Oracle, the newly reformed Bob and the SporeMother and her minions, the Eternal Emperor Amon makes contact with Jax, guiding him to use an artifact recovered in the Tower earlier. This Silverbright potion (Dragon's blood) transforms his weapon from a standard construction into a basic magical, but evolving, weapon. Jax kills the SporeMother, but is gravely wounded. Over the next day, as he is healed, the companions clear the remaining sections of the Tower, and find the creature's nest underground, along with the remains of the Golem Construction Cradles or Genesis Chambers.

They also find the Wisp responsible for the golems, name him Hephaestus, and take the time to reclaim the single working Genesis Chamber. This begins the construction of the most basic of stone golems to protect and rebuild the Tower. In the process, HeartStones are uncovered, a magical way to send a memory, as a method of communication. Most are long drained of mana, but the fragments that remain make it clear that Barabarattas, lord of one of the two nearby cities, has been trading slaves to the SporeMother in exchange for Sporelings, hoping to raise a captive army of SporeMothers.

The Wisps sense an intrusion higher in the tower and Jax explores, finding a group of slavers, heavily armed, using their slaves to loot an old armory. Jax attacks when seeing a child beaten, killing the slavers, with Oracle's help, and driving off the two airships that had been docked on the balcony. One is damaged and crashes in the courtyard below, while the other escapes to land at a nearby lake to effect repairs.

The freed slaves pledge allegiance to Jax, and while they rest, he takes one of their number, Oren, the captain of the crashed ship, down to the courtyard. He discovers that they were pressed into service, and had no desire to work with the slavers. The remaining surviving crew swear as well, and inform Jax that there is a third ship. This is the warship that was enforcing the City Lord's will, and it was still incoming, having stopped to raid a village along the way. Jax and the slaves use the weapons they have, the remains of the damaged ship and subterfuge to lure the warship in to land, while Oracle disables their engines.

Jax and Bob, aided by some of the former slaves, fight and kill the soldiers aboard the warship, capturing the crew, freeing a group of slaves taken from the villages and locking the crew in those same cages. Jax formally claims the Tower as his, and through the right of blood, having found that he is an illegitimate son of the Baron Sanguis, and therefore noble in his own right, he begins the right of Imperial Succession.

Barabarratas, like all nobles remaining in the Empire, with no Imperial House to swear to, had been unable to lay claim formally to the Imperial Throne, but once the succession has begun, sees a way to claim the throne. He threatens war against Jax, unless he surrenders. Jax, being short of patience and self-control, as well as occasionally being an asshole, in turn declares war on Barabarratas and his city of Himnel, taunting him before leading his people in a wake. The end of the book comes to Thomas, Jax's brother, languishing and injured in a jail, before being sold as fodder, the lowest caste of soldier, to the Dark Legion of Nimon.

BANE

PROLOGUE

Thomas shuffled as far back in the wagon as the chains would allow, groaning as the wagon bumped over yet another rut in the road. He was gloomily certain the bastard was actually aiming for them now.

He'd been in the back of the wagon with seventeen other inmates for just over four hours, bouncing, juddering, and shaking their way across the entire goddamn city, then out into the countryside.

He'd occasionally smelled a hint of grass and heard the wind in the trees around them.

He'd actually *seen* fuck all though, because that bastard Boris, back at the jail, had put a blindfold on him before leading the prisoners out to the wagon. He'd fallen over, had things he'd rather not guess thrown at him, and judging from the voices, groups of kids had been throwing stones at the prisoners on at least three separate occasions as they traveled. The guards had laughed and told the little shits who to aim for.

Thomas had given up weeks ago on plans of revenge…then he'd given up on hopes of escape. Lately, he'd actually begun fantasizing about the guards going too far and beating him to death accidentally.

That had come to a stop yesterday.

He didn't know why, but something had changed in the ongoing war that Himnel was waging with Narkolt. Someone new had joined in against Himnel, so even the dregs like him were getting a chance.

Details weren't important, and as he'd been in a mana 'null-zone' in the prison, surrounded by walls specifically designed to stop any and all mana, he and the others in there with him had missed the announcements, but still. It didn't matter.

He'd be used as fodder, good enough to soak up a few arrows, if that, but maybe, just maybe, he could use the chance to get away. Maybe the real soldiers would take pity on him; hell, if they killed him, at least it would be over.

Thomas fell forward as the wagon stopped unexpectedly, falling into the wagon bed and pulling others with him, the captives' wrists and ankles chained together.

"Idiot!" someone growled, and a punch rocked his head back, a mailed fist tearing the skin of his cheek, before someone else twisted his chain and yanked him out of the wagon by it.

Thomas cried out in pain and fear as he fell forward with no way to catch himself. The cry was cut off cruelly by a mouthful of cobbles.

He couldn't take it anymore.

He'd lost everything, now he could taste blood filling his mouth from broken teeth.

Tears prickled his eyes, soaking into the cloth that blinded him as he curled up as much as he could, the first spark of anger he'd felt in what seemed like forever kindled to life, fed on the shame of his own inability to escape.

This was that fat shit Boris's fault.

Thomas had found Dirik's family, taken his gear back to them, given them Dirik's cut of the loot, and told them how their son had been a hero, about the times he'd saved Thomas's life. He'd told them how they'd been friends, and how sorry he was that Dirik had died.

The last thing Thomas had seen as a free man was the look of cold hatred in Dirik's father's eyes, and the lead cosh that bastard Boris, Dirik's uncle, had swung into his face when he'd been distracted.

When he'd woken up, he'd been in a cell for "attacking a guard," with—surprise, surprise—Boris as both the victim and his new jailor.

He'd still managed three escape attempts. During the last one, he'd actually made it out of the mana-canceling field of the dungeon and had even managed to fire a few spells off, trying to cobble together a new spell on the fly with nearly two weeks of being kept magically from sleep.

It'd gone hideously wrong, the backlash scouring his mana channels and driving him to his knees, tearing entire sections of his magical memories apart and butchering his spellcasting ability. He'd been caught, vomiting blood, half-blinded and in the midst of a fit. Ultimately, it was all for nothing.

Since then, his life had become a nightmare of daily beatings, starvation, and sleep deprivation.

The tiny flame of anger had sparked again at that thought, growing slowly, before smoldering away. He took a deep breath, trying to bury it. It was dangerous; for a prisoner with no hope of escape, it came at just too high a cost.

"What is this filth?" a voice called out, carrying over the screech of seabirds and the grunts and shouts of men working.

"New recruits, sir!" came a shout inches away from Thomas, making him jump in panic, his heart racing.

"Worthless!" the first voice snarled, and the sound of steel-shod boots smashing into the cobbles moved closer. "What the hell happened here?" the voice of authority demanded, coming to a stop somewhere to the right.

"Fell outta the wagon, sir!" came Boris's voice, and Thomas flinched instinctively.

"Then you're even more of a fool than I thought, jailor. You're responsible for this scum. Don't think I didn't see who got the recruitment bonus for them, yet still you're trying to hand them over damaged?"

"It's 'is own fault, sir, tried t' escape," came Boris's voice.

A laugh rose from the man in charge. "Tried to escape? With his wrists and ankles bound? Blindfolded and a slave collar on him? Don't be stupid." Hands tore the blindfold free of Thomas's face, and he squinted in the suddenly revealed sunlight, wincing back from the glare.

"Well, boy? Were you trying to escape?" the man standing before Thomas asked gruffly, his gleaming black- and gold-highlighted armor showing that he was a Paladin of the Death God, Nimon.

"No," Thomas started, then spat out a tooth and a glob of blood onto the floor. "No…sir."

"'Sir, is it?" the man asked, snorting. "Humph…well, at least he's got a brain. Tell me, son, what were you in jail for? Murder? Rape?"

"He assaulted a guar—" Boris started, only to have the paladin cut him off with a roar.

"Silence!" he screamed, stepping forward and gritting his teeth as he glared at Thomas's tormentor. "As far as I'm concerned, you're no better than them! They committed crimes, but you pulled strings to make sure they were accepted into *my* forces and even had the sheer fucking gall to take a recruiter's purse for them! Your little ploy means I'm stuck with *them*, nearly twenty fucking prisoner scumbags I'll have to train and watch over, instead of the honest men I asked for! The least you can do *is shut the fuck up!*"

Boris straightened to attention and swallowed hard, keeping silent as the paladin turned back to Thomas, breathing hard as he tried to get his fury under control.

"Well, boy?" he snapped eventually, then shook his head. "I'm wasting my damn time…" He started to turn away.

"I took word of my friend's death back to his family, sir…and they attacked me for it," Thomas said, desperate to seize the slim chance before him.

"Yer lyin' bast—" Boris screamed, yanking his infamous cosh from his belt and lunging for Thomas.

The paladin had half-turned back, only to see the jailor smash the cosh into Thomas's side, then his jaw on the backswing. Thomas collapsed to the floor, blood spraying from the severed half of his tongue, caught between his teeth when the cosh had landed.

"Restrain him!" the Paladin of Nimon ordered and stepped forward, looking down at the blood rapidly spreading from Thomas's mouth. "Fucking idiot!" he raged at the jailor, before twisting around and shouting to a nervous-looking man in white robes nearby. "You! Get here and earn your keep!"

The priest of Issa bowed his head, rushing forwards, bobbing and calling upon his patron, even as he tried to avoid the looks of contempt that the others of the Dark Legion were giving him.

"Warrrgh!" Thomas screamed, thrashing about, his tongue regrowing, bones and cartilage popping as they shifted back into place. He rolled back and forth, as far as his chains would let him, crying out in pain as the healing spell tore into him.

When it finally stopped, he lay there gasping and staring up at the paladin, who stood regarding him thoughtfully.

"You were a soldier?" he asked flatly.

Thomas nodded, still trying to catch his breath.

"Freelance or sworn?"

"Freelance…sir," he managed to get out, gasping and blinking as the pain slowly receded.

"Interesting…"

"'E's lyin', sir!" Boris wheezed from the restraining grasp two of the paladin's guards, arms wrenched awkwardly behind his back. The guards were dressed in the black-and-gold livery of the Church of Nimon's forces, and they regarded the city guards and jailors with obvious contempt.

"Really? Well, let's look at this, shall we?" the paladin asked, his voice brittle with anger. "We've got a prisoner who's been purchased from the city to be used as a soldier by the Church, a prisoner who arrives in a sorry state, then is further injured, and almost killed.

"A prisoner *who is already the property of the Church*...yet a lowly jailor believes that he can not only damage the Church's property, but can kill it? I have to step in and have that useless fuck heal the Church's property, only after he accuses you of what would be laughed off if there was no truth to it...? Does this seem accurate to you...jailor?" the paladin asked, forcing patience into his voice as he finished with a snarl.

"I...I..."

"I have been forced to accept this...this *dross*...in place of real soldiers," the paladin continued. "And not only are they far poorer quality than the Church was promised, but you dare to injure them *further*?"

"They...they all be murderers an' such, sir! They all be violent criminals!" Boris stammered out.

"Well, let's find out, shall we?" he hissed. "You have an obvious issue with one of them, and if there's a grain of truth in what he's said against you, he's *certainly* got one with you. Release him!" the paladin barked, gesturing toward Thomas. Another of the Church's soldiers tore the keys from Boris's belt and knelt to free Thomas of his restraints.

"And the collar, sir?" the guard asked as he removed the shackles. Thomas slowly rose to his feet, rubbing at his calloused wrists and stretching out fully for the first time in months. His health was barely above half, his body atrophied through malnourishment and regular beatings. He'd been broken, less than half a man, but he'd take what he hoped the paladin was offering...oh hell, yes...

"You'd let me fight him, sir?" Thomas asked, and the paladin nodded in satisfaction.

"You're still a man, after all, eh? Good. I'll have use for that fire in your belly. If I let you fight him, will you swear the Oath?"

"What Oath...sir?" Thomas asked, shifting his jaw and probing his teeth with his regrown tongue. It felt as though some of the teeth had been replaced, but some were still sharp and jagged...he could live with them, though, as long as he got his chance here.

"Swear to obey the orders of the Church of Nimon, to follow where he leads, and to face the false gods wherever they skulk. Swear to obey the commands of the Holy Order, and one day, who knows, boy? You might end up standing as a free man again. Or you'll be kept, as appropriate to the crimes you're accused of." The paladin nodded toward Boris and the others, and Thomas paused, thinking quickly.

He'd be signing his life away, property of the Church to such a strict degree that even a slave wasn't. A slave always had the hope of escape...*but*...he'd be a soldier again. He'd be able to move around the camps, even earn his way up the ranks...if he were lucky. He'd heard the horror stories of the Dark Legion or the Legion of Nimon, but...but he'd heard the good tales as well, and at least he'd stand a chance this way.

"I'll swear, sir, if I get a chance at him?" Thomas said, jerking his head toward Boris.

The paladin grinned. "Excellent! Perhaps this morning isn't a waste of my time, after all!" He clapped his gauntleted hands together. "No time like the present. Form a ring!" he shouted, gesturing to his men, and in short order, the prisoners, transport wagons, and guards had formed a rough circle around Thomas, Boris, and the Paladin of Nimon.

"Sir…the collar?" the Church soldier asked again.

"Hmmm…no, I think not. For now, it stays on. He can earn its removal," he mused, looking Thomas in the eye. "Mage?"

"No, sir, arcane soldier," Thomas said, getting a raised eyebrow as a smile quirked at the edge of the paladin's mouth.

"Really? Well, now. There's a rare gift. How many spells?"

"Five, sir. Flame Touch, Magic Missile—"

"Best you keep them to yourself, son; perhaps we'll talk later. For now, you've got the chance to prove yourself, followed by an Oathbinding as a slave-aspirant," the Paladin said with a nod toward Boris, whose face was a mix of fear and fury.

Boris spoke up quickly, pointing at Thomas. "'E's a criminal! 'E attacked me when I weren't ready, an'—"

"Then you've got the chance to face him fully aware now, haven't you? How wonderful," the paladin said, cutting him off. "I'll admit I'm curious, though. If an arcane soldier attacked you without warning, yet you still managed to defeat him, why are you a simple jailor, rather than leading a squad now? Hmmm?" He turned to look Thomas up and down, noting his condition and dismissing it as unimportant. "If you're a real arcane soldier, boy, you'll be able to beat this streak of shit easily, even as weak as you look.

"If not, then you're a liar, and I expect this jailor will beat you to death, in which case I'm out a potential soldier. While I'll regret the loss of a man, I'll not have liars in my forces. Last chance to back out."

"I'll rip off his head and shit down his throat…sir," Thomas said, shifting from foot to foot, ready to fight. "Do I get a weapon, or do I have to do it with my bare hands?" he asked, focused on Boris with laser-like precision.

"What do you use?"

"Anything, sir. I trained in spear, sword, axe, mace, lance, and morningstar," Thomas replied, still focused on Boris, watching the sweat beginning to bead across his forehead. Thomas's injuries were still there; most had been healed, but months of beatings, deprivation and abuse couldn't be reversed in a single spell. He was weaker than he'd ever been in his life and absolutely desperate for the chance to kill his hated attacker.

The paladin nodded to the soldier who had unlocked Thomas's restraints.

He sighed, pulling his own mace from its hook on his belt. "You'd better not damage this, laddie," the soldier quietly warned Thomas, handing the weapon over before stepping back.

"Well then, let's see what you both can do." The paladin's mustachios quivered as he grinned at the two men standing before him, and he stepped back.

Boris lunged immediately. His regulation shortsword whistled through the air, the tip cutting a thin line across the ragged, filthy jerkin Thomas wore.

Thomas had judged the distance as best he could, moving back a single step and bringing the mace up to catch Boris's left forearm as the jailor tried to lash out with his cosh, trying to end the fight quickly by dual-wielding.

Boris screamed, dropping the cosh from suddenly numbed fingers. Taking a quick step back, he yanked the sword back around, only for it to clang off Thomas's hastily raised mace.

Thomas twisted his wrist, deflecting his opponent's sword to the side, and kicked Boris hard on the inside of his left knee, staggering him.

Boris half-fell backwards, the encircling men and women moving with him. He thrust frantically with his sword, rust spots standing out against the metal. Thomas leaned aside, lashing out and grabbing the jailor's wrist, pulling him forward.

With grim satisfaction, Thomas grinned into the terrified eyes of the man who'd tormented him, beaten him, and tortured him for months. Then he brought his borrowed mace around to smash down onto Boris's bared forearm.

The flanged mace hit with sickening force, bones shattering under the blow.

Boris screamed, both arms effectively out of the fight, and Thomas stepped in closer, hooking his opponent's uninjured leg with one foot, head butting him and sending him sprawling to the floor with conspicuous ease.

Dropping the mace, Thomas lunged and landed on his jailor's chest and started punching. A right hook, then a straight left, a straight right, then he grabbed Boris's hair with his left to get better leverage, pulling back his right fist with a feral grin as voices rose all around him.

Two men suddenly tackled him from behind, yanking him up and off his enemy. Thomas went wild, his fury at the interference to his justice roaring to life.

He braced himself and yanked, digging deep and using strength he'd thought long lost as he brought both arms forward, smashing the restraining soldiers together. Their heads sounded like bells as their helmets crashed into each other.

The man who'd been holding his right arm let go, staggering and mildly concussed. Thomas reacted with the speed of a man used to fighting for his life. He punched the left guard savagely, his fist actually denting his target's helmet, and he sent the man flying.

Thomas spun, tucking his foot under the mace on the floor, and flipped it up into the air, reaching out almost casually to intercept it before screaming in pain and collapsing to the floor as his collar sent a wash of agony pouring through every muscle.

"Impressive!" came a voice from above him, and Thomas gritted his teeth, forcing his eyes open. It was the dark paladin, standing over him, the restraint stone for his collar held in one hand.

Thomas growled, his fury fully awakening. Fighting through the pain, he dragged himself forward, determined to reach the stone, only to have more soldiers pile on him. They yanked his arms back, and he raged at the terrible feeling of manacles being locked back into place.

He strained against the irons and the pain, but as the world blackened, the paladin smiled down at him in approval.

"We can use that anger, son. With a little training and some reins in place, you might be an asset to the Church of Nimon yet." He turned to a corporal who quickly stood to attention under the dark paladin's gaze.

"Take him to the infirmary; get him healed up properly and evaluated. I think Sergeant Nix's squad was one short. If so, see what he can do with him." He turned back to Thomas and gave him a fatherly smile of approval before sneering down at Boris, who lay half beaten to death with his arms broken and skull fractured. "Oh, and someone clean this shit up. Nimon has no need of scum like this on his doorstep!"

CHAPTER ONE

"**D**o ye be awake, laddie?" a voice boomed from nearby, making me jerk upright, my brain going from fast asleep into panic mode as my knees hit the underside of the table I'd been sprawled over, drunk. The impact sent me flying back down to bang my forehead on the table in a splash of spilled booze.

"Arghhhh!" I cried out sharply, pushing back from the table and tangling my legs with the stool that was bolted to the deck. I fell sideways, my flailing arm tearing a coat free from a stand to fall on me as I collapsed to the floor, slumped against the wall.

"Bwahahaha!" The laughter rang out, echoing around in my skull as I grabbed my head.

"Oren?" I whispered after a few seconds, lying there trying to figure out who and what was going on.

"Aye, laddie! It be me," he forced out, still laughing.

"I hate you," I muttered, tugging the coat off my head and glaring up at him. He stood leaning against the door to the captain's cabin, shoulders still shaking as he snickered. I winced at the bright morning sunlight that streamed in through the great windows that took up one side of the room, reaching from the floor to the upper deck, one of them still shattered from where Bob had dragged his bony arse through yesterday.

"Ach yer face, laddie, and tha way ye danced around there? Ah!"

"Bastard." I grunted, blinking and rubbing my face as he looked around the room.

"Ye could have let *me* use the captain's quarters! Ye did'na even use the bed!" he said in reproach, gesturing to the undisturbed bed as I followed his gesture, looking around the room as well.

The night before came back to me slowly. After the fight for the tower was over, I'd gathered everyone together for a wake, and in traditional Northern style, it'd ended up as a party somehow.

I vaguely remembered that Oren had gotten a golem to bring some rotgut up from his ship, then we'd raided the captured ship's stores. The sudden appearance of a fuck-load of alcohol, the combination of a battle won, and the knowledge we were safe—for a few days, at least—had resulted in a lot of drinking.

"Aye, well…sorry, mate," I muttered, rubbing some life back into my legs as I looked up at him. "Any particular reason you snuck up on me like that?" The note of irritation was clear in my voice.

"*Snuck up*? I banged on tha' door twice! Thought mebbe you'd been murdered! Or mebbe ye found an elf maid in yer bed and were making tha most of bein' a hero!" He laughed, giving me a bawdy wink.

"You thought I might have an elf maid in my bed, so you walked in? Dude, seriously…we need to talk about boundaries," I muttered, grabbing the wall and hauling myself upright. I stood unsteadily as I looked around again, my memories of last night blurry and fragmented.

The room was ostentatious for a warship, even for the captain's quarters, with gilded lamps, a large table with ornate tableware, a double bed, and multiple decanters displayed in what had previously been a locked cabinet.

I vaguely remembered jimmying the lock with a dagger while shitfaced, too drunk to manage to use my Manatouch spell, and a crystal-cut decanter had sat in the middle of the table I'd fallen asleep on. A piece of parchment curled up from underneath the decanter, stained with booze and covered in what looked like chicken scratch.

"Aye, well, only one way to be sure!" Oren said, unrepentantly shrugging. "So…ye said to be here early, that we had plans to make?"

"Yeah," I said, wracking my brain as I tried to remember what I'd been thinking when we'd last spoken.

I looked around for inspiration, and when I reflexively shied away from the glaring light of the windows, I found what I needed. The parchment, torn, messy, and lying halfway in a puddle of booze, held my master plan from last night. Thank fuck.

I leaned over it, spreading it out and frowning. I'd written it while smashed out of my skull. I'd never used a quill and inkpot combination before, tearing the parchment as much as marking it intentionally, so it wasn't the easiest to read.

To do:
T…y…up…
Nottifcasuns!
Council
Rebuild t…er!
Find Tommy the twat!!
Explore!!!

I grinned as I reached the second-last one, upon seeing my old nickname for Tommy. A memory resurfaced of the first time I'd used it, when we were training during basic, and he'd lost his mind. Good times…

*I'll find you, bro, just hang on…*I thought.

"Well, laddie?" Oren asked.

I blinked, lost in reverie.

"Sorry, mate," I said, shrugging. "Righto, then. Yeah, we've got a few things to get sorted. First, and most important, breakfast! Then you and Cai are gonna help me get shit organized around here." I took a quick look around the cabin, then snorted in amusement.

"The tower, I mean. I don't need help to clean up the room. Okay, we've got a fuckload to get done, and we're at war with an arsehole city lord. Add to that, our army would just about fit in this one damn room, so we're going to need to find some new recruits. Last, and most important of all…I need a damn drink. It tastes like the ship's cat took a shit in my mouth."

Oren lifted the decanter and sniffed it before gesturing to a glass questioningly with it. "Oh, hell no, I meant water or something. Did you not get enough last night?" I said, shuddering and moving back to the cabinet.

I quickly checked the other decanters and bottles, finally finding one at the back that had no smell. Taking a tentative sip, I relaxed, tasting water. I turned around to find Oren savoring whatever was in the decanter and shivered again. The little sod must have a cast iron stomach if he was still able to drink again already after last night.

We finished our drinks, and I put the decanter back, suddenly aware that I probably shouldn't have smashed the lock open to get at the good booze.

"Let's go," I said, somewhat gruffly. Gathering up my naginata but leaving my armor and most of my other weapons behind, I led the way out of the captain's quarters to the main deck of the airship, locking the door behind us and pocketing the key.

Despite the large windows in the cabin, I was still surprised by how bright it was outside and the birds that flitted madly all around as life seemingly decided it was safe to return to the Great Tower. I wandered down the gangplank and over to the edge and stood, resting my arms on a worn stone railing, staring out at the world before me.

I drew in a deep breath as I took in the forested hills and valleys that surrounded the Great Tower of Dravith. For hundreds of miles to the east and north, it was surrounded by dense forests and fierce mountains until the land reached the coast. To the south by southeast, the forests continued almost as far as the eye could see, broken only by a pair of great lakes and a few small rivers.

Beyond the curve of the horizon were twin cities of Himnel and Narkolt on the coast. They had been embroiled in their own war, which had apparently begun before I'd managed to piss off Himnel by claiming both the Great Tower and the continent as my birthright.

Considering that, just over six months ago, I'd been a barman and odd-job dude for a few nightclubs, it wasn't bad going.

I looked down, my gaze drawn by children's laughter rising on the winds, and I grinned down at the small figures. The warship, whose captain's cabin I'd spent the night in, had a pair of massive cages on its deck. When the ship had arrived, they had been holding dozens of people the crew had captured from a village on their way here. Now they held the ship's former crew, and the former prisoners and their children were roaming through my tower.

The sight of a trio of young children, all toddlers, splashing and squealing in a pool on one of the lower floors' balconies was a balm to my soul.

I watched their lively play for a long moment, smiling at a few birds wheeling around, disturbed by the happy laughter that rose on the wind.

Yesterday, I'd led a group of former slaves to fight the warship's complement of soldiers. While we'd won, it had been at a terrible cost. Three of those brave people had died, and my mood last night while drinking had been foul at first.

It had only lightened as the night went on, as Oren and the others introduced people who we'd freed. They had been destined for a life of slavery until we had intervened, and that felt good. I drew in another deep lungful, enjoying the clear, crisp air.

Intoxicating scents rose from the gardens dotted around the tower, supported by each balcony, but this one was teeming with plants and herbs. I could practically taste mint and lavender in the air, and after living in the polluted cities of Earth, I fucking loved it.

My stomach suddenly let out an almighty rumble, and I grimaced as an unwelcome thought filled my mind.

"Do we have enough food for everyone?" I asked, recalling all of us raiding the stores on the ship drunkenly last night, and the party we'd had. I cursed myself for a fool as I realized I could have wasted a huge amount of food when we needed it.

"Food? Aye. Well, I'd expect so. No idea, really; I had enough supplies on ma ship fer a month, easy, but that were for ma crew an' me, nothin' special." With that, Oren turned and waved toward the tower, getting a wave in return as the cat-man, Cai, started heading over from where he'd been talking to someone. "The cat'd be the best one to ask, I bet. Keep hearin' people complainin' 'bout him stickin' 'is nose in everywhere…"

I regarded Cai as he jogged toward me. The description of "the cat" was accurate, even though I automatically winced at the use of the casual slur. However, I also remembered Cai and Oren drinking together last night. Considering Cai had been a slave held aboard Oren's ship a short time ago, any real bad feelings would have been evident by now. They were just two men getting on without thinking about it.

Was speciesism really an issue here? I stood watching as Cai came to a stop, nodding his head at me and Oren in turn.

He stood a little shorter than my own six-foot-eight frame, the recent unexpected physical growth that my leveling up had provided having caused some clothing issues that slightly dampened my recent enthusiasm over it. Black fur covered him head to toe, and he was dressed in worn but serviceable clothes.

His face was a mixture of human and panther, with a wide feline nose, sharp teeth, and whiskers. He grinned at us both, and rather than any instinctive fear from facing such an obvious non-human, I always found myself grinning back at him.

Cai was the unofficial leader of the former slaves and seemed to have settled himself into the role of middle manager for me. Last night, he'd been the one that had organized the food, the few people who could cook, and even limited the booze at one point.

"Jax, Oren," he said, nodding his head and gesturing expansively around us. "It is a glorious morning. The birds sing for us, and the sun shines!"

"It be unnatural!" said Oren, shaking his head. "He always be like this, too damn happy by half!"

"Ha! I know you love the sun as much as I. What can I do for you, Jax?" he said, shaking his head at Oren before looking at me questioningly.

"Food," I said abruptly. "Do we have enough of it? Oh, and good morning to you too…sorry. I was enjoying the view when I had the horrible thought that we might have wasted food we needed last night—"

"Ah! No, we have, perhaps not a surplus, but enough for everyone for several weeks at present, now that I've checked the ships over. More than that, if we are permitted to supplement the stores with the bounty of the tower?"

"The trees, and so on?" I asked, getting a nod in response. "Yeah, of course, people can have what they want from the fruit trees and gardens; don't worry."

"Ah…maybe a little caution is in order, Jax?" Cai responded, looking at Oren and getting a grimace before carrying on. "Most of the fruit trees are in bloom at this point. If we are to harvest them, we would have plenty. However, some of the trees are rare varieties, and I have already heard of people stripping them to hoard for later."

My attention snapped back to him sharply from where I'd begun to look back down at the garden below, my attention pulled once again by the laughter of the children.

"Remember, my friend, these people were slaves. Slaves don't know when they'll next eat, so they tend to think in the short-term with any opportunities they find. It's not intentional, I'm sure," Cai said soothingly.

"Well, we need to figure out what we have and what we can take safely. I don't want the trees stripped, and certainly not damaged. We need them.

"As to people hoarding, we need someone to look after the food stores, gather everything together, and store it somewhere safe," I said, grimacing.

"That was one of the things I wanted to talk to you about today. I know you'll have a lot to do, but we need to consider the future. Especially if you're planning on adding the people of the village to our total?" Cai responded, nodding in agreement.

"Do they want to join us? Where are they all, anyway?" I asked, looking around and spotting only a few faces I vaguely recognized from last night.

"The majority of them are a few floors down; They found a reasonably intact series of rooms and set up a camp in there. I'd suggest you talk to them, if you don't mind me saying so?"

"Hell, Cai, I'm new to this whole 'lordship' thing. You know that," I said, shaking my head as I met his gaze. "I know there's a hell of a lot I don't know. In fact, the only thing I do know is that I don't know enough! I'm going to need a lot of help from you, and you, Oren," I finished, looking from one to the other.

"Of course, Jax!" Cai said, even as Oren responded with a gruff "Aye, well, might as well, I guess…"

"Thanks, guys. Okay, first things first. We need to plan things out a little better than we have up until now. We had the ship to fight, and now we kinda have a war with that prick Barabarattas…" They both nodded at me, and I went on. "So first of all, we need to meet the new people. More than we did last night, I mean." I got a nod from each, and Cai spoke up.

"The majority of them were very pleased to meet us all yesterday, my lord, especially after you told them there was no debt between them and you for their freedom, and you let them out of the cages they had been kept in. I know a few were unhappy about the soldiers and ship's crew you imprisoned in those same cages and the rules you imposed on not harming them. But overall, they have an exceptionally good impression of you, and by extension, us, at this point."

"Yeah, well, let's go meet them," I said, putting the issue of the prisoners aside for now. I'd had the surviving crew and soldiers of the warship tossed in the same cages and brig that their own prisoners had vacated last night, ordering they be given some food and water and left alone by the others.

I'd always loved city and world sims in my old life. Now, though, just considering all I had to get in place made me wince.

I needed a damn system of laws and everything, and what I'd realized about myself during the long hours since I'd adopted the former slaves into the tower was that, despite how much I'd enjoyed those games, I really hated being the one who was responsible for everything in real life.

Alternatively, though, I sure as shit wasn't going to be letting anyone order me about again, so I had the choice of put up or shut up. That meant it was time to grow, which I grudgingly accepted.

We trooped across the balcony and into the tower, jogging down the stairs as I called out with my mind to the person I most expected to be there when I woke up, and the one that had been most noticeably absent.

"Oracle, you okay?"

There was a moment of silence, then the sense of her presence appeared in my mind strongly enough it almost made me miss the next step.

"Jax! You're awake!! At last! Honestly, I was starting to think you were going to sleep the whole day away..."

I grinned involuntarily at Oracle's contact. Even through this medium, I still got a feeling of the excitable wisp's happiness that I was back in the land of the living.

"Yeah, I'm awake, and what do you mean? It's barely past sunrise!"

"I've been bored for hours! Bob still won't play with me, and you were asleep, and you snore! I didn't know you snored!"

"I passed out drunk, Oracle. I've got the beginning of what's probably gonna be a horrific hangover, I'm sure. I was snoring because I was completely shitfaced. Don't worry about it. Anyway, Cai, Oren, and I are going to talk to the villagers we freed yesterday. Where are you?"

"Bob and I are helping the completed golems to fix the damaged one. It's really interesting!"

"Ah, okay...I guess? Well, we're going to be finding out what the villagers want to do. Come meet up with us when you get the chance; not sure where we'll be."

"Do you know where they are?"

"Ah, a couple of floors down, I think. Cai and Oren seem to know."

"Okay, well, I'll see you later!"

I broke the contact and focused back on the dark stairwell as we continued down. My DarkVision had activated, and I was having no problem seeing, but Oren and Cai were a bit more hesitant. *Add lighting to the list!* I thought to myself before shaking the thought loose.

Most of the tower had some kind of magic lights embedded in the walls and ceiling, but they needed mana to run, and the tower needed a fuck ton more mana than it currently had just to keep from falling over, so...no magic lights for now, as much as it annoyed me to pass the damn things sitting embedded in the wall as they were.

Admittedly, most were shattered, but fuck it, *some* looked fine.

It took a few more minutes to reach the next level, then down into the next stairwell. Soon enough, Cai was leading us through the next floor towards a section set back from the rest.

The interior walls were still standing in this section, and as we turned the final corner, the voices we'd been hearing since arriving on the floor became clearer.

There were people ahead. They were arguing, and they were getting louder by the minute, their words echoing in the previously silent rooms.

Without slowing, Oren shoved aside a curtain that had been hung across the doorway for some privacy, and I got my first look at the people inside.

The doors on the closest trio of rooms had been clearly broken into, the furniture had been removed, and what was intact had been dragged out into the common area. The other rooms showed signs that people had spent the night in them, on cold stone. I'd need to address that as soon as I could.

The rooms being broken into was an annoyance, and I'd have told them to do it if they'd asked me, most likely, or hell, just opened the damn doors, I was the master of the tower now after all. The problem was that the few rooms I'd managed to get into had contained valuables, like the silverbright potion, and I doubted I'd be getting anything back from these rooms, judging by the man in the middle.

He was a little under average height, maybe five foot six, slim but expensively dressed and flanked by two obvious henchmen types. I glanced from them back to him and across at the group that faced them. He was seated behind a desk in a stone chair with a high back, which had been dragged in from another room, considering the scuff marks on the floor.

The second group stood huddled together, fear clear on their faces as they'd been trying to convince him of something. Their combined wheedling, begging, and cajoling had clearly been falling on deaf ears.

These people were dressed in far rougher clothing, their hands and faces worn and desperate. Several had elven ears poking through their hair and other non-human features. An irrational desire to snap at them to stand up straight arose in me as they hunched back, trying to vanish as they realized who'd just entered the room.

"No! That's final!" The human snapped at the rest of the group and turned to glare at my small company as we stepped inside.

"Yes? What do you want? Have you no manners at all? The door was clearly *closed*!" he spat at me.

My annoyance rose as I stood a little straighter, setting my naginata's steel-clad base down with a solid clang.

"Yeah, I saw the closed *curtain*, and the broken doors leading to the other rooms as well. However, given that it's *my* goddamn tower, and I could hear raised voices, I decided to see what was going on!" I retorted.

I focused on him, though it didn't keep me from seeing the others in the room shrink back from my obvious ire. The only one that didn't, predictably, was the human.

"And? I met you last night, and you were thanked; what more do you expect? I am Lorek, the reeve of the village of Dannick, and I was made a reeve by Lord Asher of Himnel himself, I'll have you know! These are my vassals, and I demand some privacy while I deal with certain…internal issues." He waved at the cowering group, a sneer curling his upper lip as he went on. "I will summon you when I've dealt with this, and we will leave for Dannick as soon as you have made the ship ready."

He was looking at me as though he expected me to bow and apologize for interrupting him, when Oren spoke up. Cai, meanwhile, was glaring at the man with his ears laid back flat, his tail twitching as he tried to hide his dislike..

"Aye, well, I dinna think *High Lord Jax* cares about ye bein' a 'reeve,' considerin' ye didna bother to introduce yerself before now! Lord Jax does be the lord of this land; the tower belongs to him, and the land itself acknowledged his lordship.

"Ye musta seen the notification? Old titles in these lands don't mean shit if he dinna approve them!" Oren was visibly bristling now, the little dwarf in threadbare armor almost vibrating with indignation on my behalf.

"I saw it, and I don't care! Lord Asher of Himnel owned these lands, and his son Barabarattas after him! I bought the deed legally. I own the village *and* its surroundings, regardless of whoever this imposter is!"

"Imposter?" I snarled, before stopping myself and holding one hand up, forcing myself to speak in as measured and calm a voice as I could manage. "Stop! Okay, everyone, stop right there and take a breath. Obviously, we've started off on the wrong foot here, somehow. So, let's give it one more try to—"

"Why should I? *I* am a *reeve*," Lorek interrupted me hotly, drawing himself up to his full short-arse height, hands on his hips as he tried to look imposing. The little shit looked more like Baron Greenback from "Danger Mouse" than anything else, and I cut him off as he'd done to me.

"I don't give a shit who you are or what your pathetic title is! You're an asshole who's abused my hospitality since you arrived!" I snarled, stepping closer and glaring down at him. "Your people seem terrified of you, and your title just means you supported that walking turd Barabarattas, as near as I can tell! So…for the last time, are you going to calm down and act like a civilized man, or are you going to get the fuck out of my tower?"

The naginata began to glow as I subconsciously readied my mana for a fight, my rage clear.

"What?! How *dare* you! I am Reeve Lorek! I…" he sputtered at me, his face going white as he noticed the glowing weapon being pointed at him.

"I heard you the first goddamn time!" My voice dropped as I grew angrier. "Now, you hear *me*! I am the lord of this tower, and you're an asshole! I came here to extend an offer of protection to you, to ask if you wanted to join us, but—"

"Join you? Join this…rabble? No, a *thousand* times no! I'd sooner burn my village to the ground than allow you access to it!" he snapped, his terror overcome by the outrage he clearly felt.

"The offer isn't open to you anymore, you weapons-grade wanker!" I roared at him. "And good luck getting back to your village—it's a long damn walk! Feel free to pack up whatever you *brought with you* and get out before I *throw* you out!"

With that, I turned around and stalked out of the room, still furious. Oren and Cai followed me, even as I began to silently pull myself apart, trying to figure out why that had gone so wrong so quickly. I didn't make it a dozen steps before I heard running feet and Oren unsheathing his sword.

"Hold it right there!" he snarled, and I turned back to find a panicked elf woman frantically coming to a stop, almost falling over, raising her hands and backing up slowly, shaking her head as she tried to force her words out.

"We…no, please…it's not…I'm not…"

Cai took pity on her and laid a hand on Oren's shoulder, gesturing to him to sheathe his sword.

"It's all right, miamee. Don't fear my friend Oren, here. You just startled us. What did you want to say?" Cai spoke soothingly.

25

She took a deep breath and replied to him, her gaze flicking from him, to Oren, to me, and back, in rapid succession. "I'm sorry! Please, we're not all like him. Reeve Lorek is…he's…well…"

"He's an asshole. That what yer tryin' to say, lassie?" Oren said loudly, making sure his words traveled as he glared back toward the rooms we'd just left. The elven woman squeaked and covered her mouth with her hands, shaking her head violently before replying.

"No! No! He's a good master, is Reeve Lorek," she said loudly before dropping her voice to barely more than a whisper and shooting furtive glances at me.

"I…we…we're sorry! Please, some of us—most of us—we want to stay! Please! We're not safe out there. Reeve Lorek, he has arrangements with the local bandits, but still, please!" She was visibly shaking as she stared at me, terrified I was going to say no.

"Hell. Look, what was your name, Mamee?" I asked, trying to calm her down, even as my own blood still boiled.

Cai coughed into his hand and unsuccessfully tried to hide a grin. "*Miamee,* my lord; it means 'little dove' in the elven language, and it's not a name. It's simply a term of endearment."

"Okay…what was your name?" I said, looking from Cai to the woman.

"Isabella, my lord," she said, looking uncertain.

"Okay, look. I'm Jax—Lord Jax, if you must—but despite how that went in there, I'm usually not particularly bad tempered, okay? The offer is still open to you and your people. I *literally* came down here to meet you all and to make the offer to all of you. I need people; you look like you need somewhere to live, and as well as protection, I can offer training and a chance at maybe a better life. I need to talk to my advisors, but yeah, the offer is still open."

"We accept!" she said quickly. "I can't speak for everyone, but most of us wanted to stay already!"

"Really?" I asked her, looking around pointedly at the crumbling walls and dirt coating everything. "You sure about that?"

Cai casually stood on my foot, and while the pressure didn't get through the armor, his point was clear, and I shut up.

"Isabella, can you gather your people so that Lord Jax can make the offer to them, please? Whoever is interested?" Cai said, shooting me a significant glance.

"Yes! Thank you! Thank you!" With that, she tore off, heading back to the group she'd just left.

I turned to Cai, one eyebrow climbing as I looked down at him.

"Okay, first off, when the hell did you have time to not only meet her, but to get on friendly enough standing to be using a term of endearment like that? Damn, man, that's fast work!" I grinned, getting an eyeroll in return.

"It's not like that, Jax. I met her last night at the party; she and her friends were feeling us out about life here, and…" Cai said quickly.

"And this silver-tongued devil had her fair near into his bed before I'd finished ma beer!" Oren laughed, elbowing Cai in the thigh, nearly sending him flying.

"No! It's not like that! Honestly, Oren, you only see what you want to! She's a lovely woman, and she's well-thought-of by her people. I was trying to get her to join us!"

"Oh aye, ye were tryin' ta get her ta join ye, all right, in a wee moonlit stroll!" Oren grinned at Cai, before winking at me as Cai looked away. For a second, I'd been worried Cai was taking advantage of things, before I realized he was actually mortified by Oren's accusations.

I could see that Oren was winding him up, or at least I thought so, so I did what any friend would do.

I jumped in as well.

"Really, Cai? I thought better of you! Taking advantage of that poor girl..." I shook my head in mock disgust, and didn't even finish my sentence before Cai had spun around and was waving his hands in negation.

"No! Honestly, Lord Jax! Please, I would never do such a thing...please believe me!"

"Hmmm. Well, there is one way I could give you one more chance, I suppose...but there'd be conditions," I said, as though serious, squinting at his imploring face. "Okay, first, you stop calling me 'Lord Jax' when we're alone like this. Just call me Jax! I've told you before, after all!" I told him, grinning and clearly relaxing.

"Oh...why, you..." he growled, realizing we were taking the piss. Taking a deep breath, he shot a glare at both Oren and me. "Okay, Jax, I agree. What's the second condition?"

"Well, she seemed pretty interested in you; all I'm saying is she's pretty, so relax, man. As long as you don't use your position in any underhanded ways, have fun! The second condition is...you see what's going on there, mate!" I grinned at him and turned around, making my way back to the stairwell as Oren casually spoke up from behind as he started following me.

"One other wee point as well, Cai. Ye just told her to get everyone together to meet the 'great Lord Jax,' aye? Well, only thing is, ye did'na tell her where!"

Cai spun around and started swearing under his breath as he set off racing along the corridor in the direction Isabella had gone.

"Tell them to make it the ground floor outside!" I shouted after him, having already decided that I'd need to be in the makeshift "command center" I'd been using until now.

"Yes, Jax!" Cai shouted back as he disappeared into the mess of rooms in pursuit of Isabella.

"Oh, he's got it bad fer her!" Oren muttered, shaking his head in mock sorrow. "Barely known her a night, and already..."

"Give it a rest, man, he can't hear you," I replied, grinning.

"Aye, but ye see how quick he bit?" Oren let loose with a belly laugh as we headed downstairs. "Oh, I'm gonna have some fun wit' this!"

CHAPTER TWO

O ren and I set off jogging down the stairs, and despite the poor show he'd put on only a few days ago, he actually managed to keep up for a few more floors this time. When I asked him about it, he just winked and told me that he'd leveled after the battle and sunk a few points into Endurance, as "All the ladies love a dwarf wi' stamina!"

Cai caught up with us a few minutes later, and we continued as a group, people jumping aside as we passed. The occasional bow, curtsy, or wave from people, depending on their preferences, struck me as weird enough that I still flinched when it happened.

"How do we get people to stop doing that?" I asked after a particularly rowdy fight between two children had been cowed into fearful silence by their parents at the sight of me. We'd run on past, as I'd figured it was better to give them some room rather than telling the kids to get back to fighting.

"Stop doing what?" Cai responded, his feline grace being brought into even more prominence by Oren's huffing and puffing as the dwarf's short legs tried to keep up with us.

"The whole bowing and scraping thing. The look that woman gave us was like she thought I'd kick the kids out of the window if they made noise, for fuck's sake!" I replied, the exercise doing wonders for my hangover as I got my blood pumping.

"She probably thinks you might," Cai responded sadly. "The simple truth is that we were slaves. She wasn't one of my party, instead one of the villagers that we freed yesterday. But in these lands, the strong do as they want.

"For all she knows, her children are in danger here; it's just slightly less than elsewhere. It may seem unfair that they're afraid of you but think of what they've seen of you so far. They were captured by a warship, made slaves, and their village stripped by a dozen or more soldiers that they stood no chance against.

"They then landed at a tower that they've either never known about before, or only heard of through dark tales. They fully expected to be sold as slaves, probably assaulted, and the best she could hope for was that her children might escape into the wild alone while she sold her life to give them that chance. Instead, you led a band of frankly filthy people out of the darkness and slaughtered the crew. You're a High Lord, one who's killed a creature she's only heard of in bard's tales and nightmares, and you declare war against cities like it's nothing."

"The…damn cat's…got a point…laddie!" panted Oren. "Ye did kick…a ton o' arse…yesterday!"

"You did it with me!" I protested. "You and Cai, and the crew. Damn, I wasn't alone; we all fought!"

"True, but you were alone when you fought the SporeMother, and most of them have seen the corpse now…what's left of it." Cai shook his head. "I know what you said about being sent to this world from your own, but Jax, entire legions have fallen to creatures like that and been raised again as its slaves. One man doesn't kill something like that, not alone, at least not outside of the bards' tales."

"I wasn't alone. I had Oracle and Bob, and most of the damage was done after the fight…I was looking for alchemy components!" I protested in vain.

"You mean your bonded companion and a summoned creature? No, people don't consider either of them as 'help.' They're part of you. Look; I know what you're trying to say, I do. Just take a minute and think of the way it looks from our side.

"*I* couldn't have done what you did. If I could, I'd have been free a long time ago! Same for any of my people. Sorry, *our* people!" Cai corrected himself. "We'd have tried to do some of it, and we'd have died. The other bits, we'd have fled or hid from, but you didn't. You attacked everything you saw and beat it into submission."

"Bit its cock off…" I whispered, memories flaring to life.

"Whut?" Oren asked, looking at me askance.

"It's something my brother Tommy used to say when we were children," I explained, still lost in memories. "Whenever you have a dream of fighting or being attacked, you could choose to run. But if you started running, you never knew where you'd end up. It was always better to turn around and bite the cock off of whatever was chasing you. That's what we'd say to each other when we had a nightmare."

"A nightmare? That was your response to a nightmare as a child?" Cai asked in shock. "Well, I think I can see why you win when you fight, Jax…"

"Whut…happened…to…your…brother?" Oren gasped, before throwing his hands up in surrender and slowing to a walk. "I…give…in! Just…stop…a…wee while…okay?"

He groaned, leaning against the wall, and doubling over, trying to catch his breath.

"Wimp!" Cai said, grinning as he came to halt a few steps beyond Oren, his breathing labored, but nowhere near as badly as the dwarf's.

"He's here somewhere," I said, slowing down and walking to a hole in the side of the tower. I gazed through it, my hand idly gripping the weather-beaten stone, feeling the pits and cracks. I stared sightlessly into the past again, although to a time much more recent.

I saw the Baron, my prick of a father, as he casually informed me of Tommy's capture and subsequent compulsory fighting in the tournament. He'd forced Tommy to kill other people, to "prove his value," before casting him out of our own world and into this Realm.

I stamped down on the sudden surge of fear, the thought that I could have put Tommy in more sodding danger thanks to my declaration of war yesterday. No. I had to deal with things as they were. I couldn't ignore the shit that happened because it *might* affect Tommy.

He was a hard bastard; he'd be alright. I'd find him trying to wear out the entire staff list of a whorehouse somewhere, with no clue I was here or that I had started a war.

I drew in a deep breath. I'd decided at some point the night before that I needed to come clean and tell these people everything if they were to help me. I'd spoken about a few bits already but…I might as well start now.

I gestured to them to walk with me, and I told them about Tommy, about me, and about our world. I'd barely scratched the surface by the time we reached the command center, as I'd started to refer to it, and it took over an hour longer as we ate the food Cai had arranged to be sent down. Answering their questions and asking some of my own both gave me more details of their lives in return, until at last, Seneschal interrupted us. We'd all talked about things when we'd been working together over the last few days, but going over it again felt right now that we had a little time to relax.

The small Wisp formed himself from the mana pool attached to the creation table, straightening up as he coalesced. It was like watching a terminator being born from liquid metal as he grew. At first, there were no details, then arms and legs, a head, and a body grew distinct. Details refined as the seconds passed until suddenly a small figure stood tall, poised atop the pool of liquid mana.

Seneschal was the second Wisp I'd found, and like Oracle, he swore his allegiance to me when I awoke him. Unlike Oracle, though, his bond was to the tower itself and its occupants. While he deferred to me, his only real interest was the tower.

"Hey, Seneschal, everything okay?" I asked as he appeared and raised a hand to interrupt our discussion.

"Yes, Jax, all is well. However, I noted your offer to the villagers to join us earlier, and the request that they gather outside on the ground floor."

"Ah, shit. Yeah, I meant to ask you to watch for them; sorry, man," I muttered, scratching my head. "Where are they now?"

"Almost half of them are outside and ready. Another six are traveling through the stairwells and will arrive momentarily. There is, however, an issue."

"Go on," I said, sitting upright and taking a deep breath.

"The Reeve of Lorek has convinced two others to side with him, and they are headed to the main group now. I suspect they have been 'his' for some time, as they seem unconcerned with his orders regarding violence."

"Violence?" I growled, getting to my feet. "What's the prick done now?"

"Nothing yet, but he's instructed his two men to 'make an example' of the young woman your advisor Cai seems enamored with. They are to 'enjoy her' before disposing of her body."

"What!" Cai said, jumping to his feet, Oren following behind less than a second later. Both men grabbed at weapons reflexively.

"Where are they in relation to Isabella?" I asked quietly, holding my hand up to stop Cai and Oren before they could do anything else. My irritation and annoyance with the man went from hot to an icy cold rage as soon as I realized fully what he was trying to do.

He wasn't a petty civil servant and a prick, as I'd first assumed, trying to hold onto his power and to hell with the consequences. He'd just tried to arrange a murder and rape, and as such, he and his two friends had shown themselves to me.

"They are one floor below you now and moving quickly. They will likely reach her before you reach them; however, Oracle and Bob are headed here now, so I took the liberty of sharing the information with them. They should reach the men before the men reach Isabella."

"Well done, Seneschal," I said, letting out a long-held breath.

"Thank you, Jax. However, Oracle seems rather incensed by the knowledge I shared with her, so if you wish the men to survive…"

"I get it; I'm on my way," I said, turning and heading for the door, Cai and Oren close on my heels.

"Oracle, where are you?"

"I'm nearly there, Jax. Don't worry; Bob and I will take care of this!"

I could feel the rage bleeding through from the typically happy wisp. Something about this had driven her into a rage, and I suspected I knew what it was.

"Well, don't do anything permanent to them. We need to get the villagers onside first, then you can have them."

"Define 'permanent.'"

"Just capture them, that's it. Bring them downstairs to face their people, and I'll be there with Cai and Oren soon."

Oracle disappeared from my mind, but the silence and residual anger let me know how she felt about my instructions.

I shook the feelings off and hurried down the stairs, coming out into the sunlight on the ground floor just behind Bob, who dragged both of the reeve's unconscious and bloodied men behind himself. I could hear the reeve screaming something at Oracle as I emerged, but I wasn't in time to stop the bolt of lightning that blasted him from his feet.

I suppressed a growl as I saw the effect the magic had on the crowd of villagers gathered before the tower. Before, they'd been hesitant to make eye contact, but some had viewed me with hope.

Now they all huddled together, eyes downcast as they waited to see what I was going to do to them.

"Dammit, Oracle," I whispered under my breath, knowing she'd hear me. She hovered a dozen feet away. The villagers were hunkered off to the left, and the "Reeve of Dannick" lay crumpled and moaning to my right with her floating squarely between them.

"That…that *thing* attacked me!" he screamed at me as soon as he could get his breath. "That flying *bitch* used magic on me for no reason, while your *pet* assaulted my friends!" He tried to get to his feet, pointing an accusing finger at me as he drew in to continue his screeching, when Cai darted past me.

Before I could stop him, the humanoid panther had crossed the distance and grabbed the little man by the throat, only to send him staggering with a solid punch to the face. Oren stepped up next to me and shouted to his friend to leave him some.

I clipped him across the back of the head reflexively.

"That's not helping, you little bastard!" I growled, before raising my voice to carry across to everyone. "Cai! Leave him be! I told you to stop him, not kill him."

I bent the truth a little there, but it had the desired effect, as everyone looked to me, then back at Cai and the sniveling reeve.

Cai stood there for a second, hands held curled over strangely, shining claws visible, before straightening and backing up to stand next to me, leaving Lorek reeling.

"Yes, Lord Jax. My apologies," he growled, never taking his eyes off the trembling reeve.

"You…your…" the little man squeaked before I cut him off with a glare.

"Silence, ya stupid prick!" I snarled at him, turning to the people that stood subdued to my left. Isabella was clear among them, unharmed thankfully.

"Okay, people, this is going to take some explaining, but the simple truth is that, in the tower, you are in my domain. What I'd not made clear to you yet is what that means," I said clearly, raising my voice so that everyone could hear. Bob stomped over, depositing the unconscious men alongside their "friend" before returning to hulk behind me. Even now, faced solely with giving an explanation and without any real threat to me, my massive bone minion stood guard over me, and I gained a little reassurance from his presence.

"While you've been in the tower over the last day, you might have heard mention of, or even seen, a wisp," I said, noting a few nods. "There are three of them, each with their own interests, focuses, and responsibilities. Oracle here," I said, gesturing to my companion as she flew across to hover by my side, "…is my bonded companion.

"She is also in charge of knowledge and magic in the tower. Seneschal is responsible for the tower itself and its occupants. Finally, Hephaestus is in charge of the golems and crafting. What I haven't explained to any of you is that Seneschal *is* the tower, as much as a separate entity. I asked him to monitor your previous 'master,' Reeve Lorek." Again, slightly bending the truth there. "As such, he was listening to every word that this waste of space said to his two goons."

The little man went even paler, his right hand coming up to cover his mouth as he glanced first at the two unconscious men, then at Isabella.

"Yeah," I said, looking him in the eye as he turned back to me. "So, I know *exactly* what you ordered done to her, and how you wanted an 'example made' for the former villagers of Dannick."

I shifted my focus back to the group, passed my naginata to Bob to hold, and held onto the front of my armor, in the way I'd seen the police and soldiers do when they were trying not to appear threatening. It also had the bonus of keeping my hands busy, rather than wrapping them around the reeve's throat.

"He ordered that Isabella be murdered, gruesomely, and that those two were to 'enjoy themselves' with her before they did it. I'd rather not repeat exactly what was said, but I can't just gut the fucker without explaining this. I don't know what kind of laws you're used to, but I will not tolerate murder or rape here." I felt the leather and steel under my hands creaking as my grip tightened in fury.

"I'll be very, very clear here. That kind of thing isn't acceptable, regardless of the reason or who is doing it. Just because he was your 'master' doesn't mean he gets to get away with shit like that." The group started muttering to themselves, while Isabella held my gaze, ignoring the looks some of the others were giving her now.

"Why would he do that, my lord?" she called out, the look in her eye letting me know that she knew exactly why.

"Because you had expressed a desire to join me, Isabella, and he couldn't allow that."

"Can you prove what you said?" The reeve called out weakly, trying what he must have assumed was his trump card. "You claim you respect the lives of those who live here, but you attack refugees without proof of some kind?"

"Oh, don't you worry yourself about that, pal. Wisps have numerous abilities, you know, one of which is to share memories," I said, thinking fast and making shit up on the spot. "So, all Seneschal has to do is share his memory of your words to all here, then I think we'll deal with you the same way we dealt with the last murdering piece of shit we had here.

"We'll take you all the way to the top of the tower, and I'll see just how far out I can throw each of you. I'm betting I can beat Toka's record; what do you think, Cai?" I said, denying the reeve a chance to speak.

"Oh, I think you could manage at least double that distance, my lord!" Cai said. "In fact, I'd be happy to have a try myself, if you don't mind?"

"I…I…wait…"

"Or we go for option two," I said, cutting the panicked man's spluttering attempts off as I mentally communicated with Oracle.

"Heal the idiots, please, Oracle."

"Heal them? But they…"

"Trust me, they won't be getting away with this."

Oracle cast a simple ranged healing spell on both men, and after a few seconds, they blinked their eyes and groaned, sitting up to look around.

"Welcome back to the land of the living, gentlemen. Just to catch you both up on events so far, you've been caught plotting to kill Isabella, as well as…the rest of his instructions… I have proof, and I'm going to drag you to the top of the tower to see if you can discover the secret of flight by giving you no other alternatives."

"Huh?" one grunted, while the other just sat there open-mouthed. The only sign that he had understood was a rapidly spreading wet mark on the front of his breeches.

"That's my first, and frankly preferred option. The second choice is that you admit your crimes against someone who'd already asked to join my settlement, you apologize, and I give you a pack of supplies and a weapon, banish you, and let you go home. Just the three of you, I mean, unless any of the people from your village wish to travel with you?"

"You'd set them free?"

"Oh yeah. Pay attention to my phrasing, though; I never promised to help them get there. How dangerous would you say the forest is between here and their village? With a single shitty weapon and one pack of supplies between them?"

"I don't know, but considering the SporeMother was here and hadn't spread out? Could be lots of creatures in the area…at least I hope so!"

"Me, too. Oh, and I'm going to send Oren to go and recruit whoever I can from the village by airship. If they'll all come, he can strip it to the ground. Nice surprise for them if they somehow make it and only find a hole in the ground. Maybe I'll even leave him a note or get someone to paint a picture of me giving the fucker the finger and leave that there."

Oracle's only response was a feeling of satisfaction as she left the mental connection.

"If one of you doesn't own up to this, though, I'm going to assume you all would rather fly, so on the count of three, I'm going to have the golems drag you up to the top of the tower…One, two…"

"Aye! He…said, the reeve said we was to do 'er, just like you said!" the one with the wet breeches clamored, and I decided to think of him as Pissy-Pants from now on.

"Silence, you fool! He can't prove it!" the reeve screamed, lashing out with his right hand, and slapping the terrified man across the face.

"And what's your choice?" I asked the remaining man, who gulped, looking from one of his companions to the other before nodding and looking at the ground, barely speaking above a whisper.

"What he said," was all the man managed to croak out, but by now, the entire remaining group of villagers were convinced of their guilt, as indicated by the angry mutters that started to rise. A few had managed to find small daggers, and they wore them on their hips, hands gripping them tight.

"Last chance then, Reeve Lorek. Want to join your friends and fuck off, or do you want to fly? Because believe me, if you make me walk all the way to the top of the tower, I'll be in an *unbelievably* bad mood when we get there!"

Silence reigned for a long minute, but just as I opened my mouth to speak again, he snarled out a response.

"Fine! I told them to kill the wench, and I was within my rights! They are *my* villagers. I own them, I make the laws, and *I* decide who lives in *my* lands!" he spat, glaring at me.

"Except you're not in your lands anymore, you little prick, you're in *MINE!*" I roared at him, making everyone take a step back at my sudden blaze of fury. I closed my eyes and took a deep breath, rubbing my face with my hands as I reflected on how easily this man had driven me into a rage, before calling out to Seneschal.

"Seneschal, old buddy, you there?"

"Of course, Jax."

"Coolio. Okay, I need you to get someone to grab the shittiest weapon you can find in the tower and bring it down here, along with a pack of really crappy supplies."

"I have the perfect equipment in mind. It should take only a few minutes to have it prepared, and it'll be with you within the hour. There's a servitor close by, and it can deliver them."

"Thanks, mate."

"Okay, Bob, take those three asshats off to the side. I want them out of the way before I do something I'll really enjoy," I said, gesturing at a section of the courtyard that was the furthest from where the rest of the group stood.

Bob passed my naginata back and stomped forward quickly, grabbing the three in his multiple hands and dragging them unceremoniously as far as possible from the remaining villagers, who were glaring furiously at them, none more than Isabella, who was whispering to someone next to her and testing the edge of a blade with her thumb.

CHAPTER THREE

I addressed the villagers, grimacing as I reflected on what should have been a joyous occasion.

"Okay, people," I said, taking a deep breath and smiling at them, although it was obviously a little forced. "That wasn't the start I'd hoped for with this, but Isabella told me that some of you would like to join us here in the Great Tower permanently as citizens?"

"Yes, my lord!" replied Isabella, turning from eyeing the Reeve to offer an awkward curtsy that was quickly copied by the rest of the group, including the men, who seemed as confused as I was by the show.

"Stop." I shook my head. "Please, there's no need to bow or curtsy, not here, and not with me. Yes…I am Lord Jax, and I'm lord of the Great Tower and of Dravith, but we're a small community, and we're all going to be working hard to get things up and running together.

"First of all, is there anyone here who doesn't want to swear allegiance and join the community?" I asked, noting the looks a few of them had given the three men who had been dragged off by Bob.

"Ignore those idiots, please. Isabella asked to join my community and was already under my protection when they decided to harm her. As it stands, they can consider themselves fortunate that I'm just making them leave. If they'd managed to actually carry out their threat, getting flying lessons would be the least of their concerns."

I took a deep breath and looked around, spotting a moss-covered bench off to one side that faced an open space that was dappled with sunlight. I led them over and gestured for them to sit on the ground while I sat on the bench. "Can you all see and hear me okay?"

I received cautious nods in response.

"Okay, then. You all want to join us, and that's great. I'm happy to take you, but there will be Oaths, there's no getting around that. In exchange for your fealty, I won't just give you protection. First, I know there are some kids with you. Anyone want to tell me how many?"

Isabella spoke up hesitantly. "There are eight children, my lord."

"Righto. Well, while you can all swear, as you're adults, the kids can't. Don't get me wrong, they're very welcome here," I said, seeing the panic on a few faces. "But as they're only kids. I don't expect them to swear to something they don't understand. How old are they?"

"Between three and eleven," Isabella offered after a quick whispered consultation.

"Okay, nobody under the age of sixteen or whenever the age of adulthood is can swear. They'll be fed, and we'll sort out some kind of schooling as soon as we can. Until then, I guess they get to play and get underfoot for now. I'll not tell you what to do with them, as I've never had kids and don't know what to do with them as well as you all probably do. So, moving on, are there any of you here that have a trade or recognized skill?"

Of the group of nearly twenty adults, only four held up their hands, and I asked them to stand and tell me about themselves.

"Well, um, I'm just a farmer, m'lord," the first man said, shuffling his feet awkwardly and looking down at his hands. His clothes were simple and had clearly been mended often, but he was fit and strong, with a heavily muscled frame, green eyes, and sandy hair.

I blinked, a realization dawning as I looked over the rest of the crowd, and then considered Lorek. They were all what I'd have classed as "the beautiful people" back home: not one of them was ugly, or even average, and the few who were overweight were clearly even more attractive than the others. They'd been taken as slaves, after all, or as hostages. The ship had probably left the ugly ones back at the village…if they'd not just killed them out of hand.

I suddenly realized I'd left the man standing there as I looked around, and I had to stop myself from facepalming. *Great work, Jax. Way to make them feel valued!*

"That's fantastic!" I said, forcing a smile to cover the awkward pause. "I'm sorry, I just had a realization; it wasn't important, though. So, you're a farmer? That's going to be especially useful. After all, we all need to eat, right? What's your name?"

"Ah, Timoth…m'lord," he said.

"Well, welcome, Timoth. There's certainly plenty for you to be busy with here. Tell me, how skilled are you?"

"I'm at level fourteen farmer, m'lord," he replied proudly. "Been a farmer for seven years, grew up helpin' me da!"

"That's fantastic! Thank you, Timoth, you can sit down." I addressed the next person, finding in short order that I had a tall elven baker called Krillek, a particularly wide-bodied human leatherworker called Milosh, and that a tiny, blonde half-elven girl called Miren had just started training as a hunter, until the airship had arrived.

"An' they started killin' those that wouldn't go peaceful-like, m'lord! Me Da, he took an arrow in the knee!"

"Used to be an adventurer," I muttered without thinking about it, before grimacing at Miren's look of confusion. "Sorry, just a reminder of a…friend…from my home. What happened to the rest of the village?"

Isabella supplied the information quickly from her seat on the right of the group. I noted the reassuring look Cai had been giving her and the faint smile she'd given him in return.

"The airship stripped anything that looked valuable and captured us, m'lord, but they left those that ran away. Most of the village, the older folk especially, will still be there…those who survived, anyway," she said, a catch in her voice.

"Well, we'll be returning for them soon. My good friend Oren, here," I said, clapping him on one shoulder, "will be flying us back to the village as soon as we can get the airship up and running. This time, there will be no thefts and attacks. You will all be given the chance to gather anything you want or need and bring it back, as well as any villagers who wish to join us, provided they swear the Oaths as well."

The group looked relieved at that, talking amongst themselves before quieting down as I went on.

"There is also another side to joining my community, as I said, besides my protection and getting to live in this high-class establishment." I gestured sarcastically with a raised eyebrow over my shoulder at the crumbling and almost derelict tower. "You will also get training and opportunities that I've heard have been long gone from the land."

I'd spent hours in conversation with Oren, Cai, and the wisps, and the cache of memory crystals and skillbooks in Oracle's Hall of Memories had turned out to be a bigger boon than I'd realized. With the end of the old world, it seemed the making of such things had also more or less come to an end, which meant that it was, in fact, a treasure trove of skills that may have been long lost.

"I, and my advisors Cai and Oren, will talk to you all, discovering your skills and interests and what your attributes suggest you might be best at. We will separate you into teams, assisting the more skilled individuals amongst you to accomplish the first steps needed to bring life, comfort, and security to the tower.

"Once that has been accomplished, and I've gotten a better measure of you, we will grant a select few with skill memories and skillbooks, maybe some spellbooks too. Are you familiar with them?"

The group looked at me in shock, followed by a few mutterings, then more voices rose, until everyone was speaking at once, making it impossible to understand anyone.

I turned to Oren and Cai, catching the grins on their faces as they nodded at me, Oren, of course, being the one to clap me on the shoulder and half shout in my ear.

"I told ye so, laddie!"

I shook my head, making eye contact with Cai as he rolled his eyes at the dwarf's ostensible need to say it.

I stood, holding my hands up for silence. As everyone quieted down, I relaxed slightly, glad that at least some gestures and reactions were universal across the realms, for whatever reason.

"Yes, I see you do know what skill memories and skillbooks are, and yes, I have access to both. They are limited, and I won't be just giving them away to just anyone. You will have to prove yourselves to me and my advisors, and I will expect a lot of those who do get these things. For a start, anyone who gets one will be expected to teach others. For free!" I sat back down, looking at the now silent group.

"Teaching others in our community will always be for free, and teaching others who are not is banned, for now at least. I want to improve your lives, but I won't be taken advantage of, so let's be clear on that. Also, you won't all be learning how to do everything. As much as I'm sure you'd all like to try everything, if you split yourself too many different ways, you'll never level up or get more skilled.

"I want you all to consider what you would like to learn and what you *truthfully* think you'd be best at. I'm aware these could be two totally different things, but I'd like to know, as it'll give me a lot of room to work with you. I might let you do both, if they are things that will complement each other.

"It's my intention that we will grow and quickly, visiting other villages in the area and offering the chance to join us, so if you know others you think would make a good addition, tell Oren and Cai, and if you feel that someone won't, for whatever reason, tell them that, too.

"We will initially need food and protection most of all, so I will be choosing two teams. The first will be farmers, and they will be working with Timoth to start getting our food supplies in order, and the second will be learning to fight and to hunt.

"Normally, hunters and guards or soldiers would be separate groups, and I'm well aware of that. But for now, I want a lot of you to be able to defend yourselves and those around you in short order. Once you've got a bit of experience in those groups, and I can see where your skills lie, I'll probably separate you out into soldiers, guards, and hunters properly. Does anyone have any questions so far?"

When the other two skilled individuals, Milosh and Krillek, looked uncomfortable but stayed quiet, I grinned at them.

"Don't worry, I've not forgotten that you're skilled as well. Krillek, I want you to work with Oren's first mate, Barrett, as he's an organized bugger, and get a plan together for what you need to start baking. There have been a few people helping to keep us all fed so far, and that'll need to be expanded into a proper kitchen team. Milosh, there's going to be a lot of animal pelts coming in soon, I'd imagine. I know you're a leatherworker, but have you any skill with skinning?"

"Um, well, I did it once?" he said, scratching the back of his head with an embarrassed look on his face, one which quickly got redder when a big young man seated next to him smacked him on the shoulder and spoke through a huge grin.

"Yeah, and tell him what your master told you after it!" he laughed.

"That I'd never be allowed to butcher another animal as long as he drew breath...but he's dead now, isn't he! I'm tryin', I am! Least I got a skill; you're no good for nothin' besides chasin' Betti!"

"Hey! I didn't know!" The lad apologized shamefacedly, but Milosh shoved him hard, trying to hold back tears. He pushed back, a fight clearly about to break out.

"Enough!" I shouted, coming to my feet, and both men—boys, really—settled down, glowering at each other. "Look, it's clear what you've gone through in the last few days, but there's no need for this. First, I want five volunteers to help Timoth; anyone?"

A dozen hands shot up, and I grinned in relief, having half expected nobody to want to do it.

"Okay, Timoth, pick those that you feel will be the best match, please." He quickly picked five people, two men and three women, and I noticed they all had elven features as they stood with him, moving off to the side. I murmured a quick inquiry to Cai, who quietly assured me that elves were well known for their affinity for growing things. I looked at the remaining thirteen people and decided to do a good deed for a friend next.

"That's great. Thank you, Timoth. Cai, I think you'd better get with Isabella and get a breakdown of her people's skills in preparation for talking to them directly; you okay with that?" When I saw the surprise, swiftly followed by a surreptitiously exchanged look of relief, I moved on.

"Next, I want six volunteers for hunting and fighting training. Any volunteers?" The rest of the group immediately raised their hands, looking eager.

"Miren, you've got some experience in this, and you know your fellow villagers, so can you pick those you think will be best, please?" With Isabella and Krillek already assigned, that left five people looking disappointed until I spoke to them.

"Okay, people, I know you're all feeling a little down at not being picked yet for a job, but please don't be. These next few days and weeks will be the chance for each of you to show yourselves ready for different training. In the meantime, you will be helping the wisps and the golems put this place back together. That means hard work. Clearing fallen rubble will likely be the best of it, but believe me, while it might not be glamorous, it is needed.

"The faster we have secure quarters and a little comfort, the sooner we can start with the interesting things!"

The remaining group looked a little mollified, but clearly still felt a bit depressed about not being chosen.

I asked them all to gather around and take the Oath, a slightly different one from that sworn by Oren's people, as we'd now had a little time to consider things. Seneschal had given me a few pointers, including the use of one of the abilities afforded by being the master of a settlement.

I took a deep breath, and reached out with my mind, summoning my character sheet easily. But instead of looking it over and dealing with the stack of notifications, as I knew I needed to, I instead…twisted…my attention to one side, reaching out with my mind to the tower.

At Seneschal's guiding, a new page blossomed before me. Most of its options were greyed out, but a tab clearly visible at the top of the page was marked Citizens. Selecting it, I found it was split into two sections. The top group was marked Oath Sworn, while the second group was marked Prospective.

I chose the second group with a mental flick, and an option appeared to add all the prospective citizens of the tower, the wider land, and the country, or just selected people to the Oath Sworn category. I chose "all" for the Tower section and grinned when a prompt showed before me, allowing me to check over it before sending it out to them.

Prospective Citizens of the Great Tower of Dravith!

Lord Jax offers you the chance to join him and swear fealty to his line and the Great Tower.

If you be pure of heart and clean of conscience, then repeat these words, but be warned, there will be consequences for those who are not!

I swear to obey Lord Jax and those he places over me; I will serve to the best of my ability, speak no lie to him when the truth is commanded, and treat all other citizens as family.

I will work for the greater good, being a shield to those who need it, a sword to those who deserve it, and a warden to the night.

I will stand with my family, helping one another to reach the light, until the hour of my death or my lord releases me from my Oath.

Lastly, I will not be a dick.

I nodded, reading over the words I'd written. They covered it all, really. I wanted it to sound a lot cooler, but the popular green comic book hero's oath was all I'd been able to remember. As cool as that was, I didn't really see it fitting in here. Besides, nobody messed with Stan Lee and lived. I wasn't going to disrespect the man like that.

I took a deep breath and reached out to the tower, feeling the mana it drew in from the world. It felt like simply taking a breath of the freshest, sweetest air I could imagine, but once I started, it began to increase in volume. It was like taking a drink from a straw; you sucked it in, then found the straw was somehow pouring the liquid into you, growing faster and faster.

As the milliseconds passed, the straw became a firehose, mana pouring into me at a horrific rate, making my eyes bulge as my body began to shake from the power infusion. I'd drawn on it for less than three seconds, and I was starting to feel like I might explode, when Oracle was there.

Her mind was suddenly nestled within my own, guiding the strings of raw mana, the lifeblood of the realms, into the channels the tower held for it. Instead of the huge weight of mana about to crush me, a slim siphon existed again.

The mana returned to its proper channels, and the tower gave an almost imperceptible shudder, returning to the task of repairs as the channel Oracle had guided branched out from me, splitting into smaller and smaller strings, then threads, reaching out to link to the hearts of the people who stood before me.

I blinked, seeing the beautiful tapestry that existed all around me, the mana seeping into people and spreading throughout them as it connected them to the tower…and to me.

The sound of voices rose all around me, the people each taking a knee and pressing their right hand to their heart in salute, speaking the words in a staggered but heartfelt way, as each read at a different speed.

As the final words rang out and silence filled the courtyard, broken only by the distant mutterings of Lorek and his men, I let the latest notification pop up.

You have gained nineteen new Oathsworn Citizens!

The average morale of these citizens is: Optimistic! Adding these to your current total citizenry of 34 has resulted in an overall rise of morale to: Optimistic!

The Morale Bonus for Optimistic of 10% increase in productivity and population growth has been added to your settlement.

I frowned, not realizing the opportunity for such a bonus before, but I quickly dismissed it and the rest of the notifications, feeling a resistance like I was mentally closing a dozen virus/porn popup windows from the early 2000s. The notifications really seemed to want to be read!

When I focused on the real world again, Oracle was hovering before me, watching me.

"We need to talk," was all she said, making sure I understood how serious this was before flitting to the side to allow me to interact with the people first.

I drew in another deep breath before forcing a grin at people, making sure I'd made eye contact with all of them before I spoke.

"Thank you all for your faith in me. I, Lord Jax, do swear to protect and lead you, to be the shield that protects you and yours from the darkness, and the sword that avenges that which cannot be saved. As the tower grows in strength, so shall you." I smiled at them then, a genuine smile as I relaxed a bit more. "Okay, people, if those who have been chosen to be hunters can head straight up to the airship, you will be able to find Barrett.

"He's hard to miss, as he'll be the one making everyone clean and scrub the ship! When you get there, he'll have some gear ready for you. Farmers, I want you to head up to the first balcony garden and find out what plants we have there.

"Clear away the dead ones and see what you can do to improve the yield, as well as putting together a plan for raising the food we will need. Lastly, my workers." I looked to the five who stood in the middle of the group. "I want you to work directly under Seneschal. If you head straight to the main floor, the one that you landed on, I'll make sure he gives you direction. It will be hard, but he will also be giving me recommendations based on your aptitudes, so remember, who you will be is entirely up to who you show yourselves to be from now on."

As the groups started heading for the stairs in a rush, I sat back down, reaching out to Seneschal.

"Hey, buddy, you there?"
"Always."
"Coolio. Well, I've sent you five people to help with the rebuilding, I know they're not going to be anywhere near as useful as the golems yet, but they'll learn fast. Also, can you pass word to Barrett and have him get the weapons and armor we discussed ready for the group of prospective hunters? Lastly, ask Barrett to join Oren, Cai, and myself in the command center once he's gotten them all sorted."
"Very well. However, I remember being extremely specific on the process for drawing the mana to seal the citizens to the Oath. I believe I was exceedingly clear on how to make sure you did NOT tap the main mana collection intake?"
"Yeah, about that buddy...I was wasted. I basically only remember bits of the conversation, like little bits. The bit about 'whatever you do, don't draw from the mana collectors directly' kinda only came back to me when I was already pulling on them."
"Jax, I understand you deal with many serious circumstances using levity and a laid-back attitude, but in this case..."
"How bad is it?"
"It's not how bad it is, it's how bad it would have become! In another second, you would have begun pulling from the second channel as well, and your body would have been unable to release the siphon. Once the second draw began fully, you would have been killed. No mortal could withstand the amount of power you were about to draw, and there were two more about to make connection after that. Your physical shell would have detonated, destroying the area around you for up to a mile."
"Okay, but best-case scenario..."

"That is the best case!! The worst case is becoming a full-blown vampiric mana-infused spirit! Your mind would be wiped, and all that would be left is a desire to feed on any mana around you! You'd feed on the children with pleasure and suck on the tower collectors until you overdrew, making an explosion that would warp the land for hundreds of miles into a hellscape of twisted creatures and evil!"

"Okay, so…how about I don't do that again?"

"Definitely! Now, Oracle is waiting to 'discuss' this with you further; have fun!"

"Oh crap."

"Oh yes…enjoy!"

I turned my full attention to Oracle then, wincing as I saw the way she smiled at me. Somehow, the tiny, stunningly beautiful Wisp looked more like a great white shark watching a skinny dipper. A skinny dipper that had just pissed in her tank.

CHAPTER FOUR

I t was more than a half hour later before I escaped Oracle's tirade. She'd taken the time to berate me for everything from my lack of paying attention last night (I was drunk, dammit) to putting off reading my notifications, to my lack of planning for the future. Even the fact that I hadn't been working on my next gift from the Goddess Jenae was thrown in there.

I had an answer for everything, mostly along the lines of "I'm working on it," but I wasn't that stupid.

I'd learned long ago, when you're in a fight with someone who's *that* pissed with you, it's best to just take it. Fair enough, tell them afterwards what you've done to make up for it, but never, *ever* let them know they're too late, and you're already fixing things.

They won't stop ranting, and they won't accept it; you'll have just become defensive and have wasted the opportunity. It was always best to wait a while, then unveil what you'd been doing anyway. They'd claim credit, but you'd get an easier life.

Before I could go back into the tower, I decided I needed a little me time to process, so I sat and thought back on everything that had happened lately. I realized I was running from fire to fire, constantly reacting, and never really getting ahead of things. That needed to change.

No, dammit; I need to change…

I had been sitting for maybe twenty minutes when a golem arrived with a single bag of supplies and a tiny, rusted knife with a loose sheath. It was perfect, and I felt myself grinning from ear to ear as I thanked it automatically and took the bag, joining Bob and Oracle where they watched over Lorek and his two friends.

"Good news, assholes!" I called out as I got close to them, lifting the bag higher to make sure they saw it. I came to a stop and threw the bag at Lorek, hitting him in the face and knocking him back a few steps.

It might have been petty, but fuck it, I was sometimes, and he was an ass who deserved it.

"Wha—…what is this?!" he spluttered, shoving the bag at one of his companions, who took it and peered inside cautiously.

"It's your supplies, as promised. One bag of supplies, one weapon," I said, and I held up the little dagger, giving it a little shake from side to side. Once I was sure I had their full attention, I threw the dagger underhand to the second man, who caught it and checked it over.

"You said supplies for all of us! And weapons!" Lorek spat at me, clearly working his way up to a full tirade. "This proves you're no noble, you—"

"I promised *a* bag of supplies, and *a* weapon. Not my fault you weren't paying attention, you little bitch. Now, I also promised I'd let you go home. Guess what you missed me leaving out from that promise?" I asked, smiling thinly at them. Pissy-Pants looked at his friend then at Lorek before gaping at the forest behind them. I could see the light dawning in his eyes, even as I ignored Lorek's complaints.

"Looks like we have a winner!" I said with a wide grin. "For the slower amongst you, I never said I'd help you get anywhere, just that I'd let *you* return home. Judging from the direction your airship came from, that'd be that way," I said, pointing south by southeast. "However, if the airship banked at all, rather than going straight, well, I hope you enjoy your chance to get back to nature, lads!"

I turned to Bob and a glowering Oracle; she'd gone back to watching them after tearing me a new asshole and had been looking forward to this.

"Bob, Oracle, these dicks are not welcome in my lands. Anywhere in my lands. If you catch them within one mile of this tower, or anywhere sworn to me, I want you to kill them and do it fucking slowly. They get thirty minutes' head start, then feel free to hunt them."

I started to turn away, intending to walk back towards the tower, when I sensed more than saw Lorek move. He was a scrawny little fucker, and he telegraphed the punch so blatantly, it might as well have been a love letter sent in the post. I turned back, and held my hand up to Bob and Oracle, letting the punch land.

He hit my right cheekbone and glanced off, making him grimace and cradle his hand. I blinked at the pathetic blow and leaned toward him, whispering loud enough for them all to hear.

"You want to try that again, little man?" The unchecked rage built again, its coldness threatening to overwhelm me as I waited and the stupid bastard took me at my word.

He punched me in the stomach. I felt it, but it was a weak punch. He had no training and little muscle behind it, and I took it easily enough, hiding the small amount of pain it gave me as I grinned at him.

"That's strike two…want to go for the third and final one?" I growled at him, my tight smile fearful to behold.

He took a step back, Pissy-Pants reaching out to his former lord and trying to reason with him.

"Get off me! Remember your place, fool!" he snarled, glimpsing the sheathed knife held by his other companion.

He shoved Pissy-Pants aside and grabbed the knife free, twisting around to stab at my face left-handed in what he probably thought was a lethal strike. It wasn't.

After fighting my trainers and then the battles of the last few days, it was just pathetic on every level.

I used a tan-sau block, as I'd been taught seemingly so long ago, deflecting the strike to the side before twisting my hand around in a fluid motion. I grabbed his wrist and pulled, twisting at the same time, extending his arm out into a full lock, overextending the elbow, and forcing the little bastard into immobility as I grabbed his throat with my other hand in a vise-like grip and squeezed.

"Let me make this very clear," I whispered into his ear, pulling him in close. "I could have killed all of you at any time, and I really, *really* fucking wanted to. I wanted to show the rest of your villagers what a whining little bitch you are.

"I wanted to make you piss yourself and beg for mercy in front of them, but I couldn't. I'm trying to be a better man. I'm going to be the lord they deserve, not the man I could be…but you?" I grinned at him though he couldn't see me, close as I was.

"You just gave me a perfect excuse to give you a little present to remember me by. Enjoy your walk, dickbag." With that, I released his throat and moved back, putting my right hand on his shoulder, and stamping my left foot into the back of his left leg, driving him down onto his knees in the dirt. I maintained my grip on his wrist, keeping his elbow extended.

As I planted my foot firmly, I drew back my right knee and brought it up as hard and fast as I could, driving it into the outside of his locked elbow while yanking down, shattering the joint. It was a cruel move, one I'd been warned about when I'd been trained.

It'd get you jail time back in the UK, as it counted as "grievous bodily harm." After all, if you could put someone in the position to do that, you clearly had them restrained already…but I'd trained with some people who believed in the American tactic of shock and awe. Do that to someone in a fight, and nobody else wanted to mess with you again. Ever.

It proved its efficacy now, as Reeve Lorek screamed in pain, the brightly colored elbow of his tunic spattered with blood from the bone shards that had punched through his skin. It was clear that the way his arm now bent was unnatural as hell.

Pissy-Pants went green, backing up and covering his mouth with one hand. The other man looked terrified but was clutching the bag to his chest and looking around from me to Oracle, to Bob, to the forest.

"I suggest you grab your friend and get him off my property," I snarled at the pair, giving them a tight grin. "Once he's off my land, I think the scent of blood is going to draw some…unwanted…attention, don't you? I'd be reconsidering my options if I were stuck with him as a traveling companion. Now, fuck off. Twenty-eight minutes and counting until Bob and Oracle come to play."

I shoved Lorek backward to fall sprawling before the pair and turned around to walk back into the tower, ignoring their panicked attempts to get their little lord up and running.

I brought up the notifications I'd been ignoring on my way back to my command center, trying to bring my heart rate down and forcing myself to remember I was trying to be a better man these days.

Congratulations!

You have killed the following:

- 7x Inexperienced Soldiers of various levels for a total of 940xp
- 1x Guard, level 11 for 220xp
- 2x Elite Guards of various levels for a total of 1200xp
- 1x Elite Mage, level 19 for a total of 750xp

As leader, you receive a portion of the experience earned by troops when they fight under your command:

- 5x Inexperienced Soldiers of various levels for a total of 720xp
- 6x Warship Sailors of various levels for a total of 840xp
- 1x Warship Captain, level 12 for a total of 400xp
- 2x Warship Elite Guards of various levels for a total of 840xp

Progress to level 14 stands at 107,840/120,000

I also dismissed a significant number that mentioned my crippling injuries, broken bones, and status debuffs, grimacing as I saw the amount of damage I'd managed to accumulate over the course of the battle. The next prompt, however was quite interesting.

Congratulations!

You have led your citizens to battle for the first time, overcoming a more numerous, more skilled, and more highly-trained opposing force. As such, you have earned a Title!

Strategos: Level I
You may choose a bonus for your forces. This bonus will stack with others and will grow as you grow in experience.

Attack: All troops led by a level 1 Strategos gain a 5% boost to attack damage; this boost extends to all troops within a 20-ft radius of the Strategos.

Defense: All troops led by a level 1 Strategos gain a 5% boost to damage resistance; this boost extends to all troops within a 20-ft radius of the Strategos and must be assigned as Physical, Magical, or Mental at time of selection.

I slowed as I entered the tower itself, rereading the choices and considering the benefits. Five percent wasn't really a great deal, especially not when considering the possible fights to come, what with having declared war on a city state and all that, but still.

I pondered the options further as I wandered up the stairs, but the choice was clear, really. I selected *defense*, then *magical* before dismissing the prompt and moving onto the next.

Congratulations!

You have used your home to your advantage, overcoming a more numerous, more skilled, and more highly-trained opposing force.

As such, you have earned a Title!

Fortifier: Level I
You may choose a bonus for your forces. This bonus will stack with others and will grow as you grow in experience.

Attack: All weapon emplacements personally commanded or designed by you will do 5% more damage to enemy targets.

Defense: All defensive constructions will gain 5% integrity if you were directly involved in their construction, design, or use.

Attacking might be better, but we were always going to be the underdogs in this fight. With that in mind, I knew I'd have a better chance if I made defensive positions and let them attack us. Armor would provide physical defense readily enough, but magical damage could be anything. Defending against that was my current priority. Besides, if I'd had that bonus yesterday, some of our dead might have survived long enough to be healed.

This prompt, again, wasn't a hard choice. While five percent might make a little difference in damage to an enemy, the same amount added to the tower integrity was a huge difference, especially when a structure had the potential for tens of thousands of hit points. I immediately chose the defense option, relieved it wasn't just against one type of attack this time. Before the notification even fully disappeared, I was already lost in thought over how to increase that title further; if I could boost it to provide fifty percent in the future somehow…

I blinked, dismissing the fantasy, and opened my last notification.

Congratulations!

**Through hard work and perseverance,
you have increased your stats by the following:**

Agility +2

Constitution +3

Dexterity +2

Endurance +2

Intelligence +2

Strength +1

Continue to train and learn to increase this further…

I cheered up a lot from reading that last notification as I entered my little command center, finding Cai, Oren, and Barrett sitting on the floor on one side of the room, conversing idly. They cut off and jumped to their feet when I appeared, causing me to wave to them in irritation.

"It's all right, guys. Relax." I scanned the space, seeing that there were still only a couple of chairs in the room. Rather than one of the three sit in my designated seat, they'd all elected to sit on the floor instead.

It spoke well to me of Oren that, despite the fact that he'd been Barrett's captain until recently, and still kinda was, he hadn't just let him sit on the floor and relaxed in his own chair.

Then again, I looked more closely at the chairs that were available, and "relax" really wasn't in the cards with them. They were rickety, exceedingly old, and the cushioning had died a long time ago.

"Damn." I grunted as I straightened up. "We really need to add some decent chairs to this place."

"Aye, laddie, along wi' everythin' else!" Oren replied, gesturing around the small room.

It was bare beyond the chairs and the creation table, and I grimaced. He had a point.

"Well, we can sort that out soon, hopefully." I walked over to the table and brought up the liquid silver display to show the tower in its entirety. The other three joined me and stood watching as the tower rendered before our eyes.

"So, Barrett," I said, "I sent up a group to you to begin training as hunters. I realized that we hadn't really discussed this properly yet, not sober anyway, or the roles for each of you."

Barrett nodded and quickly spoke up.

"Yes, Lord Jax, I gave them some of the basic gear we took from the warship and set them to shadowing our soldiers. Lydia was guiding them all to start the morning workout as you taught us. I figured I'd get more information from you here and then give them some better direction after that."

I winced at the thought of the grueling morning workout regime I'd shown those that wanted to be soldiers. It was one that the Baron's men had taught me. When I'd first started, it had left me shaking and vomiting most days, until I acclimatized. Add to that, we were all drinking and partying last night? *Damn...cleanup on aisle three...*

"Well done, Barrett. Sorry about the lack of discussion. As you all know, this is kinda new to me. So, what we're going to do is split the tower responsibilities up. I can't keep on top of everything, and I'm going to need all three of you to help me with that.

"As of now...Barrett, you're in charge of the soldiers and the hunters, at least for a while. Cai, you're going to be helping me get the tower itself up and running properly and look after our people's needs. Oren, you get to be a captain still; you're getting command of the warship!"

Oren immediately broke into a huge smile, punching Barrett in the hip and getting a clip across the back of the head in return. Cai simply smiled his faint smile and inclined his head once.

"What this will mean, really, is that you all get to argue over who got the most thankless job, as it's not going to be the party you thought it was; you especially, Oren!

"We're going to be getting the ship sorted as quickly as we can. I mean in the air today, if at all possible, so we need to go through the ship's old crew and see if any of them are okay, or if they're all assholes.

"We also need to win the ship's engineers around to joining us, preferably by talking, but if not, with bribery or whatever else we need to use, in order to get them working on the ship. Once it's air-worthy, space-worthy…what do you call it?" I asked Oren, my train of thought momentarily derailed.

"Flyin', laddie; we call it flyin' or able to fly," Oren said, his gravelly voice laced with amusement.

"Well, it's feckin 'flight-worthy' from now on," I shot back at him, getting a wink from Cai as Barrett and Oren grinned at me.

"So, once it's *flight-worthy,* we will be taking a quick trip out to find your mate Decin to see if we can recruit him. This is where it gets a bit harder, though, as we can't have him returning to Himnel if he's not willing to swear to me, and that includes his crew.

"If we can convince him to join us, help us get things sorted here, and help defend the tower, that'll be great. If not, well, we might have to take measures to make sure he doesn't return to help Barabarattas. I'd prefer that be by grounding or taking his ship and making them walk back. But if it means shooting him down, then so be it. I'm sorry." I clapped a hand on Oren's shoulder and made sure he knew it wasn't my preferred choice.

"After we've got him taken care of, one way or the other, we need to head to the village that the ship raided before coming here, to see if we can help people and convince them to join us. If they won't, that's fine; it's their choice, as they're not in command of anything that's a threat to us, or—hopefully—close enough to the cities to spread any word.

"With luck, they'll join us, though, and we can take some of the villagers that have sworn with us to help convince them. Also, we need to empty the ship as much as possible, in case they want to bring furniture or larger amounts of goods. God knows we need it." I met Oren's eyes, getting a sigh from him, but he nodded his understanding at the same time.

"Aye, laddie, that do make sense. Decin do be a prick at times, but he does no' love Himnel or Barabarattas. He be doin' this fer his family, same as I were."

"Well, hopefully he'll be amenable to joining us, then. We'll be trying to get your families out of Himnel as soon as we can, after all." I turned my attention to Cai, and he straightened as I did.

"Cai, I want you to start organizing the people. Their first task is to help clear and fix the ship up as quickly as possible, then start turning the tower into a home. I want a list of recommendations from you and Isabella as soon as possible, with skills and abilities of our new people. We need to organize the farmers and get the food sorted out and get cooks to take charge of the food and arranging meals.

"We've all just mucked about in the last few days because we've had no time to do anything else. Once we have a team to begin getting a kitchen in order, then we'll need to prioritize bedrooms and comfortable sleeping arrangements. God knows our morale will take a dip fast enough if we don't take care of that soon."

Cai nodded once and spoke up quickly.

"The kitchen is being taken care of already. Two of my fellow ex-slaves were skilled kitchen assistants until they fell afoul of an employer. They've been clearing out a large room on the twentieth floor; it's close enough to the gardens on the sixteenth and twenty-third floors that it's not too hard to transport food to, and it's low enough in the tower that its manageable to get meat up if the hunting parties are successful."

He coughed and looked a little embarrassed. "As to Isabella and the skills of the villagers, well, I shall look into that. I haven't really had the chance to talk to her yet."

Oren grinned at him and elbowed him in the thigh hard enough to stagger him.

"Really? Ye looked ta be talkin' plenty afore." The dwarf would be in serious danger of losing the top half of his head if his grin grew any wider, so I stepped in to move the conversation along quickly, trying to hide my smile at Cai's discomfort.

"Well, there's a baker called Krillek in the group that just joined us from the villagers, so there's a bonus as well. Barrett, you are gonna absolutely hate me, but hell, I'll be right there with you at least some of the time. I want you to take our soldiers and make them into two teams of fighters.

"I also want the hunters training at first with the fighters, as I want them able to fight, so they can look after themselves. Then they're going to learn to hunt to feed us all. The fighters are going to be in two teams because one will be here to defend the people at any time. The other, well, they're going to be on the ship with me, or roaming the wilderness with the hunters.

"I'll be joining you each morning for the workout, whenever my other duties permit. The most important person on this side of things will be you. I need you to be the strongest, the fastest, and the meanest. Take some time and tell me what you need; if you need skills, tell me. I'll sort it out." With that, I turned back to the other two and had to bite back a smile at seeing them both straighten to attention.

"That goes for you both, as well. If you're going to be my advisors, helping me to keep everyone safe, they need to respect you. They need to know that you are where you are for a reason, as eventually more will join us that don't have personal experience of you and your shared past here. If you need skills or magic, tell me. We have enough, and while I don't want to waste it needlessly, I'd rather use it than not. Lastly, we need a healer; a real one, not just my magic and Oracle's.

"I want a dedicated healer for the tower, and they need to be someone we can power-level, as I have a personal need for them to be strong as soon as possible."

"Power-level?" Cai asked.

I grimaced at realizing I'd not even thought about the concept being alien to them.

"It's a phrase from my home; it means to push them up the ranks fast, such as taking them with us when we go to kill things and sharing the experience gains with them, that kind of thing."

"Ah! We have the concept here, though it's usually something that guards do for the nobles or richer people. I just hadn't heard it put that way before," said Cai.

"Okay then, any questions?" I asked, and Barrett raised a hand hesitantly. "Seriously, dude," I said, shaking my head. "Just speak. No need for that crap when it's just us."

"Okay, Lord J—"

"And none of that! Just Jax, unless there's a good reason to use more!"

"Okay…Jax…what about gear for the fighters and hunters? And you said soldiers one minute, then fighters the next, so which do you want? You can't have both. I served as guard sergeant before I signed on with Oren. It was a long time ago, but I remember enough. People either fight as a unit, or as an individual, with different strengths and weaknesses."

"Well, we're going to teach them differently. Everyone gets the same basic training; that's why they'll be soldiers. They'll learn to fight the same, then they get to specialize. Each team will have one dedicated healer, a tank, and damage dealers; they'll need both a ranged and a melee fighter. Last of all, we're going to train those that have the aptitude to do magic as well, but keep that quiet, as I haven't figured out all the details yet." I grimaced, thinking about how we could teach everyone magic. I made a mental note to bring it up with Oracle later.

"We've got plenty of weapons and other equipment, and the soldiers' armor, but most of the gear from the armory upstairs is junk. Literally. The metal was safe from the weather, and it'd been treated and oiled, but anything that isn't metal is useless. The leather has either rotted away, or it's so hard, it might as well be sharpened and used as a weapon itself now." Barrett warned me, making me grunt in annoyance.

"Well, you have anyone that likes working with that kind of stuff?" I asked, getting irritated. Always, there were more details. I wanted to do something, not sit around talking.

"Aye, there be Iken. He loves to tinker wi' stuff, but we need 'im on the ship! Especially if you're sayin' Barrett no be flyin' wi' me goin' forward!" Oren spoke up, looking agitated as he gestured at his former first mate.

"Iken? And no, while you'll occasionally fly together, of which I've no doubt, Barrett is now in charge of the security side of things for the tower," I said, shaking my head regretfully.

"He's the big, furry engineer, Jax. You've met him a few times, but he doesn't really speak unless you speak to him first. He's a bit...shy," Barrett said, looking uncomfortable.

"The big lad? The ginger Ewok-looking dude? Damn."

"I don't know about 'ee-wok,' but yes, the big ginger one that doesn't fight. He's a krill. His people survive primarily on nuts and berries. He's basically eating his way through the gardens at the minute. Never seen the big bugger as happy as he's been the last few days, despite the fights."

"And he's needed on the ship?" I asked Oren directly.

"Aye, laddie, ya canna take 'im! I need 'im; well, iff'n ya want the ship ta run, anyway!" Oren said, folding his arms across his barrel chest.

"Hmmm, okay. Well, we will see...For now, he's yours. Maybe see if we can recruit from the engineers or existing ship's crew. Make that a priority, please, guys. Get through them, sort out who can be trusted and arrange for them to take the Oath this afternoon. The rest, we need to get rid of, so I'm going to have a think on that. We don't have the setup, manpower, or any damn desire to have prisoners long term."

"What will ye do?" Oren asked.

I shrugged, sitting back in my chair.

"I'm not sure. Either give them some basic supplies, and we can drop them off somewhere and point them in the right direction for the cities, or maybe something a bit more permanent. I honestly don't know. I'd much rather not hurt people if I don't have to, and they did surrender, at least some of them. As I say, I'll think about it," I said, and the three of them took the hint, saluting with a fist to their chests and heading out of the room.

I sat for a long minute after they left, just thinking. I knew what I had to do, but that didn't make it any more fun.

I took a deep breath, straightened up, and let it out in a long sigh, squaring my shoulders as I put my hand on the creation table, calling out in my mind to all three of the tower's wisps.

It didn't take long for them all to respond. It felt strange as both Heph and Seneschal joined my mind. Oracle was always there, to some degree, but the other two dropping in was weird.

It felt like a mixture of sensing someone coming up behind you, making the hairs on the back of your neck stand up before you consciously knew they were there, and being on a video call when someone joined it without activating their own camera, with that weird…echo…of another line joining your own.

Oracle was coming closer. I could feel her approach, so I didn't start yet, instead relaxing as we chatted idly for a few minutes. Heph began telling me about a small child who had braved the dark at the bottom of the tower, stumbling around until he sent a golem servitor to collect him and take him out.

I grinned as Seneschal brought up a representation of the boy on the table. I knew exactly who it was, even before the visual reference had solidified. Caron. There were only maybe a dozen kids in total in the tower, at the minute, anyway, but Caron had stood up to me on the first day. He was tiny, ragged, and, at the time, a slave. Half my size, and with me covered in blood and viscera after slaughtering his former captors, he'd still stood up to me to protect his friend, a girl called Kayt.

The kid had spunk, I'd give him that, and now he was off exploring the tower on his own? Picking the darkest section of the entire place to go wandering? He either had a bright future as an adventurer ahead of him, or a truly short one as a meal for something.

I liked him.

"We're here!" called a voice from the doorway, and Oracle rode in on Bob's head. The massive skeletal minion clattered and shook like a box full of maracas as he walked, and I sighed, looking him over. We'd been in such a rush yesterday, making sure that everyone was okay and safe, that I'd not had time to fix Bob yet.

I got up and walked to him, putting one hand on his shoulder in apology, and looking into the fire that burned steadily in his eye sockets.

"I'm sorry, Bob," I said, shaking my head, "I should have helped you earlier. Once we're done here, we'll fix you, okay?"

Bob just stared at me stoically, and I turned back to Oracle, frowning.

"I know I asked you to come up when you were done, but what about that prick, Lorek? I thought you'd be a while playing with him yet?" I said.

"I decided that he'd learned his lesson, or will have soon enough. They were falling over every root and branch out there as they disappeared, and unless you actually want them dead, they're never going to get out of range before the time runs out. I let them go once they were out of sight. I don't think they're going to stick together long out there; such a shame!" she said, grinning darkly.

"I found the golem sealing up the ground floor and gave it an order to kill them if they came back; otherwise, I just let them run on." I couldn't help but grin at that mental image and resumed my seat, even as Oracle landed on the side of the creation table, blurring, and then growing to her full-size form.

She stood a little under five and a half feet tall today, with her hair blonde, a faint golden tan to her skin, and green eyes. She was slim, but very busty, with enormous, beautiful wings that slowly fluttered as though caught in a slight breeze.

She was also wearing a bikini so tiny, it was physically impossible. There was no way straps so slender could hold that kind of pressure; it would have snapped when she tried to put it on. Oracle coughed, staring at me when I guiltily met her eyes, and grinned like the crazy bugger she was.

Oracle was a wisp, but she was also bonded to me, and had decided, after watching people long ago, that she really wanted to try sex out. She'd gone through my mind when I'd met her, picking up on certain…movies…and memories, and now took great delight in shifting her shape to the most sexually attractive forms I could imagine, while casually dissolving and reforming her outfits for maximum effect.

I had only recently found out that she could become human-sized, rather than remaining a foot tall, and I was still a bit weirded out by it all. On one hand, she was literally every straight male fantasy rolled into one body; on the other, she was childlike in her innocence, bonded to serve me, and it just felt wrong to take advantage of that.

Years of being conditioned by the western world into not looking—*well, not too overtly, anyway*—and feeling embarrassment if you were caught looking warred with Oracle's blatant offer. If I gave in, that'd be it, so for now, until I could sort out my feelings for her, I was keeping my distance.

One of the few rules I'd managed to stick to over the years was "don't shit where you eat," and that translated into never having sex with someone you had to see every day, unless you were damn sure about them. I was going to behave myself…sort of, anyway. My damn traitorous eyes were roaming every chance they got, and as to other parts of my anatomy…*down, boy!*

I shook myself and refocused on the table before me, seeing Oracle's clothes shimmer and disappear, reforming slowly into a new outfit, and I focused with laser-like precision to keep from looking.

"Okay, then," I said, a roughness to my voice that I tried to cough away. "We need a plan here. I'm getting Cai, Oren, and Barrett to help me, with Cai focusing on people and organization, Oren on the ship, and Barrett on our security, and for now our hunters. I need some information on the tower now.

"I know we've talked about it before, and how it'd take years to repair it all. That's fine for things we don't need, but we need it to be safe, secure, and actually stay upright through storms and shit. What can you give me?"

"Well, the tower is primarily my responsibility, Jax," Seneschal said, appearing to grow from the liquid silver of the table until he stood straight, and a half-dozen inches tall. Heph appeared next to him, short, barrel-chested, and giving an impression of solidity, despite his also diminutive size.

"Structurally, we have two choices. I can go floor by floor repairing to the minimum realistically acceptable level, then moving on. This would result in more livable areas being available quicker. The second choice, and this is the one I favor, is that I work on the most damaged and dangerous areas first, spreading out the work across the entire structure. This means you will see less effect day-to-day, but there is a significantly reduced chance of the entire tower falling over in a high wind."

"Okay, 'collapsing tower' is definitely on my list of things to avoid," I stated firmly. "That said, we don't need a great deal, Seneschal. How about a hybrid approach? You concentrate, say ninety percent on the overall structure, then put ten percent of your available mana into making the few floors we need more usable?"

"This is your choice, of course. Simply be aware that, even with one hundred percent of the mana being invested, I cannot guarantee the tower's survival. I do not recommend resources be used elsewhere, but you are the master. I will obey."

"Look, Seneschal, I understand this, but had I not killed that thing and reawakened you all, the tower would have collapsed anyway. We need to secure the walls and ground floor at a minimum. I want you to divert five percent to the ground floor, get the walls and doors back up and safe," I said, determined to get on with things. "The other five percent I want you to use on the floor with the armory, where the ship is parked; it's what, the twenty-third?"

"Twenty-sixth," Oracle threw in lightly, smiling at me.

"Great, okay, the twenty-sixth floor. I want that floor repaired as far as possible. Not the general rooms inside, unless they need to be for structural reasons; just the outer walls, the parade ground or whatever it was, the armory, and the interior cleared out as much as possible. I want to eventually be able to use that floor for more ships, once we have them. For now, we just need some spaces cleared so that the ship, and possibly Decin's as well, can fly inside safely. I want the parade ground converted into a proper landing area for the ship, reinforced and able to hold its weight and others. Once that's done, I want the twentieth floor sorted out.

"I know Cai is organizing the kitchens on that floor, and from what I remember, it was a couple of big rooms, with a few dozen or so smaller ones. Is that right?"

Seneschal nodded.

"Good! I want that floor sorted out, walls, roof, whatever other structural needs first, then the entire floor. Convert the larger areas that aren't being used to eat or prepare food into barracks for now; if people have somewhere safe to sleep, it'll help a lot."

"And the smaller rooms, too," Oracle said quickly. "They'll need to be sorted out as quickly as possible, since it won't look right for the people to see you just sleeping among them."

"Hell, I'm fine with sleeping there; why not?" I said, my train of thought momentarily derailed.

"Jax, these people have to look at you as their lord, not the guy that's snoring and farting the loudest," Oracle said, closing her eyes and shaking her head slowly. "Please just trust me on this. The lord of the tower and his closest advisors need separate quarters."

I blinked and thought about arguing but considered how Oracle usually teased me. She was right; people didn't need to see that. I'd take a room.

"Okay, then, but we get the safety issues sorted first. How long will all that take, Seneschal?" I asked, turning back to the small figure clad in silvery armor, his cloak rippling in a nonexistent breeze. He stood there for a long moment, considering before finally responding.

"After reviewing the floors, I'd estimate nine days to secure and repair the twenty-sixth, four days to work on the twentieth, and forty-seven days to repair and secure the ground floor."

"Fuck, man, that's insane! Okay, give me options here; what can we do to fix that? Make it faster or whatever?" I asked, sitting back in the chair and tugging on my beard, disappointed.

"There are three ways we could speed this up: first, we create more golems and assign them to the task. Second, we secure more oath-bound members of the community, since they can assist in repairs, and we can grant certain skillbooks and memories to increase production. Lastly, we could seek out manastones."

"I've heard manastones mentioned before. What are they?" I asked, sitting forward quickly as a thought occurred to me. "I'm sure Oren has some on the ship; he said something about them being a fuel source?"

"That's correct. There is a simple explanation, or a more complicated one that includes the formation of geodes, interactions of mana, and physics—"

"Simple! I like the simple explanation!" I said quickly, shaking my head in negation. "I totally don't want the goddamn complicated one!"

"Very well," Seneschal said, and I was damn sure there was amusement in his voice. "Manastones are formed from crystals that are found in areas of high mana concentration. Essentially, certain naturally forming crystals store mana as they develop. They can then be harvested, *very* carefully, and used to power devices or particularly powerful spells, or they can be created by someone with the right skills, but that would require the mana in the first place."

"Okay, so we go find some of this first kind, and boom, you can use them to speed up the repair of the tower, right?" I said, getting excited.

"Ha! Aye, ye jus' tell 'im how much you be needin,' an' how expensive they be!" Heph interrupted, instantly dropping my mood.

"Crap. Okay, Seneschal, give me the bad news." I sighed glumly.

"They are both rare and expensive, Jax, or they were, in our time. If they're being used to power ships now, they may be cheaper, but they are more likely to have climbed in price. Also, to repair the entire tower fully would take hundreds, possibly thousands, depending on their size and potency."

"Well, fuck me sideways, that's unlikely to help, then!" I muttered, sitting back with a thump.

"Possibly, but maybe not, Jax," Oracle said, and I regarded her questioningly. "You let me search your memories, and I've had time to think about things. After all, I don't need to sleep the way you do…"

"Go on," I said, shifting in my chair and watching her as she brushed her hair back and smiled winningly at me.

"Well, we're at war with Barabarattas, right?"

"Uh-huh?" I said, raising one eyebrow.

"We haven't got enough of a force to go toe to toe with him. Not yet, anyway, but he doesn't know that. He's at war already with Narkolt, so he can't dedicate too many ships to come for us yet. He's probably still thinking his warship is on its way, after what he said yesterday, right?"

I nodded, and she grinned at me.

"What's the saying you like, the one about being outnumbered?"

"That it's the ideal time to charge in and bite their cocks off?" I asked, confused.

"Oh…no, sorry, it was Tommy's saying! It's your memories, they're a bit…messy…sorry," she said, shaking her head.

"Oh…ah!" I said, grinning and nodded at her. "'It's guerilla time, motherfuckers'?" I suggested, missing the crazy fucker all over again.

"Exactly! They don't know how many of us there are, but they can't afford to send more ships until they're sure Narkolt won't attack."

"So, if we can get in there somehow, we can nick the manastones and give their guards a good kicking. Then if we pull back, we can probably gain the time we need to get ready properly!" I said, grinning evilly.

"Exactly!"

CHAPTER FIVE

Oracle and I sat there, staring at each other. It was madness. We didn't even have a fighting force yet. They'd barely survived the tower assault, and that was with me doing most of the work, but if we could pull it off?

"We could put his ships out of action; he wouldn't be able to launch an assault against us or Narkolt until he'd gotten more stones! We'd solve two problems at once. Hell, if we include getting people's families out of the city and to safety, it's three!" I said, my mind spinning with all the possibilities.

"We could buy the stores we need or steal them…we'd need wagons to get them out of the city," Oracle mused, her eyes alight. "We could use Oren and the crew's families to drive the wagons, but we'd need to convince them."

"Hmmm. Maybe steal the manastones, but hire the wagons and buy the supplies; don't want to make enemies of the ordinary people, after all."

"How much gold do we have?" Oracle asked me with a raised eyebrow.

"Okay…plan B. We steal everything," I said, shrugging. "It's a shame and all, but to hell with it. Our people are my priority. I need to speak to Jenae, though. She said she could give me quests and information. I need to check on Tommy. If he's nearby, I need to get to him, and bring him here."

I felt terrible that I wasn't already headed to wherever Tommy was, but I needed to make things here as safe as possible. Add to that, I knew Tommy. If anything had tried to hurt him, it'd be pulling back a bloody stump with no body attached.

And if he were dead…well, then I'd tear this realm apart until I found whatever had killed him, and I'd fuck it up, big style. I'd done my best to ignore that possibility until now, but sitting here, comfortable, more or less, and knowing that for all I knew he was bleeding out somewhere *right now*? I swallowed hard, shaking myself and sitting straighter. I needed to do this. He'd survived this long, I hoped; he could last a little longer.

I coughed, looking around as I noticed the sudden silence, and I forced a smile, remembering where we were up to.

"Okay, so my next task is to communicate with her, but before I do, Heph, we need lots of golems, buddy, fast as possible," I commented to the stocky figure that was idly kicking the quicksilver liquid mana about like a child in a puddle.

"Wha…? Oh, aye, right! I canna do it, laddie," he said, shrugging apologetically. I frowned, and he went on quickly. "I'm no sayin' no, I'm sayin' it canna be done! I would iff'n I could. We need more cores! We also need ta repair the chamber."

"We need to make a decision, basically," Seneschal interrupted smoothly. "We can build, say, three more servitor-class golems, then shut the genesis chamber down for a full repair and rebuild. That would take three golems a week to do, but the chamber would then be able to build class-two simple golems.

"Each class two could be given orders to repair, clean, build, or for the war golems, to stand watch and defend the tower. The golems wouldn't have to be directly commanded anymore, and that would in turn allow us to concentrate on the repairs themselves, which would speed that process up."

The caped Wisp gestured toward the tower as it slowly spiraled around on the creation table. "Alternatively, we could produce two servitors and a construction golem. The constructor could continue to speed up repairs to the tower, while the servitors could search for more golem cores and materials to continue making more. It would not have as big an increase in the repairs as the first choice, and we run the risk of the genesis chamber breaking down, but…"

"Could we have the golems make another genesis chamber?" I asked hopefully, but all three wisps were shaking their heads before I even finished speaking.

"Nay, laddie. To make somethin' o' tha' complexity needs at least advanced or level four golems. We could try, but I dinna recommend it. I'd expect it ta take at least a month o' work ta build, and that'd be wi' both Seneschal and meself doin' naught else. Even then, I dinna expect it'd work," Heph said, looking depressed as hell.

"And that'd be a month without any other golems being produced or controlled, or the tower getting fixed. Okay, I get it," I said, shaking my head. *It had been a nice dream, though…*I sat and pondered the options for a minute, before nodding and speaking to Heph.

"Okay, build the servitors. We need to get the place cleaned up and repaired as quickly as possible, I know that, but if I'm going to try and steal the manastones, I'm going to need you guys to be ready to use them. Build three servitors and…wait." I came to a halt suddenly as another thought came to mind. "Where the hell are we getting these cores from? I thought we used all the ones we had?"

"Aye, laddie, we did! Little Caron was fair pesterin' me fer a job, so I told him I needed cores. He found three in two days!" The dwarven-featured Wisp was obviously bursting with pride as he bounced up and down on the balls of his feet.

"Damn, he found three that fast?" I said, shaking my head in shock, "Okay, how long will it take you to make all three?"

"Well, wi' the repairs I've already done, should be all built in aboot ten hours, thereaboots, anyway!" Heph said, looking proud of himself.

"Damn, that's great! Okay, then let's build the three servitors, and while they're in process, get Caron to keep searching. If he can find more, build more. As soon as we run out of cores, though, shut the genesis chamber down and begin proper repairs and upgrades.

"Once you get three more servitors built, get them all working on the repairs as much as you can. Once the upgrades and repairs are finalized for the chamber, begin building one construction, then a servitor, and just keep repeating that pattern until I tell you different. But make only level two versions once the upgrade is complete."

"Aye, m'lord, it'll be done," said Heph, bowing his head then flowing down into the pool as he relaxed.

"I'll speak to Cai to determine what help he needs and begin directing those you have assigned to me. Thank you, Jax." With that, Seneschal followed Heph and disappeared, leaving both the room and my mind. I turned to Oracle and grinned.

"So, fancy going and raiding a city?" I asked her, getting a laugh in return.

"Of course! I always wanted to explore, after all! But you still need to speak to Jenae, so I'll take Bob up and get a few bodies arranged for his repairs, then chase Oren along!" She hopped off the table, leaned in, and planted a gentle kiss on my cheek before straightening up. "Just don't be too long!" she said, shrinking down to her normal size and flying to Bob.

Oracle landed on his shoulder, resting one arm across the polished and cracked bone of his skull and struck a pose, pointing toward the door dramatically.

"Off we go, Bob! Onward…to the ship!" Bob, of course, said nothing and simply turned around and set off, his compromised frame sounding like a collapsing bellows and shaking as he went. "We really need to get you fixed, you know, and maybe a cushion…" Oracle's voice faded into the distance as they began climbing the stairs.

"Okay, then; just you and me, I guess," I said aloud, then paused. "Actually, I have no idea how this works…hello? Jenae? Can you hear me?" I said, receiving only silence. "Okay, so I need to work on that."

I sat for a while, thinking. The last time we'd talked, I had been channeling mana to her, but I didn't have a quest to do that anymore. There had to have been a way people spoke to her without the quest in the past, so maybe that was it?

I drew in a deep breath, and then got down on one knee for good measure, with my right fist curled and my knuckles pressed flat to the ground, left fist pressed to my chest, and I closed my eyes.

I am trying to speak to a goddess, after all, and she has saved me once already; best to try to be respectful…

I searched inside of myself, feeling the mana channels that ran through me and visualizing them in my mind. I saw my body, kneeling there on the cold, pitted stone floor of the tower, and I concentrated on the feeling of using my magic.

Seeing in my mind's eye the way it flowed from me to form the components of the spells, I imagined it slowly gathering before me, a faint blue mist seeping from my skin, as I concentrated it into a ball of magical energy that pulsed and rippled.

I realized that the light in the room had changed, the soft silvery illumination of the creation table and the sunlight that streamed in through the window to my right slowly replaced with a steady blue glow.

I opened my eyes, finding it exactly as I'd visualized it: a gentle, glowing ball of mana that slowly bobbed and weaved before me. I focused on it and said one word.

"Jenae."

The ball of mana seemed to burst, but instead of the mana splashing or falling apart, it pulsed brightly, then vanished into motes, like embers rising from a campfire in the dead of night.

"Eternal? You called to me?"

I grinned as I straightened up, relief flooding through me. I'd done it!

"Hi, Jenae," I said, suddenly realizing that I really should have put some thought into what I was going to say, rather than whether I should kneel when calling to her. Dammit.

"Ha! You don't need to do that, Jax. We agreed that for now we're allies and will treat each other as such. Just speak to me, but remember who I am; I do appreciate the gesture of kneeling…"

59

"Well, don't get too used to it," I muttered before giving myself a shake and getting on with things. *She's a goddess, remember, fucknut.*

"Jenae…first, thanks for your help with the assault, and for helping to boost my experience with the quest. I really needed the extra stats in that fight!" I said, nodding my head as I tried to make sure I didn't think anything stupid…*blue elephant, blue…dammit!*

"You're welcome…? What is the blue elephant?"

"Dammit! Look, this is really freaking me out, with you being in my head, okay? I'm trying not to think anything inappropriate, especially considering you're a goddess, not just a woman in my brain, which is freaky enough. It's taken me this long to get used to Oracle! So…look, let's start again, okay?"

"Okay, Jax…well, you called to me. Well done on that, and thank you for the mana, but I assume you need something?"

"Yeah, I do, a few things, actually. First, and most importantly, Tommy. He's my brother, and he was sent here five years ago…do you know if he's alive? Can you tell me where he is?" I asked quickly. I'd almost chickened out, mainly because I didn't know what I'd do if he was dead.

"I can look for him, but I have truly little power to touch the world now, Jax. It could take weeks, or even months, to build up enough disposable mana to search this small section of the realm. Show him to me in your mind, and I will try to help you. I can promise no more, but you will owe me the mana, or a quest!"

I followed her instruction, visualizing my brother, thinking about what he'd looked like when I'd seen him last, his personality; hell, even the way he stank the place out when we'd been eating curry. I had no idea what would be helpful, so I just…threw it all at her, receiving a mental nod of acknowledgement.

"Totally fine with that! Please, just…see if you can find him! Thank you!" I said, nervous in a way I hadn't felt in years. "Also, you said I needed five Marks of Favor to gain my first star in the Constellation of Secrets. How can I earn those?"

"You earn my Marks of Favor by doing things I like. Complete quests for me, find hidden knowledge, dedicate shrines to me, and I will occasionally gift you them when you do things I am particularly proud of you for, or when you spread worship and knowledge of me in the realm."

"Worship, right. That brings up something else I've been thinking about. I had to give you a thousand mana to contact you, right? How do your priests and worshippers contact you or pray to you if they haven't got mana?"

"All creatures have mana within them. Most never learn to tap into it, but all have it. My priests were all able to use magic, as well as abilities I granted them. The common people could pray to me inside my temples or touch a sanctified symbol of mine; both methods would slowly drain their mana to me as they prayed.

"If I had required only mana users to pray to me, I would have been a much weaker god. After all, there are many thousands of sentient creatures who have not unlocked magic's secrets, for each one that has…"

"Wait; you mean if I had symbols that you sanctified, then people could pray to you now?"

"Of course. I was hoping you'd want to spread knowledge of me to your people; after all, what good is dedicating the tower to me if that's all you ever do? It'd take centuries before I could grow my reach again without prayers."

"You mean they could pray to you now? Just because they're inside the tower, and it's dedicated to you?" I asked, my mind racing with the possibilities.

"Yes, and I see what's in your mind. Here," Jenae said, amusement and excitement clear in her voice.

You have been offered a Quest!

My God is Better Than Your God

For every two worshippers you bring to Jenae's service, she will grant you one Mark of Favor. To qualify, a worshipper must donate at least ten mana per third day to Jenae.

Will you accept?

Yes/No

"What if they donate a lot more, like a hundred a day; that goes towards my totals? You said I needed…ten thousand mana and five Marks of Favor for each star in the first ring, right?" I asked, summoning the constellation of secrets with a thought.

As before, it started with a tiny spark flickering to life before me; then, like a fire burning through dry paper, it spread, blazing through the air until it reached a meter square, and I could see into the blackened section.

Inside, a single star glimmered and pulsed. Set in a ring around it were six more stars, all dead. A faint line ran from the first star to each of the others, then beyond them I could just see the lines disappearing into the darkness, hinting at the stars hidden beyond. Some had multiple lines, and I just wanted them all! The completionist gamer in me cried out at the sight, just as it had whenever I'd looked at it since Jenae had first given me access.

I knew the names of the first six stars, but not really what they'd give me, beyond the basic details Jenae had shared:

Enhanced Construction was at the top; then rolling clockwise, it went to Magical Research, Crafting, Governance, Personal Enhancement, and Exploration. Unlocking one of the stars would grant me options for dedicating my mana, and once they unlocked, I'd get help, advice, blueprints all of it from the goddess. I needed it all!

"If your people donate their mana to me, then yes, I'll count it against the mana cost of the Constellation of Secrets. If I didn't, it'd take you centuries to unlock even a fraction of a fraction. However, the tower's tithe to me does not count. That was already bargained for and accepted."

I'd been about to ask, so I shrugged and moved on.

"So, for each worshiper I bring you, you will grant me a Mark of Favor and their mana donations count towards my total, right?" I said, quickly tallying figures in my head.

*"No, every **two** worshippers, Jax. Good try, but I've had millennia to play these games; do you really want to play with me?"*

"Ah, no. Now that you mention it, I really don't…Okay, every two will grant me a mark. Done deal. Lastly, I'm going to start looking for a healer to help with my problem and with generally keeping things together; any ideas?"

"The person you need isn't amongst your people. I took the time to examine them since we last spoke. You could force a healer, give someone the memories and spellbooks, but they'd be average at best. You need to grow your population, that's all I can tell you. Now…I have things to do, but don't forget to spread the word about me!"

The sense of her presence disappeared, and I sat back in my chair to think. Lifting one boot, then the other, I rested them on the table, crossing my ankles and relaxing, my mind awhirl with the possibilities.

I could maybe get access to a star of the constellation in a couple of days if I asked my people to do it anyway. Even if only half were willing, I still had, what, forty people at present? There were the nineteen from the warship, then there were…I thought for a minute, and an old quest notification popped up:

Completed:

Congratulations, you have made progress on your Quest: A Place to Lay Your Head.

Wisps sworn fealty: 3/3
Locations cleared and secured: 5/5
SporeMother killed: 1/1
Guardians claimed: 11/10
Workers claimed: 27/10

Reward: The Great Tower is yours to command. Surrounding area will become aware of your rightful ownership. Access to supplies and facilities. 450,000xp.

I grinned and took the servitor golem from that total, giving me twenty-six, then I took the three dead from the list, taking me down to eight guardians.

I had a total of fifty-three people sworn to me. I hadn't realized I had so many living in the tower, and I still had another twenty or more that were locked up. If half the people sworn to me would worship Jenae and donate their mana to her each day just once, say, fifty mana per person—couldn't expect people to drain themselves and get a headache every day, after all—uh…

It took a minute, but I eventually worked out that half of fifty-three was twenty-six. That'd be thirteen Marks of Favor and thirteen hundred mana…*Crap.* That was access to the constellation of secrets in just under eight days for the first star. Once that was unlocked, I could start to earn benefits from it. *Double crap…*

Math was never my strong point, and I'd refused to let the kids swear fealty, so they weren't counted yet. It just felt wrong to force them into that when they really didn't have a choice.

There were five kids out of the original slave group, and four that we'd freed from the warship, so nine in total. I had no idea what to do with them; hell, I barely had a plan for the adults!

I knew that they were basically safe in the tower from attack, as Seneschal was watching over things. But still, the damn place was crumbling. They could fall down a hole or something, and it would all be my fault, I just knew it.

I got up and headed back up the tower. Ideally, I'd have everyone and everything centralized on the bottom floors, so we weren't constantly climbing, but it just wasn't safe. I'd have to just get my head around the damn climb for now.

It took about an hour to get to the twenty-sixth floor, and as I approached it, I could hear a lot of noises filtering down to the stairs below: shouts, laughter, clattering and banging, and a final crash of falling stone, followed by a cheer that stopped my sudden panic over a collapse just as it began.

I set off jogging the last bit, anyway, coming out onto the floor to find it abuzz with people. Almost the entire contingent of the tower was there; Barrett stood off to the right, directing his security force and the wannabe hunters. He had them picking up random rocks and debris, running to the edge of the balcony, and chucking them as far out as they could, dropping to do five pushups, then running back inside. I caught his eye and he grinned, jogging over to meet me.

"What do you think? I took what you said about your own training, and thought, 'why not make them useful at the same time?'" I nodded to him, thinking back to the interval training I'd endured, and as much as I'd damn well hated it, it was bloody effective.

"How are they coming along? Do you need anything?" I asked him, and he shook his head.

"For now, it's best they have the bare minimum. I have armor we can mostly fix up from the ship and yesterday's fight, and a load of melee weapons. We'll need some bows for the hunters; we've only got four, and a couple dozen arrows, but no sense wasting them yet."

"Best to teach them to work together first," I agreed, nodding. "I don't know if you've seen Oracle yet, but..."

"You've got some batshit-crazy plan?" Barrett asked, chuckling. "I saw her come up a few minutes before you. She had a quick word with Oren, and he went stomping off swearing. Looks like it's gonna be bad."

"You could say that," I said, drawing him off to the side. "Look, it's a bit of a mad plan, maybe, but it gives us what we need—time—and it'll hurt Barabarattas.

"Plus, we might be able to get some of the crew's families back here, *if* I can pull it off...You like the sound of it so far?" I asked and got a shark-like grin in return.

"Jax, my sister is all I have left. She's stuck in that shithole of a city, probably thinking I'm dead, especially if I don't get back soon. I'll do anything that gets her somewhere safe and feeds her and her bairn." He raised one eyebrow as he looked at me. "Judging from Oren's reaction, it's not something I'm gonna want to hear, so enough sugar-coating. What is it?"

"We're going to raid Barabarattas's stockpile of manastones and steal them all, and as much gear, food, and materials for the tower as we can. I'm going to need some help to pull it off; who do we know who's still in the city?" I asked with an apologetic grin.

"Our families," Barrett said in a flat tone, frowning at me. "Look, I'm all for getting them out. Hitting that bastard of a lord where it hurts? Yeah, I'm in for that any day, but you have to understand, most of our families are working around the clock...and the guards watch them.

"They're leverage over us; you understand? Either they're at work, or they're flat-out exhausted. If you turn up, a total stranger, and try to get them to help you, it won't happen. It'd take the entire crew days to gather up their families alone, never mind sneaking them out, and that's people they know and trust. Unless you think we've got months to hide in the city in order to try to get things planned out, it'll never work."

"I'm planning on a few days, and that's it. We can't risk more than that. They'll be expecting this ship back soon, after all." I rubbed my chin, disappointment burning through me.

This was the way to do it; I knew it, felt it balls to bones. I knew it was never going to be easy, but…

"How many people are we talking?" I asked, having just assumed until now that the families would be small, two to four members, like I'd known back home.

"Well, I just have my sister and her lad, since her husband died years back. Oren's got two kids, a wife, and his father. Most of the crew have wives or husbands and kiddies, some parents and brothers and sisters. At least fifty? Probably not more than a hundred or so, maybe two when you think of friends, and more if you want to try to recruit any of the ship's crew up there," he said, pausing as he took in the look on my face. "What's wrong?"

"I…okay, we can work with that," I said, forcing myself to smile, my mind awhirl as I tried to figure out what to do. I'd had it in my head that I'd have about twenty to thirty extra people, maybe forty at the most. Just considering that, I needed to have a proper plan in place.

A hundred or more would leave the ship ram-packed, with no room for cargo, but if we got half the crew or less, the rest would soon be swept up by Barabarattas's watchers when the others vanished, along with his manastones. Feck.

"Look, I'm not saying we can't do it, Jax, just that it's going to take some work. I need to get back to my people. Go talk to Oren; he's had some time to think about it now. And Oracle is still buzzing around a like a glow bug on crack. She obviously still thinks it can be done."

"Well, here's hoping. Oh, and Barrett, I need you to get everyone together for me. There's a group of farmers on the tenth floor, in the balcony gardens, I think. Everyone else seems to be here, but if you could make sure? And get them here as soon as possible, please; I need to speak to everyone in, say, an hour or so?" Barrett nodded and grinned devilishly.

"Looks like my lads and lasses get to do some running, then!"

I nodded to him, and he saluted, jogging back to shout at someone who was taking a break in between pushups. "What are you doin', maggot! Get your lazy arse up *right now* and…"

I tuned his irate screaming out as I headed toward the ship. He was so much like a drill sergeant I'd had in basic, it was scary. It was also reassuring, though. As much as officers were the head of the army, sergeants were always the heart.

CHAPTER SIX

By the time I reached Oren, who stood on the deck of the warship, I had a smile back on my face, determination filling me again. There was a way to do this, I just *knew* it. I just had to find it.

"Aye, laddie, I bin' hearin' all about yer latest madness!" he said as I reached him, looking up at me and nodding in respect. "As usual, ye dinna do things by half!"

I grinned right back at him.

"You know me, Oren! Gotta up the game, after all. What do you think of my plan?"

"Well, the way Oracle explained it ta me, it willna work," he said bluntly, then shook his head. "I wish it would, ye ken? But the first thing tha guard will do when we land is search tha ship. We canna just hide ye aboard."

"Dammit!" I cursed. "I thought, I don't know, that you'd have a little stash somewhere, a smuggler's compartment or something." I said, thinking back to a movie I'd loved as a kid.

"Weeeeeell…" Oren said, drawing the word out. "I mighta had one on me old ship—…just in case, ye understand—…but this ship? Nah, she be clean o' such things…sadly."

"Double fuck," I muttered, when an idea struck me, and I stared at Oren. "You'd not have such a spot on your old ship unless you knew someone that would make use of such things. Tell me all about it, mate."

"Ah, well…mebbe I mighta occasionally done a wee bit o' rubbin' shoulders with the less than legal kinda people…"

"Oren, we're going to be raiding the city lord's war supplies and probably killing his soldiers to do it. I don't give two shits about legal. Gimme!" I straightened up and stretched, then led him off toward the more private upper deck.

"Ach, no, laddie, we dinna want ta be up there…Last o' the corpses are there. Oracle said ye needed 'em fer Bob. They be a bit…ripe."

With a jerk of his head, he instead indicated for us to lean against the railings, looking out over the forest with the tower at our backs.

"Well, laddie, I guess it be time ta talk a bit aboot me past. Ye ken I were a trader, along with Decin, aye?" he said, looking up at me.

"Yeah, you said; what's that got—"

"Just trust me, there be a point ta this." He lifted one hand, and I settled back against the railing, frowning at him.

"Okay, mate, tell me the whole story, then." I gestured for him, and Oren shifted his gaze back to looking out over the treetops. He was silent for a long minute before the memories began pouring out.

"It were a good life…It were hard, dinna get me wrong. I had ta go into debt to a lot o' people ta be able to afford me own ship. Me da borrowed gold from tha clan, we got investors, and I took some gold from a…friend…who said he'd just ask me for a wee favor now and then, that were all." Oren snorted and shook his head, his beard waggling.

"Oh, I was so naïve! I had contracts from t' guilds, I ferried people back an' forth to ta Narkolt and other nearby villages, not ta mention a few trips out ta the Sunken City. I thought it'd go on forever. I thought I had it made fer life." He snorted and spat over the side.

"Then t' war came. Overnight, it were treachery ta be dealin' wit Narkolt. All that were left were a few wee deals here an' there. Mostly runnin' tha scummy tax collectors back an' forth. I hated it."

"I bet, mate. I'm sorry to hear it, though," I said. Oren shook his head, continuing.

"Then me old friend, he comes outta tha woodwork. Says he knows I need gold, an' I'd already bin droppin' off a wee package here an' there for 'his friends'. I knew what it were, smugglin', but I didna care. It were only a wee bit, after all, and it were keepin' me ship in the air. A dwarf has ta pay his debts, ye ken?"

He looked up at me from under one bushy eyebrow as though waiting for me to condemn him.

I grinned back at him.

"I do know," I said.

"Aye, well, turns out tha' me old friend; let's just call 'im Mal, all right? Well, Mal happened ta ken a wee way fer me te make a wee bit more gold, an' I were already going tha' way, takin' tha taxman to the villages. Why no' drop a wee parcel off here and there, mebbe pickin' up a wee bit extra, too?

"Taxman didna care what I were doin', as he were too busy ta see. Thought I were under their thumb. It got ta be a bit o' a game; tha villages were payin' their taxes wi' gold from tha city. Half tha time, it were gold I was carryin' out on tha ship, passin' it over all subtle-like, an' they'd be turnin' around an' givin' it straight back ta the taxman."

I grinned at that, imagining the villagers laughing their asses off at the trick.

"Then came tha day me contact were late. Taxman made me take off wi' out the time ta take tha gold onboard. I gave tha villagers what I had; me own gold, ye understand? It were all I had, but it were no' enough. I tried ta reason wi' tha taxman, but he were a bastard. Stripped tha village o' anythin' valuable. He would ha' taken tha chief's daughter, too, 'cept I put me foot down an' refused, said he'd be walkin' back iff'n he did."

"Good man," I said, a thread of anger rising at the detail. This realm seemed to be so in favor of slavery, it made my damn blood boil!

"Aye, well, it meant tha' when I landed back at Himnel, I were arrested, fined, an' they took ma contract. Taxman went back a few days later wi' another ship. Tha scumbag captain o' the *Star's Glory*, Bateman, he were happy te take it, and they brought her back still. Sold her at tha slave market. So, I lost me contract fer nothin'."

"No, mate, you stood up and you did what was right, and if we ever come across that cocksucker, Bateman? Feel free to shoot him down. Especially if the taxman is aboard," I said with feeling.

"Ha!" Oren laughed. "Aye, well, I'll be holdin' ye ta that, laddie! Anyway, when I lost th' contract, I also lost th' cover ta go ta the villages we'd been usin'…Mal did pay me, fer tha gold I'd lost and me cut I'd ha' earned iff'n his lad had been on time. But it was still only fer what I'd earned up 'til then."

"Sounds like he's a good guy?" I said.

Oren snorted, shaking his head.

"Nah, laddie. Mal be a smuggler, plain an' simple. He be out ta line 'is pockets, ye better believe that, but he do be honorable. Iff'n he says he'll do it, he will. Tha weeks go by, an' I'm almost outta gold, when I'm offered tha chance ta come here. I took it, obviously. I didna have a choice."

"Oren, don't worry about it, mate. I've seen you with the former slaves. They love you, man, and you were the captain of the ship they were on. If you were any less of a good man, they'd never have accepted you the way they have. You did what you had to do, and we all know that. Let it go." I put my hand on his shoulder, giving it a quick squeeze, and he let out a long breath.

"It means a lot ta hear ye say that, Jax, it really does." He brushed a hand across his eyes and coughed, continuing gruffly. "Anyway! What I be sayin' is that iff'n ye want a way ta get shit done in Himnel, Mal be tha man ta get it sorted, fer a price."

"Okay, but how do we get to him? And what's the price gonna be? We haven't got much gold, mate," I said, frowning. I'd happily give him all the gold I had if he could help me to pull off a guerilla-style raid on the city, but we didn't have much. "I'll be honest, Oren; I don't like the idea of telling him our plans. What's to stop him selling us to Barabarattas?"

"He be from Narkolt, laddie. He'd be locked up if they found him, and all his stash took. Only reason tha nobles had no handed him over to the guard already is he owes 'em gold. Once that be paid, he'll be taken; he knows it, so I bet he be losin' deliberate-like at tha cards." Oren gave a short laugh at that, then amended his assertion. "Losin' as much as he can bring himself to, anyway!"

"Right, but…"

"Problem ye got, is tha the guards figured that the ships could be full o' troops, so they be searchin' every ship when it lands now. Ye're no a citizen. Tha guards be on lookout fer spies and saboteurs. Ye'll no get five feet afore ye're fightin', an' ye better believe they'll be ready."

"So, we're fucked, then?" I asked, my mood dropping faster than a drunken blonde's underwear.

"No exactly…ye see, laddie, afore tha smugglers were using th' airships, they be using tha smuggler's road." Oren grinned at me, and I raised one eyebrow.

"Go on."

"Well, our Barrett once be seein' a lassie who rode security on tha caravans tha smugglers used, an' he told me about it. Turns out, there's an old forgotten escape tunnel under tha walls, leads out to a place a few miles north o' tha city. It be a dark place, deep under tha ground, scary.

"An' remember, I'm a dwarf. Ma ancestors lived under tha mountains, so iff'n I say it be a deep feckin dark hole, trust me, it be that, all right?" He shook his head. "It used ta be a way fer smuggler's caravans to pass into tha city and out. It were a sweet way to avoid those who'd want a cut o' the profits. Thing be, though, there's a lot in the dark places o' the realm that likes a bit o' fresh meat.

"Sometimes people did disappear; sometimes, it be one or two, other times it be entire caravans, nothin' ever turnin' back up. Last few months, somethin's been happenin down there, and ain't nobody making it through, so they turned to me and mine."

"These tunnels, don't suppose you know where they start and end?"

"Nah, well…no really."

"Come on, Oren…gimme!" I groaned, staring at him.

"Well, Barrett, as ah said, he—"

"Wait. I just spoke to Barrett, and he said nothing about this tunnel?"

"Well, let's jus' say he does no have good memories o' the lassie, and leave it at that, okay?" Oren said, grinning at me. "Mebbe next time we get him drunk, we can get him to tell ye, and show tha scars!" He snorted and shook his head. "Mad bastard always goes fer the dangerous lassies, an he never learns! Like someone else I know!"

"Get fucked." I grinned.

"Ha! Oracle do be plannin' on breakin' ye one way or t'other; she be clear on tha'!" Oren let out a hearty laugh. "Anyway, another problem be how ye be plannin' on payin' Mal and t'other smugglers."

I smiled mischievously, and he closed his eyes and shook his head. "Oh no, I be sensin' another wee mad plan…I dinna need to hear it. No, I'll jus' stay here, safe an' warm in ma wee bed…"

"You've not got a bed, mate, but I could be persuaded to give up the captain's cabin…"

"Ye already did! I be the captain on this ship, so it be ma cabin! Dinna start tha' shit!"

"Hahaha! All right, man, I'm just fucking with you!" I said, shaking my head and laughing. "But seriously though, if there's something down in the tunnels that's been raiding the caravans, all we need to do is kill it and nick the gear back."

"Aye, tha' be true, but wha' if it be another SporeMother, or a dragon, or a bunch o' fuckin' cave trolls?" He shook his head, looking dismayed.

"Well, let's face it, this isn't a plan. It's a fucking half-baked idea. We're going to be risking our lives on it, and we could lose, big time." It was true, but even as I said it, I felt a grin tugging at my cheeks.

"Oh lordy, no." Oren muttered with his head in his hands. "Gods protect me from mad bastards like ye!"

"You love it, mate!" I said.

He shook his head in exasperation. "Well, mebbe ye can do it again, I dunno. But we need a fuck ton o' luck, and to sort those bastards out!" Oren said, jerking his thumb over his shoulder at the people huddled miserably in the cages on the deck.

"I'm going to patch up Bob first, then we talk to them. Are there any you know from before?" I asked hopefully.

"There be two lads that I recognize, but they be shipyard rats, never been out flyin' tha ships before, just fixin' 'em. Might be that some o' the reason there be so many arguments goin' on in there be because they be new to the ship. I'll go talk to 'em; willna be long…. Er…Bob be a scary bastard, so I bet they'll be happy to do anythin' I ask when he be standin' behind me, that be all right?"

Oren winked at me, and I nodded as he set off towards the cages, giving me the chance to actually inspect the inhabitants properly for the first time.

I'd made a point of ignoring the people held in them, as I'd seen them as the ship's crew. Because it was a warship, I had assumed they must all be loyal to

Barabarattas. However, now that I realized Oren's crew had been under the watchful eye of the guards, it made me wonder if these buggers had been the same?

Maybe there weren't so many loyal to the city as just too scared to step out of line? *Whatever*,... I thought, turning to look up at the raised deck and seeing the top of Bob's skull reflecting the sunlight. I headed over, taking the steps two at a time, but came to sudden halt when I reached the top.

Bob stood motionless, waiting for an order and watching over the ship, surrounded by the four corpses of the captain, the mage, and the last two guards that he'd killed yesterday. The sun was well up now, and the combination of the warmth, the dead bodies, and the sticky blood had attracted flies by the dozens, if not hundreds. Bob stood motionless near the top of the stairs, but I grimaced as I looked around.

I needed the corpses for their bones in order to repair Bob. I also needed to check them over, as these were the most likely to have decent gear. When I tore the bones apart to rebuild Bob, the flesh and internal organs tended to liquify and become a noxious mess. I didn't want the gear ruined. I'd have to do it the old-fashioned way, but that didn't mean I had to do it alone.

I walked to the side of the ship, looking down to find Lydia staggering over and hurling a rock the size of her head off the balcony to disappear into the trees below. She stood catching her breath for a second before straightening up as though she was fine, as soon as one of the wannabe hunters appeared. Before she could disappear from view, I called out to her.

"Hey, Lydia!"

She stopped, looking around a bit until she saw me waving a hand, and she jogged across to the gangplank and up onto the ship. In short order, she was up on the raised deck with me, clapping her fist to her chest in salute and trying to ignore the flies as assiduously as I was.

"Aye, milord?" she asked, her eyes watering from the smell.

"I need a little help, and you were the closest I know I can trust," I said, noting the way she stood even straighter and the faint smile that tugged at the corner of her mouth as she nodded back at me.

"'Course, milord, what d' yer need?" she said.

"Well, I need to search these bodies, I'm afraid. You mind helping me out?" I saw the tightening around her eyes at the thought, but she went straight ahead, nodding at me and turning to the corpses.

"I'll strip 'em down and get rid of 'em. Do you want me to bring the gear to you, or—"

"Don't worry. I'm not that much of an asshole, Lydia. I'll be doing it too; I just wanted a little help, that's all. We need to strip anything useful off first. Just pile it up here, okay?" I said, getting a nod in return as I went to the nearest body on my side.

It was that prick of a light mage. I had no idea what his name was, and I really didn't care, so I quickly searched him. I found a few potions; two mana ones were pretty easy to identify. The almost glowing blue syrupy content literally screamed "mana potion" to me, and when I used Identify on them, I wasn't surprised at all.

Mana Solution		Further Description *Yes/No*	
Details:		This mana potion will restore 150 mana immediately, followed by a further 2.5 mana per second for 90 seconds.	
Rarity:	**Magical:**	**Durability:**	**Potency:**
Uncommon	Yes	97/100	3/10

The only surprising thing was the strength. I slipped them both into my potions pouch with a clink of bottles and cast Identify on the third unknown potion. It was brown, and well…it was gloopy as fuck. I tilted it from side to side and watched it move with the slow viscosity of mud. I really didn't want to drink it, no matter what it was.

Earthen Ability Boost		Further Description *Yes/No*	
Details:		This potion will increase the imbiber's affinity for Earth magic by 20% for 180 seconds.	
Rarity:	**Magical:**	**Durability:**	**Potency:**
Rare	Yes	82/100	2/10

I figured it was a good potion, if you had a load of earth spells, but hell no, not for me. I stored it in the potion pouch for the moment, but immediately forgot it in my excitement when I pulled off the mage's rings.

Ring of Veritas		Further Description *Yes/No*	
Details:		The Ring of Veritas was made by the dwarven sage Bennitos. Bennitos grew so enraged one day at the sloppy lies his customers told him that he created a ring that would glow in the presence of untruths. Be warned, this ring will only react if the subject of the wearer's attention is aware they are lying.	
Rarity:	**Magical:**	**Durability:**	**Charge:**
Rare	Yes	11/100	0/150

I could see some serious uses for this straight away, but the fact that it was both out of charges and down to a durability of eleven out of one hundred meant I was shit outta luck.

I put it on, as it was fairly cool-looking, a jet-black band with a single white stone set into the top, but I figured it was useless until I found a way to repair or recharge it. Preferably both. The second ring was another plain ring of healing, almost identical to my first, but with a lower threshold needed for activation and only healing thirty points, rather than fifty, per use.

Ring of Healing		Further Description *Yes/No*	
Details:		This ring provides a 30-point healing twice per day. Minimum Intelligence to safely use this item is 7.	
Rarity:	**Magical:**	**Durability:**	**Charge:**
Uncommon	Yes	72/100	2/s

I put it in my pocket for now, resolving to give it to someone who needed it. I quickly searched the rest of the mage. His robes were well-made and had armor plates sewn into them, but they weren't magical. While he carried a pair of fair-sized pouches on him, the first was only coins. It contained thirty-seven gold, a handful of silver and copper that I didn't bother to count, and two small rubies, which, while pretty, were all pretty useless for now. They probably would help when we got to the city, I guessed, so they weren't a complete disappointment.

I tossed the coin purse to the side, getting a startled look from Lydia as she saw how little I cared for the coins. That look shifted to outright amazement when I tipped the contents of the second purse out into my hand and grinned, obviously much more interested in them.

The pouch was packed full of dried alchemical ingredients, I quickly checked through them and found:

- **16 x Labian Leaves**
- **9 x Manaberries**
- **3 x Mugrot**
- **19 x Bernicle Beans**

I ate one of each at a time, studying the notifications that popped up with each one.

Labian Leaves		Further Description *Yes/No*	
Details:		These long leaves have a minty taste and are oddly satisfying. **Uses discovered:** 1) Restore Mana 2) ? 3) ? 4) ?	
Rarity:	**Magical:**	**Durability:**	**Charge:**
Common	No	100/100	N/A

Manaberries		Further Description *Yes/No*	
Details:		These small blue berries pop with flavor and leave a refreshing minty aftertaste. **Uses discovered:** 1) Restore Mana 2) ? 3) ? 4) ?	
Rarity:	**Magical:**	**Durability:**	**Charge:**
Common	No	100/100	N/A

Mugrot			Further Description *Yes/No*
Details:			The Mugrot stems are long and sticky, but the heat they infuse into dishes is highly sought after. Beware overindulgence! **Uses Discovered:** 1) Fortify Mana 2) ? 3) ? 4) ?
Rarity:	**Magical:**	**Durability:**	**Charge:**
Common	No	100/100	N/A

Bernicle Beans			Further Description *Yes/No*
Details:			These green beans have a gritty texture but leave an unusual aftertaste. **Uses Discovered:** 1) Restore Mana 2) ? 3) ? 4) ?
Rarity:	**Magical:**	**Durability:**	**Charge:**
Common	No	100/100	N/A

I spat the remains of the bernicle bean out as soon as I got the notification. The others had been fairly tasty, but those...hell no. Never again unless I absolutely had to. They burned like chilies on the tongue but had no flavor at all! I looked at Lydia and caught her grinning before she tried to hide it.

"Did you know?" I asked her, summoning a water fountain, and trying to scrape the residue off my tongue.

"That bernicle beans are foul?" she asked, trying to keep a straight face.

"Yeah."

"Well...yes...I did. Never seen nobody eat 'em just random-like in public before!" she said, trying to keep from laughing.

"Why not?" I asked.

"Well...well, look you didn't swallow 'em, did you?" she said, looking suddenly embarrassed.

"No, why?" I asked, getting worried now as well.

"Oh, thank the lady! Well, they have certain side effects...down below...That's kinda their main use, if you get my meanin'..." She looked heavily embarrassed.

"Noooo, still not a clue.... Wait, you mean..." I said and gestured towards my crotch, getting a cough and a nod in return. I started to move on, determined to get this awkward conversation over with as soon as possible, then thought better of it. Better to find out now. I'd only end up asking someone else later otherwise, and that'd be an even more awkward conversation to start. "Okay, let's keep it quiet. I didn't have a clue what they do, so..."

"They, ah, make certain things harder? Like, longer?" she said, her face aflame with embarrassment.

"Ooookay, got it! Thanks, and we never had this conversation, okay?" I said, both of us turning away as swiftly as possible, trying to pretend the conversation had never happened.

The last item the mage had, beside a couple of rune-inscribed things that looked like sticks, which I put aside, was his staff. The staff was composed of a dark wood, about six feet in length, and was topped with a round, black orb that had several small cracks running through it.

Synergistic Staff		Further Description *Yes/No*	
Details:		This staff was created by the master of enchantments Lufthousen and gives a boost of 10% to magical experience gained while wielding the staff, as well as a 10% boost to your mana capacity.	
Rarity:	Magical:	Durability:	Charge:
Rare	Yes	35/100	43/100

I had no idea who Lufthousen was, but I loved his ability to create a staff. It was nowhere near my naginata, but hey. Setting it aside for later, I moved on to check the captain's corpse, finding two large purses of gold and silver. I didn't bother counting them, just put them with the other one. He had three rings, only one of which was magical; the other two were pretty, but far too sparkly for my tastes.

Ring of Farseeing		Further Description *Yes/No*	
Details:		The Ring of Farseeing is part of the standard equipment given to warship captains by the City of Himnel. This ring forms part of a set and grants +1 mile to visibility in ideal conditions. Five times per 24 hours, a single charge may be used to focus the wearer or another's vision for 30 seconds.	
Rarity:	Magical:	Durability:	Charge:
Unusual	Yes	79/100	18/100

I pocketed the ring, planning on giving it to Oren, and continued to search, finding a pair of boots that were enchanted to increase traction in the wet. Little else wasn't sparkly, ruined by blood, or otherwise rubbish.

I'd seen maps and other clothes in his quarters, and decided I'd talk to Oren about them later. The sheath for the dagger was on his waist, but honestly, the dagger would be worth more smelted down, after he'd practically ruined it in his attempt to stab Bob. It was crap.

I didn't even bother reading the rest of the details on the boots, just checked their title and chucked them aside to join the small pile. Lydia hadn't fared well either; between Bob's attack, the two guards had left a small amount of usable armor, two swords, three gold, six silver, and eighteen copper, and a few bits of personal junk I ignored.

"Okay, well, that's enough, anyway." I straightened up and backed away from the corpses. Lydia did the same, and Bob moved forward at my silent urging.

"Woo boy, okay," I muttered to myself. Beginning to cast at Bob, I funneled a third of my mana straight into him, using my bonus ability Bonemeld to heal over cracks and breaks in his form wherever possible. After a few minutes, he looked better. Not right, as he still had a lot of his mass missing, but not quite as freakily broken as before. I poured mana into the bodies arranged all around him, watching the flesh slough away into noxious puddles as the bones lifted into the air. As each corpse collapsed, the bones gathered around Bob, building up a stock of material to rebuild him.

I closed my eyes, seeing a mental picture of Bob hanging before me, and I slowly separated out his form.

I started with the legs, making them thicker and stronger, and reshaping some of the bones to create smaller overlapping plates designed to absorb damage, but break off before his actual structure was broken. I carried this theme up to his chest, giving him a heavier, thicker ribcage, overlapping the bones to strengthen his shoulders, then melding bones together to form a sort of cuirass.

With his shoulders so heavily reinforced, I scrapped lower pair of arms to provide extra bone for armoring. I kept the flexible, spear-like legs attached to his back as well; they were just too cool to change.

In the end, when I opened my eyes and looked at him again, he was an imposing sight.

He stood almost eight feet tall, and the combination of the naga skull and back spears mixed with the bone armor to make a hell of an impression.

I grinned at him as he shifted about, examining his new form, and with a thought, I pulled up the new notification I'd received.

You have created a new armored form for your minion.

Do you wish to save this form for easier reconstruction later?

Yes/No

I chose *yes* and was asked to name it. Easy one, that.

You have selected Knight as the name for this form. Reconstruction will require 0.53 metric tons of bone to complete from scratch.

This form has received the following bonuses:

- **+1.5 to intimidation**
- **+3 to damage against darkness-aligned foes (due to consecrated bones used in construction)**

Congratulations!

You have raised your spell Raise Weak Skeletal Minion to level 12. Once this spell reaches level 20, you may choose its second evolution.

As a Reanimator you may be able to unlock certain abilities inherent in the bones you use…

I grinned at Bob, admiring my companion as he banged one huge bone fist off his chest armor to test it before straightening up and becoming immobile again, returning to watching over me.

I turned from the corpses and saw Lydia gaping at me in wide-eyed shock.

"What?" I asked, confused at her expression.

"You...you just made 'im!" she whispered; her voice filled with awe.

"Uh, yeah? What did you think I meant when I said I needed to fix him?" I asked her, thinking quickly. Since I'd adopted everyone, I couldn't remember if I'd made any changes to Bob, and it took a few seconds of her mouth opening and closing before I got it.

I hadn't changed his appearance since the fight with the SporeMother, and people obviously hadn't realized the things I could do with him. I shrugged and gestured for him to go below and join Oren as I turned to look out over the ship.

"He's my minion, yes. I created him from bones I found in the tower. After all he's seen and done since coming to life, he's starting to become 'more' now, though. He's...well, if not fully sentient yet, he's on his way. So please, do me a favor and let people know that he's to be treated with respect, okay? Also, where did you think he came from?" I asked curiously, glancing over at her.

"Well, I...I thought he were a bone minion!" she said, still awed.

"Uh, yeah? He's made of bone?" I said, confused.

"No! A *bone minion*. They're magic, like the golems. I seen 'em before; they do some jobs in the cities, but they don't last long. I thought you'd got a load of scrolls and were using 'em!"

"No, but it's cool that you can do that," I said, only to be met with a furious shaking of her head in response.

"No, bone minions ain't cheap. They sell slaves because we're cheap! Bone minions only last a few months, then you need to buy another. I been made to do their jobs before 'til they can get another! Are ya...are ya gonna make more?" Her voice quavered as she asked me, practically terrified of the answer.

"No," I said. "I chose to only have Bob. I wanted him to grow, rather than just get more copies of him. Why?"

"I...well...yer could make a load o' gold, an'..."

"I don't give a shit about gold at the minute," I said, holding her gaze. "And as far as I'm concerned, the real wealth here is you and the others. We can always get money. We can't get people so easy, so don't ever think your place here isn't safe."

"Oh, I...uh, I didn't mean that, 'onestly," she said, looking anywhere but at me.

I nodded, certain that it was exactly what she'd been worried about. "Thanks for your help, Lydia."

She straightened, saluting me with a fist to her chest.

"Anytime, milord. And, well," she said, looking suddenly hesitant.

"Just say it. You don't have to be worried; god knows you always said what you meant before." I grinned at her. I'd seen a difference in the way she acted around me since the fight, like she'd decided maybe I wasn't a waste of skin after all.

"Well...ah, fuck it," she said, suddenly deflating and wringing her hands. "Look, when we met ya, I...I thought you were gonna be one of those ones, ya know, an adventurer. All mouth, just out fer yerself, and screw everyone else.

"I 'alf-expected you'd use us, just so ye could escape this place. I was a slave; I figured even a little chance to escape was more'n I had before." She shook her head and looked around, gesturing out to the people below in the cages, then to our own people as they walked about, free.

"I been shit on, used, and sold fer years. I was dead and still walkin'. Now I'm free. I've got food, I'm safe, a soddin' god is on our side, and I can go where I want. I been there, where those poor fuckers are. All I'm sayin', I guess, is thank you. And maybe give 'em a chance? Might be, they're shits and need taught to fly, like Toka, but maybe there's some good 'un's too."

She trailed off, shrugging as she looked at me.

"Maybe they're all twats, though. Fuck it."

I couldn't help but laugh as I saw the way she washed her hands of it all, but her honesty touched me.

"Thank you, Lydia," I said, smiling. "I, well…I try. I'm trying to keep us all safe, and I'll try to be the man you all need me to be."

She saluted again and walked off, as I looked down at the cages, noting the dejected and scared looks on the faces of those inside. Oren was standing outside talking to them, but only a few seemed interested. The rest seemed, well…resigned to things, as though they'd given up, and a few looked furious.

I shook my head, seeing too many similarities to the way the slaves had looked when I'd found them. I had to straighten this out, and I needed these people.

CHAPTER SEVEN

I straightened up and moved down to the cages, trying my best to look stern, but fair, however that was supposed to work.

"Well, ye all heard who I be, and this be the Lord Jax I been tellin' ye about. He be the one that kilt the SporeMother and all, so ye be careful, now," Oren said, straightening up and stepping aside to stand at some imitation of attention.

I stood there for a long minute, looking them over. There were two distinct groups, ten men and women of various species that wore brown coveralls—well, nine, I supposed, as the tenth was a humanoid that looked to be made of rock. I'd almost assumed him to be a golem, until I saw that his eyes were perhaps the most intelligent of the lot and that he'd had a brown coverall style of uniform painted onto him as well.

The larger second group was a lot better dressed. They, too seemed to have a uniform, but it was a simple white top and blue pants. All were human males, maybe thirty of them, ranging in age from about fifteen to maybe sixty or seventy. I locked eyes with the oldest man, and he nodded back to me in acknowledgement.

"You've all had the pleasure of Oren's company here, and you've had time to see what's going on," I addressed them, "I'm Jax, lord of the tower and this land. You've seen the announcement, I'm sure.

"I'm not interested in keeping slaves or prisoners, so I'll make this quick. Those who want more information can ask, and I'll talk more afterwards. You can join me, or you'll be set loose to return to the city. If you choose to swear loyalty and stay, you'll be free, get food and respect, and the chance to learn skills. Some of you are already skilled with the ship, and that'll be useful. I'll be clear, when I say skills, I mean *skills*. I have some skillbooks, memories, and spellbooks, and I'll be giving those out to people who impress me and earn them."

At that, the people who'd been sitting zoned out or looking uninterested joined the rest in paying attention.

There were also four that sat at the back that I'd taken special note of on my approach, though, as they'd been the angrier-looking members of the group. They exchanged sharp looks and pushed forward, shoving others out of their way. The rest of the crew moved to avoid them, all either showing dislike or fear of the small group.

"Aye, all right, we're interested!" said the one that pushed to the front. He was small, but wiry, and had the teeth missing on one side of his mouth, giving him a lopsided appearance. "What spells ye offerin', then? And what skill memories? How many ye got?"

He tried to grin at me, and I stared right back at him as Bob hulked up beside me, a low rumbling growl coming from him as he picked up on my dislike of the man.

"As I said, I'll be giving these out to those who *earn* them."

He stared at me, licking his lips nervously, then looked away.

I took the time to make eye contact with the rest of the group, noting the sidelong glances they gave the foursome. "Those who want to stay, I'll require an Oath from you, one that will be magically enforced. Those who don't want to stay, well, I'll let you go. I won't hurt you, despite you trying to raid my home. I know you were forced to come here by your captain and by that prick, Barabarattas."

"You'll let us go?" Another man spoke up, one of those in the brown coveralls.

"Yes. I've no interest in keeping prisoners, or in killing you. If you don't want to be here, you can go. I'd prefer to recruit you, reward you for working hard, and offer you a place in the tower. That goes for you and your families, but I won't lie to you, I'm at war with Barabarattas. There's risk for everyone, no matter which side you choose."

"Aye, well, we're in, ain't we, lads?" the wiry little man said, waving at the cage. "So, you just let us free, yer lordship, and give us what you promised, and we'll join ya."

Again, he tried to grin at me, and Bob stepped forward, making them all cower back in the cages.

"That's great!" I said, feigning enthusiasm. "One point, however, you'll remember I said your Oath would be magically enforced? That comes in two parts. First, you swear loyalty to me," I said, locking eyes on him. "Second, you swear to be truthful in all your dealings with me, just as I will with you. That second part means, once you've sworn and I ask you if you had any intentions to fuck me over, like, oh I don't know…if you'd planned to take the memories and skills and rob me or harm my people, you'll be forced to tell me the truth. At that point, I'll strip you of citizenship, and I either give you to my minion Bob, here," I said, gesturing to Bob, who made a point of flexing his enormous taloned hands and opening his mouth to show his pointed teeth off to best effect.

"Or, if I decide I'm really angry…I'll deal with you myself," I said, my naginata beginning to glow and pulse with power as Oren spoke up.

"Aye, an' remember tha' Lord Jax just fuckin' killed a SporeMother. On his own. Ye dinna want to see him pissed off! I'd be hopin' Bob'd make it quick, 'cos I'll tell ye, he be tha one more likely to be merciful!"

The four exchanged glances between them, then slowly melted back in the cage, pushing others in front of them.

"Yeah, I thought so." I shook my head before looking at the oldest of the ship's crew. "You have a question?" I asked, catching his gaze on me again.

"Ah, yes, lord. I was the helmsman of *Agamemnon's Pride*. I live to fly, but you said you'd give us a home? I saw you before, you and your wisp. You were healing people!" he said, stepping forward and gripping the bars of the cage with gnarled and weathered hands. "I…well…"

I grimaced, seeing his fingers, bent, and twisted with arthritis, and I held up a hand to stop him.

"Oracle, where are you?"

"I'm in the hold; be right there."

A handful of seconds later, Oracle came flitting out of a porthole and flew across to me, perching on my shoulder like an insanely attractive parrot.

"Will our healing spell, the focused heal-all, have the ability to fix his arthritis?"

"His fingers?"

"Yeah."

"It should; simple physical damage like that should be easy to fix."

"Good. I thought this would be embarrassing if it didn't work!"

I lifted my hands, slowly building the spell, making sure I had all the sections and various weaves right, investing a lot of mana into it, until I'd nearly bottomed out my reserves. I wanted this to prove a point as well as help him.

When I released the spell, it latched onto him, and his fingers gripped the bars of the cage even tighter, opening and closing spasmodically, as he gasped and shook like a fresh-landed fish. His spell-shrouded body hovered a foot off the deck, his scraggly white hair brushing the top of the cages.

The light show of the magic caused a mass stampede to the back of the cages, all ten feet of them. As each layer of the spell completed, slowly rising and falling in his body like a magical version of an MRI, tendrils of mana flowed in and out, targeting individual issues and repairing them as they went.

It lasted almost a full minute. The entire time, he gasped and twitched. I was starting to feel concerned that I'd overdone it, when it finally dissipated, and he dropped to the ground with a gasp.

Silence reigned for what seemed like forever, broken only by the gasps as he got his breath back and slowly raised his hands to stare at them.

He flexed his fingers, tears suddenly flowing down his cheeks as he crouched down, then popped back up.

"They're fixed!" he whispered, before shouting at the rest of the people in the cages. "Do you see this? He fixed my hands! And my knees, and…" He patted at his crotch and whimpered. "I'm right again, I can feel it."

Others moved around him, his friends stepping forward to examine his hands, observing the way he stretched, his hands moving to his back as though stunned, searching for a pain that had been a part of his life so long, it was no longer even acknowledged. He spun around, pushing others aside as he got to the front of the cage and locked eyes on me.

"You fixed me, you healed all of it! My old body feels like I'm twenty again! I'll swear to you…I'll damn well live and die for you for this! You don't know what you've done, but I do! Tell me the Oath, lord, and I'll swear it right now!"

Tears still ran unbidden down his cheeks, but the old helmsman stood straight and tall, practically glowing with health, and I grinned at him.

"I'm glad you like it; it's one of the advantages of citizenship!" I said. "But don't worry about the Oath. I'll ask all who want to join to swear it together soon. For now, does anyone else have any questions?" I looked at them all, searching for the one in coveralls who had asked about leaving. Before I found him, he spoke up, stepping forward.

"Lord, will you do that for all of us, for our families?" he asked, gesturing at the helmsman who now stood surrounded by his friends who were peppering him with quiet questions.

"I'll help whoever I can of our people, but I'm also going to be training a healer. They'll be free for all of our people. Nobody will have to pay for healing."

"My daughter," he said, closing his eyes and swallowing hard. "My daughter got run over by a cart. She can't walk; hell, she can't do anything. She just lies there! Only her head works, lord. Can you heal her...tell me straight!"

"I don't know," I said truthfully, locking eyes with him. "I think so, but I know there's damage my spells can't fix. I'm hoping a specialized healer will be able to do all of that and more. All I can say is I'll try; I'll not fill you with false promises."

"But you'll try?" he said fiercely. "You'll do your best for her, and any of our families we bring?"

Others stepped forward, staring at me intently, even as a woman spoke up.

"And what about our friends? Mikas, 'e fell from a ship in dock, 'is leg don't work no more; 'e can't get work. We all clubbed together to feed 'im, but you'll heal 'im? Fer' real?" she asked me intently. Others were starting to speak up, and I held my hands up to stop them all as Oracle took flight, landing on the top of the cage and beginning to examine the people.

"Listen to me; I won't let any of my people be hurt if I can fix it. If it's magic or potions you need, I'll damn well do all I can, okay? I can't guarantee how quickly we'll get your family free, but I will do my best to make sure it's soon. The rules of citizenship are simple, aren't they, Oren?" I said, looking to him.

"Aye, Lord! Number one rule is do no be a dick!" he called to the crowd. "We're all family, all o' us now as citizens o' the Great Tower. Just like ye might no like yer brother, but yer wouldna see him hurt, ye all swear to look out fer one another! Those that do be ready to swear the Oath, I'll ask ye to take a step forward. Those that do no, take a step back!"

The majority of the two cages separated out; the four men that were obviously planning on robbing me and escaping stayed at the back, as did two others, including one of the men in coveralls. I ignored the assholes, as I'd already written them off as a waste of space, but the other two, I regarded questioningly. The man in coveralls shook his head and spoke up first.

"I'm sorry, lord, but my family is loyal to the city. My father is a guardsman, and I'd end up at war with him if I helped you. I can't swear."

"I understand that and can respect it. Hopefully, there'll be a way to take care of the issue without it coming to battles between us and them, but..."

"Yeah, 'cos you'll get dead!" one of the four assholes muttered, just loud enough to hear. Silence fell, growing deeper as I just smiled at the man who'd spoken and saw him blanch.

"Another pack and poor weapon?" Seneschal asked in my mind, and I smiled wider.

"No, I didn't promise them anything. I just said I'd set them free."

"Thanks for that vote of confidence," I said to the man, and turned to the last person in the cage, raising an eyebrow questioningly.

"I can't swear neither. My family be in the city. I can't leave them to a maybe. If I had them free, I'd join you. I've no love for the city, but I can't risk them; I need to go home. Sorry."

I nodded and smiled at him regretfully.

"That's okay. I understand. I'll not be able to get you to the city, you understand, but I'll make sure I drop you both within a few days' walk of it, and I'll give you supplies to make it the rest of the way on foot, good enough?"

The relief on both men's faces was clear, and Oren stepped forward at my nod to unlock the cages. Once the majority of the people had filed out, one of the four assholes tried to leave, and Bob stepped in, one claw-tipped hand gripping him by the throat and stopping the exodus.

"Ah, ah!" I said, smiling at him and shaking my head, as though reprimanding a naughty toddler. "You didn't want to swear the Oath, and I don't trust you, so you get to stay right there with your friends."

Bob shoved him back, hard. He tripped over the bars on the floor and fell into his friends. They glared at me, but they didn't say anything until I spoke to the other two that had refused fealty.

"You've been honest with me, and as long as you promise you'll do no harm and stay in the areas I ask, you can come out." They both hurried forward, glad to be free of the cage, but the other four immediately started to swear and argue that they should be allowed out as well.

"Iff'n yer let us out, yer lordship, maybe we'll come to a deal. Just give us some time, eh? We got families back in the city, same as them, that's all," said the smallest one, lopsided grin and rotten teeth showing in what he clearly thought was a winning way.

"And maybe you'll try and rob me blind and murder my people. Fuck no," I said.

His face went red with anger, and he started to swear at me. Then Bob moved in. My skeletal minion ducked down so his face was level with his opponent's and hissed, his mouth wide, fangs and teeth grazing the skin as the men jumped backward in fear.

"Oh, and I don't recommend pissing Bob off," I said to them as I turned away. "He'll eat your fucking face next time."

Oren led the group down to the parade ground from the ship, telling the other two to stand to one side before calling out to Barrett. They held a quick, muttered conversation, then Barrett was racing away and summoning people.

As we waited, more and more people appeared, until at last, Seneschal spoke up in my mind.

"This is almost all of them, Jax. There are two more on the stairs a level below, and Cai is two floors below that. Once he arrives, that will be the entire population of the tower."

"Thanks, dude."

"Just be a wee minute, my lord!" Oren said grinning at me, and I tried not to shake my head.

It took less than five minutes before the next two arrived, and I realized the former slaves and crew of Oren's ship had spread themselves about in the new group of volunteers. When I raised an eyebrow at Oren, he grinned back at me.

"Well, it be like this, lord; the Oath ye swore to us were a lot more...simple. We felt we should be tha same as everyone else, no favorites! Plus, it do mean they can all see that we're tha same."

"Thank you, Oren," I said quietly, and I moved up to stand at the top of the gangplank where they could all see me. It had crossed my mind that I'd bound the new recruits from the village with a more formal oath, but not with the first people I'd rescued from the slavers and from Oren's ship. I hadn't really known how to broach the subject without sounding like an ass.

"Ach, we're all sworn to ye, laddie. It's nothin'," he replied, just as quietly. As he finished, Cai came running in and took up his place at the front of the group, a little out of breath. "Oh aye, at last the furry-eared bastard gets here, nothin' like keeping yer lord waitin' an' all!" Oren called out, loud enough for everyone to hear.

Cai stood straight and tall, then slowly and regally raised his right hand…and flipped him the bird. There was silence for several seconds until people started to snigger, then full-blown laughter rang out.

"Right, then! Repeat after me!" Oren took care to enunciate every word as he read from the notification that appeared before him. I felt Oracle take control of our shared mana pool, linking to the tower and reaching out to bind them all as they read aloud:

"I swear to obey Lord Jax and those he places over me; I will serve to the best of my ability, speak no lie to him when the truth is commanded, and treat all other citizens as family.

I will work for the greater good, being a shield to those who need it, a sword to those who deserve it, and a warden to the night."

"I will stand with my family, helping one another to reach the light, until the hour of my death or my lord releases me from my Oath."

"Lastly, I will not be a dick!"

As the last echoes of the chant faded away from the Tower, I held my hands up and replied to them as I had before, having felt Oracle weaving mana through the Oath as they spoke it, knowing they were sealed to me and the tower now.

"I, Lord Jax, do swear to protect and lead you, to be the shield that protects you and yours from the darkness and the sword that avenges that which cannot be saved. As the tower grows in strength, so shall you." I felt kind of pretentious saying it, but as the cheers rose from them, I knew it was what they expected to hear.

"Now then, for those who don't know already, this…is Oren." I gestured to him, and he preened at their attention. "And that's Cai!" I pointed at the large cat-man, who quickly jogged over to stand on the opposite side of me to Oren. "Oren's in charge of the ship and any others we get from now on; at least, until he's dead or I find someone better!"

That took the wind out of his sails, and he looked at me askance for a second, before going back to glowering at the new recruits.

"Cai here is in charge of tower residents and will be sorting things like food and lodging. You come to him if you have any issues in those areas. Engineers! Get with Oren; I need this ship up and running as fast as possible! We have some spare parts from Oren's old ship if we need them. Crew! Talk to Oren as well, as he's going to need to fill some positions on the ship. If you're not one of those chosen to help him, go to Cai, he'll find you a job for now."

I introduced the wisps in much the same manner, threw in a reminder about the skillbooks, and let everyone know Oren and Cai would be the ones to impress if they wanted access to special skill memories. The low murmuring that had built up instantly quieted as Barrett roared at the group.

"Silence!"

"Thanks for that, Barrett," I said, a faint smile on my lips. "I want to talk to you all about religion. I don't know if you have gods, goddesses, or beings that you follow, but here in the Great Tower, we are sworn to Jenae.

"Jenae is the Goddess of Fire, Exploration, and Hidden Knowledge, and she has granted us boons to help us repair the tower faster, as well as information, such as advice on how to fight and capture this ship."

I smacked a hand down hard on the railing that ran around the deck. "It's because of her help that you are all free to live your lives, and she still offers more. In exchange for mana, she will help us as she can, with information." Looks of uncertainty passed between people and I paused, inspecting them. "What's up, people? You look like there's a problem?" I said.

It took a few seconds, but Cai finally spoke up.

"Lord Jax, you said the goddess needs mana, but unless you're a mage or other spellcaster, you don't have mana. I'll help however I can, I swear, but..."

"Ah! No, that's a mistake right there, my friend. You all have mana; all living creatures have it. I've been assured by Jenae. Learning to cast a spell gives access to consciously use mana, but it's like a muscle. You have to learn to use it. The more you use it, the stronger it will grow. This apparently is how the first priests came to be; they gave their mana to their gods so frequently that they learned what to feel for. Once they knew, the gods granted them spells, healing abilities, and more."

A voice rose from the back in the silence that followed, and I smiled.

"How? How can we give our mana to the goddess? Tell us how to help you, lord!" It was the elderly helmsman, and his face was still alight with the joy of being pain-free for the first time in years.

"The entire tower is consecrated to Jenae; all you have to do is pray to her. I'll show you how, but first, a warning. When you drain your mana to the last, you grow lightheaded and can get headaches. Please, don't push yourselves that far. I don't want you to be in pain, but the longer you pray, the more mana Jenae receives.

"Mana also recovers over time, so if you wanted to, you could pray morning and night to Jenae, but again, you don't need to do this. I will be, and I ask for your support, but if you have a god, or you don't wish to, then I understand. If you wish to pray to Jenae, find a space, sit, or stand, however you wish, and close your eyes.

"Reach out with your mind and call her name quietly. You can speak aloud or inside yourself, but talk to her, tell her whatever you wish, and she will listen. Now, do as I do, please." I went down on one knee, clasping my hands together and closing my eyes. I heard the shuffling sound of people moving. After a few seconds, a low murmur arose from the group, and I felt Jenae's presence in my mind.

"Eternal!" her voice rang, shocked but pleased.

"Hi, Jenae, how's this?" I asked her, hope filling my mental voice.

"You brought me the entire population of the tower! I can feel their prayers, their hopes, and dreams. It's been so long!" I sensed as much as heard the emotion behind her words, and the relief that this action had brought her.

"I didn't expect them all to pray to you, but I asked them to help me, and I guess they went for it?" I said, and a low chuckle came from Jenae at that.

"You didn't expect it? You need to ask the people you trust about their lords and the interactions they have with them. To talk to them as equals and to respect them seems to have far greater effects than I suspected. It saddens me,

because it shows what the nobility has become. But as long as it plays to our favor, and you try to fix it in word and deed, I'm happy."

"I'll do what I can, Jenae, but…"

"Just do what you're doing, Jax. Follow your heart and keep on going."
The praise from Jenae made me feel ridiculously pleased for a few seconds, but I tamped it down as best I could.

"Sooo, about those Marks of Favor?" I asked, and I received a notification a second later.

Congratulations!

You have led 82 of your citizens to worship Jenae, Goddess of Fire, Exploration, and Hidden Knowledge. As such, you have received 41 Marks of Favor for use in the Constellation of Secrets. Use them wisely!

A second notification popped up as soon as I dismissed the first, and I grinned as I read it.

You have received a lesser boon from Jenae, the Goddess of Fire, Exploration, and Hidden Knowledge. This may be used at any time and will include the answer to a single question. This boon is a lesser boon and is limited to use within ten miles of a consecrated place of worship to Jenae.

"Thank you, Jax. I can feel their mana already; I will let you know when you can use the constellation. But for now, I suggest you speak to your people. Some are already approaching the threshold and are still praying to me. I do not wish for them to be drained fully."

I blinked and stood, the sense of Jenae leaving my mind, but I could still feel her all around. I looked at my people, seeing some had risen to their feet, while others still knelt. Some had tears running down their cheeks as their lips moved, communing with their goddess. A few of the group looked around hesitantly, realizing that I was watching, and quickly went back down on one knee as though to start again, and I spoke up to stop them.

"Please, everyone; I meant what I said. You don't have to do this at all, and if you do choose to help me with it, please, don't drain yourself. If you feel weak, if you feel a headache coming on, stop. That is both an order from me, and the Goddess Jenae's direct command."

With that, the majority of my people finished their prayers and stood, but a handful stayed as they were. Notably, the helmsman knelt for so long, I started to think he was going to pass out, but after another minute, his friends helped him to his feet, and he stood shakily. He laughed and hugged one of the men closest to him, and they all started talking, pointing at each other, and joking. I couldn't help but smile, thinking back to simpler times with friends, with Tommy.

"Okay, people, thank you for your help. Now, I suggest you get back to whatever you're supposed to be doing!" I clapped my hands together once, and turned away from the group, walking into the tower.

"Where are we going, Jax?" Oracle asked me quietly, and I closed my eyes for a second, taking a deep breath.

"No idea, Oracle. I wanted to get out of people's way while Cai and Oren directed them, and now I've realized I should have gone to the captain's cabin on the ship. I'll look bloody stupid turning around now, though, so we're going this way!" I whispered to her, getting a low laugh in return.

"How about we go to the Hall of Memories?" she asked after a minute, throwing it out in such a casual way that immediately made me suspect an ulterior motive.

"Okay…and why are we going there?" I asked looking up to my shoulder where she sat, my eyes drawn to her obvious assets.

"Behave. You're not forgiven yet," she said, smacking me lightly on the top of my head. But I caught the smile at the same time, and I grinned as I set off toward the floor we needed.

Bob clanked along behind me, and behind me, Oren was already explaining to Cai about the two men that hadn't sworn loyalty to me. I trusted that he'd get them somewhere to eat and rest.

"Soooo, why are we going to the hall, then?" I asked again, and this time Oracle answered seriously.

"We need to discuss the skills and spells that are available. You can't make a decision about who gets what until you know what we actually have."

We reached the hall and began what can only be considered the second most boring few hours in my life, because I once had to spend a day filling out government tax forms.

After three hours of being told again and again about how great a particular spell or memory-gifted skill was, but that I couldn't use it, I was done. My head was absolutely fucked, but at least now I had a rough idea of everything we had.

It seemed that we had pretty much one of everything for a lot of skills, which was both awesome and terrible, as the majority of them were around the expert level. I sat considering things for a while before asking Oracle about it to make sure I had it right.

"If I gave, say…Oren that memory stone on woodworking, what would happen?" I said, getting a smile in return.

"He's worked with wood on repairs to his ship frequently over the years, so he's got the basic skill already. If you gave it to him, he'd jump two whole levels in knowledge, straight to journeyman if he were a novice. But he'd still have to physically level the skill the old-fashioned way to gain the bonuses a true woodworker would get.

"If he'd never worked with wood at all, he'd gain the skill, but he'd retain very little of the knowledge, and unless he used it and started to work on wood straight away? He'd start forgetting bits of what he did gain, until eventually, he'd just have vague feelings about how he should do things, but no real clue."

"And if he was already skilled with it? Like an apprentice or journeyman woodworker?"

"Then he'd probably learn the entire memory, and he'd end up with the knowledge to make anything the creator of the stone knew," she said, smiling patiently. I sat there for a long time, looking at the memories and trying to not feel cheated again. After a while, I burst out in irritation and got to my feet, grabbing my head in my hands.

"Then it's all a head-fuck! I mean, come on! I have an entire library of knowledge that can hugely help us, but if we use it, it's wasted! That one there, the one about magical siege weapons!" I said, gesturing to one that twinkled merrily at the end of the second row. "That could be given to one of the engineers, and they'd be awesome with it, overhaul the ship's weapons, and make some really cool shit, but I need the engineers working on the ship! If I gave it to someone who's unskilled, someone I can afford to have use it, they'd have a rough idea of how to make a catapult, and that'd be it!"

"Jax, I know why you're upset, but you have to remember, these are a treasure trove, *if* you use them right. If you're offered a free horse, there's no point in complaining you don't like the color," she said, crossing her arms and staring at me in disapproval.

I narrowed my eyes at her. "Did you just tell me to quit being a whiny bitch?"

She shrugged, gesturing at all the books and stones around her. "Jax, just take the time and think, okay? If you get people to start the skills off, learn them for themselves, then you can use the books and memories to make them into amazingly skilled citizens. If you waste them, well…it's your choice."

"Fuck. When did you get so wise?" I asked her rhetorically, sitting back down and sighing.

"I didn't; I've been in charge of the magical knowledge here for hundreds of years. I get excited. I don't know much else about the world, it's true, but in here? Here, I do know things, and I can give you advice and support," Oracle said, moving across to join me on a long, sofa-like thing. She shifted to full size as she sat beside me and took my hand in hers, giving me a gentle nudge with her shoulder.

I took the hint and moved over, giving her some room. We sat in silence for a moment while I thought. Oracle seemed content just to sit, and my mana hadn't dipped that much when she assumed her full size, so I asked her about it.

"I'm bonded to you, but I also have a link to the tower still. As you're the formal master of the tower now, I can access the mana it draws in. I just slipped a little aside for my transformation and maintaining my form at this size, that's all. Do you like it?" She regarded me with a throaty little chuckle, raising one eyebrow.

I swallowed hard as I looked her over, my eyes roaming downwards from her perfect features…to her other perfect features…

"Oh god, yes," I whispered.

She smiled, leaning in for a kiss.

It seemed to go on forever, and yet ended far too soon, despite my earlier plans of behaving myself with the wisp. When we finally broke apart, it wasn't long before our lips met again. Her breath tasted of strawberries, a small fuzzy part of my mind noted as we kissed again, mouths opening and tongues reaching out, our arms going around each other…

"Jax! Ye in there, laddie?" a voice shouted through the sealed crystal doorway, muffled, but still clearly Oren. I groaned as we broke apart. Oracle forcibly pushed down a look of irritation and disappointment as we both stood a little regretfully, the buttons of her top undone and hair all tousled. I didn't remember undoing any buttons, I thought, then blinked as my brain reengaged when I heard Oren's voice again.

"Jax! Can ye hear me, laddie? Seneschal, are ye sure he be here?" I couldn't hear anything from Seneschal, but I certainly could hear some growled swearing under Oracle's breath as she began to mutter about what she was going to do to him for interrupting.

I coughed and turned back to the door, both glad and extremely regretful that we'd been interrupted. Glad, because I really needed to sort my head out about Oracle, and I didn't want to feel like I was taking advantage of her bond with me. The other side of it was…hell, I was a guy, and she was insanely hot and really, really up for it. The little head did *not* want to hear it from the big head that she wasn't to be played with.

I concentrated and commanded the tower to open the door, watching as Oren jumped and backed away as the crystal doorway dissolved into mist. He paused at finding both myself and Oracle inside, then stomped through the entrance, gazing about the large, lushly appointed room.

It had mostly survived the decimation of time, being as well-sealed as it had been. Not even air had moved inside, and the natural entropy of centuries had been held at bay. Aside from the soft furnishings being a bit weird and hard, the rest of the room looked as it had when the tower had been completed. Its walls were still covered in tapestries; the furniture was still far and away better than anything we'd found in the rest of the tower.

What really got his attention, though, were the hundreds of memory stones and spellbooks. He stared transfixed around the chamber and completely missed the first things I said to him.

"OREN!" I shouted, making him jump in shock and finally focus in on me again.

"Ah! I'm sorry Jax, I jus'—…I mean, I didna expect…" He gestured around; his hands visibly trembling. I shook my head and put one hand on his shoulder.

"Well, I've good news and bad with all this, my friend. First of all, airships didn't exist then, not like they are today, so there are no memories that'll help you with that. On the other side, though, when the time comes, if we can find something that's appropriate to you, I'll give you a stone. Or a spell, if that's your preference. You and Cai both will have earned it ten times over by the time we have the tower fixed up."

"Thank ye, laddie, I mean it," he whispered, shaking his head as he gawked around again. "I jus' never…"

"I know," I said. As annoyed as I was with the way things were—I'd had hopes for a tower full of experts—I'd been goddamn lucky. I could have been stuck in the middle of nowhere with a collapsed tower, after all, or dead. Or underwater, for all I knew.

"Come on, then, mate; what did you want?" I asked, heading for the door and dragging him along with me as he tried to look everywhere in the hall.

"Ah…oh yeah, with tha engineers an' shipyard types all sworn in, tha ship do be lookin' okay now. The main thing tha' was wrong with her was the engines bein' fucked. The lad's replaced two with spares and did some magic with the others, so she's ready ta fly again. Won't be great, but she'll get us to Decin an' back, safe enough."

"And to the village?" I asked, and he nodded quickly.

"Aye, we can reach th' village. I been told where it be, but even with the engines replaced, it'd still be a full two days there and back."

I swore under my breath at that, thinking about timescales and what we could and couldn't afford.

"Okay, how long to get to Himnel from here?" I asked, guiding Oren for the stairs with me even as I felt Oracle close the door behind us. She buzzed past us, her wings blurring as she disappeared around the bend and out of sight.

"Well, it depends, laddie. If we hammer tha engines, we could be there afore three full days o' flyin'. Go steady an' careful-like, closer to five. If we're headin' straight there, I'd be saying give repairs another day. Tha lads could replace tha other damaged engines and fix a bit more. We'd be there at nearly tha same time from today, but with a faster ship."

"You mean it'd take five days as it is, or if we give them another day, they could do more to the engines, and it'd be four days' flight time instead of five...if we're going slow and careful. Okay, makes sense. How long to Decin?" I asked, pulling out my map and showing him where I'd observed the ship's landing. Oren counted off distances with his fingers and thought for a second, nodding to himself.

"Tha' be aboot four, mebbe five hours' flight, as bad as tha ship is right now."

"Then get the ship ready. We'll fly light, nothing that's not needed aboard, and we'll need a little security force, as well. Not Barrett, though; we need him here to look after things, just in case." Oren nodded and grinned at me. "What're you grinning at, you mad bastard?" I asked.

"Just one wee thing, afore we join tha others downstairs..." he hedged, and I nodded impatiently. "Well, ye might want to tie yer troos properly."

He cackled as he kept walking. I frowned before realizing what he meant and looked down. Sure enough, my pants were undone slightly, and I hadn't even realized, between all the armor and bits, as my belt was still done.

"Oh, for..." I groaned and did myself back up, resolving to get my hands on Oracle later...and I had no clue which way round I intended to do that...

CHAPTER EIGHT

W hen I got back to the ship, it had changed dramatically from its gory, battered condition early that morning. Instead of the aftermath of battle, with bodies and blood still strewn liberally about, the ship looked clean and in fairly good repair. There were still scorch marks across the deck in places, and chunks cut from the railings, stains in the wood, and even the occasional bang and clank coming from below decks. But the majority of the main deck and the upper deck were clean and well-laid-out.

I headed toward the ship quickly, calling out to Barrett as I saw him standing with six of his team members.

"Yes, lord!" he answered, jogging over, and saluting as he came to a halt.

"Thanks, Barrett," I said, nodding in response to the salute, and he relaxed. "We're going to go to find Decin, see if we can recruit him and his people, then we're heading back. I need a team to fight alongside me if things don't go well."

"Yes, lord," Barrett repeated, gesturing to the group he'd left behind.

I looked them over and recognized them all. Lydia stood in the middle, a mace in one hand and a large heater shield resting against her legs. Her appropriated armor from the guards she'd looted suited her, and although she looked skinny, she was fit and strong.

Stephanos was off to one side, testing his bowstring. I'd caught his name, but didn't know much more about him, aside from the fact he was one of the hunter wannabes. Next to him, cradling an identical bow, was Miren, the tiny blonde girl that had some training to hunt already under her belt. Arrin stood next to her, a small firebolt balanced in one hand as he winked at Caron, who was trying to hide nearby.

I pretended not to see Caron, and instead moved straight on to Jian. I had hardly seen him since the fight, and not at all last night, as near as I could remember, but he looked...well, he looked great, actually. He looked healthy, not just because he had been near skeletal as I had first met him, but he'd filled out and appeared full of vitality.

Most of the fighters had gained at least one level, but in his case, he'd gone from barely being able to hold the twin swords he insisted on using to now looking like he'd been born with them. He'd cut the sleeves from his tunic and stood with his arms crossed, solid—if wiry—muscle covering them, and he stared at me as I appraised him. I nodded in respect, guessing that he'd piled most of his points into his Strength and Constitution stats, from what I could see.

The last of the team was Cam, a tall elf who had lost his family just before being sold as a slave. He stood there with the same thousand-mile stare he'd worn since I met him, a large wood axe leaning against his hip. He wore no armor, and his dark hair was cut short, but he nodded to me, ready to fight.

"They'll go with you, Lord Jax, and protect you and the ship," Barrett said, looking them over proudly. I smiled at them, speaking up quickly.

"Sounds good to me. Thank you, Barrett. I'm glad to know I've got this lot watching my back!" I addressed the team next, walking over to stand before them. "Is there anything you need to get? I want us to take off within the hour, so there's still time." All six stood straighter and stayed silent, so I gestured them onto the ship with one hand.

"Okay, then, get yourselves and your gear aboard." I turned to Barrett. "You're in charge of security when I'm gone. Err on the side of caution; if there's something you don't like, and you think it's a risk to my people or my tower, stamp on it hard with both feet, okay?"

At his firm nod, I dismissed him and strode across to Oren, who had come to a halt, talking to Cai.

"Cai, Oren, how's the ship looking? How soon can we leave?"

Cai spoke first. "We've almost finished unloading her. We've gotten several tons of foodstuffs and a considerable amount of armor and weapons that are being moved into the armory. The goods that the ship had in its hold are more…unusual…now that I've had the chance to look them over."

"Go on," I said, shifting to lean against the side of the ship and considering him with interest.

"Well, I've spoken with Isabella, and some of the items in the hold definitely did *not* come from her village. There are a lot of strange items aboard for a warship, bundles of cloth, a few small totems, and a large frieze that appears to have been broken in two when loading. There are at least a dozen magelights, from what I've seen so far."

He stopped at my look of confusion. "Magelights are, well…lights made by mages, I guess. Never really thought about the name before." He shook himself and went on quickly. "They are charged with mana, and they provide light throughout the night. They're not particularly expensive, but candles are far cheaper, so they're unlikely to have come from another small village.

"I suspect the ship found a traveling merchant and robbed him. The crew members seemed to think the ship was collecting taxes for the city. I believe they were collecting wealth for the captain, judging from the conversations I've had."

"So, we had a captain who was using his ship to go pirating?" I asked, grinning.

Oren jumped in. "Aye, laddie, an' judgin' from the damage we've fixed so far, he was makin' the ship look more damaged than it really be. Probl'y tryin' to get away from tha fightin'! As to the piratin', well, it no be that uncommon. Warships be expected to help supply themselves, now an' then."

"Sneaky fuckers!" I said, still grinning.

"You seem inordinately pleased about that, Jax," Cai said, leaning against the ship as well and facing me after scanning the area to make sure we weren't being observed. "What's going on in that devious mind of yours?"

"I'm just thinking that if there's no way to prove which goods are whose, we can't be expected to return anything. That means it's all ours, spoils of war and all that, and if pirating is that common, well…"

"Well, what be stoppin' us from doin' tha same!" Oren chimed in, grinning wolfishly.

"Exactly, but I'm thinking to the pirates! And if it's known that the warship has been doing this, and that others do too, well, Barabarattas might think the ship went rogue, rather than being captured…"

"So, he's more likely to be annoyed and wait a while before sending other ships after this one. And he didn't think his ships had arrived yet, so he probably thinks we're all fighting you for the tower or something now," Cai concluded.

I grinned. "Exactly! We really need Decin on our side, then, as I bet whatever we try to pull on the city to steal those manastones would work a lot better with two ships than one!"

"Damn right, laddie!" Oren said, his grin stretching his face even further.

"Time for a quick test flight. Let's go see if we can convince Decin, save anyone we can, and get his ship repaired and back here!" I said, clapping my hands together.

Cai saluted and spoke quickly before turning away. "I'll get on with things here and get the cargo sorted."

With his departure, Oren and I headed up onto the ship, dodging crew who ran and weaved about, carrying the final piles of gear off the ship, and straightening the trio of cylinders that sat on the deck.

"What are those?" I asked Oren, and he grunted as he saw what I was looking at.

"Flamin' dangerous be what they be! There be three o' them, yer see?" he said, gesturing to the two on the deck, one on either side of the ship.

The third and final one was set in the bow, heavily secured in place, compared to the other two, with a mass of metal strapping it down. "Those two, they be for fightin' ships; fire a great big rock up to a mile. Sod-all accuracy, though. Iff'n yer need to use them, yer need to be in close! T'other one, though? That's a Lightnin' Shot. Yer use that on buildin's. I only ever see'd one fired afore; well, two, but the second wen' boom an' tha ship vanished. The time it worked, though? Hellish powerful!"

"Wait…the other one exploded? What happened?" I asked, Oren eyed the explosive construct as he shrugged.

"Who knows! They be new to the fleet. Ain't nobody seen 'em afore a few years back. Some ol' design Barabarattas found in a ruin. Like tha first airships, there be a lot o' trial an' error. More error 'n not, if yer get it…"

"Fuck, man, that's insane," I said, shaking my head and inspecting the cannons. All three were totally different-looking, for all that the first two were similar in design. One of the smaller two had fanciful swirls and patterns on it, where the other was bare. The big one was clearly lashed in place to try to counter some kind of kickback.

"Wonder why they never used them on us?" I said aloud as I studied them.

"Probl'y didna give 'em time, or we'd all have been fucked," Oren said, shrugging again and moving off to shout at someone that was coiling rope on the deck exactly like everyone else, to my untrained eye. Oren yanked it from her hands and did…exactly the same thing. I frowned, trying to figure out what was going on, but I had a lot more important things to try to figure out first. *Hell with it.*

I turned around and watched as Oracle appeared from the tower and flitted over to me. She smiled, then flew straight to Bob, landing on his shoulders and folding her arms over the top of his skull as she regarded the four ruffians still inside the cages. I joined her, and she turned to me, gesturing at them.

"What are we going to do with them?" she asked with a concerned look on her face. "Lorek and his men deserved what they got. They were going to hurt Isabella, but these men haven't done anything."

"Aye, that's right; we didn't do nothin'." The weaselly little man spoke up quickly, stepping forward. "The lady's right, lord. We can be helpful. We're good workers, an'—"

Before he could say anything else, a bucket of water splashed over him, thrown from the side, and I found the old helmsman standing there.

"You jus' wait, yer old bastard! I'll get you yet! One night you'll be flyin', all right, right over the side! I'll…" the man started screaming at him.

I met the helmsman's eyes and smiled. That simple act, something that would have been a wind-up between friends, had brought out the real side of the man in the cage. I'd have understood anger, all things considered, but as the ranting went on, and got more inventive as I walked away from the cage, following him up to the raised deck, I recoiled at some of the things being shouted.

When one of them included what the four in the cage would do to the helmsman's daughter and granddaughters though, I twisted around, ready to silence them, only to see all four already shaking and crying out. Oracle had struck them with a lightning bolt, taking off from Bob's head and flying over to me.

"Jax, why are some people like that?" she asked disgustedly, landing on my shoulder and frowning with revulsion. "I was trying to help, trying to see if they could be reasoned with, or at least make them understand why we couldn't trust them yet. Then they said all that…just because of some water?"

"Some people are just broken, Oracle," I said, shaking my head, "and no matter what you do, they can't be fixed. It's best to treat them like a rabid animal and simply kill them off."

When I realized what I'd said, I paused. It had come out before I'd thought about it, but it felt right. Back home, they'd have gone to prison, come out, and been shits again, robbing and hurting people until they were caught again and sent down, again and again as the cycle repeated. I'd always been annoyed at the pattern, that these assholes continued to hurt people around them, but that was just the way the world was.

I'd accepted it. Here, though? Here, we couldn't afford that, and I'd made the decision on how to deal with them already without realizing it. Lorek and his thugs had been different, as the villagers needed to see a merciful lord.

These shits were as bad, if not worse, judging from the things they'd said. I made my way to the helmsman where he stood on the raised deck, working on sanding out a divot I'd carved into the deck with my dagger yesterday.

"What's your name?" I asked, and he straightened with a delighted smile.

"Jory, m'lord! I'm Jory Ansbach." He unconsciously flexed his fingers as he spoke to me, clearly reveling in the feeling of having a body that wasn't as damaged as it had been for decades.

"Good to meet you, Jory." I held out a hand. He looked surprised, then grinned wider, quickly wiping his hand on his pant leg, then reaching out and briefly gripping my wrist in greeting.

"So, why did you throw that water over those assholes in the cage?" I asked, and I got a guilty look in return.

"I saw you speakin' to them, an' I knew they'd all stink, so..." He shrugged, looking down reflexively.

"Whoa, none of that shit, Jory," I said quickly. He blinked and opened his mouth to speak, but I beat him to it. "Don't go staring at the deck in fear of me. Just look me in the eye and explain things. If you fuck up, I might be pissed at you, but as long as you don't hurt someone or fuck us over deliberately, I'll always listen. Okay?" Jory looked at me for a second, then straightened his shoulders, a decision clearly made.

"Aye, I did it so they'd not smell as bad, but mainly, I wanted you to see what they were like. Honut, the little evil one? He'd stab his own mother for a copper. All four of 'em were sent to work on the ships fer ten years 'cause they'd been caught rapin'. I got no time for the likes of them, sir, and I wanted you to see for yerself."

I paused, thinking through his assertion and remembering that, in my world's own past, convicts had sometimes been used aboard ships. I had a sudden sinking feeling about the people I'd given a blanket amnesty to and had accepted into the tower. I'd taken an Oath from them, one that Seneschal had assured me would protect both them and me, but still.

"How many others in the crew are like that? Criminals, I mean?" I asked Jory, receiving a shrug in return.

"Not many, lord. I think Petey was given five years for stealin', and Gimil was here fer murder of a guardsman, but he'd came home and found the fella with 'is wife, and Petey was trying to feed 'imself. The rest of us were all signed up for a life in the sky out of choice."

I nodded at that, thinking maybe we'd been lucky, then, but I'd need to speak to this Gimil.

"About Gimil," I said, only to get a sad shake of the head.

"Captain—the old captain, I mean—'e made an example of 'im to make sure we all 'knew our place.' Threw 'im over the side two days back. When we raided the village, 'e gave some of the boys and girls to those who'd pleased him. Gimil had led us when we said it weren't right."

"Some of the crew raped the prisoners?" I asked with a low growl, and Jory spoke up quickly.

"None of those that swore to you, lord! There were seven that did it, that I saw. One, well 'e hurt a little boy bad, killed 'im, and we threw 'im off the ship ourselves. Two more died in the fightin'; they were ships guards, and the last four...well," he said, gesturing to the four men in the cage.

I managed to grab Oracle's leg just before she took off, and I spoke firmly to her. "No! We'll deal with this once we're away from the tower."

She looked rebellious for a second, then quickly settled down when she saw the look in my eye.

"Thank you for telling me, Jory. I'll not have men like that in my lands. However, and I'm sure you understand this, I need to be sure of what you've said."

"I do, milord. Just tell me what you want. I can bring you others that saw it, or the girls and boys that were...used..." He faltered, looking concerned about bringing the last group to me and making them relive their experiences.

"No. I'll probably talk to you again later, but thank you," I said, walking away from him and crossing to Oren where he stood on the main deck. He regarded me as I approached, noting the twin looks of anger on both mine and Oracle's faces.

"Uh-oh, who pissed in yer breakfast?" he said, frowning.

"Nobody, I fucking hope." I drew him aside. "Look, I just found out from Jory that a few of the crew of this ship raped and killed some of the villagers. I hadn't realized before, but the two groups have made a point of staying separate since I released them. Have you seen that? And did you know?"

"Nay, laddie, I'd no seen tha', but I can believe it. It be the kinda thing that happens, unfortunately."

"No...no, it fucking doesn't," I said forcefully. "I need you to make this very, very clear to people. This doesn't 'happen,' and if it does, I'll make damn sure whoever did it regrets it for the rest of their life, both goddamn seconds of it!"

I took a deep breath and went on. "If I have to say this to our people, if this is really a rule I have to lay down, I will, but I'll be furious and disappointed that it even needs to be said. We're supposed to be family here, and that—"

"Nay, laddie, ain't needed to be said. None o' my lads and lassies would need to be told, and I dinna see anyone else that'd need it neither. It be normal fer a warship to need extra crew, and sometimes, well, mebbe they get shits like that. My ship, and Decin's, we were family ships, an' we only hired those we knew well."

"Thank god," I growled, shaking my head as I tried to tamp down on the fury raging in me.

"Can I ask a question?" Oren said suddenly.

"I've never known you to ask permission before, mate; what is it?" I said, getting an embarrassed grin in return.

"Well, you an' Oracle...yer bond, how deep does it be?"

"I don't get you," I said, looking at Oracle in confusion only to find her looking back at me in the same way.

"Argh, look. I am probl'y sayin' this wrong, but yer bond...last few days, I've seen it, an' I need to ask, are you sharin' yer emotions?" Oren cheeks were stained bright red, but he plowed on manfully. "Look, we all been seein' how she acts wit' ye, and truth be told, it be fuckin' hilarious. But yer anger...yer depression when people died, all o' it, I dinna know ye well enough to be sure, but iff'n yer sharin' emotions, well..." He shrugged, and I stared at him blankly.

Oracle took off suddenly, flying away in a blur of wings, and disappeared over the side of the ship. I followed her trajectory in confusion. After a second, though, I felt my anger die down to a manageable level, and I drew in a deep breath, even more confused. I looked to Oren and saw him nodding as he looked back at me.

"There it be." He smiled and continued quietly. "Ah did wonder, the way ye were so easily sidetracked suddenly, where before yer were a man o' focus. Me an' Cai were talkin' about it a wee while ago. I think ye need to go find yer companion, mate."

I nodded, not pleased he'd been talking about me behind my back to Cai, but understanding that, as "the boss," it'd happen.

I followed Oracle's flight over to the side of the ship, my bond guiding me. I broke into a jog, taking the stairs quickly to her floor and dismissing the crystal doorway to the Hall of Memories.

She was huddled on her manawell, shrunk down to her original size, only six inches in height. She sat with her legs pulled up to her chest, arms wrapped around them as she shook.

"Oracle?" I called softly, rushing to her, and going down on one knee so I was level with her face. "What's wrong?" I asked, afraid that she was hurt. She lifted her tiny tear-streaked face and spoke, barely above a whisper.

"I'm sorry, Jax. I'm so sorry!"

"Why? What happened? Seriously, Oracle, what the hell?" I whispered, reaching out to her, and dipping my hand into her well.

She sat on the surface as though it was solid, but my fingers felt only a cool liquid as I lifted her free. I cradled her to my chest and took a seat, closing the door with a thought. After a second, I felt her uncurl, growing to her normal size of a foot tall, as she wrapped her tiny arms around my neck and buried her face against me.

I held her for a while as she cried, with no idea what to do beyond slowly stroking her back, her wings fluttering with each sob. After what seemed like forever, she finally responded to my coaxing and spoke again.

"When we bonded, I…well, I'd never really done anything with people before," she whispered. "Oh, I'd watched them, and I'd talked to them loads, but until you let me bond you, I'd always been an observer. Our emotions are different from yours.

"They're, well…when we have our ability to absorb mana burned out, we lose a lot of the highs and lows. We still feel, but just not as much. When we bonded, I felt your emotions so strongly, and I…I wanted to feel that myself."

"Okay, that's all right, Oracle…" I whispered, continuing to stroke her back and trying to keep my voice level while imagining the things I'd like to do to someone who burned emotions out of a sentient creature and enslaved them to a fucking tower for eternity.

"So…I…"

"It's all right, Oracle, just tell me," I asked quietly, already fairly sure of what was coming by now.

"I made a connection to you that was deeper, I…I didn't know what I was doing! I could have hurt you, and I just…I…"

"No, you couldn't have hurt me. Remember, the bond prevents that," I said firmly. "You did what you thought was best for us, didn't you?"

"Yes, but I…I wanted…"

"Even if you wanted it, that doesn't make it bad. But explain it for me, please," I whispered, still holding her.

"I made our emotional connection deeper. It's helped to heal some of the damage that the spellbooks, and well, your life, did to you. You were alone for so long, and betrayed so much, so you didn't trust people very much. I…I helped you to relax."

"Okay, now tell me the downside." I didn't feel any different, but would I know?

"It's made our emotions feed off each other!" she cried out. "I don't know how to fix it!"

"Feed off each other?" I asked, but even as I said it, I knew what she meant.

I'd always had issues with my temper, and it had been getting worse. Breaking Lorek's arm was only one example. I'd been keeping my rage under control so far, but only just. If Oracle hadn't hit those guys in the cage with a lightning bolt, I would have. And I had to admit, if only to myself, I wouldn't have been as gentle. I'd have used fire.

"Every time you're angry, *I* get angry; then you get angrier, and so do I! And with the sex? I want to try it, I want to enjoy you, and have you enjoy me, then I feel you getting aroused, and I feel hotter, suddenly. Just thinking about it means suddenly, it's all I can think of! I could have killed those people, I could have…what do we do, Jax?" Oracle wailed, sitting back in my arms to stare at me, her eyes puffy from weeping.

She pulled at her long hair, making it come away in clumps. I stared as her body began to change before my eyes, going grey, her face draining and her body twisting.

She drew in upon herself, becoming a strange, ugly, naked, half-starved little creature, and I swallowed hard.

"Oracle?" I prodded, and the little figure looked up at me, a bright red spark deep in her eyes as she focused on me.

"I should be an imp," she said despondently. "I don't deserve to look pretty."

Despite it all, I had to stifle a laugh.

"What did you do to yourself?" I asked, and she shrugged, looking away.

I couldn't help but think of a petulant teenager in full swing, and just like that, the spell was broken. It started low at first, a shake in my chest, but inside of a few seconds, I was laughing openly.

At first, Oracle was clearly angry. But as I roared with laughter, she slowly began to see the funny side, until she was hitting me and shouting about how "it just wasn't funny" while giggling. After a few seconds, she grew in size and leaned in for a kiss.

"Ah, Oracle?" I stopped her, leaning back a bit.

"Yeah, Jax?" she asked, hesitant as I clearly felt differently about kissing her.

"Think you could change back?"

She started, looking down at her hands, and then burst out laughing properly. She gave herself a little shake, and she was back, growing to full size, seated atop my lap on the little sofa thingy. She was stunning again, long black hair down to her waist…and she was also still completely naked.

I coughed. Free of the emotions we'd been sharing, it was a lot easier to concentrate on things, but still…she was beautiful, naked, and straddling me.

We kissed slowly, but when she drew back, I realized our hands had been a lot less busy than last time, and we gazed into each other's eyes for a long moment before I broke the silence.

"I need to figure all this out, Oracle. We're bonded, so it's for life if we cross this line. I'm not ready for that, not until I know how I feel properly, so can we cool it a bit?" I was painfully aware that I was close to catapulting her across the room if my belt broke with the pressure it was under, Mr. Happy desperate to "meet" her as he was.

"I understand," she whispered, leaning in to kiss me one last time. "But as you say, Jax, we're bonded for life, so…"

"Oh, I know. This is a fucked-up situation in every way, and believe me, I want to. Damn, I really, really, want to, but…" I stroked the skin over her hips with either thumb, unable to let go of her silken skin, yet having to force my hands to stay where they were.

"I can see your mind Jax, your past…and the rage you feel when the strong force the weak, but I'm *neither*. Just consider that I'm your bonded companion. I'm not really a woman; I can take any form, but I'm still me. I'm not going to change how I feel about you, and I won't get jealous if you want to play with others…Well, not much…and we could always…" She trailed off, looking anxiously at me.

"Seriously, Oracle, don't finish that sentence." I took a deep breath and sat up, which had the unfortunate effect of moving her until she was poised directly over the problem area. "And please, for the love of god, don't start rocking. I'll tear through these pants at this rate," I whispered, closing my eyes as she immediately moved, sensing the disparity between my words and what I wanted, and I felt it. "In fact, please, *please*, get off me and put some clothes on!"

Oracle let out a little laugh and I felt her shift, becoming her smaller foot-high form and taking off as I climbed to my feet. I was going to have to make adjustments now, and that was dangerous with her about as well. I turned my back to her and started shifting myself around when a sudden change became clear. I paused, realizing just how much easier this was to control. Well, not easy, I was still male after all, but the desperate need…

"I know, Jax, it's a lot easier to think like this, but…I'm using a lot of mana to do *this*," Oracle commented.

I turned, accidentally sweeping a book from the table as I spun too fast. Oracle laughed from where she hovered before me.

"Oh, for fuck's…" I groaned, spinning back around and putting myself right. When I turned back, Oracle was smiling nervously, and I shook my head, knowing I'd been tricked.

"Right! So, care to explain what you're using our mana for, then?" I asked, trying to move past her cheeky maneuver.

"Ah, ummm…okay," Oracle said, still smiling. "I've suppressed my emotions and dampened down our link, a bit like the reverse of the way I bypassed that slave collar."

"I have no idea why that has anything to do with the slave collar, but no," I said firmly, and Oracle blinked in surprise.

"But Jax, this way you won't have to feel…"

"Do you still feel your emotions properly?" I asked her, and she shrugged.

"Well, some, yes. I—"

"And you're using most of our mana to do this," I interrupted her, checking the mana bar in my vision. We were hovering at less than a third of the usual total.

"Well, yes," Oracle said, wringing her hands, "but—"

"No. Undo it please, Oracle. We need the mana, and I'm not having you stunt your emotions to make my life easier. We'll both just have to watch it and try to control ourselves." I took a deep breath and shrugged. "It'll feel like being a teenager again, I guess. All I wanted to do was shag constantly, and I survived that. Guess I've got a lot of cold showers ahead of me until I figure this out."

"Are you sure?" she asked. I nodded, feeling a strange sensation inside as she released the weave she'd used to suppress my emotions. We both took an involuntary deep breath.

97

The world seemed different, and I couldn't even explain how. Brighter, the air crisper, and Oracle looked…I refocused my eyes with an act of will and saw her doing the same. Even though it had felt this way before, I had been exposed to it gradually, and I hadn't noticed how much of our bond I'd taken for granted. This would come to a head soon, I just knew it, but right now, I had a fuck ton of other things I needed to sort first, and banging my companion senseless was not going to help…*maybe just a quickie?*

I drew in a deep breath and forced those thoughts aside as Oracle and I headed for the door. It had been an hour that we'd been up in the hall, and the ship had to be ready by now. They were probably all waiting on me and placing bets on what, or who, I was doing.

I opened the door, then Oracle and I set off jogging, letting the tower seal the room behind us.

A short while later, I was on the ship, and Oren was grinning at the pair of us. Cai and Isabella stood with a dozen others, watching as Jory slowly awoke the ship under Oren's direction.

"Tha's it! Bring 'er to life again; warm 'er up jus' right now!" he called out, a deep *thrummm* of energy running through the ship, causing it to tremble. The energy began to build, slowly at first. But after a few seconds, a faint blue glow intensified around the engines, and I moved closer to the nearest one.

I leaned over the side of the ship, watching as the cylindrical pod shook slightly, and the light grew stronger. A line of runes lit up, encircling the top half of the engine and slowly pulsing with the energy that flowed through them.

"Tha's it! Now tha engines, bring 'em up!" Oren called out, and I looked over my shoulder.

He and Jory stood at the helm, hands flashing as they hit and adjusted levers and dials, two engineers standing watch over them nervously. A second line of runes ignited on the lower half of the engine pod, and the entire pod shook like a bear awakening from slumber. The light grew, shifting from a deep indigo all the way to a pale blue that was almost impossible to see. As the engine flared fully to life, the entire ship twisted and tilted slightly as it lifted from the tower's balcony.

"There! Number three! Get 'er up!" Oren shouted, three more of the engineers running to the far side of the ship to make some adjustments.

It only took a few minutes, but the bobbing and weaving of the ship evened out, and the slowly building seasickness I'd started to feel began to fade. Over the side next to the engine nearest to me, the steady, deep blue color was holding strong.

The warship *Agamemnon's Wrath* slowly began to turn, heading out and away from the tower. I had a moment of vertigo as the point where I stood passed over the edge and out into the air, and I gripped the railing tight.

I scanned around, wide-eyed as we flew forward. The flat-bottomed ship began unfurling sails to either side and above, sails that billowed and boomed as they filled with a fresh breeze. I was standing on a ship, a ship of the sky, and it was magnificent!

I couldn't help it. I let go of the railing and held both fists in the air, letting out a cry as we went.

"Whoooo, fuck yes! We're flying…WE'RE FREE!"

CHAPTER NINE

I enjoyed the sights for a few minutes before tearing myself away and going into the captain's cabin. It only took a few minutes to pull the rest of my gear on and make sure my weapons and various potions were in place. The three mana and two health I'd found could be life-savers.

In short order, I found myself outside again, jogging up the stairs and standing next to Oren and Jory, watching out across the sea of clouds.

I could have spent days at the bow of the ship. Hell, where being on a helicopter in the past was all noise and weirdness, and a plane was just sodding uncomfortable, especially for someone my size, this was…glorious. The gentle sun, the constant breeze, the sheer luxury of a sailing ship in the sodding sky…

I couldn't help but grin to myself at the thought of Tommy here. He'd be as high up as he could get, and he'd be helicoptering his cock at his enemies.

In the end, it was just under five and a half hours until we entered the valley that held Decin's crashed ship. We flew over trees for most of that time; the occasional river slipped through the verdant forest like a shining snake, but beyond the valleys and hills, the huge mountains stood silently at our back. Even with the cries of the flocks of birds that seemed to erupt from nowhere regularly, it was the most peace I'd had in days.

The air was clear, and with the sun shining down on us, despite the breeze, it was warm enough that I could have made a fortune selling tickets. Something like this would have made me a billionaire back home, I reflected as I watched the river below us. I lost myself for a few seconds, imagining a fleet of these flying through the sky in the Mediterranean or exploring the Alps.

It was a wonderful fantasy, especially alongside the thought of being absolutely, insanely wealthy and never having to fight for my life again. But after a few seconds more, I dismissed it. I'd be bored inside a week, and without the chance to fight, I'd never level again, and I damn well loved that feeling.

I grinned to myself, noticing a creature that looked like a crocodile crossed with a pitbull as it came stomping out of the shallows and bit down hard on some kind of deer. I winced in sympathy at the prey's cry, but shrugged and dismissed it, as I realized the croc needed to eat as well. Fuck it.

The river emptied out soon into a small lake, and on the far shore, listing to one side, was Decin's ship.

As we approached, I grimaced and jogged back to Oren, who stood squinting at the ship ahead.

"Dude, sorry, I meant to give this to you earlier." I pulled a ring from my bag, passing it to him.

Ring of Farseeing		Further Description *Yes/No*	
Details:		The Ring of Farseeing is part of the standard equipment given to warship captains by the City of Himnel. This ring forms part of a set and grants +1 mile to visibility in ideal conditions. Five times per 24 hours, a single charge may be used to focus the wearer or another's vision for 30 seconds.	
Rarity:	**Magical:**	**Durability:**	**Charge:**
Unusual	Yes	79/100	18/100

Oren took it, then grinned as he realized what it was. He slipped it onto his finger and frowned, his eyes turning silver as he used the ring's ability.

"Thanks, Jax, but did ye no see any other gear like it?" he asked, his eyes unclouding thirty seconds later as the ability wore off, and he turned back to me.

"Not really. The prick of a captain had some magic boots, but I kinda ignored them. I think they improved your grip, and that was it?" I said, but I gestured to the captain's cabin below. "I guess if he had any more, it'd be in there. Feel free to check; if it's for the ship, you can have it," I said, thinking "need before greed" as a loot rule had always steered me right before.

Oren chucked me the ring and set off running towards the cabin while shouting to me.

"Use it! They're no' there!"

I blinked then slipped the ring on my finger and concentrated, the ring's magic flowing into me as I focused my eyes in on the ship.

It took a few seconds to get it right, and it zoomed in and out of focus, the scene unidentifiable as though I was staring through a blurry telescope.

Suddenly, it came into focus. It was still too distant to make things out clearly, but even at this distance, I could see a huge difference from a few days back when they'd landed. The ship looked deserted, and to add freakiness to the whole thing, it was definitely listing to one side. The entire ship looked like it'd been pulled down hard on one side by something, and the ground was churned up on that side by the passage of many feet. I took a deep breath and called out to the squad that stood close by.

"Lydia!" She came running over, sliding to a stop next to me and saluting. "Do you have a rank structure yet?" I asked her, and when she looked confused, I explained. "Did Barrett name one of you to take the lead out of your group?"

She nodded quickly.

"Aye, sir, I were to stick close to you, and make sure you get back to tha tower, no matter what; the rest are to do what I say."

"Good enough. Right, look at the ship and tell me what you think," I said and passed her the ring. She blinked in surprise but quickly slipped it onto her finger, and I pointed at the ship. She frowned and activated the ring, staring at the ship, and with each passing second, what had happened there grew clearer.

"Looks like they were attacked," she muttered, then shook her head as her vision returned to normal. She blinked a few times as her eyes adjusted, and she met my questioning gaze. "It looks like they were attacked, Lord Jax. Somethin' big came out of the forest and took 'em."

"I think so, too. Whatever it was, it looks to have pulled the ship half over to get to them, so it's either big, or heavy, or both. I couldn't see any bodies, so we need to check for that first. If they're alive, then we're going to go get some practice in!" I said, grinning at her. She grinned right back, clearly up for testing her new skills. "Did you level when we fought at the tower?" I asked.

She nodded enthusiastically. "Twice; I put 'alf my points into Endurance, and the rest into Strength." It was a solid tank's choice there, and I hoped that it'd help in the fight. We'd barely had time to train together as we'd prepared for the fight for the tower. Since then, well, Barrett had given them all some help, but it was very little. I'd be carrying the majority of the upcoming fight, I already knew.

"Gather round, team!" I called to the others and went to meet them, waiting until we were all together, and ignoring Oren as he came flying out of the captain's cabin, wearing pants that were far too long and carrying a load of other gear.

"From what we can tell, something attacked Decin and his ship," I said, looking from one to another. "Whatever it was, it's probably big, and it likely came from—and returned to—the forest. We're going to check it out, but I want to cover some tactics before we get any closer." I pointed to myself and Bob. "We're the tanks for the party; we take the hits and deal them out, which means we're the front line.

"Lydia, you're going to be to the right of me at all times, but far enough aside that I don't gut you. Remember, this isn't exactly a precision instrument." I banged the base of my naginata down once, hard. "It's basically a giant stick with a damn sharp knife on the end, and I don't want to hit you with it."

"Isn't that a spear, lord?" A voice came from my left, and I turned my head to look at Arrin, who grinned at me. "A stick with a knife on the end, I mean?"

"Okay, point. This is more like a staff with a sword on the end, but…"

"So, a swordstaff? Or a polearm?" Lydia interjected.

I shot her a glare. "Okay, fuck you all; this is a *naginata*, and I don't want to hurt you with it. Or at least I didn't until now. You all got that out of your system?" I asked.

Arrin opened his mouth, but shut it quickly at a glare from me. I could hear snickering from the rest of the group, and I had to work to hide my smile as well. Cheeky bastards.

"So, moving on: Jian, you're on Bob's left. Stephanos and Miren, you're behind them; keep back a bit so you've got space to use your bows. Cam, you've got fuck-all armor. Even Miren has some, so why is that?" I asked the big, dark-haired elf, garbed in a rough tunic and pants, but he held that bloody enormous wood axe in one hand. He'd blatantly piled all his stat points into Strength, and I just had to know what he was thinking with not wearing armor. I mean, I knew we had some…

"Don't like it." That was it. That was all I was going to get, clearly.

"You don't like it?" I asked, getting a nod in return. "You don't like wearing the armor, or that it protects you, and you know, could keep you alive?!"

"Yup."

"Well, fuck me. Thanks for explaining that so well. I feel much better about things now!" I said, facepalming. "Okay—"

"You're welcome, lord," he muttered, interrupting me. I looked up at him and glared.

"Right, clearly you're either more batshit crazy than you were, which I didn't think was possible, or you're trying to wind me up. Congratulations, you get to be ass end, Charlie."

"I'm Cam."

"You're annoying is what you are. It means you're staying at the back of the group, and you're going to protect the archers until you prove that you're stable enough to trust by my side," I retorted, turning back to Miren and Stephanos. "Take shots when you can, but not until I say so or unless we get spotted. If you think there's a chance you'll hit one of us, move or hold your fire. We don't need an arrow in the back of the knee to fuck our day up further, okay?"

Once everyone knew their roles, I told Miren and Stephanos to take up places on either side of the ship and watch for anything that might be dangerous until we landed.

Then I pulled out the robes and staff I'd looted from the mage who had attacked the tower. "Arrin!" I chucked them to him. "Put these on and use the staff; consider them a loan until you prove yourself."

"I get to wear a dress?" he asked, shaking his head.

"Aye, well, Lydia told me about your tastes. I thought you'd like it!" I shot back at him and got a laugh in return, as well as a nod of thanks.

I made my way across the ship to rejoin Oren, who was half-naked on the upper deck, pulling clothes on he'd clearly looted from the captain's cabin. While they were meant for a human, he'd been both short and fat, so they weren't as badly fitted as they could have been.

After a long minute of huffing, sweating, and far more dwarven ass crack on display than I ever wanted to see again, Oren was wearing a pair of rolled-up trousers, his own shirt and breastplate, and a hat, with a large overcoat thrown on the floor and a pair of gloves that came halfway to his elbow.

"I'll have to get tha' altered; they be too good to pass up!" he muttered, kicking the coat aside and adjusting himself. "Och, these pants do be a bit tight, ye know whut I mean?"

He grunted, and I closed my eyes, rubbing at the bridge of my nose as I tried to banish the sight I'd just been exposed to. I suspected I'd be waking years from now, screaming in the middle of the night with the memory.

"So, you've nicked his pants...anything useful?" I asked heavily.

"Oh, aye laddie, tons! The full set be givin' bonuses to ma farsight, ma handlin' ability, even to the ship overall! It be five percent faster, gunners be ten percent more accurate, and the entire crew gets a bonus o' plus one to Luck!" He grinned at me as he gestured each item then to the overcoat on the deck. "As long as it be close by, I still get tha set bonus; now all I need to find is tha boots!"

"Ah, crap, yeah. Good point!" I said and pulled them out of my bag, chucking them over to him after examining them quickly.

The Forgotten Faithful

Captain's Boots		Further Description *Yes/No*	
Details:		These boots grant +2 to Agility and improve traction on slippery surfaces. These boots are part of the Himnel Airship Captain set and grant bonuses when worn as a full set.	
Rarity:	Magical:	Durability:	Charge:
Uncommon	Yes	86/100	34/100

I shrugged as I looked over the notification. They were all right, and yeah, the plus two to Agility was good, but my boots were damn comfortable, and my armor fit over them, so I wouldn't have swapped them out, anyway. Giving Oren the full set, though…he pulled them on as quick as he could, thumping down on his ass to yank them on. Despite grumbling about how tight they were, he was grinning ear to ear as he stood.

"Ye know how long I wanted a set o' these?" he queried, pulling the gloves on tighter and wiggling his fingers in the air. "Years, laddie! The bonuses alone be worth it, ten times over! No to mention, the wife loves a man in uniform, iff'n ye know what I mean!" He gave me a wink while catching the ring I threw back to him.

"I really didn't need that image in my mind, dude; thanks for that," I grumbled, but I couldn't help grinning at him.

He looked slightly ludicrous in the gear, especially as it was tight in all the wrong places and clearly meant for someone else. The thing was, though, he also really suited it, like I was seeing him in his natural habitat. I checked the notification I'd received and blinked.

Congratulations!

You have received the following bonuses due to being part of the ship's crew of the *Agamemnon's Wrath*:

+1 to Luck
+2 to Agility
+2 to Endurance

"Hell, that's a great bonus," I said, then turned to Jory. "Why didn't the old captain have this on when you arrived at the tower?"

"Well, milord, he said it enough around us so we all knew it, 'Why should I give you slackers anything?' That's what 'e used to say, said we should work harder, then we'd earn the bonuses. Don' get me wrong, he wore it when we went into battle, 'cause 'e was too cowardly not to, but the rest o' the time, nay." The old helmsman took a few steps to the right and spat over the side of the ship, returning to catch the wheel before it could move more than an inch or two.

"Fair enough; he was a prick and deserved to die. I'm fine with that." I scowled down at the four men in the cages.

"I wouldn't," I heard Oren warn, and I frowned at him questioningly.

"All I'm sayin', laddie, is that ye promised to set 'em free. Givin' 'em the freedom o' the clouds, while damn well deserved, will no make ye more popular with tha crew, an' word will get around."

The entire time, Oren had been staring forward, but he'd been watching me out of the corner of his eye, and Jory was silent as they both waited.

"Dammit," I muttered, shaking my head. I wanted to open the cages and have Bob throw them out. Hell, I wanted to do it myself, but I needed to master my emotions. I'd learned control hard over the years, fighting again and again when my smart mouth got me into trouble or someone annoyed me too much. I could do it again. I had to. As to those fucknuts though...

"I don't think anyone's going to miss them, so how about we use them instead?" I suggested, getting a questioning raised eyebrow in response.

"We need to know what happened down there, so let's use them. Send them down first to have a look."

"Use them like they be rats? See iff'n somethin' bites?" Oren clarified.

"Yeah, why not?"

He shrugged, and I got the feeling that he wasn't liking the idea, but he didn't want them around either, so...

"Okay, what can you see?" I asked him.

His eyes changed again. "The ship looks to be in fairly good nick; engines appear intact, so she probably jus' needs restartin', an' the engineers can do tha'. I can see where tha crew made repairs an' all. It be them I be worried aboot."

"Yeah, me, too," I said, nodding. "Get us over there, and we can take a look. Once we've checked out the ship, we'll follow that trail as far as we can. Keep us back a bit on the first pass, so we're out of range if there's something hiding, but don't look like you're keeping your distance."

"How do I do tha'?" Oren asked, looking at me like I was mad.

"I don't know, fly casual!" I snapped at him, walking down onto the deck below.

Something about the conversation with the hairy bastard had triggered a memory, but I couldn't figure out what it was. I shrugged and dismissed it; either it'd come back to me, or it wouldn't.

I strode forward, Lydia quickly meeting me halfway down the deck. "We're going to follow the trail, and we're going to have help," I told her, nodding towards the cages.

"Yer settin' those animals free? Lord, we can't trust 'em!" she said, alarmed.

"Oh, I promised to set them free," I said, giving a shark-like grin. "I just didn't say where, or if I'd give them anything to help them survive. Let's go give them the good news!"

Oracle, who'd spent most of her time on the trip perched at the top of the highest mast, came flying down as soon as she saw us approaching the cage, and I could feel her interest.

"What are we doing, Jax?" she asked, alighting gently on my shoulder and getting a warm smile from Lydia. Oracle had become something of a mix between a mistress of the tower and a mascot to the people over the last few days. She was loved for the way she interacted with people and especially for the free healing she gave.

Occasionally, she'd go so far as using a huge amount of mana in one go to cure a person of pretty much anything she could. On the other side, she was very clearly revered as one of the three wisps of the tower and as my companion.

As we walked closer, Oracle dug her fingers into my shoulder slightly before forcing herself to relax, and the three of us joined Bob, who'd stood guard at the cages, staring at the criminals ceaselessly since he'd taken up the station earlier. The men glowered at me, all four of them clearly feeling hard done by.

Not one of them seemed to believe this was deserved, and the dark looks they gave me, Lydia, then Oracle made my anger build. They'd begun to ignore Bob, which I supposed was fair enough.

If they thought he was an average bone minion, like Lydia had, they were expecting him to disappear sooner or later, and he was hardly the most interesting conversationalist. What inflamed my anger the most, though, was the casual way they shifted their eyes from me to Lydia, then Oracle, staring at their bodies.

Lydia was dressed normally, and Oracle was…well she was dressed normally for her, which meant an outfit most exotic dancers would have loved.

That didn't give those asshats the right to ogle her, though. Bob clearly picked up on my irritation, leaning in and gripping the bars of the cage in his enormous hands. He flexed, and the entire cage creaked, causing the men to flinch. I tamped down my own anger as much as possible, and I resolved to give them a chance. I was well aware that I had an issue with anger, even before all of this, and having Oracle's emotions reinforce my own wasn't helpful, but I'd deal with it.

"I'm going to give you one last chance," I said aloud, getting a concerned look from Oracle and Lydia. "I said I'll set you free, and I'll do that, but I'm going to give you a chance to help us, and maybe earn a—"

"Get fucked." A voice cut me off from the back of the group. The man who'd spoken was larger than the rest, heavily muscled and scarred, and he spat at me.

It hit the cage, breaking up and falling down to the ground. I swear I felt some of it, and the world went white hot with my rage.

I spun my naginata around, hammering it down into the cage, and it cut through the bars like a hot knife through butter. The runes blazed like the heart of the sun as my fury hammered through it. I made a second cut, then a third, and the remains of the cage fell apart around me as I shouldered my way inside, Bob hissing like a kettle, and Oracle…well, she was past me in a blur.

Before I could get to him, she was there, a lightning bolt slamming into him and flowing out into the other three, making them all scream in agony. I reached past her, grabbing ahold of him by the throat and drawing my naginata back, fully intending on skewering him and the bastards that shared his cage. They deserved it, after all. They were rapists, thieves, and likely murderers. There was no place for the likes of them in my new world, not the one I would build.

I rocked to one side as something hit me, and I turned, eyes blazing, only to find Oren there. He pushed himself the rest of the way inside the cage, moving in front of Oracle, Bob, and me. He shoved me back, forcing me to release the target of my ire.

"You…*dare!*" I growled, and Bob and Oracle fixated on the little dwarf as well.

"Aye, laddie, fer the sake o' who ye be, I dare!" he said, shaking his head. "Dinna lose yersel', no like this, no fer the likes o' them!"

I stared at him for a long moment, my breathing ragged in my throat, but as I calmed slightly, I saw things.

The men in the cage were huddled back, terrified beyond their wits. The crew had frozen, fearful of the animal in their midst. Most of all, I saw Oren. He was trembling; he was absolutely sodding terrified of what I was going to do to him for interrupting, but he'd done this because it was right.

Just like risking everything to feed the slaves was right. Just like risking everything to throw in with me and save the people back at the tower was right.

I took a deep breath and acknowledged to myself that he was doing what was right now as well.

They'd spat at me. I couldn't chop them limb from limb because they spat at me. I wanted to; oh fuck, I wanted to so bad, but it wasn't right.

A memory popped up then, when I was much younger, sitting in the back of a police van. Thomas sat across from me, and Jonno stood in the door, wiping some vomit off his uniform. He'd stepped in to break up a fight. We'd been force-feeding a dealer his own shit, making sure he knew not to peddle that crap to kids. Jonno and some other police had arrived, breaking up the fight between us and the dealer's friends.

He'd stopped Thomas from curb stomping some poor fucker for standing up for his mate, then he'd saved the dealer, even though he ended up covered in vomit.

We couldn't be sent to prison; we were only fifteen, and we were wards of the court anyway, so we didn't give a shit about consequences. We were cleaning up the streets in our "territory," and we were both furious about being stopped. We were doing what the police couldn't. We deserved respect for that.

I remembered it like it was yesterday, the stink of the stomach acids, the fury of the fight, the warmth of the blood we were both covered in, and there was Jonno. He'd picked us up enough to know who we were by that point, and he knew we were aggressive little shits, but that we did what we thought was…right.

No matter what it cost us, we did what we thought was right, and he was there telling us why we were wrong. We disagreed; scum like that guy couldn't be helped. They needed to be removed from society. Instead, he'd piled in there, getting fluids that could hold any number of diseases all over himself, all to help a goddamn drug dealer.

I'd asked him why, why he'd risked himself for that piece of shit, and he'd looked at me, world weary and sad as he shook his head. It wasn't his place to decide who was worth saving, he'd said. For all he knew, that man was a saint or a murderer. The police don't get to make that call, he'd said. Those entrusted with protecting don't get to decide who lives and who dies. It was his place to save who he could, and in saving a piece of shit drug dealer, he saved us from being split up and sent to separate homes.

I remembered it all, come and gone in a second, and I compared that moment with now. In this new world, someone had to make the call. It couldn't be a jury of peers, not yet. For now, democracy was going to take a back seat, and I would be the final arbiter of justice. But spitting at me couldn't mean death, or where would it end?

Would disagreeing with me be death next, or refusing to go to my bed? How short was the step from judge to murderer? I swallowed hard, closing my eyes, and forcing the rage down.

When I opened them, Oren was still there, but he was watching me with a lot less fear.

I nodded to him, and he stepped aside. Bob backed away, and Oracle returned to hover by my side. I waited, ignoring the acrid smell of urine and fear, until the men each looked up, making eye contact at the last.

"This is the last chance I'll give you," I whispered, my voice rough with suppressed emotion. "We need to know what happened down there. I will set you free, and you'll follow the trail. I'll be right behind you.

"You'll get a weapon each, and you can keep it, as well as some food. Once we've found the missing crew, you get to go in whatever direction you want, provided it's away from my tower. Or...I'll do as I promised, and I'll set you free right now. We're over the lake, so you'll survive the drop, probably. Provided you can swim, you'll probably get to shore. You'll have nothing from me, and you'll be killed on sight by any of my people. Choose quickly."

I stood there, my naginata pulsing with mana, and waited. It wasn't long before the first spoke, then the others quickly followed his lead.

"We...we'll help..."

I nodded once and stepped out of the ruins of the cage, moving past Lydia, who stared at me for a second before nodding and falling in behind me. Oren returned to the raised deck, and I drew in a deep breath as I reached the railing, staring out over the water that sped along below us. It took me a long while to speak, but when I did, it was in a voice that shook slightly.

"Do you think I did wrong there?" I asked Lydia and included Oracle as she landed gently on the railing, flicking her legs over the side. It was a few seconds before Lydia responded, but eventually, her unusually subdued voice rose.

"It's not my place te—"

"Bullshit. I asked you a question, Lydia. You've never been shy about your opinion before; tell me the truth," I snapped, and instantly regretted it.

"You were angry," she said eventually. "They spat at yeh, and yeh lost yer temper. I've seen yeh struggling with yer emotions for days; we all 'ave, and people are startin' to get worried. One minute, yer like a big brother to everyone, the strongest there is, honest and carin' for us all. The next, yer like a wild animal. Yer need to watch yer temper."

"I shouldn't have done that," I agreed. "They didn't deserve to die for..."

"Aye, they did." Lydia cut in suddenly, making me stop in surprise. "Yer the lord; if yeh didn't like their hair, yer could kill 'em. That's not what this is all about. Yer want 'em dead, yer tell one of us, an' we'll do it, or do it yerself. When yer killed Toka, sent it flying off the tower like that, we all knew why. We knew it deserved to die. Yer said to Makin that it had to be you what did it, that it had to be justice, not revenge."

I nodded, thinking back to that day as she went on.

"Since then, yeh been throwin' yerself into things, an' working like a madman. We needed that, we know we did, but now yer on the ragged edge. Yer need to rest, and yer need to decide and stick to it. If they deserve to die, it be because yer the lord, and yer sayin' it be so.

"Yeh don't need no more. People be afraid, because yer seem to do one thing, then another." She coughed, embarrassed, but pressed on. "Yer our lord. We'll do anythin' yer want, just command us. Don't go mental with rage, 'cos that's scary as hell. Most of the people back there think iff'n yer wanted the day to last longer, yeh'd just grab the sun and make it stay still."

"I'm not a god, Lydia; I'm just a man," I muttered shamefacedly.

"Yer a man who talks to the gods. Yeh don't call 'er 'the Great and Powerful Goddess Jenae'; yeh just call 'er Jenae. Yeh found a real goddess, yeh conquered a Great Tower, and kilt a SporeMother. They believe in yeh...an' so do I."

Her voice was quiet, but it held an unshakable confidence. "Yeh'll do the right thing, yer just need a little help from those of us that follow yer now and then; that's all."

I studied her face for a moment, seeing the pride and conviction in her eyes, and I smiled gratefully.

"Thank you, Lydia. I'll try my best to be worthy of that trust," I promised.

She smiled properly at me. It was like the sun coming out from a cloudy sky, and I realized she'd never smiled like that around me before. It was genuine and bright, and it made me feel better immediately.

I took a deep breath, shifting my attention up to the raised deck, and sighed. I knew what I had to do next.

"I've got an apology to make, I think. He's a good man, and I scared him," I said.

She laughed, breaking the spell. "He's a cantankerous little bastard of a dwarf, but he's all right, I guess."

I couldn't help but laugh as I agreed with her and headed towards the upper deck. Lydia called out from behind me, and I acknowledged her with a wave.

"I'll get the squad ready, my lord." she said, her footsteps heading toward the bow where most of them waited, snapping at them to gather around.

Oracle alighted on my shoulder again and spoke to me in a small voice. "This is my fault again, Jax. I'm so sorry."

I looked up to her, and we locked eyes, the turmoil in my own gaze matching the concern in hers.

"It really isn't. Yeah, what happened with us hasn't helped, it's true, but it's not your fault. I always had problems with my temper, and so did...*does*...Tommy. I just need to learn a bit of control again, that all."

"I'll help, just tell me what you need," she whispered.

"Maybe we should talk tonight, see if all that tree-hugging, touchy-feely crap helps, huh?" I said, sending her a sad smile.

"Touchy-feely?" she asked, perking up immediately.

I groaned before realizing she was winding me up. As she took off, I cursed, realizing she'd gotten me again. I knew she was trying to distract me, and I was thankful for it.

I crossed the raised deck to Oren, where he stood calmly next to Jory. As I paused next to him, we both spoke at once.

"I'm sorry, dude, I—"

"I'm sorry, Jax, I shouldna—" We both stopped and looked at each other, bursting into laughter.

"I'm sorry, man, I lost my temper. I'll do better." I grinned at him, and he nodded, replying quickly.

"Ach, yer tha lord. Yer in charge. I'm sorry I stepped in, 'specially for shits like them." He inclined his head toward the remnants of the cage, where Bob still stood guard over the four now thoroughly cowed criminals.

"Ha, thank you, man. I'm glad you did, even though a part of me disagrees, even now!" I said, shaking my head.

"I'm sorry too, Oren. This is my fault, and you were right earlier. We did bond too deeply; how did you know?" Oracle asked, and Oren grinned up at her.

"Ach, dinna worry, lass. It doesna matter…. As to the bond…well, let's jus' say tha' I've seen it happen…a long time ago, ye know. Over eighty years back now, when I were a wee nipper, but still…" He ran his hands through his beard, combing it out.

"Ma cousin, he were popular with tha ladies, iff'n ye take ma meanin'. And well, he mighta made a bond with a nymph. He wouldna say, but we all knew, ye ken? He started to get a bit…wild…chasin' anythin' in a skirt, then jus' anythin'! No one knows whut happen'd to him, but there was a rumor about him askin' about a supposed demon summonin' tome, and he were never seen again.

"Tha family were all warned after, dinna bond with nothin' that don't own a distillery!" Oren shrugged at us, and we simply stared back at him. "All tha' were ever found were his pants," he said quietly, gazing into the distance.

"So…you got that we had an emotional resonance from a cautionary tale about your cousin trying to bang a demon?" I asked slowly, and he nodded firmly. "Dude, you are so full of shit."

I shook my head, and when he started to speak up, I just held up my hand to stop him.

"I don't think we need to hear it, man. Seriously. I…just concentrate on the ship, okay? How long 'til we're ready to land?"

"Do we want to?" Oren asked, raising an eyebrow. "Canna see why we'd do tha'; can we no just let down a ladder?"

"Okay, that's far more sensible; let's do that. How long?" I repeated my question, and he shrugged.

"About five minutes, iff'n ye quit pesterin' me!"

"Fine. Let me and my team, plus those four idiots, climb down. Then you should take off and follow us at a distance while we check the ship and explore the area. We'll see what we find, then probably follow the tracks.

"Ye got balls o' brass and brains o' mince, ye know tha'?" Oren said.

I smirked, walking off down the deck towards my waiting team. "Damn right I do, mate! Damn right."

I retrieved four swords from the ship's stores and gave them to Lydia to hand out to the four in the cage once we were on land. Then I gathered up Bob, the rest of the team, and our smelly, depressed bait, directing everyone to the ladder one of the crew was preparing.

CHAPTER TEN

W e gathered around the railing, watching as the wrecked airship grew closer. We slowly lowered until we were less than ten feet from the low waves that splashed about on the lake, quickly closing the distance to Decin's ship.

I reveled in the warm sunlight on my back, the light reflected from the water below, and the beautiful view before us. Gnarled, ancient trees clustered everywhere. Some had fallen, creating bridges that led out into the water a hundred feet or more, and I imagined that this was what European settlers had felt when they first encountered the giant sequoias of the past.

These trees looked alien, they were so tall and wide, but considering the giants that surrounded the tower, I guessed these were just older versions of those that had been planted when the tower was completed.

I leaned against the railing and closed my eyes for a second, drawing a deep lungful of the sweet air. I could taste the humidity of the lake, but the combination of the speed we flew at and the gentle breeze meant it was pleasant rather than sweltering in the heat.

"We're getting' close, milord," Lydia whispered, and I opened my eyes almost regretfully. The shore was indeed closer, and I could make out the churned earth alongside the ship with my own eyes now. The toppled ship listed partially to the right, or starboard side, its stern facing the lake, and the bow of the ship pointed into the forest ahead. Large containers had been strewn about the ground nearby; some were broken open, either from falling from the ship or by whatever had attacked.

As we grew closer, and our ship began to slow, a sudden explosion of birds took off from nearby. When I looked in that direction, I discovered they'd been feasting on a body. I searched the raised deck for Oren and waved to get his attention. He raised one hand in return to signal that he'd seen me, and I made a circular motion with one hand as the other gripped my naginata tighter.

Oren nodded and gestured to Jory, speaking a few words I was too far away to hear, before signaling me with a circular motion in return. Either some things were universal, or I'd just called his mother an unflattering name with a hand gesture, and he was returning the favor.

Fortunately for universal hand signs, we were soon slowly circling the crashed ship, finding that a significant portion had been fixed up. There was still a missing engine on one side, where I'd taken it out with a lucky throw, but the damage to the sails and decking where it had impacted Oren's ship was mainly repaired.

We slowed further as we took a second lap, but we couldn't see anything besides the one body that lay between a couple of large crates. It was half-crushed by one of them and had clearly been fed upon by the birds we'd seen earlier.

I waved at Oren again and pointed down, getting another nod. He brought us in close, hovering a dozen feet off the ground. I turned to Lydia and spoke loud enough that all of the squad and our four guests could hear.

"Okay, everyone; after me, it's Lydia. If she tells you to do something, you do it, no questions. Bob and I are going first, then you four, then Lydia and the rest." I pinned my gaze to the foursome. "Lydia will give you weapons when you need them, but I don't trust you. I'll make this clear: if you try to fuck with us or hurt one of my people, so help me god, I will kill each and every one of you. And I'll make sure your own mothers wouldn't recognize what's left of your bodies, understand?"

Getting scared nods from each of them, I looked over the side at the ladder the crewman was lowering. It would never hold Bob's weight, and it was only a short distance to the ground. I ignored it and jumped, Bob following my lead.

I couldn't help it; I did a superhero landing, one fist pressed to the ground, one knee down, the whole works. I probably looked amazing, until Bob landed right next to me and clanked straight off to search the surrounding area while I slowly straightened up.

Deadpool was right; it fucking *killed* my knee, and it was only a short distance. I was totally putting more points into Constitution before I tried that shit again. I hadn't even rolled or tried to absorb the landing properly. I'd nearly *smashed* my goddamn *kneecap*. I quickly cast a healing spell as I gingerly stood there, trying to hide the fact that I was doing anything while I looked about heroically.

It took a few seconds, but by the time the foursome and Lydia had descended, I figured I could walk without crying, and I tried to hide the limp as I moved over to the corpse. Lydia and the others spread out to surround me and keep watch, while Oren moved off to scout the area further, just as we'd discussed beforehand.

I moved cautiously to inspect the remains. Whatever it had been in life had at least worn a loincloth. There were long strips of torn flesh and gobbets of…bits…where the birds had been feeding, but they hadn't been there long enough to strip the creature entirely. I couldn't make out much, given the state it was in, beyond the fact that it had been small; maybe three to four feet tall in total, if the rest of the corpse was in proportion.

Bob was there a second later, responding to my summons, and he dug his hands into the soft, dark earth that surrounded the base of the container. He creaked and let out a hissing noise as he strained, but after a few seconds, he managed to tip the crate over.

Considering the fact that it was at least ten feet by ten feet and square, it was clearly insanely heavy, and I made a mental note to get it searched.

What took most of my attention, though, was the tiny corpse revealed underneath it. It had been crushed into the dark earth, likely killing it instantly, but enough of the body remained to make Lydia hiss in anger.

"You've seen this before?" I asked her, blinking in surprise, and got a nod in return.

"Forest goblin. Little bastards usually live in the deep woods. They kill travelers and loot anything not nailed down. They also raid small villages and cabins; they eat meat."

"So, do we…eat meat, I mean?" I said, then I understood the look on her face. "You mean sentient meat, don't you?" I asked, getting a sick nod in return. Cam spoke up, disgust straining his voice.

"They need killin', lord. If we don't, they'll just keep breedin' until there's too many to face. They're like a fuckin' plague." The taciturn man grunted and spat on the small corpse before turning back to watching the perimeter.

"We came for the crew and ship first," I said, studying the nearby tracks. "If we need to kill them off, we will, but the ship's crew is our priority, not meeting the neighbors."

"I don't think we've much choice, Lord Jax," said a small voice from the left. My gaze found Miren where she knelt a dozen feet away, studying the tracks in the dirt.

She pointed at first one, then another, then a third. "This one's a cave troll; me da' taught me what they look'd like, so I'd keep well away from 'em. Most of these look like other goblins, judgin' by that one's feet. And this one?" She indicated the final clear print. "This one looks like a normal boot; might be a man or a woman. It's too short to be a goblin, and they don't normally wear boots, do they?"

"Too short?" I asked, joining her to inspect it. It took a few seconds of looking the jumble of tracks over, but I managed to make out the ones that she'd seen, and a handful of others, thanks to the tracking training I'd been given prior to being sent to the arena.

"Goblins have really long feet, Lord Jax, narrow at the back and wide at the front, and you can see the claws…here." Miren touched the ground gently, pointing out the short gouges near the end of several prints. "And here…But this one"—she pointed out another much wider and deeper print, which was almost triangular due to being particularly wide at one end—"this one's a cave troll. Nothin' like it, me da' said, an' I recognize it!"

As soon as I had the three prints fixed in my mind, a notification popped up:

Congratulations!

You have learned three new tracks and have increased your Tracking skill to level 2. Practice and learn to increase this skill further. Skillful trackers can grow in ability, until even the west wind could be traced to its home!

Once this skill reaches level 10, you may choose its first evolution…

I couldn't help but grin at the skill increase, despite being aware that it was tiny. I'd literally only reached level two, after all, but every step was an improvement. As I looked at the muddy earth leading from the forest to the ship and back again, I concentrated, and a faint red glow began to outline certain prints as my visual augmentation kicked in, highlighting important details.

"Thank you, Miren," I said, then glanced over at Stephanos. "Have you got the tracking skill yet?" I asked him, getting a shake of the head in the negative. I waved him over, asking Miren to explain it to him while we searched the site.

I followed the cave troll tracks to the side of the ship, finding scratches and gouges in the wood where it appeared that one had tried to climb up the side. Smaller prints indicated where the goblins had swarmed aboard. I climbed up the rungs that had been built into the side of the ship and paused at the top, scanning the deck quickly to make sure there was nothing waiting for me before climbing aboard.

Lydia followed me while Bob clattered around the perimeter, looking for things to hurt. Once we were both up, we edged cautiously toward the nearest hatch. The ship's deck was canted at an angle, but we were careful, approaching the edge of the open hatch quietly. As we drew near, we made eye contact and separated out to either side before moving to peer into the darkness below…

"Ere! I need that sword!" A voice called out from behind us, and we both spun around. The leader of the idiotic foursome had followed us up and was standing there expectantly. "Ya can't expect us to be unarmed, now; yer promised us!" he went on in a loud, nasally voice. A sound from below deck rang out, making it clear we'd just lost the element of surprise. I swore as Lydia grunted, shoving me aside and sending us both sprawling.

When we fell though, the steep cant of the deck became a much, much bigger issue, as we couldn't stop! We rolled slowly at first as we thrashed about, trying to find purchase, then faster and faster, until I slammed into the railing with a *thump.*

I saw Lydia coming and just managed to throw my naginata free before it impaled her, and she crashed to a stop atop me with a painful kick to my jaw.

She frantically pushed off as she tried to get to her feet as quickly as possible, shoving me again as I tried to get up. I fell back, smacking the back of my head, and had a second to wonder if she was attacking me, when I saw what had made her push me, and I cursed.

Embedded a solid inch into the heavy wood of the ship's railing was a small throwing knife, the darkened tips at each corner warning against dire repercussions if it hit me. I braced a foot against the railing and kicked off as hard as I could, flipping myself to my feet as I set off running toward the only nearby cover that I could see, a large chest that appeared to be fastened to the deck. I reached it a bare second ahead of a solid thunk that impacted the far side. I let out a breath and called out:

"Lydia, you okay?"

"Yeah, just! You?"

"Aye, I'm all right! Who…"

Before I could get any more out, something shoved me from the side, throwing me out into view. I fell, frantically kicking off and rolling forward. I heard more than felt something zip through the air where I'd been a second before, and I began jinking and weaving desperately.

I knew the direction the little weapons were coming from, but I couldn't see anything, and the nearest cover was where I'd just been thrown from. I couldn't take the time to defend myself against whoever had attacked me from that angle, not while dodging the knives. I jumped to the left, sliding on the angled deck, then dove to my right. A second hatch was open to blackness below, and I took the risk, diving forward just as I felt a sharp tug at the back of my neck.

"Jax!" I heard Oracle cry in shock at the pain suddenly radiating through me. She'd been exploring the perimeter with Bob, but she suddenly sped up, heading straight toward me like an arrow in flight as I tumbled into the darkness.

I managed to twist as I fell, tucking my head in and throwing out my right arm, which meant that I landed on my shoulder and side rather than my head. The world exploded in a shower of stars as I had the breath knocked out of me, but I managed to roll again, hitting a crate and diving behind it. I had a split second to wonder if I had the crate between me and whatever we were fighting when a loud thud from the deck above resulted in a scream of pain.

I shook myself, blinking furiously as I tried to adjust to the strange light below deck. I was surrounded by boxes, hammocks, and debris, the sunlight filtering down between occasional damaged planks, and from two open hatches.

One was where I'd entered the hold, and the other was a dozen or so meters further down the hold. I guessed that was where the attacks had started, and where my people were fighting right now. I huffed out a breath as I forced myself to my feet, the back of my helmet catching on the bloody gash across the back of my neck and making it flare with pain.

I used it; I used the pain to kick my anger into a higher gear as I set off running as fast as I could, heading for the far hatch. Footsteps thudded on the deck overhead, weapons clashing as people fought. I wasn't going fast enough. I needed to be faster!

I kicked off a small crate, using it to launch myself into the air, landing and immediately jumping again. Using the debris and storage containers as a parkour range, my enhanced Agility came to the fore as I barely managed to keep from braining myself on the deck supports. Just as I closed on the wooden ladder to the upper deck, my mana dropped suddenly as I tasted ozone; it was Oracle, casting her favorite spell.

The crackle and boom of lightning flashed through the air above me. I kicked off the ladder, redirecting my hurtling form with all the strength I could, rocketing myself up through the hatch.

As I appeared, I slammed my legs out, bracing them on either side of the hatch. I lashed my right hand up to my nearest sword hilt and cupped my left, subvocalizing the components of my own go-to spell: firebolt…before having to frantically catch my balance as a wave a nausea and disorientation ripped through me, a flashing icon appearing in my vision, warning of poison, before I blinked it away, growling under my breath.

I looked around frantically, seeing movement all around me. To my left were Lydia and the weaselly little bastard from the ship; they were spread out in a standoff with a taller figure, which had its back to me.

I barely had time to glance at the figure they faced, just enough to see that it was upright, had two legs, four arms, and a fuck ton of small tentacles that sprang from the back and sides of its head. Oh, and that every goddamn hand wielded a weapon.

Oracle cried out a warning at the exact same time as something barreled into me from the right, taking us both off our feet to tumble across the deck. I had an impression of the world spinning around us as we rolled. My sword arm was gripped in two hands, my left wrist was grasped in another, and a final, fourth hand shot up to grab me by the throat as we spun end over end.

As we rolled, I lost control of the Firebolt, the spell backlash ripping through my mind and making me scream in fury and pain. The hand around my throat tightened, and my air began to disappear. My sword eventually clattered away as my wrist was bent far enough aside that my options were to release it or have my wrist broken.

The Forgotten Faithful

We smacked into the railing, then fell through a gap, dropping roughly ten feet to the loamy forest earth below. We hit with enough force that we broke apart, two fingers snapping on my left hand as I landed badly. I screamed and forced myself to my feet, my mind filled with a red rage.

People rushed in from the sides, my people, and I roared at them to stay back.

I turned and faced the one that had attacked me. It was smaller than an average human, at about four foot six inches. I noted once again that it had four arms and two legs, and its head was weird. I couldn't find any eyes or ears on the strange oval, the back of which was covered with a tangle of tendrils or tentacles that waved and danced. Its jaw hinged apart in the middle to expose teeth that were surprisingly normal-looking; some were flat, some spiked, and others obviously for cutting, and all were a deep black that reflected the light of the sun.

I slowly moved to the left, edging away from the ship, and started to circle the creature, keeping it fixated on me. It seemed to look at the others, then focus back in on me, brandishing a short club that it pulled from its back and held it in the lower right hand.

The stronger upper arms lifted and extended to the sides; three digits tipped with black claws flexed in anticipation as it circled opposite me. Its lower left arm was cradled in close to its chest, and I guessed that it had been damaged in the fall.

I grinned at it while Oracle's heal landed on me, and I gritted my teeth and growled out my pain as my broken fingers cracked back into place. A second and a third round of healing tore through me, digging the last of the lingering poison free. My opponent froze, glancing toward Oracle, and I shouted out to everyone.

"Leave him! This little fucker's mine! Get up there and help Lydia!" My blood was up, rage burning through me and setting my soul alight. I took a deep breath and grinned at the creature once again. Oh, I needed this! I drew my sword from the left-hand sheath and swapped it to my right hand, never breaking from watching my opponent.

It backed up a little, a lot more cautious upon seeing my sword. I was about to draw a dagger with the other hand when it raised its club out to one side. I paused and watched as it wiggled the club to make sure I was watching, then dropped it to the ground. It lifted its three fingered hands out, flexing them and making a point. A point I understood, and in my rage-addled state, I totally agreed.

I hefted my sword, then stuck it point-first into the ground and did the same with my dagger. I still had others standing behind me; Oracle fired one last lightning bolt overhead, and a few seconds later, Lydia appeared at the side of the ship.

The fighting was all over now, bar me and my foe. I slowly pulled out each weapon I had, save the razor wire in my belt, dropping each onto the ground behind me before moving forward. He did the same, and we circled each other warily again. I noted Cam gathering up my weapons and moving them back out of reach, even as Bob lumbered over with my naginata, coming to a halt at the edge of the fighting circle we'd claimed.

The creature crouched, one foot ahead of the other, upper taloned hands spread wide, left lower arm kept in close, and right lower arm slowly weaving back and forth. I stepped forward as well, turning so my left side was advanced slightly, left foot and left hand forward, right foot out to brace, and right arm in closer to my chest.

115

I slowly shuffled forward, ready for the fight of my life against the little four-armed bastard, when it literally ran at me, arms windmilling. I stopped, frowned, and watched as it came closer. Its feet were triangular, as well as its hands. Two long toes at the front and one clawed tip extended backwards from the heel. I stepped back as it got within arm's reach, slapping its hands aside as I watched for the real attack.

It tried a kick, a couple of jabs, then a slashing attack with both upper arms coming in from the sides. I couldn't help it. I was holding myself back, but I couldn't ignore the opportunity. I swept down with both hands open-palmed, slapping the outside of its wrists and driving its skinny arms down, allowing me to Sparta kick forward, catching it in its solar plexus. It hadn't even tried to attack with the lower uninjured arm, and it flew backward with a cry.

I stopped, confused. I was sure I'd felt bones break under that kick. The creature was fast, and seemed like it'd be lethal, but it was…crap. On the upper deck, they'd seemed like death incarnate, so fast, and accurate, but now?

It was seriously disappointing to fight. I straightened up as I regarded the little thing. It was curled up and clutching its stomach, coughing blood onto the grass. It hacked up a thick gobbet then slowly forced itself to its feet. It lifted its upper arms again, but the lower two limbs were clutching its chest, and it was shaking badly.

"Stop," I said loudly, gesturing to the creature, and it took a step back, confused. "Can you understand me?" I asked it and got a slow nod in reply. "Can you speak?" I asked, and it pointed to its mouth, the thin dribble of blood that leaked out made its point better than the garbled words I couldn't understand. I looked up to Lydia, and she looked as confused as I was.

"How many were up there?" I asked, and she replied quickly.

"Three, Lord. One got away; one be unconscious, as Oracle shocked it so many times, it started drooling; and that one down there with ye'."

"Anyone dead?" I asked.

"Not yet, but there will be soon," she replied darkly, disappearing for a long count of five. She finally reappeared, dragging one of the four bastards from the ship. "When we were trying to get out of the way of their throwing darts, you got kicked out into the open, right?" she asked. I nodded. "This is who did it."

I switched my gaze to the little bastard and saw confirmation in his eyes as he tried to squirm free of Lydia's grasp.

"Explain," she snapped, shaking him by the scruff of his neck. He mumbled a few words before she backhanded him casually. He tried to defend himself, but she hoisted him over the side and dangled him, making him kick out in panic, despite only being a dozen feet above the ground.

"I can't…hold you long…better speak…" Lydia grunted as she deliberately shook him.

"'E's got armor! I didn't! 'E shoulda made room fer me!" he cried, frantically scrabbling at the wood as he tried to get a handhold.

Lydia looked to me, and I nodded, my face black with renewed anger as I reached up to touch the back of my neck to feel at the bloody gash. Notifications pulsed away in my peripheral vision, but I was too angry to look at them immediately.

Lydia released him with one hand and punched him in the face, dropping the weasel to the ground with a cry and a thud. His friends were all standing close together, obviously scared, but none of them made a move to help him, either. That spoke volumes, both about them and him.

I shook my head in disgust at the scumbag and mentally told Bob what I wanted. I needed to speak with this strange creature, and I couldn't get distracted by the little weasel. Bob surged forward, throwing my naginata to me. One massive hand reached down and closed over the man's head, yanking upward then to the side, hard. He shook the asshole like a rag doll as he moved, the sound of snapping bone reverberating around the shore as he stomped out of sight.

I closed my eyes and cursed under my breath, shaking my head slightly from side to side as I berated myself. I'd told Bob to take him aside to where he couldn't be seen then kill him quickly and with minimum noise. I hadn't wanted the creature to think we were evil, but hey!

I opened my eyes and considered the little thing that stood before me.

It had retreated a dozen steps until its back was pressed tight against the ship's hull, surrounded in a semi-circle by me and my men, and Lydia stood above it. Hell, even Oracle hovered nearby, and she fairly crackled with energy.

The creature had to lean against the ship for support. It had a steady stream of oily blood dripping from its mouth, and it shook as it tried to watch everywhere at once. Its lower arms were wrapped around its chest as best it could manage.

I shook my head again and lifted my right hand, palm upward, and began to cast, building the spell layer by layer until it was ready. I launched it at my target, and the little creature flinched and tried to dodge. It was far too slow.

The Focused Heal-All spell was weak. It had been cobbled together from dozens of bits of knowledge that Oracle and I had between us, including half-remembered details of medical training I'd gained over the years and spells Oracle had seen and been involved in.

All these aspects came together to create the original spell, and we had adopted a "brute force" method to its casting. We essentially just kept the connection going, pouring more and more mana into it, until we couldn't find anything left to heal.

This time, as the spell finished, I got a new burst of notifications, and I let out a sigh of relief as the little creature dropped to its knees when the weaves released it. It held up its hands in shock, clutching at its chest, its head, then its fingers roamed over its body as though it couldn't believe it.

Congratulations!

You have raised the level of your Focused Heal-All spell to level 10!

You may now choose your first evolution of this spell.

Congratulations!

You have raised your spell Focused Heal-All to its first evolution.

You must now pick a path to follow.

Will you lock this spell to a set form, and choose SPECIALIST, or will you follow the path of GENERALIST?

Choose carefully, as this choice cannot be undone.

Specialist:
You have grown familiar enough with this spell that you've noticed areas that are more effective than others. You can choose to specialize in those areas: BONE, MUSCLE, or FLESH. Specializing this spell to focus on one of these areas will result in a mana cost reduction of 50% and an increase of 5% per level of healing as this spell grows.

Generalist:
Choosing the path of the Generalist will remove the option to focus on one aspect of healing, but it will instead increase the healing effect by 2 points per second per caster's level of skill with this spell.

I tried to dismiss the prompts, only to find that they stubbornly remained, pulsing an angry red as I tried to get rid of them. I didn't have the time to consider it properly, and it wouldn't go away, so I thought for a second, then chose.

You have chosen Generalist for your first evolution.

Your spell, Focused Heal-All, has evolved into Battlefield Triage.

For a cost of 25 mana per second, you will heal 22 points of damage across the entire target creature, starting with the most grievous wounds first. This spell will improve all aspects of a creature towards its ideal physiological status.

Continue to use this spell and build upon your understanding to unlock further evolutions.

My selection satisfied the notifications, and I dismissed them to focus in on the creature I'd fought. It was watching me again, and it looked at least as scared as it had been before.

"Can you talk now?" I asked.

It aimed its face at me, tilting its head strangely as it appeared to look around, finally speaking in a surprisingly deep voice.

"I speak," it said, hands flexing as it continued scanning the area. I couldn't decide if it was looking for a way to escape or to attack.

"Who are you?" I asked, and the noise it made...well, I'd not be able to replicate that any time soon. "That's your name?" I asked, receiving a short head bob in what I supposed was confirmation.

"Okay, I can't pronounce that. I'm Jax; I'm in charge here. Where are the people from the ship?"

"Don't know," it said, still looking around.

"Well, that's fucking unhelpful, isn't it? Let's try again." I took a deep breath as I thought about the tracks. None of them matched the feet I'd seen on this creature, and they'd disappeared into the forest, while this thing looked...

"You're from the lake, aren't you?" I guessed as the thought registered, and the creature flinched, looking to the water involuntarily.

"No," it said.

I couldn't help but grin. It was a crap liar. "Okay, so, did you attack the people on this ship?"

"No."

"Who did?"

"The greenskins…goblins," it said, and I nodded.

"What do you know about the ship that landed here?"

"It crashed. Lots of people on the deck and about, making lots of noise. Never safe to make noise. The goblins came, took them; that's all I know."

"And what were you doing in the ship when we arrived?" I asked, seeing the creature hunch down as it heard my question.

"Didn't know it was yours. Thought goblins would strip it. Just wanted to try to make things better, came to search the ship…we didn't mean to steal."

That was enough, and it clicked in my mind as all the clues came together. "You're a child, aren't you?" I asked, and a second voice answered me from behind our group.

"Yes, he is. I ask you to leave him be, stranger. We will bargain for his life."

I spun around to face the water, finding a trio of the creatures slowly emerging. Eddies and ripples in the water farther out indicated there were others out there still hidden as my Perception and meridian enhancements worked together to draw my attention to the details.

CHAPTER ELEVEN

"I don't deal in children," I said after a few seconds, before gesturing to my squad. They understood what I was getting at, and they moved back, making a clear path to the aquatic group that was now striding out of the water.

They were considerably taller than any of the creatures I'd seen so far and more heavily muscled. None of the creatures seemed built for power, more of whipcord strength and flexibility, but they'd be lethal in the water and damn dangerous on the land as well.

The leader of the group inclined its head to me in thanks and gestured to the little one we'd faced. The errant boy took a hesitant step, then another, then broke into a run, flashing past us as quickly as possible before diving headfirst into the water. The leader of the group shook its head and muttered something to one of its companions, who disappeared after the child. Once its orders had been obeyed, the leader then set the butt of the spear it held into the ground, twisting it to make sure it was stable, then stepped forward, leaving the weapon behind and continuing to approach alone.

I nodded to myself, thinking that I could see what it was doing. I did the same, driving my naginata's base into the ground and walking forward to stand face-to-face.

We stood for a long second, evaluating each other before we both spoke at once.

"I—"

"We—"

We both came to a stop, and the awkwardness built until I finally started laughing under my breath. I shook my head and held out my right hand, the creature reaching out and clasping my wrist, giving it a firm shake before releasing me.

"I'm never any good at meeting people," I said, smiling. "I'm Jax, and I'm the Lord of the Great Tower of Dravith. Who are you?"

"I...ah. I am Flux. I had companions who were surface dwellers long ago, and I remember their issues with my name, so please, Lord, call me Flux."

"Nice to meet you, Flux," I said, and he suddenly dropped to one knee, splashing in the muddy shore and damn near making me punch him reflexively.

"I...we are sorry," he said quickly, before snapping something out to his companion, who hastily dropped to a knee in the fashion. "We are unused as to correct protocol amongst the surface dwellers. You are a lord; I remember such titles. We did not mean disrespect."

"Ah, fuck. No, please, Flux, don't do that." I reached down, grabbing his arm and hauling him to his feet. "There's been a misunderstanding here, one that nearly ended with me killing one of your kids. Let's just make sure that doesn't happen again, first of all; other details, we can sort out later."

"My apologies then, lord, and my thanks for your understanding. We did not know this land had been claimed by the surface dwellers, nor that the ship was yours. The younglings should not have left the depths; they knew the council was debating exploring the ship, and they decided to try to be the first. Youth is foolish, and now we have this tragedy," Flux said, shaking his head and setting his tendrils bouncing. I noticed they had colorful beads attached to the ends, while the rest of his body was covered in tight blue-black leather.

"Tragedy?" I asked.

"Five came to the ship, apparently. Three stayed to explore while two went to examine the tracks in the forest. Now only the youngling which you freed and his clutch brother, who came to get us, survive. It is a tragedy."

"We only saw three of them," I said, and looked up to Lydia, who turned and disappeared at my look before popping back up a few seconds later.

"This one is still breathing as well, Lord Jax," she called out, and Oracle immediately flew over to her, calling out behind to me as she went.

"I'll heal him; don't worry."

"So," I said, "We've got three still alive so far; what about the two that went into the forest?"

"I will call for them, but the others reacted as badly as they did to your appearance because they had lost contact with them already. Please, a moment." Flux held his head up high, standing straight and opening his mouth wide. I realized he was taller than I thought, nearly six feet when standing as straight as he could. A headache spiked suddenly as he did...something.

All my people backed away, grimacing, or drawing weapons, and I shook my head to clear it as...whatever Flux had done wore off.

"What was that?" I asked, and he spoke without turning, the tendrils around his head reaching out in all directions like a lion's mane.

"My kind can speak through the water at great distances. While this works in the air, it is...imprecise, as a way to speak...I am sorry if this caused you discomfort; it is simply a deeper noise than you are used to hearing."

I thought for a second and snapped my fingers, grinning at him.

"It's sonar! That's how you see, isn't it!" There was a long pause, but eventually Flux shook his head in reply, the tendrils still waving.

"I don't know this word, but...there!" The tendrils on one side of his head suddenly went stiff, and he twisted around to look higher up the valley away from the shore. "There! I felt it; one at least still lives!"

"How far?" I asked Flux, and he squared his shoulders in determination.

"A mile, two? I have not dealt in surface measurements in a long time, and even then, I was poor at it. It is difficult for many of my kind to go so far in the air; our bodies need the water. I will go, as will Cheena. That must be enough." At the mention of the name, the second creature stepped forward.

"Was your youngling taken by the goblins?" I asked, and Flux nodded slowly.

"Most likely, yes. There are no other creatures in the valley, save the goblins and the cave trolls that we know of. Cave trolls would have killed them and eaten them immediately, not taken them alive. The goblins have a camp somewhere farther up the valley, but that is all we know, so it fits."

"Do you know how many there are?" I asked, and Flux shook his head.

"We have no idea; they arrived sometime last winter, and in that time, they have tamed a family of cave trolls. There will have been losses from that, but goblins breed like the vermin they are. There could be dozens, or hundreds, or more. We have no way to tell."

"Well, we do have one advantage," I said, turning and looking out over the water. The others turned to follow my gaze, and we could just make out the warship *Agamemnon's Wrath* as she came around, still searching the lakeshore. She was a mile or so out, and coming in at speed, having clearly seen that something was happening. A wide wave built before her as she raced towards us, water rippling out from the backwash of her engines.

"This is your ship?" Flux asked, and I nodded, a smile on my face. "I see...perhaps we can come to an arrangement?" he queried; his head tilted to one side. "The goblins have taken your crew from this ship as well as my own younglings. Perhaps we could make a deal to rescue them all together? We do not have much gold but can pay in other ways for your assistance...fish, metals. There are also some amongst us who can craft items that are popular amongst the surface dwellers?"

"We can do a deal," I said, frowning as I looked around. "You said there's trade between you and the 'surface dwellers,' but I don't see any villages or—"

"Ah, no, lord. We used to trade with the cities to the south, but there were...disagreements about value. We chose to leave several dozen years ago and migrated up to this lake. Our goods, however, were popular until then."

"What kind of goods?" I asked curiously.

"Foodstuffs, armor such as I wear, some carvings...we also had a runesmith, but age has robbed her of the ability now."

"Age?" I asked quickly.

"She can no longer feel the shape of the world; without that sense, she cannot form her magic into the correct shapes. In the last attempt, her apprentice nearly died, and she was gravely wounded."

"Have you got healers?" I asked, a hope coming to mind. If I could recruit these people...

"No. The gift of magic is a rare one for my kind; we have had no healers in the pod for as long as I have known."

"Okay, and this is going to sound rude, but what exactly are you?" I asked.

"Tia'Almer-atic is the name we use; surface dwellers generally just call us Tia or Mer," Flux said, shrugging unconcernedly at the vagaries of the surface dwellers.

"Okay, thanks for that. Right...your people and ours are being held by the goblins, so we're going to get them back. We can talk about suitable rewards for saving your younglings later, but for now," I said, looking up toward the hull of Decin's ship above us.

Oracle had ceased to use our mana, and a second later, she flitted down to me, landing on my shoulder and inspecting Flux before looking up at the railing overhead. Lydia moved back slowly, her hand on the hilt of her weapon as the largest and previously most heavily armed Mer appeared at the railing.

It looked confused, as much as I could see from the body language anyway. But when it saw Flux, it quickly clambered down the side and strode over, going down on both knees before him. I realized he didn't have any weapons now, and I looked up to Lydia, who raised her hands, showing all four were with her.

"You, I expected better from!" Flux snapped at the creature that knelt before him, and its head lowered even further. "Return to your chambers...we will speak later!" Flux ordered, and the Mer got up and started walking quickly toward the water, pausing only when I called out, "Lydia, is everyone okay? No damage?" When I got a shouted affirmative, I went on. "Well, no harm, no foul. Throw down the weapons."

Lydia paused at that before slowly throwing the weapons down onto the ground one at a time. The young creature had been armed with two short spears and four long knives, almost shortswords. The knives, like the spears, had no cross guards and looked very alien in that they had a strange bend in them: at about halfway up the haft, they kinked slightly to one side, and Flux caught me looking with interest.

He slowly drew one of the long knives with exaggerated care from the sheath at his side, passing it over to me. When I inspected it more closely, I realized I couldn't tell if they were actually from an animal or man-made, but they'd be deadly in a fight, either way.

The points were long and sharp, but behind the tips, on the back of the blades, they had a scalloped design with small ridges that looked designed to saw flesh. Lower down, the kink appeared to be a reinforcement that made it easier for their shaped arms to pull the weapons out, causing maximum damage.

"Nasty," I commented, passing the weapon back.

"Effective!" Flux replied with a little shake of his head and a low buzz that reverberated the air around us. I shrugged and gestured to the weapons Lydia had thrown down.

"I think they're all his..."

"You would return his weapons?" Flux asked.

"Yeah, of course." I shrugged again. "As I said, no harm, no foul. I am sorry about the little one, though; I kinda kicked it pretty hard before I realized it wasn't a threat."

"Who attacked first?" Flux asked me intently.

"I really don't know which of your younglings, but it was one of them. We were exploring the ship, looking for the crew when a...member of our group called out to me. The next thing I knew, knives were flying."

"Small blades? Thrown weapons?" he asked, sounding angry.

"Yeah, short throwing knives; looked like they'd hurt."

"If they were coated when they cut you, you'd not be standing here now," Flux said with controlled fury evident in his voice. "The throwing knives are called 'ashik-tor,' and they are to be used in the direst need only, due to being coated in a deadly poison.

"That they used these weapons first? I fear they have brought more dishonor to our pod than I felt possible." He barked something at the figure that had stopped halfway to the water, and the Mer quickly ran over to the weapons, picking them up and returning to stand behind Flux and Cheena, rather than heading into the water as it had been ordered previously. "This foolish child will now earn back his weapons threefold, due to this dishonor, or he will never again return to the pod!" Flux snarled at him before turning back to me and going down on one knee again. The other two did the same, and I started to step forward to help him back up when Oracle stopped me. She grabbed a handful of hair at the back of my head and yanked sharply. I barely managed to avoid swearing.

"Don't…This is important to them," she whispered.

I cleared my throat, swallowing my irritation.

"Flux…we can…ah, we will talk of the dishonor later,…okay?" I said, I had no idea what he wanted or expected, and we didn't have time for this shit right now.

"Very well, Lord Jax. We will earn your forgiveness this day," he replied in a tight voice, coming to his feet and snapping at the others to do the same.

Oren brought the warship to a halt a dozen feet away, appearing quickly at the edge of the railing to look down at us.

"Yer done found more followers already, laddie?" he called down. "Ah saw 'em kneelin'. Damn, tha' be fast work! Whut did I miss?"

"It's not like that!" I called up to him, "Get your arse out of the way; we need to use the map in the captain's cabin," I said, striding over to the side of the ship and grabbing ahold of the rope ladder. Flux followed me, at my invitation, and a few minutes later, Flux, Oracle, Oren, Lydia, and myself were gathered in the captain's cabin, encircling the magical map I'd seen there earlier.

I'd spread it out across the table, and Oracle touched the activation rune, channeling a little mana into it to bring it to life.

Instantly, the map shifted from a flat drawing three feet by two, to a 3D representation of the same place. The major difference was that now we could zoom in on our location and expand it, making the valley and the lake fill the map.

"Okay, where do you think the goblin camp is?" I asked Flux, and he shifted the perspective slowly, obviously having difficulty with it for a few seconds until he was happy with it. Once he had it centered over where we stood, he shifted it around and waved his hand in a circular motion over a raised area further up the side of the valley.

"I think…here. There was an old ruin up there somewhere. We found it when we explored, but it was deemed unsafe and too far from the water. We left it, but knowing goblins, that'll be where they'd live given a choice."

I zoomed in, finding the controls a mixture of using a giant touchscreen tablet and a little mental prodding. Once our view hovered over the area, all we could see was a series of trees, higher than some others, but lower than many. It looked like a normal hillside to me, except…

"Is that a road?" I asked the room in general, catching sight of a line of smaller trees that followed a straight path. Looking closer and twisting the map around, what appeared to be straight lines of stunted growth appeared, running…south toward the sea and north toward the Great Tower, where it loomed in the distance.

"That was probably one of the Waystations!" Oracle said excitedly. When we all just looked at her, she huffed in disappointment. "The Waystations were built to help people moving to and from the Great Tower. When the tower was first built, this whole area was only recently freed from the Night King's control, but the only way to this side of the continent was through Terin's Pass; the mountains shielded the land beyond that.

"The Tower was built here to watch over the pass and secure the eastern side of the continent. When the Waystations were first built, the land here was wild, creatures roaming and killing, so they were secure places that people could rest. They stopped being used so much after the legions started pacifying the land."

"Well, sounds like tha legion missed a few wee beasties!" Oren muttered, getting a dark look from Oracle.

"That's enough," I said, holding up one hand and looking around the room. "Does anyone have anything else to add?" There was only silence, so I went on. "Okay, then, we can get everyone on the ship, then we can do a quick flyby over the camp, see if we can see anything. Then we'll back off and come up with a plan. Any issues?"

"Besides tha goblins knowin' we're comin' iff'n we do tha', ye mean?" Oren said, then held up his hands when I glared at him. "Ye told me ta speak up iff'n I disagree, laddie. Well...I'm tellin' ya, tha' plan will no' work. I already flew over; iff'n we go again, they'll know we're comin'. There were nothin' to see when we passed over afore, or tha map'd look different now."

"Fuck," I muttered eloquently, realizing he was right.

"I suggest we scout it on foot, Lord Jax. Goblins are notoriously lazy and stupid. They may not have scouts at all, but if they do have scouts deployed, we can find them," Flux said confidently.

"You're sure?" I asked, and he nodded.

"We can sense their hearts beating at closer range," he explained.

I grinned, realizing just how hard that would be to hide from.

"Then that'll work, but we've no idea how many there are up there...Oren, there are no clearings between here and there, just solid forest; that right?" In response, Oren just gestured at the map, as though to tell me to look at it. I glared at him. "In that case, the ship can't help us in the fight, or at least not yet. Can you get Decin's ship flightworthy?"

"I can have tha engineers look 'er over...canna see any issues meself. Most looks fixed, but I've no been on her yet," Oren grunted, glancing out of a porthole at the ship and shrugging.

"It'll take us a good few hours to get up there, I'd think. Once we're there, we'll scout out the area and see if we can get to the crew and Flux's younglings. Then a few more hours to get back down here. So...if you can't get the ship in the air in, say,...four hours, get everyone back on here and take off. We can always fix the other ship later, if need be. If we need you to use the cannons to support us, then I'll either send Oracle to you or shoot a Firebolt up into the air as we retreat. Otherwise, be ready to pick us up."

Oren nodded, then spoke hesitantly. "I could come with ye. Another fighter'd be—"

"And who'd look after the ships?" I asked, cutting him off. "No; thank you, my friend, but you're needed here, and we'll be okay." I considered my words for a second before adding, "Unless, of course, it all goes to shit, in which case we're going to need you on the ship even more than with us, as we'll either need support or an escape..." I shrugged, then clapped him on the shoulder.

"Seriously, you'll be the most help to me and to Decin on the deck of your ship, but thank you." I scanned the room, a collection of grim faces looking back to me, and I nodded to them in return.

"I'd like a word before we go?" Oracle piped up.

I smiled at her. Her attempt at seriousness was a bit strange, but hell, so were we all at this point.

"Okay, if nobody else has anything they need to say?" Lydia raised her hand, and the others paused on the way to the door.

"Well…the three idiots, lord. What do we do with them?" she asked hesitantly, and I immediately saw the problem. I could force them along with us, and they'd be essentially cannon fodder for the goblins, which would potentially save one of us, or even prove useful…although I doubted that. More likely, though, they'd get in the way, give us away at the worst point, or run when we needed them most. I couldn't risk it.

"Give them a sword each and the pack of food we put aside for them, then turn them out. I don't care where they go, as long as they choose a direction away from us and the tower, and not towards the goblins. Point them towards Himnel and let them make their own choices."

Lydia nodded and left the room, drawing Oren and Flux with her. I just knew I'd have to explain this to Flux. There was no way it looked good. I turned to Oracle and blinked, startled.

The door was swinging closed, leaving us alone. She blurred to her full size, my mana dropping appreciably as she did so. This time, she'd shifted to long, black hair again, rather than her usual blonde tresses, and she wore a simple white blouse, denim shorts, and sandals. The scent of coconut sun lotion filled the air, and her skin practically glowed with health and maybe just a touch of sunburn.

She pulled these images from my past each time, adjusting them to herself. Every single time, I was captivated all over again. She stepped forward, her beautiful green eyes staring up at me as she wrapped her arms around my neck, and she stood on tiptoes to kiss me.

It was a long kiss, gentle, but deep, and I wrapped my arms around her, too, feeling her wings flutter as my hands brushed them.

She broke the kiss after a moment, leaning back to look at me as we held each other.

"I don't like you fighting when I'm not by your side," she whispered. I smiled appreciatively, leaning forward to kiss her back. "I was trying to keep everyone alive, and I couldn't see you…I was getting really scared, especially when I felt the poison."

"I'm all right, Oracle," I whispered. "I'm a big boy, you know."

"So you keep saying," she whispered, then clearly trying to move on, she grinned up at me naughtily. "But you never seem to want to prove it?"

"Oh, you little minx!" I laughed.

She released me, stepping back and making a point of looking down at my pants.

"I mean, if that was true, surely it'd be easily proven…?" She winked at me.

"Hey, my nickname used to be 'Tripod,' and we both know it's not because I'm really fucking stable, put it that way," I boasted to her, winking before shaking my head. "Honestly, Oracle, I really want to, damn, do I want to, but—"

"But now's not the time, and you need to figure things out. I know, Jax, I just like teasing you. After feeling you get hurt when I didn't know what was happening…"

"You were scared, and you wanted me to pay you some attention?" I gently finished her sentence for her.

"When you put it like that, it sounds so childish," she complained, releasing my neck and stepping back to fold her arms across her impressive chest.

"It's not; it's perfectly normal," I reassured her, resting my palms on her shoulders and looking into her eyes. "Look, we'll talk about this later, okay? When we're back at the tower and nobody needs rescuing."

"Okay, Jax. I know…It's just…well…"

"I know," I said, smiling at her. She smiled back, and I released her. I took a deep breath as she shrank down to her usual size, flying over to hover before my eyes.

"Let's get things sorted out, then we can have that chat, okay?" she said, and I nodded, and she *shifted* again. Her clothes vanished and reformed, becoming her fighting outfit of yoga pants and sports bra, with two lines of camouflage paint on either cheek.

"Just so you know what you might have to play with later; I'm yours, and you're mine, Jax…but only if you're good," she whispered, throwing me a saucy wink and disappearing out of the porthole. I shook my head and…adjusted…myself before walking out onto the ship's deck.

I knew damn well she didn't have to be naked to change her outfit; she just liked to friggin' tease me. And worst of all, it damn well worked! My entire brain just shut the fuck down whenever she did it, like my cock was wired to the reset button. Whenever it sprang to life, my brain froze.

I took a deep breath and glanced around, letting the door swing shut behind me. I noted the uncertainty in the crew's faces as they watched the tree line and Flux. He stood halfway down the deck, talking to Oren. As I walked over, I caught the tail end of their conversation.

"…they be criminals, an' deserve no mercy."

I waited patiently for him to finish, and when he saw me, he jerked his chin toward the three men that Lydia was talking to. She was on the ground already, her squad gathering as she threw one of the men a backpack. It wasn't particularly large, but it had a few days' worth of rations for each of them, and they were in a forest, after all. There had to be a fuck ton of food around if they looked.

Next, she passed out three swords, one to each of them, and gestured over their shoulders toward the far side of the valley. The men began speaking, low at first, but then becoming more agitated. A sound made them look to their right, where Bob slowly walked out from behind Decin's ship.

There was a long moment of stillness, and Lydia pointed again at the forest behind them, then at Bob, clearly giving them the chance to choose one or the other. Unsurprisingly, after seeing their most vocal member have his head half-crushed by Bob earlier, they shouldered the pack, snatched their weapons, and started off into the forest, stopping when they were almost out of sight to shout some abuse back.

I was a bit surprised, in truth, when they did that. Not that they would want to get the last word in—bullies always did—but that this would be true in a world with magic as well. Oracle got the last word in, though, in reality, and that word was *fulgur*.

The bolt of lightning was a weak one; she'd obviously not channeled any more than the standard into it. The sight of it hurtling across the distance between the two groups and causing a small sapling to explode—which sent all three scrambling frantically into the distance and out of sight—was worth it.

It took a few minutes more to get things under control on our side, mostly because the three had been despised, and everyone was laughing their asses off.

I grinned at Oracle, and she shrugged before smiling back at me, then flying off the side of the ship to take her usual perch on Bob's head. I walked to the side of the ship, waiting as Flux climbed down and rejoined his people, and I took stock of my small strike force. There were six guards from the tower, three Mer, and a giant skeleton tank with a Wisp riding his head. I couldn't help but smile at them, and of course…do a superhero landing.

I jumped from the side of the ship, landing with one hand thrown out behind myself, the other flat on the ground. One knee was planted firmly, and I had thrown the other leg out to the side. I gritted my teeth as I straightened up, enjoying the looks of surprise from the others. I forced myself to march forward through the group, taking up my place at the front as we started into the forest to follow the tracks that disappeared into the sun-dappled wilderness.

CHAPTER TWELVE

I tried to hide the pain; there'd been a damn rock under my knee when I'd landed, and it was killing me. After a second, a gentle pulse of power spread through me, and I sent Oracle a silent "thank you" through our bond, receiving an impression of gentle laughter in return.

So, she'd caught me; that was fine…I could live with that.

"Lord, Cheena here is a skilled scout; might we…" Flux asked me, stepping up to walk alongside me and gesturing ahead. The trail was easy to follow for now; easily dozens of beings had stomped, dragged, and occasionally shit their way through the forest. The literal piles of crap that littered the trail on occasion were enough to make me want all goblins to die a painful death alone.

Flux dispatched Cheena to rush ahead in time for a foul squishing behind me as Cam started cursing. He'd just learned a valuable lesson about watching where he stepped. The smell was awful, but the occasional tracks that stood out were worse.

There was a multitude of small goblin tracks, and the occasional huge cave troll footprints, but the worst were the drag marks. I was very new to tracking, but even I could tell that Decin's crew were being made to carry a heavy load. I hoped they were carrying loot from the ship, but I was all too afraid they were carrying their dead instead.

"Spread out and keep your eyes open!" I called to the group as we moved on, following a slight incline. As we jogged along, I took the time to work on the tracks. I tried to single out an individual set of tracks, then followed that one for as long as I could, picking up the trail again and again as quickly as I lost it, pausing periodically for people to catch their breath. After a few minutes, I got a skill level notification, then another within forty minutes of that.

Congratulations!

You have reached level 4 in the Skill Tracking!

No longer will you have to hope that your date will be in touch; now you can follow them home! Once this skill reaches level 10, you may choose its first evolution.

After an hour or so, Cheena seemed to appear from the forest a dozen feet ahead of us. One second, she was nowhere in sight; the next, she casually leaned against a tree. I slammed to a halt, carving a small furrow in the covering of forest mulch, and leveled my naginata at her before I realized who it was.

"Impressive, lord," she said, her voice low and carrying an atonal thrum that I had to guess was amusement.

"Cheena...report please," Flux huffed, coming to a stop alongside me. I turned to look at him quickly, confused as to why he seemed to be flagging so badly; he seemed pretty fit and healthy? I looked back to find the massive youngling also struggling along, far in the rear. His weapons were stowed, but he had to keep grabbing trees to pull himself along. I was distracted by Cheena's voice as she spoke up.

"The camp is a mile or so further up the hill. Two scouts are outside, neither of which are worth a damn. The camp seems to be a large collapsed ruin, as you suspected. The entrance is simply a hole with maybe half a dozen goblins in and around the entrance. I can't get close enough to sense any deeper."

"Sense?" I asked Flux, and he gestured to his tendrils.

"What you called sonar earlier, Lord Jax, I—"

"Seriously, Flux, we're about to charge a goblin-held ruin and-fight side-by-side. I think we can drop the 'lord' for now, okay?" I interrupted.

"Very well, thank you, Jax. I suggest we pick off the scouts first then use your archers to kill as many of the remaining group as quietly as possible. We have no way of knowing how many are inside, after all."

"Cheena, can we get close enough to drop down behind the goblins? To stop them from running into the camp hole and warning the others, I mean?" I asked.

"I probably can, as could Flux, but you and your people...forgiveness, lord, but you are poor at woodcraft. Even your hunters."

"I know," I said, looking back up the trail in the direction of the camp. "My people are freed slaves and villagers. We can fight, but don't expect a huge amount of skill or experience yet. All we have in abundance is heart."

"We have more than that, lord," came a voice from my left, and I turned to face Lydia.

"I don't mean to question your abilities, Lydia. I'm very proud of you and the entire squad, I simply mean—"

"Yeh mean that we're new to fightin', and we are, Lord. But we're fightin' for each other, and we fight for you. We'll not fail yer, just trust in us," she said, fixing me with a hard stare.

"I do trust in you, Lydia; I trust in you all. Never doubt that, and please, I don't care what Barrett said—call me Jax. We're all in this together. When I give an order in front of others, or we're being formal, you can call me 'Lord'; otherwise, just call me Jax, okay?"

I turned to face the rest of the group squarely, and I spoke quietly, but my voice was pitched to carry to all of them. "We're going to go and rescue the prisoners up there...might be that they don't want to join us, might be they do. Either way, I'll not leave them in the hands of goblins.

"I'm proud of you all, both for the fights we've had and the trip so far. I know you're scared; fuck, I'm scared, but I'm going up there. I'm going to kill those goblins, each and every one of them, because, from what I know of them, they're evil little shits. They've captured Flux's younglings, and that alone would be enough for me. Some things, you don't let happen, and they're exactly the kinds of things goblins do to prisoners.

"This is your last chance to walk away; if you do, I'll understand, but if you come with me, if you're going to stand by my side up there, then I need to know"—I paused for a long second, making direct eye contact with a few—"...because there might only be a few dozen to a hundred goblins up there, and I saw you buggers fight in the tower. If you're all going to come up there and fight, I need to know, as I'll need to kill some quick to be able to keep up with you all!"

There were a few scattered snorts and grins, but nobody walked away, and Lydia muttered just loud enough to be heard. "...really is crap at speeches...."

I turned to Flux and his two scouts, noting how exhausted they all appeared.

"Are you able to do this? Seriously, Flux, you all look terrible." They were leaning over, out of breath still, and their skin looked...dry. "Is this because of the water? Do you need it?" I asked.

Lydia pulled out a waterskin, throwing it to Cheena, who immediately offered it to Flux. Flux emptied a little over his head, gills at the sides of his tendrils greedily pulling it in, before he passed it back, allowing Cheena and the unnamed youngling to do the same.

"We are a species that cannot live long from the water, Jax; our kind can adjust, becoming more used to the arid atmosphere you all prefer. It takes time, and we cannot survive without water for long," Flux said, a low whistle accompanying his words. I guessed it was his equivalent of a concerned sigh. "We will go on, though; we must."

"Here, will this help?" I asked, casting Summon Water to bring a gentle fountain of clean, cool water up from beneath the forest mulch. Cheena stepped forward and leaned into the water, letting it coat her head and pour over her body for a handful of seconds. When she stepped back, shaking herself, a low vibration filled the air. Immediately, Flux gestured the youngling forward and rested a grateful hand on my shoulder.

"Thank you, Jax. This will indeed make things much easier for us. I had not considered that you might know magic that could be useful to us in this way." While he was speaking, Oracle cast a second spell. A new fountain sprang to life next to Flux, who nodded his thanks and leaned into it. When he was refreshed, the other two started taking turns in the fountain as my own squad took advantage of the spell to wash hands and faces, took drinks, and generally relaxed a little.

The spells only lasted ten seconds, usually, but channeling a little extra mana into them kept them around long enough for everyone to use. The mana cost was less than forty in total, and I'd recover that in just over fifteen minutes. I gave everyone a minute to get themselves together.

"Okay, Flux, if you and Cheena can lead the way, you're both a lot better at stealth than we are. Watch out for any scouts. When we get closer, we'll take a look and come up with a plan," I said, getting a round of nods and general acknowledgement.

The last mile of the hike took about thirty minutes. The forest was overgrown heavily enough that we could only see, at most, a few dozen yards at a time. The trail the goblins had made seemed to follow the path of least resistance, always dragging left and right, heading in the general same direction. We probably walked twice as far due to the zig-zag nature of the trail.

"Hsst!" Cheena let out a hiss of warning and dropped down low, seeming to melt into the bushes and vanish without a trace. I paused for a second, then hurried to hide behind a fallen tree to one side of the trail. Looking around, I could see the others were as poorly hidden as I was, all except the three Mer.

I concentrated, searching where I'd last seen the youngling, and picked him out after an extensive search, and I only found him because he made an awkward wave at me, having caught me looking. He was crouched by the side of the trail, daggers and short spears drawn. I watched him in amazement as he slowly seemed to blend into the long grass. I cursed myself, remembering my own Chameleon spell. I cast it quickly, and a second later, saw my mana drop again as Oracle cast it on Bob.

I'd not even considered him; he was a bone-white skeleton construct over eight feet tall and at least four across. The bugger was huge, and even with the spell, he was crap at hiding. I facepalmed as I saw him; he stuck out on either side of the tree he was hiding behind, but I had no time to reposition him as the first goblin come into view further down the trail.

It was a short creature, with long, pointed ears, bald and maybe four feet tall. It looked like it'd never eaten a real meal in its life.

Its belly protruded, and it walked like a toddler in need of a nap, slowly and listlessly. Four of these creatures came into view over the next several seconds, ranging from three and a half feet to nearly five feet tall, and in color from grey to a dark green. The biggest was clearly in charge and would occasionally hit the others with its club as they walked. Every time they slowed even further down, it would smack the nearest, driving the group forward.

They were all dressed in filthy loincloths, and all had clubs, ranging from short sticks to one small goblin that was determinedly dragging a club that must have weighed half as much as it did.

I watched them, confused, as I wondered about all the concern the others had shown. These creatures were no threat; surely, they were more comical than scary?

There was a rustle further up the trail, and a few more wandered into view, the noise level from the creatures slowly rising as more and more started to appear. Soon enough, there were a dozen of them, and they kept climbing in number. By the time the first few were level with the space where Cheena had vanished, there were easily twenty, and my heart dropped. It dropped even further when the Chameleon spell on Bob was refreshed, as, for a second, he seemed to flicker. One of the first few goblins froze, staring at him. It growled something, and the entire group went silent, then finally they moved forward as one, bunching up around the one that had seen him. More were coming, turning from a trickle to a flood, and I gave up counting when they reached thirty, and yet more kept hurrying down the trail. The possibility of prey was the first spark of interest I'd seen in them.

There were three larger goblins now as well, each over four and a half feet. The tallest and heaviest of them had a spiked club and wore mismatched armor that covered most of its body, obviously the leader in the way the others deferred to it as it stomped forward, kicking others aside.

Bob was still pretty obvious where he hulked behind the tree, and the goblins slowly began to spread out, clearly planning to encircle him and attack.

"Well, can't have that, can we," I whispered to myself. Raising my hands, with my naginata laid on the ground at my side, I began to dual cast Firebolt. I continued to channel mana into it, adjusting the spell as I remembered using it what seemed like ages ago, when I'd first arrived at the tower.

As the mana built, I kept my hands spaced about ten inches apart, fingers slowly dancing as I layered the weaves one atop another.

I'd not realized what I was doing when I'd done it the first time, but after casting the normal version so many times now, I'd noticed…differences. Areas where the spell could be improved, I'd thought, but I hadn't had time to experiment consciously yet. Now, I thought "fuck it" and piled the changes in, feeling the spellform ripple and fight to be free. I forced the shape to hold together as the pressure built until I'd hurt myself if it went any further. The normal Firebolt was ten mana, but this…there was sixty mana in it when I finally cut it off and threw both hands forward in a "Streetfighter" move.

What left my hands was a different level entirely from the Firebolt. My notifications went crazy, even as it impacted the left flank of the goblin gang.

When the glowing, white-blue spell hit them, it smashed through the first few creatures unfortunate enough to be in its way before exploding. Bits of goblin bodies were hurled through the air, liquid fire covering them, and over a dozen were killed outright. I paused, gawking at the devastation before me, when Lydia struck.

She'd darted out from behind her tree as soon as the spell hit, and was shouting like a Valkyrie, rousing the squad to battle. I swept up my naginata and ran forward, jumping back onto the trail and stamping down hard on a weakly struggling, green-skinned figure, feeling the snap of weak bones as it stilled.

I lashed out, stabbing to my right, left, sweeping the haft around and breaking bones wherever it hit. In the madness of the fight, the others waded in. Cam, to my right, was using his axe like a baseball bat, hitting each opponent with a huge amount of force and sending the corpses flying in pieces.

I didn't have time to watch them all as I stabbed and swung, my naginata dancing through the air. But, in what seemed like seconds, it was over.

I spun from one side to the other, looking for another target, my naginata dripping with gore as I panted, trying to get my breath back.

"Is…is that…it?" I asked and got a grim look from Lydia in response.

"Flux and the other two are chasing the last ones down, but…we were too close to their camp, I think. They had to have heard that."

"Fuck!" I cursed, looking around. "Okay, anybody hurt?" I asked, seeing Miren raise one hand. Her left arm looked torn and bloody, but before I could do it myself, Oracle had cast healing on her. Miren hissed as the flesh knit itself back together, but soon, she was looking at her arm in wonder, the wound completely gone, and only the torn and bloody cloth of her sleeve showing it had ever happened.

"Anyone else?" I asked. Getting no response, I nodded to myself. "Good! We might have lost the element of surprise, so we need to be careful now. Keep the noise down where you can, but speed is more important."

I turned and started jogging up the trail, quickly finding a few more bodies. Clearly, Flux had caught these, at least. There was no other sign of him, so we continued on, moving faster.

It took a few minutes, but we caught up to Flux, Cheena, and the youngling fighting a handful of feet from the entrance to the camp. A dozen small corpses were sprawled around, and the sound of more enemies came from the hole that led underground.

"Shit!" I cried out as the youngling got stabbed by a goblin that leaped on his back, wielding what looked like a kitchen knife. I rushed forward, punching out with a fist. I felt the small creature's neck snap with the force, sending the body flying from his back as he collapsed to the ground, wheezing. "Oracle! I need you!" I bellowed.

She was there in a flash, landing by his side and growing to full size and flipping him over to get at the wound. "This is bad! I need more mana!" she cried to me, and I pawed at my belt, pulling a potion out as I stabbed around, one-handed, trying to stem the tide of goblins. I looked at the potion, verifying that it was a healing one, and chucked it to her.

"Use that!" I shouted to her, kicking out and sending another goblin flying, swearing as more and more came running out of the hole in the ground. There were easily fifty in the small clearing now, and more were emerging every second.

The others took up position around me, and my vision suddenly updated, my usual vision of my own health and mana bars augmented by a series of symbols that matched up with the rest of the party. Each symbol had a red ring around it, and Arrin's had a second blue ring as well, I could see them all dropping slowly, yet somehow it didn't interfere with my vision, luckily.

Bob was suddenly by my side; his symbol was grey, and the single white ring around it chipped away slowly but steadily.

I glared around as I slashed and kicked at the goblins, finally pulling out a bright blue potion and biting down on the cork. I yanked back, pulling free and spitting the cork at the nearest screaming goblin. As it closed the last two steps, I punted it in the face as hard as I could, bones breaking as it flew backwards in a spray of blood, and I chugged the potion.

As soon as my mana refilled, Oracle was draining it, piling the layers of the Battlefield Triage onto the youngling. Despite the potion she'd already used on him, his wounds were severe enough that he needed more. As soon as the mana potion was empty, I hurled the bottle into the crazed horde and started laying into them.

There were dozens all around us now, and we fought on; like a rock in the middle of the sea, we survived the waves that came, stabbing, kicking, and beating them back as quickly as we could. We'd moved to fight in a tight group with Oracle back to her usual size flying above. Miren, Stephanos, and Arrin held positions in the center of the group, firing out as best they could while the rest of us weathered the storm.

Jian was to my left, Bob to my right, and I could see everyone's health bars getting hammered. I didn't dare use my magic, more from fear of running out when Oracle needed it, as she steadily depleted it on healing our people.

I cursed myself as I swept my naginata from side to side. I had the second damn healing ring, and I'd forgotten all about it! I fumbled it from my bag, tossing it to Lydia.

"Catch!" I shouted, and she blinked in confusion as it bounced off her shield. I swore, but Oracle was there a second later, diving into the mass of bodies and sweeping the ring up. Lydia stepped back to buy time and jammed it on her finger, sighing with relief as she used it to banish her minor wounds and stepped back up to the line.

I yanked my own off and shoved it into Miren's shocked hands, telling her to use it if she needed to. We were getting slowly overwhelmed, surrounded as we were in the middle of the clearing. I figured we had one chance, but it was a toss of the dice.

"Stay here!" I bellowed at the others. I took a step back, a deep breath, and threw myself forward. Sweeping my naginata low and putting as much force as I could into it, I sheared through the goblins, sending them screaming to the floor, maimed and dying. As soon as the gaps appeared, other goblins rushed to fill them, easily a hundred in view as they kept boiling from their nest, as I could only think of it now.

I didn't give them the chance. I lunged forward, spinning my weapon in overlapping arcs, finally letting myself use a little mana as the potion replaced it, and the two healing rings gave Oracle a break.

I channeled mana into my naginata, feeling it roar to life as the blade burst into bright, crackling light. I channeled a lightning bolt into it and whipped it around in circles. Hissing sounds arose from the freshly made corpses as the blade met black blood, and I cleared even more space.

As soon as there was enough, I started to spin, getting dizzy with each rotation. But with the naginata flashing up and down, the blade carved through them in their dozens. I staggered from side to side, dizziness making it hard to keep going in the right direction. Slicing my way forward through the oncoming goblins, I forced myself forwards, sending blood and viscera flying.

The closer I got to the entrance to their home, the tighter packed they became and the harder it was for them to dodge. I could hear shouts and screams from behind me, and I sensed Oracle pulling on our shared mana, but I couldn't stop. It was our only chance.

I lashed out even though I could barely stay upright. The world was spinning wildly, and I planted my feet firmly, locking my gaze on the hole right before me, which was filled with goblins fighting over each other in an effort to fall back out of range of the madman with the glowing naginata. The world tilted, and I frantically tried to keep upright, knowing I'd die in painful seconds if I fell.

I started a kata I remembered from my training, looping the blade over my shoulders and forwards before dipping it and repeating, swapping from hand to hand in a constant loop. West had called it a "lawn mower move," and it worked exactly as he'd warned it would. It sliced and diced everything in front of me, but it left my sides and rear totally exposed. I had all I could do to keep upright and keep this up; I couldn't risk anything more complicated, and I relied on the others totally.

I stopped using my mana when I felt Oracle pull on it again, and we dipped to single digits. The mana headache bloomed, and I winced, then gritted my teeth as the taste of ozone filled the air around me. An explosion seemingly right at my feet told me that Oracle had my back.

The goblins went flying from the explosion out of the corner of my eye, screams filling the air as well as less identifiable…bits. I was frantically slicing and dicing, out of mana, almost blind with the headache, and the world was spinning like crazy. When Bob stepped up on my right, a Firebolt flew past to blast into the seething mass before me. A hand grabbed my shoulder, and hands reached past me, closing over my naginata before I could hit anyone on our side with it.

I let myself be pulled back. If Bob was there, I was safe.

Long seconds passed as I was dragged back and dropped down onto my ass on the floor, hard. It seemed like forever before the world stopped spinning, and I could focus again, but when I could, Oracle's face hovered before me. She had a vial out in either hand, a mana potion and a stamina potion. I focused blearily on my bars.

My health bar was at seventy percent, but my stamina and mana were close to rock bottom, and I realized why my mana headache had flared so badly just now…Oracle had used a healing spell to get me up to where I was.

I grimaced and shook my head again to clear it as I took the mana potion first, chugging it and dropping the bottle, quickly following it with the stamina one. I needed to be back in the fight, and as soon as the stamina started refilling, the world started making sense again.

I'd no idea that stamina depletion was such a killer, but without my team, I'd have keeled over in a few more seconds. I coughed and forced myself to my feet, staggering to one side before righting myself and looking around at the battlefield.

Miren and Stephanos were alternating between picking off stragglers and firing arrows into the nest. Arrin was taking his time and firing the occasional Firebolt into the goblins then stabbing the wounded between castings.

Bob and Lydia were at the front of the group, hammering their way through the goblin horde, and all three Mer were darting around at the sides. The youngling kept nearby and had clearly been tasked with watching over me, while Flux and Cheena were on either side of the group, slaughtering everything they could reach.

My notifications were going crazy, but I ignored them, shooting a glance at the youngling as he stood nearby, clearly torn between diving into the fight and staying close to me.

"What's your name?" I asked him. He jumped, turning to face me fully and starting to go down on a knee. "Fuck's sake, man, get up!" I growled, grabbing his arm and hauling him upright.

"There's no time for shit like that!" I snapped and pointed to Cheena. "Go help her!"

He took off running, but after a few steps he paused and turned, bowing his head to me again and called out.

"Call me Bane, lord." With that, he was back up and flying across the distance to join Cheena, diving in and fighting alongside her with a hell of a speed.

I turned and exchanged a look with Oracle. The kid had either a natural talent or he was exceedingly dedicated. He was like a machine as he fought, two upper arms blocking and deflecting the goblins' attempts at attacks, while his lower arms struck forward and pulled back like pistons.

I strode forward to join the line again, pulling Lydia back to rest as we started to push the group back further. The press of goblins had begun to weaken off. Where before, they'd been clambering over each other to get at us, driven to insanity by some instinctual need to fight, now, there were fewer and fewer joining the battle, and at last we could enter the ruins.

The roof was sagging, only the occasional section of exposed ancient stonework letting us tell that it wasn't a natural occurring cave. The lip was overgrown with centuries of moss, grass, and vines, then trampled into mush by the passage of hundreds of feet over and over.

At first, Bob and I could fight side-by-side, but as we continued down the earthen corridor, it grew narrower. I eventually had to step back and let Bob lead the way. We took turns resting and recovering, with me watching Bob's status and waiting as long as I could while my mana returned slowly.

As soon as Bob reached the fifty percent mark, I ordered him to fall back, stepping up and taking his place. I needed him, and we all would. But at the end of the day, he could be rebuilt if need be; others couldn't be. I'd repair him as soon as we got the chance, but the passage we were following had narrowed to the point where he was having difficulty moving forward.

I stabbed forward, shuffling along and using my naginata as a spear for a few minutes, stabbing and deflecting the goblins' crude attempts at fighting. The dirt and exposed rubble of the passageway suddenly gave way to a roughly broken hole into a large stone hallway, and the last few goblins backed away and ran to the right.

I paused, still in the earthen section, and popped my head out cautiously, looking to either side and finding that the left led to a solid wall of collapsed masonry, but the right was a meeting hall or barracks, old and large enough that there were several fire pits needed, each of which smoldered. The glowing embers and occasional dim magelights scattered around the room granted a mixture of light that failed to illuminate so much as create more shadows.

The goblins, however, were clearly visible as they raced away, and they weren't running randomly. Halfway across the darkened room stood a group of twenty larger goblins. Each of them wore cobbled-together armor, but they carried real weapons: swords, flails, one even had a giant cleaver. They were waiting for us, and that wasn't the worst bit.

Standing behind them were two other goblins. One was easily the biggest in the room and wore what looked like a complete set of armor, carrying a hammer and shield. The other goblin was wearing a black robe with its hood up. A single, sickly white hand was all that emerged from the garment's protection, and it clutched a wand threateningly.

I jumped down and moved into the room, the others of my squad following me and spreading out until even Bob had shoved through, dropping down to stomp up to my side. Flux and the other two Mer were nowhere to be seen, and Oracle was staying out of sight behind Bob. I grinned at the thought of the surprise to come for the nasty creatures we faced.

I checked my mana as both sides eyed each other coldly. I was at a hundred and four stamina out of a hundred and ninety. I had three hundred and sixty health out of five hundred and eighty, and at the lowest, of course, was my mana at one hundred and twenty-six out of two hundred and fifty.

I stepped forward and called out to them, the previous silence of the room broken only by the crackling fires dotted around and the panting of the retreating, smaller goblins.

"Where are my people?" I asked, and there was a long pause before the hooded goblin spoke up in a harsh voice.

"What people?"

"From the ship," I snapped back, looking around the room. I needed to delay as long as possible to let my mana recover, but...the room was lit by scattered fires and contained what looked to be old stone benches. Piles of rubbish were carelessly strewn about, but there were no cages or bodies visible. At the far end, a doorway led out of the room, and more fires reflected off the walls down that way.

"You come here for food?" the goblin asked then cackled. "You come to *be* food!"

It raised its wand and fired a bolt of solid darkness across the room at Bob, making him rock back with the force of it. He'd already lost several bones from his plated armor, and his rib bones were exposed by the impact. He dropped by nearly ten percent of his health, or structural integrity, or whatever it was…

"You'll pay for that, my son!" I bellowed at the creature, running forward, the rest of the team following me. "Kill that fucker!" I roared.

"Oracle! Keep hidden behind Bob and charge up a big lightning bolt; I want that fucker dead!"

"On it!"

I sent gratitude to Oracle, aware that she'd hidden when we entered the room. I got her response mixed with a sense of glee; she loved using that damn spell.

The armored goblins spread out to take our charge as the others spread out behind me. I picked my target, cold rage building. I'd been focused before, but now? Now I needed control, as other goblins shouted in the distance. I gritted my teeth and tamped my anger down as hard as I could.

I lashed out with my naginata, beating the nearest goblin's sword aside, jumping and spinning into a kick that snapped its head back and sent it reeling. I'd used the impact to push myself back and blocked a mace strike from my left.

Jian was there in a second, his right sword slamming into the mace as well and driving it further aside to free up my weapon, even as his left-hand sword stabbed deep into the goblin's unprotected side where it's armor didn't cover. Another blast of magic preceded a cry of pain as someone was hit with the dark magic the goblin mage was firing. I gritted my teeth again, determined to end this fight as quickly as possible.

I swept across to my right, hooking the base of my naginata between that goblin's legs and pulling it off its feet. Bob took advantage of the gap to stamp forward, one huge foot ending that goblin's worries in a permanent way. My first target staggered back toward me, glaring past a broken, bloody nose, and growled, about to attack. Oracle appeared from behind Bob, lashing both hands forwards at the mage.

At the last second, the armored goblin leaped in the way, its shield absorbing the spell and making the goblin scream in rage and pain.

The sudden, unexpected addition of Oracle caused the goblins to freeze for a second, one which Arrin, Stephanos, and Miren made the most of, all firing on the mage who cowered behind his protector.

Both arrows clattered off the shield harmlessly, but the firebolt was aimed better. It slammed into the armored goblin's leg, blasting him back a few steps and out of position. Oracle's second lightning bolt hit him directly, rather than his shield.

The armored goblin screeched at the mage and began backing away, even as the mage fired a dark blast at Oracle. She managed to dodge but called out a warning.

"It's death magic! Don't let it hit you!"

I stabbed forward, the tip of my naginata sending sparks flying as it skittered across the goblin's armor. It jumped back with a hiss of fear before slashing wildly at me. I blocked with the haft of my weapon, releasing with my right hand as the goblin's blade slipped towards it. Leaning forward, I grabbed the top of the creature's breastplate, yanking it off-balance into a headbutt that stunned it long enough that I managed to sweep its legs.

Once it was on the floor, I lashed out hard, driving the metal-clad butt of the naginata down into its face, feeling bone crunch underneath the blow as the body spasmed and went still.

I glanced up just in time to see Lydia block a sword that had been aimed at my face with her shield, then lash out with her mace. A loud crash reverberated through the air as her blow met the goblin's helmet, sending it staggering back.

The mage and armored goblin had retreated nearly to the door while we'd been killing the main group. I was about to cast a spell myself when the pair moved too close to the corridor, and the darkness resolved into three figures. The first and tallest drove two spears and a dagger into the robed figure's back while slashing downwards onto the exposed arm, nearly cutting its hand off with the last dagger.

The other two figures appeared next to the armored goblin. One yanked his shield aside, twisting the arm quickly and violently enough that the snapping of bone was heard clear across the room. The second figure grabbed its hammer and yanked back, immobilizing that arm. Both figures stabbed out rapidly with their weapons. The long, kinked daggers that seemed to be a signature weapon of the Mer punched through the weakly covered areas such as the armpits, throat, and groin, driving deep and coming out in sprays of blood.

I turned back to the remaining goblins only to find Bob smashing the last one from its feet, Arrin firing a firebolt into its face a second before. Bob drove a fist down, crushing its skull and ending its life with a messy splat.

It was over, at least for now. I could hear shouting, and the sounds of more goblins deeper in the building. Jian was laid to one side, his breath whistling through teeth gritted in pain, while Miren looked like she was going to throw up.

His leather armor was covered in blood, and his left arm...looked like it'd been hit with a hammer blow. The bones were obviously shattered. The arm hung limply, bone fragments poking through the skin, and a quickly widening pool of blood was spreading under him.

Oracle was there already. She didn't dare waste the mana on shifting sizes, and without her asking, I pulled out the last mana potion, downing it.

As soon as there was enough, Oracle started casting our newly evolved Battlefield Triage spell. It tore through the little mana we had quickly, causing me to wince as the expected mana headache bloomed. But Jian rapidly looked better, the wounds on his arm closing as the bones were drawn back into their correct places.

"He's lost a lot of blood," Oracle said quietly as I moved to her side.

"I can fight, lord. I am strong!" Jian whispered, but his face was white with pain still, and I shook my head. I didn't have the mana to spare to cast Identify to check on him properly. Hell, I'd wanted to use it so many times since this fight began, especially on the last two goblins that had tried to escape the room, the mage, and its protector. I just didn't have enough. The triage spell had pulled him back from death's door, but he looked terrible, and it had run out of mana before he could be healed fully.

I could see the glowing red "1" symbol in the emptied-out mana bar, and I shook my head sadly at Jian.

"No, mate," I said quietly, gripping his other shoulder and giving it a gentle squeeze. "I know you're strong, but you can't keep going, not wounded as you are."

I checked on the others, finding that Miren was trying to hide a blackened side, the skin appearing grey and rotting. I ignored her weak protestations that Jian needed help more, and I looked her over, pulling my last health potion out and forcing her to take it.

She downed it after only a little protestation and shuddered as the grey and rotting skin fell free, sloughed off as fresh, pink skin replaced it, floating up from below.

"Do we have any charges left on the healing rings?" I asked, getting negative head shakes as my only response. I swore, low and fervent, and looked the others over.

None of them were in good shape, save the Mer; even Lydia was trying to hide a long gash on one cheek, and I growled to myself. I checked my mana and did a quick bit of math...

With one point of mana left and a regen rate of two point six per minute, bolstered by the mana potion by an extra point, it would take me about fourteen minutes to regenerate enough mana to cast Cleansing Fire, and I had no idea if I could alter the spell to not harm my party, or what it would cost.

I looked over the team's details in my vision; the Mer and I were the only ones above half health, though Miren's health was starting to tick back up now that she'd taken the potion.

"Okay, let's get the stone benches over to the doors," I said, coming to a decision. "We need to create a barrier so we can hunker down and rest for a bit, then we'll move on."

As soon as I said it, Bob was off, dragging what looked to be a solid ton of weight across the floor. I shook my head at the strength of the skeletal construct, damn glad he was on my side and not against me.

"Jax..." I turned at the sound of my name to find Flux. He was spattered with blood, and clearly tired, but beyond that, he was okay. I needed to get him and the others some fresh water, as well I knew; yet another thing to add to the list..."We can't wait. I'm sorry."

"What? We don't have a choice here, Flux. Only you three and me can still fight, and I'm out of mana. We need to—" I retorted, confused.

"They'll kill the captives if we wait," Flux said sadly.

I groaned, clutching my head and swearing under my breath.

"Okay, explain that please," I said, tired and annoyed, my mana headache not helping the situation.

"Goblins live an existence filled with hate and fear. Right now, they're afraid of us, but as soon as enough of them are together, they'll get angry again and come for us. They'll kill the prisoners rather than risk us freeing them. I can't wait; I have to try to save the younglings."

"If you three go in there without help, you'll all die as well," I stated flatly, shaking my head. "You know that, mate. We don't know how many are still alive—"

"Exactly, Jax. For all we know, there could be only a few dozen left."

"A few dozen? And can you handle a few dozen goblins, the three of you? Considering that's the best-case scenario here?"

"No, we probably can't...but we've agreed, and we're going ahead. Please, come when you have rested enough," Flux said, turning his back and starting to walk towards the door that led deeper into the nest.

"Oh, that's a fucking low blow, mate!" I snapped, but Flux just kept on walking.

I considered the group scattered around me. There was no way they could fight. They were all on the ragged edge, especially as, for some of them, it'd been their first fight. I sighed and called to Flux.

"Wait by the door," I snapped, then I turned back to the group, gesturing for Oracle and Lydia to join me in walking toward the corpses of the mage and his protector. I was silent for a few seconds.

"You're not going to like this, either of you," I muttered in a low voice, by way of starting the fight off. "But I'm going with Flux, and you're both staying here."

Immediately, both of them started arguing. Lydia was respectful, if blunt, but Oracle was anything but.

"Lord, you're in hardly any better shape than the rest of us; we can't afford to lose you—"

"Don't be an idiot, Jax! You—"

"That's enough," I said quietly, the cold, serious tone cutting them both off. "Flux is right; if the goblins have time to rest, to regroup and come for us, we might survive, we might not…but the prisoners definitely won't."

"They're not your people, Jax," Oracle said, hovering right before my face and locking eyes with me. "I know you. You want to stand up for the weak, for the oppressed, but you don't know these people. What if they're like the assholes we just sent off into the forest? You're risking your life for people you don't know! We need you!"

"I know," I said quietly. "I know I'm needed at the tower, and here with you. Hell, *Tommy* needs me, but I won't abandon these people. Flux and his team are going forwards regardless. I can help them; I *have* to help them."

"No! No, you don't. You just—" Oracle snapped at me, shaking her head before drawing in a deep breath and looking around. "Fine, okay. You know what? If you're going to do this, at least Bob and I can—"

"Stay here," I finished for her, and she frowned at me. "You need to stay here, and you need Bob to protect you. If there are other goblins, they might counterattack. Hell, they might be out on patrol now and walking down the passageway as we speak. You need to stay here. Once you have enough mana, you can heal our team and get them out safely. You'll need Bob to protect you until then, and you'll need him to move the tables, anyway; nobody else can."

"You need me Jax, I—"

"I need you to protect them," I said quietly. I hated doing this, but…"Oracle, that's an order. I need you to protect our people, heal them, and get them home safe if I don't come back." I turned to Lydia.

"I go where you go," she said simply.

"Oh, for…Lydia, seriously you need to—" I started, and she cut me off.

"The tower needs you, Jax; we need you. It doesn't need me. I can go with Flux and the others…"

"And you'd get killed straight away. You're barely above half health, and I can see the way you're holding yourself; you've broken ribs at the very least, haven't you?" I asked, seeing the guilty flare of acceptance in her eyes. "Look at me, both of you," I said quietly, continuing once they both complied.

"I need you both to look after them. Bob can't understand anyone but us, Oracle, and he's needed here. Lydia, you're in no state to move far. But if you can fight? Stay here and protect them; if goblins come, they'll need you. If it makes it any easier on both of you, it's an order," I finished, anger written all over both their faces. "You don't have to like it," I said finally. "You just have to do it."

I got a short nod in confirmation from Lydia, and Oracle spun around and flew off towards Bob.

It wasn't a win, but they would be safe, it was enough.

I crouched down, quickly searching the goblin mage, hoping I'd find something I could use, ideally a potion or two. After a quick and rather disgusting search—...the damn thing was naked under the robe, and it wasn't a sight I'd ever wanted to see—...I found that, apart from a necklace of bones, a few coppers, and the small wand, it had nothing. I didn't waste time checking the armored goblin over; I just stood and called out that, when one of them had the strength, I wanted the goblins searched for anything that could be salvaged. Then I headed to join Flux and the others. Bob had blocked off the far entrance to the room and was dragging another table to barricade another opening when I nodded to Flux.

"Let's go do something stupid," I said and walked into the hallway, all three following me closely.

CHAPTER THIRTEEN

"...thank you, Jax," Flux said to me in a quiet but firm voice.

"I'll not let some kids die if I can help it," I muttered and got a nod in return.

"Cheena, scout ahead, please," Flux requested in a low tone. As she started off, he spoke to me again. "We'll add this to our debt to you, Lord Jax. It will not be forgotten."

I just shrugged, creeping forward as quietly as I could.

The corridor was short and filled with debris and literal crap, the goblins clearly having no concept of hygiene, and it reeked. At the end was a cross-connecting corridor that led to the left and right, and Cheena had barely paused when she reached it. The left had been clogged with collapsed masonry, while the right led into a square room with a low fire burning in the far-right corner.

We snuck up to the doorway and peered inside, seeing nothing moving and a second doorway that led to the left. We took that one, entering a second small room that was similarly abandoned. As I started forward towards the far door, Bane grabbed me and yanked me back hard. Before I could ask him what was going on, a hand was clapped over my mouth, and Flux was by my side, staring into my eyes, waiting.

I had a moment of panic. *Was this a betrayal? Had I given myself up to be slaughtered like a lamb?* Movement shifted the shadows in the far corner of the room, and I focused on it with a frown.

Flux, seeing that I was aware something was wrong, nodded, and Bane released me. I crouched and waited, staring at the pile of debris that I was sure had moved. After a second, another pile nearby gave a twitch as something moved in it.

I froze as Bane hissed out a single word...

"Spiders!"

It was as though the word were a call to arms, and suddenly a dozen spiders the size of cats erupted from hiding across the room, barreling towards us with a horrific skittering sound, dozens of chitinous legs tapping across the floor. I backed up straight away. I wasn't scared of spiders; I just hated the horrible bastards. They made my skin crawl...and the sight of a dozen of the largest ones I had ever seen heading straight for me...*nope!*

I lashed out with my naginata at the nearest while Flux and Bane moved up to either side of me. I cut through a handful of legs on one side of my target, sending it flying, and a gout of ichor poured out.

An angry chittering rose, and the remaining spiders started moving faster. Panic reared its ugly head as they sped up, and I slashed out again and again, screaming involuntarily when one bunched its legs up and leaped through the air at me, flying at my face.

I had a long view of its approach, legs spread wide, foul head facing me, and long fangs extended…when Bane smashed it from the air with one of his spears.

The spider hit the wall with a crunching sound and fell to the ground, its legs spasming before curling up in death.

I took an involuntary step back again before gritting my teeth and stepping forward again, slashing and stabbing. The tip of my naginata punched through the chitinous shell of the last spider and glanced off the ground below it, filling the air with a scraping sound.

I panted, searching around and, seeing nothing left to kill, I spun on Flux instead.

"What the hell was that?!" I snarled at him. "Where's Cheena? She's supposed to be warning us about shit like this!"

Flux bowed his head in apology. "She wouldn't have considered this something to warn us of, Lord Jax. All of our kind can sense the spiders and their kin. We can generally slip through without them sensing us or kill them with ease, usually. With only a dozen, she would have considered them a minor annoyance and simply continued on.

"I didn't consider it myself, until you almost walked into their trap…" He shook his head and clapped Bane on the shoulder. "If not for Bane, you could have been seriously injured. Our debt to you climbs further. I take full responsibility….I…"

"Oh, fuck off." I turned away from the room, wiping my hand across my face, getting my breathing under control. After a couple of long seconds, I turned back to them and spoke up quietly.

"I'm sorry, Flux. I shouldn't have snapped at you. I've got an…issue with creatures like that. Fucking SporeMother was the same, freaked me the hell out," I said. I hadn't let anyone know about it, hiding it even from Oracle so far, but I'd been having nightmares of fighting that damn thing ever since I'd killed it. I kept imagining it at full strength, capturing me and impregnating me with its spawn. Freaked me the fuck out.

"SporeMother?" Flux asked, turning to face me again, ignoring the room ahead. Even Bane had jumped, spinning halfway around before he caught himself and turned back to watching the room ahead.

"Yeah…there was one in the tower, fucking thing nearly killed me," I muttered.

"You escaped it? Has it bred? The Tower has long been considered a site of ancient evil, even by the soldiers I knew. Adventurers were sent over the years to clear it out, but none returned."

"It had bred…yeah. Maybe a dozen sporelings were loose in the tower when I arrived; they're nightmare fuel as well. As to the adventurers, I found a few inhabited by DarkSpore, so if you knew them, I'm sorry," I muttered, shaking my head and shrugging apologetically.

"Then this area isn't safe, either…We will gather the pod after this, and we will move to…*wait*, you said you were Lord of the Tower…the notifications…you *killed* it?!" Flux asked me, clearly shocked.

"Yeah, and believe me, it wasn't easy." I gestured at the rooms ahead of us. "Let's get a move on; we can talk about it later."

Ignoring the low barrage of sounds Bane and Flux exchanged, I forced myself to walk forward. Stepping over spider corpses I intellectually knew were totally dead, I still worried at a deep level that they were just waiting to bite me.

"Thank you," I said to Bane as I passed him, putting my hand on his shoulder, and squeezing once before letting go and moving on.

We went back to moving as stealthily as possible, which meant Bane and Flux were utterly frigging silent, as near as I could tell, and I just tried not to clatter and clank too much. My notifications were still going nuts, but I tuned them out. We crossed the spider room and found Cheena waiting for us in the next corridor, gesturing for us to move back a bit to talk.

"The end of this corridor, there's a hallway. The right leads to a single room, and a handful of goblins are barricaded inside. At least, I think they're goblins; they sounded small, and the air tastes foul." She shrugged. "The left-hand side leads to two more rooms. One is the kitchen; there are a lot of dead bodies in there, but otherwise, it's abandoned. The final room…" She paused, taking a deep breath.

"It's where the boss and its guards are all holed up, waiting for us. There's maybe a dozen of your people there from the ship, and T'lek is there as well. The…the rest of the crew and little Gaul are in the kitchen, dead. What's left of them, anyway."

"How many guards, and what's the boss look like?" I asked, feeling sick that so many had died already. I thought back to when I'd viewed the ship through the arcane eagle's vision. There had been several more crew than that on deck alone at that point. I didn't want to know how many were dead in here, killed by goblins. I tried to keep my rage tamped down, but it bubbled away, building beneath the surface.

"Maybe twenty goblins in the last room, but the boss is…huge. I think it's a matriarch," she said meaningfully, evoking a growl of horrified rage from Flux. I turned to him.

"What's a matriarch?" I asked, and Flux shook his head in disgust, his tendrils waving in agitation.

"Goblins breed like wildfire. Clans either have a nursery with a handful of breeders that constantly drop more of the vicious little bastards, or—"

Cheena cut him off in a flat tone. "Or they have a matriarch, a single greater female that has mutated. It births fewer goblins at a time, but they can pass on genetic traits from the creatures they eat to their spawn."

"Wait, so…"

"So these goblins we've been killing were normal goblins, the base species. Matriarchs are thought to be responsible for the creation of orc and hobgoblin tribes; they're slaughtered whenever they're found, with good reason!" Cheena said.

"And those twenty goblins in the final room?" I asked, a sudden horrible thought occurring to me.

"They're mutations, bigger, stronger looking…she's eaten sentients and birthed whatever she's using as her personal guard."

"Why only twenty? And hundreds of the weaker ones?" I asked, and it was Flux that answered.

"Either she ran out of the…genetic material…or they mutated in ways she didn't like…and she ate them."

"Okay, so I suggest we kill that fucking thing before it can whip up a new batch, then!"

"Definitely!" Cheena agreed, then looked back to the end of the corridor where Bane had moved to keep watch. He was gone.

"Oh no…" she whispered, and she and Flux set off running. I scrambled after them. At the end of the corridor, the doorway to the next room was barricaded by wood and stone. I dismissed it and set off running towards the other end, arriving just in time for Cheena and Flux to dart into a room on the left. I followed, noting that the last room, the boss room, must be to the right, at the end of the corridor.

I slowed down, moving cautiously into the room, and found Bane on his knees, clutching what looked to be a Mer's leg in his hands. He was rocking back and forth and keening. Cheena knelt beside him and started to speak quietly to him.

"What…" I asked before Flux gestured to me to stop.

"Gaul was one of Bane's companions, his friend," Flux said quietly to me, as we quickly checked the rest of the room. "We need to—"

Bane suddenly roared with rage. He threw Cheena aside and took off running down the corridor.

"Bane! Wait, you fool!" Flux cried out. We exchanged a stricken look, then we were off, Cheena forcing herself to her feet to follow us.

We hurtled down the corridor just in time to see Bane disappear around the corner to the right. We'd certainly lost the element of surprise, but Bane running in like he was and us hot on his heels? I just had to hope we all survived this.

I hurtled towards the corner, taking it fast enough that I had to jump and kick off the far wall. Digging deep and pushing off as fast as I could, I passed Flux and was drawing closer to Bane when he ran through the open doors ahead.

I had a split second to check my health, stamina, and mana, finding that my health had climbed to eighty percent, stamina was nearly full, but my mana…my mana was at thirty-six,…As I watched, it dropped to eleven.

Fuck. Oracle had clearly needed it, but…I shook my head, resolving to do this without mana if need be, then dismissed the thought and ran on. Seeing Bane leap to the left, I angled myself to do the same.

As I ran through the large double doors, I realized the room was larger than all but the first we'd fought in. It was easily fifty meters on a side, square, and had a vaulted ceiling. A large fire crackled in the far left back corner, casting flickering shadows across the walls. There were piles of debris still, but they seemed ordered. At the right, embedded into the wall, was a row of dust-covered figures. I dismissed them as soon as I saw they weren't a threat, in favor of the twenty goblins that stood between Bane and the matriarch.

I took in the cages on the rear wall, dozens of poorly constructed stone and metal sections that had been twisted together to hold a rag-tag bunch of beings. Nowhere amongst them was a purple robe, the one I'd seen Decin wearing.

"Oren's gonna be pissed…" I groaned, coming to a sliding halt next to Bane, who was already fighting two goblins. Lashing out with my naginata, I deflected a third goblin's attack from taking Bane in the side.

I twisted my grip, lifting my back hand and pulling my forward one down, dipping my weapon down and punching the impossibly sharp tip of the naginata through the upper thigh of the goblin facing me. I twisted it viciously and yanked it back, ignoring the screaming, falling foe. I knew it wasn't going to live; the artery in its leg looked like it was around the same place as in a human, and it was spraying hot, black blood across the floor.

I moved further to the right, gaining some space to use my weapon more effectively, and frantically ducked, wove, and stabbed as I faced three more goblins. I used the base of the naginata as a club, deflecting blow after blow, and I soon took dozens of small cuts. Battle raged all around me, Flux and Cheena as sorely pressed as I was.

The goblins we faced weren't the barely conscious animals we'd fought before. These creatures were bigger, around five to five and a half feet, well-muscled, and covered in armor. They used a variety of weapons and gear, obviously scavenged, but of far better quality than those we'd fought so far. The worst thing was that they fought as a group.

They used shields and advanced when we looked in the other direction, they attacked in pairs and trios, and they were fast.

I sliced my naginata across at throat height, making two in front of me jump back. A thrown dagger almost took my eye, and I cursed, backing up and switching to one-handed slashes while I wiped blood free, clearing my sight. The distraction of me backing up let another goblin jump forward, slashing at Bane's leg. He frantically blocked the attack but missed the chance to strike against his own opponent, who stabbed at him, giving him a glancing wound across his hip.

I let go of my face, feeling a flap of skin shake with the movement, and I raised the naginata overhead. Bringing it down as hard and fast as I could, I smashed it into the goblin's helm, driving it to its knees.

We fought back and forth, frantically trying to take the other side down, blood flying from dozens of light cuts. Flux shouted to me suddenly.

"We have to kill her! It's our only chance!" I shifted my focus to the enormous creature that reclined on a handful of benches pushed together. I'd done my best to ignore her so far, trying not to get bogged down in details.

The matriarch was huge. While she was probably only eight to ten feet tall, if she could stand upright, she was at least that wide as well, almost round. And she held in her hand...a mirror image of the leg Bane had been clutching earlier.

She stared at me, her piggy little eyes locked on mine as she bit down, tearing flesh free and chewing it with sharp, pointed teeth. The leg was clearly small, smaller even than the first Mer I'd fought, and while I'd always known that Bane's group were young, and even had a few children amongst them, fighting with Bane had made me assume they were all like him: strong, deadly, and fast.

The first one I'd fought wasn't deadly at all, once it couldn't get away. The thought that something had slaughtered an even younger one? That this *fucking* thing was *eating* it and *enjoying* it?

That we were a fucking cabaret act for it to watch while it ate our people?!

"*NOT TODAY, MOTHERFUCKER!*" I screamed, my rage finally bursting past all the boundaries I'd tried to impose. An answering shriek of rage exploded in the distance, and I just knew Oracle was losing her shit as well.

I lunged, going from a balanced fighting style, mixing defense and offense equally, into an insane, all-out attack.

I felt Him awaken, watching as he always did, silent, but his mind seemed to link with mine easily, as it had since we had shared memories back in the tower when fighting the SporeMother.

We didn't speak; there was nothing to say to each other, just an extension of awareness. He took over watching out of my peripheral vision, enemies seeming to pulse when they moved in my direction. Their weapons were glaringly obvious, allowing me to dodge, weave, and in one case, to kick them aside.

There.

I stabbed, driving the nearest goblin back, the tip of the naginata kissing the underside of his chin and slicing his rough skin like butter. The blade slid in and out and away, cutting down on the inside of my next target's arm, opening the wrist before the first had time to clutch at its ruined throat.

Behind.

I twisted, pivoting around, and struck out with the heel of my left foot to connect with the side of another goblin's helm, sending it reeling long enough for Cheena to end its life with a thrust of both spears.

I smacked the tip of my naginata down on the ground, speeding my pivot, and I crouched down low, spinning the weapon over my head and swinging the bladed end around. Dipping low again, I sliced through another goblin's ankle, sending it toppling to the ground with a scream.

Now!

I popped upright, lifting the naginata overhead and swapping my grip in an instant, the chance I'd been waiting for given to me with that goblin's fall.

I threw the naginata as hard as I could and had the satisfaction of seeing the piggy eyes in that bloated face go wide in fear. Then the blade hit, punching through the rough skin high on the right side of her chest. A screech of pain was quickly followed by a burbling cry that told me I'd scored a good hit.

I grabbed my swords, a hilt over each shoulder, and I pulled hard. I'd had to practice this maneuver so many times; despite what the movies showed, it was difficult, but I brought both swords down just in time to block the nearest upright goblin's attack.

Left!

The world shrank into a frantic blur of steel, bronze, and teeth as all the goblins seemed to fixate on me, attacking with manic ferocity.

You put your left foot out…

I cried out as a blade got past my defense. The voice in my head's nursery song distracted me for only an instant, when I needed its help the most. I hissed as the hit tore into my right upper arm, glancing off the bone and making me drop that sword from suddenly numb fingers.

I roared in rage and punted the goblin in the balls; I didn't know much about their reproductive capabilities, but from the way it lifted into the air and the high-pitched squeal that came from it, I'd just ended that aspect of its existence. I then slashed out, determined to end the rest, only to have a mace crash into my sword, deflecting it enough that it skittered off my target's chest plate.

I roared in pain again as a hammer hit me in the left wrist, the bracers barely cushioning the impact. My second sword flew from nerveless fingers.

I stepped back quickly, finding that there were only three goblins left, and that Bane, Cheena, and Flux were battling two of them now. All three Mer bore various injuries, blood streaming from them. The Matriarch was squealing and pulling herself across the top of her cradle, frantically trying to drag herself close enough to grab a pack that sat nearby.

The last thing I noticed was something that I'd missed in the ferocious melee: the prisoners.

They were screaming encouragement! They were pounding away frantically at the makeshift cages that held them, bloody fists and feet ignored as they tried to get free to come to our aid, determined to stand on their own two feet and help.

I grinned at the goblin I faced, my mental passenger focused in tight on it as well; he'd kept me alive this long. Imperfectly, sure, but there was only so much that was possible when the fight was that fast and vicious, or when my passenger was so deranged.

Now we both focused in with laser precision. The goblin growled, its jaw a mix of under and overbite working from one side to the other, yellow and black teeth interspersed with rotting…bits…made a concoction of halitosis that would kill a dentist just from looking at it. The goblin glared at me, shifting its grip on the hammer that had broken my left wrist and licked its lips nervously, nearly cutting its own tongue off.

I shifted to face it fully, teeth gritted as I glared at it, daring it to attack. It let out a growl that was mixed with hatred and fear and swung the hammer two-handed at me, aiming for my chest and swinging right to left.

I stepped back, my useless arms dangling. My capoeira sessions suddenly came to mind as I began to move lightly, balancing on the balls of my feet and shifting from one foot to the other. I made sure it was watching me, readying for another swing. I could feel my companion getting closer, going faster and faster, our twin rages feeding each other and spiraling higher with every beat of my heart.

It swung the weapon again, right to left, then yanked it back as fast as it could, aiming to catch me with the spiked head on the back of its hammer. I dodged, barely quick enough, and I grinned at it as I leaned back. The hammer beat through the air in front of me, close enough that I felt the wind of its passage.

I'd bent back as far as I could, keeping my left foot planted, and I brought my right up as fast as possible, smashing my heel into the goblin's face and causing it to stagger backwards, lashing out blindly with the hammer. I backed up a step, waiting for it. As it focused on me, hatred twisted its face, then its forehead shot up in confusion as I dropped to one knee and ducked.

Both emotions were wiped from its face by the terror that followed as Oracle shot over my head at tremendous speed. She used the mana I'd regenerated to make herself solid at the last second as she hit its face, fingers shifting to claws that drove deep into its eyes and burrowed into the brain behind it.

The goblin gasped in pain and collapsed, a momentarily insane Wisp shredding its face while screaming incoherent swearwords. The goblin was dead before it hit the ground, but Oracle's fury lasted much longer.

I stepped around her victim, finding the matriarch panting in panic as she managed to get her pudgy claw into the backpack at last. It came back out clutching a gleaming red potion, but before she could raise it to her slobbering mouth…Bane was there.

He slapped the potion aside with his lower right hand, the upper hands each grabbing a wrist and holding the matriarch still. She squealed in terror again and tried to wrench herself free. But despite her huge size, there was little muscle. She had a second of uninhibited writhing, then Bane's lower arms went to work.

He clutched a dagger in the left and slowly dug it into the creature, making her cry out in pain as it slowly cut through layers of fat.

"Bane!" I called out, and he turned furious eyes on me. I stepped in close and nodded toward my belt. He found the dagger there, nodding in thanks as he reached down and yanked it free. I spoke for his and the Matriarch's benefit.

"It's called the Dagger of Ripping...have fun." Turning at that point, I was just in time to see Oracle lift herself from the corpse of the goblin I'd been facing. She searched around the room, her rage clear in her eyes, and I made sure the enemy were all dead. Once I had no doubt, with Flux and Cheena moving to free the captives, I closed my eyes and went to work at tamping down my anger, getting control over myself and feeding Oracle a sense of calm as well.

It took several minutes of careful breathing, and it wasn't surprising how difficult that was, what with the Matriarch screaming in pain behind me. But eventually, she wheezed out her last, and Oracle and I grew calm.

I opened my eyes again, having heard Flux and Cheena talking to the prisoners, but I'd blocked the words down to a buzz. The freed prisoners had all gathered around Flux; he was helping a small Mer to walk, clearly having to half carry them; they were that badly injured and dehydrated.

The people went silent, even Flux's words drying up as I stepped forward. I was covered in blood again. Oracle hovered over my left shoulder, liberally covered in the goblin's black blood, and Bane appeared on my right, facing the group.

"Who *are* you?" asked one of the elves amongst them, barely speaking above a whisper.

CHAPTER FOURTEEN

"He's your lord,…Lord Jax," Flux said, confusion clear in his voice. "We swore to Barabarattas," The elf said slowly, "He'd never come for us; nobody would."

"*He* did," said Bane simply, nodding towards me.

"I thought they were your men?" Flux asked me, looking over.

"No. I want to recruit them, though," I replied, catching the looks of awe on their faces.

"You went through all this to recruit people you don't even know?" Flux asked wonderingly after a few seconds of silence.

I shook my head. "My friend Oren vouched for them; that's enough for me. Besides…I told you I'd not leave a child here to the goblins."

"You want to…recruit us? You came here, killed the goblins and…you just want to recruit us?" the elf asked incredulously before a dwarf moved around to stand by his side.

"Ye knew Oren? Prove it," he said, eyes locked on mine.

"I *know* Oren," I corrected. "You Decin? He said the story about the lich is bullshit."

Decin swore, shaking his head and looked around at the other prisoners. The elf beside him started to laugh, going from a snigger to full-blown shaking as Decin drew in a sharp breath.

"None o' you fuckers believe him. It were a lich!" With an indignant glare at the lot of them, he turned back to me as the group seemed to relax. "Ye say yer *know* Oren…when'd ye see him last?" he asked hopefully.

"About four hours ago. He's sworn to me and is flying a warship now. He's my right hand, in charge of all the ships I command…You want to see how high you can rise?" I asked.

"Depends…how many ships yer got?" he said, a grin flashing across his face.

"I've got two, a warship and a nice little abandoned one by the lake outside; my engineers got her fixed up," I said, hoping I wasn't lying through my teeth.

"Ye stole ma ship an' expect me to swear loyalty?" The dwarf growled.

Flux cut him off. "He came here with a team of six to face hundreds of goblins to save your life, dwarf. What did your old lord offer?"

There was a long silence as the prisoners looked at each other. The elf who'd been laughing clipped Decin across the back of the head, hard.

"You've always been a bloody fool, D," he said affectionately, shaking his head. Then he looked at me. "We come as a package, Decin and I. Is this a problem?"

I noted the way his hand quested down, and Decin's lifted to grip it without a thought, the automatic response of a long-term couple seeking reassurance from beloved partners. I couldn't help it. I grinned at them, glad to see that someone else in this shithole of a place had a partner they were drawing strength from.

"I'm happy to have you both. How about your crew?" I asked, looking at the rest and receiving firm nods in return. "Glad to hear it! Now, how about someone finds me a healing potion before I bleed to death? We can cover all the Oaths and shit once we're out of here and have a beer in hand."

I turned and staggered a little as I walked toward the corpse of the matriarch. My health wasn't too bad, sitting at a third of its maximum. My stamina was at a quarter, but my mana was in the single digits still. Oracle flew over to me, sitting down on her usual perch of my shoulder and gave a little shiver that caused all the blood covering her to fall straight through her...onto me.

"What the...thanks, Oracle," I muttered.

"Sorry, Jax! I didn't think," she whispered, cheeks turning red as she realized what she'd just done.

I smiled gently up at her. "Ah, don't worry about it. Thanks for coming for me." I'd felt her drop everything and speed straight to me when I'd lost my temper.

"Anytime," she whispered back, leaning down to kiss my cheek before taking off, flying to inspect the bag the matriarch had been rooting in.

Bane was there almost as quickly as Oracle, and he dug in, pulling a few variously colored potions out, dropping them aside and moving on as Oracle directed. It took hardly any time before he pulled out a deep crimson one and jumped to his feet.

He was at my side quickly, popping the cork out and raising it to my lips carefully so that I could take a drink. It felt a bit weird having someone else literally giving me a drink, but considering the heavy cut on my right arm and the broken wrist on my left, it was the best and quickest solution.

"Thank you, Bane," I said after I'd finished it, and Oracle called him back to the bag, indicating a mana potion she'd spotted.

"This one next, Bane. It's a weak one, but it'll be enough to start with." I felt the healing potion spreading out and starting to work, my arms tingling at first, before the bones in my left started shifting, and I hissed in pain.

The potion must have been a greater healing potion or something similar, because it had me feeling great in under a minute, bones fixed, blood regenerated, and wounds almost all closed.

Bane had held the second potion for me again, while my arms were healing. I soon confirmed it was a weak one, unfortunately, as it only restored twenty mana and barely boosted my regeneration in that area at all.

It was enough, though.

I quickly assessed the people that were standing around. Mainly, the things they needed were a hot meal, a bath, and a metric fuck ton of booze. They all had minor wounds, and one guy had nearly shredded the skin on his arms trying to get free to help in the fight. I resolved to watch him, as anyone that determined was either going to be an asset or a nightmare.

"Does anyone have an urgent need for healing?" I asked, and received a chorus of head shakes, noting the concerned looks Bane, Flux, and Cheena were giving the little Mer they'd freed.

"Flux, in a few minutes, I'll be able to use that water spell and channel it long enough to be useful. For now, though, there's still that last group of goblins."

"Where are the green-skinned little bastards?" one of Decin's men growled, reaching down and pulling a shortsword free from a goblin corpse. The rest of the crew immediately armed themselves and clamored to join in the fight.

"There were only a handful, hiding in a room they'd barricaded at the end of the corridor," Cheena said, and in seconds, the room was mostly empty. Almost the entire crew had gone running and limping, determined to cleanse the area of the goblin infestation. The only people left in the room now were Decin's partner, who was called Hanau, the four Mer, Oracle, myself, and an older elven woman who'd started examining the dust-covered figures embedded in the wall, while totally ignoring me.

I looked between her and Hanau with a raised eyebrow, and Hanau laughed briefly.

"You'll soon find that, while I love the battle of wits in trade, I have no interest in physical violence, Lord Jax. Riana there loves to learn. She's our chief engineer, mainly because she's always digging into something she shouldn't, or she'd still have a job in the city—"

"That ship'd be lucky to get anywhere by winter, if not for my fixes, Hanau; don't think I didn't hear you," Riana replied, shooting Hanau a glare that could have frozen a lake solid in summer.

"Why did you ask if there was a problem with you and Decin coming as a package?" I asked Hanau quickly, trying not to smile at the two friends giving each other grief to relax.

"Well, Lord Barabarattas issued a declaration that cross-race relationships were an abomination, and I wanted to see where you stood on it."

"I don't give a shit who you're boinking," I said honestly. "All I care about is if you're loyal and trustworthy. Where you're sticking whatever is up to you."

"It's true...Jax doesn't care about that kind of thing; besides, he likes me!" Oracle said, bouncing up and down on my shoulder and damn near giving me a concussion with her impressive chest.

"I wonder why," Hanau said with an open smile.

"Oh, it's because I went through his brain, I found out what he likes, and—"

"I think Hanau was being sarcastic, Oracle," I said, cutting her off and getting a laugh from the tall elf.

"It is! It's a relic!" came a shout from the corner.

Riana had climbed atop a pile of rubble to examine one the dust-covered figures more closely. Our conversation effectively derailed, we gathered around Riana as she finished wiping a section clean of dust and the funk of centuries.

Revealed under her hand was a diamond set into an ornate pattern in the middle of the figure's chest.

I blinked, recognizing a sight I'd not expected to see here, and Oracle took off with a flutter of wings. She landed on the figure's chest and grabbed onto the diamond, her hand sinking into the stone effortlessly. When she pulled it back, my mana dipped by ten points.

"They're intact!" she cried, meeting my gaze with a huge smile on her face. I looked from her to the stone, remembering similar designs I'd seen strewn about the tower. I frowned, then blinked, my eyes going wide as I studied the row of figures.

There were ten of them; three stood with enormous crossbows braced across their chests, five had huge shields resting on the ground against their left sides and hammers brandished in their right. One had a sword and shield similar to the others, but its carvings were markedly more ornate, and the final one was different in almost every way.

Where the other nine were bulky humanoids covered in armor and carrying weapons, the tenth was slimmer, with four arms spaced equidistant around the torso and three legs making it look like a tripod. The head was weird as well, making me think of an Indian deity I'd seen depicted; it had three faces, each looking in a different direction, so that it covered the full three hundred and sixty degrees of vision.

They were golems, nine war class and one servitor. They weren't as ornate as the broken ones I'd seen in bits around the tower, not most of them, anyway. But these were intact, and judging from the dip in mana when Oracle touched the first, they were able to absorb mana from a direct source.

"They can be fixed?" I asked, and Oracle shook her head, still staring at the line of treasure.

"They don't need to be fixed, Jax. They're intact, they're just sleeping. All they need is mana to reawaken them…maybe the collectors are also intact! They must have shut down when the tower did. Seneschal probably shut down *all* the collectors, not just the Tower's…do you know what this means?"

I shook my head, and Oracle went on.

"It means there are more out there! This was the fourth waystation, one of the closest to the tower and used as a rest point and place for people to stay when they visited the lake…which means there are four other stations like this out there, and their golems might be intact as well. We *need* to find them!"

My head was suddenly filled with visions of golems. We wouldn't need that great an army if we had dozens of these, surely? But the next second, Oracle ruined the wonderful dream.

"They have huge mana requirements when they're in battle, but if we can get the local collectors working, that would charge them up, then we could send them to the tower. They could refill their cores completely and help so much! And I think this one is a complex or level three servitor; it'd have to be able to operate independently to be here, so it must be!"

"You're sure it's not a level four?" I asked quickly, my hopes of upgrading the genesis chamber leaping to the front of my mind.

"No, I don't think so. It doesn't feel the same. Until it's awake, though, only Heph would know for sure."

"Dammit…okay, how do we reawaken them?" I asked, trying to dismiss the flaring disappointment. There was no use complaining; these were an amazing find!

"We need mana, basically. To reawaken a fully dormant golem takes about a thousand mana for the most basic. It doubles with each level, so the 'king' or level seven would take about sixty-four thousand mana."

"Feck," I muttered, "How do we go about reactivating the mana collectors?"

Oracle started scanning the room in confusion.

"If they are here…the control room must be here too, or nearby. I know they were built to a template, but I never saw it. Sorry, Jax. All I know is that they wouldn't be far from the control room in case they were needed."

"You know what these are?" interrupted Riana suddenly. We'd forgotten all about her, and she'd been practically bouncing on the balls of her feet listening to us. "You know about the relics?"

"They're golems," I said absently, gesturing to them. "We've a load of damaged ones back at the tower, and we've built some of the lowest or basic-class constructors and servitors. What do you know about them?"

"You've got more? And you can build them?!" she gasped, flying across the room in just a few steps to grab my arms and stare into my eyes intently. "I need to see them. I'll swear anything I have to; just let me work with them!"

"You're an engineer, right?" I asked her, getting a fervent nod. "And an archeologist, I guess. You'll need to speak to Heph and Seneschal, but I've no issue with it."

"Who are they, and what's an archeologist?" she asked firmly. "You *will* tell me everything you know about this."

"Riana!" snapped Hanau, stepping in close and grabbing her arm to tug her free before turning back to me. "I apologize, Lord Jax…. Riana is an asset to the crew, as skilled as she is with both ancient magics and modern technology. She sometimes forgets herself, however."

Riana's face blanched when she realized what she'd done, and she started stammering an apology.

I held up a hand to stop them both. "Honestly, it's all right. I like that enthusiasm; I can certainly use it! I'll make this same offer to the rest of your crew later, it's the one I make to all my new people. Join me, swear loyalty to me, and I'll support you.

"That includes, for a select few, gaining access to our Hall of Memories. We have skill memories from before the cataclysm, several hundred of them, and depending on the abilities, desires, and loyalty of people, they may be given one or more of these." I paused. Instead of listening with the rapt attention I expected, Riana was focused on the golems still, stroking the gem in the center of one's chest as she listened to me with half an ear.

"To answer your next questions, yes, I'm Lord Jax, the one that's at war with Barabarattas, and yes, I claimed and cleared the Great Tower, making me the ruler of these lands. Riana was vaguely nodding and Hanau was cradling his head in his hands, so I went on. "We tend to do ritual sacrifices in the morning and group sex in the afternoons. That work for you?"

"Uh-huh…" She mumbled absently, before Hanau burst out laughing. "What?!" Riana asked, jerking around.

I sighed, going back to the beginning. Hanau helped to keep Riana on track, and I went over the basic structure of the tower and people.

"…lastly is Oracle, mistress of the Hall of Memories. She's in charge of the skillbooks, spellbooks, and all the memory stones and so on we have. She's also my companion," I said, gesturing to Oracle where she perched on the golem's chest still. She grinned at them and lifted off, starting to search the rest of the room.

"You...I mean,...actual memories,...and...and..." Riana sputtered, trying to decide what to ask first.

"Well, I never thought I'd see the day!" Hanau said, clapping her on the back. "Riana actually speechless and not through apoplexy!" He laughed and gestured to the room. "What should we be looking for, Lord Jax?"

Before I could answer, there was a crash from the corridor and a series of screams followed by the sound of battle. I swore and turned, sprinting for the fight. Realizing at the last second that my naginata was still buried in the matriarch's chest and altering my direction to grab it, I yanked it free with a *shlurp* as the lungs released the last of their hold on the weapon.

I kicked off the opposite wall again, maintaining my speed as I turned the corner then slowed to a walk. The barrier at the end of the corridor that had been up earlier was down, and Decin and his crew were cheering at the sight of the last few goblins that had been hiding inside. They were dead; hell, they were very dead, from what I could see, and the room itself was open to see now.

I spotted what looked like a furnace and forge combination and a dozen other bits of equipment I had no names for. Riana was behind me, and I turned to her as we stopped near the door, Hanau cheering his partner happily.

"What can you see in here? That's usable, I mean?" She pushed a few people out of the way and started hunting around. The loot stripped from the ship appeared to have been haphazardly dumped across the floor, making it difficult to pick anything out.

"See what you can find, then come find me in the last room," I ordered Decin, turning to walk away. Oracle hovered nearby, and I quickly spoke to her.

"Was everyone okay? I should have asked before," I said, getting a brilliant smile from Oracle that set my mind at ease and my heart racing.

"They're fine. Well, they're all still wounded; I healed them as much as I could without using all our mana, but..."

"Well, it looks like the goblins are all dead now. We need to scout this place out, make sure it's safe, then go get Oren and the ships to come up here, even if they have to use the cannons to clear a space to land," I said, grimacing as I thought about blind firing the cannons to make space.

"We can search the ruins quickly, lord," came a voice from my left. I spun around to see Cheena standing in the shadows.

"Fuck's sake, I nearly crapped myself, Cheena! I swear I'm gonna make you guys wear bells or something!" I snapped, my heart racing. I took a deep breath and shook my head before speaking again. "I'm sorry, I shouldn't snap at you. Yes, if you could scout the area that would be fantastic. Oracle, can you bring everyone up here? I'd feel a lot better if we were all together right now, and if we can restart the mana collectors, it'll take a while to reactivate the golems, or reawaken, I suppose I should say."

"Bane will stay with you, and T'lek, Flux, and I will scout the rest of the ruins. Not a single creature that isn't loyal to you will survive, lord," Cheena said.

She seemed to vanish into the shadows, and I had a sense of a second movement nearby. I spun, barely spotting a blur as Flux disappeared with her into the next room.

I looked around and found Bane standing nearby, his friend T'lek half hidden behind him.

"Ah, are you okay?" I asked them both, unsure of who I was asking myself. Bane had myriad small cuts covering him and was covered in black blood, but he looked far better than little T'lek, who kept Bane between us.

"I am, lord. Thank you. If you had not done as you did, we would not have survived. My friend would be dead," Bane said, starting to lower himself to one knee again before I snapped at him.

"For...stop! Seriously, Bane, we already covered this. There's no need, especially not when we've fought side-by-side! Just talk to me, man, and call me Jax!"

Bane straightened up but paused before he replied.

"I know what you said before, Jax, but for what you did, Flux was right when he spoke earlier...what lord of the land would do as you have done? I have heard the tales of the cities, the warnings of how we must always be on our guard against them. They and their people will always seek to take what is ours. We can recognize them by the way they will give nothing but words and take all that isn't nailed down—"

"And take the nails, too," T'lek muttered.

"Ha, yes! We were warned of this, and it's not just old tales. It's confirmed by those like Flux who lived amongst the city-dwellers. He was beaten and captured, lost friends and family to the city dwellers, looked for missing friends, only to find their remains for sale in the shops of apothecaries he trusted.

"We are taught from an early age that, while not all are bad, that the other races are not necessarily born evil, we must nevertheless be on our guard constantly."

"Sounds like you've had a shit experience with them," I said.

"Yes; one that has been repeatedly reinforced. Then we meet you. You ask for nothing and give us back our weapons, forgiving our attack. You heal those who harmed you, and you fight at our side." He shook his head, tendrils rising and then falling in rhythmic patterns. "You confuse us, but we trust you, not because of your words, but your actions."

"Good job, really, since my words are usually wrong," I muttered self-consciously, then realized he'd heard that and had to explain. "Where I come from, actions matter more than words as well, Bane. I'm not good with words; I always say the wrong thing at the wrong time. I've had a lot of experience of people who stab you in the back," I said, thinking back to my ex and the last time I saw her, naked with her "friend" Martin. A quick blur of faces and memories scrolled through my mind. She was far from the worst, just the latest in a long list of reasons to distrust people.

"Look, I helped you because it was the right thing to do. I'm not going to let a child get hurt, not if I can help it, and I wanted to recruit Decin and his crew, so I was getting something out of it."

"You risked your life to save those who might have refused you, Jax, because you wished to give them a home? It is not a gain to only you," Bane said, entirely dismissing my point. He strode alongside me, half-carrying the smaller T'lek. I looked over at him and checked my mana. I'd wanted to do this before but had decided to wait until my mana had recovered enough to help all of the Mer. Now that Flux and Cheena were off scouting, though...

I waited until we were back in the main room, then spoke to them both again.

"I'm going to summon some water for you. It'll only last about fifteen seconds before I need to let it go, so make the most of it, okay? You both ready?" I asked, getting quick nods from them both and I cast Summon Water beside Bane and T'lek. The purified cool water bubbled up from the stone floor to form a spring five feet high like a small fountain. There was a moment of shock from T'lek before Bane pushed him forward into it.

The smaller Mer stood reveling in the water, breathing it in and seeming to absorb it as fast as drink it, his gills fluttering like crazy. Eventually, Bane gently shifted him and leaned into the water in his place, catching the last few seconds I was able to extend it by. When the spell died, and the water fell to the previously dusty floor, T'lek slumped despondently.

"Don't worry," I said reassuringly. "I'll summon another as soon as we get people healed and the control room activated. We just need to find it!"

With that, a much livelier Bane began striding around the room, poking and prodding at the seemingly arranged piles of debris. Hanau and Riana joined me, and the four of us started searching the room, T'lek jumping to help when Bane snapped at him.

We soon realized the piles of debris were actually loot, or at least what goblins considered to be loot. Some were totally worthless, shiny pebbles and weird-shaped wood, small piles of what looked like birds' wings, and in pride of place on one heap was a pile of broken glass. There was also, thankfully, some actual loot: a pile of copper and silver coins, the gold ones from a bag near the matriarch, a set of cooking pans, and some shells that shone strangely, but that Bane insisted were valuable.

There were also a handful of gemstones, three flasks that bubbled even when kept totally still, which reminded me of lava lamps, and a pair of manastones. Both were inert, completely drained of mana, but they were intact, placed atop a pile of stones that were shattered into pieces. I guessed either they could be recharged or put to some use.

When we were nearly finished searching the room, Riana finally called out from where she'd been examining the far wall.

"Is this something?" she asked, and we all dropped everything to crowd around and look at it. The wall itself looked the same as the others, composed of simple carved stone blocks that stood one atop the other in an offset pattern. Typical brickwork, I thought…then a sense of wrongness tugged at me.

I examined it closer, trying to figure out what it was, Oracle joining me. We searched it for a few seconds before feeling a throbbing that made me shake my head. It felt like we were coming in for a landing too fast on a plane; the rapid pressure change lasted only a few seconds before stopping, and I looked at Bane questioningly.

He stared at T'lek, who had all his tendrils extended out like a lion's mane. The pair of them spoke quickly.

"There, it's—"

"Solid, it's not—"

"It's a door!" T'lek finished as they cut each other off in their excitement.

"Where?" I asked, and both of them pointed at the wall where we'd been looking.

At first, I couldn't see it, just observing an unbroken wall, but after a few seconds, my meridian enhancement finally activated, and a faint blue glow outlined a symbol carved into the wall.

There were dozens of them. Carvings dotted the room, all coated in hundreds of years of dust and, more recently, soot from the goblin's fires gradually leaking smoke through small cracks in the ceiling.

What made this symbol different was the glow; as near as I could see, it was identical to two others carved into the other walls. As I studied them, the glow started to build on them as well, but…it was red.

My instincts mixed with my trap knowledge to inform me that using the wrong symbol would be a fatal mistake. I was fairly confident in the blue glowing symbol, but I still ordered everyone else from the room while I examined it, just as Oracle arrived, calling out that the others were on their way.

Riana muttered complaints at having to leave the room, but Hanau clipped her across the ear. She quieted down, casting irritated glances at her friend as she rubbed the side of her head. I reached out, took a deep breath, and brushed as much crap off the symbol as I could, revealing a starburst pattern with a stylized tower in the middle. I pressed the tower gently, then applied more pressure until there was an audible click followed by a much louder clunk, and a cloud of dust was expelled from the wall.

I jumped back, covering my mouth with one hand and trying not to breathe the dirty air in. It didn't take long for the dust to settle, thankfully. When it did, there was a clear, rectangular outline visible in the wall. Riana stepped forward and put to words what we'd all seen without realizing it.

"The door was hidden, but whoever made it never considered hundreds of years of dust! They'd filled in the lines to look like it would have when it was new, which meant the dust couldn't fill them! I knew there was something wrong with it!"

"Well spotted, Riana," I said, then coughed as a little dust got into my mouth. "Everyone, keep back, please. Oracle, can you get in there? Take a look around?"

She flew over, going partially insubstantial as she passed through the crack. A whoop of joy resounded on the other side.

"It's here; it's the control room!" she cried out, and we moved forward again, waving the dust out of the way until it was clear.

By this time, Decin and the others had joined us and were happily digging fingers into the revealed cracks along the door. Hanau called out as we were all getting ready.

"Okay, people! On three, you pull, move back one step, and release!" he called, and the crew, obviously used to following his orders, responded in unison.

"Hup!"

"One, two, aaaaand…THREE!"

We all strained together, pulling at the seams with our fingers driven into tiny cracks. Just as we were about to give in, there was a creak, a pop, and a loud crack, followed by the door grating slowly open a foot. We dropped it then, all of us panting and trying to get our breath back, when a sudden scream made us all stagger back to our feet.

One of the crew had been facing the entrance to the room and was pointing frantically. People began panicking and readying weapons, and…I started to laugh.

"Stand down, people; the cavalry is here!" I said, gesturing to people to lower their weapons. "How are you doing, Bob? Everyone okay?" I asked as the hulking skeletal minion stomped into the room, the rest of the squad trailing behind him. Several were limping, but Oracle had healed the majority of their major wounds already. I turned to the crew and T'lek, who all remained concerned, and spoke up again.

"Seriously, he's my minion. Relax, people." I walked over to Bob and clapped him on a huge, armored shoulder as I looked past him at the rest of my squad. They really did look battered; they were dirty, had streaks of blood covering their clothes, and were clearly worn out, but they also looked triumphant. I turned back to Decin's crew and T'lek and waved to the newly arrived group.

"Are you all okay?" I asked them, being met with nods and smiles before I turned back to the room. "These are my people; they came with me and stood shoulder-to-shoulder to kill the goblins and rescue you. You only saw the fight in here, but how many goblins do you remember seeing here?" I asked, getting grim looks from the crew. "Well, this small squad—these fucking *heroes*—stood strong out there, and we killed them. As near as we can tell, we've killed *all* the goblins now, literally hundreds if not thousands of the little bastards. They did that, so they damn well deserve your respect," I said, a proud smile covering my face as I looked at them. Lydia stepped forward and spoke up, tired but firm.

"And you were there with us, Lord Jax. We fought for you."

"Yeah, but I'm fucking fantastic," I stated casually, giving a quick wink and a shrug. "I'd have not been able to do any of it without you, or without Bane, Cheena, and Flux."

"Think a lot o' yersel' don't ye...lord," Decin said, a grin on his face. He ducked reflexively as Hanau's hand flew past overhead. "Ha! Ye missed!" He grinned at his partner, who gave him a black look before muttering something that made him grin wider and unrepentantly back at him. "Bah, it be worth it!"

"You won't think so later!" growled Hanau before turning back to me. "I'm sorry, Lord Jax, he's always been trouble."

I just grinned and shook my head. Bob stomped over to the jammed doorway and glowered inside, checking for any threat.

"Bob, open the door, please," I said, gesturing to the crew to all back away. Bob braced himself against the wall and heaved, the sound of several bones cracking under the strain clearly audible.

Bob's health—or structural integrity, or whatever—meter dropped a noticeable amount, bringing him to twenty percent overall, but in a few seconds, the door was open far enough to easily get inside. "That's enough!" I called out, and Bob released it, stepping back with a hiss as several sections of bone fell away from him. I patted him on one armored shoulder.

"Thanks, buddy. Don't worry, I'll get you fixed up again soon." I stepped past him through the opening, Oracle flying into the room with me.

The room was small with a single, large seat placed in the middle of it. Dead magelights hung on the walls. I sat in the seat facing a small table and the entrance to the room.

"Be warned, people, this could take a while," I said.

As soon as I sat down, I felt a resonance from the seat and table, and I recognized the sensation of my mana being pulled from me. I remembered the discussions I'd had with Oracle and others, including Xiao, and I closed my eyes, concentrating on my breathing as I began to meditate.

I sat there for what seemed like forever, yet simultaneously like mere seconds. At one point, Oracle was speaking to the hushed group, telling them I was meditating and reactivating the ruin. Even with my mana regenerating slightly more rapidly through meditation, it was sucked away faster than I could regenerate it.

It took a thousand mana to reactivate the interface, Oracle helping me to sense what was needed. But even with the meditation, it took just over four hours to complete it. I finally blinked my eyes open, my constant state of headache beginning to dissipate as I looked around, finding the table humming with energy and Oracle grinning at me. My notifications activated on their own, a single popup blazing to life before my eyes, golden letters flowing from nowhere to fill my vision.

Congratulations!

You have cleared Waystation Four and have the prerequisite authority and abilities to claim this structure and the surrounding land, adding it to your territory as a claimed location. As this territory holds less than 10% of sentients that are actively hostile to your rule, it can be claimed.

Do you wish to annex this territory now?

Yes/No

"Flux, you there, buddy?" I called out, hearing a few sounds, and he stepped into my peripheral vision.

"I am here. What is it?" he asked calmly.

"I've been offered the choice of annexing this territory to my already-controlled lands. It's telling me that there are less than ten percent of actively hostile sentients in its area. How will your people react if I claim this?" I asked, concerned, as I didn't want to piss off my new neighbors.

"Bah, they will be fine with it. I sent Cheena, Bane, and T'lek back to them several hours ago with Gaul's remains. Your ships now hover above us, so I know that Bane passed the message onto them as well. My people will regard you as a valued and powerful friend at the very least. Your claiming of this territory matters not to us; we already knew you were the rightful liege of the land from the earlier notifications. Go ahead and claim as you will."

"Thanks, mate. Okay…here goes!" I said and mentally selected *yes*. There was a slight pause before a new notification sprang to life, swiftly followed by a second.

Congratulations!

You have annexed new lands into your own, providing the following benefits if the land is worked:

Fishing Rights: You own a large body of water that is teeming with life. +5 to food production in all this territory.

Mining Abundance: This territory has two ancient abandoned mines within its borders. Gain +10 copper ingots and +13 iron ingots per day once these mines are cleared out and mining is at full capacity.

Supportive Population: You have gained the trust of some of the residents of this territory, and the others believe you to be benevolent. +2 per day to loyalty of the population, provided you take no hostile action against them. This bonus may change due to events.

Attention: Citizens of the Territory of Dravith!

High Lord Jax of Dravith has expanded his territory and has claimed an additional three hundred and twelve square miles of lands by defeating the previously hostile occupants!

All Titles, Deeds, and Laws in the Territory of Dravith are held for review, and can be revoked, altered, annulled, or approved.

All Hail High Lord Jax of Dravith!

I took a deep breath. By the golden edges on the second prompt, along with the gleaming red letters and the fact it required reading all the way to the end before I could dismiss it, this was a territory-wide announcement.

I dismissed the prompts, resolving to discuss the bonuses with Oracle and the team later. By the looks on everyone else's faces, that thousand-mile stare, they were looking at something only they could see. Yup, they'd all got that again. Last time it had happened, I had a momentary mental image of someone having sex...then that jumped up in the middle of their vision.... I knew I wouldn't be happy, but it amused the hell out of me as the one who caused it. I turned to Oracle, and she looked at me expectantly.

"Okay, so the waystation is awake. How do we find out if the mana collectors are intact?" I asked, and she grinned at me.

"Concentrate and ask for the status of the waystation, of course!" she replied.

I frowned. "I never had to do that with the tower."

"Of course not. You have Seneschal for that. Without a wisp, all you have is the interface. This one is a more basic one than the creation table in the tower, but it's also in better condition, so..." She shrugged and gestured to the table before me, and I got the hint, concentrating and visualizing what I wanted the table to show me.

Since activating the ruin, the one thousand mana that I'd donated to it had filled the shallow well that sat in the center of the table first, then had spread out to bring life to the structure as best it could. The liquid mana that remained in the well had taken on the consistency of quicksilver, and as I concentrated on the waystation, it began to shift and eddy.

The waves quickly came together, forming lines that first grew into a small box that related to this control room, complete with a miniature table and chair. Then it rippled out, the room shrinking as other rooms grew, a top-down map building up. Collapsed sections of the corridors and rooms lay beyond them.

The rooms we'd explored already showed a corresponding outline of equipment and debris, while the remaining unexplored rooms showed a wireframe diagram instead. It took less than a minute to build that floor out. The next higher floor, including the stairway to reach it, was filled with rubble almost entirely. There was also a lower floor that shifted and shook strangely until Oracle made the connection.

"It's full of water!" she exclaimed, and those who could see the map murmured as it became obvious to us all.

At the edges of the map, I found five damaged pillars. Three were shattered beyond all use, pulsing then melting away when I looked at them. But the remaining two shook and started to move when I concentrated on activating the mana collectors. One of the two shuddered after a few seconds and vanished from the map, showing as debris suddenly. But the final collector continued to grow.

A full five minutes passed as the collector slowly shifted into position, and ominous creaks echoed around the underground structure. But eventually, the lights in the room gave a sudden pulse before strengthening to full daylight.

As we looked around, the walls began to shudder faintly, dust, dirt, and debris cascading from them as the structure began to repair itself. In the distance, I heard a crash as falling stone announced that not all the repairs would be smooth, but after a short wait, nothing else seemed to happen.

I concentrated again, and a new screen appeared before me.

Greetings, Lord of Dravith and Master of the Great Tower.

This interface is limited by damage and capacity.

Please select from the following options:

System Repair:
Current condition: 27%
0-100% of mana allocated

Structural Integrity:
Current condition: 42%
0-100% of mana allocated

Golem Recharging and Maintenance:
Current charge: 0.01%
0-100% of mana allocated

I read over the options and allocated ten percent to System Repair, twenty percent to Structural Integrity, and seventy percent to charging the golems, receiving a final popup. There were more notifications waiting, and I resolved myself to working through them as quickly as possible.

Allocation of mana resources confirmed.

Estimated time to completion:

System Repair: 142.6 days

Structural Integrity: 383.7 days

Golem Recharging and Maintenance: 1.25 days

I blinked at the timescales and resolved that I would get the golems up and running, then redirect the mana to repair the mana collectors. Once they were fixed, it shouldn't take long to fix the rest…I hoped. To be fair, I was only really interested in the golems at the moment. The bonuses for claiming this structure and the surrounding land were just an added extra. I focused and managed to redirect the charge going to the golems to prioritize the servitor, getting a notification that it would take six hours for that one alone. I figured it'd be the most useful to us in the short term.

"Oracle, can I use the mana collectors here to refill my own mana? Or use it to heal everyone directly?" I asked suddenly, a thought coming to mind. But Oracle was shaking her head before I'd finished speaking it aloud.

"No, Jax, not without a resident Wisp to direct the other end. Even if I were to bind to here, you'd still need someone on your end to stop you from drawing too much. I'm sorry."

"Ah, well, worth a try." I sighed. I slowly stood up, my back cracking as I realized I'd been seated in an uncomfortable chair for hours without moving. As the blood rushed back into areas starved of it, I bit my cheek to keep from groaning and concentrated on staying upright until the feeling passed.

While I fought through the pins and needles, I brought up the notifications, reading through them and dismissing them as quickly as I read what they contained.

Congratulations!

You have killed the following:

- 267x Basic Goblins of various levels for a total of 4,320xp
- 13x Goblin Fighters of various levels for a total of 390xp
- 7x Evolved Goblins of various levels for a total of 250xp
- 4x Spiders of various levels for a total of 60xp

A party under your command killed the following:

- 611x Basic Goblin of various levels for a total of 36,750xp
- 27x Goblin Fighters of various levels for a total of 3,100xp
- 1x Goblin Matriarch for a total of 1,500xp
- 13x Evolved Goblins of various levels for a total of 5,150xp
- 6x Spiders of various levels for 1,100xp

Total experience earned: 47,600xp

As party leader, you gain 10% of all experience earned

Progress to level 14 stands at 117,620/120,000

That goddamn experience drain! Jenae had warned me about it, saying it was partially because I'd broken myself by using too many spellbooks at once, and partially because of who and what I was. I *needed* a goddamn healer! A real one!

It looked like I was getting literally ten percent of the experience that I would be otherwise. For my part in that fight, I'd have earned…I stopped myself before I could work it out. I settled on the fact I'd earned far less than I should have, my anger and frustration begging to boil over again.

I dismissed it and went onto the next notification in the backlog.

Congratulations!

You have raised your spell Weak Lightning Bolt to its first evolution. You must now pick a path to follow.

Will you choose the path of the STORM, or concentrate on the INDIVIDUAL?

Choose carefully, as this choice cannot be undone.

STORM:

The storm does not discriminate, but you can. Following this path will fundamentally change your Lightning Bolt spell into an AOE or Area of Effect spell, rather than a single target. You must now designate an area to create fear of your attention. As you grow more experienced with the spell, you will learn to make changes, increasing or decreasing the area covered and the duration. Beware distractions, as the Storm will only spare those you force it to, and will kill any it can.

INDIVIDUAL:

Individuality is what separates all things from one another. You know this, and you can choose to follow this path, adding secondary effects to your Lightning Bolt spell at the cost of removing its ability to spread.

Choose one of the following three options:

Cleansing Light: Clears away status effects on the target. While this can be used on friend or foe alike, don't expect to keep any friends you target with a spell this painful.

Stun: Grants a 10% chance to stun the target for between 3-10 seconds, depending on resistances and abilities.

Spreading Wildfire: Adds a 10% chance that this spell will cause combustible materials to ignite, creating secondary and tertiary damage.

I read the options over for a few seconds, then frowned. I didn't really use this spell that much, but to Oracle, it was a favorite…

"What do you think?" I asked Oracle. She frowned prettily, reading over the options as I went on. "It's basically your go-to spell, so you choose," I said, and she twisted to look at me, a brilliant smile on her face.

"Are you sure, Jax? I mean, this is—" she started, and I cut her off.

"I'm sure, Oracle. I use Lightning Bolt occasionally, but you love it. You can pick; I trust you."

Oracle gave me another brilliant smile, going silent for a few seconds in thought. Eventually, she reached out and touched the box where it floated in my vision. She somehow made it shimmer, the option she'd chosen pulsing brightly for a second before fading back to normal.

"I choose Stun, then. I like the others, especially the Storm option, but being able to add a stunning effect to our normal Lightning Bolt would be hugely helpful. To get that otherwise, we need to add water to it, and the chance of it activating Stun is still low, even then."

"I'll be honest, the fact it doesn't spread concerns me a bit. I like using it with the water."

She smiled, patting the top of my head reassuringly. "Don't be silly! This is an evolution of a spell; it's not changing physics! If we use water, it will still spread. It just won't do it on its own anymore! The original spell had a five percent chance to spread, and now it won't; that's all it means!"

"Besides, if you really want a Lightning Storm spell, we can make one. It'll be really heavy on the mana and have a weak effect for a while, but we know enough to make a rough one, and it would get evolutions at level ten as well."

I blinked as I processed that. It was pretty obvious; after all, I'd made enough changes to spells already. I still had the knowledge in my mind, it was just that the Weak Lightning Bolt I'd been using for ages had become familiar enough to me that I could choose an evolution of it. I could literally cobble together another one and start using that, if I wanted, getting that to its evolution at ten and choosing a different option then.

"Good point!" I said, selecting the Stun option.

You have chosen Stun for your first evolution of this spell.

Your Weak Lightning Bolt has evolved to Stunning Lightning Bolt, and now has an additional 10% chance to stun your target for 3-10 seconds, depending on mana channeled and your target's resistance to Air magic.

I smiled at Oracle's obvious pleasure at choosing and dismissed the last few notifications, finding that they were welcome increases.

Congratulations!

Through hard work and perseverance, you have increased your stats by the following:

**Agility +1
Constitution +2
Dexterity +1
Endurance +2
Intelligence +2
Strength +1
Wisdom +2**

Continue to train and learn to increase this further.

The Forgotten Faithful

I grinned to myself as I read the changes I'd achieved, feeling them consciously for the first time, and I couldn't help but pull up my stat sheet to compare how I looked overall.

Name: Jax

Titles: Strategos: 5% boost to damage resistance, Fortifier: 5% boost to defensive structure integrity, Chosen of Jenae

Class: Spellsword > Justicar	**Renown:** Unknown
Level: 13	**Progress:** 117,620/120,000
Patron: Jenae, Goddess of Fire and Exploration	**Points to Distribute:** 0 **Meridian Points to Invest:** 0

Stat	Current points	Description	Effect	Progress to next level
Agility	40	Governs dodge and movement.	+300% maximum movement speed and reflexes, (+10% movement in darkness, -20% movement in daylight)	7/100
Charisma	11	Governs likely success to charm, seduce, or threaten	+10% success in interactions with other beings	89/100
Constitution	32	Governs health and health regeneration	620 health, regen 36.3 points per 600 seconds, (+10% regen due to soul bond, -20 health due to soul bond, each point invested now worth 20 health)	3/100
Dexterity	21	Governs ability with weapons and crafting success	+110% to weapon proficiency, +11% to the chances of crafting success	30/100
Endurance	21	Governs stamina and stamina regeneration	210 stamina, regen 11 points per 30 seconds	66/100
Intelligence	29	Governs base mana and number of spells able to be learned	270 mana, spell capacity: 17 (15 + 2 from items), (-20 mana due to soul bond)	43/100
Luck	17	Governs overall chance of bonuses	+7% chance of a favorable outcome	96/100
Perception	23	Governs ranged damage and chance to spot traps or hidden items	+130% ranged damage, +13% chance to spot traps or hidden items	85/100
Strength	22	Governs damage with melee weapons and carrying capacity	+12 damage with melee weapons, +120% maximum carrying capacity	73/100
Wisdom	28 (23)	Governs mana regeneration and memory	+180% mana recovery, 2.8 points per minute, 180% more likely to remember things	81/100

Yeah, I'd take that, finding I was only a few levels away from gaining an evolution for Firebolt as well. I guessed that was because, even though it was my go-to spell, like lightning was for Oracle, since I kept altering it so much, I'd delayed the evolution. I shrugged, looking around at everyone.

The rest of my party had basically spread out and gotten as comfortable as they could. While I was busy with the notifications, someone had even arranged for the corpses to be removed. I grinned and had a little internal bet with myself over whether it was Decin and Hanau or Flux who had done it.

"Okay," I said, clapping my hands together. "Leadership group, I need a word…That's you, Flux, Decin, and Lydia, in case you didn't know."

Each of the three got up and hurried over to me, and I led them out into the corridor, passing Arrin, who was sitting on watch at the entrance to the room. I spotted Jian stationed at the far end of the corridor, watching down the next hall.

"I can move, Jax, if you want privacy," Arrin quickly offered, starting to get up, and I waved him down.

"No, it's fine. Nothing secret, just a chat here," I said. My little group, accompanied by Oracle and Bob, moved down to the middle of the corridor, where I sat and motioned for the others to do the same.

"We need to wait a dozen or so more hours here; basically, the first golem will be up to charge then, and we need it and the others back at the tower. They will activate over the next day or so, and once they're all awake, we can order them to head to the tower by foot if necessary and take up position. Until there are at least a few awake, though, I don't want to leave the area. I plan to use my mana as much as possible, as soon as it regenerates, anyway, and I'll be healing everyone up in that time.

"I'm not sure what use we will have for this location, but we do need to clear the bodies out regardless. The goblins can burn, as far as I care, but the crew and your own dead, Flux, we will need to remove and care for. I don't know your customs, so what do you want to do with them?" I asked, looking from Decin to Flux and back.

"We have returned Gaul to our home already. He will be buried with honor there, with his family," Flux said firmly

Decin spoke up next. "I appreciate the thought, lord…We lost dozens to tha bastards. Best iff'n we take all that ain't goblin an' make a pyre. I know we're burnin' 'em, same as the goblins, but the lads will feel tha difference. Th' goblins be scum, but we don't need their diseases, neither."

"Okay, then, that's simple enough," I agreed. "As soon as the golems awaken, I'll set them to work removing the bodies. We will have to clear a way to the surface that the golems can use. The entrance the goblins were using won't do; it's too narrow, so if we need to dig anyway, they might as well start clearing the passageways and shoring up the walls as they go.

"That will open up buried sections of the building to us, so we may yet find something worth looting. We also need to loot the goblins. I'll be very clear on this, Decin, and I'm sorry if this upsets you and your people, but whatever is found belongs to my squad and Flux's group.

"It will be shared equally, although I reserve the right to claim anything I feel is needed. Coin will be shared out equally between all combatants, and if anyone can use the weapons or armor they find, they can claim them. Everything else goes back to the tower and goes into stores. We need everything, unfortunately."

Decin grunted, and I waited.

"Aye, we understand, lord. It just be a bit annoyin', seein' loot tha' we canna take a share o'; yer know how it be," he explained after a second, realizing I was waiting on him.

"I do, and I'll not be stealing your ship from you entirely, to be clear. I have claimed it, as part of the tower, and it is now my property. Fuck with me, and I *will* take it from you, but I want you to captain it. I'll provide upgrades and repairs, give you missions, and reward you when you do well. You are master aboard your ship, second only to myself and Oren. Do you understand?" Decin didn't look happy, but he nodded, and I turned to Flux.

"I'd like to see if we can work together in the future, Flux. Our settlements, I mean," I offered, watching him carefully. "I think we worked well today, and I could use the help in the future. You've probably already guessed, but I'm a bit crap at all the fancy talking, so I won't even bother. I want to try to negotiate a deal with your people. We need food, crafting, and basically all the rest of the bits that make a city work."

I shifted, trying to get comfortable, and explained who I was, how and why I ended up in the UnderVerse, and what the current condition of the tower was. I held little back, hedging only on the defensive capabilities of the tower. I guessed Flux was the key to his people, by the way the others jumped when he spoke, and the way he acted without thought. I needed him and the Mer.

"…now we're at war. It's a war I would not have gone looking for, but if someone treats his people that badly and tries that shit with me…it was always going to happen," I finished with a shrug.

"Tell me truthfully…Do you think you can win?" Flux asked me after a long break while he and Decin digested what I'd said.

"I wouldn't be here if I didn't," I said calmly. "If I thought I couldn't win, I'd have gotten everyone on the warship, and we'd have looted the tower and fucked off. I would never risk lives without reason, but we've found a home here.

"The tower is damaged and decrepit at the minute, but the potential! Once it's repaired, it will be a powerhouse. The ability to literally build our own golems ensures our productivity. The tower will be our bastion and our capital; we can secure the local area, gathering what we need, and keep our people safe. I can't imagine a more secure or better start to a nation than we have. It'll be tough, but nothing worthwhile is ever fucking easy, mate."

I straightened, knowing I could be saying all of this better, but I didn't know how. "I can get materials; I can get the physical things we need. What I don't have is the most valuable resource of any nation: I don't have enough people!"

"And you want us to what? Join you?" Flux asked slowly.

"Ideally, yes, I do. I want you to join me, but if that's too much to ask, then I want us to at least trade. Tell me what you need, what you want in return, and I'll buy food and goods from you for my people."

As Flux listened, his tendrils were fully extended, and an almost uncomfortable thrum filled the air, as if he was studying me minutely.

"I think you've got a good measure of me from today, but if not, then come and help me. I'll take you at your word if you swear you mean me no ill will.

169

Come to the tower and help me to make it a home for both our peoples, and you can leave whenever you want."

"I'll discuss it with my people," he said finally. "I will return in the morning to the shore where we first met. That is the best I can do at this time."

"Thank you, Flux," I said, smiling at him.

He nodded, letting his tendrils relax as he got to his feet. I stood as well, and we gripped each other's wrists, shaking once and releasing. With that, he turned and set off walking through the ruin, disappearing around the corner, and I let out a sigh. I liked Flux, and I hoped he'd accept my offer, or at least not dismiss it out of hand when he spoke to his people.

I finally turned to Lydia, noting the way she sat, exhausted despite the hours of rest.

"You haven't had any healing, have you?" I asked her, getting a shrug in return, and I shook my head at her. Sitting back down, I drew in a deep breath and cast Battlefield Triage on her.

It focused on the most grievous wounds first, moving through her body in stages, fixing each injury as far as it could before I ran out of mana three seconds later. She wasn't fully healed, but she looked a hell of a lot better than she had before.

"Oracle," I said suddenly, as a thought occurred to me.

"Yes, Jax?" she asked.

"At the end of the battle yesterday, you asked me if it was okay to give out a healing spell…who did you give it to?"

"I gave it to Ardbeg; he's one of Cai's people, and he had the best affinity with Life magic. It wasn't much, but…"

"Can you get up to Oren? Tell him to get back to the tower and bring Ardbeg back with him as fast as he can?" I interrupted her, and as my stomach rumbled, I added, "and bring back enough food for everyone. Hell, bring back a golem, too! And tell Cai I want as many alchemy ingredients gathered as he can manage. When we get back tomorrow, I'm going to start teaching someone basic alchemy, and we're going to make sure we have enough damn potions in the future!"

Oracle spun in place and blurred away at high speed, disappearing down the corridor as I turned to Decin and Lydia, who were both watching me.

"Well, let's get started. I know we're all wounded to one degree or another, but for the next few hours, let's get the main room cleaned, as best we can. Once that's done, we can shift to removing the dead. By then, we're going to have at least one golem to help us, and it can do the truly gruesome bits."

CHAPTER FIFTEEN

I t had taken Oren about ten hours to make the round trip to the tower and back, and he brought an extra handful of people with him to help. Oracle had returned to my side, assisting me as we all worked, trying to return the ruin to a livable condition. We knew Oren had arrived, because there was an almighty crash from above, dust suddenly falling from several places as the ruin creaked ominously.

He'd apparently decided that the best way to clear a space for the warship to land wasn't to use the cannons, but instead to drop the golem off over the side in the area he'd thought was near the ruin. He'd, in fact, dropped it directly on top, and it was only blind luck that it hadn't done more damage or killed one of us.

Oracle had found a way through to the surface at one point, an enterprising badger having cleared some of the way before being eaten by goblins. She immediately used that route to get out to see what had happened.

Once she finished berating Oren, she took control of the golem and commanded it to clear the immediate area of smaller trees, then the larger. Thankfully, a few hours ago, the servitor golem had finished charging as well. It had stepped from the recess in the wall where it had been stored, causing the room to explode in panic for a few minutes.

Once I'd settled the room, I took control of the servitor golem, glad it was a higher class than the other ones stationed in the Great Tower. Those golems needed to be directly controlled when they were as simple as the first level or basic versions. In the tower, Seneschal or Heph usually controlled them; here in an outpost, however, they either needed a local commander or to be semi-autonomous.

The servitor was a level three or complex-class golem. All I had to do was give it orders, and it would obey, returning to me if there was an issue. Much of the condition of the waystation was beyond its ability to fix properly, as the structure was magical in part, but the walls and floors, it could do, and the magical nature of the building could repair the rest.

I had ordered it to clear the goblins' kitchen first, sorting the bodies into three categories: goblin, animal, and sentient. I was worried it would need more direction than that, but it clattered away happily.

It took it less than an hour to do a job that would have taken us days, and when it was done, it was immediately redirected to begin clearing a way out of the ruined waystation. Oren landed as soon as he could, and Ardbeg and a team from the tower worked their way through the corridors to us from the old goblin entrance.

By the time the sun rose again, the building was partially uncovered, and the simple or level two war golems that were charged were being commanded by their unit commander, a complex warrior. The commander golem took charge of the lower-leveled versions effortlessly and directed them to clear out corridors, shoring up sagging roofs and walls, and generally uncovering a building that had been entirely lost to time until now.

Riana was running from one section of the building to another, examining uncovered walls, carvings, and the occasional rusted hulks she swore were important finds. I just left her to it and sat on the warship deck, talking quietly to Oren and idly flicking through the intermittent notifications I received from the waystation, when I found one I'd earned a few hours before and missed.

Congratulations!

Through hard work and perseverance, you have increased your stats by the following:

Perception +1
Wisdom +1

That made three points my Wisdom stat had jumped in twenty-four hours, which seemed insane, until I thought about the fact that I'd essentially been casting healing spells continually for the entire night. I'd scrapped the notifications that told me about a spell leveling up, keeping only the ones that told about reaching an evolutionary point. When I looked at my stats, I found that not only was I close to reaching that point with my Firebolt, but I was at level twelve with my summoning spell. Repairing Bob alone had been enough to bring me to that stage, since I'd had to basically rebuild him entirely, twice over, in the last forty-eight hours. I'd only recently finished the most recent repair to his form, using hundreds of goblin bones to convert him back to his knight form.

"Well, laddie, ye ready to head down to tha shore? Meet up wit' yer Mermates?" Oren asked.

"Yeah, let's go," I agreed, grinning at him until he shot me an askance look. "Hey, back home we had legends of mermaids. You made me think of them when you said that; are they real here?"

"Mermaids? Ye mean tha female Mer? Aye, how else d'ye think ye be gettin' wee Mer kiddies?" Oren replied, confused.

"No, I mean…oh, forget it. In my world, mermaids were half human, half fish, supposedly beautiful women who would lure sailors to their death."

"Aye, still female Mer, laddie," Oren said, turning to shout orders to the crew. Oracle and Bob began heading over from the ruin, where Bob had been working to clear a section with her direction.

They clattered up the makeshift gangway that had been rigged to lift the loot aboard. Bob took up station halfway down the ship, watching everything, while Oracle flew to me.

"I don't know," I muttered, thinking about Cheena. "They were supposedly beautiful creatures, made sailors jump over the side of their ships, drowning willingly to die in the arms of the mermaids while boinkin'."

"Ha! Ye dinna know many sailors 'til now, did ye! I tell ye, most o' ma crew would no say no to a tumble wit' Cheena after a week's sailin', and after months? Ye'd be beatin' them wit a shitty stick just to get their attention!"

I grinned at him, remembering my time in the army, and reconsidered Cheena for a second. I couldn't see it myself, but after months on deployment…yeah, the world looks incredibly different, far more than any civvie would ever understand. I shrugged, making my way to the upper deck near Oren and Jory, the ship's old helmsman. I leaned forward, resting on the railing, and watched as the ship slowly raised itself, lifting through the trees that surrounded the waystation and into the clear morning sunlight. We slowly turned, the lake coming into view, and began to head down toward the shore. I stayed there for a few minutes as Oracle sat by my side, neither of us speaking as we enjoyed the other's company, the fresh morning breeze bringing the smell of the forest mixed with the clean scent of the lake.

I'd never really thought about being able to smell water before, but it had always been there, and here, surrounded by the forest, it was clear when the breeze brought it to us. We watched the morning fog gently rolling off the water, and I relaxed.

It was beautiful, and even though it only lasted a few minutes, it felt fantastic.

All too soon, we were coming into land on the shore, touching down close to Decin's ship. It was as fixed as we could make it now, the engineers taking advantage of the extra time we'd given them to fix a few other issues.

As we came to rest, Decin walked out of the captain's cabin, and he gave a little wave as he saw us. He'd found the damn purple robes Oren had told me about and was wearing them proudly already.

Flux was there as well, waiting in the shallows with a dozen other Mer, and I recognized both Bane and little T'lek among the group.

I climbed down, deciding that a superhero landing wasn't needed right now, although I got a few curious looks from the crew when I did that, and I cursed internally. Clearly I was *supposed* to leave the ship like that now. My knees were going to be so fucked up…

I strode down to meet the Mer on the shore. I couldn't see Cheena anywhere. As we came to halt, and Flux and I gripped wrists in greeting, she emerged from the water as well.

"Well met, Lord Jax," Flux said.

I glared at him, immediately feeling the subsonic vibrations I'd come to associate with laughter amongst his people as he released me and held up all four hands in apology.

"I know, I know, my friend; you don't like the rank unless it's needed, but let's get the formalities out of the way first, shall we?" Flux gestured, and several older Mer stepped forward, each bowing their heads to me. "These are the leaders of our pod. The closest you will get to pronouncing their names are Yuti, Ja'la, and T'mon. T'mon is father to T'lek and demanded to be part of this meeting." T'mon stepped forward first, dropping to one knee and bowing his head low.

"This one owes you the life of his only child. I will not forget; ask, and if it is within my power, it is yours," he said simply. I reached out, taking his hand and gently pulling him to his feet.

"No, as much as I want and need from you, I'll not bargain for a child's life," I said. "There is no debt."

The Mer exchanged looks, and Flux laughed again, speaking to them.

"You see now, he is not like the lords we have encountered before!"

173

"We thank you for this gift, then. Flux has told us of your adventures, both before meeting him, and together, and he put your proposal to us," Ja'la said, stepping forward as the other two moved fluidly to flank her. T'mon nodded while the one introduced as Yuti, heavily scarred and missing a lower arm, continually watched in all directions, as if expecting a threat.

"With regret, we must refuse. We cannot bind ourselves as a people to one so new to our world or allow ourselves as a people to be drawn into your war."

I gritted my teeth, pushing my disappointment down as she went on.

"However, we are not rulers as you are. We are elders to our people, and while our word is respected, it is not law. We have given our recommendation to our people, and advised we wait. We will learn more of you, and we will reconsider in one year's time. This is against the wishes of some of our pod. They have declared that they will follow you, if you will have them.

"We ask that you treat them well, should you accept them, and have brought gifts to show our thanks to you." She stepped back, both her companions moving back at the same time, and she gestured to the water where another group of Mer waited. They slowly began walking out onto the shore, and as they left the water, they were dragging a large net between them.

"First, food," Ja'la said, gesturing to the flopping fish caught in the large net. It looked like something a small trawler would pull, and I guessed several tons of fish being presented. It took almost a dozen Mer to pull it onto the shore, and they returned to the water as soon as it was done. "Next, goods. We have several sizes of armor that we had completed for sale to the cities. These and the weapons we would have sold are here for you."

"We have also included some of our alchemical ingredients, as they are highly sought-after, and Flux made us aware that you have a need of them." A second group of Mer walked out of the water, bearing these items in three large chests, placing them carefully before returning to the depths.

"Finally, people," Ja'la said, gesturing to the third and final group of almost a dozen Mer. As they moved forward, I noticed that several had to be helped along, having obvious difficulty. Flux stepped forward then, gesturing to a female Mer who stood several feet back and faced off to one side aimlessly. "This is Ame, the runesmith I spoke to you of. She and several others are skilled crafters, but their age or infirmities have robbed them of the ability to practice their craft. They have offered to swear to you if you can make use of them," he explained quietly.

"Of course I will, and gladly!" I said, a grin on my face as I looked at my new crafters. I would have healed them without them swearing to me, but, well…I needed them.

"Last of all, there are a couple of other Mer who wish to join you in your adventures. We cannot spare many; we are a small pod, after all, but equally, we will not hold them against their will," Ja'la said, and she gestured to the remaining Mer who stood with Ame and the other infirm. Cheena and Bane were among them, and I felt my heart lift. I liked them, and hell, I trusted them, and that was saying a lot for me.

"Cheena and Bane you know already; the others that are armed are Jana, Hel, and Katerin." Flux clapped me on the shoulder, "Also, seeing as I can't let such young and inexperienced warriors as them out of my sight, I'll be coming along, too."

I couldn't help but grab his hand. My smile ran from ear to ear as I looked at him and the others.

"Thank you! Thank you, my friends. You've no idea how much I hoped you would join me," I said. As the elders and other Mer began making their way into the lake again, T'mon waded over to me and held out a pouch.

"It's not much, but take this and use it well," he said. "I will be watching, and know that in a year, if you've kept faith with us, you'll have more than one friendly voice speaking for you amongst the elders."

With that, he turned and set off into the water with the others. I opened the pouch, shaking a handful of small black pearls into my open palm.

"They're beautiful," I said, and Oren grunted from where he stood.

"Aye, laddie; they also be worth a small fortune! They be tha same as a hun'red gold each, so use 'em well!"

"I will," I said, tipping them back into the bag and putting it carefully in my pocket. I greeted the small group that wanted to join me and helped to lead them to the ship, finding myself escorting Ame to a seat on the deck as the ship readied to take off. I called to Oren to wait a few minutes, and Oracle and I prepared ourselves.

I needed these Mer, and I needed to make a good impression on them. As near as I could tell, Ame was the only one that couldn't "see" or "sense" or whatever; the others had various other issues, arthritis mainly, as near as I could see. But I wasn't having Ame's first airship ride be in the dark with no idea of what was happening.

"I'm going to help you, Ame. Please relax as much as you can," I said gently, and she responded in a surprisingly strong and vibrant voice.

"You are our new lord?" she asked, and I started to nod before catching myself.

"Yes, I'm Jax, Lord of Dravith and the Great Tower," I said, and she nodded to herself.

"Then I stand ready to swear the Oath. I will try to instruct your people as best I can." she said matter-of-factly. "Although I cannot feel the world around me anymore, I can still teach, and I will…arghhhh!"

She cut off with a loud gasp as Oracle and I released the spell we'd been building. We poured our entire mana pool into the spell; two hundred and seventy mana was infused into the Battlefield Triage spell, and it soaked into her like water into sand. She was lifted from her feet in the first seconds of the spell, suspended in midair as the spell went on, until at last, it cut off with a sound like the ringing of bells. I closed my eyes against the bright flare of a mana migraine as I took deep breaths. When I could see again, I looked at Ame, seeing what I could only assume was shock. Her tendrils were out, waving around frantically, and the rest of the crew and I flinched as repeated low vibrations washed over us. They made my teeth ache, but only lasted a handful of seconds before dying away.

Ame stood there, her hands outstretched, shaking as she waved them about. Then she started reaching out and touching things; the deck of the ship, the people around her. She finally spun around to face me.

"You? You did this?" she demanded, reaching out and grabbing my arms.

"I did; well, *we* did," I admitted and nodded to Oracle, who came to land on my shoulder. "And I'll do the same for all of you in the coming days! It takes a lot of mana, so please, bear with me, but I'll do it," I said louder, speaking to the entire group.

The air erupted with a barrage of low-level sonic vibrations as the group examined Ame minutely, and I tried to back away.

"No!" Ame snapped as I tried to pull my arms free. "Explain this; I must understand! Will this fade? Will I return to what I was?"

"I...I don't think so," I stammered, blinking at the ferocity of her questioning.

"You don't think so? But you don't know?" she asked, then shook her head. "I must know! I have been locked away from the world, locked away from my life! I will *not* return to that!" Ame snapped at me, releasing my arms as she stalked to the side of the ship, pushing others aside and gripping the railing as she muttered to herself. I turned to Flux, who shook his head as I opened my mouth.

"Don't ask. I have never understood females, my friend, and that one least of all!" he admitted, the last bit under his breath, eliciting a small chuckle from one of the crew who stood nearby. I glanced over and saw him shaking his head. He froze when he realized I'd heard him and started to apologize until I grinned at him.

"I'm the same; never understood a woman yet, and I don't think species matters like that!"

"He should understand Ame by now!" Cheena chimed in from where she leaned against a nearby crate. "How long have you loved her for now, Flux?" she teased, and Flux gestured sharply at her. "What, you think she doesn't know?" she asked, a low burble escaping her, and I guessed it was her version of a laugh.

"She is the runecrafter of the pod. She would never—"

"Bah! 'She' is no longer 'of the pod,' and I've not been any use as a runecrafter for years!" Ame snapped, not bothering to turn around. "'She' will discuss this with you later, Flux, and you'd better not try to hide! Things have been put off too long."

The fierce Mer woman turned back to me and strode over, the other Mer jumping aside. It was move or be walked over, considering the determined way she went.

"Flux said you have offered skill training, memories, and more. You can heal us, but you have no idea if this is permanent...I will be your runecrafter, but I will need access to items to do this. I have brought what I have, but I will need more soon, depending on what you expect of me.

"I will also teach my secrets to others you choose, though this will come at a cost," she said firmly. "I have been cut off from the world entirely for too long. My worldsense was lost first, then I began to lose the feeling in my body. I knew not what I touched or where, being left with only a hint of the sounds others made.

"I had planned to let go, as soon as my apprentice learned enough that the pod would not be left without a runecrafter, when she was almost killed by her experiment, and she quit. I had nothing left and had resolved to give myself to the darkness, and had been planning this for the last few days," she stated bluntly.

"Now that I am here, I feel the world again. I have been granted a second chance. A chance to learn, to grow beyond my dreams. I will swear to you, but I will need support, information, and most of all, access to magic to make sure the darkness never returns!"

You have been offered a quest!

Teach the Teacher:

Ame was the greatest Runecrafter in a dozen generations of her people, but the encroaching darkness has changed her. She demands training to become all she can be. She is determined to learn and will not accept no for an answer.

Accept?

Yes/Yes

I blinked at the notification before dismissing it and frowning at Ame.

"I have the materials to teach you just about anything, Ame, but I'll not waste the strongest healing spells and memories on you. I'm sorry, but you're already skilled in something that could be insanely useful. I'll give you some, and you can teach yourself from there, though."

"Who else will be as dedicated or driven as I am?" she replied flatly. "I need to know. My people gradually suffer from this deterioration as they age. I began suffering far earlier than I should. What if others have begun to decline? No, I will not accept this. You want assurances? Give me the basic tools, teach me, and I will prove myself! You need a healer? For your brain?" she asked, and I growled, moving forward until we were inches apart.

"What do you know of that?" I asked her, my voice a low rumble, Oracle gripping my shoulder tightly in warning as she felt my anger and fear rising.

"I can sense damage in your brain, child," she replied, equally quietly. "What made me an excellent runecrafter was my attention to details, my manapool, and most of all, my worldsense. I sensed your injuries when I reached out, glorying in no longer being trapped inside the decaying husk of my head. Teach me, and I will do all I can for you, *I swear it!*" Ame said fervently.

I looked at her for a long time, well aware that we were being watched by the crew and the rest of the Mer, my anger and fear over the damage to my brain warring for dominance all the while.

"Fine. I'll give you access to healing spells, the basic ones…but you prove to me you're worth more than that before you get anything else!" I snapped, then took a deep breath and softened my tone. "I'm sorry, Ame. I don't like even considering the damage done to my brain, let alone discussing it aloud where all can hear."

She paused for a long moment, then stepped back and knelt smoothly.

"No, Lord Jax, I am sorry. My fear and excitement drove me to demands when I should be thanking you and swearing forever to serve. I will earn your trust and your forgiveness." She stood slowly, nodded respectfully to me, then her right upper arm shot out and she grabbed Flux by one tendril, making him grunt in surprise as he bent close, dragged by her inexorable will as much as her grip. "Now, with your leave, lord, I will take care of something else that's been left for far too long."

I grinned at Flux and Ame and stepped back myself.

"Fine by me, Ame. I'll go make preparations for our return to the waystation then home. Have fun!" I turned and started walking down the deck, leaving Ame and Flux to their "conversation."

Oracle gently kissed my cheek before she took off, darting up into the rigging of the mast, ready for the flight. She'd spent hours up there on the way over, glorying in the sight of the world flying by.

I walked up onto the raised deck and stood with Oren, nodding to Jory as I propped myself against the railing.

"How long?" I asked Oren, and he shrugged.

"Iff'n yer ready now, we can be back at tha waystation in a few minutes, then soon as tha golems be sent on their way, we can be off. We do no be as fast as Decin's ship; she be built fer speed, a courier an' scout, an' we have damaged engines to boot, but they be better than they were. Mebbe another five hours to get back to the tower, wind willin'." I nodded to him, gesturing upwards, and he grinned, shouting orders.

It took less than a minute before we lifted from the sand where he'd landed, the ship creaking as the engines took the strain. Sails slowly extended and boomed as they caught the wind coming off the lake. We picked up speed, the ship tilting gently as we lifted higher and higher, more engines coming online, driving us into the air.

Oren took us up slowly, circling around and heading to where the ruined Waystation Four stood. We weren't even halfway before Decin overtook us, his smaller ship built, as Oren said, for speed.

I'd hardly had the chance to see Decin's ship before, but as it passed us, I watched it. It had four engines on the sides, two front and two back that lifted and directed it, one large engine at the back for thrust, and three sails, one on either side and one above like a traditional ships mast.

She was almost entirely wooden, a deep golden oak color with a blue line painted diagonally across the hull halfway up her side. The name that stood out proud on her rear was *Libertas*, and I frowned, trying to remember the meaning. Liberty? Liberate...no, *Freedom*, I translated.

I'd never been taught Latin at school, but Xiao had battered enough of it into my thick skull that I remembered that, at least.

"So, laddie, yer got yersel' a new hanger-on, eh?" Oren asked, and I looked at him quizzically. He gestured behind me and I turned, my eyes almost skipping over him, until he moved.

"Bane?" I asked, and he straightened up, no longer seeming hard to see. Instead, he was a heavily muscled four-armed warrior again, who casually stepped forward from where he'd been crouching. "What are you doing here?" I asked.

"You saved my life, forgave my assault, helped me save my friend's life, and healed me when I was injured. Where else would I be, Jax?" he asked me, gesturing as though confused.

"Well, you could be anywhere; explore the ship...talk to your friends, hell, watch Ame kick Flux's ass, if you want. I mean, why are you *here*, specifically why were you skulking around behind me?"

"Ah!" Bane said, thrumming in understanding. "I'm here as your bodyguard."

"I don't need a bodyguard," I replied, and Oren called over, interrupting me.

"Aye, ye do, laddie, and no' just Bob, neither!" I turned around and gave Oren the finger, making him laugh as Bane went on.

"You are our leader, and you are at war. You need bodyguards. Flux, Cheena, and I have discussed this. We will take shifts until a proper team can be arranged," Bane said matter-of-factly, moving to look over the side of the ship, then back to watching everything around me.

"What do you mean, you 'discussed this'? Look, mate, I need people, yeah, and I really need fighters, but a fucking bodyguard? I don't need that," I said flatly.

Oren spoke up again. "A lord needs bodyguards!"

Bane nodded in fervent agreement. "It's true; how else would you survive assassins?"

"I..." I was about to tell him to fuck off and that there weren't any assassins about, when I remembered the bastard in the stairwell, right before I met Oren, and the assholes that were keeping the others as slaves. Bane would have been insanely helpful then. And he'd have been awesome help in facing the slavers...and the SporeMother, actually.

"See, you know you need a bodyguard," Bane said, noting the expression on my face and gesturing around us. "You can't defend against all sides, and especially not when you sleep. You need us, and we already agreed to serve you. You earned my life thrice over in the goblin battle...you helped us, now let us help you."

I still wasn't sure when Oracle spoke in my mind.

"He's right; we need them...and we trust them, don't we?"

"I do. I like Bane and the others, but—"

"But it's 'just you,' and you don't need a bodyguard?"

"Well, yeah, basically. It seems wrong."

"But throwing yourself into battle to save them wasn't?"

"No..."

"We need them, and they need us. Let them help. It's important to them. They're an honorable race, and you helped them."

I forced a smile and clapped Bane on the shoulder.

"Thanks, mate; glad to have you with me," I said, trying not to growl. I'd be talking to Flux about the matter later. I did *not* need a goddamn twenty-four-hour bodyguard. Fair enough when we were out and about, some help would be great...but not all the time, and not at the tower!

I was about to say something else when the ship started to descend, gently lowering itself through the surrounding trees to come to a rest in the clearing before the ruin.

I strode down the deck, taking pleasure in the low voices of the Mer as they discussed their first airship ride. It seemed they'd enjoyed it, judging from the lack of screaming and vomiting, anyway.

I passed Bob, who stood calmly on the deck watching everyone before slowly walking along behind me. Oracle flew down from above and landed on my shoulder, and I sensed Bane following along, more than seeing or hearing him.

I took a deep breath, resigning myself to the situation, when I caught sight of Flux and Ame. He was gesturing toward me, an edge of panic in his voice as he explained that he needed to go and help me.

179

"No, no! Don't you worry, mate! You stay here and sort things out with Ame; I'll be fine!" I called to him, grinning evilly. *Got you, you bugger!*

We'd had to spread the engineers out on Decin's ship to fill the spaces of crew that had been killed, and I'd had Lydia, Jian, and Arrin take up station on his ship as well, just in case. That had meant that Hanau and Riana had been able to stay in the ruin with the golems, watching over them as the new ones activated and joined the effort to repair the structure.

The complex war golem, the one that was directing the others, I decided to call Sarge, on the grounds that anytime you needed anything done in the army, you got a sergeant to sort it.

Sarge was standing at the top of a flight of newly uncovered stairs in the middle of the ruin, working with the servitor that was slowly sealing three walls around the entrance. Off to one side lay the large slab I'd ordered it to build to close off the entrance to the ruin.

As I walked up, Oracle went flying past me, landing on the servitor's shoulder and reaching down into the clear gemstone embedded in its chest. She blurred for a minute as she lost concentration, her form going out of focus until she straightened up and flew back to me.

"It's almost done," she said, hovering before me and nodding happily. "The servitor and the golems have cleared a pathway down to the main areas. They've taken the bodies and piled them up in preparation to be burned, and the ruins can be sealed off whenever you want. Once the slab is in place, nothing will be able to get in easily to interrupt."

"Sounds good. Let's get everyone out and have the funeral, then the last golem should be finished charging, and we can head back to the tower." Oracle gave me a last grin, then flipped over and sped toward the ruin, diving in and searching far more quickly than I could have for anyone remaining inside.

"Oren!" I called, and his face appeared a few seconds later over the side of the ship in response. "Get the crew together! We're going to have the funeral as soon as the others are here." He nodded in response and whistled up to Decin's ship, waving him in to land as well.

I walked over to a large uncovered slab of stone and sat relaxing in the sunshine for a few minutes, Oracle landing next to me within moments. We talked quietly, enjoying each other's presence, and I had just started to wonder if her top was actively growing lower cut as I looked, or if it was my imagination, when a loud roar ruined the mood.

CHAPTER SIXTEEN

jumped to my feet, people all around us doing the same. I felt the ground shake, and Sarge, followed by three other golems, rushed over to take up station between us and whatever had made the noise.

A few minutes passed, with screeches and roars coming closer…until we got our first look at what was making all the noise.

The rest of the golems had formed up around us, the servitor and construction golem from the tower loaded aboard Oren's ship, just in case, as were almost the entirety of our people. My squad had surrounded us with the golems forming a second ring farther out.

At first, all we could see was movement between the trees, then flashes of a huge grey creature surrounded by smaller, faster ones. As the minutes passed, they came closer and the screams became clearer. One group was composed of goblins, chanting and screeching randomly, punctuated by the pain-filled screams of a human male. He was being dragged along by the creature that made the loudest noises, and as it came into view, I used Identify.

Adult Male Cave Troll

This is the last surviving Cave Troll from a family that was tamed by the Goblins. The Matriarch has eaten one, and the other apparently fled, rather than be tamed.

This creature has the very dangerous combination of high muscle density combined with an extremely low level of intelligence.

Health: 999/1100

I scowled at the goblins, watching them freeze as they saw us. The cowardly little monsters pulled back to the middle of their group, screaming in rage at finding us arrayed before their home. One of them, sporting a bone headdress, screamed something at the cave troll, who threw the human down and stamped on him. The crunch of his skull made it clear he wasn't going to be getting back up.

"I think that was one of the three idiots," Oracle said quietly.

I nodded. I hadn't wanted them to die, necessarily, but they were assholes, so I wasn't particularly concerned about it.

The cave troll started to run forward, smashing saplings aside as it went. The goblins following close behind, brandishing weapons and screaming, the air filled with their bloodlust.

"What do you think?" I asked Oracle, a smile tugging at the corners of my mouth. "Do they think the golems are just statues?"

"Probably," she said, an evil grin appearing on her face. The cave troll was maybe ten feet tall and heavily muscled. The golems ranged from nine feet tall for the general fighters, to eleven for Sarge, and they all had to outweigh the troll easily.

"Sarge," I said, my own grin splitting my face. "Wait until they're about twenty feet away, then slaughter the fucking lot of them. I want you to rip the troll's arms off and beat it to death with the wet ends."

The golems shifted slightly, an air of readiness palpable in their stances.

It took maybe thirty seconds for the troll to close the distance to the point I'd specified, and as it crossed that imaginary line, the golems blurred into action.

Sarge hadn't bothered to draw its sword from the enormous sheath across its back. It simply went from standing still to what looked like a dead run in two seconds flat. The rest of the golems followed its lead, and I had the chance to see the look of confusion on the face of the cave troll...right before Sarge's shield smashed into it with the force of an out-of-control semi.

The troll catapulted backwards, cracks sounding as bones were broken, and Sarge discarded its shield, crushing a pair of goblins under its ridiculous mass.

The rest of the golems spread out, the ranged ones firing mana bolts from their huge crossbows that flared into existence, then blasted multiple goblins into bits. The melee-armed golems barely got to touch the goblins before they were all dead. The last thing the goblin in the headdress saw was Sarge pinning his supposedly invincible cave troll to the floor with one foot, then grabbing both of its arms by the wrists and tearing them off.

I watched the carnage in stunned silence. The only sounds, beyond the echoes of the explosions returning to us from the surrounding hills, were the meaty *thwack*s as Sarge hammered the arms down onto the already dead cave troll, and Stephanos's retching behind us.

"Okay...note to self, golems and metaphors don't mix," I said, swallowing hard.

I pulled the golems back, ordering them back to their regular duties, once they'd gathered the fresh bodies for burning and gestured for the ships to land, everyone left a little uneasy by the amazing prowess of the war golems.

I didn't even get any experience, as it was that much of a one-sided slaughter, apparently. I just shrugged and wished we'd had the fuckers when we went to clear the nest out.

It only took a few minutes for everyone to gather; we'd had a large area cleared for the ships to land and two other areas as well. One was to the left of the ruin, the other to the right, with the goblins and all the general refuse piled to the right. We dug a trench around it all to prevent the fire from spreading and the entire heap doused liberally in whatever we could find that was cheap and flammable.

The section to the left, on the other hand, was for the bodies of the dead from Decin's ship and the other corpses that the golems had found. Anything that wasn't goblin or animal was placed here. Due to the condition of the bodies, there was no way of knowing what was from who, so they were placed with as much reverence as we could manage, then they were covered in naphtha from the warship.

I stood to one side, listening as Decin led the funeral. He spoke of the dead with long familiarity, reminiscing about fights, families, and what good people they'd been. I stood for a long while as he spoke, the thought that nobody ever said that the dead were assholes occasionally running through my mind as people stepped forward to speak. Then I realized they were all looking to me.

I stepped forward, clearing my throat and frantically running the last few seconds through my mind, realizing I'd missed my cue.

"I…I wanted to say," I said, trying to cover my mistake. "I wanted to say that I was sorry I never met you. I'm sorry that you were lost before I could help you. I don't know if you can hear us, if you're comforted by the things that have been said, but there's only one thing I can offer you to help. I'll make the same offer to your families that has been made to your shipmates; if they want to, they'll be allowed to come to the tower. I'll protect them as best I can and give them the chance to be all they could be." I looked to Decin, who nodded once, and I began.

I cast Firebolt, the simplest version of the first spell I had learned, firing a small patch of ground in front of the bodies that I'd deliberately left clear and had soaked in naphtha. It impacted with a solid '*wumph*' as the flames burst to life, spreading rapidly and flooding the corpses.

We stood there for almost an hour, nowhere near enough time to reduce the bones fully to ash. Short of a much hotter fire, Decin had warned me that it'd take the entire day or more to destroy them fully.

I gestured to Oren and Decin, and they got their people moving, filing slowly onto the ships. While we'd stood vigil, the final golems had finished charging, and Sarge had set them to work. The items we felt we could use had been loaded onto the ships, and the golems had closed off the ruins with the large slab of stone. I walked over to Sarge with Oracle and waited while the people made their way onto the ships.

"Bane?" I said quietly, and the tree beside me moved. Bane slipped silently into view, and I sighed. "Honestly, mate, you don't need to guard me here. What do you think is going to attack me? Horned bunnies? Squirrel knights?"

"I won't know until they try," was his only response, and I shook my head, turning to Sarge.

"Watch over the pyres. If they start to spread, then put them out; if not, then leave them to burn out on their own. Bury the remains of the crew together but show them respect. As to the goblins and the trash, cover it with whatever you need to. I want the fires completely out in twelve hours if they've not finished on their own, the pyres covered.

"Then lead the others to the tower as quickly as possible. Once you arrive, you are to report to Hephaestus and take on whatever duties he assigns. Do you know where the tower is, and do you understand your orders?" I asked and Sarge turned slowly, scanning the horizon through the trees until we could both see the tower. He pointed at it, then turned back to me and clapped his fist to his chest in salute. I returned the salute and walked over to the piled goblins and crap, casting a second Firebolt.

This one, I slammed into the middle of the pile, blasting some of the bones flying. The fire spread out, noxious fumes beginning almost instantly from the mixture of rubbish, unwashed goblins, and the flammables we'd piled in there.

We backed away quickly and went to join Oren on the raised deck of the *Agamemnon's' Pride*. He got us lifting off quickly, everyone happy to get away from the fumes.

It took another four hours for us to get back to the tower. Decin flew alongside, occasionally exchanging insults with Oren about his speed and ship handling abilities. It didn't take long until the tone was lowered to his "handling" of himself and his wife as well, and I couldn't help but smile. The sound of friends exchanging good-natured insults and abuse was universal, and I was damn glad about that.

When we were on our final approach to the tower, I confirmed the orders I'd given Oren earlier, at which point, he walked to the side of the ship and shouted over to Decin, going through details with him. They dropped Flux and his people, the new complex servitor golem, Oracle, and myself off on the twenty-sixth floor before taking off again and flying down to ground level to land outside.

The parade ground looked much better than it had; it'd been cleared and cleaned, all the various refuse and debris was gone, and the twisted wreck of the old doors, which we'd virtually destroyed by shoving the remnants of Oren's ship into as a trap, had also been cleared away.

Instead, two huge doors were slowly growing out of the surrounding mass of the tower, and a smaller door was forming off to one side. I headed inside, smiling and waving at the various people milling around on the floor, counting down until…

"Is that…"

"It be mine!"

I'd been waiting for them, wondering who'd spot the new golem first; no surprise that they'd both started off at near the same time.

"Now you listen here—"

"No, you listen! Do ye know whut I could do wit' that? You would'na even know how to use it properly!"

"That's enough, the both of you. The ships are going to land outside the tower on the ground. I want golems to unload the heavy gear as quickly as possible, then we'll talk about the new servitor."

"But the servitor is clearly to be used to repair **my** *tower, isn't it, Jax?"*

"Ye fool! Ye know—"

The sound of Seneschal and Heph arguing washed over me, and I banished it from my mind as Barrett and Cai approached. I left the Mer with a promise that I'd be right back and headed over to intercept them.

"You've been busy!" I said to them, gesturing around the floor and receiving proud smiles from both of them.

"You don't mind, then?" Barrett asked. "Cai and I were worried we'd overstepped our authority when we suggested it to Seneschal, but he just went ahead with it."

"Hell no. I told you to do what you needed to do, and to look after things in my absence. This project was a conversation I'd already had with Seneschal. The fact you've got this much done already?" I said, looking about in amazement.

The twenty-sixth floor was the highest of the large floors in the tower. From this point on, they shrank considerably, staying high ceilinged but growing smaller with each level. As I admired the improved space, I was amazed by the size of the floor itself. They'd somehow managed to not only get all the internal walls in this section of the tower removed, save for the armory on the far side and some huge support struts, but they'd used a lot of the stone to begin to make berths!

"Well, Seneschal and Hephaestus needed stone for the other repairs; apparently, the stone composing the tower is better to work with than quarrying more elsewhere, so stripping this floor was a priority. There are two servitors working on this floor constantly," Cai said, gesturing to a corner where I could just make out a blur of arms stacking and sealing stones together. A handful of people were running back and forth from a large pile of stones, taking them to the servitors and clearly working together to keep them supplied. "There are three servitors on the third floor, reconstructing the genesis chamber, and one is working on sealing the command room off for now, at my request."

"Yeah, the door there locks, but only just. Considering the importance of the creation table, and how rare and powerful they are? It just made sense," Barrett interjected.

I nodded approvingly. "Once we've got the basics, so that we're safe and people can rest in a little comfort, we'll make a change to that, anyway. I think the command center will become a suite of rooms all close together on a single floor, probably with the majority of the soldiers and war golems stationed around there."

"I'd recommend having that done soon, Jax," Barrett replied. "If someone were to injure or kill the wisps and get access to that table…" He shook his head.

"They could shut the tower down, change its priorities." Oracle shuddered. "They could lock you out, Jax, or they could order it to concentrate all the mana in an unstable area, flooding the mana channels and causing an explosion that could collapse the tower. There's no limit to the damage they could do."

"But they couldn't do any of that with the wisps in control, right?" I asked her, concern filling my voice.

"No, but that's the point. The tower is a structure, that's all. We wisps look after it, but if we're killed off, then the tower can only be controlled by the creation table. That's why it was kept at the top of the tower, in the most secure area we had."

"Why wasn't it moved to the Hall of Memories? Or, hell, why didn't the SporeMother use it?" I asked. Oracle shook her head.

"We didn't have time; all the golems were fighting its creatures, but the SporeMother couldn't use the creation table anyway; Seneschal cut it off when he shut the tower down."

"So, we could shut it down then, if we needed to?"

"It's a magical construct. Draining it entirely then repowering it is damaging. It had to be done like this before, but now? No. Best if we just keep it safe. Posting a war golem with it would probably be enough; there are eight, after all," Oracle said, and Barrett perked up immediately.

"Ah…eight war golems, Jax?" he asked quickly.

I grinned at him. "Yeah, mate, we found an old waystation of the tower. It was full of goblins, but once we'd cleared them out, we found ten golems. There are five basic melee class, three ranged, one command golem—it's a level three complex one that can control the war golems and fight alongside them, as well as take orders."

I turned and gestured to the large Servitor that had stopped a few feet back. "And there was also this monstrosity, a level three servitor, capable of carrying out simple requests and commands, especially for repairing and rebuilding."

"It's very different to ours," Cai said, walking around it slowly and inspecting the ornamentation.

"I know; we've concentrated on building them as fast as possible, and we've been manufacturing the very basic models. This one's a lot more advanced, and the ancients clearly cared more about style than we can afford to."

"I noticed you've brought some new recruits as well, and with the second ship, I can only assume…" Cai asked, lifting one eyebrow, and I took the hint.

"Yes, Decin has joined us, although nobody has sworn yet. We've also been lucky that a handful of Mer we encountered agreed to join us as well. In fairness, they agreed as much for the promise of healing as anything else. There's a lady called Ame that I would recommend you watch your step with; she's very determined. She's also a runecrafter and wants to be a healer. The Mer are generally led by her or Flux; they're the two at the front of the group. The one currently getting his ear chewed off is Flux."

"A runecrafter that wants to be a healer? Why—"

"She wasn't well before; I healed her, and now, boom! Wants to be a healer. Incredibly determined lady, so I suggest not annoying her, unless you want your head bitten off. That being said, all the best doctors and nurses I know have a total lack of patience for fucking about, so she'll probably make an amazing healer…if she has any aptitude for it. Come on, I'll introduce you." I turned to the golem, speaking slowly and clearly.

"You are to begin strengthening and repairing this floor. You will accept orders from the wisps of this tower. Oracle here, you already know; the other two are Seneschal and Hephaestus. You are also to accept commands from Cai, Barrett, and Oren, the dwarf from the ship we just left, provided their orders do not contradict my own, or the orders of the wisps. Nod if you understand and accept these commands." There was a momentary pause, and the servitor nodded, turning and walking over to the area where the other golem was working. The servitor paused, communing with it somehow, before grabbing stones and starting to work alongside the first, its four arms working in a seamless blur.

"Damn, that thing's fast!" Barrett said. I had to agree, nodding along with Cai. I led them back across to the group, seeking out Flux and Ame in particular as I introduced my advisors to the Mer.

"I know I haven't had the chance to really meet you all before now, so please don't be upset that I've not learned who you are and your skills and abilities before now. I wanted you to meet two of my advisors first.

"This is Cai, who deals with people and the tower itself, and Barrett, who is in charge of security and our fighting forces. They will be able to help you all with most things as we go on. As you can see, and as I'm sure Flux told you all, the tower is slowly being repaired and made to be more livable."

The group all nodded, with a few giving out the strange, low-frequency hums that I took for a form of sonar.

I noticed that, while it only looked and felt like two on the outer edge of the group were giving the signals off, the tendrils of the entire group were shifting in response. There was a long silence as I processed this, when Ame stepped forward.

"Very well; we understand this and forgive the rudeness. First, I am Ame, healer and runecrafter," she said, introducing herself to Cai and Barrett, while I blinked in shock. "This is Flux, or at least that is the closest your kind is likely to come to his true name, so it will suffice. He is my mate and a warrior. He patrolled our waters and killed those who threatened the pod. He will do this here as well.

"With him are Cheena, his second, who is also a warrior, and Fenir, her mate, who is a hunter. Bane is the Lord Jax's dedicated bodyguard, with Jana to assist until a proper cadre is chosen."

As each was named, they stepped forward, clapping a fist to chest, and stepped back. Jana was a slender female with a collection of long blades in place of the spears-and-daggers combination that Bane and Flux both favored. Jana nodded to me, then Ame, and finally to Cai and Barrett, before stepping off to one side.

"Uh, you've got bodyguards? And where's Bane?" asked Barrett quietly, only to jump when Bane spoke from behind him.

"It was decided that Jax required protection; as I already owed him my life, I volunteered," the big Mer said quietly, and I grinned at Barrett, enjoying seeing him jerk in shock.

"Good at that, isn't he?" I grinned as Ame continued. If she'd had eyes, I had no doubt they would have held a coolly reproving look.

"Next are Hel and Katerin, both hunters and warriors as well. Byat is a carver of weapons and armor. Lastly, we have brought Amoth and his mate, Esse. Amoth is a farmer, most skilled at establishing new populations of fish, and Esse is an herbalist. We are all the most skilled in our trades in the waters of our homes, it is true, but we will adapt," Ame said firmly.

I inspected the group, finding that they were clearly separated into two categories, younger and older, many in the older group having obvious infirmities or injuries. The warriors all had injuries, except for the three I'd originally fought with. Hel was missing both arms on the right side, Jana stood with an obviously deformed left foot, and Katerin was twisted and hunched over, her breaths coming in quiet gasps.

"Oracle, are you ready?" I asked, and she nodded, a brilliant smile on her face, growing to her full humanoid size. She reached out and took my hand. Drawing a deep breath in, she spoke to Ame and the others.

"We're going to heal you all one by one over the next few days, but as you saw earlier, it takes a lot of mana, and we may have to do it several times to heal you as far as we can. Who is the most injured among you?" The group looked at each other then parted for Amoth, who stood in the middle of the group, leaning heavily on his mate, Esse. He limped forward slowly, his skin a pale grey with dark lines marking his veins. His tendrils hung mostly limp and flaccid, his steps faltering and obviously pained.

I instantly felt guilty, thinking I should have gone to them as soon as my mana regenerated and healed another then, but it was important to do this right. I needed them to accept that I was in charge and associate the tower with their new lives. As much as I hated playing games like this, it was necessary.

Just like this was, as I held Oracle's hand in my own, feeling her cool fingers gripping mine as she cast Battlefield Triage over Amoth. The expanding rings of healing magic slowly flooded the elderly Mer's body, scanning and finding the most damaged areas, gradually healing them, purging infection from her, and repairing and replacing cells that had begun to die in ever-increasing numbers.

When we were finally done, Amoth slumped to the floor, only to be caught by his mate. Oracle and I almost collapsed as well, the mana drain and resulting migraine of using our entire pool in one go leaving us shaken and weak. Oracle didn't need to breathe, but she drew in mana as fast as she could while I pulled in shuddering gasps of air. I felt a hand take my right one, my arm being pulled across shoulders that helped to steady me, and I grinned weakly at Barrett.

"Thanks, man," I whispered, allowing myself a few seconds to recover before forcing myself to straighten up and step away. He stepped back as well, but he, Cai, and Bane were all close by, ready to step in and help if I needed them. The other people on the floor had appeared as well; they stood in a loose ring around us, ready to help and step in if I needed them.

I looked over at Esse, holding Amoth in her arms. Amoth's tendrils waved freely, if clearly in exhaustion. The Mer all clustered around, helping each other to stand. They all reached out and stroked their companion, celebrating in his newfound health. Not one of them appeared jealous of the gift; all simply wished to share their happiness.

I looked from face to face, reading body language as best I could. Glancing from sentient being to sentient being, I could see no boundaries, no distrust between any of them.

My eyes traveled from Cai, a humanoid panther, to Flux, a Mer, a creature clearly adapted to live in the water, to the dwarves, humans, elves, and other species who stood around. There was even the goddamn pacifist giant fucking Ewok-looking dude, whose species I couldn't even remember...They were all obvious in their pleasure, seeing one of their people being healed. Seeing more coming to join our community.

I looked about, and I saw our family growing.

Tommy, you dick, you better be alright...I thought, wishing he was here with us.

CHAPTER SEVENTEEN

I got Ame's attention and drew her aside, asking Cai and Barrett to get the rest of the people settled. I emphasized that the Mer would all need unfettered access to water, and I made a mental note to ensure that their quarters were figured out as a matter of urgency. They'd need the water to rest, after all.

"That was a good thing done there, Lord Jax," Ame said to me quietly. When she continued, there was no heat in her voice, even if she did rebuke me. "Despite you waiting until others could see it all."

I paused before answering her, knowing I was being judged on every word.

"I waited until my mana refilled, but then decided it was better to wait until everyone was here safely, and we could do this properly. I wanted your people to understand that they are part of this community. We will gather everyone together in a few minutes, once the ships have docked, and I'll take the Oath from you all. Once that's done, you, Cai, and I will be going to the Hall of Memories.

"I'll grant you one spellbook and one skillbook. One could be healing based, but I'm going to give you the choice now and some time to think about it. If you really want to learn healing, I'd be over the friggin' moon to give you some healing texts and spells, but I also need a runecrafter, Ame. Hell, I need *everything*." I sighed and scrubbed my hand over the back of my neck as I thought how to phrase this, then just went for it.

"Flux explained some of what a runecrafter can do, and I truly do need that. My people need that badly. I'll give you access to a healing spell, and you can use that to learn, the same way I did, and I'll give you a skillbook for runecrafting, one that can increase your level of ability hugely. Or…I'll give you a single memory crystal, one from a master enchanter.

"If you don't have the skill, you can lose a lot of the knowledge, but from what I can see, enchanting and runecrafting are two sides of the same coin. I think your knowledge will fill in most of the gaps there, and you'd keep more than you'd lose. Take some time to think about it."

There was a long pause as she considered my words.

"The spell you used on me and my companions; you learned this from a spellbook?" she asked me finally.

I shook my head. "No, Oracle and I created the spell together, using knowledge of my past and Oracle's memories of the ancient world, along with a basic healing spell. If you are to learn to help as a healer, you'll have to experiment and teach yourself as much as you will have to teach others to discover runecraft.

"I'll need you to train others up as you promised, and you'll need to explain your runecrafting skill to me as well. There's apparently a way for Oracle to use my memories and knowledge to teach others…but we're just not confident in our ability to do that just yet. We're still figuring it all out, and I don't want to risk magically inflicting memories onto another until we're damn sure about how we do it."

Oracle had been involved in it in the past, she'd told me, but it was always led by an experienced mage, not her, and while we could probably do it? The damage if we failed, especially with my existing brain damage? It was a definite no.

Ame was silent for a long time, and just as I was about to leave her to her thoughts, she spoke again.

"I have decided, Lord Jax. I will take the spellbook and skillbook; I will seek ways to augment my own knowledge with the knowledge of healing magics. I will become the healer you and our people need. I will heal any who need me, but I will also teach others my skill.

"The two skills will complement each other, do not fear. Runecrafting is the art of making a spell into a solid form. A runecrafter is rare; I know of no others in the land now, although my kind rarely have magical skills. A properly created rune can be powered and repowered over and over.

"If you could teach me your healing spell, and I was to figure out a fully functional rune for it, any with mana could power it. The possibilities of runecrafting are matched only by your wits and ability. My manapool is just over four hundred, and I regularly used the entire pool. I say this not to show off, but so you understand that I recognize the signs of mana exhaustion in you. You will rest after this is done, yes?"

"What spells do you know? To make them into runes, I mean, you have to know them as spells, right?" I asked excitedly, nodding to acknowledge her query.

"No," she said flatly, shaking her head. "I was never taught specific spells; I learned to runecraft from my grandmother, as she learned from her mother. I have experimented with my own runes; some worked, some nearly killed me, but I have a greater knowledge of runes than even my grandmother's notes speak of," Ame said proudly.

"Okay, soooo, how many?" I asked.

"Eleven." She sounded unsure whether it was a great achievement or not. "I created three of my own; I also managed to make eight of my grandmother's creations work."

"Okay. So, these…eleven. What can you do with them?" I asked, trying to keep my face straight. I'd hoped for more, but…

"The runes are used in groupings, depending on their use, and can form many different spells. I am versed in Add, Grow, Heat, Mana, Shield, Shock, Slow, Strength, Track, Trigger, and Weaken. I have created runes that create shock or heat damage when weapons harm their targets, increase the strength of the wielder of a particular rune, and many more."

"Magical symbols, basically, then?" I whispered, recognizing the concept. "What about size? Does it matter?" I asked, my brain roaring ahead.

"Well, of course! It takes more mana, and the runes need to be the appropriate size for the intended usage, why?" Ame asked.

"But that's it? What about the runes themselves; do they need to be made of anything in particular?" I demanded, moving on quickly and ignoring her question.

"It depends on the use. Different runes require different reagents, or they use much more mana. Runes can also burn out or fracture."

"What about healing; would healing damage done to a rune remove it or repair it?" I muttered, asking myself more than Ame.

"Healing? You can't heal a rune. It's not alive!" She snorted, then gripped my chin, turning my head to make me face her and pay attention. "You've thought of something, haven't you?"

"Oh, yeah; I'm thinking of a new way to use your runes and wondering if trying it will kill me."

"Explain!" she snapped.

I pulled my head free of her hand, shaking it in negation.

"No; at least, not yet. I want to think about this, and we can experiment to see if it works before I let anyone else know about it. You *will* keep this discussion to yourself, Ame; understand?" I said, glaring at her.

"I...very well. I will keep this between us, but if you want my help to use my life's work, you'll explain this to me, and soon!" she said firmly, receiving an affirmative nod in reply.

"I'm fine with that. Runes don't need a spoken trigger, right? Just mana?" When I got a confused nod in response, I grinned. "Excellent!"

I sought Oracle and found her standing a few feet away. She was watching me, still full-sized. Gliding over to me, she exchanged parting pleasantries with Ame and put her arm through mine casually, guiding us out to the balcony and leading me to the farthest side from everyone, where we could speak freely. Just as she opened her mouth, she narrowed her eyes and pointed to one side, speaking as I followed her finger.

"Get your ass back inside, Bane. This is private time, understand?" Bane straightened up, appearing from stealth and strolled away quickly with an apologetic nod of his head. "We need to talk, but you need to sort that out, as well. I agree you need a bodyguard, but they need to know when we need privacy."

I grinned at her, and before I realized it, I'd leaned in and kissed her, feeling her soft lips against mine. There was a second of hesitation before Oracle responded, having been clearly caught off guard. She wrapped her arms around me, returning my kiss with a fervor that left me breathless when we finally broke away.

I grinned as I gazed into her eyes, then let my vision travel downward, well aware that she didn't need to breathe, so the hurried rise and fall of her spectacular chest was done for one reason, and one reason alone.

To draw my eyes and show me what she wanted me to look at.

I coughed, looking back up at her eyes after a minute of admiring, a minute in which her top slowly but noticeably shrank in size, her exposed cleavage deepening until I'd been forced to look away. My brain, as ever, was short-circuited by the combination of her beauty, her kiss, and her very willing demeanor, so it took a frantic wracking of my brain to remember where I was and what we were doing.

"Soooo, I take it that wasn't why you wanted the privacy?" I asked and got a grin in return.

"Well, it *wasn't,* but now?" she replied.

I laughed in spite of myself. "Okay, come on then; what did you want to talk about?"

"I heard some of what you were saying, and I can sense your surface thoughts, Jax," she said, growing suddenly serious.

"How many of my thoughts?" I asked, thinking back to what had just been in my mind while I enjoyed the view. My question drew a throaty laugh from Oracle, and she patted my cheek.

"Oh, I felt those thoughts, and the mental images..." She looked down first at her cleavage and then at the floor, before eyeing where Mr. Happy was barely constrained by my pants. "That I can definitely, and very happily, do...but that's not why I brought you out here."

She shook her head, becoming all serious as I tried to bring my mind back under control.

"No, Jax...I meant the other thoughts. I don't know if they're possible, but there's only one way you can be sure. You'll need to speak to Jenae, and for the love of all that is light, don't experiment with it until we know." I grinned at her, and she smiled back, leaning in for another kiss. We stood there blissfully, enjoying the feeling of each other's bodies pressed together, the sweet heat of our melding lips, the scent of her filling my mind, until Seneschal spoke, interrupting the moment.

"I hate to interrupt, Jax, but you need to either behave yourself, or accept that Oren and his crew will see far more of Oracle's form than you seemed to want her showing. He's coming in to land now."

I blinked, pulling back from the kiss, and straightened up, removing my hands from Oracle and feeling her hands disengage from me, regretfully. I tried to straighten myself, while her clothing blurred slightly, and she suddenly appeared pristine again.

"That is so not fair," I whispered to her, turning away to rearrange myself out of anyone's sight.

"You started it," she whispered back. "Besides, we can always continue this later...alone." She shrank back down and flew out to buzz around the warship as it approached the huge hangar that was being created for it.

"That sounds good to me," I muttered to myself, conscious she couldn't hear me, but also conscious of the line I was crossing. Going from teasing and her willing offer, to actually taking her up on it, was a very big, irrevocable step. Once it was taken, well...I'd had issues with it, mainly because our bond was for life, and if things changed between us, it could be an exceedingly long problem.

The other side of it, though, was...it could be amazing. Not just the sex, which I had to admit, even if only to myself, I desperately wanted. The companionship was also great; since I'd come here, I'd built relationships like I'd never imagined in my old life.

I wanted Oracle, and I knew she wanted me. The last issue was the bond. I still needed time to get used to the fact that Oracle was permanently bonded to me. She had to obey me, and that left a bad taste in my mouth. I didn't believe that she acted the way she did because she felt she had to, but I had to know.

I'd ask her outright later, then, if it truly was something that she wanted, and she actually had grown to understand what she was asking for, as I suspected she had, then hell yes. I'd try to break her with it.

"They don't call me Tripod for nothing," I muttered to myself, finding I still had a smile plastered across my face as I watched Oren slowly glide the ship inside the tower.

The mast had lowered somehow, and the ship fit in through the widened opening with a few meters to spare on either side. I was certain Jory was sweating like crazy, maneuvering such a huge thing into such a small gap. Then I grinned again at the obvious innuendo, and the fact my brain was still wired up that way from the kisses. I laughed and waved to Oracle as she led the way for Decin's ship, *Libertas*.

She gestured imperiously for him to slow, then stop, hovering in place as Oren and Jory turned the *Agamemnon's Pride* inside the cavernous bay. They slowly backed her into the central berth that had been laid out for her. There wasn't a full scaffolding in place for the ship: hell, there was barely an outline to reference the various berths. But still, Jory managed it, landing with a quiet thump when the engines powered down.

As soon as Oracle saw that the warship was in and settled, she gestured to Decin and slowly led him inside as well.

His ship was considerably smaller and slid in easily, twisting around and settling in the second berth with a light touch.

I strode inside, a smile on my face as I admired the two beautiful ships. They were a little battered, a little beaten, but they'd soon be a lot more than they had been.

Especially with our very own runecrafter to help.

I reached out to all three wisps at once, half expecting an argument over the servitor to still be raging between Heph and Seneschal.

"You all there?"

"I am," Seneschal's smooth, refined voice confirmed.

"Aye, laddie, I be here." Heph sounded gruff as ever, but at least he wasn't yelling.

"Of course!" Oracle chimed in cheerfully.

"Great; it's time to get started on the next stage of the plan. I've had plenty of time to think over the last few days, as well as asking questions of our people. I'm going to take Ame, Oracle, and Cai to the Hall of Memories as soon as we've completed the swearing in, and then I want to get people moving. I'd like you all in the command center in a couple of hours; we've got an operation to plan, repairs to make, and a fight to win."

"Very well."

"No bother, laddie; lookin' forward to it!"

"Sounds like fun!"

They all left my mind, Oracle leaving a slight sense of trepidation and amusement behind. I gestured to Cai as he stood talking to Oren at the foot of the warship's gangplank. The pair of them trotted over, meeting me halfway. I grinned at them and waved to the ships settled in their designated areas.

"It's a hell of a sight, isn't it!" I said, getting a mixed response from them both.

"It's impressive; I'm just glad we managed to get the room cleared enough in time for your arrival," said Cai, while Oren grumped, looking around the room.

"All I'm sayin', laddie, is tha' we could o' fit the *Grace* in right over there…!" I frowned, my gaze following where he pointed, and he growled at me in annoyance. "The *Grace* were ma ship! Tha one ye butchered!"

"Ah, sorry, mate…but thanks to her, we survived, and you got this nice, new, shiny warship, didn't you?" I replied, giving him an apologetic clap on the shoulder.

"Aye, but she be *slow,* laddie. Oh, so slow! She needs the repairs ye promised!"

"How slow is she in comparison?" I asked, and he spat on the floor, getting a glare from me that turned his face white.

"Sorry! Ah…sorry, Jax," he mumbled, pulling a handkerchief from his pocket and wiping it up quickly before going on in a much more respectful tone. "Well, ye see, the issue be that she were built as a heavy scout.

"She be neither something, nor nothin', iff'n ye understand? A scout should be *fast*, nimble; but a 'heavy' is the opposite of whut a scout should be. She be great fer missions away on her own, but she be one o' the first o' a new breed, an' they always be a bit…weird. A tester, iff'n ye will."

"A prototype, we'd have called her. Okay, I get that. So does Barabarattas have more like her?"

"Aye, laddie; Himnel has a full twenty o' her, along wit' two cruisers and one big bastard tha' be in dock, still bein' built."

"Okay, and what about Narkolt?" I asked, wondering at the "big bastard."

"About tha same; they only got four scouts, but eight cruisers. It's less in numbers, but more in firepower, Barabarattas has better defenses around Himnel, so it be a standoff. Both sides send out raidin' parties, fight it out, and flee back," Oren said with a shrug.

"Okay, but if she's built off a scout's design, why do you say she's slow?" I asked.

"Her top speed do be about eighty to a hun'red miles a day. Tha's it, and she be nowhere near that now. She be able to do barely half that; her engines need to be properly fixed, not jus' a swap out o' some parts, an' even then she be beat hands down by the *Grace* or the *Libertas*. They both be makin' a hun'red to a hun'red and thirty a day!" Oren shook his head in exasperation as he looked the warship over, watching the way the engineers were already poking and prodding at her. "I do be needin' to tell them whut to do, an' where to start. How long do we have?"

I considered it and shrugged. I'd been keeping watch all the way back and had only seen a few ships in the far distance, so I knew we had at least two days before even a "fast" ship like Decin's could reach us.

"You've got four days," I said firmly. "That's the maximum, though; you need to post a watch and make sure nobody is coming. If they are, I want the ships able to fly at least twelve hours before anyone can reach us. If nobody comes by the four-day mark, we'll reevaluate it. Is that enough to get much done?"

"Four days? Aye, laddie! We can do a lot wi' tha'!" He grinned widely. "Now, do ye need anythin', or can I…" He gestured towards the engineers and Decin, who'd just come down his own gangplank.

"You can play with the engineers afterward!" I told him, trying not to laugh. "We need to get everyone together to have a swearing in first. Gather Decin and his people together for me, okay?"

"I've already started gathering our people, as well, Jax." Cai nodded over to over a dozen people who were waiting patiently, Isabella amongst them as she spoke to Ame and the other Mer. Even at this distance, I could see her brilliant smile and the way people seemed to congregate around her unthinkingly. I shifted my gaze between Cai and the group as Oren stomped toward Decin, shouting random abuse at him.

"So, how are things with Isabella, then?" I asked him quietly, feeling Oracle as she flew over to sit lightly on my shoulder. Cai started as he realized he'd been staring, and he looked around, making sure Oren was out of hearing before he responded quietly, shooting us a quick smile.

"They are...surprisingly good, Jax, thank you. We are enjoying each other's company. I don't know how things are done where you came from, but here, especially with my kind, we are very cautious with matters of the heart. We have enjoyed meals together, and she assists me with my work. I am...content, and I believe she feels the same way."

"Have you told her how you feel?" I asked him, and he shook his head.

"At this stage, it is too early. We are interested in each other and have both made that clear. Now we wait, we spend time together, and we see what grows from those seeds. It is our way."

"Okay, I get that's *your* way. Is that *her* way, though?" I asked bluntly.

"I—"

"I don't want you to lose her because this isn't the way things are done for her, mate. She's from a small village that was recently raided by an airship who took her as a slave. Some of them were taken and...used...by the assholes on board. She's very beautiful, so you need to be careful. I can't imagine they'd have missed her." I observed the way his ears flattened, and he glared at me. "Whoa, dude. I hope I'm wrong. I'm just saying you need to be aware; she might have issues that—"

"I don't care if she was taken by them! That's not all she is!" he snapped.

"No," I said gently. "No, I don't mean like that. If she was assaulted, all I care about is making sure that she's okay; those that hurt her already got what was coming to them. What I meant was—"

"What Jax meant is that she will need you to understand her, to be patient, but also to show her how you feel," Oracle cut in, clipping me lightly across the back of the head. "He says it terribly, but his heart is in the right place, you know that."

Cai shifted his glare to her for a second before closing his eyes and exhaling slowly. When he opened them, he had visibly calmed, and when he spoke, the anger had been tamped down in his voice.

"I know. I am sorry, Jax, Oracle," he said. "Amongst my kind, things are very different. Some like to have multiple partners, while others do not. Some, like myself, have one and only one, until death separates us, and some maintain harems.

"It is a personal choice, but the one thing that is never accepted amongst us is force. If one was found to have forced another, they become clanless. They are sold to slavers or put to death. The victim is given all the support they need and more, as the entire clan becomes their family, looking out for and protecting them. My father was made clanless for such a crime. The clan raised me and guided me. That I was forced into slavery, too, even if by a crime, will forever stain my soul by association."

"A crime?" I asked him, and he shook his head sadly.

"I was starving. I had been robbed and beaten, left for dead in the streets like the fool I was, and I had no choice. I stole food; I managed to escape a few times, but then I was caught and made a slave."

"Fuck, this conversation took a miserable turn," I said without thinking about it, then I froze as I realized I'd said that aloud. There was a long pause as my brain frantically cast around for a way to take that back…when Cai began to laugh.

"You are subtle as always, my friend!" he said, wiping a tear from his eye. "You are right; it was a depressing topic, and do not fear. I will speak to Isabella, make it clear how I feel, then I will let her make the next move, as the signs I have given her are clear to my race, but perhaps not to a human or an elf."

I drew a deep breath and let it out slowly, shaking my head in relief. "Sorry, mate. That didn't come out as intended. If you want to talk, I'm always here, you know."

Cai nodded his thanks and gestured to the group of people that was slowly growing.

"I know, Jax, and thank you. I suggest we get on with 'swearing them in,' as you put it. Then we have much to discuss."

I nodded at him and smiled.

"You're damn right we do, mate. We're going to take Ame and Oracle, and the four of us are going to choose her path as best as we can, then we're going to choose the best spells and skills to give out to people, and kickstart the tower to life!"

"Excellent! I have a few suggestions as to who would do well with certain skills, although…might we include Isabella? She has been instrumental in creating the list of villagers and their skills."

I paused thoughtfully for a minute; if I allowed her to come along and help to make that decision, I was essentially letting her join the "inner ranks" of my council, but if she was the best person for the job…

"Not right now, Cai. I know she's good at what she's doing, but I'm not ready to have her involved at that level, not in the Hall of Memories directly. We will see for the future. I'd rather not have Ame in there either, but with her skills…she might be more important than she knows."

"Of course, Jax; it was only an idea." Cai forced a smile and nodded his head in acquiescence.

"Okay then, let's get them all together," I said, and Cai nodded again, moving off to gather the stragglers.

"Why don't you want Isabella in the Hall of Memories?" Oracle asked me quietly, and I looked up at her.

"It's not so much about Isabella, as that it's too much, too soon. If Ame is going to be our only magical crafter, and have a second line as a healer, she's going to have a voice on our little council. We're going to need to be very careful about who we bring into that, as it's a position of power.

"We're also going to have to be careful who we *exclude*, as it'll piss people off. For now, Cai, Oren, and Barrett make sense, as they cover each logistical side of things: Cai for resident management and the tower, Oren for the airships and Barrett for the fighters, guards, and soldiers. Once we add in Ame, we'll have a crafter and healer rolled into one as well, but what then?

"Do we have a farmer, someone from each other crafting group we'll need? What about scouts; do they come in separate to the fighters? Hunters? It's growing too fast, and we need a plan," I murmured to her. "I miss when it was just us and Bob."

"I know," she said softly, looking over to where Bob hulked silently off to one side, watching everyone. "I don't think he's happy, you know?"

"Bob?" I asked, surprised, looking over at him.

"Yeah; remember, Jax, you created him, gave him life and a soul, of sorts. He's your guardian, but you've got more people watching out for you now. I don't think he knows what to do with himself.

"He seems fine most of the time, but then…"

I made my way to Bob before she'd even finished her thought. *I wasn't having this!*

"Hey, Bob!" I said as I came to a halt before him, looking up into the glowing sparks of his eyes. Even now, he towered over me, a hulking skeletal creation covered in bone armor, a nightmare to face in a fight. But he was a damn good friend to me, and had been since I'd created him. I wasn't having him feeling discarded, not Bob.

"I'm sorry, buddy; I've been caught up in everything, and I've not given you the time you deserve. I need to ask you a question, though, and I want you to think as hard as you can, okay? Nod once if you understand me." Bob stood motionless for a long while, and just as I was about to speak, he nodded slowly. "That's great. Okay then, Bob, you nod once for yes, and twice for no, okay? Do you understand that?" Again, there was a long break, then he nodded once.

"Whoo boy, I really hope you actually understand me," I muttered, then I straightened up and looked him in the eye sockets. "I need to know if you want to stay with me, if you want to keep doing what you've been doing, acting as my bodyguard and tank in fights. I need you to nod once if you don't want to, then nod twice, okay?"

There was a long pause as Bob seemed to consider, then a nod. I was just about to relax, when he pointed to the side, directly at the people mingling about, waiting on me. I looked over at them, then at Bob, who kept pointing at them, then slowly pointed at me, then at them and nodded firmly again.

"Okay, I've no idea," I muttered, and looked at Oracle, who sat with a huge grin on her face. "What, you get what he means?" I asked her.

She leaped from my shoulder, coming to point to the left of our small group. Bob slowly pointed to me, then to her, then across to the far side at the people gathered there.

"Of course!" Oracle cried out, flying across to land on one of his huge shoulders, leaning in and kissing the polished dome of bone.

"Well don't keep me in fuckin' suspense, Oracle, give me a clue here!" I said, exasperated.

"He wants to be a bodyguard still; he wants to protect you, but he also wants to protect us all!" she said, flying back to hover before me. "Think about it, Jax. His mind is based on your own, and what's the strongest impulse you feel?" A proud smile played on her lips.

"I…I don't know?" I muttered, thoroughly confused.

"It's the impulse that brought you here, the one that drove you through all the dreams you had. It's the one that made you take all these people in and declare war on Himnel and Barabarattas, despite it being 'just you'," she said, flashing to full size and landing gently.

She stepped close, placing her right hand over my heart, and smiling at me, tears welling in the corners of her eyes.

"The need to protect, Jax. You always stand up for those that need it. You'll fight anyone to help those that need a friend, and Bob…?" she said, half turning and reaching out to him. He slowly reached a massive hand out to her, and she patted it, her smile growing even wider.

"Bob feels what you feel; he wants to be a bodyguard, but not just for you. He wants to protect us all; isn't that right?" Oracle said, looking up at Bob. As I watched, he slowly nodded his head a final time, before lifting his right fist and smacking it into his chest in salute, the dull boom echoing back from the vaulted ceilings and around the quiet hall.

"Then that makes things even easier, my friend," I said quietly, smiling up at him. "Thank you. You're going to be busy, though! Come on, let's get this started."

I returned the salute to Bob, and the three of us turned, walking over to where everyone had gathered.

"I'll make sure everyone who hasn't already sworn gets the Oath pushed out to them…and I'll make sure there's enough mana ready for when they swear."

Oracle spoke in the silence of my mind, and I smiled at her, nodding a thanks as we came to a halt before everyone. Not all members of the tower were there, but enough were, and more were trickling in every minute. There were enough here to get started, though, and I began speaking to all who were gathered, waiting on me.

"Thank you all for coming here. I know that some of you have gone through this before, but I think it helps our new recruits to see that you all did the same. We're going to take the Oath now, and after that, you'll be citizens of the Great Tower. Once that's done, we'll get you somewhere to call your own, a job, and we'll get on with the day!"

Oren emerged from the mass of people, assuming what he'd decided his role in all this was.

"Right, you bunch o' buggers! You'll be seein' a notification from th' tower right about now! I want ye all to take a deep breath, and repeat after me:…*I swear…*"

"I swear to obey Lord Jax and those he places over me; I will serve to the best of my ability, speak no lie to him when the truth is commanded, and treat all other citizens as family.

I will work for the greater good, being a shield to those who need it, a sword to those who deserve it, and a warden to the night.

"I will stand with my family, helping one another to reach the light, until the hour of my death or my Lord releases me from my Oath.

"Lastly, I will not be a dick!"

I felt the mana flowing from the tower again, directed entirely by Oracle this time. I'd not been involved at all, beyond being the focal point, and I felt an awareness of their mana streams all joining my own. I could feel where each of them stood in that moment, before the feeling died away. I opened my eyes again, unaware I'd closed them. I smiled at them all, seeing that more had arrived dirty and sweating during the Oath and had rushed to take part, a smile on all their faces.

"I, Lord Jax, do swear to protect and lead you, to be the shield that protects you and yours from the darkness and the sword that avenges that which cannot be saved. As the tower grows in strength, so shall you," I said, ending the Oath and giving them my promise in return, the last threads of magic reaching out from me to touch them all, binding us together.

There was a long, solemn moment that was, of course, interrupted by Oren.

"Right then, ye bunch o' buggers, let's get back to work!" he shouted to the engineers, setting off gleefully towards his ship. Decin started to follow after him, only to be grabbed by the back of his armor by Hanau, who redirected the pair of them over toward me. Ame, Barrett, and Flux followed closely behind, while Cai took the chance to draw Isabella aside for a quick chat.

"Ah, righto, then," Decin said, rubbing the back of his neck self-consciously. He glanced up at Hanau and took his hand when it was offered, looking back at me as though embarrassed. "Ah, well, we, the crew and I, well..."

"What he's trying to say, Lord Jax, is that we'd like to work on the *Libertas* as well as the warship; she still needs work. Is that all right?" Hanau stepped in, looking put upon. I couldn't help but grin as I responded to them both.

"Of course it is; feel free to work on the ship whenever you want, but I'd like her to be ready for a flight in another day. We'll be heading out to check on the village that the warship raided on the way out, and I'd rather not leave our people worrying needlessly, after all. Oren said your ship was a lot faster than his, and it took us five hours to reach the lake, a trip which Oren said would have taken a full day before the repairs were done."

"How long would you say it would take the *Libertas* to reach?" Decin looked at Hanau, and Hanau looked at me with a gentle smile.

"If you hadn't guessed, I also work as navigator on the ship, lord. I'd say about three hours, if we go carefully; two, if we go all out."

"I think I should have just made you captain and had done with it, Hanau," I said, half-jokingly. "I mean really, what does Decin actually do?"

"He's great at making the crew work, and gives amazing back rubs, but yeah, that's about it, in all honesty," Hanau replied, a smile quirking the edge of his lips as Decin started growling.

"Fair enough; I suppose we should leave him as captain then, for now," I said slowly with a straight face, winking at Hanau where Decin couldn't see. "But if he loses his edge any more..."

"Don't worry, Lord. If he doesn't give me a backrub on time tonight, you'll know about it."

"...And you'll be captain from tomorrow," I finished for him, as Decin elbowed him in the thigh and glared up at me.

"Ye better be careful there, laddie, or he'll be looking to trade up fer a tower next!" he grumped, and Hanau and I laughed. He couldn't help himself, joining in after a few seconds, before the pair walked away together, calling their ship's crew over and arguing good naturedly with Oren over the allocation of engineers. I turned to address Ame, Barrett, and Flux, who had been standing nearby and waiting patiently.

199

"Okay, then, it's time for a serious look at skills and spells. Ame, you'll be coming with Cai and myself to look at the options. Flux, Barrett, what do you need?" I asked.

Barrett spoke up quickly. "It's not much, Jax, but the addition of Flux's team makes a huge difference to our forces; also, they're skilled hunters and scouts. I want permission to spread them out amongst my people and the hunters, and I want to start sending them out to explore the surrounding area, maybe bring back some fresh meat."

"Are you good with that, Flux?" I asked him, receiving a nod in confirmation. "Then that's fine. Keep a team close by, so we have some fighters in the tower at all times but start pushing the teams out in a rotation to explore the surrounding area. Also…" I turned and beckoned to Bob, who stepped forward. "Bob here wants to take a more active role in defending our people, so perhaps you could plan to integrate him into the groups going forward?" Barrett blinked, then grinned at Bob.

"That would be amazing, but can you do that? I thought you could only communicate with Jax and Oracle?" Bob stood still for a minute, long enough for the excited smile to start to fall from Barrett's face, before the skeletal minion pointed at him and slowly nodded.

"What he means is that he can communicate with others. It's not as clear or as simple as when Oracle or I give him direction, but he can understand. Essentially, make the orders as simple as you can.

"He understands that 'yes' is one nod, and 'no' is two, so tell him what you want, carefully, and ask if he understands. We only just realized he could respond like this, so go slow, but try it and see how it works." I felt a little sad that Bob would be out fighting without me, but I was also proud of him.

"Okay…yeah, we can make this work!" Barrett said, his smile back as he clapped the skeletal construct on one armored shoulder, having to stretch to reach it.

"Be careful with him, though. If he dies, he's dead and gone, understand?" I said firmly, "Don't risk him for no reason."

"I won't," Barrett said, nodding soberly. "I know Bob is there to help, not to do all the work, and I'll make sure everyone understands that. He's there to protect us if we need him."

"Exactly," I said, and Flux and Barrett saluted, deep in discussion before they'd gone a handful of steps. Bob looked to me, nodded once, and followed them.

"They grow up quickly," Ame said. I turned to regard her, one eyebrow quirked quizzically. "Our children; I've heard it said they grow up quickly, and judging by the way you look at that creature, you obviously created it yourself."

"I did. Well, no, I summoned and built him. I gained the option of sentience for him, and as he grows over time, he becomes more self-aware, so I suppose he's his own as much as he's 'mine'…ah, fuck it." I shook my head, dismissing the confused thoughts of Bob's sentience and looked over at Ame. "You ready for this?"

"I have never been more ready for anything in my entire life," she stated quietly.

"Glad to hear it. We're just waiting on Cai; he's confirming a few details with Isabella, so why don't you go over and wait with him? I need to speak to someone, so as soon as you're both ready, head up to the Hall of Memories together, okay? He knows the way." She nodded and walked over to him as Oracle and I set off toward the stairs.

"Where are we going?" she asked me.

I shot her a grin. "Well, there's one more person we need to speak to, remember, about both the runecrafting and about the healer...Jenae!"

Oracle smiled back at me, twisting her flight into a roll in midair and heading for the stairs, well aware both that I intended to relax a bit in the Hall while I spoke to her and that I was getting a terrific view of her legs and cleavage as she flew around me. *The teasing little sod...*

It didn't take long to jog up the stairs to Oracle's old home, and we strode in, relaxing as the crystal doorway closed behind us. Oracle had resumed her full size, and the sight of both her naughty smile and the little black cocktail dress she'd summoned from somewhere was hugely distracting. I took a seat on one of the sofas, and she hopped up to sit on the arm of the one opposite me, showing an incredible amount of tanned leg in the process.

I groaned and closed my eyes, well aware that she was getting exactly the result she wanted. When she laughed, I reopened my eyes, and she had shifted again, back to her diminutive usual form and dressed in jogging bottoms and a halter top. It wasn't covering her as much as that outfit would any other woman. She'd somehow altered it to stick like rubber in places, but it was a lot less distracting than she had been a few seconds before, at least.

"You just do that to get a rise out of me, don't you?" I asked her, getting a grin in return. "Thought so. Okay, I'm going to talk to Jenae."

I closed my eyes and drew in a deep breath, pulling mana in and concentrating. I felt it build and build, until I was sure there was enough. For the second time, I imbued it with Jenae's name, and a sense of who she was. I knelt, pressing the knuckles of my right fist flat against the ground and my left to my chest and released it.

There was a soundless wave of pressure that spread out from me, and a second later, the sense of her presence was there, filling my mind.

"Jax, you called to me?"

"Hi, Jenae. I wanted to ask a few questions, if that's okay?" I asked her, getting a sense of amusement back through the contact as she replied. I stood up, moving back to my seat.

"You may ask, Jax; I'll answer what I can, but if it involves specifics, I can't, and you understand that you'll have to use the boon I granted you?"

"I do. Look, I'll just tell you what I need to know, and you answer what you can, okay?"

"That seems sensible. Go ahead."

"Ame, a runecrafter from the Mer village, has joined us. However, she also wants to learn some healing...I need to know if she's a good choice for the healer we need. I need to know how we can get runes from spells, and I need to know if Tommy is still alive...Anything you can tell me about those, first?" I asked her, conscious that there was one more question I needed to ask.

"As far as Ame is concerned, that's a choice you need to make. Magical aptitude is different among the races of the UnderVerse. The Tia'Almer-atic are rarely gifted with any use of magic beyond their natural uses in camouflage, but those who do have it tend to be powerful.

"I would, however, suggest that you think on it very hard. Runecrafting is a rare art, and to have an extremely skilled individual give it up to become a healer? Consider well. Also, runes are specific magic and can be hugely powerful. They are, however, a form of crafting...*and as such, perhaps researching something in the Constellation of Secrets would help you. That's all I can say on that, unless you want to use the boon?"*

"Gotcha. I'll have a think, and I'll save the boon. Thanks, Jenae...and my brother?" I asked cautiously.

"I have seen no sign of him yet. I am sorry, Jax."

"Okay then, there's one last question I need to ask..."

CHAPTER EIGHTEEN

A few minutes later, I heard the muffled sound of a fist banging on the crystal doorway to the room. Having just finished my conversation with Jenae, I'd been idly admiring the view as Oracle contrived excuses to show as much flesh as possible while pretending she was doing no such thing. We'd both started to get entirely too interested in the game, and the arrival of Ame and Cai threw some much-needed cold water on our increasing ardor.

I concentrated, and the door vanished just as Cai tried to knock again. I had to grin as the usually reserved catman staggered and let out an involuntary yelp of surprise.

"Hi Cai, Ame," I greeted them, standing up and gesturing for them to come inside. They both entered cautiously, looking around the room with eyes and sensing-tendrils wide in shock, the true wealth of the Great Tower on display.

"I—I never would have believed…" Ame whispered, slowly turning around, gaping at the book-covered shelves, the beautiful carpets and seating, and most of all, the hundreds of memory crystals where they lay in their individual niches.

Cai was having a similarly hard time as he attempted to stare everywhere at once. I'd never get anywhere with them in the state they were in now.

"Both of you can have a quick look around before we start. I can see I'm not going to get anything from you until you've had that, at least!" I said, returning to my seat and closing the door. I concentrated as a stray thought crossed my mind, and I began looking around the room carefully, until I spotted him. Crouched down, almost invisible against the wall beside a bookcase, was Bane. I'd not seen him enter, and I'd damn well certainly not invited him along to this meeting.

"Bane," I said flatly, and he straightened up, his reflexive camouflage relaxing as he arose.

"Yes, Jax?" he asked, and I shook my head.

"Bane, you're a great friend, and a hell of a bodyguard, which I can see already, but you don't need to be this close all the damn time. I need privacy, and when I call a meeting somewhere like this, unless I invite you, I don't expect you to be here, okay? We're in a sealed location in the center of the Great Tower. This is literally the most secure place we have; I don't need to be guarded here!"

"That's exactly how I'd want you to feel if I was an assassin," he said stoically.

"What?" I asked, my train of thought derailed by the assertion, and I paused, letting him continue.

Jez Cajiao

"If I was going to kill you, I'd want you to believe you were in the safest place you could be, so you'd let your guard down and get rid of your bodyguards," Bane continued.

I shook my head again. "Okay, look, mate, I'm going to be in here for a while, then I'm going to be in the tower for the next two days, probably. A day, at the least. I don't need you in here, so please, go explore, relax and pick out quarters, do whatever you want...*except guarding me!"* I added as I saw him start to return to the corner where he'd been hidden. He stopped and stood there for a long minute, and I sighed, giving in a little.

"Look, Bane, seriously, I'm safe here, and even if I wasn't, you can't guard me literally around the clock. It'll drive us both insane. Go explore; if you want to find something useful to do, you could go out and kill something we can add to the food stores, or hell, explore the local area.

"There could be all sorts of things to find out there; we haven't explored any of it yet. Just go, okay?" Bane hesitated for a second then clapped a fist in salute and headed to the door. I opened it and let him out, breathing a sigh of relief when the door had fully closed, and I wasn't being watched over anymore.

"You know he's right, don't you?" Ame spoke from right behind me, making me jump.

"Fuck's sake, Ame! Not you, too," I said, shaking my head and sitting back down.

"He has a point, though; if an assassin wanted to get to you, this would be ideal. After all, you've trapped yourself in here now with me, and how well do you really know me?"

I grinned back. "I killed a fucking SporeMother alone and cleared this entire tower before I even met any of you; how well do you really know *me*?" I asked, forcing my grin to take on a hard edge. She took a step back, the instinctive fear of creatures she'd heard tales about all her life coming to the fore.

"Exactly," I said, sitting back in my seat and looking at her. "I try to be nice to people, Ame, and I try to be patient, but remember, I'm the one who fought the creatures from your nightmares. I'm also the one who will do it again.

"I might act kind, but if I have to, I will fuck up anything that threatens me or my people." My voice was hard, cold, and Ame stepped back again, aware of the change in the air between us. Before it could grow too intense, I straightened and gestured to the seat across from me, letting a softer smile return to my face. As she stepped between other furniture and took the seat offered, she nodded to me with respect.

"I understand. Best to show the steel under the glove sometimes." It was all she said, but we both understood. When Cai moved out from between the shelves to join us, I could tell he'd witnessed the interaction as well. I felt a touch self-conscious about it, but it needed to be done.

"So, Cai, Ame, we're going to start a plan today to use the tower resources properly. There's a risk to using too many spellbooks and skillbooks in a short time; you both know this, right?" I asked and got a snort from Ame.

"Of course! Everyone knows that," she said, and I winced as I shook my head.

"Yeah, well, nobody where I came from told me that, so I'll be clear about this. I used eight spellbooks and a handful of skillbooks, to get to where I am now. When I tried to use another, it backfired, opening a series of wounds in my brain and damaging other areas in here." I tapped my forehead lightly as I made eye contact with them both, noting their shock over the amount that I'd used.

"Jenae, our patron goddess, has told me that there are specialization paths for healers, much as there are for all professions. A 'reconstructor' is the specialization I'd need our healer to take. However, the thing is, Ame…that's not going to be you."

"What?" she demanded.

"You're not going to be the tower's healer, Ame," I repeated, shaking my head. "Don't get me wrong, I think you probably could become one, if you really wanted to, and you'd probably be amazing at it; I accept that.

"The thing is, though, you'd need to spend a fuck-load of time training up a replacement runecrafter for us, since someone as skilled as you could make huge improvements to the tower, to our weapons, hell, you could do all sorts of things. It makes no goddamn sense to retrain you, and have you retrain someone else to take your place, all so you can be a healer.

"Tell me truthfully: do you actually want to give up runecrafting and spend all that time retraining to be a healer? Or are you afraid of the darkness you were trapped in, and you just want to make sure that doesn't happen again?"

Several minutes passed in silence before Ame sighed heavily.

"I wanted to make sure it doesn't happen again; that's all. I loved being a runecrafter," she admitted, sitting back, and seeming to relax for the first time since I'd met her.

"Glad to hear it," I said, smiling. "To be clear, I'm not saying no to you learning healing magic, or any magic. Instead, I'm going to give you one spellbook, and one skillbook. The skillbook will be for your runecrafting, and the spell will be healing. I know I'd suggested enchanting, but that was before I'd had time to look at things, and before Oracle and Jenae explained the realities of life. If you find you like healing, and you want to go that way, then great.

"You can help, as there's always going to be a need for healing magic here, I think. I'll also want you to take on at least one apprentice, as I think your runecrafting skills are going to be massively in demand. Lastly, I'll need you to help me with a little side project." Almost on cue, Oracle approached, the books we'd discussed in her hands, and she laid them on the table between us before disappearing into the depths of the hall again.

"One last point," I said as Ame reached out tentatively for the books, and she froze. "I've also spoken to Jenae about the runecrafting. She's informed me that there's a way for us to learn the runes for spells through her, so eventually, my Battlefield Triage spell, the one that Oracle and I used to heal you and rebuild your body in several places, will be able to be made into a rune."

With that revelation, Oracle put two more books down on the other side of the table, and Ame gasped in shock as she identified them. A single memory crystal had also been set down with the pair of books.

"Now, you need to choose, Ame, as you know far more about your skills and path than I ever will. The two spellbooks are Lay On Hands, which allows you to heal others through physically touching them, and will teach you the basics of healing magic. Identify allows you to gather information on whatever you're looking at.

"I've found that channeling additional mana into Identify can be hugely beneficial when you need to know about a target. The memory crystal is from a master runecrafter from before the cataclysm, so I'd imagine there's a lot of knowledge there that can help you. The two skillbooks are firstly for Mana Coalescence, which will allow someone with the required skill to create a solidified mana crystal, in any shape they desire.

"It'd take a while, but with your manapool, you could literally create perfect runes with this skill once you'd leveled it up. The second skillbook is called Mysteries of a Runic Mind and apparently teaches the theory behind runecrafting." I shrugged and leaned forward. "I'm sure you know a lot of the theory already, and have most of the knowledge this could teach you, but these skillbooks are both journeyman level. As such, I have to think they'll be able to provide you with some kind of benefit." I watched Ame as she moved her head from side to side, a low *thrummm* filling the air as she examined the items minutely using her worldsense. Her tendrils danced in weird, slightly disturbing patterns.

"What is this?" she asked me eventually, sitting back hesitantly. "You are aware of the damage that absorbing too many spellbooks can cause, so this is what? A test?" Annoyance clearly tinged her tone, mixed with desire.

"No," I said honestly. "It's not a test at all. All of these are available to you, although I'll stop you if you try to take them all at once; that's true. I want you to make a choice of which you want...Oracle?"

"We've discussed your path between us, Ame," Oracle chimed in, returning from the depths of the shelves and taking up the conversation at my invitation. "The thing is, though, I don't know a great deal about your species or your limits, and the only person who knows what's truly best for you...is you." She smiled and sat next to me, gesturing to the contents of the table.

"We'd like you to choose what you wish to learn. I would recommend the memory stone last of all, and it is true that there are other books, both magical and skill based in here, but these are the ones that we feel would suit you best at this time, based on the knowledge we have."

"I think a mixture would suit you best, personally," I said picking up the conversation again. "I'd choose the healing spell, as with it, you can aid our people. It is a very basic spell and can only heal basic injuries. It'll save a life, don't get me wrong, but it'd take a long time and a hell of a lot of mana to do any more than low level healing with it.

"I included Identify, as it would enable you to examine people and objects. I believe over time, you'd be able to use these two spells together to improve your ability to heal hugely. This would only really help you if you wanted to focus on being a healer as well, though. The Mana Coalescence skill will enable you to form physical objects of pure mana, essentially forming mana crystals at will. Oracle has told me, however, that a huge amount of mana is needed to make even small objects, so your manapool of four hundred will be used damn quick."

"However, being able to create a pure crystal in any shape you desire, and eventually make it entirely flawless?" Oracle cut in, quirking an eyebrow at Ame, whose fingers flexed involuntarily.

"My runecrafting would be both far cheaper and far more powerful," Ame admitted.

"Exactly," Oracle replied, then reached out and tapped the final book with one perfect fingernail. "Lastly, the Mysteries of a Runic Mind…this is a theory book, which means you'll quite possibly know many of the details in it already.

"However, training delivered by one person, who passes it to the next, as you said your training was given, may have missed important details. This, while only a theory book, covers the basics of all aspects of runecrafting, including how to make new runes."

"So this book could teach you either a way to discover hundreds of new runes, or a lexicon of them, or it might teach you nothing you don't already know," I said. "As I say, this needs to be your choice."

There was a long minute of silence as I watched her, seeing the way the tendrils twitched and feeling the low-level constant *thrummm* of her senses working on overdrive.

"I want *you* to choose, Ame, so please, take your time and think. You can take two books or the memory crystal. Whatever you leave will be available for you to use at a later date, should you want to, so there's no rush. I'd recommend leaving the crystal for now, until you're sure you will be able to use it to its maximum potential."

Ame sat for several long minutes, reaching out to touch the books twice, lightly caressing them with the tips of her fingers. Her black claws were gentle as they brushed the leather bindings, almost reverent. She touched the crystal just once, as though to confirm it was real, before looking up at me.

"I may never forgive you for forcing me to make this choice, but I'll also never pay off the debt that I earn by accepting this gift and receiving your healing already. I will be the one that you and our people need. I will be the runecrafter of the Great Tower. I will be worthy of this." With that, she selected two of the books from the table, and Oracle stepped in to remove the others and the memory crystal, setting them back in their places on the shelves.

"What books did you take?" asked Cai, and Ame spoke softly as she looked them over. The blue bindings on both books were as pristine as the day they were made, protected by the magic of the tower for centuries, the golden and silver embossing's glittering as she spoke.

"This spellbook is Lay On Hands, which allows the user to heal any person they touch for twenty points of damage over sixty seconds, while the skillbook is Mysteries of a Runic Mind. There must be a reason you suggested these?" she asked.

"There is. I only know one healing spell that was taught to me. The spell that I used on you and your people is one that Oracle and I created, and it is only through constant use that it has evolved into as powerful a version as you have experienced. I think that, between us, Oracle and I can guide you to use Lay On Hands to create your own more powerful version.

"Also, it's a spellbook that is supposedly fairly simple. It's not as likely to fuck your brain up, and hopefully you can use the theory skillbook to make a runic version of it. I'd like you to try to make a hospital area with these runes in bays, ready to be activated if our people need healing, until we can get a real healer for the tower, anyway.

"Add to that creating runes that cleanse the area of disease and accelerate healing would be fantastic. Once you've had some time to absorb these books, Oracle and I will attempt to teach you the spell we created. It might not work, but she tells me there's a much better chance of us being able to teach it if you've already learned some healing magic…if you want us to try and teach you?"

"Very well, but also…hospital area?" Ame asked, clearly confused.

"Yes, in my…land…a place where the injured were gathered together was called a hospital. They would receive treatment there. I intend for us to make the same thing here," I said, and Oracle surprised me by speaking up as she returned to sit next to me, still full-sized.

"Think of it by whatever name you wish, Ame. Jax is used to hospital, and the wisps remember various terms, such as valetudinarium. What did your people call such a place?"

"We had a healer's hut, that was all. Without a magical healer, there was a member of the pod who made potions and cleansed wounds, but it was well known that she was too low a level to earn the bonuses that a village could gain from such a building."

"Bonuses?" I asked, and everyone turned to me. "Okay, clearly another thing I should know, but I don't. Make it quick, please?"

"Different buildings can grant bonuses to a village or city. A healer's hut, as Ame explained, would have granted bonuses to the entire village if the healer in residence had been a high enough level. The plans we have for the tower included some variations for healers; we had rooms, floors, and entire sections as options, with dedicated growing areas for the medicinal plants and other requirements they had. Or they would have had, once we'd been fully inhabited, anyway," Oracle said, looking sad. I sat dumbfounded.

"You've got plans for these things? That we could be building in the tower right now?!" I asked, shock lacing my voice.

"Ah, no. Sorry, Jax," Oracle said apologetically, turning to me and holding her hands up to forestall my barrage of questions. "We have plans for the tower; there were other Great Towers, after all, and we have the plans from each.

"In theory, we could make anything you wanted; we've discussed the malleability of the tower structure before, after all. The issue we have is that the various buildings and specializations can't be built when the tower is in this condition. There was a tower magus long…well, *exceptionally long* ago now, and he forced his tower to begin altering itself while it was still growing.

"He altered the magical construction to such a degree that it warped, the tower collapsed, and the surrounding area was devastated, as the mana used to grow something like this is, well, a lot." She shook her head, staring far into the past. "The emperor was furious; so many died. Due to the loss of the tower, additional legions needed to be brought in to stabilize the area. There was a war going on at the time, and the resulting movements of troops, well…let's just say, it didn't go well. All because the magus wanted 'his' tower to be more opulent and to grow his quarters first. The emperor issued a commandment to all future buildings, one that his magical architects wrote into the programming of each spell creation.

"There can be no focused growth, no access to designs, and no additional bonuses earned until the tower is at ninety percent complete."

"Yeah, but the tower is complete, it's just—"

"No, it's classed as 'derelict' now, Jax. Until the repairs move along, the best we can do is build the features we want ourselves. We can build a healer's hut—well, rooms, I suppose—and we will gain some bonuses from having that, provided we build it ourselves. If you want access to the plans for the tower that we had, and to use the tower's mana to construct them, we need to repair the tower from 'derelict' to 'damaged,' at the very least."

"What do we need to do to reach that?" I asked. Oracle closed her eyes for a second before the small pool of mana that she'd been reborn in began to bubble up. In a few short seconds, Seneschal stood there, a foot-tall figure clad in shining silvery scale mail, a reflective helm covering his face, and a long black cloak that swirled in an imaginary breeze as he nodded to each of us before speaking.

"Oracle has made me aware of your questions, Jax; do you wish me to answer them here?" he asked. I nodded, having no concerns about the pair before me knowing any such details.

"Very well. The Great Tower is currently at approximately sixty-seven percent integrity. To use the plans and reconstruct floors to maximum efficiency, we require the tower to reach structural integrity of ninety percent. Understand that this is integrity, and reflects the outer and load-bearing structure, not cosmetic or internal enhancements.

"This will take a minimum of eight months to reach at the current speed of repair. If we created more golems and used them exclusively on the repairs, it would drop significantly. But that would change, depending on how many golems we had access to. All I can guarantee is that, as things stand right now, it will be eight months."

"Okay. How long if we gained another couple of the servitors like the one I brought in today? You could map out the locations of the old waystations, and I could find them, right?" I asked.

"Each additional servitor that was class three, or complex, and above would bring an additional seven percent to the overall total. If you found two and gave me exclusive use of the one you brought today, that would cause a twenty-one percent increase in repair speed.

"Add in three more general use golems to provide assistance with tasks such as clearing and placement of stones, and we would cut the total from eight months to perhaps five. That would be the most likely scenario. Some waystations had more golems, but they also may have been destroyed entirely."

"Yeah, I might spend days searching and find fuck-all, or I might find dozens. Okay, this conversation has gone wildly off-topic, and as much as it's useful information, it's no use right now."

"Perhaps this would be a good time to discuss the best use of the level three serv—" Seneschal began, and I lifted a hand to stop him.

"No. At least not right now. We can talk about that after this is dealt with, Seneschal," I said. "Ame, I want you to read those books, absorb the knowledge, and tell me truthfully if you feel you can accept another book without damaging yourself. Better to be safe than sorry right now. Then I want you to consider what you've learned. You can take either the second spellbook or skillbook whenever you feel you can handle it.

"The memory crystal will only be given once we have a resident healer, and they and Oracle agree you are ready to use it safely. Lastly, I'll be talking to you later about that additional project. It's more of a concept at the minute than anything else, but Jenae has assured me it's possible, if slightly insane."

Ame nodded and stood, recognizing that she was being dismissed, and she was clearly ready to get to work. I waved to her and opened the door, closing it after her, and turned to Cai.

"Okay, mate, I know you've been itching to discuss what you've found, so hit me with it."

"You choose the strangest phrases, my friend," Cai said, shaking his head and pulling a small booklet out of a pocket. "I took this from the warship; it's made things a lot easier. You don't mind, do you?" I shrugged and he went on. "Good. Making notes is much easier than trying to remember everything and everyone's names. So…"

"Ah, you've got everyone in there?" I asked cautiously, my heart sinking.

"Yes, Jax, the entire population of the tower," Cai said proudly, "And I've made notes on their skills, their aspirations, and where I think they'd be best utilized."

My worst fears were realized as Cai flicked through the book, showing me page after page filled with tiny, cramped notes. This was going to take forever!

"Ah…wonderful," I said, forcing a smile.

"It wasn't easy, I can promise you, but I think you'll find it was worth it."

CHAPTER NINETEEN

I t was nearly five hours later when I realized that my brain had totally shut down, and I'd been staring at Cai blankly while he spoke. I'd been lost in the pleasant daydream of banning all paperwork forever, when Cai stopped and looked at me.

He was clearly waiting for something.

"Ah, that's…great?" I tried, and the frown I got let me know I'd totally buggered that one up.

"What's great, Jax?" he asked, and I frantically cast about, trying to remember his last words. After a minute of obvious struggling, I gave up, sitting upright and looking Cai straight in the eyes.

"Okay, mate, I'll be honest. I totally zoned out there; the infodump was just too much. Sorry, man."

"What?"

"I…I'm sorry, Cai. The massive amount of information was just too much for me to absorb. I was paying attention, I just drifted for a minute. So, any chance you have a summary for me? Recommendations?" I asked hopefully, and Cai snorted, shaking his head.

"Jax, the last half-hour *was* the summary."

"Oh…"

"Okay, then," Cai said, letting out a rueful little laugh as he looked at the book in his hands. "I suppose it is a lot of information. How about I give you the short, short version?"

"Thank you, Cai, that would help," I said gratefully.

"Okay," he said, quickly sorting through a couple of pages and marking them for quick reference. "I'd suggest we split the farmer group. There's ten now in total, including Amoth, one of the Mer who've joined us. I recommend keeping six as dedicated farmers and asking four to become gatherers and growers.

"One of the people from the group overall could be chosen to train in magic that will help, if you have any." He looked at me as though to make sure I was listening. I nodded, holding up a hand, and turned to where Oracle had made herself comfortable on the end of one bench.

"Oracle, what spells, skillbooks, or memories do we have that would help? Narrow it down to the most appropriate three, please, and choose ones that we can afford to give out to help them grow. We won't be using the higher ones for a while yet." Oracle smiled at me and dove into the shelves, rushing from one to another and checking titles, pulling a book here and there only to replace them a second later. It took less than a minute, all told, then she was back with us, three books in hand.

"Okay, this is a spellbook called Nature's Boon; it enhances the growth of any plants inside the casting area by ten percent, it lasts three days, and it can be stacked up to five times over before it expires. The second spellbook is called Gizmo's Growth and gives a chance for exponential growth, provided there's enough water in the surrounding area.

"This spell can be recast every two days, needs a hundred mana per cast, and gives a ten percent chance to create five more plants similar to the first with each casting…There's a warning at the back of the book, though, something about not letting them get too wet, but it's unclear."

She shrugged, put the first two books down, and moved to the third and final. "This is a skillbook, called A Time to Sow, which teaches the skills any good farmer needs. It covers the various soil types, what kind of plants grow best where, and how to take cuttings and increase their yield. We've only got one copy of the skillbook and of Gizmo's Growth, but we have three of Nature's Boon."

"Okay, then, who do you recommend for each of these, Cai?" I asked.

He spoke up right away. "I'd suggest that Timoth be given the skillbook, as he'll retain more than any other. As the highest skilled, and only professional farmer we have, he'll be in charge of the entire group, for now at least. D'rin would do well with Gizmo's Growth; she's the halfling and has the highest Intelligence of any of the farming group.

"Tel has the second highest and is particularly interested in herbs and learning some of the alchemical side of things, so I'd suggest giving him Nature's Boon. He can split his time between working with the growers and working with Esse, the Mer herbalist."

"Sounds good to me," I said, pushing the stack to one side and deliberately not referring to Esse as the 'merbalist'.

"Make sure they understand these come with the expectation that when they get skilled enough in their use, they'll teach others."

"Of course. When is that, usually?" Cai asked, and I turned to Oracle.

"It depends on the individual, but most can teach a spell they know to another after they've reached level twenty in that spell. It's a basic version that can be taught; the student always gets a weaker spell than the teacher, as they don't understand the little bits that the teacher knows instinctively. The only way to learn a spell as the caster knows it is to have the caster create a spellbook, and learn it from there, as the caster must pour all their knowledge into a spellbook."

"Wait, so when I teach Ame our Battlefield Triage spell, she'll only get a weak version of it?" I asked, and Oracle nodded.

"The spell she learns will have the same basic capabilities, but the overall spell we use is compounded by our joint knowledge, so ours will do more than she can with it. The greatest spells are always self-created. Those learned from others, even if from spellbooks, are always another's knowledge grafted onto you, and some bits just don't stick."

"Crap. Okay then, I guess we can leave it at that for now for the farmers. Who else are we looking at today?" I asked Cai.

"Warriors," he said bluntly, flipping to another section. "They can be a lot more expensive to train. I've spoken to Barrett, and he's told me about his training. It seems the best way to teach a group of warriors is by a warrior, basically. If a soldier is trained to teach their skills, then they can, over time, teach a group to use them as well.

"That's common sense, I know, but certain abilities, such as Recover or Charge can also be taught, provided the trainer is a high enough level in both teaching and in the skill needed. I'd suggest we talk to various fighters, mainly Barrett and the Mer, and see what abilities they have."

Oracle moved out from the shelves again, carrying a single small black skillbook. I glanced at it and nodded to her in approval.

"I suppose we might as well include this for now. We have several skillbooks on fighting styles, mainly armed, but some unarmed as well. As soon as we can get things a bit more secure here, and get my brain fixed, I'm going to use at least one of these books, and begin giving classes.

"It'll be a small cadre at first, probably only to three or four people, but they'll then assist me as we teach more. While I want everyone to be able to fight primarily with a weapon of their choice, I also want everyone to be able to defend themselves. Unarmed Combat is about learning to fight without relying on anything else.

"In my world, I studied a lot of different arts over the years, and many taught you to take the enemy's weapon and use it on them. I want everyone that lives here to be able to do that and more. I won't have them being victims, not again."

"I believe you will have a lot of volunteers for that, Jax," Cai said quietly.

"I hope so, my friend. Now, Barrett and Flux; I know they've both got a background in fighting, and some training. Has either of them got any experience—"

"Flux has experience both in training small groups and in teaching particular fighting styles," Cai interrupted me with a smile. "He's actually asked when you train, as I think he's decided he's going to help you."

"Oh crap," I muttered, having seen Flux fight. While I had a lot to learn, I also just knew training under Flux would be painful. Everything he did had an economy of movement that was just beautiful and terrifying to watch. If he was a machine, fighting simply and perfectly, regular, exact movements, and all...I was more of a pissed-off cat, full of hissing, spitting, manic energy.

"Yes, he asked me to tell you to be sure to meet him after you're done to discuss training together, and that he was looking forward to payback for leaving him to 'that woman.'" At that, Oracle burst out laughing before covering her mouth quickly and trying to pretend she'd done no such thing.

"This is gonna fucking hurt, isn't it?" I muttered, dropping my head into my hands and shaking it slowly. "Just when I had gotten free of the training, as well. Dammit. Okay then, I guess I'll speak to him myself about training our people and teaching them some skills."

"I imagine so, yes...moving on!" Cai said with a wide smile on his face, and I glared at him. "I think the crafting group is next. We have a lot of my former fellow slaves that have expressed an interest in learning to craft. Some, such as Elan and Frank, will be useful, as they wish to set up a tanning and leatherworking area between them.

"With Milosh being a leatherworker already, I think they will make a good group, once the hunters begin bringing in skins for them to work on. I'd suggest kinning primer for them if you have one?" Oracle spun away and returned quickly with a pair of skillbooks that covered the basics. I ordered that one be kept back and passed him the other.

"Okay, I'll ensure the right person gets this. The other crafts are mainly ones they can learn the basics of themselves, such as woodworking or ones we would be better off waiting on. The trip to recruit from the village might save us from using a valuable skillbook on someone less suited to it.

"The only group that I'd still like you to consider, though, is the engineers. They have pledged loyalty and are highly skilled individuals, but most of them are self-taught. The mana engines and other flight systems of the airships are constantly being refined, as they've only been really in use for the last twenty or so years. Do you have anything that might be useful to them?"

Oracle had already gathered an armful of books and was staggering over with them.

"Well, we will soon see, I guess," I said, getting up and helping Oracle with the stack. "Also, before we get into this, I need an artist. Do we have any?"

"What kind of artist?" Cai asked, a little nonplussed.

"Someone who's great at drawing and painting, preferably," I said with a grin.

He frowned in thought, nodding slowly. "I think I might have just the person; why?"

"Just a little secret side project. Not sure if it will work yet, but I'm going to give it a go. You sort out the artist for me and send them my way, okay?"

"Very well. So, to the engineers?" We both turned back to the pile of books. I sorted through them, putting the more advanced volumes aside to return to later and narrowing it down to three that I was both interested in seeing what the engineers could do with, and very wary of letting go.

"These are the only copies we have of these skillbooks, and they're all fairly advanced. Journeyman skills, each of them," I said, looking from one to another.

"True, but giving them these books? You'll have them for life, that's for sure," Cai said, shaking his head slowly as he read and reread the titles.

"That's one point, but I'm considering their long-term usefulness at least as much as their loyalty," said Oracle, separating out the books and naming them from left to right. "We've got Magical Structures, Overpowered Engines, and Secrets of Mana and Metal. The first is a basic guide on producing magical structures; it should be helpful to any of the engineers, but mainly the general ones, I think.

"The second, despite the name, is not really appropriate for the engines. It's the second in a series of five books around siege weapons, and it deals exclusively with the basic magical siege weapons. The authors didn't include information on magical cannons in this volume, but I'm thinking whatever knowledge they did provide could be used to improve the ship's weapons?

"Last of all is Secrets of Mana and Metal. It's another one from a series, and it deals with using various metals to conduct mana, amongst other things. The series is aimed at enchanting and making magical weapons more than anything else, but Elaine, the magical systems engineer, might be able to make the best use of this…"

I looked over the pile of skillbooks off to one side and back at these three. Each was the only one of their kind, and I didn't think they'd be easy to replace. Neither did I think they should be hoarded forever, as they'd be bugger-all use to me then.

"You honestly think they could make good use of these, Oracle, Cai?" I got a fervent nod from Cai along with a smiling one from Oracle.

"I think that making our engineers more skilled and their use of those skills in making our ships better can only be a huge help to us, but these books are treasure beyond compare. Only you can decide this."

"They do us no good sitting here, Jax. I've watched over them for hundreds of years, and I think it's time they were used," Oracle said.

"Okay, then, guess it's time to give them out. Cai, I need you to gather the relevant people together, maybe bring everyone to the garden on the fortieth floor? The small one that's got the grassy area with the pool?" I said, looking over at Oracle, who confirmed that I had the floor details right. "Bring the artist, too, please. What are they doing currently?"

"She...it's Renna, from my old group. She's been clearing rubble and helping the crafters with odds and ends and drawing in chalk in a few of the rooms that have been cleared whenever she has the energy. The children love her creations," he said with a gentle smile.

"Perfect; bring her as well." I straightened up and stretched, letting my back crack and pop as I relieved the damage done by hours of sitting and listening instead of doing things.

I gathered up the books, asking Oracle to get me one final selection, and I set off to climb up to the fortieth-floor garden.

About twenty minutes later, I heard the sound of someone running behind me. I'd stopped for a break and was resting the pile of books on the edge of a pile of debris when Flux appeared from the stairwell.

"Ah, Jax!" he called out, smoothly jogging over to me, hardly seeming out of breath at all. "I'm glad I found you. Oracle said you were ready to discuss training?"

I groaned. "That little traitor."

Flux let loose with the subsonic I'd come to assume was his equivalent of laughter.

"Well, she said, and I quote, 'Better to get this out of the way now...' and I agreed with her. I owe you a lot for your help with the goblins, and I think it's best to make sure you survive, don't you?"

"I'd like to survive," I said warily, picking the books up again.

Flux reached out, taking half of the stack from me and walking alongside me. "Excellent! Well, now that we're in agreement, I think two hours in the morning and in the evening should help. I'm thinking weapons practice for an hour of each, with a ten-minute warmup and cooldown; how does that sound?"

"And the other forty minutes each session?" I asked, my heart sinking.

"That'll be sparring, of course!" he said, and an evil edge bled into his voice. "We'll start tonight, and I'll be your first partner. Also, just so we're clear, I need to...*thank you*...properly for leaving me with Ame earlier."

"Great," I muttered, closing my eyes for a brief second. Then I drew a deep breath and spoke up, thinking *in for a penny, in for a pound!* "Actually, I wanted to speak with you about training anyway. I need training, I know, but so do my people. I want you to help me teach them to fight and to defend themselves."

"To do this properly will require a lot of effort on my part and that of the other trainers." He was quiet for a long time, and I was just about to break the silence when he finally spoke again. "I will be your trainer, and I will organize with Barrett to teach the fighters, the hunters, and the scouts, as you need them badly. However, you will attend these lessons in addition to your own, you will owe me a favor, and—" He broke off, as though unsure how to proceed.

"And...?" I prompted him.

"And you'll take me out of the tower with you to the city, before Ame can stop us!" he replied quickly. "She's got some harebrained plan that we were meant to be together. She's insane, and I have to get out of here before she can do anything about it!"

He was so agitated, and spoke in such a desperate rush, he nearly dropped the books. Then the realization of the value of his armload struck him, and he nearly dropped them all over again. "Jax, she..."

"I thought you liked Ame?" I said, confused.

"Of course I like her!" he snapped, settling the books properly and shaking his head. His tendrils raised as he checked the area for anyone else close enough to hear us. "I...I've loved her for most of my life, Jax, but that's not the point! She's a runecrafter, and now she's going to learn the magic of healing. Do you have any idea how rare the talent for magic is amongst my kind? We had two in the last four generations, that I know of.

"Her apprentice came to us from hundreds of miles away because it was known that Ame was willing to teach. The girl was the only other known to us that had been born with the gift of magic. Ame is...Ame! She's the rarest flower of our kind, and she's determined that I will be her mate, but it's a mistake. She deserves better!"

"Why is it a mistake? And what do you mean about magic? We have spellbooks, and as far as I can tell, they work for anyone. Sure, they sometimes fail, but that's a really rare occurrence, right? And if you need to, you can always improve your Intelligence and Wisdom score?"

"You ask questions like beavers chew trees: randomly and irritatingly! And no, not all can learn magic, because spellbooks are horrifically expensive. Yes, all beings have some capacity for magic, but unless one is born with the ability or finds such a book, they will never learn to harness it."

"But, using their mana, by somehow, say...granting it to a deity a couple of times a day, that would unlock the ability to use magic much more easily, right?" I asked, another link forming in my mind.

"Yes, if we were willing to travel to the Dark God's temple in Himnel. We are not. We will not follow a being that helped to destroy the realm!"

"What about the other gods, though?" I asked cautiously, a hope building as we spoke.

"There were altars to all the gods across the land long ago; now, there are none. They were all lost or destroyed. None but the worshippers of the Dark One can grow that way now. That has nothing to do with Ame, though; she—"

"And if you could pray to...oh, say...a Goddess of Fire and Hidden Knowledge, and devote your mana to her, you'd have a better chance of unlocking your ability to do magic, right? And so would your people?"

"Well, yes...why?" he asked me suspiciously.

I shot him a grin. "Because I'm the Chosen of Jenae, and this whole building is dedicated to her. My people pray to her and gift her a portion of their mana most days. It's helping both her and me, and it's certainly helping them as well, by the sound of it," I said, bragging slightly.

"How?" Flux asked me, coming to a dead stop. "How did you do this?"

"When I explored the Great Tower, I found the altars. There is one for each of the gods up there. I felt…no, I *chose* to follow and ally myself with Jenae, as her outlook matches my own. I guess I was just lucky, really."

"And you are sure that she still exists, that the strength you send to her is helping her?" he asked intently.

"Yes. Look, we're only a few minutes from the garden now. When we get there, I'll show you something, okay?" We headed off, circling the tower through the final stairwell and out onto the grimy fortieth floor.

I looked around and nodded; it was as I'd remembered, silent and abandoned. The main floor was made up of dozens of rooms, almost all sealed, and the gardens were nearly invisible behind the crap-covered glass and stone piled up around the doors. I led him over, finding the opening where I'd struggled through previously. I carefully set the books down, pulling and heaving at the rocks until I'd cleared enough of a space to walk out easily.

Now that a way had been cleared, the gentle light of evening fell inside the tower. I realized how dark the last few floors had been.

I had my Darkvision ability, and clearly Flux, coming from a species that lived deep underwater and had no eyes, had no need of light, either. I fumbled out one of the magelights and set it down by the top of the stairs, determined that I'd make lighting a priority for everyone…as soon as the tower was unlikely to collapse, anyway.

I picked up the stack of books again and led Flux out into the small balcony garden. He stopped in surprise.

The air here was full of life, even this close to the SporeMother's lair. The balcony was only a few hundred feet square, but it was covered in lush trees and grass. There, at the center, as I led Flux through the low-hanging branches laden with fruit, was the pool.

I didn't know why it had originally been stocked with fish, but over hundreds of years of storms and buildup and breakdown of the plants and general growth, there was now a small, secluded grove. The ground was carpeted in lush grass and moss, and the pool had been surrounded on all sides with overly full fruit trees.

It was beautiful, and now, with the sun slowly sinking in the west, the red-tinged sky made it even more so. Flux and I sat down on the banks of the small pool, carefully stacking the books well back from the edge, and we relaxed for a moment. Flux shifted forward, slipping down into the pool, and dipped under, sinking all the way to the bottom where an explosion of fish and sediment marked his impact.

He slowly rose back up, stretching himself out and doing a quick lap of the pool before he returned to the side closest to me. He half-lifted himself out, leaning on the grass, and faced me fully.

"I've given you the time you asked for, Jax, and I enjoyed the feel of cool water again. But I must know…were you being truthful about your access to the goddess?" Flux asked me, his tendrils raised and fixated on me.

217

"I really wish I understood your body language better, mate," I muttered, before shaking myself and going on. "Yes, I'm the Chosen of Jenae, and if you'd like, I could arrange an introduction."

Flux considered me silently before slowly pulling himself out of the water and facing me.

"You are an enigma at times, Jax. I hear the words you speak, but it's as though the meaning of them escapes you. We are talking about one of the greater gods, one of the creators of the Infinite Realms, and yet you talk about introducing me as though she is a particularly attractive cousin. I ask again, and I need you to understand how important this is: do you really have the ear of a goddess?"

I frowned at him as I thought through what he'd said. I'd found the altar, and just as I always did, I had taken a gamble. Somehow, I had contacted a being that apparently helped to create reality as I knew it. I dug my nails into the grass I sat on and felt the soil beneath it.

The thought of the countless billions of sentients who had lived across what little I understood of the Realms spun through my mind's eye, and I stiffened, unconsciously pulling some of the grass free with a jerk that brought me back to reality.

Yes, she was a goddess; no, she was not all-powerful, and I had to wake her up. She was weak at present, and it was thanks to me that she was getting stronger. She was my ally, and maybe my friend? Either way, she was just another being, as far as I was concerned; a powerful one, even.

But I was from Newcastle, and we didn't back down for anyone.

I'd had our people compared to the Nac Mac Feegles of Sir Terry Pratchett's creation by a friend, and fuck if that weren't accurate. We loved to fight, drink, and shag anything we could. I'd be respectful to Jenae, but that was all she was getting, and fuck it if she couldn't take a joke. I straightened up and grinned at Flux.

"Yeah, good point; means she's almost as important as the queen. I'll be polite when I introduce you, mate," I said, going to one knee. I closed my eyes and concentrated, drawing in the mana and focusing on Jenae. I built up until I had enough ready before I opened my eyes, facing Flux across the glowing ball of mana I'd called into being between us. I gave him a wink and called out in the silence of my mind, the mana infusing the call as the glowing ball burst into a thousand motes of light that slowly settled to the ground, winking out.

"Jenae!"

She connected to me, the shift like the opening of a door into a vastly larger room. I stood on my side of the doorway, but I could feel the space beyond and the presence that lived there, the heat of the fire, and the far hotter desire to *know* that defined her.

"Hello, Eternal," she said into the silence of my mind.

"You always call me that." An involuntary smile tugged at my lips. *"Why?"*

"You are blessed by Amon, the first emperor. As such, some of him is within you. He is Eternal, and so are you. You'll know more when the time is right; don't worry."

"Okay, mysterious much? Anyway, that's not why I reached out to you; I have a friend here who'd like to meet you…"

"Really? You called out across the immeasurable distances of space and time to say 'Hi, want to meet my friend?'"

"Okay, when you say it like that, maybe it's a little weird, but hey, you're here now. Want to meet Flux?"

"We really need to talk about realities and the gulfs between them at some point, Jax, but at this stage, yes. I'd like to meet any prospective follower, thank you," Jenae sighed in my mind.

I opened my eyes to check on Flux, seeing him suddenly jerk and drop to his knees, all four hands pressed to the ground as he let out an unconscious subsonic *thrum* of awe.

I straightened up and grinned at my prostrate friend, knowing that Jenae was talking to him. A thought I'd had at the back of my mind since this conversation with Flux had started gave a wiggle, and I spoke to Jenae without thinking about it.

"So, wasn't one of your siblings all about water?" I asked, flinching when I felt the displeasure in Jenae's mental voice.

"Yes."

"Okay. Clearly this isn't going to be a fun part of the conversation, but didn't you say you wanted me to help bring the other gods and goddesses back?" There was a long silence, during which the others began to filter in, looking embarrassed as they found Flux on his knees with me standing over him.

"Don't worry; we're just talking to Jenae, that's all. Take a seat, and I'll be with you in a few minutes, okay?" I said, and Jenae's mental snarl nearly drove me to my knees.

"You're JUST talking to me...'that's all'?" she snapped, *"Just talking to the GODDESS WHO SAVED YOUR LIFE?"* Pain bloomed in my mind even further, a hot, wet feeling on my upper lip making me reach up instinctively. When I pulled my hand back, it was covered in blood. I could feel my ears and eyes joining my nose as blood began to trickle out, and the pain grew horrific.

I turned, struggling as I tried to face away from the others, and I bit the inside of my cheek. My rage roared to life over the pain that filled my mind. I felt Him wake with it as well, our twin angers feeding one another, even as Oracle blasted out through a lower floor window and hurtled up toward me.

The pain vanished as suddenly as it had appeared, and I staggered, blinking as I straightened again. I wiped at my face and held my hand up before my eyes, seeing the blood smeared there.

"That's twice you've done that, bitch. Want to try for a hat-trick?" I whispered, knowing she could hear me, as the world around me seemed to shift into somewhere...else, a realm that lived in the space between our atoms and the beating of hearts.

"I...I..."

"You attacked me, again! All because I tried to follow your requests!" I roared at her in the silence of my mind, and I felt a presence filling the mental space behind me. It was disjointed, confused, and angry, made of a thousand memories more than a mind, but it was powerful, and it was filled with rage.

I mentally faced her, the rage behind me swelling, growing like a cloud of smoky fury, rising to surround me.

JENAE'S REALM

I n a second, the world had finished changing, and we stood elsewhere, a new place. The sky was dark overhead, with heavy, purplish-grey clouds that roiled and flashed with hidden lightning. The land all around us was dead and barren, soil and sand intermixed across the scrublands, broken only by the howling winds that filled this place. All around us in the distance were huge mountains; they towered higher than I could see, disappearing into the clouds. Before me stood a single figure.

She was older than I, but not past her prime. Dark red hair fell in waves down a face that would never be called stunning. Her jaw was too strong and her cheeks too wide, but her eyes blazed with the Fire of Knowledge, and she was outlined in flickering, crackling flames.

This was Jenae, I realized, the goddess as she was now. I glanced behind me, looking up at the growing wall of rage that had my back.

It was filled with darkness and light, roiling clouds and brilliant sunshine burst through, screams of fighting and death, cries of laughter, cheers of celebration, and the sweet giggle of children. The cloud of righteous fury grew, spreading around me and enveloping me. It clothed me in armor of madness, and I knew what it was.

This was the remnant of Amon, First Emperor, Eternal. This fraction of his soul was all that was left of him in the realms of life. Hundreds of years had passed, his mind and soul shattered anew with each generation that was born of his genetics. The crazed and tangled web grew, taking more and more of him, spreading his consciousness out until it broke, and all that was left were impulses, memories…

He'd never live again and couldn't die; the torture of seeing his descendants committing the very crimes he'd created his empire to defend against driving him deeper into insanity, until at the last, he'd found us.

The remains of Amon had flared to life in Tommy and myself, some twisted fate of genetics pulling more than the usual amount of himself together. He'd found more than kin when he'd found our twin rages. He'd found enough to regain some of his mind again, but it was still broken and could never be rebuilt properly.

All of this blazed through my mind in a second, leaving understanding behind.

I reached out, curling my right hand into a fist as I looked at it. A glowing gauntlet pulled itself together from the void and covered my fingers, joining to me seamlessly.

I looked up at Jenae, a shiver of pleasure running through my body as the armor flowed up to cover my head, my vision restricted momentarily as the metal flowed over my face, then it cleared. I could see through the protective cover of metal, felt it encompassing me everywhere, yet it flexed and moved with me.

It felt as though I had donned stiff silk, yet it would provide protection better than the finest steel could ever hope to.

"No!" Jenae cried out, taking a step back.

I glared at her, knowing she could see me even through my armor. "You did this. You started this!" I growled at her, the heat of righteous anger filling me.

"No, please, Eternal!" she repeated, taking a step back. In her right hand, a sword suddenly appeared, and she gripped it. I held out my right hand parallel to my chest, and I closed my fingers around a naginata that hadn't existed before now. It glowed an unearthly silver, and a second presence appeared beside the madness, a huge yet confused mind reaching out. It recognized Amon, and it touched him, tasting his madness and recoiling, even as it also took up a protective guard at my back.

"AMON?" it questioned, fear and sadness filling its mental sending. There was a burst of communication from the madness, a disjointed pulse that carried the taste of hundreds of years of terror and fury, the knowledge of a world being destroyed, and a soul being unraveled. I was hit with it, and it left a series of memories, but I couldn't take it all. The second presence, though, took it easily, absorbing everything.

"NO. THIS MUST NOT BE. WE AGREED TO AID YOU. DESPITE ALL THAT HAPPENED, OUR BOND HOLDS. WE WILL INTERCEDE." The huge presence behind me moved forward, and an enormous claw-tipped foot, longer than I was tall, crushed the earth beside me as a fathomless voice echoed through my mind.

"HEAR ME, ETERNAL. THIS MUST NOT BE. AMON MUST BE PROTECTED. HE CANNOT BE LOST, WASTED LIKE THIS. PULL BACK HIS RAGE, BURY HIS MADNESS, AND LET HIM SLEEP ONCE AGAIN. I SHALL AID YOU IN HIS STEAD."

I glared up, looking into an eye that I could comfortably stand inside, which regarded me from a scaly head the size of a truck. It was a dragon, one that I recognized dimly from Amon's memories. I struggled for a second, and a name sprang to mind...

"Tuthic'Amon?" I whispered, and he nodded slowly, the memory I'd seen him in flaring to life and dying as he rumbled acknowledgement.

"THAT MEMORY SHOULD NOT BE KNOWN TO YOUR KIND, BUT I ACKNOWLEDGE THE DEBT AND THE OATH, REGARDLESS. STAND DOWN, AND PULL BACK WHAT REMAINS OF AMON. I WILL AID YOU IN THIS FIGHT."

I scowled at him for a moment longer then turned my furious glare onto Jenae.

"You see what you've done...you see what you've started!" I growled at her, confusion warring with anger even as I tried to control the rage flooding me.

"Please, Eternal!" Jenae begged. She looked down at the sword in her hands and cast it aside, the blade vanishing as soon as it left her fingers. "Please, let me try to fix this!"

"JENAE? MISTRESS, YOU HAVE DONE THIS? YOU ATTACKED THE ETERNAL?" *Tuthic'Amon asked in confusion, each syllable echoing like lead blocks dropped in a cave.*

"I lashed out in anger, and now I cannot fix this. Please, Tuthic, aid me!" *she cried. The ground shook below us, the mountains in the distance seeming to shift.* "We must get him out of here. He cannot be found; we cannot be found! If Nimon senses us…"

The enormous dragon looked upward as though his eyes could pierce the skies. He growled in anger, before ducking his head down to be level with me.

"ETERNAL, THIS CANNOT BE. SEARCH YOUR FEELINGS; EVEN IN YOUR RAGE, YOU KNOW ME. TRUST IN WHAT I SAY. YOU CANNOT BE HERE, AND NEITHER CAN I. YOU ENDANGER US ALL FOR YOUR RAGE, AND MY CHILDREN MOST OF ALL.

"I TASTE YOUR ANCESTOR'S OATH UPON YOU. WILL YOU HONOR IT, AND STEP BACK? I WILL GUARD YOUR MIND FROM ALL. JENAE WILL NOT HARM YOU AGAIN; I WILL SWEAR IT ON MY SOUL IF NEED BE, BUT YOU MUST STEP BACK!"

I glared at him, then at Jenae, but I remembered the oath we (HE) had sworn, and I took a single step backwards. My mind remained filled with anger, even as my body shook with the need to fight.

CHAPTER TWENTY

I blinked, back in the world. The vision I'd seen had gone, and seemingly not a second had passed. I glanced down at my hand, and a glimmer of ghostly armor vanished like fog in the heat of the sun.

I could feel him in my mind; I could feel them all. Amon, the Eternal Emperor, Tuthic'Amon, the enormous silver dragon that had been Shustic's mate, and Jenae. The relief from the last two was palpable, even as confusion in what was left of Amon's mind still scrambled my own.

The anger was still there, bouncing around in my head, but now it was only mine and Oracle's rage as she arrived by my side and observed the blood that covered my face. I trembled slightly, and Oracle landed on my shoulder. Pressing her hand to my temple, she caught up on everything in my mind. Her anger reinforced my own, each feeding off each other. As before, I contained it, compressing it down, forcing it into submission.

The rage that the pair of us felt was a candle beside the sun compared to Amon's rage, and I knew that I had done the right thing in stepping back. I needed Jenae, but damn, I wanted to gut her right now for this betrayal.

"THAT IS UNDERSTANDABLE, ETERNAL." The voice that echoed in my mind made me wince. Oracle curled her tiny hands into fists as she whimpered at the ancient dragon's mind touching ours. **"I apologize. I have not spoken to one of your kind in long ages,"** Tuthic said, clearly trying to modulate his tone. **"I have spoken with Jenae, and while I think there is a need to explain this…it is best to come from her. Will you speak with her?"** I drew a deep breath and nodded, replying to him.

"I will, Tuthic'Amon. I…thank you. It is an honor to speak with you." I was speaking mind-to-mind with a dragon that flew through the skies when my own people were still exploring our world's oceans in tiny wooden ships; that knowledge was helping me be respectful.

"And yet you brave the lion in his den in facing Mistress Jenae? How strange. Still, I appreciate the honor you show me, Eternal. Your ancestor was different from most of your race; I liked him, even though our final words to one another were said in anger."

"Jax…I am sorry." Jenae's voice came through. *"I lashed out when I felt your seeming dismissal of me. I regretted it as soon as I did it, but still, my shame is my own."*

"Yeah, you're good at that," I said to her, my anger ticking over once more.

"She is a Goddess, Jax the Eternal. She deserves your respect," Tuthic admonished.

I shrugged, feeling like a petulant child.

"This was my fault, though, and I accept that. Jax was attempting to help me, to carry out an earlier request, and I let my fear and greed feed my anger. I lashed out. I should not have. Will you let me explain, Jax?" Janae asked.

I drew in a deep breath before letting it out with a sigh. *"I will, and I'm sorry as well. I didn't show you much respect there, did I?"* I directed the thought to her, a feeling of shame blooming within me.

"No, you didn't. But we had agreed to be allies, not mistress and servant. Despite our relative experiences, the realities of our situation mean that we are far closer matched than we would otherwise be. We are allies." There was a pause as Jenae gathered her courage, and I felt Tuthic watching and waiting.

"For a god or goddess, there is no greater shame than to fail your people, and my brothers and sisters and I did this. When we were ripped from the realms and cast out, we wasted much of our power raging and trying to return. Nimon grew stronger on the devastation that his cataclysm brought about, and we became...lesser.

"When his curse eventually expired, and we returned, none who worshipped us still lived. Any temples and altars that could be found had been scoured from the realms, and we were alone and weakened. The last of our altars, like the ones you found, were hidden away in only the most dangerous of locations.

"We slept the ages away, too weak to fight him without our champions and our faithful. Then you awoke me, and I saw the slimmest of chances to return to what we were. I took it, and I asked you to return my family as well. I asked it, believing it would be easy to give up potential followers, as it's easy to give up future wealth, when you have it not.

"When you bought me another potential group of converts, then casually asked about giving them to my sister...my jealousy raised its head, and I was filled with greed. Then you so casually dismissed talking to 'just' me, and my fear and anger over my weakened state...I'm sorry, Jax. I should not have lashed out."

"Jax, do you wish to speak?" Tuthic asked calmly, and I had a mental image of a headmaster standing over a quarreling pair of pupils and making them behave and shake hands.

I couldn't help it, and I started to laugh, the last of my anger passing as I did. There was a startled silence in my mind, until they both understood the imagery that I shared mentally with them. The feeling of gentle amusement and relief filled my mind from both of them.

"Yes. I am sorry, Jenae, and I'm sorry you were pulled into this, Tuthic'Amon," I said. *"It was my casual disrespect that caused this. Please understand, it's not intentional; in my...land...it was the way we generally spoke to each other. I'm sorry."*

"Then this matter is resolved," Tuthic said, **"All that is left is an explanation of why that was dangerous, and an exchanging of gifts."**

"Gifts?" I asked, and Tuthic explained.

"In the old world, before the Cataclysm, when an agreement such as this was reached, a gift was exchanged to each of the wronged parties by their peers. In this case, we have all done wrong.

"Had I been watching for you, as I should have, I might have explained matters to you and offered my advice before now. Mistress Jenae should have held her anger and spoken with you, rather than lashing out, and you should have shown the proper respect.

"As such, I will give you the gift that is most needed. I will grant you an ability, one that will protect your mind from all that seek to harm it. In doing so, I can again begin to honor my oath to Amon, as it will protect him as well. Prepare yourself."

With that, a second blinding pain that flooded my mind, and I cried out, feeling strong hands gripping my shoulders supportively as voices rose in fear and confusion all around me. A golden notification appeared before me, overriding my usual preferences. I blinked at it, reading it quickly before dismissing it.

Congratulations!

You have been gifted an Ability! You have received Aegis, an ability gifted by the Elder Dragon Tuthic'Amon. This ability will consume health, mana, and stamina in equal measure at a rate of ten percent of each per second. While this ability is active, no being can reach your mind. Increasing your skill with this ability will reduce the cost.

I took a deep breath and replied gratefully to Tuthic. Gifting such a thing across whatever distances existed between us couldn't have been easy.

"If I could give more, I would, Jax the Eternal, but I must protect my children as well. If you have need of me, call, and I will come. Please, consider well before you summon me, though."

"I...I will, Tuthic'Amon. Thank you. I don't have a gift to give you," I whispered, and I felt his laughter shake me.

"You have returned the Eternal to us and taken up his mantle, and still you think that you have given me no gift? Jax, you have given me and my kind a gift beyond measure! Trust in yourself and grow your strength. Give Mistress Jenae a chance, and work to return the Greater Gods, and you will have given more to the realm than could ever be repaid."

"This is true, Jax. My gift to you is this: I know your needs and your most fervent desire. I have not the strength to do both, but I can either grant you knowledge of a healing rune, or...I will cast a spell of detection. It will give us a general location for your brother, or at least the last place he used magic. I can do no more without more time to accrue more mana."

I didn't need time to think on that. I knew I should take the healing rune, but I'd come here for one thing, and one thing only. I was over here screaming at gods with a hole in my chest the size of half my heart without my twin by my side. Tommy. It could only be Tommy.

"I'll take door number two, please, Bob," I whispered, a game show from my childhood momentarily springing to mind as I answered.

The feeling of warmth from Jenae increased. *"I will cast the spell tonight, then, Jax. It will take some time to prepare, but at least I can do this for you in apology. Will you dissolve our alliance?"* the goddess asked hesitantly.

"No," I said squaring my shoulders. *"I need you, and I think you need me, too. Allies still, but this is the last time you strike out at me or mine. I've given you two chances, Jenae; the third time you do this, we're enemies."*

"I understand. We also need to discuss the place where you addressed me. That is an extremely dangerous place for your kind. It's a dangerous place for mine, now, but for a mortal? It is a place your soul would be destroyed by, were you any less than you are."

"You keep calling me Eternal, but I'm mortal as well, and Amon was the Eternal, but he died…what the hell?"

A pulse of rage from Tuthic'Amon rippled through me and disappeared a second later. Jenae replied, a hint of sadness lending a heaviness to her presence.

"Your ancestor, Amon, was the Eternal Emperor. He was gifted by all of the gods to protect the realm. He was not supposed to be able to die, until Nimon took a hand in events. His descendants have some of his abilities, as shown by their long lives…you and your brother, however, would have developed only some of these abilities, until you came here.

"The acceptance of you by what is left of Amon has granted you certain abilities; they are, as yet, unformed and in their infancy. I cannot explain or define them, as such an act by a goddess may trap them into a form that may be less than they could evolve into.

"For now, accept that you are becoming…more…and leave it at that. As to the place we were, it is the realm of the gods. The mountains you saw are the bases of our thrones, and you saw my power and size in comparison now to my simple seat as it was then."

"Nimon has claimed our realm and has seen fit to raise many lesser gods and demons to roam the realm to amuse him and to form a pantheon of his own, tied to and subservient to him." She growled as she spoke, her anger clear.

"I must bide my time, build my strength, and reawaken my brethren so that we may pull Nimon from his throne and return the realms to what they should be. Your display of stolen power nearly drew the attention of others, and it would have been costly for you, possibly deadly for us both."

"What do you mean 'stolen power'? I don't even know what I did!" I protested, standing straight and looking around. Bane had appeared from somewhere and was the one supporting me. The others I'd asked to come were standing well back. I had Bane on one side, Flux on the other, and Ame had appeared from somewhere. Cai moved around carefully on the far side of them, examining everything for any possible threat. They all had weapons drawn, and I blinked as I realized what was happening.

Flux and the others had thought I was being attacked; they'd drawn weapons and gotten ready to protect me against anything that might be coming.

"I…I'm all right," I said, then cleared my throat and spoke up louder. "It's okay, I'm all right. Sorry to have startled you all. I…received a gift; it just wasn't one I was expecting, and it hurt a bit, that's all. Give me a minute to clean myself up, and I'll be with you."

People relaxed slightly, but I could see how finding me staggering around and bleeding from my mouth, nose, eyes, and ears had clearly freaked them the fuck out. Hell, it'd freaked me out, and it was yet another reason I needed to find someone who could make and clean clothes. Mine were covered in blood, fucking again!

"It's all right, Jax. What you did…you used power from Amon, power that should have been long gone. I don't know how he did it, or how you used it, but you came to me and you stood on your own feet in a realm that should have crushed you mercilessly. I'll try to figure out what and how you did what you did, as I'd certainly like to know myself. Again, I am sorry. I will make it up to you."

"I think it's time we introduced another of your brethren, anyway," I said to her. *"Not because of all this, but it was something I was thinking about before. I considered that the Mer could do with some help, after all."*

"I agree, and I will consider who will best suit them. Goodbye, Jax. We will talk later."

"Yeah…bye," I muttered and drew in a deep breath as I clapped my hands together, forcing out the lingering feelings of worry and concern and compelling myself to smile.

I rubbed at my face, my hand coming away sticky with blood, and I made a face. Looking around and holding my hand up where people could see it, Bane, Flux, and Ame gave me room, but still stayed close as I walked to the pool.

"Well, guess I'll be needing a bath tonight!" I said aloud, trying to drum up a laugh, but the best I got was a series of wary half-smile, half-grimaces.

"What happened?" asked Flux, and Ame and Bane moved a little closer to be sure they could hear.

"I got a gift, like I said," I said to them quietly. "Ah…on a totally separate note, does the name 'Tuthic'Amon' mean anything to you guys?" I asked. When they all looked at me blankly, I went on.

"Big silver dragon, probably in charge of them all, from what I remember?" I wracked my brain, trying to remember where the memory had said Shustic and Tuthic had lived. "I think they said they lived at Dragon's Reach…but that might be wrong." I caught the looks Ame and Flux were exchanging, while Bane glared at everyone indiscriminately, and I spoke up.

"What? You know something…"

"Dragon's Reach was said to be somewhere in the south, thousands of miles out to sea. There was a legend of the Greater Dragons retreating to there after the Cataclysm, that it was closed to all the races…No ships that have sailed south have returned," Ame said slowly. "It was thought that there was simply nothing there, and that the ships were lost at sea, but if you believe the Greater Dragons truly still exist, and real dragons at that, not wyrms, then…"

"They exist; take it from me," I said, holding my fingers up for emphasis. "This is what happens when a mortal gets a gift from one."

It wasn't entirely true, but I had felt fresh blood after Tuthic had given me his gift, so it wasn't totally a lie either. It'd do for now.

I moved forward, leaving them with as many questions as answers, and I crouched down, cupping the sparkling clear water in my hands and throwing it over my face, scrubbing as best I could and rinsing repeatedly until I felt a bit cleaner. I finally staggered to my feet, the sun now closer to setting, and a definite chill beginning to fill the air.

I noticed that the group had a few magelights spread out between them, and I asked them to spread them out a bit farther, making sure everyone had plenty of light.

I promised to talk to Cai, Flux, Bane, and Ame later, once everyone was taken care of, and I stood up where everyone could see me.

"I've got a few small gifts to give out, as so many of you have been good boys and girls…" I looked around at the confusion on their faces, and I shrugged.

"Or not. Fuck it, moving on! So, as I promised you all earlier, I'll be giving out certain skillbooks and a few spellbooks to those Cai and I believe are best suited to them." I gestured encouragingly, and Cai started to call out names.

As each person stepped up, a variety of emotions, ranging from shock and awe to tears to a kind of desire I'd never known danced across their expressions.

The three engineers were the last and strangest of the group. They held onto their own books fiercely, while trying to bargain with the others for theirs, promising anything they had, years of work, assistance in their projects, anything they could do. I couldn't help but smile, and I stepped in when they started to get more frantic.

"Seriously, people; Cai, Oracle, and I gave thorough, intentional consideration to whom we were giving which books. This is also not all we have. In fact, these are essentially the 'primers' and basic manuals only.

"You are a test group, but you're one that has earned the books you hold. Learn what you can and reflect on what you can do better. There will be more in the future for those who earn them, and for those who excel, multiple books and even memory stones holding the knowledge of the past may become available to you."

The group before me froze, turning to stare at me almost mechanically. I grinned at the three engineers.

"Yes, even you. But not right now! Show me what you've learned from these books, and we'll talk again, okay?"

"Cai?" I called.

He stepped up, frowning as I took a small book out of my own bag and handed it over to him. "I know you're constantly running around after everyone. Not sure how much this will help, but…well, I think you'll get more use out of it than me."

He took the book, fingers gently brushing the lightly damaged corners of the Undead Servant spellbook, before looking back up at me with confusion crinkling his forehead.

"Jax…I…"

"Look, mate, it conjures an undead servant, apparently an incorporeal spirit or a physical skeleton, depending on your preference, or so Oracle said. Basically, if you summon a spirit, you can send it to give messages and shit, and a skeleton—" I broke off, running my fingers through my hair and shook my head.

"I don't know, man, it just seemed like it'd be useful to you, you know? You can have others, spells or skillbooks, that's no worries. But I was going to put this in the Hall of Memories, and I thought you'd be able to make use of it. Hell, you can send it to fetch your pipe and fuckin' slippers if you want."

The Forgotten Faithful

"I'm sure it will be very useful Jax, thank you," Cai said reassuringly, the edges of his mouth rising in a faint smile.

I glared at him suspiciously, not sure if he was taking the piss out of me or not. "Fine, well, yeah, you're welcome," I muttered, turning to Renna where she stood hesitantly at the back of the group. With a gesture, I took her to one side.

Cai hadn't called her name, but he had asked her to come at my request, and I spent a few minutes talking quietly with her before handing over a single thick volume that she clutched disbelievingly.

She swore to do her best and to come up with a plan for me, as well as swearing to dedicate herself to mastering this new path if it couldn't initially do what I wanted it to. I just grinned at her and told her to enjoy herself, and that when she was ready, she needed to go to Ame and speak with her about my idea.

Cai stepped in and started fielding questions and directing people away as I moved to sit on the grassy bank by the water's edge. I was exhausted, and despite doing my best to cover it, Ame, Flux, and Bane all knew it.

Ame didn't even pause, crouching down next to me and gripping my head in two hands, while her others grabbed my own to keep me still. She faced me square on, all her tendrils extended wide, and let loose a subsonic *thrum* that made my teeth ache. I jerked my head free and glared at her as she sat back, both sets of arms folding as she spoke.

"You will tell me all that you just experienced, then you will teach me the spell you have promised me. After this, you will rest until I am satisfied you are strong enough to not collapse in front of the people who need you so much!"

"So, you don't need me?" I asked rubbing my jaw to try and work away the residual feeling.

"We all need you, but I am also a healer now, so it's my place to keep you alive to do what you must."

"How did you do with the books?" I asked.

She shook her head. "That is not important right now; what is—"

"No," I said flatly. "I asked you a question, Ame, and I expect an answer. How are you after using the books? Are you able to use more, or do you need some time? I'll try to teach you my spell regardless, as I don't think it has the same kind of issues being taught like that, but I need to know."

"I…I am sore, and it is unwise to use another book now. I want to learn, but…" For the first time, she seemed unsure, embarrassed almost.

"No, Ame, that's what I needed to hear. You have to be realistic about this, and for the love of god, don't damage yourself the way I did! Oracle?" I called out, and she was there in an instant.

She'd been only a few feet away, talking quietly with Bane, but in a flash, she was by my side, hovering as she looked into my eyes cautiously.

"I know you're okay; I know it, but…" she whispered.

"I am, honestly, Oracle, and I understand, you weren't expecting that to happen. Neither was I. We can talk about it another time; for now, I need your help. We need to teach Ame our spell, if you're sure we can do this?"

"Okay, got it," she said, her jaw flexing determinedly as she blurred, suddenly growing to her full size. "I know that it's normally done differently, but I think with being in the tower and having me bonded means we have an option to teach that you wouldn't normally find. I can form a bridge between your minds, and that should make things a little faster. But it's still going to take a while, a few hours at least, so make yourselves comfortable."

I shifted around to face her and Ame, the three of us making a triangle with Oracle hovering over the water. The tips of her toes lightly touched the surface and created ripples as she bobbed up and down, the gentle breeze from her wings caressing my face.

Ame sat cross-legged, her hand clenching and relaxing as she tried to wait patiently.

Flux took up a position on the far side of her, and I sensed more than heard Bane doing the same behind me.

Oracle reached out to us both, taking a hand in each of hers, and closed her eyes.

Do you wish to allow Ame access to your mind and magic?

Yes/No

I took a deep breath and selected *yes* and felt the sensation of another mind touch my own. It wasn't like it was with Oracle, the other wisps, Jenae, or even Tuthic'Amon. This was far more limited, and I paused for a moment, shocked as I realized how many beings had recently had access to my mind.

That thought was blown away in the next second as my magic reacted. It was different from how it normally felt, as I wasn't actually trying to use it; instead, I was pulling it up to show it off.

It felt like lifting something sluggish from my body. I drew it out slowly, the words and gestures needed to direct the spell coming to my mind awkwardly as I focused on it. I had to work at it, as I constructed the basic form like a scaffold in the air between us. It felt so strange, but as the minutes passed, the first sections stabilized, and I moved upward, climbing slowly. As the structure of the spell grew before us, the magic glowing bright and illuminating the encroaching night, I began to understand.

I was showing someone something that I did because I had a huge amount of background knowledge. That knowledge was entirely missing on her end, such as the inclusion of a mana-based variant of an MRI that Oracle and I had created from my memories to allow us to find the issues, let alone fix them.

It also explained one of the reasons that Ame's version would be far more basic than my own, as she had none of the hundreds of hours I'd spent watching medical programs on TV, the basic biology and medical sciences I'd studied at school, the hours and hours of first aid and enhanced medical training I'd had when training for the army, the arena, and my life here.

All of that, combined with the spells I had learned, had enabled me to create the spell. Ame had none of that, but her own abilities and background knowledge would help her with creating new magic of her own.

Spellbooks, on the other hand, had a huge amount of additional knowledge included in them.

The basic healing spell included knowledge on basic anatomy and more, as well as a way to subconsciously examine the correct "pattern" for how someone existed before the injury, so you didn't accidentally grow back scaled skin or claws or something.

All of this ran through my mind as I slowly constructed the entire spell between us, and I felt Ame struggling to comprehend it all. This spell had aspects in it that she'd never seen or imagined. But as she concentrated, with Oracle's help, she was learning in minutes what would have taken hours, and in hours what should have taken days.

Her mind flitted from detail to detail. Questions blurred between us, answered in a millisecond and more knowledge growing, the individual aspects of fire and earth, water and air, light and dark, life and death all coming together to create this one spell.

When Oracle finally released the bond, I fell backward, my back slamming into the grass and my head actually bouncing off it. The hand she'd been holding splashed into the water, her own answering splash much louder as the semi-corporeal body she'd constructed from her mana hit the water with a startled oath.

I forced myself upright, struggling, and groggy, only to find Ame doing the same across from me. We both looked at the soaking-wet form of Oracle as she bobbed to the surface, splashing frantically as confusion warred with exhaustion.

I was tempted to watch for a minute, especially as she'd been wearing a white T-shirt that was going see-through in all the right places, but it wasn't fair to her.

"Oracle!" I shouted, and she looked at me in confusion and panic, then went under and popped back up again, desperately slamming her hands into the water as her wings flailed about. "Fly!" I called to her, trying not to laugh. It was a bit ridiculous, really.

As her tired mind made sense of what I meant, she suddenly stopped thrashing around and sank, then just as easily, she rose up through the water, fully incorporeal again, her clothes back to pristine.

"Well, I...yes," she muttered, shaking her head as she shrank down and flew to my side, clearly embarrassed.

"What happened there?" I asked her. She just shook her head furiously, glaring at me and getting a little grin from me in return. "Okay, I can take a hint. I'll drop it."

I shifted my attention back to Ame, who had sat back up and was massaging her legs slowly. The half-hearted effort she was putting in made it clear that her attention was elsewhere.

"Well?" I asked after a minute. "Did you learn it?"

Ame turned to face me fully, her tendrils waving in excitement, and she lifted her hands, about to cast.

"Whoa!" I said, holding my hands up, and she froze. "You know how to channel more power into the spell as well, right? So, you can power it for longer?"

"Of course; it was part of the spell," she said.

I grinned at her. "In that case, rather than wasting your mana on me, why don't you get your arse down to the rest of your people and start fixing them? It'll be good experience for you!"

Ame paused for a minute, before scrambling to her feet and heading away at speed. She'd almost disappeared into the trees when she remembered where she was. She turned, bowing low and calling out.

"Thank you, Lord Jax, I will put this gift to good use," she said with forced calm, then spun and raced away again.

"That woman will be the death of me," muttered Flux.

"The best of them always are, mate," I said with a grin. "You sure you want to go to the city with me? I think you'd be better off here; fuck knows, you'd be more use training them than wandering around with me."

"But at least there, I'll have some time to get my head and my heart to decide how they feel," he replied.

A snort startled us from the darkness beside an old tree.

"What male ever truly understands a female?" came Cheena's voice from where she'd been watching over me. "That being said...I think Ame will be interested to hear that you're planning on escaping her clutches, Flux. Might even make a charm for me if I tell her the news right..."

"You'll keep your words to yourself!" Flux growled, raising one hand and pointing one crooked finger at her. "You'll be helping me to train the fighters here. I haven't decided how, though; trainer or victim?"

There was a long pause, broken only by Bane calling out "trainer" a second before Cheena said the same.

"Looks like I've one more trainer than I need...watch your words, Cheena!" Flux said, and he turned to me. "Are you sure you're okay?" When I nodded, he continued, "In that case, I will return to the lower floors and see if Ame needs any help. Excuse me."

Once he was gone, there was a long pause as we all waited to see who'd make the next move. Eventually, I got bored of it, and I stretched out, letting out a low groan as I straightened myself out and rested my head back on the grass.

"Jax?" came a voice into my mind, and I almost groaned. I did not want to hear from Jenae at the minute. not at all. Certainly not. Unless it was about...

"Jenae? Did you find him?" I asked quickly, sitting up.

"Not yet. I have released the spell, and it is currently mapping the continent, but it will take some time to finish. I'll be in touch when it's done. I just...I wanted to apologize again, and to let you know I was doing as we agreed."

Her voice was much quieter and calmer, but seemed a lot sadder as well, which made me let go of a little of the residual anger I felt towards her and myself, considering it was my casual disrespect that had started the whole thing off.

"Thank you, Jenae, and I'm sorry as well. If I'd been a bit more respectful, this would never have happened." There was a sense of acceptance, then she was gone, and I lay back again with a groan.

"Well, I'm going to have a nap here; I can't be bothered to find my room. Go do whatever, okay, guys?" I mumbled, my eyes already closed as I enjoyed the peace of the garden. The breeze made the leaves rustle all around me, the occasional *clop* of disturbed water only serving to lull me into sleep faster.

I barely registered Bane and Cheena agreeing upon a watch, not even remarking when Oracle shifted back into a more or less corporeal form to snuggle into me. I didn't stir as, hours later, she got bored and flew off to cause mischief somewhere. I just slept on, exhausted.

CHAPTER TWENTY-ONE

I woke slowly, stretching luxuriously as I gazed at my surroundings. I was still in the small garden on the fortieth floor, thankfully, and as I slowly sat up, I tried to work out what had disturbed me. I could just make out the change in the sky from the rising sun, and the birds were raising a cacophony of songs all around me, but…

"He's nearly here," a voice whispered. I glanced in the direction of the call, making out a Mer crouched in the deeper shadows under a tree.

"Uh…thanks?" I murmured slowly, wracking my brains for her name. "Jana, right?"

"That's right, Lord Jax," she said quietly.

"Who's coming?" I asked.

"Flux. He's ordered that everyone who needs training should gather in just over two hours on the parade ground at the twenty-sixth floor of the tower. He also said he was going to be spending the first and last few hours of the day with you, so that means he'll be here any time now. I thought you'd rather wake up without his help."

"Definitely!" I said, clambering to my feet and cracking my back, even as Jana moved out of the darkness. "Thank you for that," I said.

She shrugged. "I'm to be your guard at night; better if we get along, after all. Besides, Flux trained me. I know what an evil bastard he really is and how much not getting to wake you up will annoy him!"

"And yet, you still did it," Flux's voice came from directly behind her. She spun, all four arms suddenly brandishing daggers. She froze a second later as Flux stepped out of the trees and nodded to her. "Better. You always did get distracted too easily, but it was better than you could have responded before. We will talk about it later."

"Dammit!" she muttered, slinking back into the shadows. As she was going, I noticed that she no longer limped, and I spoke up quickly.

"Jana, your foot…"

"Ame fixed it last night. She said you taught her the spell so she could help us all, so thank you again, lord."

"No, you don't need to thank me for that. Ame did it; I'm just glad she managed it, and I'm sorry you had to wait until she learned the spell first."

"Still, thank you," came the reply from the night.

"Sooo, how bad is this going to be?" I asked, turning back to Flux. The subsonic thrum of his laughter was my only answer, joined a second later by Jana's. "Crap," I muttered, shaking my head.

The next half an hour passed in a blur. We started with gentle stretches, which slowly grew faster and more challenging. We moved through a variety of poses, some modified for me with having only two arms, others clearly deliberately chosen to make me shake with exertion.

Once our warmup was complete, we slowly began to pick up the tempo, moving from one position to another until I was bathed in sweat. I thought I was getting fitter and healthier, not to mention stronger every day. But this was a struggle even for me, and I'd dumped a fuck ton of points into my Agility.

Flux finally called a break and slipped into the water, immersing himself for the shortest two minutes I'd ever experienced while dressed.

Once he drew himself back out, he nodded to me and gestured to two spears waiting on the grass to one side. His lower arms bent around and clasped hands behind his back as the upper ones took up one spear, throwing the second to me. He positioned us both as mirror images of the other and began to teach me a new kata.

We started out with a series of simple sweeps and blocks, many of which I already knew. But, as he sped up, I started to fall behind, his spear flashing in stabs, ripostes, and sweeps I could barely see, let alone copy.

As the second hour began, he broke the kata up into sections, making me do each move ten times before moving onto the next. It took the full two hours to get it locked into my muscles and mind, but at the end, I finally managed to do a full run-though, right before I collapsed panting onto the floor.

"You...are...trying...to...kill...me," I whispered raggedly as I tried to catch my breath, and I felt the thrum again.

"When I feel you're ready to move on from the basics, then I'll start to teach you properly, but for now? A solid base will keep you alive longer than fancy tricks, Jax. Trust me on this."

"I...do, but...really...did you...have.... to...?"

"Break you? No, but I needed to see what you were made of. A lesser man would have given up long since. From what I can see, your main issues are stamina and skill; you lack nothing in the heart. That, I can work with. A weak man can get stronger, a broken man can heal, a lazy man will be forever lazy until he defeats his own inner demons."

"Lovely...thanks...for that...fortune cookie...crap." I groaned, forcing myself to sit up and slowly get to my feet, hoping that walking and gently swinging my arms would aid my recovery.

"Now, we have eight minutes until we are due for the first lessons with your fighters. It will reflect poorly on you to turn up late, wouldn't you say?"

I glared at him, my breaths still coming in shallow gasps as I remembered where they'd be waiting for us.

"That's fourteen floors...at least a mile...or two from here," I whispered.

"Just under three, as the tower winds. Try to keep up!" And he was off. He didn't even start with a bastard jog; he just went into a full sprint practically from a standing start.

I groaned and stuck the practice spear into the dark soil, trading it for my naginata before following him. The knowledge of the small book that rested in my bag of holding as I ran after him came back to me, and I regretted not giving it to him earlier.

It was a training manual; it covered the basic unarmed kata which the Imperial Legions had used in their special forces, and I wanted everyone in the tower to master it eventually.

I wanted to learn it, too, but I just knew giving it to him earlier would have resulted in me being a test dummy.

It took just under twelve minutes to reach the twenty-sixth floor, and when I finally staggered out onto it, wheezing and barely able to walk because I'd pushed myself that hard, I caught Flux bending over, his head in a barrel of fresh water as he drew in the refreshment he needed.

I staggered across to him on wobbly legs and collapsed to the floor, getting an unwanted shower when he finally pulled himself back out and looked down at me, water dripping from him.

"You did well, Jax!" he praised. I gave him the finger, getting a thrum of amusement from him in return.

"I don't...get how you...managed to...push yourself that...fast, when you got...so worn out...in the forest," I muttered.

He reached down, taking my hand, and hauling me to my feet. "My kind are able to live above and below the waters, it is true, but any heavy exertion requires that we rehydrate quickly. Without using the pool before we set off, I'd have collapsed on the run; now, I am merely tired. But you will keep that to yourself."

"Okay," I whispered, moving into a stretch. He nodded to the congregating people out on the main balcony.

"When we train, I must push you, and push you hard," he said, clapping me on the shoulder. "But just so that you have something to look forward to, tonight we will start to spar for real, now that I know more of your capabilities."

"Fuck," I whispered and grabbed his arm as he started to walk away. "Here. If you're going to do this, better to do it right, eh?" I asked, pushing the book into his hands as I straightened up again. "I intended to give it to you last night, but with everything..." I shrugged and left him staring at the small volume as I ambled over to the group, only to have Barret intercept me.

"Hey, man, how's it going?" I asked him, my heart finally getting back under control from its frantic hammering.

"Things are good, Jax," he replied. "I spent time consulting with Flux and a few of his people, and we've come up with a training regimen. I just need you to approve it. To make it as quick and simple as it can be, the hunters and fighters will all attend morning classes here, given by Flux and those he designates.

"The first hour will be focused on a general fighting style that all people can use, mainly unarmed and daggers. Then the groups will split up; hunters will move to the ground floor and practice archery and tracking, with classes on skills like skinning and harvesting corpses. The fighters will be split into three groups: sword, spear, and axe. They will spend an hour on their chosen skill, then train for an additional hour in their individual small units."

"And after that?" I asked, and Barrett grinned.

"After that, one unit joins the hunters and patrols, getting to fight out there in the real world. The others get to spend the day split between helping to clear the floors and more fighting practice."

"People will get sick of practice pretty quickly; how many small groups do we have?"

"Six now, but we've only the two healers still. Not sure how you want them allocated?" he asked.

As I took a moment to consider, I noted that Ame stood off to one side of the group, watching me. I waved to her on our way over. "Who's the other healer?" I asked….

"Ardbeg. The dwarf that you gave the Lay On Hands spell to, he's been using it whenever anyone gets so much as a cut or a sprain, but he's…well, he's trying, is what he is."

"Explain," I said curtly. Barrett took a deep breath as he considered his next words.

"Ardbeg…well, he's a good lad. He's trying to be as helpful as he can be, but he's a fucking coward as well. He wanted to learn to heal people because he thought it meant he could be in a nice, safe place, dealing with people who are sick, and he'll always be valuable.

"He's not going to be much use with the teams. He came running when we needed him back at the battle for the tower, and he was trying to help, but he was also almost outta his mind with terror," Barrett said bluntly.

I gritted my teeth. I'd been in no state to pick who was given the spell, and Oracle had directed that it be "given to someone who wants to be a healer and has the highest affinity for Life magic." From what I remembered of that day after the fight, he'd been pretty desperate to help people, so he'd gotten it.

"Just because he's afraid doesn't make him less useful; we're always going to need extra healers here, after all. Plus, he did come to help when we called for it," I said, trying to be as optimistic about it as I could, just as we reached Ame.

"Yes, and I take it you mean the dwarf?" she said, and I nodded shortly. "He tries. When I met him and realized how desperate he was to be a healer, I was confused as to your choice of teaching; now, it is clear. He will make the true healer an able assistant, however, and there is always a need for a healer here, as you say."

"Well, I'm glad you're taking it so well, as it means you're going to get to increase your healing skills as well, Ame," I said with a forced smile. "I'm going to need you to go out with the hunters and patrol groups, keeping them as safe as you can and healing those who get injured. Can you do this?"

I almost got my head taken off my shoulders when she replied.

"Go out with them? Of course I will be going out with them! What possible use would I be as a healer if I didn't? What of those that would die before they are returned to the tower? I must be there with them; I will need to be out, fighting alongside them!"

I nodded, thankful that she wanted to do things that way and chose not to reply to the comment about the usefulness of a healer who didn't.

"What is the old fool doing now?" she asked, clearly looking past us towards Flux. He had the book in his hands; it was open, and as I watched, he activated it.

The words on the pages seemed to catch fire, visible even from this distance, lifting from the pages, crisping, and fluttering, before turning into glowing ash that broke down into smoke. The smoke flowed into Flux, sinking into his head, and making him shake. The book suddenly crumbed to dust, and Flux arched his neck, throwing his head back and flinging his arms wide before the transfer was finally done. He collapsed to his knees, panting heavily.

We rushed over to him, helping him to his feet. Ame checked him with her sonic pulse before scolding him thoroughly over the lack of respect he'd paid an artifact and why he should have told her first. He turned slowly to face me, and I couldn't help it.

"Let me guess, you know kung fu?" I asked, a vision of Neo flashing through my mind, gone in an instant as he shook his head slowly.

"I don't know what 'kung fu' is, but I know the Art of Asha'tuun...I must...I..." He shook his head as though in shock.

"Sounds freaky," I said, shrugging. "Is it any good?"

Flux slowly nodded.

"It...it will take some time to work this into our training, but by tonight, I will have a plan," he assured me shakily.

I gave him a smile. "Seriously, Flux, if you think it's worth studying, then that's great; we all need to be a lot better at fighting, but if it's just another style, or you think that another style that you use would be better..."

"No. You don't understand," Flux said, shaking his head. "A master of this art would be practically unstoppable; you gave me a *primer*. It covers the absolute basics and was created to give new members of the Special Forces Legion a very bare bones understanding of the art before they began to train. We *have* to find more of the series." He spoke adamantly, and I turned to scan the space. Not finding Oracle anywhere, I reached out to her with my mind. She'd turned up while Flux and I were training and had gotten bored and wandered off again since then.

"Oracle, do we have any more books on Asha'tuun in the Hall of Memories?"

"Hi, Jax, how're you?"

"Sorry...Hi, Oracle. Are you okay?"

"Yeah, I'm having sooo much fun with Bob. We're exploring the forest, just outside the tower!"

I got a mental image sent by her that showed Bob absolutely covered in flowers. She'd even pushed them into the gaps in his armor. *Poor bastard...*

"I know you and Bob are having fun, but about the Asha'tuun...?"

"Okay, yes...there's a memory crystal and one more book in the Hall of Memories that references it, but I wouldn't use them yet. The book is an advanced one, and the memories are from a member of the Special Forces Legion. She was a hunter-killer for the emperor, and we haven't got anyone that I know of that's even looking to be an assassin or bodyguard beyond Bane, and he'd have no chance of understanding the details."

"Okay, thanks, Oracle."

I turned back to Flux and shook my head.

"Sorry, mate; that was the only lower-level book we had for that art. We have memories for a hunter-killer, whatever that is, and one advanced book. But until you're more experienced, I'm not going to consider using those. It'd just be a waste," I said.

"Hmmm, well, I understand that. It would be a waste,...but..." He shook his head, and I clapped him on his shoulder, nodding.

"I know, mate. Look at it this way: as soon as you can level your skill high enough, it's yours. Okay? Besides, doesn't teaching help to level your skills?"

"Not as much as you'd hope." He shrugged. "But I know more than I did, and I have a goal now, so thank you, Jax."

"No worries. Shall we?" I asked, nodding toward the group that was milling around, waiting for something to happen.

We joined the rest of the group. While I got a lot of strange looks for joining in with them all, once Cai, Oren, and Barrett also showed up, people seemed to accept that it was training for everyone.

Flux separated us all out until we surrounded himself, Cheena, and Bane in a giant ring. Each of the three faced a different direction, and they guided everyone through a series of basic stretches, jumps, and exercises for the first ten minutes.

Once everyone was warmed up and sweating, he introduced a series of moves that were practically dances, fluid steps forward and back, a low, high, and side kick, and two different punches, one high and fast, one low and aimed at center mass. We spent the next forty or fifty minutes following his instructions before a long slow cooldown that was almost exclusively stretches and lunges.

By the end, combined with the morning's two-hour intense workout, and the insane sprint down the tower, I was absolutely exhausted. I walked away on wobbly legs as I tried to hide just how hard the workout had been.

The group part hadn't been so bad at first; it was when those three murderous bastards began to circulate through the group, pausing to order people to go faster, kick higher, and to work to their absolute hardest level, that it got worse. No matter when I tried to slow, to just take it easier a bit, just for a minute, one of them was there by my side.

They'd just pause, looking at me, then looking at the others, and they'd draw everyone's eyes effortlessly to me. I was stronger than most, and faster, and if I just did the same as they did, well…I worked harder.

I was filled with the thoughts they might be having, concerns over my abilities, and I pushed harder. And harder. And even harder.

As I stood at the railing of the balcony, looking out over the miles of forests and mountains spread out before me, I gripped the enchanted stonework as hard as I could and tried to project relaxation, even as I frantically tried to keep my legs from buckling.

I had notifications waiting, and I opened them after a minute. I felt optimistic, having seen the smiles from the dispersing crowd and heard their oaths of delighted surprise.

Congratulations!

Through hard work and perseverance, you have increased your stats by the following:

Endurance +1
Charisma +1
Strength +1

Continue to train and learn to increase this further…

Congratulations!

Through dedicated training with a skilled instructor, you have increased your Unarmed Combat skill. Continue to train and learn to increase this further…

Congratulations!

Through dedicated training with a skilled instructor, you have increased your Spear Wielding skill by two points. Spears are a subset of Staffs, and as such, your Staff Wielding skill has increased slightly. Continue to train and learn to increase this further.

Those notifications had made me smile again; increasing skills always cheered me up.

For the first time in what seemed like ages, I summoned my stat sheet and read it over, my heart finally coming down from its frantic rhythm to a more normal one as I examined my levels.

Name: Jax				
Titles: Strategos: 5% boost to damage resistance, Fortifier: 5% boost to defensive structure integrity, Chosen of Jenae				
Class: Spellsword > Justicar			Renown: Unknown	
Level: 13			Progress: 117,620/120,000	
Patron: Jenae, Goddess of Fire and Exploration			Points to Distribute: 0 Meridian Points to Invest: 0	
Stat	Current points	Description	Effect	Progress to next level
Agility	40	Governs dodge and movement.	+300% maximum movement speed and reflexes, (+10% movement in darkness, -20% movement in daylight)	36/100
Charisma	12	Governs likely success to charm, seduce, or threaten	+20% success in interactions with other beings	2/100
Constitution	32	Governs health and health regeneration	620 health, regen 36.3 points per 600 (+10% regen due to soul bond, -20 health due to soul bond, each point invested now worth 20 health)	17/100
Dexterity	21	Governs ability with weapons and crafting success	+110% to weapon proficiency, +11% to the chances of crafting success	60/100
Endurance	22	Governs stamina and stamina regeneration	220 stamina, regen 12 points per 30 seconds	13/100
Intelligence	29	Governs base mana and number of spells able to be learned	270 mana, spell capacity: 17 (15 + 2 from items), (-20 mana due to soul bond)	57/100
Luck	17	Governs overall chance of bonuses	+7% chance of a favorable outcome	99/100
Perception	24	Governs ranged damage and chance to spot traps or hidden items	+140% ranged damage, +14% chance to spot traps or hidden items	42/100
Strength	23	Governs damage with melee weapons and carrying capacity	+13 damage with melee weapons, +130% maximum carrying capacity	22/100
Wisdom	29 (24)	Governs mana regeneration and memory	+190% mana recovery, 2.9 points per minute, 190% more likely to remember things	98/100

I was about to pull up my skills sheet next when a cough drew my attention. I dismissed the page and looked around, finding Barrett and Oren standing nearby, clearly waiting for me, while Ame berated someone within hearing distance.

"What's up?" I asked, and Barrett gestured to the people as Bane, Flux, and Cheena split them into individual groups.

"I wanted to confirm that what we'd planned before was okay; you remember, the training schedule we were talking about?"

"Yes, sorry, mate; I approve. The only concern I had was the healers, and Ame agreed to go out with the groups, so that's fine. I'd suggest you have the hunters work from a set location that they all agree on, then split off to hunt. That way, they can bring back anything they catch to that location, and Ame and the fighters can be waiting there, in case they're needed. They'll be close by, but far enough back that the hunters can get some experience as well. Does that work?"

"Yes, that makes sense. One more thing, though…we need to talk about Himnel and the people we left there. You were talking about a trip to get supplies and to try to get our families out. Each day we delay means that things will get worse for our families. Not all of us can afford to wait. I—"

"I know it's not ideal—"

"No, Jax, please, listen to me," Barrett pleaded, shaking his head as he interrupted me. I stopped and frowned, gesturing for him to continue. "Look, some of the crew's families, hell, some of our closest friends and the people who we'd most like to recruit, they can't afford for us to wait much longer.

"When we talked about it, I thought it was just two of my friends, and I figured it was better to wait until we had a proper plan, rather than risk it. I figured they'd be able to survive. I've asked around, though, and a lot of our people are in the same boat. At least a third of the people we're most wanting to recruit are the ones that will be in the shit, now that Oren and Decin's ships are 'missing.'

"People relied on us, on our wages, on us being able to get cheap food on our trips…when word spreads that we're gone, whether it's because people think we're dead, or whatever, our families are going to spread out. They're going to need to go looking for work in places they wouldn't normally consider.

"The mines, the Arena, the Pits…some will end up taking contracts for adventuring, then they'll never come back. As it is, our people will be scared, wondering where we are. Another day or two, and they'll be getting frantic. We don't have the weeks and months it'll take to do this properly, Jax. Do you understand?"

"I think so. How long?" I asked, my mind going into overdrive. I'd wanted to get things set up here first, get the tower running better, maybe take Decin's ship out for a trip to Isabella's village and recruit some more first…

"Literally a few days. I've also asked around, and without including the engineers and shipyard rats and their families, there's nearly three hundred people that we'd be looking at trying to get out of the city."

"Fuck!" I cursed, running my fingers through my hair, and glaring at him. "Seriously, man, three fucking hundred? Plus, the engineers and their families, so it'll jump to what, three-fifty, four hundred? How the hell am I supposed to get them out of there? Plus, how the fuck would we feed them? I bet none of them are hunters or anything useful like that!"

"No, but they're a cross-section of a city, Jax. Some are crafters, guards, cooks, and cleaners. Also, two of those who'd want to come are prostitutes, but they're some of the nicest people I know, so—"

"I'm not gonna look down on someone for being a hooker, for fuck's sake; I used to drink with a couple. Weirdest drunken conversations I've ever had, but still cool as fuck people," I muttered, shaking my head. "No, I'm not being an arse here, Barrett. I want to bring anyone who wants to come. But to increase our little group by three or four times its size in one go, and to have to smuggle them out of the city, along with food and supplies, plus the goddamn manastones that we desperately need…"

"I know," Barrett said, taking a deep breath and shrugging. "I needed to let you know, though, because as the days pass, those people are going to start starving, and when your people here know it and compare their new lives to their friends and family starving to death back there because of their choices? It's not going to go down well. My sister and her bairn are back there, and thinking of either of them starving…well, it makes me want to leave you and go help them, despite my Oaths."

"Fuck!" I spat, shaking my head. "All right, leave it with me. I wanted more time to come up with a plan, but that's not the way the world works. I'll have a think and come back to you soon, okay? It's the best I can say right now. I'm sorry; I *know* you're worried, but we only have the most basic plan in place.

"We need to figure this out more, then we can go in and make sure that we save them. If we just go rushing in now…we could lose more than we save, mate. We're not ready to fight Himnel's forces in a head-on war." I motioned them to come closer as I dropped my voice.

"We need to prepare; if we can damage their infrastructure somehow, maybe bomb their shipyards or something, and then get people out with supplies, it'll make a huge difference. We have to take our time and do this right, though."

I looked from one to the other, sympathizing with the torn expressions on their faces, and I nodded toward the ships.

"How's the rebuild going on them?" I asked and got a surprising mix of looks in return. Oren looked depressed, while Barrett looked annoyed, when I'd been expecting a much happier mood.

"Wait, what am I missing here?" I asked.

"Well, laddie," Oren admitted, "tha truth be tha' we hit a wee problem." He shook his head and gestured to the ship. "C'mon, it be better iff'n I show ye."

The three of us set off walking toward the ship, moving quickly through the groups of people training. I had to look twice when I noticed virtually Decin's entire crew in one group, learning to wield spears.

"What's going on there?" I asked, and Barrett smiled as he followed my gaze.

"They asked to be trained as well. In fact, by the time we were done with the first session this morning, almost the entire population of the tower had turned up to join in. It seems a lot of the people wanted to learn to defend themselves, even if they don't intend to be fighters outright."

"Glad to see it, then. I can't complain at people for that; god knows they've all learned what happens when you can't defend yourself, after all. Maybe we need to speak to Cai about shifting things slightly, have people do the workout in two groups, with everyone having a day off in between.

"I don't want people to burn out or hurt themselves by pushing too hard. If people do a morning of exercise and fighting training, followed by the afternoon, and next day doing their normal routine, their bodies will adjust faster."

"I'll talk to him because that makes sense. The original plan was fine when it was just going to be the fighters, but not if it's going to be the entire tower," Barrett agreed.

"Thanks, mate. Okay, Oren, so what's the...problem...?" I asked, but as we moved around the far side of the warship, I saw where the engineers were all congregating. There was a long, dark line that snaked from around mid-deck to near the stern on the starboard side of the ship, and the engineers were busy removing the engines from the entire starboard side.

"Well, now ye see tha problem, laddie. Some fool dinna use the same wood fer tha entire ship. Inside there, under tha claddin', ye see, is a bunch o' green timber. We found it las' night. It's warped and cracked tha outside. One good hit, or a particularly hard turn...tha'd be all it'd take to change ma ship into a pile o' scrap full o' screamin' sailors."

"Well, fuck." I articulated my feelings as clearly as I knew how, while Oren waved one of the engineers over to join us.

"This here be Derik, an' he's done got some options fer ye, but I'm warnin' ye, they do no be good," Oren said, blowing his beard out in irritation.

"Ah! Lord Jax! Sorry, I be a wee bit o' a mess here," Derik said, wiping his hands frantically on the front of his coveralls. He was short, even for a dwarf, which, combined with his massive arms, chest, beard, and eyebrows, gave the impression of talking to a silverback gorilla in a jumpsuit. A very stained, and, in places, torn, jumpsuit.

"Hi, Derik. Don't worry about it. I'm more worried about the ship! What happened?" I said, looking up at the side of the ship and the team of engineers crawling all over it. Some were leaning over the side, while others hung suspended on ropes as they examined the damage.

"Well...basically, it be like this: some *G'stucnik asshole* cut corners an' put a load o' green timber in the ship; it be in the armorin', between the inside o' the ship and the outer hull. It's warpin' and slowly shiftin' as it dries, crackin' the supports around it, and startin' te crack the outer hull. We need to strip it out and put in some fresh, properly seasoned wood, then rebuild her, an'—..."

"An' it'll no be quick," Oren said, taking up the conversation. "It be at least a few days to do, mebbe a week, an' that'd be iff'n we had seasoned timber, which we dinna have."

"So, you're telling me that the warship, the most powerful weapon we have, is basically fucked, unless we take the time to practically rebuild her from the ground up. Is that it?" I growled, running my hand through my hair as I glared up at the ship.

"Aye, well, tha'd be one way o' lookin' at it," Oren hedged, and I turned to him, raising one eyebrow in irritated query. "Ye remember whut ye said t'other night, about wantin' to fix tha issues with the ship? Like replace the shitty wood they'd used with good, thick wood, tha kind that'd shrug off a cannon blast?"

"You mean when we were talking about the ideal kind of warship we'd build, given the wood around here? And using the weapons I described from my home?

The shit we don't know *how* to build?" I asked him, and he colored slightly under his beard.

"Ah, well, mebbe it were a slightly diff'rent conversation ah remember, then. Anyhoo…how about we make tha best o' it? After all, ye did give Derik here tha' book…"

"Aye, Lord Jax! The skillbook ye gave me on magical structures ha' given me sooo many ideas! I can use some o' the knowledge to make the ship much stronger. She'd be heavier, much heavier, but we could mebbe make some changes, or add extra engines."

"She's already slow as shit; adding extra engines is a great idea, but if it's only to make her as fast as she is currently, I don't see it.

"As to the extra armor, yeah, it'd be great, but seriously, that was a plan to make an entirely new ship, and it was a 'maybe someday' plan, not a 'let's do it right fucking now' plan!" I said, shaking my head.

"Look, you've obviously had time to think about this. Get with Ame, Lun, and Elaine, the engineers who I gave the other books to. You've got a few hours to come up with a basic plan, then I want you all working on it. We're going to need this ship up and running to protect the tower and get me and my team to Himnel soon, not to mention the village of Dannick."

The pair of dwarves raced off with barely a second glance, and I turned to Barrett, who grinned at me.

"Not long ago, it would have been me getting told to 'sort it out' by Oren. Gotta say, it makes a nice change!" he said, walking off to discuss the training updates with Flux.

"You need to relax, Jax," Oracle's voice sounded in my ear. I turned my head to find the diminutive Wisp hovering close by, watching me.

"I'd love to, Oracle, but I don't know what the hell I'm doing most of the time. Every time I turn around, something has just gone wrong or needs me to look at it," I muttered.

She flew in closer, landing on my shoulder and reaching down for my hand. I reached up to her, feeling her solid, warm skin as she gripped my hand tightly.

I could never get my head around the fact that she was incorporeal one second, then seemingly fully flesh and blood the next. I wrote it off ninety percent of the time as magic and her nature, really, but it still weirded me out on occasion.

"How about we go explore?" Oracle said. "You, me, and Bob can go out for a wander, explore some of the local forest, and see what trouble we can find?"

"God, that sounds good," I said quietly, observing the hustle and bustle of people training, working on the ships, or running from one place to another.

"Bob's still downstairs; I asked him to patrol the outer wall. It's pretty ruined and overgrown, but it makes him happy to have a goal he can understand. Walking around the wall and killing anything that attacks him is pretty simple," she said. I laughed, a bit of my building irritation dispelled by her comments.

I was about to suggest heading down, when Jenae made contact, her sudden arrival in my mind flooding out every other thought. I saw a map projected before me, a map with a pair of glowing sections.

"Jax! I've found a trace of Thomas." Her voice crackled with emotion, and I grinned in spite of myself, my sudden sour mood banished easily as I looked over the map.

"It's not recent; the two spots I've highlighted are a cave system in the lower mountains to the southwest. He used a lot of magic there, over, and over, but that was about a year ago. The other trace I found is in the city of Himnel; it was a collection of spells, followed by something else, a failed and backfired spell, if I had to guess.

"The last one was powerful, and it was about six weeks ago. He's either not used magic since, or it's been somewhere well hidden enough that I can't sense it with this tracking spell. I tried casting a second, more specific spell at Himnel, but found no trace of him. I don't have the strength for a third yet, not for days to come, at the least."

"You're sorry? Jenae, this is wonderful! This means he's still alive, and he's not even that far away! This is fantastic news!" I blurted out loud, and Jenae was quick to reply.

"No, it doesn't, Jax. It means he was alive six weeks ago; that's all. I don't know where in Himnel he is, or even if he is still there.... I—"

"He was alive six weeks ago, Jenae, which means he still is. If he's survived this long already, he can survive until I can get to him. I need to get the warship put back together, and..." I said, directing my mental voice to her.

"Jax, please...stop," Jenae said. I froze, her tone of voice finally getting through to me. *"There's more. I can't tell much of what he did, since it was too long ago, but the spells he cast...he was suffering when he cast them, gravely injured, and his mana channels were damaged. The trace is full of pain, so whatever spell he was casting...it damaged his ability to cast spells, and he did it anyway. You have to be prepared for the worst."*

"I..."

"I'm sorry, Jax. I wish I had better news. I swear I will try again as soon as I have enough strength."

"No," I said. *"No, Jenae; you don't know my brother. He's not dead, and I'm going to find him. Thank you for doing this. All is forgiven. Rest and get yourself back together. I'm going to Himnel, and I'll need you to cast that spell when you're ready."*

As I ended the connection, I felt something I'd not done in days, not since the fight with the goblins. I knew what I had to do and where I had to go! I wasn't an administrator or a teacher. I was crap at that side of things; I knew I was. But the thing I could do? I could fucking well fight, and I could have my people do the rest of it. I could battle my way to my brother.

No fucker ever expected Conan to hold people's hands and explain what they needed to do. He said "do it," and they found the way. That was going to be my path from now on. Although I'd probably wear more clothes generally and chop off fewer heads.

"Cai, Oren, Barrett, Ame, and Flux, I need you! Lydia! Get your team together! Decin! You and Hanau get your arses over as well!" I bellowed, making everyone around me jump as I headed straight for the warship and the captain's cabin inside it.

It took a handful of minutes to gather everyone together, and even the wisps used the tower's mana to create projections of their forms. The small room was cramped with everyone inside, but it had the one feature I needed; it had the map.

I stood on the far side of the mapping table, looking down at it as Oracle tapped the activation rune, and the map flared to life.

I felt a pull on my mind, similar to the way the notifications appeared. This time, it was Oracle pulling something out, and as the map blurred and updated, I nodded grimly.

The small map that had given basic details of the continent up to the mountains then very patchy information on the other side, was suddenly far, far more detailed. The continent was longer than it was wide, with the mountain range that ran down its length being wider and longer than I'd realized. The mountains alone must be at least five hundred miles in length, and while the land was heavily forested on our side, there were far fewer trees on the west. A huge marshland and great plains and hills rolled over most of it, with several castles clearly marked, as well as dozens of sites of ruins and other symbols I couldn't identify.

What really mattered to me, though, was the city of Himnel, south by southeast from the tower, established on the coast. There was no sign of the highlighting that Jenae had added when we spoke, but the cave that Tommy had been in was maybe a hundred and fifty to two hundred miles further southwest from where we were, so I dismissed it for now. Tommy had left there, and had clearly headed to the city, where something had happened. He'd been hurt then had vanished.

"Hold on, Tommy," I muttered, glaring at the map. "I'm coming!"

CHAPTER TWENTY-TWO

The others gathered around, murmuring in awe. Oren, Decin, and Hanau in particular were stunned by the map, especially the level of detail, much of it thanks to Jenae sharing it with me. They immediately started muttering amongst themselves as they pointed out details to each other.

"Right, people!" I said loudly, and everyone went quiet, looking to me. "I've spoken to Jenae—the goddess Jenae, I should say, sorry. She's told me that my brother was in Himnel, and he was hurt badly. This was six weeks ago, and I've lost too much time already.

"Barrett has told me about how desperate our people's families are, so fuck it. We're leaving today, even if I have to pick up and throw the goddamn ships to get them in the air! Give me options." I looked around the room, concentrating on Decin and Oren primarily, but surprisingly, it was Barrett that spoke first.

"There's no way that the warship can be made…flightworthy…in that short a time, lord. It simply can't be done," he said earnestly. Both Oren and Decin spoke up in agreement.

"Okay, what about the *Libertas*?" I asked, and Decin nodded.

"She be ready, Lord Jax. We can get her in tha air sharp; the work we be doin' were minor, no stress there."

"Then it's settled. We're going to be taking the smuggler's route."

"Ye'd be takin' a risk there, laddie," Oren said, grimacing.

"Yeah, well, what's new there? You got a realistic alternative?"

"Ah…well…"

"Then suck it up, buttercup," I said, moving on.

"Buttercup? Ah…look, Jax; ain't nobody survived tha' route in months. I'm just a wee bit concerned tha'—"

"Do you know what's down there?" I asked.

He frowned. "Don't know, don't nobody tha' still lives knowin' neither. Those few tha' lived through tha last caravans did it by bein' sneaky and abandonin' their friends to whatever lives down there. They ran, and they lived, but they didna see shit, they said."

"Well, if anyone has a better idea, now's the time to speak up…" I waited a minute, then went on when I was only met with uncomfortable silence. "Then it's settled. There's an old saying in my home: 'When you've got a problem, it's shit. Two problems, and you're fucked, but when you've got a bunch? You've got some solutions, too.'

"Cai, get with Decin and Hanau, and get that ship loaded for a flight to the smuggler's route. We're going in at night, which means you can drop me and my team off outside and bugger off. Decin, once you've dropped me off, head straight to the village of Dannick.

"Take Isabella with you and call in. Talk to the people and get them recruited. If they're up for it, strip the village and head back to the tower. If they're not, take whoever is and whatever they'll let you take, but get back here as fast as you can."

"My ship only be a small scout, lord, an'—"

"Make extra trips; just do what you need to," I cut him off. "Oren, I need someone your crew's families will trust, someone who knows where they'll be and can recruit them...not you!" I said, holding a forestalling hand up as he tried to volunteer. "You're going to be getting your ship in order. Seneschal, how much would assigning the class-three servitor to the ship rebuild speed things up?"

"Considerably; work that would take weeks would take days instead, especially if we assigned a class-one construction golem to assist, as well."

"Do it. I'm not sure how soon we'll need it, but if we need it, we'll really need it. Take the time to get the ship outfitted right. Fix what you can and strengthen it. Wisps, can I communicate with you from there?" I asked.

They exchanged a long look.

"It's possible, but it'll take a lot of mana," Oracle hedged. "And I'll need to be up high. Like, really high."

"Okay, then when we need the ships, we'll let you know. For now, plan on not being needed before a week's time, so you've at least that long to make repairs and upgrades. How long does the smuggler's route take to cross?"

"A full day and a night, at a minimum," Barrett offered. "I don't know exactly where it was, but I had a 'friend' who used it a few times. She said it must have been an old escape tunnel from the city, and it was somewhere in the forest here..." He tapped the map just north of the city where the trees were heaviest.

"Sounds like fun, Barrett. The crew's families, will they trust you?" I asked, and Oren spoke up before Barrett could.

"Aye, laddie; he'd be better loved than me, if no fer the bonuses I paid out. They know him."

"Good; then you're coming with me, Barrett. Flux, I've not got time to fuck about right now. Can Bane continue to teach me like you have been?"

"He can; he's less experienced, but he's dedicated and skilled," Flux acknowledged calmly.

"Good, then he's coming with me, and you're staying here." When Flux tried to object, I cut him off, hardly looking away from the map. "Leave it, Flux. If I could, I'd take you all. But as a group, you'll draw too much attention, and I need someone I can trust to watch over the military side of the tower if I'm taking Barrett."

"You're to continue to train people and help them to get fit, strong, and deadly. As of now, you're folded into the command structure of the tower, as commander of the hunters and stealthy fuckers. We'll come up with a title later. In Barrett's absence, you run all security for the tower; understand?" I fixed him with a glare, and after a second, he bowed his head and stepped back respectfully.

"Yes, Lord Jax," Flux said, and I turned to Ame.

"Ame, you'll work with Cai and make sure people are fit and healthy; you'll also be in charge of any medical issues. Train up those you'll need and go out with the squads. Level your healing as fast as you can. When this meeting is over, I need you to get Renna and bring her here. Tell her to bring along whatever she needs. I'll explain when you're both here.

"Barrett, tell Lydia what she needs to know and get the squad together. They're coming to the city with me, so have them prepare as much as they can. Oracle, I want a skillbook for each of them, something geared towards their abilities, and get two spellbooks for Arrin; it's time he got a bit more useful.

"Decin, how long will it take to get to Himnel on your ship?" I asked, turning to him and he rubbed his chin in thought, doing a little calculation with Hanau.

"Well, we could make it in a day, but we'd be pushin' tha engines hard. Dangerously so."

"Damn, I knew your ship was faster, but…" I said, shaking my head.

"It be the rear engine," he explained. "Most of the ships, they use their engines on tha sides fer lift and thrust, but tha *Libertas* were a test. She's got a single larger, more powerful engine at the back tha' do just be fer thrust, no direction at all. Makes it more dangerous; if we lose the lift from the others, we could smash into the ground, hard, but we be much faster!"

"Damn, right you are," I muttered, thinking. "Okay; plan is for a day and a half. We get as far as we can before nightfall, then slow down or stop or whatever you'd normally do. I want us to arrive in the middle of tomorrow night at the forest north of Himnel. Is that a problem?"

"Nay, laddie, we can do tha'."

"Good!" I looked around at the room full of people all waiting on me, and I straightened up when none of them had anything to say.

"That's it, then. Dismissed!" They clapped fists to chest in salute and filed out quickly as I turned to Seneschal and Heph. "Keep things together, guys. Make sure my people are safe and the tower is still standing. I'll get anything I can to help us.

"Build the golems as we discussed, and I'm sorry I can't give either of you the class three now. Once it's finished with the ship, it goes to work on this floor, to repair it and make it safe. Make use of the war golems when they arrive; I'm only sorry I can't grab one to take with me."

"They are fairly obvious as to their nature, Jax. You'd be spotted straight away."

"Doesn't mean I don't want one, though," I retorted. "Seriously, though, guys, work with Cai, Ame, Flux, and Oren, keep things together, and I'll see you soon. I hope. Now, I need to get my gear together, and you need to get back to work."

The pair of them clapped a fist to their chests and vanished.

I dismissed the map and left the room as well, I sent Jana running back up to the fortieth floor to make sure I'd not left anything anywhere, and I set off with Bane to round up the rest of my gear. Once I'd gathered everything, I took it back to the ship and spread it out in the captain's cabin, sorting through what I had. I'd really wanted to spend a few days at least making potions, but I just didn't have the time.

I stuck my head back outside and shouted to Cai to make sure that Tel came with us, as he was going to get some alchemical training on the ship, but to tell him that he would be staying with the ship, not coming to town.

He was also expected to gather any of the ingredients he could find to bring with us. I needed a fuck ton of potions, and a nice, relaxing holiday…a trip on a flying fucking ship to sneak through a monster-infested sewer into an enemy-held city so I could rob it of people and gear would have to do.

"Oracle bring a basic alchemy book as well, and one on herbalism. Fuck holding everything back until we need it; we need it now."

"Ooookay, Jax…I'll be there soon."

I felt the annoyance Oracle didn't bother to hide from me as she turned back and returned to the Hall of Memories. I didn't think she'd gotten far from it; it was hard to tell at this distance, but I had no doubt I'd be paying for it in some way.

I shrugged and returned to my gear, examining each piece's condition. What I found wasn't bad; my mostly complete Night's Embrace set had dropped a bit on its durability, but the rest still in decent shape. I pulled up the stats for them, checking each over quickly:

Cuirass of Night's Embrace		Further Description *Yes/No*	
Details:		This chest armor is made of vertical strips of blackened highsteel laid over toughened leather. It gives a bonus of +5 to stealth. All attacks made when undetected will do extra damage.	
Rarity:	**Magical:**	**Durability:**	**Charge:**
Rare	Yes	68/100	N/A

Greaves of Night's Embrace		Further Description *Yes/No*	
Details:		These greaves are made of vertical strips of blackened highsteel laid over toughened leather. They give a bonus of +2 to stealth.	
Rarity:	**Magical:**	**Durability:**	**Charge:**
Rare	Yes	73/100	N/A

Pauldrons of Night's Embrace		Further Description *Yes/No*	
Details:		These pauldrons are made of vertical strips of blackened highsteel laid over toughened leather. They give a bonus of +2 to stealth.	
Rarity:	**Magical:**	**Durability:**	**Charge:**
Rare	Yes	69/100	N/A

Boots of Night's Embrace		Further Description *Yes/No*	
Details:		These boots are made of vertical strips of blackened highsteel laid over toughened leather. They give a bonus of +3 to stealth and reduce the sound of footsteps made when wearing them.	
Rarity:	**Magical:**	**Durability:**	**Charge:**
Rare	Yes	74/100	10/100

Dagger of Ripping		Further Description *Yes/No*	
Details:		This dagger is enchanted to tear a wound wider than normal, ensuring the target bleeds heavily.	
Rarity:	**Magical:**	**Durability:**	**Charge:**
Rare	Yes	79/100	56/100

Ring of Pain		Further Description *Yes/No*	
Details:		This ring is enchanted to inflict 20% more pain on damage done by weapons held in this hand.	
Rarity:	**Magical:**	**Durability:**	**Charge:**
Rare	Yes	66/100	10/100

Naginata		Further Description *Yes/No*	
Damage:		24-40 +17	
Details:		This two-handed weapon was built from a combination of modern Earth techniques and traditional Japanese skills, creating a weapon that is truly deadly in the hands of a skilled user.	
		Enhanced; This weapon has been enhanced through silverbright and has absorbed some of the souls of its victims. Current capacity: 17/100	
		Bonus ability: Magical infusion: Casting your spells through this weapon will infuse it with that ability for the duration of channeling and cause X damage where X is equal to the damage done by the cast spell.	
Rarity:	**Magical:**	**Durability:**	**Charge:**
Unique	Yes	86/100	N/A

Dragon Shortsword		Further Description *Yes/No*	
Damage:		12-17	
Details:		This shortsword is made of L6 tool steel and is far stronger than its traditional counterparts, gaining a +6 to damage done with it. This sword will bend, not break, and has been engraved on one side with a dragon motif by its creator. This is part of a set of two but grants no bonuses at this time.	
Rarity:	**Magical:**	**Durability:**	**Charge:**
Rare	No	98/100	N/A

Phoenix Shortsword		Further Description *Yes/No*	
Damage:		12-17	
Details:		This shortsword is made of L6 tool steel and is far stronger than its traditional counterparts, gaining a +6 to damage done with it. This sword will bend, not break, and has been engraved on one side with a phoenix motif by its creator. This is part of a set of two but grants no bonuses at this time.	
Rarity:	**Magical:**	**Durability:**	**Charge:**
Rare	No	98/100	N/A
Bracers		**Further Description** *Yes/No*	

Details:		These bracers are made primarily from leather and have been reinforced with thin steel bands. Each bracer has a short punch dagger concealed within it.		
Rarity:	**Magical:**	**Durability:**		**Charge:**
Common	No	72/100		N/A

Belt of Concealment		**Further Description** *Yes/No*		
Details:		This sturdy leather belt is wider than commonly worn to allow for the loops of razor wire concealed within. Dual wooden toggles are artfully disguised as ornamental latches at the front, while providing grips for the hidden wire.		
Rarity:	**Magical:**	**Durability:**		**Charge:**
Uncommon	No	86/100		N/A

Assassin's Helm		**Further Description** *Yes/No*		
Details:		This a black full-face helm with interwoven steel reinforcement. It provides basic protection while covering the face, leaving only the eyes uncovered. The lower face-concealing panels can be hinged back if desired.		
Rarity:	**Magical:**	**Durability:**		**Charge:**
Unusual	No	56/100		N/A

Basic Bag of Holding		**Further Description** *Yes/No*		
Details:		This basic Bag of Holding reduces the weight of any item placed inside by 75%, has 24 slots, and enables multiple items to be stacked up to 99 times in a single slot. This item was created in a low-mana location, and as such will deteriorate faster than a normal Bag of Holding.		
Rarity:	**Magical:**	**Durability:**		**Charge:**
Common	Yes	43/100		N/A

Bow of Accuracy		**Further Description** *Yes/No*		
Damage		8-10 DPS		
Details:		This bow grants the user a 10% increase in accuracy when used.		
Rarity:	**Magical:**	**Durability:**		**Charge:**
Uncommon	Yes	72/100		N/A

Dagger		**Further Description** *Yes/No*		
Details:		This dagger is made of L6 tool steel and as such is far stronger than traditional counterparts, gaining a +4 to damage done with it.		
Rarity:	**Magical:**	**Durability:**		**Charge:**
Rare	No	98/100		N/A

I'd finally taken the time to check out my gear properly, something I'd not done in seemingly forever, and I found two things I should have looked at long since. First was my naginata; it'd absorbed some of the souls from the goblins, thankfully not many, but some of their weak-ass souls had taken up slots in it, and I hated that.

I thought about the fights and realized that it had also absorbed that asshole human's soul, the mage slaver. It probably meant that it would only absorb souls if I was actively channeling into it when I killed something, but I'd need to be careful from now on to make sure that was the case, and I didn't waste any more slots.

The second thing that I'd rediscovered was Ora's bow in my bag of holding. I'd completely forgotten about it, and it had a quiver of arrows with it, including some arrows clearly designed for hunting animals, while others were tipped with the heavy chisel tips of armor piercers. I looked the bow over quickly. I was no archer, after all, and while I'd been trained to use a bow, this would definitely be put to better use by someone that didn't have magic as an option.

I lifted it closer, peering more carefully at the runes that covered the surface, seeing something that tickled at my memories. It made me think of the spellbook I'd wasted with Oracle, Airblade. There was something…

Congratulations!

You have taken your first step toward a greater world of mystery. Basic Runes Skill has been learned. With this skill and your existing magical knowledge, you have a 3% chance of understanding the meaning behind runes you encounter, provided you know the corresponding spellform.

I blinked, the notification's appearance distracting me, and the moment of epiphany was lost. I growled in irritation; I'd allowed myself to be distracted by the flash of the notification, and I'd then actually opened it and read it, which had cost me the chance to learn whatever the rune was.

I slammed the bow back down and stripped off, pulling cleanish boxers, jeans, socks, and a long-sleeved black undershirt on, as I resolved to find somewhere that I could clean my damn clothes soon. I pulled my armor on and settled my weapons, leaving the helm in my bag for now. It was cool-looking, and it'd kept my skull intact a load of times so far. But the stitches Justin or Helena had put into it in between bouts in the arena were clear to see, and I didn't think I needed it here.

A tentative knock reverberated the door to the captain's cabin, and I quickly jerked it open to find a human woman standing there. I froze for a second, confused, as my mind had been elsewhere, then I grinned at her. It was Renna, the artist I'd given the magical infusion book to, standing and waiting with Ame, Flux standing not far away.

"Great to see you, Renna. Come in, please. Ame, Flux…you too," I said, stepping back and making sure they closed the door once they were all inside.

"Did you study the book?" I asked Renna.

She nodded, a smile coming to her face.

"And my request? Will it work?"

"It should; I'll need to study a lot, though. For now, I only know the one rune that Ame taught me."

"That's fine." I bade them all sit, and I stripped my armor and top off again, showing all three of them the torn and damaged containment rune that the Baron had etched into my skin, seemingly so long ago.

"Wha—what is this?" Ame asked, stunned. She pushed Flux aside and struggled around the small table to sit close with me, the vibrations she emitted as she examined me setting my teeth on edge. I saw they were affecting Renna just as badly, but she was fascinated as she tried to look without getting in anyone's way.

"Renna, you're free to examine this as well," I said, gesturing her forward. When the pair had looked it over, they finally took their seats again. Renna was already making drawings of it in a sketchbook she'd been given by Cai.

"No, see here, the lower Dantian linkage? It must be longer," Ame said, quickly comparing my scarring to the drawing and correcting it. I gave them a few minutes to discuss it before explaining what it was and why the Baron had given it to me. It immediately sparked a new discussion between Ame and Renna as to the magic that had been used and why it had included a trap, a discussion which I suddenly had visions of raging out of control, until I put my foot down and stopped them.

"You can discuss this in your own time; for now, I need you to do as I asked, Renna. Ame and Flux, you're here both to help with this, considering your skills, and your manapool, Ame, and to plan how we could use this to our advantage in the future, Flux."

Renna gathered her gear together, and I sat in the middle of the room, directing her as to positioning, though I left the style to her. Ame looked over the drawing as she worked, instructing her, and guiding to make sure it was as well-made as possible. It took a few hours, but in a surprisingly short time, I was buttoning up my top, and Renna was staggering out of the door, exhausted.

"She will make an excellent runecrafter," Ame said, looking to me, and I nodded, wincing as my body shifted.

"Well, teach her, then. So, how long does it take to learn a new rune?" I asked, pulling the bow out of my bag of holding. I couldn't help but grin at how cool it was to do that, but it wasn't until Ame let out a pulse of surprise and snatched the bow from my hands that I saw any reaction. Clearly, the bag wasn't anything special to them, but the bow?

"Where did you get this?!" Ame demanded, lifting the bow and examining it from multiple angles.

"I won it in a tournament; I take it that it's good?" I said, grinning.

"It's trash," she replied, examining it closer and twisting it this way and that.

"Oh…right," I said, a bit stunned by her dismissal, and the fact that she was still examining the bow so carefully. "So why are you still looking at it?"

"The bow is of poor craftsmanship; certain materials I don't recognize were used, and the crafter's skill is…disappointing. The runes are carved in perfectly consistent depth, and the material used to fill them is…clear. There are no blemishes in the material at all, but the skill of the runecrafter is pathetic. I could do better while drunk! Look, see here?" She tapped on one of the lines of a symbol and I looked at it, seeing nothing different from the rest. "This is too short! And here…" She stroked another section, digging the tip of a nail into the wood and peeling a section up without effort.

"This wood is too weak to survive the magic that would be drawn through it; it would be lucky to survive a hundred arrows." I grimaced, but she went on, examining it before clutching it to her chest. "I must have it," she stated.

"I thought you said it was shit?" I asked, frowning in confusion.

"It is," she replied brutally. "But there are two runes on here I do not know, considering how the crafter butchered the rune of addition. I can only imagine the months of work…of experimenting and researching to fix the errors I have ahead of me, but still! These are two *new* runes, three, counting that containment rune, which is more than I have seen in almost a decade. Add these to what I have learned from my books? I can use these runes in a dozen ways that I can think of already."

"Why is it so rare to find new runes, anyway?" I asked her, and she tapped at the runes clearly visible on the bow.

"Have you seen other runes like this?" she asked me, and I shook my head.

"I've not been looking. I've got a few magical bits of gear, and—"

"Do they have runes on show, like this?" she interrupted quickly, her tendrils all extending and that now familiar subsonic thrum shaking my teeth as she examined me.

"No…not that I've noticed," I admitted, and she gave up after a few seconds of examination.

"No, they don't," she muttered, clearly disappointed. "The runes on the cannons on the ships are partially hidden as well, warped to hide sections so they cannot be copied."

"What's the difference?"

"When an enchanted artifact is created, they are created one of two ways: they are enchanted, which is by far the more common way, or runecrafted. Enchanting is both easier to learn and more reliable for most purposes because a script is used, instead of runes. This may sound similar, but it is not! A script defines the use of the magic in a very specific way, fire to heat the blade, for example.

"A rune is far more general, and as such needs to be adjusted to the specific requirement. The fire rune on a blade must be adjusted to specify the blade, and not the hilt, to activate only when used as a weapon, and not when in a sheath and a hundred other minor alterations. These are all written into the rune; each rune I know has dozens, if not hundreds of qualifying details on it."

"Why the hell would you choose runecrafting over enchanting, then? Seems like enchanting would be the better choice," I asked curiously.

"It may seem this way, but an enchanter is limited far more than a runecrafter. I can take my knowledge and create runes that will work on armor or shields, airships, or even the walls of this tower; an enchanter will spend their lives working only on a sword or a shield, over and over again."

She paused, looking again at the bow more closely.

"The rune is etched into it through the use of magic. As part of the rune's creation, a secondary section is overlaid, to hide all or part of the rune from the eyes of all who see it, except the creator and their teacher. This means that the runecrafter or enchanter can keep their secrets. Whoever created this bow decided not to do this; I cannot imagine why, but I will gladly learn their runes!"

I was struck by a sudden insight and spoke before I thought about it.

"No, they didn't," I said and grinned at Ame. "They didn't have the choice to hide the runes because the bow was created in my world! There's much less mana there, so they didn't have the mana to spare to make it!" I grabbed at my bag of holding, untying it, and holding it out to her. "What about this? Can you sense anything on here?"

She took the bag and started examining it. I stood there for a few long minutes as she pored over it minutely, before slowly nodding.

"There is a hint of the rune still visible, here, you see. They tried to hide it, but not well enough," she said, tapping at one side of the bag. I looked closely. There was nothing I could make out, and Flux shrugged when I looked to him, clearly not seeing anything either. "Blind fools," Ame muttered, before going on. "Here there is a resonance to my touch. My mana follows paths woven into the structure of the bag. It is not enough for me to make a bag of holding, even one so basic as this. But if I were to study it, I might be able to glean the rune that is visible…I will keep them both," she stated suddenly, and I fixed her with a glare.

"You damn well won't," I said. "I need my bag, and as to the bow, I was going to give it to Miren or Stephanos!"

"But lord—"

"And call me Jax!" I snapped.

"Jax…I must study this! If it were lost or broken, we would lose the chance. But if I learn it, I could make more. I could use these runes to improve a dozen weapons easily if they are what I think they are! Please, I beg of you, we must examine this," she said, holding the bow like it was her firstborn, while I took my bag back, securing it to my side.

I looked at her as I thought about it and finally I pulled the arrows out of the bag and passed them to her as well.

"Okay, learn what you can, *but* I know you've got a fuck ton of work on already, between helping the squads and researching into runecrafting. Take your time, and don't fucking burn yourself out. Rest when you need to. Flux, I expect you to make sure she damn well does that, okay?" I insisted, waiting until I got a nod in response from each of them. "Good. Examine the bow and see what you can learn, then. Although, out of curiosity, how the hell do you learn new runes if everyone hides them?"

"You have to destroy the artifact," she said simply. "You have a chance to learn the rune as you destroy it, but it is a slim chance, and few manage it. Beyond that, you must apprentice yourself to a teacher, serving many years to learn a single rune. In such ways are the balance of power maintained; after all, the greatest armorers will only entrust their creations to the greatest of enchanters. In this way, those of us who are not sworn to a lord or crafting association can never grow to compete," she said bitterly.

"Well, you're sworn to one now, so I guess I'll have to get you some more runes, then." I shrugged. *Enough of this crap*, I decided, heading to the door.

I stalked out of the captain's cabin, shrugging to settle the pauldrons in place and trying to ignore the sting of Renna's work.

I stopped in my tracks, a grin coming to my face at how quickly people were running, determined to make the *Libertas* ready for this trip.

Lydia and her team were gathering on the deck of the ship, the crew running back and forth as they completed last-minute tasks.

"Bane?" I said quietly, testing, and a second later, I heard a quiet response.

"Yes, Jax?" he said. His stealth skills and natural camouflage had allowed him to hide in almost plain sight next to a pile of barrels by the door.

"Nothing, mate; I just wondered where you were," I said when a thought struck me. "I didn't actually ask you about this, but are you okay with the idea of training me?"

"Do you want the honest answer? Or the nice one?" Bane replied after a few seconds, the subsonic of his race's laughter reverberating through me.

"Don't blow sunshine up my arse, mate, just tell me straight. I'm a big boy, I can take it," I replied, grinning at him.

"I'd rather you learned how to fight before we go anywhere. So far, you have survived on a mixture of insane aggression, luck, and what seems to have been very basic training. But to anyone who actually studies your fighting style, you have huge gaps in your knowledge. Have you chosen your specializations yet?" he asked.

"I don't think so; what are they?" I replied, shaking my head in confusion.

He let out a low groan. "I knew it. Okay, Jax, this is simple, but oh so complicated at the same time." He stood up and moved over to stand at my side, watching around the ship as he did so. "Not much point in my staying in stealth when we're in a conversation, I suppose," he said, shrugging. "So, when you reach level ten in any discipline, you gain a specialization. I don't know about the other aspects of life, but in fighting, you can choose a way to improve your skills. When I reached level ten in my daggers, I chose to improve their piercing ability. I gained an extra ten percent of the overall damage done by any dagger I use, and it bypasses my target's armor."

"How the hell does that work?" I asked.

"I hit harder and cut faster; not by much, but as skilled as I have become with daggers, I would have been surprised if I had not improved somehow."

"Okay, give me a minute," I said, concentrating as my skill matrix appeared. It flared and changed, the details shifting as I concentrated on only what was important to me right now.

Skill	Sub-Skill	Level	Bonus	Specialty Knowledge
Ranged	Archery	1		Bowman (0/100)
	Throwing Knives	3		Small Blades (20/100)
	Throwing Axes	1		Axes (0/100)
Melee	Axes	1		(0/100)
	Dual Wielding	4		Twin swords (50/100)
	Daggers	5		Daggers (90/100)
	Maces	3		(40/100)
	Swords	6		Swordsman (40/100)
	Staffs	8		Naginata (70/100) Spears (50)
	Unarmed	6		Unarmed (50/100)

The skills list, once I'd dismissed the details for anything not weapons-related, was short and to the point. I read it out to Bane, and he laughed.

"Well, at least you're close to your first specialization for your weapons, then; one more fight will probably do it. Considering the way you fight with that naginata, I'm surprised you're so low, still, but we can fix that."

"When we spar, does that increase the level?" I asked and got an immediate shake of the head.

"No. For whatever reason, the gods decided that such skills only increase with actual combat, but the act of training does make a difference, and not just to your chance of living through the fight. If you train in a skill, then use that same skill in combat, you will increase the skill much quicker than without training first."

"So, basically, train my ass off, and it'll all be worth it later. Gotcha," I muttered, dismissing the screen.

"Essentially true, Jax; we will work on it together," Bane said reassuringly, before easing back into stealth and vanishing.

"Fuck it, then," I muttered, watching Flux and Ame finally leaving the cabin behind me. Oren and Cai walked over, and I waved to them to join us.

"Okay, guys," I said when we were all standing together, "take care of things here, get our people trained as best as you can, and don't let the damn tower collapse while I'm gone. I trust you, so for now, act as a council for me. You deal with any issues you have to, and I'll check in with Seneschal as often as I can I guess; you can give him messages for me."

With that and a round of wrist clasping and nods, I turned and marched up the gangplank onto Decin's ship instead, finally ready to go. I could feel Bob somewhere below me; I'd sent him a command to protect the tower, but it felt weird to not have him by my side. I'd considered taking him to the city; people have seen skeletal constructs, after all, but he'd draw too much attention even then, and I needed to be as stealthy as possible. Lastly, I needed him to protect my people here, so as much as I wanted my buddy with me, he was staying behind.

Oracle flew down to me, full-sized, and her arms were full of books which drew the eye of everyone that saw them. I took them and slipped them into my bag of holding, thanking Oracle and getting an excited grin from her as she felt the engines roaring to life below us.

"Are we off?" she asked me. I grinned at her, unable to help myself.

"Yeah, Oracle. Fuck all this town-building shit; we're off to kill people," I said, feeling the last of the weight of the tower sliding from my shoulders. I'd spent too much time on building the infrastructure up. I knew I could have sorted it out in half the time, if I'd known what I was doing, but I just didn't know enough.

I'd have to rely on Cai and the others more than I had been; I'd had conversations about what I wanted to see happening with the tower, we'd all thrashed those ideas out. But still, it had ultimately been me telling everyone what to do and where to go.

No more.

From now on, I decided I'd be giving Cai, Barrett, Flux, and Ame orders, and they could be the ones who made shit work. I was going to do what I was best at.

Fucking monsters up and stealing their lunch money.

CHAPTER TWENTY-THREE

"Lydia!" I called over to her. "As soon as you've got them sorted out, come join me, okay?"

She nodded and started getting her people moving. They had bags of gear, weapons, bedrolls, food, and other equipment. With rushing them as I had, they hadn't had time to sort it all out yet.

I smiled to myself as I saw a pile of rope amongst it all. *Can't be an adventurer without some rope…*

I sat on the edge, watching the forest below gliding by, as I reveled in the breeze, the feeling of standing on the edge of a cliff and looking down, combined with the fresh, beautifully clear air to make me feel amazing, despite how concerned I was about Tommy.

I had a half-baked plan to get into the city, fighting my way along the smuggler's path and hopefully raiding, in turn, whatever the fuck had been raiding them. Then I'd use the smugglers' stolen goods to pay for a fucking criminal to help me get a fuck-ton of people out of the city. If I was lucky, we'd get some gear as well, and if I was *really* lucky, I'd find my damn brother while I was at it.

I thought over the plan again, taking it apart piece-by-piece. There was still too much left to chance. Maybe we wouldn't be able to find the entrance; maybe we'd be caught; maybe there'd be a fucking cave in, or the smuggler that Oren knew of would sell us out.

There were a million things that could go wrong, but I'd find a way, because at the end of the day, all most people wanted was an easy life. I didn't have that luxury; I had too many people relying on me to not succeed. I'd fucking do it. I knew I would, even if I had to leave the streets of Himnel running red.

My chances were slim; hell, they had to be in the single digits, but I didn't give a shit. I'd make it work.

"What're we doin', Jax?" Lydia asked me a few minutes later, moving up to stand by my side at the railing as we looked out over the trees below as they sped away, the speed difference between Decin's *Libertas* and the *Agamemnon's Wrath* strikingly clear.

"We're going to Himnel; we're going to kick some ass and find my brother, free the crew's families, and hopefully get some gear to help ourselves as well," I stated quietly, a sardonic smile lifting the corner of my mouth as I looked at her.

"Oh, and I thought it'd be 'ard," she muttered, grinning at me.

"I should have said this before, but if there's anyone you or the rest of the team want to bring along as well, if you can trust them to keep their mouths shut, then they're welcome," I said, just realizing all the focus had been on the ships' crews until now.

"Thank yer, but yer don't tend to end up as a slave if yeh've got family that care about yer," she replied quietly, digging the edge of a nail into the wooden railing and refusing to meet my gaze.

"Well, if there are any slaves you want to bring along and free, then?"

"And how will we pay for 'em? I don't see much gold. I know ye got some from the battles, but yer'd need a lot."

"Truthfully, I don't know, Lydia," I said, shrugging. "But leave that to me to worry about. I'm going to have a lot of things to sort out, not least how I'm going to convince a smuggler that helping us is in his best interests, so buying a few slaves is a minor issue. Whatever happens, though, I know I can rely on you and your team to watch my back. So if you need something, just tell me."

"We will," she said, smiling genuinely. I sensed that she felt she'd found where she was supposed to be in life.

"Good." I turned, looking around and frowning until I spotted him crouched beside a pile of gear. "Fuck's sake, Bane, I swear I'm gonna make you wear a bell or something," I said, shaking my head. "Get your bony arse over here." I gestured for him to join us by the railing. "Right, I've got a couple of skillbooks for you both, and then there's some for the squad, as well." I reached into my bag of holding.

The first book I gave to Bane, then two to Lydia, before piling the remaining handful on the top of a barrel that was handily close.

"Bane, this one's for you, mate. It's an assassin's skill, but I think that'd be useful for you?" I said, giving him Midnight's Kiss.

"It's a dual dagger technique?" Bane asked, looking the book over, and I nodded.

"It requires stealth to use it properly, and I guessed you'd be the best for that; besides, you can use it twice, I guess?" I said, looking at his two sets of arms dubiously.

"Thank you!" he replied, turning the book over and over reverently. I could feel the subsonics as he examined it, and I grinned at him.

"Don't thank me yet, mate; you just got a new job. In addition to helping to train Lydia's squad and me, from now on, you get to keep watch for others you think will be suitable. I need a cadre of assassins and stealth types."

"I'll see what I can do then, Jax. Thank you," Bane repeated quietly, nodding and stepping back to watch over the ship, making sure there was nobody nearby before he used the book.

"And for you, Lydia," I said, handing her the second and third books.

"Heavy armor and mace usage?" she read, looking the books over. "But I don't have any heavy armor...The mace, I'll take happily, and thank ye so much, but—"

I cut her off with a shake of my head.

"You've more than proven yourself to me. I know it's not going to fit you properly; after all, regardless of what people might think. Armor doesn't fit different people the fucking same, but I had a full set of the heavy armor from one of the elite soldiers brought onboard. It should be belowdecks on an armor stand that was being cobbled together by one of the engineers. Go check it out, read the book, and take what you can wear comfortably from there, unless you think someone else would be better suited to be the tank for the group?"

"Tank?" she asked, only half paying attention as she looked at the books in her hands.

"The way I and Bob fight are tanks' roles. We step up and take the center of the line, fighting and keeping the enemies' attention, so that the rest of the team don't have to. On this trip, we don't have Bob, and I've seen the way you fight. Want to step up and take his place?" I asked.

The sudden grin she gave me was all the answer I needed.

"Hell, yes!" she said.

"Glad to hear it! So, why don't you sort your squad out? Bane can watch over them while you read your own books and check out your new gear."

"I…I will, thank ye. I don't know what else to say, just…thank ye, Jax," Lydia said again, shaking her head as she looked at the books.

"Like I said, you earned it. There are these books for the squad, as well," I replied, gesturing to the books, and she nodded to me, a genuine smile brightening her face. A second later, it was gone, as she turned to find some of her squad clearly trying to listen in.

"Did I tell yer to stand around lookin' cute, or to sort yer gear?" she growled at them. "Because there's a shit load of gear 'ere, and yer all fugly, so yeh've failed on both counts! That's it! Bane! D'yer think ye could teach these idiots a lesson for me?"

"Happily!" Bane growled, stepping forward.

"Well, let's have a little challenge, shall we?" Lydia snapped out, looking over the disorganized rabble as they tried to look busy. "I say they're weak, but might have a chance of being more; what do ye say, Bane?"

"I say they're too weak, worthless!" Bane snapped back.

"Well, then!" Lydia replied, clearly playing her part to the hilt. "I'll bet ye the gifts that Lord Jax set aside for 'em, that you can't break 'em in say, an hour? I'll leave 'em in yer hands, and ye see what yer can do. If they're all still standin' when I return, they get the skillbooks and spellbooks Lord Jax picked out for 'em. If not, they go back to 'im until we can find a squad that's worthy of 'em!"

"Sounds like a deal!" Bane replied. "In fact, if they lose the books, I might see if I can persuade Lord Jax to give some to me; no need to waste them, eh?"

"Deal!" Lydia snapped, glaring at her squad. They stood like rabbits, heads jerking from her to Bane to the pile of books on a barrel by the edge of the ship's railing, the wind ruffling the pages as we flew.

"They've got potential!" Barrett whispered to me, having walked over during Lydia's performance, and I grinned at him.

"Was that your doing?" I asked.

He nodded. "Mine and Flux's; he spent a lot of time adventuring when he was younger, and it sounds like his team was pretty much military, through and through. He was a scout for them, much as Bane will be for us. The two of us had a chat with Lydia about leading her squad."

"Looks like she's the right choice for leading them," I said quietly, and he nodded.

"She's got the gift for it, that's for sure." We both glanced back over our shoulders, seeing Bane spreading the group out and ordering them into a series of kicks and punches we'd all learned this morning. Lydia glared at her squad for a while before turning away and heading below decks, the two books I'd given her held tight.

I nodded to the group, grinning as I saw the way they all tried to do the exercises they'd been taught, while Bane separated books out as I'd directed, putting them next to each member of the group.

The funniest was Arrin, the mage support, who kept tripping and falling into the others as he desperately tried to read the titles of the pair of spellbooks set on the deck before him.

Bane had deliberately put them down upside down, and I could feel his laughter as Arrin tried to read them.

"I'll be claiming these books back soon, but I wanted you all to know what you were going to be losing," Bane informed them, starting to speed up the exercises.

I shook my head, grinning at the evil tactic, before saying goodbye to Barrett and stepping over to where Tel stood nervously by three large bags.

Tel was a large man with heavy, sloped shoulders and massive fingers, clumsy to the point of being laughable. But, for some reason, he became graceful when he worked with plants, those massive fingers gentle and assured in his movements.

When Cai had told me about him, I'd almost dismissed it out of hand. The thought of this huge lump of a man using the alchemy set? Then I'd caught a glimpse of my own reflection, and I'd paused.

I was bigger than he was, considerably so, and if I could do it, however badly, then surely he could, too.

"Tel," I greeted him as I approached.

"L—Lord Jax!" he said, bowing and almost falling over as the ship lurched on an air current.

"Whoa, there!" I said, catching him by the shoulders and steadying him. "Let's not worry about that right now; no need for bowing and all that shit. Let's just concentrate on why you're here, okay?"

"Y—Yes! Cai said you wanted me to help you with some alchemy, but I'm not sure…"

"Yes and no, Tel," I said, cutting him off. "You're here to help me, and for me to help you. I've heard you've got a gift with herbs and alchemical plants, is that right?" I asked.

He nodded hesitantly. "Yes, lord, I've always been good with plants. They…well, they just seem to like me. They grow real easy, and I can sell them easy enough. I always wanted to learn more, but nobody could teach me, so I sort of just made it up as I went along…I guess?" he said shyly, wringing his hands in embarrassment.

"Well, today you get to learn, then. I'm going to be making as many health, stamina, and mana potions as I can over the next day of travel. You're going to be reading these and helping me," I said pulling out a Basics of Alchemy and Bartlebee's Excellent Herbalism Primer skillbooks. I had no idea who Bartlebee had been, but he'd clearly thought a lot of himself.

"My lord!" Tel squeaked, clutching the books as I passed them to him.

"Get them read, then I want you to start sorting through the alchemy ingredients," I told him, gesturing to the three bags. "I'll set up the basic gear I have, over there, I think," I said, pointing to an area to one side where it didn't look like we'd be in anyone's way, "…and I'll get started on the health potions first, so I suggest you hurry."

I reached down to grab the first bag, intending on shifting them over, only to have Tel sit on it in his excitement to get started. He jumped up quickly, the combination of realizing what he'd done and the sharp spike of a thorn helping him along.

I couldn't help but laugh, and I pointed at the corner nearby.

"Sit there and read; I've got these," I said, grabbing the bags. They were the size of rubbish bags from back home, stuffed with herbs and seemingly random plants I guessed had alchemical properties. But they were light enough, and in a few minutes, I had them sorted out.

I spent the next twenty minutes picking through the plants, taking anything I didn't recognize and trying it. I got a dozen new alchemical ingredients added to my internal list, and a combination of wonderful side effects, one of which resulted in Oracle having to use a healing spell on me while I chugged one of my old basic cure-all potions.

Whatever else althem blossoms were capable of, they were fucking lethal poison as well, and I couldn't get the damn taste out of my mouth. I ate a couple of thulin berries that I'd identified earlier, discovering that they had a stamina boost effect, just to get rid of the taste.

"O—okay, L—Lord Jax…" The hesitant voice spoke up.

I looked over at him, popping another handful of berries into my mouth and munching on them.

"Tel, you ready?" I got a nervous smile in return. "That's great," I said, making room for him in front of the alchemy gear. "So, did you get a healing potion recipe as part of the alchemy book?" I asked, and he nodded. "Great, and with the herbalism one, can you identify these ingredients? No, not all of them? Then let's go over them."

I spread a sample of each out on the deck as I went. His hesitation disappeared as we talked about the various plants and their properties. Some of his knowledge was different from my own, and I made notes as we went, adding the extra properties to the ingredients in my list.

The day passed quickly taking turns using the alchemy set I'd brought. I spent my turn teaching him my methods and making sure he understood how and why I did things, and he did the same. Our basic knowledge was nearly identical, but coming from two different skillbooks, we got slight differences.

It took a few hours, but eventually, I got the notification I'd been hoping for:

You must now pick a path to follow.

Will you choose the path of IMPROVEMENT, or concentrate on CREATION?

Choose carefully, as this choice cannot be undone.

IMPROVEMENT:

Choosing to specialize in this direction will result in a 5% increase in potency of your learned potions, and you will have a 5% chance of a breakthrough when being tutored by an alchemist of higher experience.

CREATION:

Choosing to specialize in CREATION will result in a 5% increase in your chances of creating a new recipe from unconventional ingredients. Following in the footsteps of others will result in a 10% drop in potency of all potions you make, but for each potion you create without others' assistance, you will gain a point in Intelligence.

I didn't pause in the slightest, not when stat points were on the line, as I preferred going my own way anyway. I selected the path of Creation and felt a shudder run through me.

Congratulations!

You are now a Creationist Alchemist.

A path trodden by few means that greater rewards could await you.

I grinned and dismissed it, resolving to make the most of the trip. It'd take a full day and a half to arrive at the city of Himnel, and for obvious reasons, we wanted to arrive in the dead of night. It was starting to get dark now, and Decin had made the decision to head east by southeast from the tower, meaning we'd approach from the side least likely to be heavily guarded.

I looked down at the lake that was approaching in the distance, and I hoped that this one didn't have thousands of goblins pissing in it.

I'd wanted to try to find more of the waystations as well. The golems that Waystation Four had provided were a huge help, but searching for them on the way would have meant heading more towards the south and Narkolt. Approaching from anywhere that Himnel was already at war with wasn't likely to help our attempts at stealth at all.

I shivered suddenly with a feeling like someone walking on my grave, and I turned around. Lydia's squad was long gone, which meant that Bane...

"Well?" Bane said from beside me, and I turned to look at him.

"Well, what?" I asked him, and he shook his head at me, making my heart sink.

"What, you think I'd forget our agreement already? Because we will need the potions, I left you to play with them until your alchemist had learned enough to make them, but now? Now, it is time to start training."

"Fuck," I muttered, already knowing that I was going to regret this.

Bane had me strip out of most of my gear, setting all but my naginata aside, and bare to the waist.

I caught the looks my bandage-wrapped chest and arms got me, but I ignored them, standing opposite Bane as he stood holding one of his spears.

He guided me through a basic spear kata that he knew, slowly. The influence of being an aquatic species was clear, as his movements were far more fluid than my own, and the kata seemed…slow as hell at first. I just knew it wasn't going to stay that way.

We began with a slow sweep upwards, pausing, then pulling down, the butt of our weapons striking the ground. We pulled them in close, hands well-spread, and held the weapons to our sides, our feet steady and braced. I slowly brought the naginata up until it was horizontal before sweeping it down slowly to my right. Once the point dipped below my knee, I spun it slowly, arching around behind me until it returned to the horizontal. I repeated the move, switching my grip to dip the blade down on the left, spinning it and returning to holding in on my left side now.

It was a simple kata, meant more to make sure that my footwork and grip were both firm. But as Bane made me repeat it, over and over again, slowly increasing the speed of my movements, I became less jerky and more fluid as I went.

He made me repeat the kata for two turns of the hourglass, missing the evening meal as it was served, continuing on until it grew dark enough that the crew lit lanterns around us.

Eventually, he let me take a break. My stamina reserves had bottomed out, and I collapsed to the floor, wheezing and covered in sweat.

"Are you okay?" Oracle asked me as she landed beside me, back to her usual diminutive size.

"No," I managed to gasp out, and I felt Bane laughing. I managed to lift one shaky hand and give him the finger, resulting in multiple voices raised in laughter from my right.

I turned my head and saw that the majority of the ship's crew were seated there, having finished their evening meal and just watching me.

"How…how long…have they…been there…?" I managed to gasp out, and Oracle gently stroked my face as Lydia replied from my other side.

"We've been watchin' for the last hour or so, milord."

"Feck," I groaned, my stamina slowly starting to return, and I could see that I was surrounded on three sides by people who'd just been watching my kata and the way that Bane kicked my ass on every mistake.

Just what I needed.

"Thanks for that, Bane," I said as I forced myself to my feet, my muscles aching as I stretched and pretended that I was fine. "I think that was a good bout."

"It was; you did well, my lord," he replied. I looked at him, considering the fact he called me Jax normally, at my insistence. I just knew the fucker was being sarcastic.

"So, ready to give in for the night like a normal person, or can you keep going?" he asked me, and the low murmur of voices that had begun to climb immediately silenced.

Goddamn evil…sadistic…motherfuc—

"Yeah, I can go a bit longer," I said, forcing the words out with a fake smile. I hadn't felt this bad with training since I first started with the Nigerian. Even Flux's workout this morning had been gentler, and I'd only done one damn kata!

"Excellent! Perhaps it would be better taught without lights, however. We don't need to be seen here, hmmm?" I quickly agreed with him, and people moved to put the lights out, the mid deck where we stood vanishing into blackness.

A low grumble rose from the spectators, even as Decin and Lydia started chivvying their people away, forcing everyone below decks or back to their stations now that the entertainment was over.

"Oh, thank fuck," I whispered, slumping over my naginata. I drew in a few deep breaths and straightened, facing Bane. "Come on, then, let's get it over with…"

He shook his head firmly.

"No. I wanted to see if you'd push past it and continue, that's all. Flux gave me very specific rules for your training. Relax, Jax, we will do half an hour cooldown and stretches, then sleep."

"You're a fucking legend, mate," I whispered, moving to lean against the railing, while Oracle summoned a spring of clean water to fountain up and bubble over next to Bane. He dipped his face into the water, drawing in long lungful's until it dissipated. He slowly straightened up again, shaking the water off, and bowed to Oracle.

"Thank you, Oracle," he said.

She replied with a sunny smile, landing lightly on the railing next to me. She reached out and slowly stroked my back and neck, the tips of her nails caressing my skin in a way that made the hairs rise and caused me to shudder. She grinned at me, and I snorted, shaking my head at the sight of her.

She'd conjured up a grey low-cut top that barely held her in and yoga pants that were surely sprayed on, they were that sheer.

I was too exhausted to really appreciate the view, but I remembered the way the sailors had looked at her ass as she bent over to check on me after training, and I laughed again.

There was going to be a lot of studious "remembering" going on in the crews' bunks tonight over that image, I had no doubt.

I staggered over to Bane, and we worked through the cooldown, ending with a series of stretches and lunges that made my back pop, but I felt better immediately.

I didn't bother going down into the hold and finding a space. I'd refused the offer from Decin and Hanau of taking their cabin, and I'd insisted I'd just sort somewhere out. Now, I couldn't be bothered to try and instead put my bedroll on the floor and laid down right where I was.

Bane put his gear down nearby, and a few minutes later, Lydia join us, a little hesitant at first. But when we included her in the conversation, she relaxed.

I finally got my evening meal, and as soon as I finished it, I was asleep, not even noticing when a sailor came to collect the bowls.

DREAM THREE

As soon as I fell asleep, I felt it, that falling sensation that was so familiar, plummeting as if from a great height, only to be yanked sideways instead. Miles blurred like I'd been strapped to Concorde's nose cone, before the impact shocked me back to wakefulness.

I coughed, forcing gummy eyes open, and frowned. The room before me was lit by flames that danced and spun in bowls of polished bronze. The reflectors positioned behind the pools sent the blazing light out to fill the small room, and I shifted, my body subtly wrong as I sat up.

"Mana wight," I whispered to myself, the reality of my situation slowly filtering through the cloudy exhaustion that filled my mind.

The room was empty of supplicants but fully stocked with all the armor and weapons it should have. I leaned forward, staggering when I put my right foot down, only to find the muscles wasted and atrophied. I grabbed the side of the sarcophagus, my grip slipping as I staggered again.

I looked at my body in shock. As always, I was naked when I arrived in a summoning hall, but instead of the powerful form I usually inhabited, this body was…weak.

I looked like a victim of a famine. I lifted my fingers and curled them slowly, the muscles and tendons creaking and popping.

I stared in shock, looking down at my body. The bright blue current of mana flowed along channels usually hidden by skin, skin that seemed paper-thin now.

I was still staring when a crash sounded from outside, the doorway at the end of the hall shaking, and a cloud of dust billowing through the cracks. I flinched and almost fell before I got ahold of myself, closing my eyes. When nothing happened after a few seconds, I drew in as deep a breath as I could manage and reached out with my senses, pulling at the mana I expected to find in the air all around me.

My eyes shot open in shock when I found nothing; no mana at all.

I blinked, trying to understand what had happened, when a second crash echoed down to me, and I growled in frustration.

Clearly, something was going on, and I'd better go find out what it was.

I tottered around the room, stretching my arms and legs as I went, gathering up armor first. It was over a thousand years old, but whatever magic kept this body intact and ready had preserved it as well. The leather jerkin felt soft and supple as I pulled it on; the thicker areas that would usually have supported the armor I'd wear over this would have to make do as my only protection.

I just didn't have the strength to carry more, not if I wanted to use a weapon. But I had an advantage I'd never managed to make use of before, if I could reach somewhere with mana...

I picked up the matched pair of mage gauntlets and pulled them on. The interwoven links of steel and quicksilver that covered the gauntlets were inert, rather than humming with power as they should be, but unlike every other time I'd had access to these...I now knew how to use spells.

"Jax?" A faint voice called, and I spun around, almost falling over. There was nobody nearby, but... **"Jax, can you hear me?"**

"Oracle?" I whispered, and I felt something change as the sense of her grew stronger.

"Jax! Where are you?" she asked.

I shrugged. Realizing she couldn't see me; I spoke up a second later. *"I don't know, I'm in a mana wight body, somewhere without mana, as near as I can tell. How can you reach me?"*

"I'm bonded to you, Jax. I can't sense much, just that you were pulled from your body. Lydia and Bane thought you were under attack; the entire ship is at battle stations."

"Dammit, no, I'm all right, Oracle. Just relax and be ready to heal me, okay? Usually these dreams only end when I die, and I'll have a lot of wounds usually. Better to not let anyone see."

"When you what?! I'm not letting you die, Jax! Hell, no!" she screamed into my mind, and I worked to project a sense of calm to her.

"It's not like that, Oracle. This form is a wight, remember? We've talked about them; once it's destroyed, I'll come back to my body."

"I do not like this, Jax! Not at all!"

"Ha! Believe me, neither do I!" I said, and pulled a shortsword from the rack, belting it to my waist with a dagger on the opposite hip.

I'd usually tool myself up a lot more, but right now I couldn't carry it. I could barely carry what I had.

I slowly moved across the floor to the stone door. I'd seen this enough times to know that the supplicant usually had to give a donation of their blood on the other side. It wasn't a large one; it was just meant to show humility, from what I'd been able to make out over the years of inspecting the glyphs on the walls.

Instead of a supplicant begging for aid, though, there was a sealed door, and it sounded like explosions outside somewhere.

I reached out and searched the inside of the door for a latch when my fingers slipped into it.

I blinked and pulled back, shocked. After a second, I reached out again, my fingers sinking into the stone effortlessly. I reached in deeper, at first concerned that it was to do with the gloves, but my arms continued to pass through, so I took a deep breath, pushing myself into the stone.

The deeper I moved into the stone, the more resistance built up, until, as my fingers waved in clear air on the far side of the passage, it felt like I was walking through quicksand.

I pushed myself free on the opposite side, but when I touched the stone again, the lustrous shimmer that had covered it had drained to a bare hint of glitter. My fingers, instead of passing through, gouged patterns in rapidly solidifying stone.

I yanked them back, as my brain caught up, and I realized what was happening: the loss of mana was affecting the stone! If I'd waited any longer, or moved any slower, I'd have been trapped inside.

I stood looking at the stone, my eyes wide as I processed the thought of being trapped inside the stone for who knows how long, as the last dregs of mana drained, and I suffocated.

I started to shake, my artificial heart speeding up as I panicked. My one true terror from childhood reared its horrific head before me, until I heard Oracle's voice.

"Jax, are you okay?"

"Ye-yeah…sorry, I'm okay…Why?"

"You…your body, I guess…it just tensed up and started to shake."

"I…I'm okay, just a bit of a bad experience. I—" An explosion from further down the hall interrupted me, and I spun around, crouching low as I fumbled my sword out of the sheath.

"I've got to go," I told her, setting off down the corridor. I was used to being out in the middle of nowhere, but here, it looked like a city, an old one.

The floor I crept along was slanted slightly; it took a few seconds to realize it, but I had to work to walk in the middle. As I went on, another faint crash sounded in the distance, followed by a scream of rage.

I sped up, coming to a T junction at the end of the corridor. To my left was blackness and cold seeping into my bones, but to the right, in the distance, was a light, as I'd nearly left the light from two glowing bronze bowls outside of my sanctuary.

Wherever I was, I didn't even have the mana available to use my DarkVision, and I cautiously moved toward the light.

I sniffed as I walked, a scent filling the air strong enough to get through even the weak senses of the mana wight. These creations I usually rode had fantastic vision and hearing, but smell, taste, and touch were always off. So if I could smell it, I knew it was bad.

It was coppery and tangy, like salt…sea salt, I realized a few seconds later. As I turned the next corner, passing a single room that was filled with debris, the back wall collapsed in, and grey shale covered most of the interior.

I couldn't see much inside, but the white of bones stuck out from under a large slab as I staggered past. I took another turn, going to the left this time, and the light grew much brighter, bright enough that I had to cover my eyes to look at it, and I came to a wobbly stop.

The room before me was broken; huge rents ran across the floor and walls, and the mosaic-covered ceiling had cracks running across it. One crack had water flowing through it, running down across the sharply tilted floor. I squinted at the silvery-white light that illuminated the space, reflecting from the collected seawater that lapped at the sides of a circular pool filling the center of the room.

I stood transfixed as I looked into the room, the floor sloping away from me at a low angle. Debris had been piled against the far side of the room, and I realized what I was seeing, why the air tasted so strongly of the sea and blood that I could taste it through the sense of a mana wight.

I was in a sunken city, a city from who-knew-when, and the creatures that battled around the pool at the center, their blood staining the blue of the ocean, were its terrible residents.

At least three species were battling it out: a merrow, a six-armed, serpentine monstrosity, stood on one side, a half-dozen smaller variations of its species surrounding it and battling tall, blue-skinned humanoids with jet-black eyes. The second group held scavenged clubs and stone daggers as their only weapons in webbed fingers tipped with onyx claws.

They were being slowly driven back, battling against the merrow on one side and heavily armored crustaceans on the other. Their bodies littered the ground for each step they took backwards from the pool.

The creatures in the third group were short but wide, covered with thick armor plates that moved as they did, reflecting the light. Glittering spikes covered the crustaceans' armored pincers. They looked like lobsters, grown to horrific size and possessing terrifying sentience.

I gritted my teeth, looking the groups over, until one of the blue-skinned second group tried to cast a spell. It wove its fingers through a pattern I thought I almost recognized, until the large merrow lifted a huge pearl into the air, and the blue-skinned creature screamed in agony as the mana was ripped from it.

The pearl pulsed with dark energy, and I gritted my teeth. That thing, which every instinct screamed at me was evil, had clearly brought such a device here to steal the mana of what was left of the city. The minor detail that the only ones I'd be able to speak to without my balls curling up into my stomach in fear were also apparently the inhabitants of the city, also helped.

I stepped forward, my feet passing slowly across a deep crack in the floor that bordered the entrance to the room, and the slant of the floor beneath me increased. With every step I took, I weakened, my hands beginning to shake as I snuck along, trying to keep to the shadows.

I watched the merrow leader, noticing some of the city's inhabitants rush out of a doorway on the far side of the room, carrying heavy slabs of rock and facing off against the crustaceans…even as I examined her, my body weakened as I used mana I needed to animate it for the ability.

Critical success!

Your opponent is unaware of being observed and has no defense against your ability.

Deepwater Merrow Chieftainess
You have found a creature hated and reviled by the surface world. A Merrow Chieftainess is a creature so thoroughly steeped in dark magic that it can create, use, and alter artifacts from the great void that her master resides in.

Merrow Chieftainesses are well aware of how hated they are and tie the life-force of their minions into themselves, gaining their abilities and immunities for themselves. This ability weakens their minions and creates a festering hatred that would consume their nests, if only they could break free.

Weaknesses: Fire, Earth, and Life magics are all doubly effective against creatures of the Deepwater.

Resistances: Water, Darkness, or Death magics used against this creature suffer a 75% damage penalty.

Critical Weaknesses: Neck, Eyes, Liver, Lungs.

Level: 37

Health: 410

Mana: 16/70

I blinked as I read the details focused on the creature, my meridian-aided vision helpfully highlighting the creature's weak spots. I reached out in the silence of my mind, a desperate plan coming to me.

I had no mana to speak of, and with none in the air or anywhere about, anywhere…except…

"Oracle! I'm going to need mana!" I called out to her within my mind. A second later, I felt her suddenly closer, the awareness of her filling my mind as she somehow reinforced our link even further.

I staggered forwards, my determination and sheer stubbornness overcoming the weaknesses of my flesh.

I pushed myself, rushing forward from cover to cover, ducking behind fallen pillars and piles of rock until I was close to the battle, then hurried to put my back to a large rock just within running distance.

I rested for an all-too-short time, my body shaking with the exertion, and the faint blue glow of the veins tracing my limbs grew steadily dimmer as I grew closer to the artifact.

I edged my eye around the corner of the rock and looked, seeing the battle slowly pushing back from my location as more and more of the blue-skinned humanoids fell.

The merrow chieftainess had risen up on her coiled tail, looking over the battle and screaming something in a language I didn't understand. She had a hood that flared out and covered the back of her head. From where I stood, the line of spines flaring from the tip of her head and running down between her shoulders looked perfect for my plan. Two of her six arms gripped the artifact high overhead, while another two pointed and gestured to her subordinates. I took a deep breath and blew it out slowly, then pulled in another sharply and sent Oracle a last message, setting off running.

"Now!"

I kicked off another rock nearby, forcing myself to go faster, my sword already growing heavy in my rapidly weakening hand, but I pushed myself to go on. My boots, made of supple leather undamaged by the ages, kept my approach quiet, and the battle served to cover any last noises that I made.

I was less than two dozen steps away, but as weak as my body was, I nearly didn't make it…until a sudden infusion of mana hit me.

It was like getting a double espresso made with an energy drink instead of water then injected straight into the heart. Everything changed as my body flared to life, limbs strengthening, muscles bulging. My flesh grew thicker, and my skin lost the texture of old parchment. I covered the last few steps just as one of the rearmost merrow turned, the now-brightly gleaming mana in my veins drawing his attention before the skin thickened enough to hide them.

It had time to hiss a warning in shock before my sword, short and heavy-bladed as I liked it, lashed out, cutting halfway through its neck. It fell back, blood fountaining out of the severed arteries, and the second one tried to bring its trident around.

I grinned as the trident moved slowly, too slowly, and I leapt over it, landing and kicking off in the same maneuver to leap for the chieftainess's back.

She must have been over eight meters in length easily, with her upper body raised over the coils of her tail. She twisted around, turning to her right. I went to her left, reaching out and grabbing a thick spine where it jutted from her lower back.

I held on tight, using the spine to brace myself, my feet slamming into her back and I twisted, using not only my arms and back, but all the momentum of my waist as well to drive the sword upwards.

The chisel-thick tip of the blade, designed for punching through thick lamellar plates of armor, had no issue with her scales. It drove in and up as I angled the hilt in close and rammed it as far as I could.

She screamed in shock and pain, thrashing wildly as the battle paused. The combatants were all stunned by the appearance in the middle of the room of a fourth party, one that was riding the most fearsome creature there.

"Yippie-ki-ay, mother…" I growled out as she spun and thrashed, frantically trying to throw me off. Her arms flapped wildly, trying to get enough of an angle to reach me. I held on, bitterly determined to kill this bitch. Twisting the blade, I yanked it back and forth, imagining an egg scrambler inside her lower chest.

She screamed in pain and finally managed to grab my wrist in one huge clawed hand. She yanked, breaking my grip and throwing me free easily, my sword still embedded in her gut. I cartwheeled across the room to smack into a fallen section of stonework, my bones shattering with the force of the impact…

I collapsed to the floor, the stabbing feeling of dozens of fragments of broken ribs piercing my lungs enough to let me know I was out of the fight.

I barely had the strength to raise my head, but when the world stopped spinning long enough to focus, I saw the blue-skinned creatures had counter attacked. They were driving the crustaceans back on one side; dozens of cracked and shattered corpses covered the ground near them. On the other side, they were beating back the merrow.

I grinned at the chieftainess as she collapsed, the floor shaking with the impact of her enormous bulk. She managed to look at me, her all-too-human face staring at me across the room, as blood ran from her mouth.

I lifted one shaking hand, slowly extending a single digit. The fury that flashed across her face made it clear that, whatever else was different between the realms, this insult at least seemed to have transferred well.

She collapsed fully, life going out of her and blood pouring across the floor as the merrow bound to her screamed in rage and fell on each other. The blue people backed up, slabs of rock and stone knives held ready as they waited for the merrow to kill each other. The crustaceans were fleeing now that the tide of battle had turned.

I lay there, bones shattered and life leaking out as they fought, the local inhabitants falling on the weakened survivors of the merrow. I could feel Oracle in my mind, her panicked focus as she tried to heal the wounds that were showing on my real body even now.

I slowly slumped to one side, losing the strength to hold myself upright, blood pooling around me. Then I felt a presence nearby. I managed to lift my head, my arms weakly flopping, and I looked up at one of the locals.

He crouched before me, his head tilted to one side quizzically. He had a ridge of fur that arched back from just above his jet-black eyes, growing from a point to a thick band that disappeared over the back of his head. His blue skin was made up of thousands of tiny iridescent scales, and his teeth were a mix of sharp points and thicker molars.

He opened his mouth and made a sound at me, a series of clicks that made me think of a dolphin, before nodding in satisfaction…then his right hand flashed out, the sharp claws ripping out my throat.

You have died.

CHAPTER TWENTY-FOUR

I gasped, sitting up and clutching at my chest and neck as I felt myself back in my own body. I coughed, blood frothing in my mouth, and turned to my side, spitting it out. Footsteps vibrated the floor as people ran about, voices raised in anger and confusion. I coughed again, spitting more blood out, and groaned. The cuts across my throat left my hand bloody, even as my mana dipped precipitously, Oracle using it to heal me as quickly as possible.

Before I could speak, something was rammed into my lips, and I almost choked as liquid flooded my mouth.

"Drink it; trust me," said a familiar voice, and my gaze trailed up the arm holding the potion to find Bane crouched there. I swallowed, trusting him immediately, waves of pain running over me as my abused body rebelled against the damage.

It only took a handful of seconds, Oracle pushing as much mana as I had left into the Battlefield Triage spell, before I was healing over, bones popping as they restructured fully, flesh knitting together and organs returning to good health.

I finished swallowing the dregs of the potion, and hands laid me back, legs behind me propping me half-up, and something soft supporting my head, and I looked up to see Hanau.

I glanced about, my mind slowing from its frantic post-battle crash to take in the scene around me.

I was laid out on the deck, blood pooling around me, with my upper half laid across Hanau's legs. He braced my head with a rolled-up shirt and was whispering to me to not panic, that it was all okay. His voice gentle and kind, even as Decin's deeper tones barked out orders nearby.

Bane rose from his kneeling position by my side, the empty mana potion tossed aside as he switched between watching me and the surrounding deck. Opposite Bane stood Lydia, and in a tight circle around us were her squad, all dressed to one degree or another, but their weapons out and ready.

I forced myself up, Bane and Hanau helping me as I coughed and cleared my throat of blood and potion one last time, before calling out, even as Oracle swept me with another run of healing.

"It's okay!" I said, waving to them. Now that I was upright, I could see the entire ship at battle stations. Its two small cannons had been rolled out and armed, mana flickering over the runes that covered them. The crew that weren't needed at battle stations, and even Isabella, who'd been practically hiding from me since coming aboard, all had weapons in hand and formed a protective ring around me.

"It's okay," I said again, warmth filling me as I realized the way they'd all come together, determined to protect me. "Thank you, all of you, but it's not an attack. You can stand down."

I gingerly made my way to the railing and leaned against it, reaching up to touch the ridged, faint scars on my neck from the claws. I grinned at Oracle self-consciously as she landed before me, her beautiful, perfect face marred by a frightened scowl.

"What the hell just happened, Jax!" she cried out, lunging forward and wrapping her arms around my neck, hugging me tight.

"It's all right, honestly," I whispered to her, hugging her gently, before raising my voice to the others, figuring the truth couldn't make things much worse than whatever people would come up with on their own.

"Okay…looks like it's time to let you all in on another little detail. You all know I'm different," I began. "What you don't know is just how different. This is a little complicated, but basically…"

I spent the next hour telling the history of the empire and the Emperor Amon, as I understood it. I explained that he was my ancestor, that he created special places with bodies that could call to me and others like me, such as my brother. That we were called to protect and to defend people until the legions could arrive, and now that the legions were seemingly no more, I was all that was left, besides Tommy.

I answered a few questions, but mostly I talked, and they listened. By the end of it, I was feeling weak as a kitten, having had my body pushed to breaking point before I'd gone to sleep. Instead of the restful nap I'd needed, I'd instead fought for my life and died in a sunken city. The mental strain and blood loss combined to leave me exhausted again, despite the healing.

Decin had shouldered his way through people and sat nearby, holding Hanau's hand, the blood covering his partner's clothes showing just how bad it'd been as I spoke.

"So laddie, whut yer tellin' us, is tha' yer a prince o' tha old empire? A hero? Do tha' be right?" he asked, and I paused.

"Yes, and no, I suppose," I said, rubbing my chin in thought. "Yes, I'm of the emperor's bloodline, but my father, the shit biscuit that he is, is a Baron, or was, and he's been on Nimon's side this whole time. I don't really know where I fall in the whole nobility thing. And I'm no hero, I just…I just kinda do what has to be done."

"You'll be an imperial prince when you finish conquering the continent," Oracle said, and I swore I could have heard a pin drop after that statement.

"Yer gonna conquer tha entire continent?" Decin asked after a minute.

I drew in a breath, thinking fast. Did I want to do that? Hell, I didn't particularly like being in charge of the people back at the tower. It was far more hassle than I liked, and I really wasn't very good at it…but if the alternative was assholes like my father, or Barabarattas, being in charge…

"I don't know," I said eventually. "I hadn't planned that far ahead, I'm not interested in being in charge, but equally, I'm not going to leave Lord Fucknut ruling Himnel, so it might come to that, yet."

"And if you're going to conquer the continent…where do we go after that?" asked Barrett quietly, watching me carefully as a sailor pressed a steaming coffee into my hands.

"We'll see. For now, let's just get a society more interested in helping each other get built. Once we're safe and strong, we can look at the empire again."

"What happened in the dream?" a voice called from the back.

I leaned back, taking a drink from the coffee. I told them a sanitized version of the dream, having discussed the past and what happened generally to them before. By the time I finished, Hanau, Decin, and Bane were looking at each other intently.

"What is it?" I asked them.

Bane shook his head. "Perhaps it's something better discussed in private, my lord," he said, and I took the hint.

Decin nodded and turned to the crew, getting people moving with a few shouts and good-natured light kicks that made people laugh. In short order, Lydia's squad went back down below to get fully dressed, now that the sun was beginning to rise in the east. I called her over to join us as Decin began to speak.

"Well, laddie, it be like this...there were a load of old cities tha' were lost, wiped off tha face o' tha realm in tha Cataclysm. Some o' them be normal, and some no; some did be floatin' in tha sea or even flyin' cities. The stonework ye described, and tha pool, it be makin' a case fer it bein' a floatin' city tha' be lost to time.

"There be one a good week's flight to the south; tha bits ye can reach all be long plundered now. Tha rest be sunk to tha bottom o' the ocean. The races ye describe, though, I never heard o' them, except tha merrow."

"I've heard tales of the other two." Bane spoke up. "The armored figures sound like a variation on the coastal Chaa. I've seen them before; as spiked and evil-looking as you say they were, I'd think a deepwater variant. They usually raid anything they can, so other races tend to kill them whenever possible, as the Chaa only respect strength. The other, maybe a species of sea elf? I don't know. The black eyes and skin don't sound right, but the actions, maybe..."

"The fucker tore my throat out," I said touching the ridged scars.

"Would you prefer to die slowly, or have it end quickly? The few sea elves I've heard of were very...blunt and practical. Flux warned us about them when I was young; he used to tell tales of the oceans, and that would fit with them. Of course, it could be that they just didn't like you and wanted your gear as well."

"They had fuck-all," I said, nodding my head. "They were fighting with clubs and rocks."

"They were gifted mages, I've heard. If something had stolen their magic, they'd have grabbed whatever they had to hand," Bane said, shrugging. "At least, that's what I'd do. You might have found a sea elf nursery; the local group would have been intent on slaughtering anything they'd see as a threat to their children."

"Or something totally different," said Hanau, shaking his head. "There's really no way of telling, unless you can go back?"

"Not as far as I know," I said, finishing my coffee and setting the mug aside. "Who knows what there was?"

"So, you could be pulled somewhere like that at any time?" Lydia asked me.

Oracle spoke up quickly. "No! He can be called when he's asleep, as he relaxes, and his guard is down. I'll see to it he's protected from it from now on."

"No, you won't," I rebutted her. "Normally when this happens, I'm all someone has. I've seen hundreds of villages destroyed, innocents slaughtered, and children killed over the years. I will not leave them to face the night alone, not when I could help them. You can prevent me from being pulled to them when it's dangerous for us, like when we're resting between battles or while we're in the city, but otherwise, no. I'll not let people die when I could help them," I said.

"You could have died if I hadn't been here," she said, a touch of anger and fear in her voice.

"I've survived hundreds of these dreams over the years, Oracle, all without healing magic. Believe me, I'd have survived. My body heals the injuries somehow. I don't pretend to understand how, even in my old world, but it did it."

"I still don't like it," she said, frowning.

"You don't have to like it," I said. "You just have to do it. I'm sorry, Oracle, but I won't let someone face the creatures I've seen alone, not if I can help it. That's an end to it," I said the last bit firmly while looking around, fixing the others with a glare as they were about to speak.

I got a round of nods, even though some were unhappy. The happiest of them all seemed to be Hanau as he gazed at Decin, and I couldn't help but quirk an eyebrow at him, where he sat smiling faintly, patting Decin's hand.

"You heard something you like?" I asked him.

"Definitely. We both did, didn't we?" he said softly, smiling at Decin, who had tears in his eyes.

"What?" I asked confusedly.

"Ach, hell, ye'd probably no remember. Hell, it may no have been ye; iff'n I understand it right, it were mebbe yer brother…but I grew up in a village in tha forest. Miles from anywhere, a proper shithole it was…but it were home, yer know?" He sighed and shook his head in remembrance.

"It no be there now. It were attacked by a creature when I were only a wee laddie. Great big thing, like a hairless wolf with six legs and scales. It tore through the village when I were a bairn, killed half o' us before this big eejit appeared. 'E were naked, runnin' around wit' a great big mace in both hands. 'E jumped on it, an' fair nearly beat tha crap out o' it before it even knew he were there."

Decin scrubbed at his face and snorted loudly, shaking his head before going on gruffly. "Me da, he led us, and we ran. Left everythin' in tha village, an' jus' ran. The crazy bastard fightin' it kept shoutin' fer us to go, while kicking twelve shades o' shit outta it. Never saw nothin' like it."

He grinned at the memory. "Big bastard swinging his cock at it, darin' it to try and bite it, while singing some crazy song about bein' too sexy fer his shirt."

"It was Tommy," I said immediately. "That guy could piss anyone off, and that song…I hope it killed him." I shook my head as I thought about it, remembering that phase he'd gone through, singing shit like that just to wind me up.

"Well, me da went back a few days later wit' a huntin' party; they found the creature, but no sign o' the mad bastard. The corpse looked like it'd been hit by a mountain by the end. It were tha final straw, an' we all moved to tha city after tha'."

"When the job is done, our bodies tend to last a few hours, then that's it. We just…fall apart, becoming dust. There must have been someone in your village who knew about us, who made a sacrifice of blood to the altar and woke us," I said, smiling. "I'm glad it worked." I thought about it for a few seconds. I realized the vast drop-off in Dreams over the last few years must have meant that Tommy was responding to them. With him being here, it probably pulled him in first.

"Well, there's the family quest fixed!" Hanau said, grinning at Decin as he clearly read something from his own notifications.

"Aye! It's changed!" he said. I looked at Hanau questioningly.

"Decin's entire clan swore to find the man that saved them; more than half the village swore along with them." His lips quirked upward at the memory. "I got it when we handfasted. It was one of the reasons we managed to get the funds together for the ship. Everyone chipped in.

"We've been asking questions for years, then you go to help someone, literally from our deck. It's fate lending a hand." He grinned widely as he realized something else. "Well, if you can find Tommy, then you'll definitely have a few more villagers from Decin's side, as most of them have been searching for him for the last ten years!"

"Ten years..." I whispered, thinking back to it, and realizing it was about right. We were in our early teens then, learning how to control the fear and just starting to get good at manipulating the mana wight bodies. They were far stronger and more flexible than our own.

We'd come to realize that, except for the pain, it could be fun, especially when we were summoned for a minor monster, like that one sounded. I snorted again at the mental image of Tommy shaking his cock at the monster and singing "I'm Too Sexy" at it as a taunt. It made me miss him more, but knowing he was around here somewhere, and that I had a place to start looking, made it worthwhile.

We talked for a little longer, me sharing a few memories of Tommy acting like an idiot, before we drifted apart, the others returning to their respective jobs— Decin and Hanau to tend to the ship and get us moving, Barrett and Lydia to chivvy her squad to begin training and checking their gear, and Oracle making a fuss over me. Bane waited until Oracle had calmed down again before gathering up my naginata and passing it to me.

"Again?" I asked, my heart dropping, and he nodded.

"Again. An hour until the first meal, then we will rest and meditate for an hour before working until lunch. After that, we can prepare for tonight."

I groaned, but I knew it had to be done, and looking like a pussy before my bodyguard was not going to help me at all.

I used some of my regenerated mana to summon a pair of springs, one for Bane to relax, and one so that I could scrub the dried blood off myself. As soon as I was clean, we started again with a short warm up before repeating the kata from yesterday.

After a cooldown, we ate a quick meal of gritty brown bread and mellow white cheese which we washed down with summoned water, and we meditated.

The remainder of the morning flew by as Bane added in a few strikes and sweeping deflects before we started to spar. The sparring was frustrating, since we could only use the stabs and blocks we'd trained in that morning. My usual combination of grappling and kicks couldn't be used, so he solidly kicked my arse.

I then spent a couple of hours using the last of the potion ingredients we had with Tel, making a good stockpile of potions before we eventually gave up and retired for a few hours' sleep, while the crew watched over us all.

I was roused as midnight came and we reached the outer edge of our search zone. Our potions had been divvied up, as per my request to Tel. Each member of the squad and Barrett had four healing and three stamina potions, Arrin had four mana in addition to his potions, and I carried ten of each in my bag of holding. The remainder, a couple dozen of each, was to be taken back to the tower and used however they were needed. It would be better for the tower if I sent my alchemy kit back with Tel, as, if I decided I needed another one, I'd be able to get one in the city, I had little doubt.

We gathered on the deck, speaking quietly as Barrett and Decin discussed possible landmarks from half-remembered conversations he'd had years ago.

Eventually, I managed to corner Bane about that bone-rattling sonic pulse of his. It didn't take long to establish between us that his worldsense was going to be amazingly useful. He growled about having to explain things to a child, before going on at length how his 'thrummm' echoing off rocks and moss was endlessly better than silly human sight.

Most of all, *we* could use it to figure out the lay of the land around us, including things like cover for our travels or smugglers' tunnels. It took another hour of low flying, an hour that stretched many nerves almost to the breaking point as the wind blowing through the tops of trees close below us stressed us all.

Eventually, Decin called a halt, and I moved back to him, everyone getting themselves ready.

"This be as close as I can get ye, even wit' all the other lights out; the engine flare be too noticeable te go much closer," Decin said apologetically, and I shook my head.

"It's okay, my friend. This is close enough. We were always going to have to land and search this section on foot." I clasped wrists with him and got a hesitant hug from Hanau, which he returned with a laugh before heading down onto the main deck, gathering up my team.

"Lord…"

I paused, seeing the one person who'd avoided me most on this little jaunt so far, waiting to one side.

"Isabella?" I greeted her, seeing she was clearly nervous in the way she waited. "Is everything okay?"

"I—I just wanted to thank you, that's all? And to wish you good luck."

"Thank you," I said simply, feeling the awkwardness.

"I—I'm sorry, Lord Jax, I didn't want to be a bother, but thank you, for all that you've done for us, and now, for letting me return to the village and bring more of our people back to the Tower! You've no idea what a relief it will be for my friends and family."

"It's fine, honestly!" I assured her, thinking I was definitely getting the better end of the deal in all of this. "Look, bring anyone you trust, and who aren't like that dickhead reeve, back to live at the tower. As long as they're happy to swear the Oath and to join us? I'm happy to have them, but I trust you, Isabella. If someone is a dick, and you think they'll not fit in? Or they're like reeve whatshisface, you can tell them to get fucked and that they're not welcome."

She blushed and nodded her head in thanks as I turned and moved on.

I looked at Barrett, and he nodded firmly. The rest of the team spread out behind him, so I let him lead the way over to the side of the ship, waiting as the rope ladder was unfurled. Jian went over first, Lydia and Bane next, then me, Miren, Stephanos, and Cam, with Arrin bringing up the rear.

CHAPTER TWENTY-FIVE

Once we were down safe, in the forest, I summoned a Firebolt to my hands and waved it up at the ship, before dismissing it, and they moved away slowly, turning and picking up speed as they flew.

In just a few minutes, all was silent in the forest, and I looked around at the others, aware that only Bane and I could really see very far.

"Use one of the magelights, but keep it low-powered," I said.

Lydia gave Arrin a whispered warning as she handed it to him. The gentle light soon illuminated the small group.

Bane moved off quickly, as agreed, while the others waited with me, staring into the darkness and listening carefully, hoping against hope we'd not landed near anything too dangerous.

Twenty minutes passed before Bane returned, leading us to the east quickly and as silently as he could. The group strung out into a line, occasionally tripping over branches and staggering when the ground dipped unexpectedly.

Eventually, we reached the cave his sonar sense had picked up, our little band clambering awkwardly up a steep incline until we carefully walked inside. I held a Firebolt in my hand to guide the others who couldn't see as clearly as Bane and me.

"Is anyone home?" I asked Bane, and he shook his head.

"Not now, but there's signs of it being occupied recently. We should be safe enough here, for a while."

I dismissed the Firebolt, letting Arrin take over light duty, and I sat at the entrance to the cave, looking out at the forest before us.

The steep slope led down from the cave's mouth to a shallow stream. Trees surrounded us, the cave itself being little more than a dozen meters deep with a sharp kink to the right a handful of meters in. I considered what could have formed such a strange cave, then shrugged, realizing I really didn't care.

Bane appeared at my side and nodded to me, Barrett taking a seat close by and drawing his sword, ready for whatever might come.

"I'll get started, unless there's a reason to delay?" Bane asked, and I shook my head.

"No, better you go now; see if you can find any of the landmarks that Barrett remembers. I'll keep watch here, and Oracle will go in the opposite direction, see if she can find anything."

Bane should be able to use his worldsense on any hidden entrances, even if they'd managed to hide the tracks of the carts and caravans they'd used.

Oracle, on the other hand, used magical senses anyway, and could always find her way back to me. So the darkness was no issue; neither was getting lost, and she could both fly and was fast at it.

I nodded to them both and watched them disappear into the darkness. Oracle had taken the time to change into her "work clothes," namely black yoga pants and a strappy top today, and two lines of camouflage paint on her cheeks. I snorted as I watched her vanish into the darkness, feeling the amusement and excitement filling her.

As usual, she'd torn the images from some deep recess of my mind, leaving me to wonder where I'd seen that particular combination. I lived in a state of constant dread of her deciding to wear a particular outfit from a movie around other people, leaving me to explain it to them.

The dread wasn't so much from the thought of the explanation as it was from the worry over which film she'd choose. All the movies I'd ever watched were hidden away somewhere in my mind, and as my wisdom score increased, my memory had started to grow far more easily accessible. This morning at one point she'd been a tiny Freman from *Arrakis*. I knew it was only a matter of time before she changed into the outfit Kelly le Brock wore in *Weird Science* at the end, then I was screwed. Or she would be, anyway…

I shook my head as Barrett coughed lightly nearby, suddenly aware I'd been staring into the forest aimlessly while that mental image circulated over and over…

"So," I said quietly, "you've a sister and a nephew back in the city?"

Barrett smiled into the darkness.

"Aye, Senna and Darin, a good pair. The dad died a few years back; mine collapse. Darin would have been joinin' me on the airship in another year or two. He's six now. Senna works as a seamstress; she's crap at it, but it was all she could find, so you know how it is."

"Didn't she want to join you on the ship?" I asked, and he snorted.

"No chance. She's terrified of heights. Strange how it gets her, and not me or Darin, but still."

"I had a friend like that, scared of heights," I said, and we chatted quietly, watching the forest as we waited. Lydia made the others rest inside in preparation for the next day.

When the dawn finally began to stain the sky, I stretched and reached out with my senses to Oracle, knowing that she and Bane would take the rising sun as the sign to return, as we'd agreed.

She was some distance to the south, a good few miles at least, but the sense of disappointment was easy to feel. She'd found nothing. We'd all finished a cold breakfast by the time Bane arrived back, tired and dirty. He waved to me then dunked himself into the stream at the bottom of the bank, staying submerged for a long time as he recovered from his exertions.

By the time he returned to the cave proper, the first two groups had gotten ready, and they passed him as he came back to rest.

Lydia led Miren and Arrin, and Barrett took Stephanos and Cam, while Jian watched over Bane and me as we slept until lunchtime.

At lunchtime, the others returned, tired and hungry, and we all ate together before we mixed the teams up, going back out and searching again.

When the teams returned at dusk, I set up by the cave entrance again, and Bane and Oracle went out to search again. It took two days before we'd cleared all the area to the point that we were sure there wasn't anything here. We moved five miles further south, finding a new cave and starting the search again.

It was boring work, mostly because Bane had the best chance of actually finding anything, and we needed a guard to watch out for the group. My nights were generally dull as hell, watching the forest while the others snored enough that a thunderstorm could have been missed.

It was in the early hours of the fourth day, when Miren had just woken Cam for farting so loud, it'd echoed in the cave, that Bane finally returned with good news.

As soon as the group realized it was Bane approaching, and not a threat, they all went back to watching as Miren beat Cam with a branch for being "...the most goddamn disgusting person in the entire Realm."

Bane walked up to the cave and collapsed next to me, gesturing to his face. I took the hint as he panted, magically summoning a spring of pure water for him to refresh himself while I summoned Oracle back.

It took him a few minutes to catch his breath, and I let him take the time to rest, not pushing him or asking questions.

"I've found the caravan trail," Bane said finally.

"You're sure it's not a regular caravan trail?"

He shook his head. "It heads directly towards an area I know I scouted last night. It must stop somewhere between here and there, and there's nowhere else around here, so..."

"...So it's probably our trail to the smuggler's entrance. Got it," I finished for him, nodding. "Rest and recover, mate. We can set out at first light."

I quickly filled Oracle in on Bane's find, and she headed straight over to the area Bane had described. It took another hour, but she eventually got back to me, excitement clear in her voice.

"I've found the trail! It's overgrown, but there are signs it's been used recently. I'm following it now, and..."

......

"Oracle, you there?"

"Jax! There's four of them th—urk!"

"Oracle?"

...

"ORACLE!"

There was no response from her, but I could feel the direction she'd been in and roughly how far away she was when she'd disappeared. I grabbed my naginata, jumping to my feet.

"Up!" I cried out, everyone grabbing weapons and looking around frantically. "Oracle's been attacked!" I shouted, my naginata blazing to life as I subconsciously channeled mana into it.

The cave was suddenly as bright as noon, and everyone scrambled to their feet as I screamed at Bane to bring the others. I yanked my mana back from the naginata and set off, diving into the forest at a full sprint.

I could still feel her, but she felt weak...and wrong, somehow. I sprinted as fast as I could, my DarkVision and enhanced eyes helping me to move through the forest with ease. I could have slowed down. If I had, I'd probably have been far stealthier, but I wasn't thinking straight.

Oracle had been attacked, *my* Oracle, and I was going to gut anything that hurt her.

I jumped another fallen log and saw the forest open up; a patch of cleared ground was obvious ahead as I started to sprint up another incline. I was halfway up it when something flashed out of the darkness and cut into my cheek, making me dive to the left. I rolled and came to my feet behind a tree as a notification began to blink, a sickly green color infecting my health and mana bars.

Beware!

You have been poisoned. You will lose 3 points of health, and 4 points of mana per second for the next 10 seconds.

"Motherfucking sneaky rogue bastards!" I growled out, starting to cast a Firebolt as I stuck my head around the edge of the tree, pulling back as something flashed toward me from the right. I dropped low, hurling the Firebolt in the direction the throw had come from, and I heard a snarl of annoyance.

I surged upright, breaking cover and sprinting in the direction I thought the cry had come from, seeing nothing at first, until a patch of darkness flowed around the tree to face me, the narrow, grey-skinned face, high-pointed ears, and bone-white hair letting me know my opponent was an elf...a dark elf.

He growled something into the darkness, and two others stepped out, simply standing watch, as he drew two swords and grinned at me.

I rushed him, my naginata blurring as I tried to hit him, stabbing first for his face, then dipping low towards an ankle, then wrapping around his left-hand sword, trying to batter it aside...and I failed spectacularly each time.

The drow barely seemed to move, a light slap of his blade against mine here, leaning to the side there; a shift of a foot. I was staggering off-balance and frantically following him, trying to catch the bastard as his friends laughed. Their high-pitched nasal amusement echoed through the trees as I fought on. The first minute or more, he just dodged, then he began to counter. A stinging slap here, a kick there, a smack of the flat of one blade against my arse as I staggered past him, making me limp for a few seconds as my leg went numb...

The entire time, his cronies were laughing, and my fury grew.

These assholes had done something to Oracle...I could feel her drawing further away from me, a faint sense of her letting me know she was terrified, and these *fuckheads* were keeping me from her!

I growled as I slashed and stabbed, the three drow dodging as I changed my target, trying to catch one of the watchers.

I realized that was a mistake as soon as the other two immediately started tripping, kicking, and smacking me with the flat of their blades. I'd evidently crossed a line in attacking a second one of them, and now I was fair game for all three.

I was slapped, kicked, punched, and had a needle-pointed stiletto knife driven through the chainmail of my thigh, when it all became too much.

I screamed in rage, my passenger jolting awake, the echoes of my fury filling the forest as I gathered my mana. I didn't try to do anything with it; I didn't cast a spell or channel it into my naginata. I just held it, the feeling of its power flowing through me, back and forth, building.

I twisted, going low, and spun the naginata around behind my back, flashing the point out as it came close to the nearest drow, before pulling back and doing the last thing they'd expect...throwing it with all my might directly behind me. I pulled all my mana into myself; I didn't know what I was doing differently, but I somehow forced the power through myself, submerging it in my very atoms.

The nearest drow's eyes widened, a gasp escaping I speared his companion straight through. As if in slow motion, his eyes tracked back, focusing in on me and narrowing in a glare before widening in alarm again.

I'd used the distraction of throwing my naginata, a move I'd hoped would hit one of them, but hadn't really expected, in reality, to cover for my shifting of stance.

I'd gathered my legs under me, and I leaped at the drow, his swords moving back from their casual arcs a second too late as I grappled him to the ground.

He tried to stab at me, his swords clattering off the sides of my armor as I grabbed onto his silken tunic, leaned back...and nutted him as hard as I could.

His eyes rolled back in his head as his nose shattered, blood spurting across his face as his right cheek cracked under the impact, deforming inwards. I hauled back and did it again, and a third time, before a boot slammed into my helm from my left. I rolled, dragging my opponent up on top of me and straight into his companion's second kick, releasing the stunned and now-fugly drow to fall to the side as I swept the leg from the one who'd just kicked me.

I yanked him closer and drove my dagger of ripping down hard, punching through the thin, aristocratic asshole armor just above his knee. No crude steel for this dickhead; oh no. It was a mixture of chitin and some amazingly soft, supple black silk. It wasn't strong enough to stop my blade as it slammed home, though. When I yanked it to the side, then back, widening the wound, before using it to haul myself up his body, he screamed in pain.

I yanked the knife free and slammed it home in his eye, smashing the fresh drow corpse backwards as I forced myself to my feet.

I felt stronger. Blood roared through me, thundering in my ears. Naked disbelief and shock radiated from the drow that sat a dozen feet away, my naginata sticking out of his stomach. I looked over at the one I'd been grappling with; he was hissing in pain, trying to pour a healing potion into his mouth, but it looked like the combination of a broken nose, crushed inwards cheekbone and smashed upper jaw was slowing him down. I grinned at him as I stomped over to the one I'd skewered.

I stopped, standing over him, and looked down. He was shaking, both hands on the shaft sticking out of his belly, and when he looked up at me in shock...I Sparta kicked him in the face. Bones cracked as his head slammed backwards, and I caught the naginata's base as it rose, stamping on his shoulder to keep him still as I yanked it out.

He screamed in pain, and I made eye contact with the one with the ruined face, maintaining it as I stabbed downwards, twisted, and yanked my naginata back up in one fluid motion.

I stepped away from my second drow corpse and stomped towards the last one living. He was frantically pouring the liquid into the ruin of his face now, trying to scuttle backwards.

I stepped forward, spinning the naginata around and bringing the steel-clad base down hard on the arm he was using to support himself. The crack echoed through the dark forest, until a heartbeat later, a second one joined it, rising along with his agonized screams.

I slammed the naginata down hard, the blade tip punching through the armor of his leg and deep into the loamy earth beneath, and I leaned on it casually, snorting and then spitting a wad of blood out onto his cheek as I looked down at him.

"Now, you fucker," I whispered, "...you and I are going to have a little chat about who you are, where you live, and *WHERE THE FUCK MY WISP IS!"* I roared the last at him and punched him in the face, rocking him back and making him scream as the naginata cut deeper with his every movement.

I crouched down, my dagger of ripping in hand, hefting the blade in my hand as I glared into his one intact eye. The other was covered in blood, face broken in around it and I doubted he could focus with it anymore. I looked at the slowly regenerating wounds, and I grinned evilly, all the nice little things I'd been wrapping myself in, the kindness, the compassion, the understanding...all falling away.

All that was left was a cold little core of control riding the wave of my roaring fury.

"You might think you're healing...maybe even hoping to escape...but guess what's really happening?" I whispered to him softly, almost lovingly, as I pressed the tip against his intact cheek and slowly increased the pressure until it pierced the skin, blood welling up around the blade. "Oh no...what it means is that you'll last longer while I play. I've got questions for you, you cocksucking piece of shit, and you're going to beg me for the release of death," I said, madness eating through me.

I'd gone straight through anger, past fury, and into that cold, dangerous rage where anything was possible. Amon lurked behind my eyes, watching. He'd been an emperor once, true enough, but I had some of his memories. Now, as he fed me more, I knew how he'd built his empire.

He'd built it by being honorable in victory, patient, and kind...and by using any means necessary when someone fucked with him. He'd made sure nobody fucked with the empire twice; they either lived nice lives, safe and good, or demons would weep in terror over the shit he pulled. Now I had him riding along on my shoulder. He'd grown to like Oracle; she was sweet and kind...exactly the kind of creature he'd done all the shit he had to protect.

He'd stained his soul black with blood again and again so creatures like her could sleep safe at night, and he'd been worshiped as a single step below a god for it. A damn small step, one that even the gods had recognized by giving him their gifts and loving him, until that fuckhead Nimon conspired with the Baron and the others to overthrow him.

The Baron and his siblings hadn't been alive when the vast majority of Amon's work was done; they'd not believed the tales, or they'd never have dared to cross that line.

Now I had him guiding me. Advising me.

I saw the figure before me differently in an eyeblink. It wasn't a man, or a woman, a parent, or a child. It was a monster, one that had harmed my friend.

Amon showed me things about my target, how thin the skin really was, how little pain it could withstand, and how to make it scream in agony and terror it had never known existed, while keeping it alive.

I stabbed my dagger down into its right hand, pinning it to the soil, and reached out casually, flipping the latches on the armor it wore, tugging it off and slipping it into my bag, then its shirt and the weapons it had been wearing.

"This is nice gear," I whispered, the light of madness shining bright as I looked into its terrified eye. "Don't want to get it all covered in blood, now do we?"

"Please," it whispered back, and I reached out with my left hand, putting my finger to its lips.

"Shhhh," I responded, then yanked my dagger free of its hand, making it whimper. "Speaking, unless it's to answer my questions, is not a good idea, now is it?" I asked, and lifted the dagger back to its cheek, idly carving a smiley face into its creamy, soft grey skin.

"I'll tell you...I will," it whispered, eyes screwed shut against the pain.

"Oh, I know you will.... I don't doubt that," I whispered back, finishing the arc of the mouth. "Now...you took my friend, and I want to know where she is, where she's being taken to, and who's there...and I really, *really* don't recommend lying to me...but that's a choice a man has to make for himself, isn't it?" I smiled at it, my rictus snarl stretching wide into a grin as I let Amon direct me.

Oracle was drawing farther away from me, headed downwards; her fear and her rage fed my own. My mana bar glowed, constantly ticking down. Whatever fusion I'd managed to make of flesh and magic that had sped my reactions and strength up to match theirs consumed it.

The others came crashing through the undergrowth, closer and closer. They didn't need to see this. I'd do what needed to be done so they could sleep and enjoy sweet dreams at night, safe.

Oh, yes.

The drow began speaking, eyes screwed tightly shut against the pain as tears leaked out, sobs interspersed with gritted teeth and cries of agony, as I pressed for clarification, pressing with my dagger, deep and slow...

CHAPTER TWENTY-SIX

The others had arrived while we talked. Bane, having led the way, had seen what I was doing and told the others to hold back.

He'd moved up, making sure I knew he was there, then had checked the bodies and spread the team out, searching the area and giving them something to do besides listen in too closely.

When it was all done, and I stood up, wiping the blood from my dagger before I sheathed it, Bane stepped in close and faced me, the rapidly cooling meat on the ground laid between us.

"Are you okay?" he asked me. I nodded slowly, so filled with fury, I might burst if I moved too quickly, except to hunt, react, or hurt something…

"Jax, I need you to do something for me; can you do that?" he said.

I nodded slowly, feeling the tension in my neck, the tendons standing out like steel wires.

"I need you to close your eyes and breathe…don't do anything else. Use the meditation techniques we discussed; put all emotion in the box. Hate, fear, love, all of it. Visualize the box in your mind and pour your emotions inside."

I frowned. I needed to be off; I knew where Oracle was headed, where they were going to take her, and—

"Jax!" Bane snapped.

I jerked, glaring at him, my left eye twitching, blood thundering through my veins. My heartbeat; it was so loud…

"Listen to me…. You know me…and you trust me, right?" Bane asked.

I stared at him for a long time before nodding jerkily, once.

"Then you know that I'll always do what you need me to do, right?" I nodded again. "Not what you want, but what you *need*."

That sounded right. He was good like that, a good friend.

"Now, come with me, just over here." He led me to the side, guiding me to sit down, and handed me a drink. "Just rest. We'll take care of it all in a minute; you just fill that box for me."

I sat there, eyes closed, and slowly pushed down all my emotions, feeding them into the box he'd taught me to visualize. It seemed to take forever yet be over in only a handful of seconds…before I felt tears tracking down my cheeks.

I slowly opened my eyes again, looking at the mess of trees before me. The sunlight that filtered down through the gently swaying branches high overhead gave the glade a gentle light, the green and red leaves fluttering, and the smell of wild garlic and lavender growing somewhere nearby filled the air, as did the scent...of blood and death...

I looked down, flexing my fingers and feeling the drying blood cracking. I slowly turned my hand over, distantly observing the patterns it made. A tiny voice in the back of my mind was moaning in fear at what we'd done, but...I couldn't remember all of it, not exactly...just bits, and...

I looked over my shoulder, searching for the body, and saw that it and the others had been dragged away into the bushes, a foot sticking out at the end of a smear of blood marking the location. Bane was walking towards me, a small pouch in one hand and a collection of swords and daggers hanging from belts held in his other hands.

"Bane," I whispered, looking at him.

"Are you okay, Jax?" he asked me quietly, tossing them aside and crouching next to me as he held out a waterskin and poured it over my hands...and my arms, and wiped at one of my cheeks with a finger.

I saw the bloody mess he cleaned away, and I remembered...I blinked, my brain having seen something, a memory of screaming and blood spraying, then it was gone.

"I—no. No, I'm not sure I am," I whispered to him, slowly shaking my head. My mana had started to refill after I'd released it, and I conjured a pair of fountains for Bane and me with barely a thought, splitting the magic for the first time, but too dazed to realize what I'd done.

Bane ignored his fountain until he saw me start to scrub at the blood, then he dipped his head in gratefully, opening his gills to the lifegiving water.

When I finished washing, and I was sure Bane had finished, I cut the mana to the spells and let them fade away, wringing the water from my top and shaking my head when it still came away bloody.

I'd stripped off my armor and scrubbed it, then rinsed my top, assuming it'd be okay, but man, it was drenched, and inside, that voice was still screaming that we'd done something terrible.

I muted it, feeling like my emotions were wrapped in cotton wool as I spoke to Bane.

"She's gone, mate; the drow said that he'd sent his fastest runner with her down into the tunnels. She's being taken to their leader, some drow-spider thing. He said that they have a way to move faster underground, that there's no way I can catch her, and...and I believe him.... I questioned him, and he—"

"No." Bane gripped my chin and made me look at him. "No, Jax, don't concentrate on what happened. You were angry and hurt, and you did what you had to do. Don't think about how you asked the questions; just answer this: do you think the drow lied?"

"No," I said adamantly.

"Do you want to do that again to another sentient being?"

"Definitely not," I said, but then I paused, considering it.

"No, Jax. I know you *could* do it; I'm asking if you *want* to," Bane repeated.

"No, I really don't."

"Then that's all you need to remember about this. They caused it and would have done the same to you if they'd won, and they would have enjoyed it. In the future, if you need me to, I'll do your questioning. But for now, all that's important is that you got the information. Do you know where the entrance to the smuggler's path is? I take it they're why no smugglers have made it through in a while?"

"Yeah, they moved in a few months back. They've got a city on the other side of the mountains and found a way through the caves to here. This is a scouting force; they're here to check it out and to steal what they can, then send back reports. Their queen will decide if they're to come and take the city."

"And the path itself; we can't catch a drow underground, not when they've got a head start, but we can track them, if the path is clear?"

"It's filled with concealed traps, but only in a few places, and I know where," I muttered; my mind drawn inexorably back to the whimpers from the drow.

"You have to stop, Jax; you can't concentrate on that now. Only one thing matters. They have Oracle, and we have to get her back," Bane said. "Do you want to wallow here or save her?"

I glared at him, and he nodded.

"In that case, pull yourself together. We need to leave. I suggest you change your top before you put your armor back on."

I looked down at the soaked fabric and gave it an experimental squeeze, getting a red-tinged stream of water for my effort. I grimaced and stood up, stripping it off and throwing it aside. It was one of my few tops from Earth, but I really didn't want it anymore.

I looked in my bag, finding only one top left, the one I'd taken from the drow in my maddened state. I swallowed my bile at another mental image of what I'd done to him, and I pulled the shirt out, examining it.

Gloom Spidersilk Tunic		Further Description *Yes/No*	
Details:		This spidersilk tunic is woven from the strands of the Gloom Spider, a species bred by the drow to create these specialized outfits. This tunic grants a +5 to armor, is resistant to cuts and tearing, and has additional padding sewn into the shoulders and chest.	
Rarity:	Magical:	Durability:	Charge:
Very Rare	No	98/100	N/A

I shook it out and looked it over, the subtle grey and black shimmer of the material making me swallow as I dismissed the memory. I steeled myself, deciding it was just loot, and I'd taken a fuck ton of that already. No need to be suddenly squeamish, even if I had peeled a sentient creature like a grape during questioning.

I saw a series of notifications blinking for my attention, and I pulled them up, swearing as soon as I read the larger one.

I'd managed to create or discover a new ability, it seemed, but it was one with some seriously shitty consequences.

The Forgotten Faithful

New Ability found!

You have supercharged your body with mana, creating a hybridization of your mana channels and musculature. You now have two paths before you and must choose one.

This choice cannot be undone or postponed.

Full Mana Channel Conversion:

Altering your mana channels to fuel your musculature completely will result in an increase of +10 to Strength, Agility, Dexterity, Endurance, and Constitution. You will begin to change to a new form, one that is far stronger than any human. Each additional level you will gain +2 to each of the aforementioned stats.

Beware!

You will no longer be able to cast spells beyond those that are internally focused; all mana in external use will be cut off.

Current Conversion Status: 1/100

Mana Overdrive:

This ability will allow the supercharging of your physical form, increasing your physical stats in Strength, Agility, Dexterity, Endurance and Constitution by +20, but will last only so long as you have mana. Once this ability ends, your physical characteristics will drop by -10 until a full healing has been carried out.

Choosing this will result in a single increase of +2 to Strength, Agility, Dexterity, Endurance, and Constitution, and a onetime increase of +5 to a stat of your choice.

Beware!

Choosing this ability will result in a permanent altering of your mana channels. Until your mana manipulation skill reaches 10, any sufficiently advanced practitioner of the magical arts will be able to sense your approach by the mana leakage you emanate. Your mana regeneration will drop from 2.9 points per minute to 1.4 until your mana channels are fully sealed at level 10. Excessive use of this skill will drain you of mana and health.

Mana Overdrive Skill: 1/100

I re-read it twice to make sure and sighed. There was no choice to be made here, not at all.

If I chose the first cool-as-fuck option, I could be a hell of a fighter. I could scrap my casting ability and concentrate on the fight, growing seriously stronger, and I'd have both a massive jump right now and a serious one with each level. Hell, I'd go to gaining nine points per level up, rather than five as I did now. I'd also pull my mana from Oracle and Bob, killing them both. Not going to happen.

I selected the Mana Overdrive skill, groaning as my mana channels shifted, and pain rippled through me. I fell forward with a gasp, my eyes flaring wide. It felt like my veins were on fire, my muscles being torn from my tendons and flesh. I could literally feel my mana channels writhing and shifting under my skin.

Bane was there in an instant, Barrett, Lydia, and her squad going into full freak-out mode as they searched for a target.

"It...it's okay," I ground out, forcing myself to speak, even as I dug my fingers into the ground, squeezing as I tried to crush the earth below me. "Just get anything you can. Strip the bodies, if there's anything...worth taking."

Bane shook his head and gestured to the pile of weapons. I looked over at them, panting in pain.

"There's nothing else worth taking. The basic, low-level armor is little better than anything our people wear now, and it's either damaged or bloody. I've taken the weapons and wealth already."

"Give them the weapons...if they want them," I forced out, and he gestured to Lydia, who separated out the swords and gave them to those who wanted one.

There were six swords in all, and while they were an upgrade to Jian, who spun and flicked them about, loving his new blades, to the others, they were a secondary weapon and an extra weight.

Barrett's sword was huge, a great two-handed affair, and he wasn't interested in another one. Neither was Cam, but Lydia, Arrin, Stephanos, and Miren each took one. The daggers were passed around as well, while Bane kept the throwing knives.

Eventually, the pain ceased, and I collapsed to the dirt, panting and trying to slow my heart rate. I looked at my HUD and saw my health and mana bars were drained to barely above half. I groaned and pulled out a healing potion, knocking it back, and casting Battlefield Triage on myself at the same time. I'd managed to assign the five points to Wisdom while I was changing, thinking it was better to get it over with in one go, and I pulled up my character sheet when I could see again.

Name: Jax

Titles: Strategos: 5% boost to damage resistance, Fortifier: 5% boost to defensive structure integrity, Chosen of Jenae

Class: Spellsword > Justicar	**Renown**: Unknown
Level: 13	**Progress**: 117,620/120,000
Patron: Jenae, Goddess of Fire and Exploration	**Points to Distribute**: 0 **Meridian Points to Invest**: 0

Stat	Current points	Description	Effect	Progress to next level
Agility	42	Governs dodge and movement	+320% maximum movement speed and reflexes, (+10% movement in darkness, -20% movement in daylight)	49/100
Charisma	12	Governs likely success to charm, seduce, or threaten	+20% success in interactions with other beings	5/100
Constitution	34	Governs health and health regeneration	660 health, regen 39.6 points per 600 seconds, (+10% regen due to soul bond, -20 health due to soul bond, each point invested now worth 20 health)	38/100
Dexterity	23	Governs ability with weapons and crafting success	+130% to weapon proficiency, +13% to the chances of crafting success	69/100
Endurance	24	Governs stamina and stamina regeneration	240 stamina, regen 14 points per 30 seconds	66/100
Intelligence	29	Governs base mana and number of spells able to be learned	270 mana, spell capacity: 17 (15 + 2 from items), (-20 mana due to soul bond)	61/100
Luck	18	Governs overall chance of bonuses	+8% chance of a favorable outcome	11/100
Perception	24	Governs ranged damage and chance to spot traps or hidden items	+140% ranged damage, +14% chance to spot traps or hidden items	81/100
Strength	25	Governs damage with melee weapons and carrying capacity	+15 damage with melee weapons, +150% maximum carrying capacity	32/100
Wisdom	34 (29)	Governs mana regeneration and memory	+240% mana recovery, 1.7 points per minute, 240% more likely to remember things, -50% mana regeneration until mana manipulation reaches level 10.	99/100

Jez Cajiao

Congratulations!

Through hard work and perseverance, you have increased your Luck by one point. Continue to train and learn to increase this further.

Congratulations!

You have killed the following:

- 1x Drow squad leader, level 31 for a total of 3,500xp
- 2x Drow soldiers of various levels for a total of 4,000xp

Progress to level 14 stands at 125,120/120,000

I was gutted. My mana regeneration had been halved until I could level the mana manipulation skill up, and it had effectively removed the opportunity for me to use stealth around any magic user at all.

I seethed inwardly while I forced myself to my feet, snapping directions out as I led the way to the entrance to the smuggler's path, which was now a drow home. It wasn't far, maybe twenty meters through the trees to a large mound, overgrown with rocks. I'd clearly drawn the drow away from covering the entrance with my wild approach, as we could see a handful of plates of food and a campfire that smoldered away merrily just inside the entrance.

As we walked, I brought up the last notification, realizing suddenly what I'd missed in my irritation before…

Congratulations!

You have reached level 14!

You have 5 points to invest in your stats.

Progress to level 15 stands at 5,120/140,000

Well, I was glad to see I'd finally hit level fourteen, and was climbing towards fifteen, but I now had to decide on the allocation. Did I continue to "fix" myself by dumping points into the weaker areas, such as putting all five into, say Charisma, or Luck, or did I keep building my stats? I considered what my Charisma was doing to me so far. I'd probably have been able to turn the Reeve of Lorek to my side if it was higher…but he was a fucknut, and I'd wanted to smash his teeth in as soon as I'd met him.

I could concentrate on building my Charisma organically; maybe try chatting some random people up when I reached the city, and pile the points into Luck…or I could fix some of the damage my new ability had done and bring my mana regeneration back up a bit.

I flicked my eyes from one side of the character sheet to the other, picking reasons to choose different things each time, until I sighed, and gave in to what I knew I needed to do.

My training with Flux and Bane had made it clear; I'd be able to raise my purely physical stats through practice. As such, piling points into them right now could be classed as a waste, especially as each level was harder to earn than the last. The problem with that was that I had to survive long enough to make use of those methods.

I sank four points into my Dexterity. It was the stat that directly affected my weapon handling and the likelihood to fumble a move, which brought it up to twenty-seven. Then I dumped my single remaining point straight into Charisma.

I *hated* doing it; it felt like I was wasting the point, but for all I knew, I'd need it, and it galled me that my lowest stat was directly related to my looks and popularity. I'd never had that much trouble getting laid, after all…admittedly, I usually went out in Newcastle, so it wasn't hard, but still.

I stomped straight inside, watching out for the signs I'd been told about. As we walked into the darkness, Lydia's squad lighting torches behind me, I soon found the first trap.

I'd begun to calm down by the time I found it, which was lucky, as I almost missed it, despite the drow telling me exactly what to watch for.

I paused, crouching down as I spotted the faint tripwire close to the ground, at the beginning of a field of rippled dirt. I grinned, liking the simplicity of the trap.

The rippled effect made it much harder to see the tripwire, and you instinctively moved closer to see what had caused the ripple, pulling in close enough to both trip the wire and to be hit by the poison flechettes that would be fired from the concealed, heavily modified crossbow.

I had everyone move back, and I slowly examined the bow, finding a poisoned needle hidden in the grip right where you'd lay your hand to disarm it.

"Sneaky bastards," I whispered, avoiding the needle and disarming the trap carefully, a notification springing up once I was done to tell me that my traps skill had increased by one.

I dismissed it quickly, too busy checking to see if there were any more traps to pay any real attention. The drow hadn't warned me about the needle, and I wasn't sure if it was because he'd forgotten, which was unlikely, or if it was a last attempt to kill me.

"To the left," Bane whispered, and I looked up at him questioningly. "The ground to your left has something hidden in it; I can sense it," he said. I crouched down further, examining the ground. Sure enough, there was a hair-thin strand of silk that led to a second needle trap, and I disarmed that as well, stashing away the various parts and passing the crossbow to Bane to examine.

"It's an assassin's weapon all right," he commented, rumbling voice tinged with approval.

"Keep it, if you want," I replied, and then shook my head, calling out to the others. "I'm sorry for back there, people. I had to deal with something, and I'm worried about Oracle."

I received a series of nods and shrugs, and I turned back to Bane.

"You're probably going to be better at this than I am, and we need to move quickly. How close did you get before you spotted that tripwire?" I asked.

"A dozen feet or so, before I was sure," Bane replied. "I would have warned you, if I'd not known you had seen it already."

"Yeah, I saw it like a foot or two away. You lead, Bane. We don't have time for me to learn the hard way," I said, checking my mana again and shaking my head. I couldn't afford to put up with this, and I popped open a mana potion, gulping it down and healing myself for a final time, making sure that I was at full health, and the debuff from using the mana overdrive skill was gone.

Bane slipped past me, and I quietly filled him in on the traps the Drow had told me about; he spotted them both within minutes, and we jogged along the smuggler's path at speed.

I looked around as we went, seeing the traces here and there of old stonework, bracings to secure the ceiling and walls, and repairs that had clearly been done, both ancient and recent.

It took over an hour before we came to the first branching of the path, where a second, more recent path joined the first. I closed my eyes and searched for Oracle, finding her still far in the distance, but stopped at last, and below us to the left.

"The new path," I said, and Bane took off at once. Where the first path was hard ground, compacted over the years by the passing of countless booted feet and small caravans, this second path was far narrower and clearly not the work of smugglers. We saw boot prints regularly and occasionally other, stranger signs, areas where the path had been swept clean by something wide and low.

Segments had been reinforced by a sparkling, ridged material, strands of something that braced entire sections, and an awful smell began to build.

We paused to rest after two hours, and I summoned a pair of fountains again for the group, this time realizing what I'd done so thoughtlessly.

You have discovered a new Ability: Multi-Cast.

You can now cast two spells at the same time, provided they are either the same spell cast twice, or complementary spells that you have at least reached level 10 in.

"Well, shit," I muttered, reading the notification that had appeared. I'd done it without thought, so used to the feeling of Oracle casting a second spell and using my mana that I'd replicated it, not knowing it was something strange. I also didn't realize just how damn expensive the spell was; instead of costing me ten mana, it was costing me ten for the first one and thirty for the second, plus an additional forty to keep them both going every ten seconds. I cut the second fountain immediately, explaining to my team and letting them share the first.

Once everyone had drank their fill and refilled their canteens, Bane rested in the water for a few seconds. We took off again, jogging for another hour almost before Bane slowed to a halt, his right upper hand waving in warning.

We gathered around and the torches were lowered, hands raising to shield them as much as possible.

"Up ahead," Bane whispered to me. "I can sense something vibrating; I think it's some form of spiderkin."

I cursed and passed the word on, turning back to him as he continued.

"I'll go ahead and scout. Wait here." I nodded, and he was off, his natural camouflage allowing him to blend in with the tunnel as he went.

Silence reigned as the minutes ticked by, my naginata resting in my right hand, loosely held, while I toyed with the dirt, idly drawing patterns as I stared into the tunnel. Long minutes passed, then more, slowly ticking on and on. I frowned suddenly, a single soft sound seemingly out of place in the silence of the tunnel, and I listened for it again.

It sounded like sand shifting, or soil…I concentrated on it, a noise from behind distracting me. I turned to shush Miren, the youngest of the group who'd just started to whisper a joke to Stephanos.

Lydia growled a warning at them all to be silent, and I turned back to the tunnel before me, freezing as a quartet of eyes stared back at me.

The creature was long and low, maybe three feet tall, oval in shape, and running back around the tunnel's bend to disappear into the distance. It was at least four feet long with a bulbous form like a pale-skinned cross between a worm and a gelatinous blob. It had paused as soon as I turned back around, its almost silent approach on dozens of small spiked legs arrested as its black, orb-like eyes stared at me. Slowly, just below the eyes on its rounded, bulbous head, a jaw hinged open, and a proboscis slipped forward, a hollow tip pointing straight at me.

My eyes widened, and I dove to the side, roaring out a warning as a stream of white liquid sprayed the area I'd been crouching in.

A scream rose from behind me, and a hissing, bubbling noise. I rolled back from my left to the right, jumping back to my feet in the middle of the corridor and stabbing out with the naginata.

Someone behind me sobbed in pain, others stepping up. Lydia was on my left, and Barrett on my right, a trio of small missiles flashing past me to embed themselves in the creature as it pulled back from my blow, exploding a second later and spattering small sections of the tunnel in goo.

I yanked back on the naginata, feeling resistance as the flesh of the creature flowed around the wound I'd made, tugging back at the weapon and pulling me closer.

"Be careful!" I managed to get out, before the creature lunged forward, its jaws snapping shut inches from my arm, Barrett shoving me aside. He dove back, the creature's pale flesh brushing against his hand and eliciting a groan from him.

"It burns!" he warned, frantically waving his hand and trying to shake off a layer of slime that covered the creature, even as Lydia smacked her mace into it with a dull squelch.

"Fall back!" I ordered him, and Arrin stepped up to take his place, firing a Firebolt into its face.

Where Lydia's and my weapons had barely registered on the creature, the fire did. It spread quickly, flashing across the surface of its flesh as the acidic slime burst into flames. The creature made a high-pitched mewling sound as it shook itself from side to side, trying to shake the fire off.

I grinned as I channeled my own Firebolt spell, not into my hand to throw, but instead into the naginata.

It immediately burst to life, the length of the weapon glowing a red that cycled all the way from a dark red as it began, to a bright, blazing white as I plunged the weapon deeper then slashed it from side to side, eviscerating the creature and cutting its head free.

I stepped back, pulling my mana back into myself and letting the naginata return to its normal color as the creature collapsed to the ground, seemingly dead.

The remains twitched as the flames still coating it caused pockets of fat to pop and crackle, but as soon as the small death's head floated up from the corpse, I relaxed. For all of a second.

Whimpering cut the silence from behind me, and I spun to see Miren on the floor of the tunnel, Stephanos holding her arms down as Jian poured a healing potion over the raised and bubbling skin of her face and neck.

Whatever caustic shit the creature had spit at her, it was steadily burning through her skin, making it bubble away as it sank deeper.

I had a few potions I'd made when we'd been experimenting, but as I frantically checked them, there was nothing that would act to counteract the acid. I growled at myself, mentally adding more potions and counter-agents to my list to learn.

Still muttering, I cast Battlefield Triage on Miren, channeling it for over a minute before the crap burnt out. Barrett luckily had a spare shirt and had wiped the majority of the slime off his hand with it before it dissolved. He was using a healing potion on it and didn't need my help.

"Where's Bane?" Arrin asked.

My blood ran cold. There was no way that thing should have been able to get past him, so something must have happened.

"Fuck," I whispered, looking at the corpse that filled the tunnel before me.

It was slumping even lower to the ground now, as whatever muscles had kept it in its semi-inflated shape released in death. But it was long, and whatever had burned Barrett could still be covering it, despite the flames that had spread.

"I'm going after him," I said after a second, only to have Barrett and Lydia speak up immediately.

"No, you can't—"

"I'll go—"

"No," I said, cutting them off. "I've the best chance to get around there. I can run, jump off the walls, and…"

"And probably die when you fall on its back and dissolve," Barrett finished for me. "We've no idea how long the thing is; what if it's hundreds of feet long?"

"I—" I broke off, knowing they were right, but Bane was out there somewhere, and something must have happened for this thing to get past him. I needed to get to him; I needed to get to Oracle!

"I'll burn it."

I turned to see Arrin standing next to the corpse. I regarded him thoughtfully, and he grinned at me.

"You gave me FlameShield and Magic Missile, remember? So, all I've got to do…is walk forward while I channel into the shield, right? It'll burn the corpse, won't it?"

I paused for a second before grinning back at him and passing a mana potion over.

"Do it!" I told him.

He started to cast, walking forward as we moved back, his gestures inscribing a circle around him, three feet out from the ends of his fingers. As his hands moved faster and faster, the flames that appeared at the tips of his fingers dripped, falling and flowing in the air as he moved. They swirled, drawn into a pattern as though being blown by the wind to coat the outside of an invisible bubble, and he slowly took his first step forward.

The minute the outer edge touched the corpse, it began to blacken and shrivel, the skin crisping up and curling back as fats inside the body began to pop and crackle.

Arrin moved slowly, a single step, then a pause and a second step. I had to resist the urge to shout at him, but I knew he was going as fast as he could. Long minutes passed as he took the corner, finding another dozen or more feet of the corpse ahead of him, only partially burnt.

I exchanged a long look with Barrett and nodded, admitting that he was right.

"Glad to see we agreed, Jax," he whispered. "Just think how lucky you are that Oren isn't here; he'd be telling you 'I told you so...' but not me. I don't need to say it. I'm a bigger man than that."

"Not by fucking much you're not, mate. He's a bloody dwarf, and you're still only what? An inch taller?" I whispered back, forcing myself to grin at the black look he gave me. "Don't worry, though, just like you'd not say, 'I told you so,' I'd never draw attention to your *short*comings."

With that, Arrin released his FlameShield, the corpse withered and blackened to such a degree that we could walk across the top safely, and he chugged the mana potion I'd given him.

"Let's go!" I said, pushing forward. I clapped Arrin on the shoulder in congratulations and started to run, taking the twists and turns of the tunnel at speed. My meridian-enhanced vision worked in concert with the tracking skill to occasionally highlight Bane's distinctive three-digit toes where he'd left a print.

It was only a handful of minutes before we passed a side tunnel that the creature had clearly come from. I checked the ground, finding Bane's prints leading onwards on the main path. We ignored the side tunnel and continued on until we came to a widening in the tunnel, as the five-by-ten-foot tunnel grew out to a cavern dozens of feet across at the narrowest, and the ceiling hung high overhead, covered in spiderwebs.

I skidded to a stop. The clattering of the rest of my group as they caught up was more than enough to ensure the awakening of the few giant spiders I hadn't already woken with my own arrival. I looked up at them as they slowly lowered themselves down, ranging in size from the size of my hand to over a dozen feet tall, long legs flickering and twitching as they shifted on their webs and lines to surround us.

"Back away, slowly," I whispered, looking up at them, well aware that with the limited light given off by the magelights behind me, the rest of my party had no idea what was coming.

"What is it?" Miren squeaked as Stephanos grabbed her arm, having seen a hint of movement in the darkness.

"Spiders," I replied. Just as I was about to throw a Firebolt into the webbing, in the hopes of injuring them and killing a few, a cocoon in the middle twitched and thrashed.

On the floor, directly below it, lay a pair of spears, and I knew I'd found Bane. Dozens of smaller spiders crawled across his thrashing, thick-webbed cocoon, bloodstains coloring it.

"...and Bane," I whispered. I saw the way the spiders gathered themselves, and I yelled in warning.

"Back! Get back!" I shouted, shoving the party. They fell back quickly, but not before several spiders shot their webs at us, with more being released repeatedly.

Instantly, it became a mess of screaming faces, yanking arms, and flashing weapons as we all tried to cut the dozens of strands that hit us, yanking us off our feet, even as smaller spiders jumped across the room or fell from above us.

I felt the pain of tiny bites on my neck, the back of my wrist, on my cheek…

Beware!

You have been poisoned.

You will lose 1 point of health, and 1 point of stamina per second for the next 10 seconds.

Beware!

You have been poisoned.

You will lose 1 point of health, and 1 point of stamina per second for the next 10 seconds.

Beware!

You have been poisoned.

You will lose 1 point of health, and 1 point of stamina per second for the next 10 seconds.

Beware…

I felt the bites as they continued, and I saw the notification flash up, the warning getting my attention straight away, as I realized just how dangerous this was.

I had one spell that I could use here, but didn't have anywhere near the time to cast it, considering how long it took for Cleansing Fire to activate. Ten seconds wasn't long, but when a single mispronunciation would cause the spell to backlash and harm me more, and I had dozens of venomous spiders covering me, I didn't have the time or control to cast it.

I had one chance, and that was to embrace my new ability.

I pulled my mana in and shoved it into my muscles, my tendons, my…

"ARRRRRRRGH" I screamed as my body was suddenly flooded with vitality. It felt like I'd had a pint of strong espresso injected into my brain directly, as time seemed to slow around me. The drow I'd faced before had been stronger and faster than me, until I'd boosted myself.

The spiders weren't; they weren't even close.

There were lots of them, but they were only dangerous as the ambush predators they were, especially when facing me in my newly enhanced form.

I spun my naginata through the air, a touch of mana spared to flare it to life and imbue it with fire as I cut through all but one of the cords holding me.

I smashed down with my other hand, swatting the spiders that covered me. They exploded in tiny pops of gore, and when my feet hit the ground, the last connected web yanked on me, trying to pull me back up, even as other spiders readied themselves to fire another salvo of webs at me.

I grinned up at the spider connected to me, and I gripped the thick webbing with my left hand, yanking…*hard.*

The spider came loose from the wall where it had crouched. It'd been bracing to pull me up, not prepared for a tug of war with a being far stronger than it.

It fell forward, legs windmilling as it tried to secure itself. Its thrashing legs hit a second spider and pulled it free, the chitinous forelegs punching deep into its unfortunate brethren, who immediately counterattacked, sinking its fangs into its supposed attacker.

I was moving now; I'd cut the cord connecting me to the spider that was battling for its life against another of its kin, and I started to dance. I jumped and sliced, cut and tore through webbing, my people falling free.

Lydia cursed as she smashed down nearby, but yanked a potion out and chugged it. Arrin tumbled down next, his FlameShield spell a nasty surprise for the spiders that had covered him and even more so for the ones that fell all around him. He quickly drank a health, then mana potion, and started running around giggling as spiders fell, bursting into flames as they hit his shield.

Barrett grabbed Stephanos as I freed him and started dragging him from the room. Arrin leaped up and grabbed onto a spider easily ten feet tall that had landed nearby. As he grabbed handfuls of coarse hair, pulling himself upwards, his FlameShield burrowed into the creature, killing it in a gory explosion of superheated chitin.

I spun and jumped, my health and mana dropping steadily, as well as my stamina, but as my blade licked out, piercing and slicing, skewering and deftly freeing my party, I couldn't help but grin at the world around me.

These were spiders, giant fucking killer spiders, in a cave deep underground, and I was going to be giving any survivors fucking nightmares after this.

Arrin canceled his FlameShield, firing a handful of Magic Missiles upwards. A second later, the struggling cocoon fell from the ceiling. Lydia caught it, staggering under the weight.

"I've got him!" she screamed, running for the exit from the room, and the safety of the others.

I spun my naginata, flashing out again and again as they fled, and more spiders landed all around me.

My mana was getting low, and I frantically spun, lashing out and slicing a leg from the nearest spider, then pivoting and driving the point forward to crack upwards, piercing through another spider's open maw. The tip crunched into its brain and sent it to the floor, spasming in death. I popped another mana potion, swallowing it as fast as I could.

I started to grow frantic, spinning and kicking, sweeping the blade forward and disemboweling one then flipping it over and swinging the metal-clad base around like a baseball bat, another spider practically exploding from the impact.

"ENOUGH!" roared a hoarse voice, and the spiders fell back, slowly clambering up the walls and returning to watching me from their webs.

"What do you want, fleshling?" came the question.

I stared as enormous webs that had coated one entire wall slowly withdrew, and the creature that hunkered behind them was revealed.

It was a spider, grossly oversized, and old as sin. Where the others were grey and black, with haphazard patterns and markings, this creature was midnight black with red patterned across it. My every instinct screamed that nature always marked things with warnings, and that this red was a hint to make sure I stayed the fuck away from it.

It slowly moved forward, a leg as thick around as I was, touching down with a crunch as it impacted a bone and smashed it into oblivion, and I realized the floor was covered in them. I was in a nest that had seen thousands of deaths, and I was almost out of mana, like seconds left...if that.

"Well? Why have you come, now of all times? Your kind never comes without cause!" it bellowed, and I felt the hot, fetid breath wash over me, the stink of carrion thick in the air.

"My friend was taken," I forced out, my mana reserves bottoming out. I felt the boosted stats leaving, my muscles deflating. I forced myself to stand straighter, knowing I couldn't win this fight.

"And now you have it back. Leave! Leave my children, before more die!" it roared at me, and I shook my head.

"No! He is my scout, and a friend, yes, but the drow took the friend I am chasing...I hunt them." I tried not to let it show, but I'd grounded the base of my naginata, frantically trying to stay upright as I gripped it with all my waning strength, the last effects of the spiders' bites bottoming out my stamina, while my health wasn't much better.

"Drow!" the spider spat, disgust clear in its rumbling voice. "Always they curse us, use us! We want no part of your fight with them; you will leave some of your number to make up for my losses, then go to hunt them."

"Get fucked," I said, not pausing to think.

"What?"

"I said, you can get fucked!" I growled. "You attacked my scout, attacked me! I'm not at fault here." I frowned, earning a vicious pulse from the mana migraine I was trying to ignore as I used my Identify spell on the spider.

Ashrag the Old
Greater Ancient Cave Spider

Ashrag was young when the city of Himnel was built, a creature steeped in blood and death even then. Ashrag was once counted an imperial servant, but she exists for only two reasons now: to protect her young, and out of hatred for the drow spiderkin that forced her species to the brink of extinction.

Health: Unknown
Mana: Unknown

"...Ashrag." I finished, forcing myself to stare into the same eye continuously. I figured that trying to look at each of them would only show weakness.

"Mageling. I should have known," Ashrag spat. "I am old. I've seen your kind come and go, be born and die; why shouldn't I command you to be slaughtered now? Give me a reason or die screaming like so many of my children have," she snapped bitterly.

I took a deep breath and let it out slowly, deciding to risk it all on one more flip of the dice, making it up as I went along and hoping the details I had weren't leading me astray.

"Because you swore an Oath to me and mine, Ashrag. You were an imperial servant once…I am Jax, High Lord of the Great Tower, ruler of Dravith. How deep is your honor? Who are you, under the cloak of age: are you Ashrag the Honorable, or Ashrag the Oathbreaker?"

Silence reigned across the cavern as she slowly moved closer to me, her eyes flaring in rage. I forced myself to glare right back. I'd never be able to win this fight, not as I was. I'd have a hell of a time when the entire party was prepared and rested, and now they were clinging to life in the tunnel, while I was surrounded.

"You dare…you *dare* to accuse me…*I* broke no Oath! It was *your* kind who abandoned *me* and mine! Thousands of my children perished; we were forced to flee when the moon struck the realm, when the seas turned to flame and the skies to ash. *Your* kind turned on *us*…you *hunted* us, *laughed* at our Oaths, *slaughtered* my *children* until I fled…and now you DARE CALL ME OATHBREAKER!"

The cavern shook with the rage that filled her voice, and I felt Amon staring out from my eyes.

We have wronged you…failed you…abandoned you…

The voice that filled my mind was a whisper, but it echoed, building until it became physically painful, the words thundering over and over, until I spoke them aloud. I opened my eyes and looked up at Ashrag, repeating Amon's words as he spoke.

"I was murdered by those I loved, the Gods themselves banished through Nimon's black arts, and my people, from the lowest to the highest, suffered for it."

Ashrag paused, her enormous bulk hovering before me, her pedipalps each longer than my legs, twitching uncertainty, even as her fangs shook with repressed anger and a need to lash out.

"Who—who are you…?"

"I am Jax, High Lord of Dravith," I said, swallowing hard, before going on. "I am Amon's descendant, and I claim his Oaths as my own." I said the last at his prompting, but I knew it was going to be a mistake.

I was right.

My meager mana reserves bottomed out instantly, and the world shook, light erupting around me as my world vanished. I fell backwards into darkness, a single notification filling my vision:

You have resurrected the Oath of Imperial Allegiance!

Due to lack of mana and territorial control, Oath range is limited to 6 miles' radius. 11 Imperial Citizens have been found inside this territory, and their Oaths have become active, tied to yourself as High Lord of Dravith and Scion of the Empire.

"I swear upon pain of death, to faithfully execute all that the emperor decrees. I swear upon my soul that I shall stand for the empire when it calls. I shall be strong when the weak need me, generous when the poor are at hand, and merciless when my fellow citizens are threatened. I shall worship the gods of my fathers, respect my elders, and raise up my children to stand tall.

I am an imperial citizen. I claim the right to call upon the legion in my hour of need, to hold those who wrong me to justice, and to be avenged if I cannot be saved."

Those who swore the Oath in truth can now sense your location and are pulled to you by its Power.

You have taken your first step on the Path of Imperial Right.

Be wary, for there can be only one end in sight:

you must rule or you must die.

CHAPTER TWENTY-SEVEN

I woke slowly. The first thing I could feel was pain, horrific pain that filled my body. It roared through every bone as they screamed with agony, their marrow pulsing. I groaned, straining, and felt myself shift slightly before my restraints stopped my movement.

I struggled weakly, pulling against whatever held me, and a sticky strand caught the suddenly exposed skin on the back of my left wrist.

As I coughed and forced my eyes open, I realized that the ceiling high overhead was moving as I was carried along, before sagging to one side as the creature carrying me began to descend a wall, carrying me effortlessly downwards.

It took a while for any of it to make sense, my mind pulsing crazily with pain, but eventually I focused in, seeing a blurry patch close to my face that shifted and moved.

It resolved suddenly as it moved closer to my face to examine me, and I jerked back. A bright red and black spider the size of a pitbull was squatting on my chest, staring at me from dozens of jet-black eyes.

"What the…" I snarled, trying to back away. I realized that I was webbed down, and my instincts flared. I opened my mouth, about to try to bite the spider, before it could bite me, when Amon spoke.

Wait…

I froze. The usual madness that filled his voice was gone, leaving only a bone-deep weariness. Somehow, that one word carried a sense of hope as well.

She is no threat to you, scion of my line.

"Can you hear me?" I asked mentally, not really expecting an answer.

I can, Jax.

"Well this is freaky as fuck, but right now, I'm about to be a spider buffet, so…"

The Children of Ashrag are no threat to you.

"Clearly you missed the fight, then…"

I saw some of it. I think…the world is different, and I lose my place in time on occasion. We don't have long, Scion, so listen well.

"Okay."

Be silent.

The voice carried no anger, but it was full of authority. I froze again when it commanded silence, the sarcastic comeback dying in my throat, the words never uttered.

We have no time but the present. Listen if you wish to survive. Ashrag felt her Oath to the empire become active when you took my Oaths as your own.

Your mana was too weak to claim all my oaths, and if it weren't, you'd be dead from the shock, so be thankful.

For now, just accept that those nearby who swore to the empire have had their Oaths called upon. They can feel you, can sense your lineage, and are compelled to come to you, to serve you. Ashrag feels aggrieved, abandoned, and ill-used, but she recognized the truth of the Oaths becoming active. She will not harm you or allow another of her brood to do so. If you would claim more from her, it will be on you...

"Look, I don't know what the fuck just happened. I just know that I feel like I was hit by a fucking bus, and you're spouting shit I don't understand. So, any chance you could run through that again in English?...Hellooo...Amon?...Fuck."

I groaned as Amon's presence vanished, and I tried to sit up again, only to collapse a handful of seconds later when it was obvious I couldn't move. I flexed my hands as best I could, the surrounding webbing pulling at the skin.

Body heat emanated from the spider under me, trapped by the long, coarse hairs that covered its body and the shifting chitinous plates that lifted and dipped as it clambered down the wall. It was warm, and I was...riding it?

"Anyone there?" I called out weakly, and the spider under me froze momentarily before continuing, but it moved cautiously now, as though afraid.

"Jax?" A weak voice called out from behind me, and others rose to join it.

"Lord Jax?"

"You crazy bastard! Whoot!" The last I recognized as Arrin's voice. The trainee mage was clearly loving life at the minute, I realized, as I managed to twist my head to get a look up at them. The rest of my party were all strung out above me, webbed onto the backs of spiders that climbed the sheer face of an underground cliff.

"They are safe," came a tiny, rough voice, and I twisted my head around. The smaller spider that hunched on my chest stared at me, its voice interrupted by a nervous clicking of fangs. "The queen commanded you are not to be harmed. We are travelling to the central nest, where she will summon the others."

"What others...tiny spider?" I asked, hesitating over the name.

"I am Horkesh," the spider said proudly. "I am the Queen-in-Waiting of our colony; my sisters travel with your servants." I coughed and tried to shift again, the spider under me freezing, and I felt it start to shake in fear.

"What"—*cough*—"...What happened...Horkesh?" I asked weakly, and the spider shifted on my chest, scuttling to one side to say something in a language I didn't understand, before dashing back to stand on my chest, its fangs flashing inches from my eyes as she spoke.

"Your mount fears it has given offense. Do you wish to eat it?" Horkesh asked.

I had to fight down bile.

"No. No, I really don't fucking want to eat it. I want to get where we're going and get the fuck down," I replied, swallowing hard.

"We are less than a turning of your sand glasses from the nest. Be patient, please, lord." With that she darted away again to carry out a hurried discussion with the spider acting as my mount, and it resumed the trip, this time notably faster and more bumpily. "I have ordered your mount to hurry," she said. I drew in a deep breath, unsure if I was really in a rush to get wherever I was going after all. I was webbed to the back of a giant fucking spider, I reflected.

I checked my mana and health, and saw they were both steadily rising, but far slower than I'd have liked.

"How long was I unconscious?" I asked, and Horkesh considered for a long while. I was about to ask again when she spoke up at last.

"You were unconscious for, I think, a full arc of the daystar. The queen allowed your servants to administer the red and blue waters to you, then she bit you, to ensure you would sleep deep and dreamlessly."

"You think...wait, she fucking bit me?" I snarled.

Horkesh backed up slightly before shaking herself and moving closer. "It is difficult to understand your references to time. We have a sand glass in our nest. I think it is accurate, but I am unsure how long your daystar takes. It changes. It is very strange in your land above the sweet darkness."

"The darkness?" I asked. The fact that the "queen" Ashrag had fucking *bitten* me was still going round and round in my head. Her goddamn mouth had to be nearly my fucking size, how the hell...

"The darkness," Horkesh repeated, gesturing with her front legs all around us. "The darkness is our home, safe and secure. Light brings danger, but darkness is safe."

"Darkness, tunnels, and underground; okay, got it. Now, why the hell did she fucking bite me?!" I snarled, my voice getting louder as my frustration and disgust rose.

"To protect you." Ashrag spoke from somewhere ahead. The spider beneath me trembled in fear again before darting forward.

"You bit me, knocking me out, to fucking protect me?!" I snarled back at her.

"Typical!" She huffed in amusement. "Yes, lordling, I bit you to protect you, the injury to your body from taking the Oaths on, even as weak as they were. Despite how few Oathsworn as there must be within reach, it was still more than your wounded body could take. So, I bit you, slowing your body down, and putting you into a restful, dreamless sleep while your servants used their potions on you."

I lay there in silence for a long time, considering her words. What details I could remember about the conversation with Amon and Ashrag slowly came back to me, and it lined up with Amon's assertion that taking the Oaths on had been dangerous.

"I'm sorry, Ashrag...*Queen* Ashrag," I said finally. "I have broken memories of the past, and I'm from a realm far from here. I don't understand a lot of what has happened, and I tend to react...badly...to surprises. My friend, Oracle, my companion...was captured by the drow. In chasing her, I nearly lost another friend to your children. Today has been a fucking terrible day so far."

There was a pregnant pause as I waited to see if I was going to be stabbed, bitten, or just plain stood on, before Ashrag's voice rumbled back to me.

"Admitting you were wrong was rare even when the empire was strong; in the years since its fall, it is even rarer. Many have come to us, for we are among the eldest of the races; most have tried to kill us. Some come to steal our young, others for our bodies or our treasures...perhaps you come to us for a better reason. We will talk soon; rest now."

I could hear the steady tap-tap-tap sound of her bulk moving away.

I shrugged as much as I could, restrained as I was, and forced myself to look around. Wherever I was, it was deep; the way I sagged against the webbing let me know that I'd probably have fallen off long since, if I was free.

"Where is the nest?" I asked Horkesh, and the spider rushed back across to stare at me before answering.

"It is ahead. Deep, deep in the earth, far from the light and any who could try to steal from us."

With that enigmatic and entirely unhelpful answer, she disappeared again, racing over the side of the spider I rode.

I tried my best to get comfortable, giving up after a few minutes, as every movement caused the spider under me to panic and either rush forward or freeze, neither of which felt good when climbing down a cliff.

I closed my eyes and did what I should have done when I had first woken up. I called out to Bane. I thought I'd heard his voice before, when I first woke, but I needed to be sure.

"Bane?" I called, and there was a second in which my heart froze, before I heard a response.

"I'm here, Jax. I'm weak, but I'm here."

"What happened?" I asked, sagging back with relief.

"I sensed the great spider…Ashrag…and I focused on her like a child on his first hunt. I ignored the signs around me until it was too late, and I was taken. Dozens of spiders were everywhere I turned, my jaws webbed down before I could even shout a warning. I failed you," he said bitterly. "I will admit my fault, lord; I will stand down as your bodyguard. You deserve better."

"Quit that shit," I snapped at him, my relief turning to annoyance. "So, you made a mistake, you got caught by a nest of frigging enormous spiders. Well, so did we, and am I gonna be safer with you as a bodyguard…or without?"

There was a long pause before a grudging sound of agreement floated down to me.

"Besides, who's going to keep me from going fucking mental, if not you? I doubt any of the others want the job, do they? Barrett, Lydia?" I called out, getting a series of snorts and strained chuckles in response.

"No chance."

"Not going to happen!"

"Hell, no; that fucker's crazy!" I heard Arrin call out, clear laughter in his voice. I let loose a low chuckle as I realized the crazy bastard was having no end of fun. I shifted enough to look up at him and he waved to me, having somehow managed to get himself webbed in place upright, when the rest of us were horizontal.

"Look, Jax! No hands!" he called and waved again.

I couldn't help it, and the low chuckle began to build, with others joining in. The laughter was strained at first, but it soon spread, and a little of the blackness that had consumed me since Oracle's kidnapping fell away.

I still had friends. I still had people that had my back. I wasn't alone, and I was going to get Oracle back, find Tommy, and seriously fuck up Barabarattas's Tuesday.

Even if it was Wednesday, or whatever.

"What day is it?" I asked aloud, and Miren replied.

"It's the third of Distan." I waited for her to go on, and when she didn't, I shrugged as best I could.

"Doesn't matter what day it is; got it."

I took a deep breath, trying to calm myself as I reached out to Oracle and got no response, so I pulled up my notifications instead, trying desperately to distract myself…

Congratulations!

You have killed the following:

- 11x Cave Spider Soldiers for a total of 2,500xp
- 10x Cave Spider Hunters for a total of 12,500xp
- 27x Immature Spider Drones for a total of 405xp
- 1x Cave Wurm Larva for a total of 3,000xp

A party under your command killed the following:

- 7x Cave Spider Soldiers for a total of 3,500xp
- 2x Cave Spider Hunters for a total of 5,000xp
- 86x Immature Spider Drones for a total of 2,580xp

Total experience earned: 11,080xp

As party leader you gain 10% of all experience earned.

Progress to level 15 stands at 24,633/140,000

I'd also managed to raise my Mana Manipulation skill to two out of one hundred, so at least I had that going for me…even though my last notification let me know I still desperately needed to heal myself up properly…

Beware!

You are suffering from mana manipulation fatigue: you currently have a negative ten (-10) modifier to all stats. This will continue until you have been healed fully.

Current health 274/460

Current mana 128/170

Current stamina 128/140

I tried reaching out to Oracle again and again, but all I could sense, besides the facts that she was alive and that she was growing weaker, was that she was stationary, slightly above and to my right. She was closer than she was before, but no matter how much I called to her in the silence of my mind, she wouldn't—or couldn't—answer. The more I tried, the blacker my mood became. When we finally stopped, and my spider mount lowered itself to the ground and froze in place, I was coldly furious again.

Ashrag might be a spider queen and an old servant of the empire, but right now, she'd gotten between me and saving my friend.

A pair of spiders scuttled up onto my mount, their bodies covered in blue and black patterns, and they spat something on the webs that held me.

The webbing hissed and spat, dissolving in seconds and freeing me. I growled in pain, jerking upright and yanking my hands away from the corrosive spit, feeling it burning my skin. But it died out in seconds, and I jumped to my feet, stripping the remaining webs from my skin. Weakness plagued my body from the wounds, from the taking of the Oaths, and from using the ability again.

I quickly cast Battlefield Triage on myself, the burst of light that emanated from it illuminating the ledge I was standing on. More accurately, it illuminated the ledge the spider beneath my feet stood on. I realized it was still shaking in fear, with my right foot crushing its face into the stone floor, my left being firmly stuck to a patch of webbing that covered some of the ledge.

I grimaced but stepped off the spider, my asshole clenching up reflexively as it scuttled away.

Nothing the size of a small horse should have that many legs or be that fugly.

I looked around the darkness, still channeling the spell until my health was fully restored, and the debuffs vanished. I let the spell go and watched as the others came down the walls, being freed and climbing onto the small ledge beside me.

I knew Ashrag was there. I could feel her presence, watching us, even if for some reason, I couldn't see far, despite my DarkVision ability. I ignored her, checking my people over and making sure they were all okay.

Bane was the last to be set down on the ledge, and he staggered. I grabbed him and looked him over; his health was full, but his stamina was still low. Then I did what he least expected, and I pulled him into a hug, clapping him on the back and grinning at the shock on everyone's faces. He froze for a second, then awkwardly patted my back in return.

"Look, you fuckers," I said, releasing him and looking the group over, "I don't care what anyone thinks of propriety. You're my friends, as well as my people." I looked to Bane directly and put one hand on his shoulder, feeling the dry, calloused skin under my grip. "And that includes you, you daft sod; I thought I'd lost you."

I summoned a spring of fresh water for him, and once I was sure he was resting and breathing the water deeply, I turned back to the darkness beyond our little ledge and raised my voice.

"Now I can't see shit, Ashrag, and that means either my abilities failed, which seems unlikely, considering I can see these muppets behind me, or you're playing silly buggers."

My voice echoed strangely for several seconds before the magical darkness abruptly vanished, magelights around the cavern springing to life and illuminating a huge cave that vanished back into the side of the underground cliff.

Ashrag sat in the middle of the cave, a huge web supporting her bulk as other spiders moved here and there, running along strands that vanished into the distance. Dozens of smaller spiderlings clambered and shook on the webs everywhere I looked, and possibly hundreds of cocoons hung from the ceiling. I frowned as something glittered under Ashrag, and I focused in, realizing what I'd missed in my first glance.

The cave wasn't empty.

Besides the multitude of spiders, it also housed buildings, dozens of them. They were coated in webs that hid much of the shape, but the occasional glittering reflection of the magelights made it clear that the doors at least were metal and hadn't rusted. Judging from Ashrag's age and how deep in the earth we were, I could only guess that meant they were bronze...or gold.

"Welcome, Jax, Lord of Dravith and Scion of the Empire; welcome to the forgotten outpost of Isthic'Mirtin." Stunned silence reigned behind me as we viewed the outpost. A narrow path ran from the ledge down into the cavern, and I slowly walked along it, ignoring the sounds of spiders moving all around me. I caught peripheral flashes of a black and red body close by, but I faced forward, determined to show some strength.

"I honored the Oaths, little lord," rumbled Ashrag's great voice, the web trembling with it as I moved closer, constantly having to yank my feet free of the webs that sought to trap me. "Now explain why you did what you did."

"Which part?" I quipped.

Ashrag growled, the sound like a tiger in a subway.

"The Oath! Tell me why...why would you bind yourself to Oaths you had no part in creating? Why would you renew them? Are you stupid or simply too arrogant to know better!"

The air stirred in response to her irritation, the spiders that surrounded us slowly moving closer.

"I...well, I did it on a hunch, to tell you the truth," I said, having reached the cavern floor proper. I gestured to a mound of stone that was coated in webbing. "Mind if I burn that off? I think this is going to take a while, and I'd rather sit while I tell you the tale."

There was silence for a long minute before Ashrag shifted, looking to a spider to one side. It moved quickly, darting into one of the web-encrusted buildings, and a handful of heartbeats later, it returned, a stone chair clutched between its mandibles.

"Thanks," I said, taking the seat. I glanced over at my companions, but got a few headshakes from them. They were still too freaked out to sit yet, and none of them, bar Arrin, likely wanted anything to do with Ashrag and her kin.

"Well, Ashrag, it's like this..." I started with my story, who I was, and where I was from. Then I moved on to my mental passenger and my ancestral line. "...So now you know how I got there, but..."

"I know where you came from and why. I know nothing about the Oaths! Don't seek to hide things under webs of words; tell me straight!" she snapped.

"Shut the fuck up...and I will!" I retorted, then took a deep breath. "Amon was a lot of things, including a fucking *mental* bastard, but what he wasn't was an asshole without cause. He thinks you're all right, and that you suffered because of what those fucks did to him and everyone else. He thinks you're honorable. He thinks you deserve better than a life down here, hidden, and now, so do I."

Silence greeted my words.

"How long have you been down here, Ashrag? How long have you been in the dark, and why the hell were you in that cave back there, if this is your nest?"

"The drow." She spat. "The drow rule the underworld. They war with the deep dwarves and kobolds constantly; all other creatures either pick a side or get consumed. I was forced to accept their trespassing, as there are too many of them for my children to kill easily, and they hide in places my soldiers cannot reach.

"We were given the choice: guard their paths or be destroyed, yet still they take my children for food and silk. I ordered my brood to spread out, and we pretended that the higher nests were our only ones, keeping this place safe."

"Have you sworn any oaths to them?" I asked, still unsure as to the power of the Oaths.

"You know so little for one with so much to lose," she muttered. "The Oaths I swore mean that I cannot swear to another, not without being released first. The drow simply ordered my soldiers to guard the cave from all intruders or be destroyed. I moved up so that they would not come looking for this nest."

"So, they don't know how many of you there really are? Or that you aren't a normal spider?"

"Define 'normal', little lord," she rumbled.

I couldn't help but grin. "Okay, well I've never known spiders that could talk; put it that way!"

"We can communicate; even my lesser brethren can do this, but my kind...we joined the empire because we were sick of being hunted and hated for our forms. I was a lesser princess; when my queen tied us to the empire, we were being hunted by the vampyres for our silk, our venom.

"Others wanted us for alchemical uses. When your body is more valuable to others than it is to you, you make deals with the strongest you can. We swore to the empire, agreed to guard it against those who would harm it, and in return, we were given sanctuary. Hunting us was punished by death."

She shifted, her mandibles and pedipalps quivering as she looked back across the long ages, remembering.

"Entire broods of your people were given to us when they were caught harvesting us. We were fed, given territory. I was permitted to walk the streets of your cities, to talk to your kind under the daystar. I sold my silk and gained sweet meats I'd never tasted. Life was good, until the empire fell.... Mere days after the ground shook and the heavens fell, we were attacked. Hundreds of my kind were killed or captured. We hid, protecting ourselves. We waited until the legion appeared, and we sent our fastest runners to them, calling for protection. We were denied!" Her voice climbed as she spoke, until she spat the last with naked anger. "The legion refused us, said they had more important things to do than to protect the 'beasts of the underworld.'"

"Fuck," I muttered, a sudden mental image of soldiers after the Cataclysm.

Oracle had said that the legions would have returned to the capital as fast as they could, to protect the emperor or avenge him first and foremost. I was freaked out by Ashrag as it was, but I was trying to get past that. For someone that had just seen the world ending in fire and death, to have a spider come running and tell you it needed help, when your family could be dead, and the empire you'd sworn your life to was collapsing? Yeah, I could see the legion telling her to get fucked.

"What did they do?"

"They kicked the princess aside, broke her legs, and left her in the gutter to be taken by her 'fellow citizens.' She was gutted and sold before we could reach her."

"And what did you do?" I asked, already fearing the worst.

"We killed them all: everyone who had harmed her. The legion had fled on ships in the port, but the citizens that killed her were easy to find, her musk still coating them.

"We killed them all, as per the Oath, we could harm other citizens only in self-defense or in punishing murderers, but others attacked us, so we retaliated…hundreds on both sides died. We retreated as soon as we'd killed those responsible, but the damage was done. We were reduced to less than a third who could fight. Our strongest had died, and all we were left with were the very young, the old, and my fellow princesses.

"Our queen, Atalaya, sent us into hiding, declared our Oaths broken, and she faced the ones who came. We saw her slaughtered, her body carried away by cheering citizens we had befriended. I watched a merchant I'd sat with, who I'd spun the finest silk I could for…I watched her laughing as she gutted my mother for her spinnerets."

The mood dropped as Ashrag and I looked sadly at each other, and we both reflected on the past.

"I don't know what to say, Ashrag," I said finally, sitting forward. "The legion shouldn't have abandoned you, and certainly shouldn't have harmed your princess. But their first duty, as was yours as a citizen of the empire, was to the empire. Their Oath meant they had to return to the capital, to try to hold the empire together. The citizens, well…they were afraid. I'd imagine the ones who hurt your princess were probably criminals, but when people saw you attacking them, they would have tried to help, and the whole thing boiled out of control."

I shook my head, getting up and walking forward slowly, the spiders all around me clacking their mandibles and fangs warningly. I was acting on instinct entirely now. I didn't know what else I could do, but I had to try to make this right, or none of us were walking out of here alive. I stopped before Ashrag, and I slowly went down on one knee.

"I'm sorry for the things our people did to you and yours, Queen Ashrag. You deserved better, and you were failed by those you relied on." I took a deep breath and met her pained gaze. "Your Oath to the empire states that you have the right to protection from the legion, the right to hold those who wronged you to justice, and the right to be avenged, if you cannot be saved," I said, the notification with the Imperial Citizen's Oath coming to me easily, the words imprinted on my soul.

"The empire failed you twice; the legion didn't come to your aid, and you were attacked when seeking justice. I can't change that. These things happened hundreds of years before I was born. But I can fulfill the third section of the Oath. You have been attacked, your children taken, just like my friend has been. I can avenge and give you what you are owed: a home, food, and my protection." I lowered my head, exposing the back of my neck, knowing that if she chose to attack now, it was all over. "I offer myself in apology. I give you the chance to strike, to claim my life in redress."

Silence greeted my offering before her webs shook again, her enormous bulk shifting as she moved forward.

First one, then another, and gradually all of her legs appeared before and around me, and she towered over me. I could hear the rest of my party shifting uneasily, but they didn't say anything.

A sword was unsheathed in the eerie quiet, and Lydia barked an order to sheathe it again, then everything fell silent.

Ashrag lowered her huge head until it was before me, and I looked up at her, waiting as her eyes searched my own for long seconds.

She said something in a language I didn't understand, and a soldier scuttled forward, moving with horrific speed as it shot across the floor to me. I forced myself to stay still, my muscles shaking under the strain.

A hot, searing pain radiated across my right cheek, then Ashrag crushed the spider, a long leg smashing down with stunning force to pierce its abdomen, killing it instantly. She threw the corpse aside effortlessly, and it fell, twitching, into the darkness of the chasm.

I kept staring at Ashrag, even as hot air entered my face through the slashed cut that separated my cheek into flaps.

"I accept your apology, Lord of the Empire, and I accept my Oath's renewal, on the conditions offered," she said eventually, straightening up and returning to her web.

"You will destroy the drow that infest these paths, then we will accept you as our lord. You will provide safety for my children, food, and the chance for them to grow. Do these things, enable us to stand tall and free in the world above again, and we will consider the debt paid. But be warned: do not fail us again, for we will not be taken by surprise a second time."

You have received a Quest from your Goddess: Keep Your Word

You have given your word to an ancient Greater Cave Spider Queen. Kill her enemies, grant her and her brood safety and food, and she will consider her Broken Oath to be renewed, binding her and all her brood to your orders and laws. You must kill 35 drow and their leader.

Drow Killed: 3/35
Locations Cleared: 0/3
Drow Leader Killed: 0/1
Reward: Oracle's Freedom, Sworn Allegiance of 1 Greater Cave Spider and her Brood, access to Cave Spider Silk, Isthic'Mirtin's Treasury, and 50,000xp

I grinned in spite of the pain it caused as I stood up, my legs shaky as I relaxed slightly, knowing that the riskiest part of being here was over. Now all I had to do was what I was going to do anyway: gut the fucking drow for taking Oracle.

The notification that had popped up let me know that Jenae was watching over me as well, especially with the experience boost her latest quest was offering me. I accepted it and dismissed the screen.

I looked up at Ashrag and her brood. It was going to give me nightmares every time I remembered how close I'd come to being killed, but I was alive! Dancing on the edge of the razor still, just like I had been since I'd been picked up by Daphne. I spared a grin, thinking of how pissed he'd been when I renamed him. I wondered idly if the name had stuck, after all.

"Thank you, Queen Ashrag," I said formally. "So, is it going to be an issue if I heal myself now? Because this is fucking stinging," I asked, pointing at my face.

"Do what you wish," she replied, uncaring, and I healed myself again, stifling a groan as my skin knit back together. The feeling of veins reaching out and reattaching made me think too much of things burrowing through me after everything had happened so far today.

"How far away are we from the drow?" I asked, resuming my seat and gesturing for my people to come forward. "And why did you kill the spider that cut me?"

"You are an imperial citizen, as am I. Harming you would have harmed me, but there are ways around the Oaths. As long as I defended you, it was sufficient. When all is restored, I could not do this, so do not fear," she rumbled.

"Well, there's a different Oath that my people take, so we will have to talk about that later. It's simpler, but more personal, based around the one rule of 'don't be a dick,' but we can discuss it," I said, grimacing.

"We will see. The Imperial Oath was enough for us. As to the drow, the nearest clutch of them is just over a mile away. It has grown concerning to us how close they are coming."

"How far is it to the city?"

"Three or four miles from here, or so I think. I remember the measurements, but whether an imperial mile and your own are the same, I neither know nor care."

"Fair enough. The drow, then; if they're a mile away, can you get us close to them? We sure as shit can't climb back up without help, after all. We could use a few of your soldiers, a few scouts, and a princess to communicate between them all," I asked, trying my luck.

"No. We will return you to a close point to them and carry you that far, but none of my brood will help further. If you are so weak that you need more, then we are better off without you. If you die, this costs us nothing, yet," she said, a growl in her voice as though she was getting sick of the conversation.

"Fine," I snapped back at her. "Carry us up, and we'll kill them, but you keep one of your princesses close to us and some of your brood nearby. When I finish the drow, I don't expect to have to come back down here to discuss it! I'll have need of your help, and I'll not have time to fuck about."

"Very well. Now go. I have lost enough to your incursion," she rumbled, spitting out commands as she slowly moved backwards into the outpost, a large building soon swallowing her up.

A familiar-looking small spider scuttled out of the mass, along with a group of spiders that moved towards each of us, crouching down and waiting.

"Horkesh?" I asked, and the spider bobbed excitedly.

"Yes! You remembered! I am to be your companion, to help you and carry your words to the queen!"

I couldn't help but be freaked out by the jerky sort of movements she and her brood made. I'd never liked spiders before meeting the SporeMother, who only slightly resembled one then meeting a huge freaking brood of them, including a queen who was bigger than a fucking bus, had only cemented that feeling.

I decided that Horkesh was a puppy, that was all. I was going to think of her as a puppy...not a spider that made my skin crawl and I wanted to hit with a hammer. A puppy...a puppy...a...*oh, for fuck's sake!*

I gritted my teeth and climbed aboard the nearest spider at her direction, swallowing the bile that rose in my throat when another larger spider began to web me in place. I held myself upright, and it stopped at my waist instead of trapping me fully, but I fucking hated it.

I could tell by the mutterings and grumblings behind me that nobody else liked it either, except for Arrin, who started petting and talking to his mount immediately, chattering away happily. As we all moved out from the cavern onto the wall of the chasm, I had to clamp down hard onto my stomach, as I wanted to be sick. At least one sound behind let me know that someone hadn't managed to hold their bile down, but again, Arrin showed his batshit self, as I heard his voice echoing around from below.

"Whoooo-hoo!" he cried out, and I had visions of him being one of those mad fuckers who jumped out of perfectly good planes for fun back home.

I shook my head and held on tight, the walls of the chasm slowly drifting by, hour following hour as we climbed, taking passageways above raging rivers, through tunnels that disappeared at crazy angles. A section of fallen masonry served as our entryway, faint light from the surface glittering down to land on fast-rushing waters that poured over the side of the cliff to disappear into the chasm below.

After endless hours of travel, the spiders stopped on a path that was open to the air on one side, and I tried not to think of how deep the hole below us was.

We dismounted, minor burns covering us again as we were freed from the webbing. The larger mounts scuttled away into the darkness, and a dozen small spiders clambered onto the wall nearby, awaiting my orders. Horkesh took up station by my feet.

I checked on my crew, healing any injuries, and drew a deep breath, making sure the others were ready.

It was time to hunt the drow.

CHAPTER TWENTY-EIGHT

I got Horkesh to send a spider ahead, figuring if the drow saw it, it wouldn't be an issue. Another trailed behind us, just in case, and I ordered Bane to lead our party, his worldsense a definite advantage in the tunnels and paths. We traveled for maybe half an hour before pausing by a small underground pool, letting everyone have a short break, with the magelights illuminating a small space around us.

We'd been passing through a huge underground chamber. Occasional faint light filtered in from high overhead, a slim path winding across crumbled rock and moss covering the floor all around us. I figured the team deserved the chance now that we were away from Ashrag's brood. I was enjoying the light filtering down, leaning against a pillar of carved rock, and we'd rested. It was a short break, maybe twenty minutes, just long enough to eat, drink, and give Bane the chance to breathe in a small pool we'd found, when he surfaced, carrying something.

He waded to the edge of the water, passing it up to me as Jian took his wrist and helped him out.

"What is it?" I asked shaking the muck from it, only to see a small skull staring up at me.

"There's dozens of them down there, maybe hundreds," he replied, gesturing towards the water. I frowned. There were clear bite marks on the bones, and they didn't look that old.

"What were they, and what the fuck killed them?" I wondered aloud.

Horkesh spoke up excitedly. "They're gnomes! There was a whole group of them down here," she said, bouncing excitedly.

"What happened to them?" I asked, my stomach dropping.

"They died," she said simply.

"How?" I asked, and she spun around to look up at me, legs clattering on the stones.

"It was many turns of the daystar ago. Queen Ashrag said it happened because they were weak. They all died."

"Did you kill them?" I asked, gritting my teeth.

"No, creatures from above. They followed them down, hunted them, killed them, stole their stuff, and went back up. Left the bodies here. We ate them and put them in the water. I was only a hatchling then."

"You ate them?" Miren asked, sounding sick.

"Yes, good meat. Why waste it; they didn't care?" Horkesh replied. I closed my eyes, fighting down my anger.

It wasn't their fault, and it made perfect sense from a certain point of view; after all, they were already dead, and the bodies would only be wasted otherwise.

"I...no, Horkesh. To us, it's not a good thing to eat other sentient creatures," I whispered sadly, slowly shaking my head. I put the small skull down gently, dropping it into the water and watching it sink back down to join other grey piles at the bottom of the pool. The muck stirred up briefly as it landed, before settling slowly again, the skull disappearing from the world once more.

We moved as quickly and quietly as we could, passing collapsed forgotten buildings, old camps, the remains of caravans, and occasional piles of bones discarded in the darkness. My people were adjusting as best they could to the oppressive darkness as we left the large cavern. I knew I'd asked too much of them when I heard a short, quickly stifled sob from behind at one point.

I grimaced at the thought of Oracle, alone, in the dark with the fucking drow and...

No. I stooped that thought dead, I couldn't think like that, not now, not yet, if I gave into it, imagined her state too vividly I'd go insane, I'd just race straight at them all, and they'd slaughter me.

Then she'd be stuck. I had to be cold, calm.

Thankfully, it wasn't much longer before Horkesh spoke up, a small spider appearing and then scuttling away again.

"The drow are in the next set of caves; they killed the scout that approached them and are stripping her body now."

"Motherfuckers," I muttered, shaking my head in annoyance. "Is there any light in there?" I asked. To my surprise, Horkesh answered that there was. The drow were apparently seated around a small fire, their lookout having opted to sit with the others in order to consume the spider's prized leg meat, while another packed away the more valuable alchemical components.

I gathered my small team around and gave them their orders.

With Bane in the lead, we moved slowly into the next set of caves, creeping along the tunnel until we could see the light and hear the low echo of melodic voices.

Once we were sure of the layout, I let Stephanos and Miren move forward, their bows already drawn and heavy arrows nocked.

We crept forward as a group, Bane and I directly behind the archers, ready to take point, with Barrett and Lydia flanking us and Jian and Arrin bringing up the rear with Cam.

As soon as they could be sure of their targets, both Miren and Stephanos fired, the thrum of the bows echoing and making heads spin to identify the sound. The four drow sitting around the fire jerked to their feet rather than dodging.

For two of them, that was a particularly painful error, as the heavy arrows I'd directed them to use punched through the light armor the drow wore, sending them crashing to the floor.

One was killed outright as the arrow neatly bisected his heart, while the other took it high in his left lung. The tip exited through his back, and he staggered back with a pained scream.

Both Miren and Stephanos drew and fired again, before ducking back behind us as Bane and I ran forward, our party following close behind.

The second volley of arrows made the drow duck and dive aside, their freakily heightened reflexes allowing them the brief time they needed to dodge.

We closed the distance between us as fast as we could, the sounds of our party running echoing around the chamber. Snarls of anger twisted the faces of the drow as we closed, and they saw our party.

As the first group had with me, these drow clearly believed we were their lessers, disgust twisting their faces. The dismissal they showed to their injured and killed brethren made me grin momentarily, as our own people would be concentrating on healing, bringing the injured member back into the fight as soon as possible. The writhing, bleeding-out drow on the floor was getting no help from his friends, though, and I loved it.

The pair of drow who were still standing took up positions on either side of the fire, one facing Bane with two swords while the one I faced held a shortsword and a long dagger in either hand, grinning at me evilly.

A trio of Magic Missiles blurred past me, and my drow opponent frantically wove its blades in the air, trying to deflect them. He caught two of them, but the third snagged his left ear and exploded, sending him staggering, disoriented.

He lashed out at me with his sword, trying to keep me back, even as he dropped his dagger and clutched at his ruined face, the grey skin and most of his hair blackened and burned. He screamed in rage; even injured, surprised, and stunned, his blade wove a deadly dance in the air. I caught it on my own, yanking the base on my naginata around, then forced his sword down, grinning at him as an arrow blurred over my right shoulder to bury itself in his eye.

I didn't waste the time waiting as the freshly made corpse gave a twitch, collapsing like a puppet with its strings cut.

Instead, I lunged forward. Bane's opponent was covered in thin cuts as he skillfully deflected its attacks. The drow had just dodged another arrow and had been in the middle of some evil villain monologue I'd not even bothered to listen to when the tip of my naginata pierced his side and glanced off his spine. Something under tension gave way with a twang, sending the now-paralyzed drow crashing to the floor with a scream of disbelief.

I spun around to search for other enemies, only to see Jian yanking his sword out of the chest of the one with the punctured lung.

The fight was over in seconds, all of us standing around and panting with the sudden exertion. I caught sight of a small spider darting past us into the tunnel leading from the cave, as Horkesh stepped up to dance and skitter alongside me.

"I sent the drones to search for more of them," she told me matter-of-factly. "May I eat this?"

She climbed onto the dead drow's leg.

"Uh, yeah, sure; just let us loot him first," I said, and gestured to Lydia, who snapped orders to her squad.

I looked around, making sure none of my team were injured, before turning back to Bane, who stood examining the drow's camp.

"What's up?" I asked.

He gestured to the bedrolls and gear. "There's little here; it looks like there were only four stationed in this cavern. I'm wondering why."

"To watch the tunnel, I guess," I said, shrugging.

"Yes, but if you believed the spiders would protect the tunnel, then why leave guards? And if you didn't trust the spiders, why only leave four?"

He rifled through their bags, chucking some of it aside as rubbish, while useful things were placed in a small pile. I joined him, and we gathered the gear from the camp together, finding two bedrolls that were of "uncommon" quality, silk sheets, no less, and well-crafted eating utensils. I shrugged, figuring I'd been getting lots of good gear lately, and let the others divide them up how they would. I just wanted to get a move on.

I only took the contents of their money pouches: three sapphires, two rubies, twelve gold, fifteen silver, and three copper. I slipped them into my own money pouch, conscious that I was literally carrying a fortune in gemstones now, especially considering the pearls the Mer had given me.

As soon as the others were ready, I set off again, Horkesh warning me that the scout drone hadn't returned, and we went cautiously, traveling for nearly an hour. Most of the time, we were in pitch black for the members of my team who didn't have vision-augmenting abilities. We didn't dare use the magelights now that we were so close to the drow. We walked slowly, occasionally warning each other of stones or dips in the path, each person bracing a hand on the shoulder of the person ahead of them, with Barrett bringing up the rear, and Lydia holding onto me. Bane scouted ahead as Miren began to sing softly.

I knew why she was doing it, her fear of the dark clear, but as Lydia shushed her, I knew I couldn't expect them to follow me somewhere like this again. I resolved to get a spell as soon as I could to help them, gritted my teeth, and moved on.

The hours dragged as we marched, Bane and the spiders occasionally reappearing to warn of groups ahead, or of the lack thereof.

We took out two more small groups, including one set of guards like the first, a trio seated around the fire drinking wine. Miren and Stephanos killed two outright before they knew we were there, and Arrin and Bane took the last one down. A Firebolt to the face ended the drow's interest in pretty much anything but stopping the pain, followed by a stab to the heart from one of Bane's daggers.

The second group was harvesting mushrooms in a small grotto; well, their servants were. A dozen small, wizened kobolds labored while the overseers stood laughing. Two of them restrained a struggling kobold while the third tried to draw a picture on its back. Using a stiletto.

The two holding the kobold died fast, while Bane and Lydia made sure the one who had been cutting into the poor creature died much slower. I healed the tiny beast, and it ran back to its fellows, terrified.

I examined one out of curiosity.

Critical Success!

Your target has no defenses against your magic, and as such, more details are available:

Midnight's Cave Kobold Minion
The kobolds of the Midnight Cave were a proud mountain clan once, but as the centuries have passed in subjugation to the drow, their history, knowledge, and secrets have been long lost.

Weaknesses: Physical damage is doubled, due to a lifetime of abuse. Magical damage is doubled, due to a lifetime of abuse.
Resistances: None
Level: 4
Health: 11/11
Mana: 4/4

I could only shake my head as I looked the creature over, its pitiful condition clear, even as it reveled in its sudden good fortune. My healing had done more to redress the systematic abuse it had endured all its life than anything else it had ever encountered. The kobold now stood taller than its hunched companions, its long snout and tail making me wonder if they were truly descended from dragons, as the games I'd played back home had suggested. I couldn't imagine any dragon pointing at this creature and claiming kinship, that was for sure. I pulled up a pair of notifications that had popped up while I looked the kobold over.

Congratulations!

You have raised your spell Identify to level ten.

You may now choose your first evolution of this spell.

Congratulations!

You have raised your spell Identify to its first evolution.

You must now pick a path to follow.

Will you augment your own abilities to EXAMINE, or will you pick the path of the INVESTIGATOR? Choose carefully, as this choice cannot be undone.

EXAMINATION:
As your spell has developed, and your understanding of the world with it, you have discovered startling similarities between the creatures of the realm. You suspect that powering the spell with more mana may give additional information. Gain further details on your target for each second you Examine it; spell cost increases by ten mana per second while in use.

INVESTIGATOR:
The world around you fascinates you, but the creatures of the realms less so. Perhaps focusing your abilities on the artifacts, creations, and details around you would suit you better? Gain further details on all inanimate objects you examine, including a one-off boost of 5% to your crafting ability. You will suffer penalties to Investigating living creatures.

I grinned as I read over the details. I was tempted for a few seconds to take the Investigator path, mainly because there had to be so much out there that I could find, treasures that dated back to the time of the empire, but I knew what would actually be more useful.

I chose Examination then dismissed it. I watched the kobolds as the bodies of their former masters were stripped of any valuables.

The one who'd been doing the carving had had a pair of black spidersilk trousers that had looked beautiful, but considering the state in which it'd died, thanks to Lydia's hatred of its actions, there was no way I was going to be putting those pants on.

Even I had standards, and I had spent a few days wearing greaves that an adventurer had died in then spent the next few years walking around and rotting through.

I checked out the quest I'd gotten for the drow and nodded in satisfaction as I saw the progress.

You have received a Quest from your Goddess: Keep Your Word

You have given your word to an ancient Greater Cave Spider Queen, kill her enemies, grant her and her brood safety and food, and she will consider her Broken Oath to be renewed, binding her and all her brood to your orders and laws. You must kill 35 drow and their leader…

Drow Killed: 13/35
Locations Cleared: 0/3
Drow Leader Killed: 0/1
Reward: Oracle's Freedom, Sworn Allegiance from 1 Greater Cave Spider and her Brood, access to Cave Spider Silk, Isthic'Mirtin's Treasury, and 50,000xp

We'd managed to take a third of them down so far, and once we'd checked the kobolds over, we set them free, giving them strict orders to go the other way down the tunnel, to find somewhere they could live comfortably, and to enjoy their lives.

They didn't exactly object, glancing at each other, then vanished in a blur of dusty scales, skittering claws, and bad smells. They'd been farting nervously the entire time we'd been there, and the subject of what they ate that could make such foul smells kept the group quietly entertained for the next half an hour.

The smells in the caves changed gradually as we moved along. At first, there'd been little besides a dusty, moldy stench interspersed with copper heavy in the air in some of the sections with more water. Now, though, the air changed noticeably.

The further we walked, the stronger the strange smell permeating the air became. It was heavy and sweet, cloyingly so. We slowed further and further, until we were creeping along, when Bane returned from one of his forays ahead of us. He gestured and we all gathered round.

"It's a garden," he muttered, as quietly as he could. "A garden made up of some flowers I've never seen before, but they give off a strange shimmer to my worldsense, so be very careful. There are six drow in the gardens, two to the left as we walk in, crouching and working amongst the flowers. Three more are in the middle of the cavern, making potions, and they appear oblivious to anything else. Lastly, there's a guard sitting at the far side of the cavern, close to the tunnel that leads out."

"Well spread out," I muttered pensively.

"They are; I could scout no further, so I don't know how far away the main camp is. It could be in the next cave, or miles from here; either way, we have to keep the noise down and kill as many by stealth as we can."

"It's the guard who worries me," said Lydia. "How far away is he?" she asked Bane.

He shook his head. "Too far for a guaranteed kill from the bows; there are too many stalactites and stalagmites between there and here."

"Shit."

"Quite," he quipped, a slight subsonic giving the impression of a chuckle.

"Okay, so the three in the middle of the room—could we sneak someone past them?"

"Unlikely. Perhaps if…"

"I can go," came a small voice, and we all turned to look at Horkesh. We'd practically forgotten about her, as her only real use that we'd considered was to pass messages to the spider drones, but now...

"Could you kill him?" Bane asked, even as I spoke up as well.

"Are you sure? I thought you were supposed to just watch over us, then return to the queen, not help us?" I asked. I'd been deliberately not asking her about anything until now, knowing she was supposed to have guided us to the drow and watched only.

"I will be queen one day; I have to learn about the world," she said steadily, but the nervous clacking of her mandibles showed her real emotions.

"Okay, could you kill the guard?" I asked her.

She bobbed excitedly.

"My venom is like my mother's!" she said, clacking her fangs together in enthusiasm. "I can change it or alter its strength. If I use my most potent, the guard will be dead within five steps, or paralyzed if I use a weak form of it."

Bane and I exchanged a long look and nodded at each other.

"Paralyze him," we said in concert, and she bobbed excitedly again, turning, and darting away.

"Hsst!" I hissed at her, but Horkesh wasn't listening, and her dozen spider drones went with her.

"Fuck!" I swore, turning quickly to the others, "Stephanos, Miren, Jian, Barrett, and Lydia, concentrate on the group of three with me. Bane, Arrin, and Cam, get the two off to the left. We attack as soon as Horkesh does."

We hurried along the tunnel, surprised at how quick the spiders were as they vanished around the corner, climbing onto the walls and ceiling.

When we reached the entrance to the cavern, we took turns moving close to the entrance and looking around, making sure we knew what was where, then falling back to discuss it. I asked the others, but none of them saw Horkesh or her spiders once they'd entered the room, so we relaxed slightly.

I'd had visions of them being spotted as soon as they entered the room, so every second we got to prepare was valuable.

Bane waited until the drow were all out of sight before slipping into the cavern, vanishing amongst the vibrant blue and green flowers that filled it. I was watching the three in the middle as they moved around, clearly working on alchemy. I was curious both as to what they were making and to the quality of their gear, when Miren gagged next to me.

I frowned, looking over at her, and caught her staring at the soil a dozen feet into the cavern, where a root was exposed in the dark earth. I looked back at her and saw the anger on her face, so I crouched and looked more carefully, creeping forward with the others as we started to move into position.

There were dozens of patches of the flowers, each with thick black soil around the base, and here and there, the roots were exposed. I moved slowly closer to the nearest root, trying to decide why my instincts were screaming that there was something very wrong.

I reached out, moving on all fours, the flowers above me seeming to shift and turn with me the closer I came, until a hand grabbed my wrist, pulling me to a halt.

I glanced over at Miren, who shook her head slowly, fear clear in her eyes as she inclined her head upwards. I glanced back and froze instantly.

The flowers were all facing us now, and they gave off an impression of intent, malevolent focus as they seemingly watched us.

I slowly backed up, and they gradually returned to slowly fluttering in a non-existent breeze. I glanced back at the roots and swallowed hard as I finally realized what I'd been looking at. It was an ankle, the leg poking above the soil in places and the foot sinking back down...it was bone-white and had clearly been drained of blood. The plants growing over the mounds that I now realized were piled corpses, covered in soil, were gently swaying, turning to follow the drow as they moved around.

As soon as Miren knew I'd realized what the plants were, she released my arm, drawing back on her bow again.

I peered around the garden, taking the time to spot our people as they moved closer to their targets. I took a long breath, releasing it slowly as I spotted a movement on the wall above the drow guard.

It was Horkesh, and she was gone in a second, dipping back into the shadows cast by the flickering blue-green light given off by the plants. I kept staring at the same spot and gradually made out movement as she slipped down the wall, moving closer and closer...

Until one of the two drow off to the left spotted Cam and cried a warning, causing the guard to jump to his feet, drawing his bow and sending an arrow flashing across the cavern a heartbeat later, drawing a cry of pain.

"Fuck!" I grunted, driving myself up and forward, moving as fast as I could towards the three in the middle. Lydia and Barrett set off running as well, but with my heavily boosted Agility, I passed them easily, pulling ahead as my naginata pulsed to life, my anger flowing into it.

The air parted around me as an arrow passed on either side of my head, a tiny thought in the back of my mind that I was glad I hadn't stepped slightly to one side or the other. I dismissed it as I let loose with a roar of anger, releasing the curb on my simmering fury.

These fuckers had taken Oracle; they'd kidnapped my friend. For all I knew, it was the ugly fucker in the middle who had done it, the one that dodged the arrow so fluidly while his friend took the other in the eye. He spat something out at his companion and brought his hands up, a sickly green glow appearing as he began to channel magic.

I leaned into my manic sprint even harder, picking up more speed as I closed the gap between us. As I charged, I pulled the Stunning Lightning Bolt spell into my left hand until my hand vibrated with the repressed spell, then I powered even more into it. I leapt into the air, jumping over a small ridge and landed, skidding on loose scree and lashing out with my naginata at a flower head that swayed too close. As I skidded closer, I released the spell at the drow in the middle.

It flashed across the intervening space, energy hissing and spitting loose from the bolt as it covered the distance...before being absorbed into a black shield that flashed to life before the mage.

The lightning simply crackled across the surface harmlessly before pouring into the ground and vanishing, gone. Over a third of my mana, I'd piled into that one spell, planning on cutting through him like a knife through butter, and...I went hurtling through the air, pain screaming through my nerves as he released his own spell that hit me unerringly and seemed to fry every neuron with an overload.

I hammered into the ground a dozen yards from where I'd been hit, rolling with the impact to come to a halt, smoke rising from my body as I twitched uncontrollably.

Inside my body, I felt the changes his spell was trying to carry out. Cells died by the score, a rippling effect that was growing exponentially as I shook and trembled, the pain growing by the second.

I managed to trigger my healing ring once, then twice, barely enough to push back the wave of destruction, but it was enough to get control of my right hand. I frantically forced my fingers through the forms needed for Battlefield Triage; it blossomed to life in seconds, but still, I barely managed to cast it before I would have lost control.

While I fought my battle frantically, lying in the warm, blood-soaked earth just out of reach of a flower that was trying desperately to reach me, my companions were battling for their lives as well.

Miren and Stephanos were concentrating on the mage, hammering arrow after arrow at him, while Barrett smashed his greatsword in great overhead strikes into the shield the mage had created.

With each blow, the strain on the mage's face grew, and the arrows got closer and closer before being deflected. Lydia and Jian battled away with the other drow; she had only a single dagger, her other hand holding a pair of pruning shears. But she moved like she had been born in the fight. The two of them could barely keep up, a pair of cuts on Jian's torso showing how close he'd come to being disemboweled already. Lydia's heavy armor was all that was keeping them going at the minute.

The other fight was going slightly better, mainly because Bane was a blur of frantic battling insanity, all four arms blurring as he slashed, stabbed, and cut, kicking and spinning as he moved in a cyclone of death. Cam had struggled back to his feet, the arrow sticking from his right shoulder meaning he was less useful. But his axe wasn't exactly a precision weapon anyway, and each mighty swing forced the pair of drow back from him, swearing.

Arrin waited until they were totally focused on Bane and Cam, then hit the faster of the two, a drow armed with a pair of silver scythes with three Magic Missiles in the back. They exploded on impact, sending the dark elf staggering forward as he cried out in pain and shock. Bane spun, his blades slicing across the drow's stomach, chest, throat, and face, ending him in a red mist of pain.

The other one fell quickly to the combined assault of all three.

The drow guard, seeing the way the fighting was going, swore viciously and fired one last arrow, then turned to run. He only made it two steps before a red and black blur the size of a pitbull leaped from the wall above him. As Horkesh landed, she bit down hard, her fangs sinking deep into the unarmored section at the junction of his neck and shoulder.

She forced her venom into him, pushing it hard, then leaped backwards, landing near the flowers and disappearing as fast as she could into the undergrowth.

He screamed, staggered, and started to run, tugging at his belt and trying to get a potion to his lips. But as he collapsed forwards, he knew it was too late. He hit the floor hard and watched the potion slowly pour out into the soil, inches from his face.

I lay there on the ground while the battle raged around me, frantically flooding my mana into the healing spell as I tried to outpace the damage, and I stared at the timer, ticking down. I could see the drow mage refreshing the spell, channeling more mana into making sure he killed me.

Bane and Cam ran at him, forcing him to back up, growling in anger at them.

Arrin hammered at the drow with spell after spell, Magic Missiles exploding against the mage's hastily raised shield, I breathed a sigh of relief. He'd thankfully switched from pushing his death spell on me to maintaining that instead.

The spell backlash of terminating his channeling so abruptly staggered the drow, and Horkesh was there, ready to take advantage of the disruption. The shield the drow had cast was directional, as she bit down hard on the back of his leg, causing him to scream and bat her aside.

I let out a relieved groan as the spell vanished. My healing spells, which had been barely holding back the onslaught, suddenly raced through my body, repairing and refreshing at an incredible rate.

I rolled over, forcing myself to my feet and staggering toward the fight, only to watch Arrin blast the last drow from her feet, the mage rolling on the ground screaming as Horkesh's venom did its work.

In seconds, it was over; the only living drow lay by the exit to the tunnels on the far side, paralyzed.

I stumbled over to the group, my breathing ragged as I tried to come to terms with just how quickly everything had gone wrong. The others gathered around, most of them with minor wounds. Cam, the exception, had two arrows sticking out of him.

I made it to him just as Lydia slapped him.

"Hey!" he complained, grabbing his cheek with his uninjured left hand, and Bane ripped the arrows out of his right shoulder and thigh. Cam gasped in pain, collapsing backwards. Stephanos caught him, lowering him gently down, as Lydia popped the top off a healing potion and poured it down his throat, grinning at him.

"Got you!" she said, and Cam glared at her, shaking his head, and gritting his teeth as the flesh re-knit.

"Next time just kiss me. Fuckload less painful," he muttered, then went bright red as he realized what he'd said.

We all burst out laughing, and Lydia stiffened, her eyes blazing even as her cheeks reddened.

"I think he got you back, there," I said, clapping her on the shoulder. Everyone started checking over minor wounds and their gear, while I scanned the cavern. "Horkesh?" I asked, several spiders moving into the tangle of roots under one of the larger flower beds nearby.

I moved over, the flowers coming to life for my approach in a way they didn't for the spiders, so I sliced the head off the first to move too close, and the rest pulled back...exposing Horkesh crumpled on the ground. Half of her legs were broken, and a thin green ichor dribbled from her mouth, her breathing labored.

"Shit!" I said, moving forward quickly. The others gathered around, slicing through the flowers until the plants got the message to back the fuck up.

I crouched by her, checking the little spider over, and quickly cast my healing spell on her. It brought her back from the brink of death, but before it could do more, I ran out of mana. I tried giving her a healing potion, but when she almost bit me, I gave up on that, instead chugging a mana potion.

Bane darted off down the tunnels but came back a few minutes later, shaking his head; the next tunnel led into a deserted cave system, and there was no sign of any more drow nearby.

I waited until my mana reached fifty before pouring it all into her again. The tortured little sounds she made as her legs popped back into place were drowned out by the howls from the drow guard, as I'd sent Bane to "discuss" the cave system with him, and what they were doing here.

He'd dragged him out of sight of the rest of us and stripped him before his paralysis wore off. Now and then we'd hear him cry out, but most of the time, we only caught occasional quiet words.

Eventually he returned, and Horkesh was healed. I discussed quietly with her why she shouldn't rush off to attack, and she agreed to wait for my lead in the future.

We gathered and rested, waiting on mana to refill, while a much more cautious Horkesh sent her drones out to search the surrounding area. We examined the loot from the six drow; everyone who wanted one now had at least a sword and a dagger of drow design and most had more than one. Jian was experimenting with the twin scythes and looked to be loving every second of it.

I grabbed the alchemical kit, finding it to be considerably higher quality than the one I'd had before, and I disassembled it with familiarity, slipping the alembics and tubes free and stashing them in my bag. I also examined one of the flowers that lay on the table.

Deathbloom Flower		Further Description *Yes/No*	
Details:		This flower from the rare deathbloom plant can only be grown in darkness. Light from any source other than its own bioluminescence will cause the plant to begin to decay. Deathbloom plants must be fed on a mixture of fresh soil, decomposing flesh, and highly oxygenated blood to ensure the greatest chance of the plant putting forth flowers. **Uses Discovered:** 1) Poison 2) Increased Virility 3) ? 4) ?	
Rarity:	Magical:	Durability:	Charge:
Rare	Yes	99/100	N/A

My improved Examination skill and increased alchemical skill meant that I now saw two uses for the ingredients, and I sniggered at the fact that such a deadly plant could also be used to put a little peck in the pecker. I looked around at the corpses of the fearsome drow and grinned as a new thought came to mind: maybe the reason they were such assholes was that, as a race, they suffered from whisky dick?

It made their general hatred of all other races and their massive superiority complex so much more understandable. I decided to pass around the good news and got a wide variety of grins in return. The conversation changed to reasons the drow were such assholes immediately, such as why they were all so skilled with their weapons…after all, they had to be used to "handling things" and trying to do the most with what little they had…

We rested for a few more minutes, all of us feeling a little better, and I checked over the notifications I'd been ignoring so far.

I just looked at the bottom line; having had little real effect in that last fight, I'd gained a huge sixteen hundred experience in total on my own, and as I was in a party, I'd gotten a further two thousand experience from that.

It wasn't much, considering how hard the fighting had been. I casually asked Miren about her gains, biting my tongue when she happily admitted to rising by three levels in the last few days. She and the rest of the squad were gaining bucketloads experience more than me, including a quest to protect me!

Everything they killed gained them more than double my experience, then they got the same again in bonus!

I sat there, my jaws aching from clenching them so hard, as they all chatted happily about how hard, but rewarding, the fights were.

I was getting hosed with the rewards! I knew that Jenae had said I was going to get far less experience than I should, due to the injuries I'd sustained in using all the spellbooks, but fuck, seriously? I was going to be leveled past by my own team soon.

I forced a smile…I was happy for them all, I really was. I just had to get a healer up to the level I needed sooner rather than later, or this was going to get *embarrassing*.

I started stripping the flowers in the cavern while I waited for my mana to regenerate. The rest of the team, seeing what I was doing, spread out and helped, netting me eighty-seven flowers, which improved my mood considerably. The real prize, though, was that the drow mage had a rather nice silver bracelet that increased the wearer's maximum mana by fifty points, as well as a much more impressive bag of holding than my own.

I'd hefted it when Lydia had passed it to me, looking it over nonplussed, until I examined it.

Bag of Holding		Further Description *Yes/No*	
Details:		This journeyman-level Bag of Holding provides 50 spaces for storage. Each slot is capable of holding up to 99 identical items before filling a second slot. Weight reduction is 84% and there are 47 slots currently available.	
Rarity	**Magical**	**Durability**	**Charge:**
Rare	Yes	82/100	N/A

I couldn't help but let out a whoop as I checked the grid, finding there were thirty-six gold coins, two magelights, and a trio of vials of deathbloom poison.

Deathbloom Poison		Further Description *Yes/No*	
Details:		This poison is one of the most reviled in the realm. Not only does it commonly kill its victim, doing 100 points of damage on contact, but it also lowers the target's health and mana pool by 10 points per second for sixty seconds. This reduction is permanent and cannot be healed through normal means.	
Rarity	**Magical**	**Durability**	**Potency:**
Special	Yes	100/100	10/10

This was a weapon I didn't want to fall into the wrong hands, and by that, I meant any hands but mine. I called across to Arrin and tossed him the bracelet, getting a grin in return, and I went through the rest of the loot, finding that the two bags of ingredients held a combination of sweet thyme and chamomile. Knowing they'd obviously been planned for use with the deathbloom meant I either had part of the recipe for that poison, or possibly a way to give someone a hard-on they could beat a dragon to death with.

I shrugged and figured I'd find out when I had time and gathered the rest of the loot together.

I chucked the guard's bow and arrows to Miren and told her and Stephanos to sort out between them who got it, and to spread out the weapons so that anyone could take what they wanted. Jian was allowed to keep both scythes as the panic on his face had been comical when he realized he'd just grabbed them, and he thought he might have them taken away.

There was also a ring of health, which boosted someone's health by a whopping twenty points and a ring of improved sneak. I gave the sneaking ring to Lydia; it wouldn't fit on Bane's fingers, and she was undoubtably the loudest of the group and needed the most help.

I left the others to argue over the ring of health as Bane and I walked off to discuss the information he'd gotten from the guard.

"There's an hour to go to get to the main camp," he told me without preamble. "You said there were thirty-five in total, according to your quest, right?"

I pulled the details up and found that the locations had been updated as well.

You have received a Quest from your Goddess: Keep Your Word

You have given your word to an ancient Greater Cave Spider Queen. Kill her enemies, grant her and her brood safety and food, and she will consider her Broken Oath to be renewed, binding her and all her brood to your orders and laws. You must kill 35 drow and their leader.

Drow Killed: 19/35
Locations Cleared: 1/3
Drow Leader Killed: 0/1
Reward: Oracle's Freedom, Sworn Allegiance of 1 Greater Cave Spider and her Brood, access to Cave Spider Silk, Isthic'Mirtin's Treasury, and 50,000xp

Clearly, the garden had been one of the areas I had to find and clear, so that was a relief.

327

Bane nodded as I finished relaying the information. "That fits with what the guard said; he called this the 'Bloom Garden' and said there were dozens more drow in the main camp. I think he was trying to scare us, as he kept on about how they'd almost killed us with six. He did let slip that this was their only mage, though, and I believe that, considering how I *asked* to be sure."

"What are the other locations?" I asked, and he shrugged.

"He said that there were only six of them in the bloom garden, some in the stables, and the others were spread out across the camp and the paths leading to it. Maybe there's something that the quest considers a location which the drow don't?"

"Yeah, it's from Jenae, so it's probably more that the drow don't consider it, but we would. Anything else you managed to get from him?"

"Just that they're only an exploratory force, so they're made up of fighters and scouts mainly, a single mage and leader, no noncombatants." I let out a sigh of relief, having not even considered that the drow might have their families with them.

"Wow dodged a bullet there, then," I muttered and led him back to the others. "Okay people, according to the quest I have, there's only sixteen left to face, plus the drow leader. We've killed nineteen so far, but this is likely to be the end of the easy fights now. Anything you can do to make yourself more deadly, now's the time to do it. Here!" I said, passing the vials of poison to Stephanos, Miren, and Bane.

"This stuff is nasty shit; it'll permanently lower your health and mana by ten points per second for sixty seconds, as well as doing a hundred points of damage when it first enters your victim. Be incredibly careful when you use it, unless you don't mind losing six hundred health and mana permanently. This shit is for the boss, and I suggest you dip your arrows and coat your daggers with it when the time comes."

I passed around the rest of the potions I had, making sure to restock those who had used their health potions already. Thankfully, a few of the drow had some as well, meaning we were all back up to three potions each. I also had four mana left after Arrin, and I had shared what we had equally. Lydia got the only stamina potion we had left, as she drained hers the fastest, fighting in heavy armor.

We took a few minutes to talk, getting ourselves ready before setting off, Horkesh leading the way with her drones.

We passed though caves that showed more recent signs of passage now, the older occasional cart marks or long-abandoned camps disappeared below the signs of regular footfall. Small side caves occasionally popped up. These were ignored out of hand, the spiders having searched them before we reached them. We went on, the party occasionally muttering to each other as we progressed.

Horkesh warned us that there was a branching in the tunnels up ahead, one path leading down and the other up. The path that led down had much more movement along it, as well as signs of life. She dispatched spider drones to explore the two tunnels and skittered along the wall with us as we crept along.

It didn't take us long to reach the split in the tunnel, the foul air rising from the lower tunnel, along with the majority of kobold prints that led that way, making it clear who was most likely to be down there, as opposed to the tunnel that rose instead.

We waited, and after nearly half an hour, the spider drone from the lower level returned, chittered at Horkesh, then rushed up to join its brethren on the ceiling above us.

"There are more of the smelly ones down there, many more," Horkesh relayed. "There are three of the drow down there; they keep the smelly ones in cages."

"What does the room look like?" Bane asked her and got a confusing jumble of words in reply.

The room was apparently both long and short, with lots of hiding places and none. Bane looked at me, and I facepalmed.

Apparently, spiders didn't look at a room the way we did.

Bane slipped into stealth and crept down the tunnel, leaving only a series of swearwords lingering in the air behind him.

I really liked Bane, especially considering the fact that, as an amphibian with highly limited contact with the outside world, he'd usually be expected to be a bit stunted in his conversational style. He'd picked things up with amazing speed, and his creativity knew no bounds, considering the lack of the internet in his past.

"Ass-eating fuck-nuggets" floated back to me before he went silent, and I grinned at the darkness. Those hours spent in quiet discussion of insults from home hadn't been wasted in the slightest. He was gone maybe fifteen minutes before returning and hurrying to me, interrupting me as I sat worrying over Oracle's ongoing silence.

"We've got a problem," he said, shaking his head. "There are only three drow down there, but there are easily fifty kobolds. They also have either the creatures the drow used to carry their goods here, or the smugglers' caravans were using weird mounts."

"Why weird?" I asked, and he gestured over his shoulder into the darkness of the cave.

"There's a bunch of different creatures in pens: a pair of salamanders, easily ten meters long and looking as dumb as rocks; a tiger that looks to be half-dead; and at least three other things farther back in the cave that I couldn't make out. The drow are playing some sort of table game with cards. They have whips and spears close to hand, as well as a trio of nightwolves close by."

"What are nightwolves?" I asked.

"They're a species of wolf that's adapted to hunting in the dark places of the realm. They use a form of worldsense to hunt, as their eyes have atrophied. Good sense of smell, as well. They don't have the pelts of their forest cousins. Instead, they have pale, thick skin with ridges of bone. I'd expect one of the drow to be a beastmaster class, or they'd have already been eaten, so we need to take them out fast, as they'll buff the nightwolves and guide their attacks."

"What's the layout?" I asked, and Bane sketched it quickly in the dirt of the tunnel.

"The drow are on the far side of the room, sitting around a table that's been pushed back against the wall, maybe fifteen meters away, directly opposite the entrance. The mounts are on the right side, with the kobolds on the left. Their cages are in a half circle, with the nightwolves in the center. Looks like the drow give any kobolds that annoy them to the wolves, as they're fighting over some scraps now."

"Well, at least they'll be distracted, then," I said, looking over the sketch, and deciding that it had to be done, despite the time it was going to cost us, and Oracle. "Okay, Miren, Stephanos, you're going to be the first to attack. I want the drow closest to the wolves dead. Both of you target the closest one; then once he's down, step back and let us through.

"I'd bet the beastmaster is the closest to his pets. Then the pair of you and Arrin are to concentrate on the wolves as soon as the rest of us are inside. Lydia, Cam, and Jian, you're on my right; Barrett and Bane, my left. Your targets are the two drow that will be hopefully left. I'll take the drow that's full of arrows then the wolves. Once you've killed your targets, help whoever you can. Everyone good with that?" I asked and received a round of nods.

"Okay then, let's go. Quiet as possible, please. Turn off the magelights, and Bane, you lead us in."

The lights disappeared in seconds, and there was a general shuffling of feet and muffled swearing as people adjusted to the dark, with a few mutters of "That's my foot!" and "I said grab my shoulder...that's *NOT* my shoulder!" that caused a few snorts of laughter, relieving the tension.

I'd seen the grab that caused the complaint; Miren had been grabbing Stephanos's arse, and I couldn't help but grin about it, as Stephanos, despite being a man who looked like he should be wrestling bears in his spare time, had a surprisingly girly squeak when it came to Miren teasing him. Plus, he really wasn't sure if it was Miren or Barrett...which amused those of us that could see even more.

We crept along the tunnel, all humor vanishing as we moved closer and closer to the fight. Soon, the floor leveled out from the steep decline we'd been struggling down into a weaving and meandering tunnel that ended in a dog leg.

The flicker of firelight up ahead reflected off the walls, the rest of the team relaxing marginally. Those without any form of DarkVision were really having a shitty time underground when we had to put the magelights away.

I understood it, and I'd turned my vision off at one point to see how bad it was for them, and I'd lasted about two seconds before ramming it back on. I did *not* like the dark down here, especially when all I could hear, besides the heavy breathing of my companions, was the occasional scrape of Horkesh and her drones moving over the walls and ceiling all around us.

It freaked me the fuck out.

We gathered up just around the corner from the next cave and looked at each other, making sure everyone was ready. Miren and Stephanos drew back on their bows and stepped up to the entrance.

Stephanos had gotten the bow from the drow, and he'd chosen an arrow from the quiver that looked like it was meant to give someone nightmares. It was triangular with serrated sides and jagged points on the outer tips. I just knew it was gonna hurt like fuck when it came to be being removed.

Miren didn't look happy as she slipped past me to join him, standing at the corner and ready to step out. Her bow looked cheap as fuck in comparison, and the regular arrow looked like it'd be an annoyance rather than anything lethal.

Conversely, Stephanos looked like he couldn't wait to fire his, and they both looked back at me one more time. I gave a sharp nod and they moved, stepping out into the open. They paused for barely a second to aim before their bow strings hit the inside of their bracers with a sharp *thwack*, followed a second later by a meaty smack as Miren's arrow hit its target, and Stephanos's swearing as his missed. We rushed forward, Stephanos getting in the way as he tried to get a second shot off to make up for his miss, while Miren stepped aside as ordered.

The confusion in the entrance as we surged forward slowed us all, and by the time we got through and into the room, all three drow were on their feet. The drow closest to the nightwolves spat an order at them, and they lunged to their feet, rushing us.

It was chaos as we entered, and I barely got ahead of the group in time to bring my naginata up across my chest.

The closest nightwolf was in the air already, but my companions were too close, and I couldn't twist my weapon around in time. I barely managed to get it high enough to stop the damn thing from tearing my throat out, and I twisted from the hip as much as I could, tossing the wolf aside. It landed, rolled over, and howled, the air seeming to shake as a wave of sound poured over us. A flashing symbol appeared on my HUD.

Fear the Pack:

You have been afflicted with an AOE: Fear the Pack, and suffer a 10% Agility and Strength debuff for the next 10 seconds...9....8...

I barely had time to make sense of it as I was already bringing the metal-clad base of the naginata around. I tucked it behind the third wolf's front leg as it lunged at me and lifted as hard as I could, flipping it over and drawing a surprised yelp from the wolf as its world spun out of control.

The first wolf crouched, ready to jump at me, only to find Bane blurring out of stealth and sinking all four of his daggers into its side. He ripped upwards with the first two and down with the other pair in an alternating pattern that turned the wolf's budding snarl into a wet yelp of confusion and pain. One that ended very quickly.

I stepped forward and, wincing slightly, punted the wolf before me as hard as I could in the side of its head, causing it to roll over and into the path of the onrushing drow. I had a split second to think about how stupid it was to feel like I'd just kicked a dog, instead of the damn horrible thing it was, then I moved on. The assumed beastmaster was standing at the back of the group now, frantically yanking the table up and over to use as a shield. The other two were sprinting forward, spears lifted.

Lydia had taken her nightwolf's jump on her shield, using it to batter the wolf out of the air. Jian had stabbed it twice in rapid succession, the silvery scythes dipping in and ripping back out with a surgeon's precision. The blades slipped easily past the ribs, before tearing back out, the jagged rears of the weapons taking a much larger cost in health as they left than when they entered.

Stepping forward, Cam brought his axe down hard, the thick ridged bone that covered the nightwolf's spine doing little to stop the massive axe's impact. The bones fractured with a crunch and a sickening whistle as he levered it back out, the air rushing into the severed windpipe as the body flopped around.

Arrin blasted a trio of Magic Missiles into the table, but the thick material held. The beastmaster was screaming orders at the animals in the pens. Most roared in response, slowly shuffling forward, but at the back of the pens, a pair of silver-shod hooves smashed a thin wall into kindling.

"Fuck!" I said concisely. "What in the name of Odin's left nut is that?!" I pointed to the back of the cave, where a huge, red and black metallic creature surged forward.

It looked like a horse, but one made of black steel, red and gold highlights marked the spinning discs and pistons that flashed and glowed as it barreled forwards.

"Shit!" cried Barrett. "Kill him, fucking kill him now!"

I gritted my teeth and sprinted, filling my naginata with lightning magic and jumping over the still-stunned wolf as it rose to its feet. I trusted the others to deal with it as I slashed wildly out, blocking a spear aimed for my groin.

I landed, skidding, and reached out, grabbing the nearest drow's shoulder guard as he spasmed, my lightning having discharged down his spear and stunning him.

I yanked him forward, growling, and rammed the tip of my naginata up through his jaw and into his skull, the tip crunching as it punched through the soft palate and sank into his brain.

"Sneaky cocksucker!" I growled, his point of aim removing any lingering dislike for killing sentients I had left.

I shoved him back, then met the flashing hooves of the horse, sending me flying across the cave and into the wall.

I flailed about as the world seemed to shift. I'd hit the wall then fallen to the floor, but my chest wouldn't move. I looked down, frantically trying to breathe, and saw the dent in the middle of my breastplate, the Cuirass of Night's Embrace deformed and blatantly badly damaged. I'd lost my naginata at some point during my flight, and I frantically grabbed at the hinge and clasp under my right armpit, tugging as hard as I could.

It took three attempts, but eventually it came loose with a soft *boing* and I felt a little air rush into my lungs. Before I could reach the other two clasps, Miren was there, her smaller, nimbler fingers slapping my hands away and freeing them.

I groaned in relief as she pulled the armor free, before wincing at the cracked ribs crunching as the armor's support was removed.

My groan was interrupted by a wet cough, and I spat blood out onto the dusty cave floor before greedily drinking down the potion she brought to my lips.

As I swallowed it, I looked over at the fight, realizing that it was rapidly going from bad to worse.

I had to get back in there.

Bane was facing off against a creature that looked like a four-legged velociraptor. I knew they had two arms and two legs normally, but this fucker was built low to the ground and moved as though greased lightning and the embodiment of hatred had a fucking scaly baby.

Cam and Jian were trying to damage the horse-thing while Lydia kept its attention. Barrett was desperately trying to fight the remaining drow spearman, and Arrin and Stephanos were firing at the drow beastmaster whenever he popped his head out of cover to direct his creatures, but they were having fuck-all luck.

I glared at the horse and used Examine…

Fenris Heavy Automaton

This Fenris-class heavy automaton battle steed was created by the gnomish mastermind Glonkill. All gnomish battle creations are imbued with both magical and mundane control methods, in case of theft.

Health: 1048/2000
Mana Charge: 412/1000

I wracked my brain trying to make sense of the information; clearly, it was a construct, and it was made by gnomes...cool, that's great...but what the fuck was the control method?!

I looked back at the beastmaster and used my Examine again, growling to myself as I saw little that was useful. The "Unknown" markers on the only really sodding useful bits just pissed me off.

Drow Beastmaster Dalael

The drow Beastmaster Dalael was dispatched to support the expeditionary force in capturing the fallen city of Mis'rak Ak Thun and was sentenced to death by Kismeth Hatchlings for his part in the assault's failure. Dalael escaped and was eventually discovered under a false name in the outskirts of the City of Eternal Night. Due to his expertise in beast mastery, he was given a final chance to aid an exploratory force, but was bound to a rune of control to prevent his escape a second time.

Health: 582/600
Mana: 100/100
Stamina: 112/500
Weaknesses: Unknown
Resistances: Unknown

I shrugged out of the rest of my chest armor and gestured Miren back to the fight, giving her a weak grin in thanks as I drank down another potion. I grunted in pain as my ribs snapped back into place, my hands already weaving around a small but rapidly building ball of flames. I might not be able to hit the fucker with a Firebolt, and I didn't have a spell like Magic Missile, which looked like it could be guided in the air, at least to some degree, but what I did have, thanks to fueling it with naked fury in the past, was a mortar.

I'd accidentally created the spell when I was new to the realm, pouring an insane amount of literal firepower into a regular Firebolt spell, overcharging it to a massive degree. I rolled to my feet, both hands too busy to push with, and I pulled my hands back to my right side, feeling like I was swinging a bowling ball that grew heavier by the second.

I swung it back forwards and threw, the spell faltering as it flew through the air, missing the target I'd set for it by less than an inch as far as I could see, but it still had spectacular results.

The spellform was broken when it impacted the rim of the table the beastmaster was hiding behind. Since it was on the outward side of the table, most of the explosion went in that direction, hammering into the back legs of the automaton and sending it staggering as flames washed around it.

The majority of the shrapnel and fire damage was confined to the metal horse, but enough hit the drow spearman that it staggered him, letting Barrett dodge a blow that would have killed him. The horse fell back to face Lydia, and one enormous silvery hoof slammed down on the drow spearman's leg, turning it to paste filled with shards of bone.

The spearman screamed in pain, and Jian spun past him, his dual scythes flashing out and slicing through his neck, cutting off the cry with a wet gurgle.

I'd been shoved back by the impact, but I was back up in seconds and charging forward. I didn't know where the naginata was, but I knew where the last fucking drow was, and I just prayed that killing him would stop the automaton's rampage.

The impact of the mortar spell had slammed the table backward, smashing it first upright and second into shards that had fired all over. Most of the incredibly hard wood had been caught by the back of the spearman and the horse, but enough had gone in all directions that it'd caused a lot of minor injuries.

One not so minor injury it caused, due to the size of the splinter in question, was to the drow beastmaster, who was screaming as he pulled an inch-long fragment of wood out of his right eye. He was braced on one arm, half-seated, half-lying under the now-upright table, frantically patting at his pouches when I arrived.

He looked up just in time to see my boot swipe his bracing arm out from under him and I slid in, grabbing him by the shoulders and yanking him forward. I rolled, twisting him over me and using our joint momentum to bring myself on top of him.

"Surprise, motherfucker!" I shouted before nutting him as hard as I could. Then I released him with my right hand, pulling back and making a fist, which I smashed down into his nose with as much force as I could manage.

The delicate cartilage snapped, and I did it again, and again. Using my left hand for leverage, I punched him as hard as I could, the back of his head impacting the stone floor under him.

He lashed out frantically, stabbing me with the only weapon he had, the inch-long splinter. With as sharp as it was, and the strength of the drow, it sank into my flesh.

The fucker had managed to get it into my left shoulder, right in the dip between the muscles, and it'd gone deep enough to send that hand spasming. He grabbed at my left hand with his right and pulled me forward, twisting and sending us both rolling as we fought, though I finally maneuvered myself back on top as the fight continued.

The next few seconds passed in a frenzy of punches, attempted eye gouges, and knees that flew everywhere...until I felt his hand tug at my belt.

Through some combination of our movements he'd found my Dagger of Ripping and yanked it free, slicing a line across my unarmored chest that stung like a bitch.

I grabbed his right wrist, and he grabbed my left. For a handful of seconds, we strained against each other before his greater strength overcame his crappy position for leverage, and he started to bend my arms back.

"Now you die!" he hissed at me, his bloody ruin of a face glaring up at me.

"Not today…mother…fucker!" I growled, as a sudden blur resolved into Bane, sliding to a stop close to us, a pair of daggers stabbing out and sinking into the beastmaster's chest, angled downwards on either side to puncture both lungs, even as they shredded muscles and flesh.

I had a split second of connection as the drow's eyes widened in shock before the pain registered, and I used it, one final nut smashing his skull back against the floor, before I released him and rolled over.

Everything seemed to hit me at once, and I gasped in pain and kicked the dying drow's leg off mine as it flailed about. I laid back on the floor and let out a weak groan as Bane started quickly searching the beastmaster.

"Didn't…know…who he was…fucking with," I groaned out, and looked over at the rest of the party, frantically trying to defend themselves from the horse.

I groaned again and reached out weakly, my right palm flat against the floor, and I forced myself to roll over. The fucking thing was still going. I made it to my feet and staggered, grabbing the table's remains for support, and started to build a lightning spell as Lydia was smashed from her feet as the damn thing reared up and lashed out with both front feet.

"Got it!" Bane shouted from beside me and pushed something at me. "Tell it to stop!" He shoved something into my hands, and I screamed as my movements were interrupted, his grab having broken both the pattern and my already addled concentration, to send the spell backlash roaring through me.

I collapsed to the floor, my hand clenching spasmodically around whatever he'd pressed into my palm, and a screen filled my mind.

Do you wish to take ownership of the Fenris Heavy Automaton?

This control crystal is tied to model 017 and will become soul-bound on acceptance.

Yes/No

I squinted at it, trying to see through the pain of the spell feedback, but as soon as I could read it, I mentally mashed the *yes* and cried out as another pulse of power washed through me.

"Stop!" I screamed, falling to the floor, and I screwed up my eyes trying to focus. Was I too late?

A chorus of swearing, groans, and relieved moans reached me from the injured, as well as muted grumbles and squeaks from the kobolds.

The rest of the creatures that had been advancing on our party, single-minded in their determination to smash us into interestingly colored paste, seemed to suddenly wake up. The two longer, thicker-bodied lizards immediately lost interest in the fight at the beastmaster's death and were hissing at everything around them. Bane had stabbed the "Jurassic Park" reject through the throat, and whatever had been at the back of the makeshift stables next to the Fenris was staying there, dead, or playing it.

The last beast that had been in the stables was a giant tiger, but it was close to death already. It had ignored the call from the beastmaster and even now, it lay there, watching us rather than attacking.

"Is everyone okay?" I asked when I could manage it, looking up at the Fenris. It stood there, directly over Barrett, one silvery hoof still raised, ready to crush his skull. He rolled out from under it and backed away. All of us slowly grouped up as far from the collection of corpses and blood splatters as we could, and we forced down more healing potions and smiled at each other grimly, knowing how close we'd come to death.

"What the hell do I do with it now?" I muttered, looking at the Fenris, only to have a new notification pop up. I ignored it for a second and spoke to the others. "Does anyone need healing?" I got a chorus of "No" from most of them, but a weak voice called out from my right, and I dismissed the notification for now, looking over at Lydia. She'd managed to get to her feet, but she wasn't walking well.

I had her sit down and cast Battlefield Triage over her until my mana pool was empty, my head spinning and my last meal trying to escape.

"We're gonna have to rest here for a bit. I know we're too close to the main settlement to rest properly, but we've no choice," I said quietly to the others.

"Horkesh, I need you to send your drones back up the tunnel, see if the main settlement heard any of that, and warn us if anything starts coming this way."

"Yes," she said simply before vanishing again, chittering at her spiders. They flowed away from her as a group, only one staying with her. "They will watch for anything coming," she said. I had a momentary thought wondering how they'd communicate it, before I remembered they were fucking spiders and had webs they could shake or some such shit.

I was too tired to care and just nodded acceptance.

We broke out some rations, I conjured a fountain for Bane, and we all rested for a bit. While we recovered, I pulled up the notifications I'd received, starting with the one that'd popped up when I was wondering about the Fenris...

Congratulations on your purchase of Model 017 of the Fenris Heavy Automaton!

Please note that the Fenris, while limited in scope compared to our premium models, has been created with a large number of additional features. These include voice command and...

I winced as a high-pitched noise tore through my mind and the prompt disappeared in a wash of pain, before a second prompt appeared.

Warning!

Cranial damage detected. This manual cannot be deployed, due to physiological and mental restrictions. Please seek immediate healing and request a new manual from your dealer...ceasing installation...

I fell onto my back from where I'd been sitting, clutching at my head and gritting my teeth as pain rippled through me. It seemed to build, then retreat, like the tide coming in and out. I curled into a ball, clutching my skull, and tried to master the pain as it built. It was like before, when Oracle had given me the Airblade spell, only worse. This time, it wasn't esoteric magical knowledge. No, this time it was a full-on goddamn instruction manual for a god-damn horse that ran on mana crystals, which meant the manual was a mix of heavy engineering details and how to polish out scratches in the damn paint.

There were details on command structures, trees of how to link together command words for maximum efficiency, and how to adjust the color of its eyes so that it matched your outfit.

I thrashed as the pain continued to build, feeling something hot and wet running from my nose, my ears, my eyes…I tasted blood, and I felt hands grabbing at me, holding me down and frantically forcing potions into my mouth again.

I coughed and choked on them, starting to shake as the pain began to build past my ability to take it…

"Jax!"

The voice echoed around inside my skull like a fart in an empty bathtub, making me wince as the sound added to the pain.

"I'm sorry…here…"

The voice came back, much softer this time, and something changed, a burrowing in my brain, a shift that was both horrifically painful, and…calming…

The pain was building on my side of a door, like there was a physical blockage in a line suddenly, rather than a pressure cooker that was building, closing on self-destruction.

"That's it…just a little more…"

As the seconds passed, the blockage transformed. I could suddenly visualize it, and I was somewhere else. The world around me that had been so shut out by my pain suddenly was replaced by the place I'd met Jenae before.

I was curled up on the floor, shivering with pain, but she was there. Jenae crouched beside me, lifting my head. She held out a hand, and a glass appeared in it, filled with crystal-clear, cool water, which she lifted to my parched lips.

I drank greedily, and she smiled down at me, little more than my own height. She helped me to my feet, holding me under my arms and supporting me as my legs almost gave out.

"Where am I?" I asked her, and she snorted, shaking her head.

"Somewhere you have no right to be, yet still, you're here…again."

"Well…" I sniffed, tasting blood and feeling it coating my face. "That's a spectacularly unhelpful answer, you know that?" I croaked, then grimaced as I saw the blood that stained the front of her clothes. She was dressed in a robe that crossed over the front and ran down to open at her knees, with creamy leggings underneath. The beautiful patterning of runic symbols that ran across it was marred only by the straps of her backpack…and the garish smears of my blood. "Shit, sorry about—"

"It's all right…and yes, I know it's not helpful. This reflects the Realm of the Gods. You've been here before, remember? When we had our…falling out?"

"Dangerous," I muttered, looking around.

"Yes, it's very dangerous, especially for you, as weak as you are, but this place is also the best place I can think of to reach a threshold, as you have."

"What's a threshold?" I asked numbly, pain still buffeting my mind. I blinked and forced myself to focus in on her face. Her lips quirked up as she watched me.

"It's the first step toward growth to real power, and not something you should be experiencing for a long time yet. But it was that or let you die, and I don't want that. You're my Chosen, after all, so it's only a short step to make you my Champion as well…"

"Champion?" I asked, confused, forcing myself to look around. I studied the cracked desolate earth of this realm, and the foothills in the distance that were the base of the gods' thrones.

"No!" Jenae snapped, gripping my jaw, and turning me back to look at her. *"Don't pay attention to anything else here; you will only force it to become aware of you, and that's not something we can risk right now. Look only at me…and listen."*

I nodded, and she went on. *"I've opened up a pathway for you, but it's one you're not ready to use yet. When I return you to your realm, you need to focus on breaking through it and reaching towards your evolution. It won't be easy, but one of the advantages to evolving is an increased capacity to learn. You'll still need to be healed, as we discussed before, but this should keep you alive long enough to find someone to do it."*

"Thank you," I muttered, screwing my eyes shut against the pain again. She shook her head, a gentle laugh coming to her lips.

"Oh, Eternal, you're very welcome. If you can survive this and bring back my brothers and sisters, you'll have earned my help a hundred times over. Again, I am sorry for hurting you before," she said, her voice tinged with sadness and regret.

"I was an asshole," I whispered.

She laughed again. *"You* **are** *an asshole, Jax, but not a bad person, for all of that. Now hold on and push forward. I've opened the pathway, but only you can walk it."*

I smiled at her weakly, and the world dissolved again. I found myself on my back on the floor of the cave. My team, my *friends*, all clustered around me. Lydia, Bane, and Miren were next to me, and the others were all facing out, weapons drawn.

"It's all right," I whispered, forcing the words out through a blinding pain in my skull. "I…just need some…time."

With that, I closed my eyes again, the wash of pain flowing through me, back and forth, building again like the sea crashing against the shore. With each wave, it grew higher, the pain threatening to overwhelm me as I searched frantically.

After a minute that felt like it lasted a year, I found it…a single thin line that pulsed and beat along with my heart. It was inside me, and at the same time, it lay behind the crashing waves, a single hair-thin line of golden light that pulsed faster as I focused on it. I reached out, and inwards…

I could feel it; it shook with my heartbeat, power flowing through it in the same way blood passed through my veins, and I followed it with my mind, looking for a blockage, a problem, a weakness…none of them were there, as far as I could tell. As I flashed along the length of it, another wave of pain hit me, and I was back on the shore, catching my breath, watching another wave build.

I tried again and again, feeling myself becoming weaker by the second.

I threw myself at the pulse of power, rushing blindly down it, hoping against hope that I could travel far enough along the golden thread that I'd find the end, before…

When I could see again, I panted, forcing the air out through gritted teeth and I looked at the thread, really looked at it. I kept thinking of it as a vein, and I was trying to get far enough along to find the blockage, or whatever was stopping the pain from draining away through it, but what if…

I shifted my perspective in an instant, not looking at the far end of the vein, but instead the beginning…

I looked back inside myself, realizing that if I could feel it inside and way, way over *there*...then there had to be a connection, a point where the two met.... It only took a few seconds of searching, tearing through my mind frantically, until I found it again...

It was the wall I'd visualized before and the door in it. My vision changed, and the pain-water began smashing into me on my island, then retreating back to smash against the door, making it creak before rebounding and heading back to me.

I watched it for a second, then gritted my teeth and *pushed*. The flood seemed to batter against it harder this time, and less so when it flowed back to me. So I did it again, pushing harder, faster.

I bit down on my fear, and I imagined the assholes. All of them. Pricks like Barabarattas and my father, the slavers, and that freak Toka...Lorek, and the asshats from the ship, all of them were on the other side of the door, eating fucking cupcakes and drinking cold beer.

The bastards had a goddamn burger from Five Guys and they were using it as an ashtray...they were pissing on my fucking cornflakes and calling it milk, and I...WAS...NOT...FUCKING...HAVING...IT!

I gathered myself, all my anger, all my hatred, and I shoved so hard, I almost passed out.

The door didn't just open, the entire motherfucking wall was smashed into pieces.

The floodwaters of my pain carried the world away with them, and as I sagged backwards, the sun rose over the water. It was beautiful. The first warming rays of the rising sun made my skin tingle, and I drew a deep breath, sweet and invigorating, before closing my eyes and sleeping.

When I opened them again, I was laid out on the floor. The shitty stench of animals, kobolds, and corpses filled the air, and my face felt wet. I shifted, feeling a rock under my shoulder blade move, and I tried to sit up, only to be immediately grabbed by Bane.

He helped me to rise slowly, and I frowned around at the room. The insane pain that had filled my world seemingly only seconds before was gone now, and instead, there was a feeling of...relief.

It was like I'd only ever taken half-breaths before now, but suddenly there was more, like a belt that had been wrapped around my chest had been moved. It had been shifted only slightly, a millimeter or less, but the air I could pull in.... It felt...better.

My mind felt clearer, and as I shifted, my muscles felt smoother, like I'd unknowingly spent my life with a restraint clamped to me in every way, only now, it was releasing. Like an elastic band that's been stretched too far, it was slowly losing its grip.

"I'm all right," I whispered to Bane's questions, the others breathing relieved sighs as I explained distractedly about the manual while I pulled up the notifications.

You have taken your first step into a wider world.

Beware, mortal.

Binding your soul to your physical form is not a step undertaken lightly.

You have gained the following bonuses:

- 2% increase to all stats
- 5% increase in experience earned
- plus a one-off bonus of ten points to distribute as you choose.

You have been elevated from Chosen of Jenae to Jenae's Champion.

As the right hand of a goddess, you have gained the following bonuses:

- +2 to Intelligence and Wisdom per level
- 1x Random Blueprint or Spellbook
- 1x Map Marker.
- Additional Bonus: 10% increase in experience earned.

"The drow have made no move to come closer," a voice chittered close to my ear. I flinched as I made unexpected eye contact with Horkesh.

"Thank you, Horkesh," I muttered, forcing myself to smile at her as Lydia and Barrett gave Stephanos a dressing down off to one side, making it very clear why he was the reason we'd all had such a nasty fight, and I pulled the remaining notifications up.

Congratulations!

You have killed the following:

- 2x Drow Squad Leader of various levels for a total of 5,950xp
- 1x Drow Beastmaster, level 38 for a total of 5,500xp
- 5x Drow Soldiers of various levels for a total of 2,850xp

As leader you receive a portion of the experience earned by troops when they fight under your command:

- 13x Drow soldier of various levels for a total of 27,000xp
- 1x Drow Mage, level 18 for a total of 4,500xp
- 1x Goregaon, level 23 for a total of 1,100xp
- 4x Nightwolves of various levels for a total of 1,800xp

Total experience earned: 34,400xp

As party leader you gain 25% of all experience earned

Progress to level 15 stands at 51,133/140,000

You have received a Quest from your Goddess: Keep Your Word

You have given your word to an ancient Greater Cave Spider Queen. Kill her enemies, grant her and her brood safety and food, and she will consider her Broken Oath to be renewed, binding her and all her brood to your orders and laws. You must kill 35 drow and their leader.

Drow Killed: 22/35
Locations Cleared: 2/3
Drow Leader Killed: 0/1

Reward: Oracle's Freedom, Sworn Allegiance of 1 Greater Cave Spider and her Brood, access to Cave Spider Silk, Isthic'Mirtin's Treasury and 62,500xp *(Recalculated...)*

Congratulations!

Through hard work and perseverance, you have increased your stats by the following:

Dexterity +1
Endurance +2
Perception +1
Strength +1
Wisdom +1

I found myself grinning as I finished with my prompts. A point in Perception and Wisdom, as well as the rest was always going to be welcome. Fifteen percent increase on top of the original ten I'd been getting from the party overall to my experience meant I would level much faster, and that was a fucking relief.

The two percent increase to my stats was awesome; not that it was much now, but considering my Agility was in its forties, that meant I'd increase it soon enough. That boost applied to all my stats as well, so while I didn't have any stats over fifty, which meant I wasn't seeing any increases yet...I would soon. I had ten points to distribute as well, which could be lifesaving, considering how close I'd kept coming to dying over the last few fights.

I pulled up my character sheet and considered my options while I washed the drying blood from my face absently. My health, mana, and stamina all slowly ticked back toward full.

I'd reached a familiar point, back to the old fight of min-max versus a balanced build. There were so many places I could invest the points, especially as they were essentially freebies, so I wouldn't miss them in that regard. That being said, there was nowhere "bad" to put them, either.

I took a deep breath and did what I really didn't want to, even though I knew I had to:...I used them to "fix" my weakest areas, putting seven points into my Charisma, two points into Luck, and a single point into Constitution, finally bringing all of my stats out of their teens and into the twenties.

I looked over the finalized character sheet and nodded in satisfaction. As much as I wanted to bung the entire ten points into something, making a superhuman increase in a single bound, like I had with my Agility, I had to be realistic.

Jez Cajiao

My Charisma would be my undoing when I met the smugglers if I didn't increase it, and I couldn't afford that.

Name: Jax				
Titles: Strategos: 5% boost to damage resistance, Fortifier: 5% boost to defensive structure integrity, Champion of Jenae				
Class: Spellsword > Justicar			Renown: Unknown	
Level: 14			Progress: 51,133/140,000	
Patron: Jenae, Goddess of Fire and Exploration			Points to Distribute: 0 Meridian Points to Invest: 0	
Stat	Current points	Description	Effect	Progress to next level
Agility	42	Governs dodge and movement.	+320% maximum movement speed and reflexes, (+10% movement in darkness, -20% movement in daylight)	61/100
Charisma	20	Governs likely success to charm, seduce, or threaten	+100% success in interactions with other beings	22/100
Constitution	36	Governs health and health regeneration	700 health, regen 42.9 points per 600 seconds, (+10% regen due to soul bond, -20 health due to soul bond, each point invested now worth 20 health)	88/100
Dexterity	28	Governs ability with weapons and crafting success	+180% to weapon proficiency, +18% to the chances of crafting success	78/100
Endurance	25	Governs stamina and stamina regeneration	250 stamina, regen 15 points per 30 seconds	92/100
Intelligence	29	Governs base mana and number of spells able to be learned	270 mana, spell capacity: 17 (15 + 2 from items), (-20 mana due to soul bond)	74/100
Luck	20	Governs overall chance of bonuses	+10% chance of a favorable outcome	38/100
Perception	25	Governs ranged damage and chance to spot traps or hidden items	+150% ranged damage, +25% chance to spot traps or hidden items	14/100
Strength	26	Governs damage with melee weapons and carrying capacity	+14 damage with melee weapons, +140% maximum carrying capacity	38/100
Wisdom	35 (30)	Governs mana regeneration and memory	+250% mana recovery, 1.7 points per minute, 250% more likely to remember things, -50% mana regeneration until mana manipulation reaches level 10.	17/100

I dismissed all the prompts and scanned the cavern. The kobolds were still huddled fearfully in the corner, and the surviving animals remained in their pens. The tiger had apparently found a friend in Barrett, who was slowly and gently feeding it.

I forced myself to my feet and spoke, drawing every eye and ear immediately.

"Thank you all. That was a hard fight, and the side effects of the manual for the horse, well, that kinda sucked…but I'm all right now. I know the drow haven't moved to come down this way; with some luck, they don't know about us, but we have to be clear. We've made a fuckton of noise. The only reason they won't know we're here is if they're as self-absorbed and assholish as we really think they are. So, let's fucking hope for that."

That got a grin from the others, and I noticed the pile of gear set to one side, and more importantly, my chest piece. While I was out cold or fighting for my life in a weird fucking magical dreamworld, someone had beaten as much of the dent out of my armor as was possible. I pulled it back on, and Cam gave me a slow nod.

"Did you do this?" I asked him, and he gave another nod.

"Thank you, Cam," I said with a smile. "I'll be more careful in the future."

I pulled the armor on, pretending the dent wasn't uncomfortable, and looked through the pile of loot: a few nice spears, some daggers, a couple of non-magical rings, and a handful of gold and silver. All would be useful at some point, no doubt, but for now, the best items were the last bits: three health and a single mana potion, which I handed out to those that were the lowest in the party, wishing I still had the majority of my ingredients with me.

The only potion I could probably make right now was one that'd stiffen the old trouser snake, thanks to the drow's ingredients, and I really didn't think that'd help in the next battle.

Admittedly, I could use it as an extra weapon and beat them to death with it, but I'd just end up in therapy later.

We checked everyone over, healed up any injuries, and pocketed anything we thought would be useful later. Then I went to speak with the kobolds.

"Do any of you understand me?" I asked. Several of them perked up at my words, but I didn't know if that was because they understood, or if they were trying to look attentive in the hope of avoiding a beating. "If you understand me, put your hands on your head," I said, and after a few seconds, they started looking at each other, a barrage of words I couldn't make out followed, then the entire group put their hands on each other's shoulders, looking confused.

"Well, fuck," I muttered, shaking my head. They clearly understood slightly, but fuck it. "Okay, we already freed a bunch of your friends and let them escape further down the tunnels. You can go find them and do whatever you want, just stay here until we've gone, okay? Then, just go do whatever, and try not to get eaten, I guess."

I shrugged and turned back to the rest of the group and gestured to them.

"Come on, guys, let's go get this over with," I said, stretching awkwardly and trying to get rid of a knot in my shoulder as I looked at them. "Horkesh, tell us if anything changes with your drones. Bane, lead us out of here."

With that, my team started moving, and I took up my usual position as second in line, the group behind me gripping shoulders or asses, as per their taste, and we set off back to the main tunnel.

Once we reached the split in the path that we'd entered from, I made sure we were all ready, and Bane started us off along the higher tunnel again, each step taking us closer to Oracle, and every one making me worry about her more.

CHAPTER TWENTY-NINE

W̲e hid in a side tunnel, waiting as the spiders explored and came back, Horkesh and her drones communicating, then Horkesh relaying the twists and turns ahead of us. Finally, half an hour later, one of the spiders didn't come back, and we knew we'd found the drow camp.

The spiders bunched up around Horkesh, and she hesitated, hanging from the wall close to me at head height. It was a mark of how used to her I'd grown that I didn't try to bat her away, but deep inside, I still instinctually wanted to Firebolt her in the face.

"We can't go on. If you die, and the drow find us, they will attack the queen, we…I…want to help, but…"

I nodded to her in understanding.

"It's okay, Horkesh. Thank you for your help so far; I know it's not been easy, especially after you were injured. Return to Queen Ashrag. She will know when we kill the drow and the quest is completed, so you don't need to risk yourself any further."

She looked at me for a handful of seconds before spinning in place and darting away, her drones going with her.

We all paused momentarily, then shrugged at each other. "Spiders are just weird" seemed to be the general consensus.

It didn't take long to find the remains of the spider that had gone missing, or at least to find some bits of it. The area looked like it was supposed to be a guard post, but it'd been abandoned, the arrogant drow wandering off with the spider's corpse. As we snuck along a tunnel a few minutes later, we could see a light up ahead. Here and there on the floor were sections of chitin that I thought I recognized as the spider drone's carapace.

Voices murmured up ahead, and Bane slunk past me, creeping to the corner, and peering around, before slowly returning to where we waited around the previous bend.

"We've found it," he confirmed. "The tunnel up ahead opens out into a large cavern. There's a handful of small tents spread out, and a building being constructed in the middle. I could spot maybe six or seven drow, all arguing about the spider that went missing; one of them is on the floor with a dagger in its back. Looks like they don't like to share." He gave off a low thrum of amusement.

"What about the boss; what about Oracle?!" I asked quickly and he shook his head.

"Can't see it anywhere, but the upper reaches of the cavern are covered in webs, and I can't sense anything at all from there…I'd assume it's either hiding up there, or it's inside the building. There's no sign of Oracle either, far as I can see. The present drow appear to be regular soldiers, mainly armed with swords and shields, a few with bows. They're all gathered around a cook fire in the middle of the cavern. There are piles of equipment and loot dumped against the walls, and I'd guess they're what remains of the caravans that were taken."

He paused, then shook his head. "There's also a cage against the far wall. A handful of prisoners are in it, with one stripped of its skin on a table nearby."

I froze, watching Bane, shock filling me as I considered what he'd just said.

"They're alive, or at least they were recently, judging by the blood. It's still flowing, but I think they're unconscious. It might be a mercy to kill them."

"No," I said straight away. "We're not killing someone we might be able to save. Anything else you can tell me?" I asked, and he shook his head. "Fine, then; this is how it's going to go down. Bane, you're the stealthiest motherfucker amongst us. Think you can get into the cavern and hide?" I asked him, getting a nod.

"Great. Your job…your *only* job, is the boss. I'm going to make an explosive spell; it'll be a big one, and I'm going to chuck it at the group that's standing together, see if I can take them all out. Arrin, you be ready with a fuckload of Magic Missiles, and target anyone who looks like they might be trouble after that goes off, but stay behind me with the others. Lydia, Barrett, you're with me.

"We're going to spread out in the mouth of the cavern; nobody gets past us. Cam, Jian, you're right behind us, you support us, striking when we can't. If we get injured, you step up and take our places. There's only seven of them, but I don't doubt that others will come running once the fight starts. Miren, Stephanos…I want you ready with the poisoned arrows. Get the boss when it appears. This is its home, so I don't think it'll be far away. Any questions?"

Lydia immediately spoke up.

"What about the prisoners?" she asked.

"We deal with them once we've killed the drow. Trying to protect them sooner is just putting us and them at more risk." My crew wasn't happy, but they couldn't argue with my logic. "Time to nut up or shut up," I said, hefting my naginata before passing it to Lydia. "I'm gonna need both hands for this, so do me a favor and hold that for me, okay?"

She nodded.

I took a deep breath and closed my eyes, deciding at the last minute that if I was going to try to take out the entire group, this was going to need to be a beast of a spell.

I relaxed the walls I'd built around my anger, relaxing the forced control I'd been exerting through Bane's meditation techniques. I thought about what they'd done. They'd taken Oracle; they'd taken someone I *loved*, and I did love her, I admitted that to myself now.

They'd taken her from me. They'd put everything I had at risk; they'd endangered my people, and now they stood between me and Tommy, too. They were scum, and they deserved everything I was going to bring to them.

I felt him stirring. Amon. As always, my extremes of emotion brought him out. He'd been watching, waiting, and now he was ready. I felt it, the bloodlust rising from him, fueled by the fury that one of his citizens had been taken, harmed.

I also knew Amon better now, and I understood what I hadn't before. He wasn't just the last remnants of a long-dead emperor, my ancestor. He wasn't just a ghost of a ghost that demanded I protect the weak and stand as their shield.

No, he was a fucking animal in his own right, a monster amongst monsters. The only thing that he'd ever feared was what he would truly become if he went all out and gave in to his darker side.

He'd instead made a set of rules, the rules that governed the empire. When something broke those rules, he could let go of the reins and fucking murder everything that crossed him.

He was a man who spent his life preventing the fight, ruling carefully and justly, but secretly lusting for war.

Now, he was in my mind, and my anger was feeding his.

He made little suggestions, tweaking my understanding of the Firebolt spell that I'd already started to cast. I was planning on using the unstable Firebolt spell I'd made up before, but that wasn't going to be enough. It wasn't enough, because that might leave some of them alive.

I kept building it as I snuck along, getting to the cavern entrance and looking inside. The original seven drow had shifted; five of them were still hanging around the corpse of the sixth, while the seventh had moved over to the half-skinned person on the table, sharpening their blades, getting ready to go again.

The five drow that stood near the fire were finishing off their snack and talking, laughing as one of their number imitated their fellow they'd already murdered, making gestures of them carrying the spider and getting ganked.

I grinned as I changed the spell at Amon's suggestions, weaving in the outer ring segment of the Cleansing Fire spell, but using it to contain the spell in ways the original hadn't.

I added in segments of the Firebolt, specifically the targeting, expansion, and heat. I took the sections of Airblade that hadn't been lost and added them to the lightning spell, forming the containment sphere from hissing, crackling lightning. I wove it all together and began to sink my mana into it, pouring fifty, then a hundred, then a hundred and ninety, stopping only when I hit two hundred mana.

I'd have gone further, such was the righteous fury that filled my mind, but I couldn't hold the spell anymore. My arms were shaking and crackling. Seething lightning streamers suddenly erupted from the ball of molten hatred I'd created, the light that flashed in the tunnel entrance drawing every eye in the cavern as I stepped out into full view.

"Hadouken!" I screamed at them, slamming both arms forward and locking my wrists together like I was in "Street Fighter."

Before they had the time to dodge, my spell flashed across the intervening distance, the sound of its passage a high-pitched whine that hurt the ears. It slammed into the fire standing in their midst, and it detonated, the writhing, twisting mess of lightning suddenly unravelling to form a mesh that flashed out, covering the ground and surrounding the drow.

From impact to full extension was less than a full second, then the second phase of the spell went off. The compressed air that was part of Airblade instead formed a dome, a shield that trapped the drow inside as the spell entered the final phase.

Flames roared to life, turning it into a pressure cooker of flame and lightning, one that shrank by the second. The compressed walls of air drew in quickly and crushed them in, as Lydia chucked my naginata through the air to me.

The spell wasn't powerful enough to kill them all outright. I was too new to magic, and too inexperienced to craft something that powerful, even after pouring so much mana into it...

But it was enough to give all five severe burns, stunned debuffs, and break multiple bones, not to mention causing panic in the oh-so-superior drow.

When the spell expired twenty seconds later and evaporated, all five of them were hunched around the fire in the center, burned, stunned, and forced into the firepit by the pressure. Once it expired, all they wanted to do was get the hell away from it, and they sure as shit weren't thinking about us.

I had led the charge into the room, Barrett and Lydia on either side of me. Cam and Jian flanked them, Stephanos and Miren following in the middle as they waited for the boss to show itself.

Arrin was in the very center of the group, Magic Missiles flaring to life and hurtling across the intervening space to hammer, one after the other, into the right leg of the torturer.

He screamed, his shock making him miss the chance to deflect or dodge them. As his knee exploded, the cap hanging from a shredded section of cartilage, he collapsed to the floor.

I'd told Arrin to focus on the main group, but I didn't mind his change of target, as I saw the state of the group in the middle. One fell toward me, the skin on his face running like candlewax, eyes a milky white that would never know sight again, short of major magical assistance.

My naginata flared to life, fire filling it. A hissing erupted as the blood in his heart boiled, the blade piercing through his now crisped and ruined clothes to bisect it. I gave it a twist to be sure, then yanked it back, flipping it over and bringing the metal-clad end down hard onto another drow's skull. A loud crack filled the cavern as the bone fractured. A third drow fell to the floor from where he'd been hunched over, his limbs twitching, the smoldering remnants of the campfire going to work on his dying form.

Barrett was past me in an instant, his greatsword flashing out to chop into his target, dipping and twisting to rise again, blood spraying from a severed artery as the drow fell back, almost decapitated.

Lydia was past me as well as I looked up, vaulting over the body of the drow they'd killed themselves, only to land and smash her wicked flanged mace into the upraised arm of another of the group. The crack of his forearm was audible, joining the dying echoes of mine's skull to fill the cavern. It overtopped even their screams and shock, followed by her shield slamming into his face with an echoing *bong*.

Past our guttural roars of anger, determination and hatred, and the screams of shock and pain of the drow, the cheering of the prisoners rose in the room. They had been crouched, terrified, three of them left more or less intact as they watched one of their companions being skinned.

Now they saw their hated enemies getting slaughtered, the tables turned in seconds as we tore through them, and they roared their approval. The drow who had fallen close to their cage was grabbed by two of the captives, pulling him tight against the bars and holding him as he thrashed.

He'd lost his knife, but the drow's superior strength showed itself as he grabbed the bars and tore himself free with a scream of pain and fury, glaring at the lesser beings who had dared to touch him with a look that promised retribution.

The look lasted only a second, as the next barrage of Magic Missiles, guided by Arrin's will, landed unerringly, one after another, in the back of the drow's neck.

Exploding a millisecond apart, they took out the upper layer and fat of his neck first, then fractured his spine, and the final one severed the spinal cord, causing him to collapse to the floor, the prisoners grabbing at him and yanking him forward. They viciously beat his skull, the only part they could reach with any force, until it cracked, then they kept on going.

The final sight that drow saw was the very prisoners that he'd excitedly dismembered and skinned for so long, beating his pain-wracked skull in.

Lydia had managed another blow to her target, dodging the clumsy stab aimed at her by her still-stunned opponent. The drow she faced had lost an eye to the flames and now had a broken right arm, the bone sticking out through the split skin of his forearm. It didn't take her long to smash him in the face with her shield a second time, knocking him back onto his arse. Barrett rushed around the other side of the fire, getting the final drow's attention and circling him, forcing his back to the blaze.

I grinned as I glanced over the guttering flames and saw Barrett neatly backing his target towards me. The blade of my naginata speared forward to take the drow in the back, erupting from his chest between a pair of ribs in a spray of blood.

Barrett wasted no time and swung a great blow, his two-handed greatsword flashing left to right and relieving his target of his head, while Lydia smashed the rim of her shield down and crushed the final drow's throat.

She spat down on the panicking, slowly asphyxiating creature, then left it to die.

We looked around the room, confused. There was nobody else here, but as the prisoners went silent, hunching down in fear, I noted the direction they stared so intently, and I looked up.

In the darkness above us, clear to my DarkVision, had I only thought to look, was the web. It was smaller than Ashrag's, but still huge by any normal sense of scale, and three sets of eyes glared down at us from it.

The web shifted as the centermost figure moved, a huge drider, a drow from the waist up, in the form of a beautiful elven woman with long white hair, pale grey skin, and covered in silver and black leather armor. From the waist down, she was a spider with eight long legs that shifted her along effortlessly, the tips giving rise to a clicking as they touched the nearest wall. Her bulbous abdomen lifted and dipped in excitement as she slowly circled us.

A movement from one of the other two occupants of her web drew my attention, and I bit down hard on my revulsion.

They were drow as well, but they had been horribly mutated somehow. In addition to the regular humanoid form, they each had several spidery legs coming out from their backs, additional eyes spread across their heads, and fangs.

I practically shit myself looking at them.

I'd been doing my best to get over my entirely fucking reasonable hatred of spiders after making the deal I had with Ashrag. After all, I was going to need to deal with her and her kin on a regular basis, but this? Fuck this shit.

When I looked back at the drider, I caught what I'd missed in my original freakout: she held a whip in her right hand, and in her left…

"Oracle!" I cried out at seeing her tiny form trapped inside a cube the drider held. She looked terrible; she'd changed to the smallest form I'd seen yet, less than three inches high, and she glowed with a sickly green light that pulsed and wavered.

"You like my pet, trespasser?" the drider asked, her voice light and relaxed, the tone far more suited to a conversation in a summer garden about a puppy. I glared up at her, my already tightly wound nerves twanging in fury at the sight of the creature that kept Oracle from me.

"Let her go," I growled up at the drider.

She laughed at me, daintily walking down the wall opposite to come to a rest atop the large building in the middle of the cavern.

"Now why would I do that? Hmmm?" she asked playfully, hanging her whip on a bony spike on her hip and tapping lightly at her ruby-red lower lip. The contrast between the grey, almost lifeless skin and her lips was jarring, not to mention the flicker of bone-white perfect teeth flashing as she spoke, long incisors visible. "You trespass here, in my home, kill my servants, and demand I give up my pet? I think not."

She smiled evilly at me, the incisors flashing as they lengthened noticeably, her pupils glowing red.

"You took her, bitch. Give her back, or I'm gonna stick this somewhere you won't enjoy!" I warned her, hefting my naginata, a touch of mana channeled into making it glow.

"Pretty," she hissed; her eyes fixed hungrily on my weapon. "I will take that from you, child. I will feed on you, let you recover, and feed again, before slowly stripping the skin from you, inch by inch, to make a blanket for my nest. You will join all your kind who trespass in the deep places of the realm, as playthings for your betters!"

I looked where she pointed, noticing piles of cloth that had been laid on the webbing, where they'd been tossed carelessly. I frowned and spat as I realized what they were. The crazy bitch had made her drow skin people, and she collected them.

"I'm gonna enjoy this, bitch." I glared up at where she crouched before focusing on Oracle. "Hold on, Oracle; I'm coming for you," I said.

I twisted, a slight movement from my left warning me just in time to avoid a small triangular blade that flashed past my face. I looked back along the line of the throw, finding that one of the mutated drow had slunk down to hang from the wall off to one side.

I threw out my left hand, a Firebolt flashing to life. My go-to spell was now almost effortless in its casting. Another notification pulsed in my vision, and I ignored it, along with the others, shouting back to my team as the spell burst against a previously invisible shield that appeared over my target.

"Kill those two; I'll take the bitch," I snarled, only to hear mocking laughter float down from the top of the building.

Her whip flashed out, cutting a furrow across my chest. The wicked barbs that tipped it flashed in the reflected firelight as it flowed back to her.

"Can you even reach me up here, mortal?" she gloated, her voice dripping with condescension. "Your kind are good for little, beside the worth of your hides, which are silkily soft, when treated right. I'll make sure...gah!" She cried out, spinning and smashing her right hand out with blurring speed, batting Bane from the air as he leaped at her.

She sent him hurtling to the floor across the room, her enhanced strength evident in the speed and force of his descent.

She lifted her right hand, staring at the cut across her forearm in disbelief, before howling in rage as she realized what had happened.

"Deathbloom!" She howled in fury, dropping Oracle's prison to the floor and spinning around, searching the webbing above her for something. In the time that it took her to identify what she needed, I'd chugged one of my more powerful mana potions, feeling my mana jump by a hundred and thirty points, then set off running, the sounds of screaming and fighting roaring to life behind me as I went.

I sprinted and jumped, planting one foot on a pile of stacked boxes to kick off and smack against the wall of the building she stood on. She was off, her legs flashing as she fled to her nest, just as I grabbed the edge of the roof, pulling hard. I dragged myself upwards, swinging my naginata over the edge to clatter against the flat roof.

I scrabbled against it, slowly sliding backwards, until I released my weapon and used both hands to pull myself atop the building.

By the time I maneuvered myself over the edge of the roof to lie on my back, the drider was in her nest, screaming abuse down at us as she frantically scuttled across it, headed towards an alcove high above the ground.

I lay there and grinned, casting Firebolt again, putting the minimum mana into it as I cast and threw it upwards, casting again as fast as I could. Firebolt after Firebolt flew true, the drider spitting acidic hatred at me as she fled, promises of what she'd do to me and mine, and laughing at my poor aim.

I grinned up at her as I fired the last two Firebolts off and whispered, "Too bad I wasn't aiming at you."

The final flaming spheres barreled through the air, passing over her head to smash into two more patches of webbing, their flames flaring out and spreading wildly. The fires were typically short-lived, but in webbing, they had found a perfect fuel: air on all sides, dust and debris stuck to it, and the silken strands went up like rags doused in gasoline.

When the last two patches caught, the tension was too much, and strands began to snap, first one, then two, then six, then dozens. The end flashing backwards under the pressure of the Drider's weight, the web came loose. She screamed in rage and fear as it fell, curling up around herself as her weight sped the end of her nest.

I had a split second in which I grinned up at her, satisfaction radiating from Amon, until reality caught up with me, and I realized what rested directly underneath her.

"Well, fuck me sideways!" I grunted, my hand moving practically of its own volition to grasp my naginata, lifting it and bracing its base against the roof. I curled up around my weapon and shoved my last few points of mana into it, causing it to flare to life, flames licking up the blade to meet the body that fell towards me.

***

Bane groaned as he shook himself, scowling up at the creature that had batted him away so easily. He hissed in pain as a row of broken ribs made their presence known. Light flared from atop the building before being snuffed out as the enormous drider smashed through the roof, vanishing inside with a scream and a crunch of falling masonry.

The walls shuddered and swayed for an eternity before falling inwards to collapse one atop the other, burying the drider as well as the one he'd sworn his life to protect.

He roared in panicked anger as he forced himself to his feet and staggered when his leg gave out, falling to the floor and staring in shock at the cloud of dust and debris that marked the collapsed building.

***

Lydia and Cam rushed at the closest of the drow mutations as soon as they'd moved down the wall. Miren sent arrow after arrow flashing through the air, only to be batted away by its impossibly fast limbs. It screamed in rage and flung itself forward through the air, a serrated silver sword held in each fist, black and silver accented armor flashing in the dark cavern.

It landed lightly, darting forward almost faster than Lydia could see. The force of the impact against her shield staggered her, before the second blade smashed her sword aside. The drow leaned back and kicked her in the chest, sending her crashing to her back.

The freakish thing spun, its long, white hair streaming behind it as it twisted, leaning back to allow Cam's massive axe to flash through the air overhead.

Cam grunted, staggering back as the drow flipped itself back upright, barely brushing the floor with the pommel of one sword and an additional chitinous leg to propel itself. As it straightened, it stabbed out, the wicked blade kissing Cam's cheek and slicing effortlessly through the flesh.

Lydia rolled, trying to get back to her feet, only to have her leg kicked out from under her, sending her crashing to the floor again in a clatter of heavy armor.

The drow easily dodged first one, then a second arrow before stabbing out and driving its sword deep into Cam's chest.

Cam let out a gasp of pain as he dropped his axe, the sight of the sword standing out from between his ribs shocking him into immobility.

Barrett and Jian were having little more luck with their drow as it flashed across the intervening distance between them. It threw tiny, three-sided daggers at them, each cutting the air with a ripping sound like silk being cut with a razor, shredding Barrett's cheek, shoulder, and upper left arm. The throwing knives sank deep into his flesh, the poison that coated them paralyzing him as he fell forward and began to bleed out.

Arrin and Stephanos fired Magic Missiles and poison-laden arrows at the mutated drow as it closed the distance between them, its magical shield flaring and dying. Just as it closed with Jian, Arrin ran out of mana, while Stephanos didn't dare fire for fear of hitting his friend.

351

Jian and the drow exchanged blows, his two scythes flashing and barely beating back the drow's single blade. It grinned at him and lunged closer, flowing past his guard like water around a boulder. One of its spider-like legs suddenly flashed out, stabbing him in the left forearm and piercing his leather bracer with ease.

He grunted and dropped that scythe, his fingers spasming as the drow lunged forward, mouth opening wide, fangs aimed for his throat.

Jian closed his eyes reflexively only to hear a hiss of displaced air as something passed over his shoulder at tremendous speed. A thunk announced its impact into the drow's open mouth, the quivering fletching of Stephanos's arrow brushing Jian's shoulder as his eyes flared open again.

The drow stood motionless, the arrow embedded deep in its throat. The tip pierced the base of its brain and quivered, the mutant creature's forward momentum vanishing as suddenly as a sparrow hitting a window.

It collapsed backwards, and Arrin frantically chugged his remaining mana potions, one after the other, flinching at the pain of the mana migraine that threatened to drop him to his knees. Stephanos stood rooted in shock, his bow string still vibrating from the killing shot.

"I—I—he was—" he muttered, and Miren screamed at him.

"Help me!" she begged, sending another arrow flashing forwards, only to be batted aside derisively by the drow standing over Cam.

Stephanos shook himself out of his shock and fumbled another arrow from his quiver. The drow-made bow granted just enough of a boost to his archery skill that he'd known he could make the shot, releasing it to blur through the air. The projectile had barely missed slamming into the back of Jian's skull, instead killing the drow as they danced their dance of death.

Now Stephanos growled, heaving back on his bow and taking aim at the drow. It slowly twisted the blade in Cam's chest, tearing his last breath free before shucking the suddenly cooling meat that had been their friend off its blade and onto the floor.

***

The creature had started to spin its blades in the air, one passing where the other had been a second before, flashing from left to right, over and back, twirling and spinning in a blatant demonstration of his skill over those he faced. A scream of rage and fear echoing from above drew its attention to its drider master as she fell, wrapped in her own web, to impale herself on my naginata, smashing the building I stood atop into rubble.

"Mistress!" it howled, a blur of light drawing its attention just in time to block a pair of arrows that split the air, hurtling towards it. It blocked one, then the other, just barely, but as it growled its hatred at them, it missed Lydia and Arrin.

***

Lydia kicked out, putting all the additional Strength points she'd invested to become a tank to good use, buckling the drow's knee and sending it crashing to the floor. It lashed out, one arm bracing itself and the other sword crashing down to skitter off her hastily lifted shield in a shower of sparks that lit the cavern briefly. A spidery limb landed wrong underneath it, snapping with a cracking sound that made it hiss in pain.

As the sparks died, Arrin's Magic Missiles lit his target back up. He'd downed two potions, both granting him an immediate jump of sixty points of mana. Combined with the boost in his regeneration, that had left him with sixty-four points. He'd forced all of it into his spell, overcharging the usual requirement of thirty mana by more than double. The resulting trio of missiles had blurred the air as he fired them straight up, only to flip over and smash down again with tremendous force.

The drow had been wearing a conical silver helmet that ran down its cheeks, leaving its mouth exposed. That's where the missiles struck, one after the other.

The first smashed his lower jaw open and down, lips blasted free, teeth shattering. Its tongue was blown backwards, its foremost roots tearing free. The second missile tore the lower jaw free of the cheek muscles that tried to restrain it. The explosion sent its teeth slicing into its face as they shattered under the force of the impact into miniature bony fragmentation grenades.

The third and final missile shredded the last remnants of the lower jaw and punched downward, piercing its throat and burrowing deep before exploding. The resulting blast sent the drow onto its back, blood fountaining upwards from the severed jugular.

It thrashed frantically, discarding its blades and grabbing at the pouch at its waist, desperately yanking a ruby-red potion out, even as others fell from the torn fabric, followed the tinkling sound of glass breaking and bouncing across the floor.

With considerable difficulty, it pulled the vial up, its head unable to rise on its own, as damaged as the muscles were. It frantically checked the potion before tugging the stopper free...its eyes widening in sudden horror in the split second between Lydia's mace swinging into view and the weapon smashing into its face. The full might of her now-two-armed swing battered its hands aside and crushed its skull in with a final, wet crunch.

The arms fell back and its right leg spasmed twice, final signals sent from the remnants of its brain spreading through the corpse. Then it was still, silence falling as the party turned to look at the still-settling rubble that marked where I'd been seconds before.

Silence filled the cavern for a heartbeat, until a groan of effort burst from Bane as he ripped the top from the small cage that held Oracle. She burst free in a flare of light and fury, flashing across the cavern to disappear into the pile of rubble, vanishing from sight.

"Cam!" screamed Miren, rushing to him and dropping to her knees, desperately tugging a healing potion out of her bag and pouring it into his mouth, pulling his head up to stare into his lifeless, glassy eyes.

The potion ran down his throat but did nothing, the life already gone from him. Stephanos crouched next to her, pulling her free and wrapping her in a grieving hug, tears running down his face as he rested a hand on his dead friend's shoulder and squeezing once in sorrow.

"Jax...Barrett," Lydia said, then coughed, dust entering her lungs as she forced herself to her feet. Staggering over to Barrett, she watched Jian moving to where Bane lay. A puddle of rapidly spreading blood lay beneath Barrett, and as she rolled him over, she winced. He was alive still, but his skin was ashen white with blood loss, and the multiple daggers that had sunk into him had been driven deeper when he'd fallen atop them.

Lydia went into automatic mode, the basic first aid she'd learned running through her mind as she worked to remove the blades. They were slowing the bleeding by blocking the damage, so when they were removed and the bleeding intensified, she moved as quickly as she could, pouring a healing potion into Barrett's frozen-open mouth, helping him swallow then spreading another out, pouring it into each of the bloody wounds.

She frantically wrapped as many injuries as she could, desperate to stabilize him before she dared move to the pile of rubble. A pile that slowly shifted, as something moved beneath it.

Arrin staggered toward the demolished structure, a mixture of desperate hope and fear filling him as he went.

He had no mana left for another spell, and the dagger he held in one shaking hand was little better than a glorified letter opener, but he was the closest, and the only one who was neither injured, trying to save a life, or comforting a grieving friend.

Stephanos and Miren forced themselves to their feet, readying arrows. Lydia tugged bandages tight on Barrett's prone form, then stood, leaving several wounds still slowly leaking blood. She moved forward, hefting her mace, and Jian joined her, his remaining healing potions used up on Bane, who lay slumped next to the remnants of the cage he'd freed Oracle from.

As they closed on the rubble, it shifted again, and they spread out, weapons at the ready.

CHAPTER THIRTY

I shifted slowly, my head foggy from pain and the multiple blows from stones I'd endured, pain tearing through me, and I froze. I felt cold, so cold, except for my right foot. I could feel it pulsing with a familiar warmth and pressure as I slowly shifted my toes, which let me know that my boot was full of blood. Well, it was that or I'd pissed myself, so I was kinda hoping it was blood, really.

I groaned again as something moved close by, and the weight pressing me down grew suddenly heavier. I tried to take a deep breath and found that I couldn't. Whatever was pressing down on me was too heavy.

I closed my eyes for a heartbeat, consciously slowing my breathing, and forced myself to focus. I slowly re-opened my eyes and began taking stock of my situation.

I remembered aiming my naginata at the drider as it fell. I'd charged it with the remnants of mana I had left, and I'd seen it pierce the bitch's chest. The impact of her body slamming into me had smashed us both through the roof, with stone falling atop us, Then the walls had toppled inward, and that was the last I'd seen for a bit.

I'd blacked out, I guessed. I could feel a lump on the back of my head, and when I brought my fingers forward, something dark stained them. It could be blood, it could be mine or hers, or it could be from the cut on the back of my hand. I swallowed hard and slowly reached out to brace myself as I figured out where I was.

I closed my eyes, feeling my heart aching when I saw the blacked out image of Cam in my interface, the sense of loss, raw and terrible. I forced them open again after a second, gritting my teeth and determined to get out of here, to reach the others, and *Oracle*.

I was face-down, my legs were lower than my chest, and I was laid at a shallow angle. I had a mound of stone under my chest, and I couldn't move my left leg. I was bleeding, and, according to the symbol on my health bar, I was down to thirty-seven points left, losing four a minute.

I had nineteen mana and figured just a few more points, and I could give myself a little healing. Then it vanished, a mana migraine flaring to life and making me gasp with the suddenness of it.

I saw my health drop by the same, and I grunted in shock, my situation suddenly far more precarious than it had been.

It was…at least, until Oracle flashed through the rubble to appear before me, and I felt her tiny arms become solid as she pressed herself against my cheek.

I sagged, a tension I'd been filled with for what felt like forever dissipating into nothingness as I lifted one shaking hand to hold her.

She was safe, she was free, and she was okay. I lay there, rocks pushing into my skin, blood seeping from a dozen wounds, and pain radiating through my body with every breath. Broken ribs scraped against each other, and tears slowly made their way down my cheeks. She was safe, and nothing else mattered at that moment.

"Jax, I'm sorry," she whispered.

I gazed down at her, a smile briefly lifting my lips as she moved back so that I could see her. The gentle light that she emitted was enough to change my vision from the greens and blacks of DarkVision to actually seeing her properly. She rested there on the palm of my hand, drawing her knees up to her chest and staring into my eyes. Her perfect face was a tear-streaked mess, her hair looked like she'd been dragged through a hedge backwards, and her clothes were simply weird. She always summoned them on a whim anyway, but she'd clearly not put any thought into making them, so her body was covered in a mixture of the outfits she normally wore, a yoga pants leg, a jeans leg, a low-cut top that abruptly transitioned into a fully decent shirt halfway across her chest. I stared at her, and I couldn't help but smile fully.

"Why?" I whispered quietly, trying not to move too much even as another point of my health dropped away.

"This was all my fault. I saw them, the drow, and I remembered. I remembered them taking me before, capturing me and taking me from my family, selling me to the empire, to be bound to the Great Tower.

"I hated them so much, and I tried to get closer to them, to see what they were doing. The next thing I knew, I was trapped. They were laughing at me, they— they—" Tears streamed down her face, and she seemed to suddenly realize where we were, and the condition I was in. "No! No, you're not leaving me!" she snarled, and she blurred away from me, leaving me in darkness. My DarkVision slowly reactivated, though my exhaustion and injuries were impacting even that. Her voice returned from somewhere beyond me.

"…inside! He's bleeding out, move it!" she snarled, before diving back down to me, slipping and flitting through gaps in the stone.

"Oracle," I whispered, and she was there, one tiny hand reaching out to stroke my cheek. "Is it dead?" I asked.

She frowned, her expression changing to one dominated by hatred as she flashed away. She sank deeper into the rubble as she searched, twisting around the enormous form I could dimly see part of, though most of its bulk was covered by the stone nearby.

Oracle returned to me a few seconds later, fear on her face.

"She's alive. She's injured, badly, but she's alive and conscious. We have to hurry."

She slipped around the rubble, vanishing up to the surface to warn the others before returning and disappearing down toward my waist. I couldn't twist around to see her, trapped as I was, so I whispered to her, a grin on my face as I pictured her face.

"Really, Oracle? Now? Can't you control yourself?"

She snorted, and I groaned as half of my slowly regenerating mana was used up again. A second later, she was there flitting back into view before me.

"I'm sorry, Jax. I know how much it hurts, but I need to use your mana to move things. I've got a potion out of your pouch; can you move your right hand down?"

I shifted slightly, pushing my hand downwards, only to shift one of the rocks I was pressed against, causing those above me to shift and press in against my chest tighter. I groaned, huffing out a breath; then I thought about the creature slowly shifting above me, testing the stability of the wreckage nearby. I growled in fury at the thought of that fucker surviving all of this and capturing Oracle again, not to mention harming my friends.

I drew as deep a breath as I could, then I twisted. The rocks shifted over me, their weight increasing as things moved. I forced my hand down, and I felt my potion pouch being pressed into my hands. The world was white with the flaring mana migraine as I yanked the pouch up, my left hand being trapped and fingers being clearly broken only drove me to greater effort, as I yanked the first potion out with my teeth.

"Drink it!" Oracle's voice came to me, a flare radiating as she used my mana to pop the cork. I guzzled it down, the headache dying in seconds as my vision cleared. Oracle blazed with power as my mana bar jumped. Thirty points appeared in seconds, then vanished as she started to heal me. I tugged out another potion, seeing the red I needed, and I chugged that as well, groaning as bones shifted, realigning and healing at tremendous speed.

"Again!" Oracle said, and I obeyed, tugging another potion out, only to have it slapped from my hand.

"No!" she cried. "This one."

And I did as I was told, my heart beating faster as I heard the drider shifting nearby. My mana jumped again, and I pulled out my final health potion, Oracle popping the cork and the improvement to my health flooding me.

My mana and health were both over fifty, and I shook my head at Oracle as she went to heal me again.

"No," I said to her. "Get back and get the others back; this isn't over yet."

She started to argue, then saw the look in my eyes and decided to trust me, flitting back up through the mess of stonework to tell the others to fall back. Then, because she knew me so well, she also told them to search the corpses for anything I could use for healing, because I was going to need it.

I braced myself, peering through the bricks and fallen stonework, and I sensed the drider shifting, gathering herself to do the same, hearing the clatter of the stones.

I took a deep breath and forced my mana back into my body, flooding myself with strength and vitality. Slamming my back against the stone that held me in place, I heaved, straining. I could feel it shifting upwards, slowly, oh so slowly.

This was draining my health and mana with every second of use, and I needed more. I still wasn't strong enough. I gritted my teeth and remembered Tommy standing over me, his hand held out to me as a gang of lads surrounded us. His nose was broken, his shirt ruined with blood, his tooth chipped. I'd been hit from behind with something, then they'd all moved out to surround us. Seven on two. All of them carrying something, a length of wood, a broken bottle, a brick. Tommy and I had been out on the lash all day, drunk as rats, barely able to stand, we were that wasted.

He'd looked down at me, holding his hand out to help me upright, and said the words.

"Go hard or go home," I whispered, then screamed as I forced my mana channels to flood my body even further, doubling the rate of use and the effect, my health dropping even faster.

"LEEEEEEROY JENKIIIIIINS!" I screamed, surging up through the stone; slabs that a normal human couldn't have budged, flung aside like cardboard.

I saw my rapidly plunging health; mana that was leaking out of me like beer from a shattered bottle, and I moved, pushing upright and lunging forward. Staggering across the uneven ground, I locked my fingers on a section of rock the size of a desk, and I *heaved!*

I lifted it above my head and looked down to see the suddenly uncovered drider glaring back up at me, her face a mess of scrapes, blood, and bruises, her fangs chipped and broken, her hair matted with blood.

I'd skewered her through the lower chest with my naginata but missed most of her organs. She floundered, trying to get to me, hatred clear on her face.

I slammed the slab down hard, driving it edge-first into the space I'd uncovered. The rock smashed her humanoid form and made her spider thorax burst.

I stepped back, the skull symbol I'd managed to hardwire into my interface somehow floating up before me in unequivocal proof of death. I screamed down at the body of the creature that had tried to take Oracle from me, had tried to kill my people, and had managed to kill Cam.

"BOOYAH, BITCH!"

Then I turned to the cavern, seeing my team circled out around me, Bane and Barrett sitting up, the prisoners gaping at me in shock.

"WHO'S YA DADDY!" I roared at them all, grinning and flexing my insanely big muscles that were even now bulging through the torn remnants of my top, like Schwarzenegger flexing as Conan…before my mana bottomed out, and I fell forward, the world going black, my health dropping back to single digits that were ticking away like a gas pump's counter in reverse…

CHAPTER THIRTY-ONE

"Jax!"

I opened my eyes. The world tilted and swam as I tried to focus, my health, mana and stamina bars all pulsing a deep, warning red. I blinked and felt hands lifting me and setting me down on something hard. A weak healing potion was being fed to me as my health bar jumped slightly.

Shapes were moving above me, and I looked up, seeing them resolve into faces, faces I should recognize, but as fast as they swam in and out of focus, I just couldn't get my brain into gear.

"JAX!"

I blinked again, focusing on a face that hovered over my own, emerald green eyes holding my gaze. I tried to make sense of what she was saying. I knew her, knew she was a woman, and important to me...but...

"Argggggh!" I roared, thrashing, as pain ripped through me from my leg.

"Jax!" The voice came again, those eyes holding my own. "We need to set your leg. It's going to hurt. I'm so sorry...this is all my fault," she said, reaching out to stroke my cheek.

Soft fingers caressed my skin. They felt cool, and strangely familiar, even as my mana bar blared another warning, the mana depletion migraine flaring again.

"I'm sorry!" the voice said, and this time, I recognized it. "I shouldn't have used our mana...I just needed to touch you, to..."

"Oracle," I whispered.

With that one word, the dam seemed to burst. Everything that had happened suddenly seemed to catch up in one go, and the noises around me finally started to make sense.

"Yes! It's me. I'm so sorry, Jax," she said. I forced myself to shake my head as I remembered everything.

"It wasn't your fault. I asked you to scout, I sent you out there, Oracle. It was my fault," I whispered to her, closing my eyes and trying to breathe through the pain as my leg was fully straightened and someone braced it in place.

"No, I—"

"I could tell you it's both your faults and neither, if that would help?" came a croak from my side, and I turned my head to find Bane watching me.

"Well, don't you look like hammered shit," I said to him, forcing a smile as Oracle disappeared off to the side.

"I hope I look better than you," Bane said.

"Never gonna happen, dude. Hate to break it to you, but you're not exactly a pretty sight...more of a Picasso."

"I'm not going to bother to answer a man who shits himself when he sleeps," replied Bane. I sat up quickly, the sudden movement making the world spin.

"Seriously?" I asked, my mood plummeting, until I saw my pants, and I felt...normal. No unexpected additional space taken up down there,...so..."You asshole," I growled, looking over at Bane, who let loose with a subsonic *thrummm* of amusement.

"You're such a dick, Bane," I added, shuffling myself upright and wincing as Oracle returned to my side, leading Lydia to me.

"You need to relax, Jax," Oracle said, landing on my shoulder.

I smiled at her and nodded at Lydia. "How did we do?" I mumbled in question, the words barely dropping from my lips in my exhaustion.

"We lost Cam." She shook her head in sorrow. "One of the drow got him. I...I'm sorry, lord, I should have been there. I should have protected him better, I—"

"No," I said, remembering the heartache of waking and seeing he was gone. I shoved myself upright and gripped her by the shoulders, forcing her to look into my eyes. "Cam's death was not your fault, you hear me? There's only one dickbag who's responsible for his death, and that's the drow. Also...maybe me. I led you all down here. I made you come with me. The buck stops here," I whispered, tapping my chest.

"He died doing what he wanted to," Barrett said, crouching down next to me and passing over a weak mana potion, which I greedily downed.

"Thanks, man," I said as the mana migraine dissipated. I drew a deep breath and looked around, checking to see if anyone else was injured. But Oracle hit me with a healing spell before I got the chance to do anything else.

I gritted my teeth then sighed in relief as the last of my broken bones realigned and bound themselves together, beginning the long, slow healing process.

"I'm going to go check on the prisoners," Lydia said, pushing herself to her feet wearily.

"So, what do you mean 'he died doing what he wanted to do'?" I asked Barrett when I could get my breath again.

"He was sick of being pushed around, of being a big man, but not being able to look after those he cared about. You took him into the team, taught him to fight."

"I didn't pick him, you did," I said. "And Lydia taught him—"

"Look, do you want me to try to make you feel better or not?" Barrett sighed, frowning tiredly.

"Sorry, dude."

"Yeah, well, look, he wanted to protect people. He wanted to feel that his life mattered, and that he wasn't weak anymore. Thanks to you, he got that. He fought drow and spiders, goblins and fucking weird lizards underground. He died as well as he could, and while he was alive, he felt valued. There's not much more you can ask for."

"Yeah that...kinda makes me feel better. Thanks, Barrett," I lied, shrugging and examining the cave we were in, all the while feeling Oracle's bond pulsing with our twinned relief and exhaustion.

The cave was about thirty meters on a side, roughly square, with a load of supplies, boxes, and other random shit piled up everywhere. In the middle of the cave was a huge pile of rubble, the remains of the structure the drow had been building. It had been a bit rough when we arrived, but me dropping their giant fucking spider-drow hybrid thingy leader through the roof kind of fucked it up, considering the walls then fell inwards.

I'd been on that roof, then in the middle of the collapsing stonework at the time, and had been buried along with her, so I felt I had a right to be a bit worn out right now.

"You know, I think I'm gonna have a little res—"

"Jax!" came a shout from my right. Lydia started over, her shout cutting me off mid-mutter.

"Feck," I whispered, and Barrett snorted in laughter.

"Hey, you wanted to be in charge," he said.

"No, I fucking didn't!" I snapped back, shooting a glare at him. "I was literally kidnapped, forced to fight in an arena, then kicked through a portal to this shithole of a realm. I had to fight a monster that made you crap yourself when I got here, and—"

"Yadda yadda yadda," Bane interjected, waving his hand and cutting me off. "We get it, 'oh, woe is you,' yadda yadda. Do you want to quit, make someone else the lord?"

"Well,...no," I grumbled.

"Then shut the fuck up and deal with it. Put your big girl pants on. You can't have it both ways...*my lord.*"

"I hate you."

"Jax!" Lydia repeated, coming to a halt and looking down at me, catching Barrett, Bane, and me trying to hide grins.

"Yeah, what's up, Lydia?" I asked. She gestured over her shoulder at the last major feature of the room, besides the tunnels that led in and out...the prisoners in their cage.

I reached up a hand and Lydia pulled me to my feet, drawing a groan from me as newly healed bones creaked in protest.

"They're the smugglers that led the last caravan, Jax, and the one they were skinning...I think she's still alive."

"What?" I asked, looking over at the flayed body. It was laid across a table, wrists and ankles secured by straps, and the skin from the back of the neck had been peeled down to the waist in one long, single sheet.

The amount of blood on the floor and lack of any sound or movements from the victim had meant we'd just ignored them so far, assuming they were already dead.... It didn't help that we'd taken a lot of injuries ourselves, which meant we'd not had time to look to the prisoners yet.

I hurried over, Oracle still sitting on my shoulder. Since she'd been freed, she'd barely moved away from me, then only to check on our people. Bane had been laid out next to me, his injuries and Barrett's being the worst of the group besides my own. Oracle took turns steadily using my mana on each of us, healing us all as quickly as she could.

Jian stood guard over the prisoners, his scythes sheathed on his back, and now twin swords on either hip, which made him look like either an utter ninja badass or an idiot, depending on how smooth the drawing of weapons went.

Despite the fight scenes in movies I'd seen, using two swords or scythes wasn't easy. Neither was drawing them from your back. I'd spent hours practicing, and I still occasionally caught the tips of my shortswords when I tried it, making me look a right dick.

"You've got to let us out!" called out one of the prisoners, and Jian growled at him.

"Be silent! Our lord nearly died to rescue you; the least you can do is show some respect!" Jian snapped at the speaker, an older, grey-haired man who gripped the bars of the cage weakly.

"You're letting her die!" he snapped back at Jian, before switching to gaze pleadingly at us as we examined the woman strapped down on the table. "Please! She's my granddaughter!"

I waved a hand at him absently to be quiet as I continued to examine her, speaking only to Oracle.

"Do you think we can put the skin back and heal it?" I asked.

"I don't see why not; we can make it regrow, so..."

"But what if it regrows the skin fully? Then she'd end up with the flap of skin; it'd hang off her."

"Cut it away, maybe? No, if we could smooth it back into place, it might heal properly, and it'd use a lot less mana."

"Why isn't she moving?" I asked suddenly, crouching down, and brushing her hair away from her face. She hung there, completely limp. Her eyes glared forward, staring at the ground fixedly. I waved a hand in front of her eyes, but there was no reaction, just a slow run of tears down her cheeks.

I checked my mana; it was sitting at seven points, far too low to heal her, and not even high enough to enable me to use my Examine spell.

"Maybe she's been poisoned? Or paralyzed?" Oracle guessed. I straightened up, moving over to the cage to look into the eyes of the grey-haired man.

"I'll make this quick, as seconds could count here. I don't have the mana to heal her, or even to examine her properly. What happened to her?"

"One of the two with the spider legs on their back bit her. That's what they did to all of us. It makes you stop resisting; you can't move or speak. When it wore off, we were all in here, and they'd take us out one-by-one, skinning us."

"How long until it wears off?" I asked.

"I don't know." He shook his head. "They did it to all of us, then we woke up here. Each time they take someone to skin, they kill them after, so nobody ever wakes up."

"Great. Okay," I said, looking around the room for inspiration. My eyes alighted on a box full of silks, and I spun back to him. "Healing potions!" I snapped, gesturing to the stacked boxes. "Did you have any?"

"We had a few, but...I don't know what happened to them! We didn't have a lot to sell anyway, it was just the couple we always took in case we needed them. For all I know, someone used them."

"Fuck," I muttered, looking around and wracking my brain for another solution. "What about herbs? Alchemy ingredients?"

"There were a few, but I don't know..."

"Everyone!" I called out, smacking my hands together hard, getting the attention of the entire cavern. "I need this place searched. we're looking for healing or mana potions, any herbs or plants, bandages, or anything else we can find. Get looking!"

"Ummm, we were already looking to use them on you and the others, Jax," Lydia whispered.

I grimaced, shaking my head. "Well, keep looking, I guess." I turned back to the people in the cage. There were four of them, three men and a woman, all naked, filthy, and starving. I looked them over and wished I had the mana for a fountain for them, but I needed all I could get.

"Okay, I need my people searching the cavern, not watching over you, so for now, until it's safe and sorted, you're staying in there. Sorry," I said, and I turned away, walking over to the remnants of the fire. The meat they'd had there was pretty messed up, having been hit by my spell, but maybe…

"The meat's human," the older man called out, and I looked at him. "The meat, the stuff that they had roasting…apart from that spider they found, all the meat they ate was…us."

I swallowed hard and backed away from the meat I'd been reaching for, my plan of giving it to the prisoners well and truly derailed.

"Okay, thanks for the heads up," I muttered and turned to the drow bodies nearby. I started searching them quickly, as did Bane and Barrett. But as Lydia warned us, they didn't have any potions, and while they had a handful of likely magical rings and gear, I'd need to Examine it to work out what it was, so they were out.

Instead, we moved on to more bodies and the rest of the cavern. The only one of us to find a potion was Miren, and that was a glowing ruby red, drawing a relieved sigh from us all. The cavern went quiet as she handed it over to me. My obvious wounds, combined with those of my teams, made the girl's grandfather speak up quickly, unaware I was communicating with Oracle already.

"It should help her, if we can smooth the skin back into place and it's not died yet…I'm sorry, Jax; I just don't know if it'll work…"

"We can give it a shot. If it doesn't work, then we'll have to cut the skin free again, then heal her up…wait, will she be able to swallow the potion, though?"

"No, as heavily paralyzed as she is, it could drown her…We'd need to wait for her to come around first."

"Please! Look, I don't know who you are, but she's half-skinned, for fuck's sake…please, she's my granddaughter. I'll do anything!" he begged, interrupting my conversation. I frowned at him before deliberately smoothing away the obvious irritation on my face.

"She's paralyzed, so she can't drink it. It'd drown her if we tried."

"I'll buy it from you!" he said quickly, cutting me off.

"For…what the hell are you going to pay for it with? You're in a fucking cage, and you're naked…anything you managed to keep back is in the 'prison wallet,' so I don't fucking want it, pal." I shook my head, and as I started to explain what we were going to have to do, he cut me off again.

"Look! I'm a wealthy man, okay? In Himnel, we're directly under it!" he said, pointing upwards. "Give her the potion, free us, and take us back to the city; it'll be worth it for you! What do you want? Weapons? Gold? Magical books? I've got them, and I can get more, I swear!"

I stopped and stared at him. I'd always planned on giving it to the girl, but fuck it, I did need help up there.

"I give this to the girl, instead of one of my team, and you'll do what, exactly?"

"What do you want?!" he growled back at me. "She's my only family; she's all I have left! Tell me what you want, and it's yours."

"I have people I need to get out of Himnel, and I need supplies and manastones," I said.

"I can arrange it! I can make it happen. I've been using the smuggler's path for years. I can lead you out. I can get you anything. I swear it. Just please, help her!"

I nodded and stepped forward. My mana was nearly high enough for me to make a single Oath, and I felt Oracle's unhappy approval as she sensed my intent.

"Then you'll swear to it with an Oath?" I asked him.

He stiffened, sagging against the bars of the cage.

"I can't," he said slowly, shaking his head. "I'm a smuggler, I already swore Oaths to the Guild. I can't swear another; they'd know, and as soon as they see me, they'll kill me…"

"Convenient," I said, stepping away from him and moving to check on the girl strapped to the table.

"No, you don't understand! You want help up there? You want me to get you gear, smuggle you out of the city? How would I do that if the Smugglers Guild are hunting me? All I'd do is draw a target on both our backs…. The Guild will reward you for this anyway—wait…here!"

He got a faraway look on his face and his lips moved soundlessly for a few seconds before my notifications flashed again.

"There! Now you know you can trust me," he said and gestured to the girl. "Please, whoever you are, she's all I have left."

Unshed tears stood in his eyes as he waited, and I shook my head, straightening up.

"Fucking hell, now I've got to work through these goddamn notific—"

I broke off, the first of the notifications just popping up into my vision, as I caught movement in the tunnel leading out of the cavern. I frantically swiped the notifications away, the resistance caused by there being so many resulting in a feeling like a porn popup in the late nineties. As soon as one began to close, another took its place, then another, as shouts and screams filled the air around me.

I finally managed to get rid of them, just in time to see the drow aiming down his bow at me, and the arrow as it took flight, speeding at my unarmored heart.

CHAPTER THIRTY-TWO

twisted at the hip, with no time to move properly, and turned to take the arrow sideways on, making as small a target as possible. I had one chance, and that was down to my insanely high Agility. I concentrated, the cavern shrinking down to the three of us: the drow archer, his arrow, and myself.

The fletching shuddered as the arrow flew towards me, the silvery metal of the arrowhead glinting with reflected firelight. Time slowed to a crawl as my miniscule amount of mana was forced into my body instinctively, the time coming closer...

In my peripheral vision, my mana ticked down from four points, to three, to two...and my left hand flashed forward, even as my right yanked the dagger on that hip free and brought it up behind my back to head-height.

The final point of mana vanished, and as time sped back up,...my left hand slammed into the arrow, fingers closing tight. I yanked backwards, the arrow's tip slicing a thin line across my right pectoral muscle as I caught it.

A look of shock crossed the drow's face at what I'd just done. I brought my right hand around, straightening my body and snapping my hips to give extra force to the throw as I'd been taught oh so long ago.

The phantom voice of West shouted at me from my memories, *"Twist and pop! Your hips ain't just for the ladies, lad! Use them, use the power in them to surprise your target, and it'll be the last fucking thing they see!"*

The dagger blurred across the room, almost too quickly to see, flipping end over end to hit the drow in the eye...hilt-first.

"Fuuuuuck!" I ground out, running forward and dipping low to sweep up a silvery drow sword from the floor on the way, wincing as my mana migraine flared anew. The goddamn throw had been perfect; the aim, the force...but to land hilt-first!

I closed the distance towards the door, Jian running ahead of me to engage another drow. I blinked, forcing myself to take in the rest of the room.

The tunnel they'd come from was close to the corner of the room, hemmed in by boxes and stacks of gear from the caravans, which made it hard to surround.

There were four of them...one archer and three melee types. One had a short spear, the other two had swords, and the archer was just starting to straighten up, clutching his face, which was blotchy with fury.

Jian parried the first stab from his drow, getting to him just ahead of me. The other two had stepped up next to the first, standing shoulder to shoulder and waiting for us to come to them. Lydia and Barrett came up on my left, while Jian was on my right. We filled the small space between them and the rest of the cavern.

The drow archer behind them glared at me, teeth gritted. He pulled back on his bow, aiming and releasing in one sure, smooth movement that cut the air between two of his companions. I dove to the ground, barely in time, sliding to a halt in front of the entire group.

The others closed in, rushing to us to help. But with the limited room and their relatively low level of skill, our own archers, Miren and Stephanos, didn't dare fire.

I rolled across the floor, a clang ringing out next to my head, letting me know just how close I'd come to dying of "damn shiny sword to the face" poisoning.

I came to a stop, then twisted frantically, lashing out with both feet and taking the furthest left drow to the floor. That gave Jian and Barrett time to face the remaining two. The archer stepped forward and drew back on his bow, aiming at me with a wicked grin as the drow I'd taken down rolled back to his feet, and I scrambled backwards.

Just as the arrow left the bow, a second, smaller dagger sprouted from the drow archer's eye, making him scream and jerk back. The blade sank up to the hilt in the eye, and I *felt* Bane's proud grin as I recognized the blade.

I'd had one thrown at me before, and I knew they were both insanely sharp and usually coated with a deadly poison.

I twisted, dodging the arrow that clattered off the stone floor next to me, and rolled back flat onto my back, bringing my legs up as high as I could before thrusting with my hips and bringing my feet down, hard.

I used the momentum to flip myself up to my feet and stabbed out, getting a glancing blow on the nearest drow's thigh before barely parrying a thrust from my left, where the drow whose legs I'd swept got back into the fight.

The goddamn drow were too fast; in close combat, without the element of surprise, one-on-one just couldn't work, not without an equalizer...

I had only one point of mana and couldn't use my newly learned Mana Overdrive...it'd be over before it was useful, and I frantically tried to think while parrying a second and third attack.

Barrett screamed in pain as his opponent dodged his swing; the short spear the drow wielded lanced forward and sank into his shoulder, punching through the gap between his breastplate and pauldron, making him drop his sword and grab at the wound.

I shoved Barrett back with my shoulder, pushing him back out of the way and off the spear, before lashing out with a quick snap kick at the drow I'd been fighting. He took the hit, grunting as it connected with his leading knee and slashed down into my leg as I pulled it back.

I staggered. The links of blackened chainmail in my leg armor crunched and split under the impact. I backed up, gritting my teeth against the pain. Oracle screamed in fury, flying forward to distract the drow and making him swing at her reflexively.

She dodged and backed up, hovering between us and hissing at them like a scalded cat as I backed up further.

Blood ran hot down my leg. I couldn't put my weight on that leg properly now, and the bleeding debuff appeared in my vision again, making me grit my teeth and check my mana...two points. It wasn't enough!

I moved back again as the drow I'd been facing off against lashed out with his sword. The spear-wielder moved to flank Jian as Lydia appeared, having been on the far side of the cavern when the fight started.

She barreled between Jian and me, screaming in fury as her people were beaten back. The tank in her soul rose to the surface as she jumped at the spear-wielder. Leading with her shield, she smashed her opponent from his feet as she put all of her armored bulk behind it.

The *boing* sound of metal hitting the drow echoed around the clearing. Lydia grunted as her target fell to the floor and rolled back. He regained his feet with a growl of fury as he stepped into the tunnel, fumbling in his pouches.

"Squad UP!" Lydia screamed, stepping forward and taking the sword strike from my opponent on her shield, while striking out at Jian's target with her mace.

Her sudden arrival turned the tables for Jian drastically, as a raging wall of pissed-off tank joined the fight.

The drow she was facing dodged the mace strike but couldn't dodge both of Jian's attacks, as he used a skill he'd gained from the books Oracle and I had given him.

Icewind's Fury coated his blades in a layer of magical ice for a handful of seconds, magical winds speeding up his attacks as he landed a half-dozen minor cuts in less than four seconds. His opponent leaped back, cursing as each cut added a chilled debuff, reducing his speed by two percent.

I backed up farther, gripping my thigh as blood ran from the wound. Bane threw another dagger at the spear wielder. The dark elf ducked then threw something back that landed just in front of his companions, shouting something that made them disengage immediately.

All three fled down the tunnel away from us as noxious green smoke rose from the shattered vial. Everyone backed up immediately, Jian swearing up a storm as his ability ran out.

"Stop!" I shouted, gritting my teeth as I spoke through the pain.

"Poison!" Lydia confirmed as she coughed and backed up.

"How bad?" I asked. She spat on the floor, backing away further.

"Ten points a second for twenty seconds…almost half my pool," she managed to get out around a hacking cough. I stared at her in surprise, realizing that meant she had over four hundred health. Considering she was only level twelve, that was impressive.

"Okay, people, everyone stay back, but be ready!" I called, and I looked over to Oracle, who hovered nearby, as a thought occurred to me. "Oracle, that bitch of a drider was desperate to get somewhere. Is there anything up high she could have been headed to?"

Oracle spun around, searching the ceiling and walls until she spotted a recess high up on one side.

"There," she said, pointing. "There's a lot of webs over there, but she kept the other two away from it. It might be—"

"Her stash," I finished for her, nodding. "Get up and check it out, please. If anyone had healing or mana potions in here, it'd be her."

As Oracle vanished up into the web-covered darkness, I turned back to the rest of the group.

"Barrett!" I said, and he looked over at me. "Are you okay?"

"Not so much," he replied, gritting his teeth. I checked my mana, five points…nowhere near enough.

"Miren, get the healing potion and give it to Barrett," I ordered, and immediately the prisoners started to complain, the older man going so far as to try to grab the potion before she could get it.

Bane was there in an instant, blades drawn and ready. Like Lydia, he'd been too far away to get involved in the fight and had to make do with throwing knives. Now, he slashed at the hand that reached for the potion, and the older caravanner jumped back with an oath.

"Are you crazy?!" he snapped at Bane, before turning to plead with me as Miren scooped up the potion and ran to Barrett. "Look, we can do a deal, okay? She needs that!"

"I can heal her," I said, cutting him off with a shake of my head. "I've not got the mana right now, but when I recover it—"

"She could be dead by then!" he snapped.

"And if we lose this next fight with the drow, she will be! Barrett…drink the potion," I ordered through gritted teeth, knowing the old man could see my leg and the spreading puddle of blood forming around my boot.

"Aye, sir," Barrett said before downing it. He stiffened as the healing rushed through him, knitting muscles and flesh together, pain flooding him for a few heartbeats before he sighed in relief.

"Now everyone get ready; those dickbags are out there somewhere, and we need to kill them," I ordered, then called up to Oracle. "Anything?"

"I can't tell. There are so many webs covering the entrance, and they've got magic in them, so I can't just pass through."

"Bane," I snapped. "Get your arse up there and help her."

"Yes, Jax," he said with a nod, rushing across the room to kick off the wall, grab onto a rocky protrusion, and start the climb.

"Lydia, Barrett, and Jian, get ready by the tunnel. Miren, Stephanos, either side of them with your bows ready. Arrin, I want you with these assholes. If they try something like stealing a fucking healing potion we *need* again, burn them." I snapped the orders out, making sure the caravanners heard the last ones. Some of them swallowed hard, while the grey-haired older man just looked pissed.

I hobbled to a stool that had been knocked over during the fighting and straightened it, sinking onto it with a groan as my leg bled some more. I looked down at my pants, seeing the bloody footprints I'd left in my wake, and the continual bleeding status that told me I was losing one health per second until I dealt with my wound.

I pulled the cinches on either hip and forced myself to my feet, dropping my pants and getting a low whistle from Lydia.

"Yeah, yeah," I muttered, forcing a grin, knowing she was doing it to try and raise spirits after our little ass-kicking.

Before I could do anything else, Miren was there, setting her bow on the floor and pulling a bandage out of her pack to wind around my leg, pulling it tight and getting another groan from me.

"Best I can do…," she whispered apologetically.

I shook my head, forcing my breath out between my teeth as I stood, letting her help me into my pants again as the bleeding debuff vanished.

"It's what I needed, Miren...thank you," I replied, forcing a tired smile and catching my naginata as Arrin threw it over to me, having recovered it from the corpse of the drider on his way to the prisoners.

"Cheers, dude," I said, nodding to him. I forced myself to walk over to stand closer to the webbing that Bane was climbing up to.

I checked my mana, finding that I was up to...six points of mana now, and I ground my teeth at the slow regeneration. The debuff from using the Mana Overdrive was there, along with my lowered regeneration, and it was kicking my ass!

I moved back to stand with the others by the entrance to the tunnels and hefted my naginata, hoping we'd have time to get the team up to strength before the next round.

Bane reached the thick webs covering the recess and started cutting into them, swearing as he tried to saw them apart. Aloud whine sounded from the tunnel the drow had fled down. Flashes in the distance, then a loud explosion, echoed off the walls. Dust blew into our faces as the air hurtled towards us and screams of pain and fury rose in the distance.

We looked at each other in confusion before I started snapping out orders.

"Jian, Barrett...get those crates over here and arrange them in front of the tunnel. Lydia—you, Stephanos, and Miren keep watch...Bane! Get that stash found! Arrin, I want one Firebolt down that tunnel right damn now. See how far you can get it before it hits something."

Arrin fired his Firebolt off without his usual flair, the loss of his friend clearly weighing on him. It flew down the tunnel to impact on a wall over a hundred meters away, illuminating a bend in the path.

"Okay, nothing coming yet, but be ready," I muttered.

I stood alongside Lydia, naginata lowered and pointing toward whatever might try and attack us, when my notifications started blaring again, the sped-up flashes and additional numerals on the image letting me know I'd just received several more...

I growled at the timing, but waited until Jian and the others had formed a small defensive wall out of the stolen shit in the tunnel, before moving out of the way and leaning against the wall behind some boxes to start pulling them up.

Congratulations!

You have killed the following:
- 1x Drider, level 43 for a total of 11,000xp
- 2x Drow Soldiers of various levels for a total of 1,260xp

As leader, you receive a portion of the experience earned by troops when they fight under your command:
- 1x Drow Torturer for a total of 2,000xp
- 6x Drow Soldiers for a total of 9,600xp
- 2x Drow Spiderkin for a total of 10,400xp

Total experience earned: 22,000xp

As party leader, you gain 25% of all experience earned

Progress to level 15 stands at 68,893/140,000

Congratulations!

You have cleared the Smugglers Path and have the prerequisite authority and abilities to claim this hidden location, adding it to your territory as an occupied base. As this location holds less than 10% percent of sentients that are actively hostile to your rule, it can be claimed.

Do you wish to annex this territory now?

Yes/No

The last notification had me blinking in surprise, and I pulled up the quest notification...It'd credited me with the deaths of the last three drow, but comparing the experience list, I realized that we'd not gotten experience for them.

Congratulations!

You have completed a Quest from your Goddess: Keep Your Word

> You have given your word to an ancient Greater Cave Spider Queen. Kill her enemies, grant her and her brood safety and food, and she will consider her Broken Oath to be renewed, binding her and all her brood to your orders and laws. You must kill 35 drow and their leader.
>
> **Drow Killed**: 35/35
>
> **Locations Cleared**: 3/3
>
> **Drow Leader Killed**: 1/1
>
> **Reward**: Oracle's Freedom, Sworn Allegiance of 1 Greater Cave Spider and her Brood, access to Cave Spider Silk, Isthic'Mirtin's Treasury and 62,500xp

Someone else had killed them, damn fast and noisy, and who or whatever it was, was headed this way.

At the end of the tunnel came a blue light, as a shimmering form stepped into view and started towards us, at the exact moment that Bane shouted down to me.

"I'm in! There's a load of gear up here, including some potions, and—"

"Just get them and get down here!" I snapped at him, readying myself for another fight. The notifications had said there were less than ten percent actively hostile to me. Was that a general notice or a hint about how many were down here? I shook myself and dismissed the prompts without making a choice.

We had a half-circle of boxes arranged a few feet back from the tunnel, giving us something to hide behind. I moved out ahead of the boxes to stand between them and the tunnel, with Arrin in the middle behind me, Miren and Stephanos on either side of him, and Lydia and Barrett flanking my right and left directly.

Now that we had a chance to fall back behind cover if need be, I felt a little better about things, but judging from the swirling blue-white radiance that was approaching down the tunnel, we were facing at least one magic user...hence us being on this side of the barrier. At least we would be able to rush the fucker if we needed to.

I stood waiting, naginata in hand, breathing deeply as Bane clambered down the wall. Oracle had come to hover just behind my shoulder, and I listened to the quietly ragged breathing of my teammates while we watched the fucker approach.

It took just over a minute for the swirling light to resolve into a mage shield. The length it had been held alone served as a warning to the depths of their mana pool, when they stopped, and a calm voice called out.

"We seek a truce!" The words echoed for a second, while I considered. Could this be a trick? A trap?

"Fuck it," I muttered before raising my voice and calling out, "Then drop the shield and let us see you!"

"Do you give Oath that you do not intend an attack? Do you agree to a truce?" The voice came again. I blinked, having never thought of this use for the Oaths. I looked to Oracle, who seemed shocked.

"What's wrong?" I asked her, and she moved up alongside me.

"Ask them to swear their Oath by their name and by the empire," she whispered. "Offer yours as Acknowledged Scion of the Imperial Line."

"I...I ask you to swear by your name...and by the empire? I am Jax, Scion of the Imperial—"

"Acknowledged!" Oracle hissed, and I glared at her, before going on.

"Jax, *Acknowledged* Scion of the Imperial Line."

There was a long pause, and I could hear muttering behind the shield before a different voice called out.

"I am Yen, Speculatores of the Dravith Cohortes Praetoriae, and I give Oath to a truce of one hour with Jax, who claims Acknowledged Scion of the Imperial Line."

"Say you accept the Oath and offer your own!" Oracle snapped quickly to me.

"I...uh...accept the Oath given by Yen, and I offer my own, as Jax, Acknowledged Scion of the Imperial Line, to one hour of truce."

The dregs of my mana were ripped from me, and Oracle hissed in pain as some was taken from her as well. I coughed blood up, staggering as pain ripped through me, my health dropping by a third. But as I straightened, wondering what had gone wrong, the shield between us was dropped.

Three people stepped forward, two tall elves dressed all in greys and greens, layered over armor that looked damn well-made, and a thing that looked like an eagle with legs and leather armor. I stared at it for a long second before Oracle hissed at me, and I straightened up, looking back at them all.

They stepped forward into the cavern, stopping and looking at our ready weapons pointedly until I shook myself and snapped out an order to my team.

"Stand down, people. Bane, where the hell are those potions?"

"Here," said Bane, stepping out from behind a box near the trio and walking over, ignoring their glares. He passed me a mana potion first, and I bit down on the cork, pulling it out and spitting it onto the floor before chugging it. Oracle went to work almost before I'd swallowed the last drops, channeling Battlefield Triage into me with tremendous power. I stared in shock as my mana bar barely dipped before refilling to full. I grinned through gritted teeth as she went on, hitting Barrett and Bane next.

"It's considered bad form to cast spells under a flag of truce, friend," the first elf said, glaring at me.

"Aye, well, is it better or worse form to let people die while we talk?" I asked, gesturing to the wounded girl.

"Hmmm..."

"Exactly. Look, I don't know who you are, beyond one of you is called Yen, but I've had a pretty shitty day so far. So why don't you fill me in on who you are and what you want while I heal her, or we can just cancel the whole 'truce' thing and go back to killing each other?" I said, gesturing towards the girl strapped to the table at the back of the room.

I turned without waiting for an answer and walked in her direction, checking my mana levels.

"Bane, how many—" I started to ask before he threw a second potion to me. I snagged it out of the air and looked at it, noting the filigreed silver chasing on the bottle and the thicker glass it was made from.

Greater Potion of Mana		Further Description *Yes/No*	
Details:		This mana potion will restore 400 mana immediately, followed by a further 20 mana per second for 90 seconds.	
Rarity:	Magical:	Durability:	Potency:
Rare	Yes	99/100	9/10

"Damn," I muttered, seeing the strength of the potion. My mana was rising steadily and close to full again. I pocketed the potion and drew in a deep breath as I walked over to where the girl had started to make faint sounds, her grandfather crouching down next to her.

"Oracle, you ready for this?" I asked, and she flew over to land on the table by the girl's side. She began to examine the damage again, and I motioned the older prisoner to step back. "You owe me for this, you old fart."

"I'd have done it anyway, but you offered payment and then acted the arsehole, so now you'll be helping me get my people out when we get to Himnel, right?" I snapped at him.

"Now, see here!" the second elf said, stepping forward before being shushed by the first, who watched me with calculating eyes.

"We can wait…Jax," the first elf said.

I looked into her eyes, recognizing the voice as the one who'd spoken earlier. I mentally tagged her as Yen and went back to the girl.

"I'll be with you soon," I said, before gently easing the peeled skin back into place on the girl's back.

I pressed it down, shifting it to rest as close to where it would naturally as I could, hisses and whimpers of pain coming from the girl as the paralysis began to wear off.

"I'm sorry," I apologized, crouching down to meet her gaze, her eyes tracking me for the first time

Oracle and I began to cast Battlefield Triage, focusing on her head at first, purging her of any damage as far as we could. We slowly moved down, the first few seconds building up a picture of the greater damage as the spell attempted to fix everything at once. We examined the injuries to her back, guiding the skin to knit together, flowing like thick cream to join up with the careful slices that had been used to peel her skin back in one intact section.

I sank my consciousness in deeper, feeling the skin on her back as I did so. It'd begun to die, being without blood for so long, but as we worked, the cells began to spread, slowly rebuilding. The cells that were totally dead began to slough off, while healthy cells grew in their place. Injured cells stayed, gradually repairing, and Oracle and I went on.

She provided the majority of the specialist knowledge that made the spell work, combining her own magical knowledge with the spells she had known details of, while I brought the actual power and ideas from my own past.

Skin regrew, sealing the peeled slab back down, even as a band of fire whipped out, passing between the skin and the muscles, making her scream in pain but removing anything that was alien to her body.

The drow had left all sorts of crap behind: hair, crumbs of food, and worse when he'd been working. The only thing he'd cared about was clearly making sure the skin was perfect. Her body would have died from infection just as surely as blood loss and dehydration if she'd somehow survived the experience.

Minutes passed, and I chugged the second potion; still, I was gasping as the final sections reattached. I fell to my knees, totally drained.

It was done. Her body was repaired, and judging from the trembling and sobbing, she was both alive and conscious.

I forced myself to my feet, shakily drawing in great gasps of air, as Lydia and Miren undid the leather restraints and helped the girl free.

After everything that I'd just done, the last thing I was expecting was the slap that sent me staggering.

"I hate you!" the girl screamed, running into the waiting arms of her grandfather.

"Are you shitting me?" I growled, rubbing my chin and glaring at her. The previous inhabitants of the cage were glaring right back at me, and I threw my hands up in annoyance. "I just saved you all, and I get this?"

I turned back to the waiting three, noting they looked unconcerned by being surrounded by my people, and I wondered if that was down to the Oath or…

"Don't!" Oracle said in the silence of my mind, and I turned to look at her in confusion.

"If you use a spell on them under a truce it'll be broken!"

"I was just going to—"

"To cast a spell on them!"

"Yeah,…Examine, not fucking Firebolt!"

"Is it a spell?"

"You know it is!"

"Well, do you want to die?"

"Noooo…"

"Then don't! Besides, if they're who they say they are, you need them. Be nice, and for all our sakes, don't annoy them!"

I shook my head, turning from Oracle and looking the three over again before gesturing to a handful of chairs that had been knocked about during the fighting.

"Let's take a seat, then," I offered, and the eagle-looking motherfucker snorted through some truly impressive nostrils on the top of his beak.

"Arrrrrk! I do not…'sit'…!" he screeched, then shook his head like a dog, turning on the horizontal, and fluffed his wings up. A huge, flanged mace clattered against his armor where it hung from his waist.

"Well, no offense, but I'm going to," I said and walked over to the chairs. I could feel Oracle facepalming, but I was past being sociable today. "Nice mace, though," I told the bird in passing, and he patted it in response.

"You have a good eye," he said, nodding jerkily.

"I'm a fighter." I smiled faintly. "I know the difference between something that's built to look pretty and something that's a real weapon."

"Hmmm," said the second elf, stomping over and turning a chair over.

He sat down with a smooth grace that surprised me. I'd heard in fantasy that elves were graceful, but so far most that I'd met had just been regular people. These fuckers, though, they moved like silk. While he sat, the first elf, Yen, pulled up another chair and reversed it, sitting down facing me.

"Why do you do that?" I asked. She blinked, glancing down at the chair.

"Sit like this?" she asked, and I nodded. "Makes it harder for someone to stab you in the belly."

She had clearly done it so many times, it was reflex now.

"Sooo, you've either not a lot of faith in the Oaths, or..."

"A bit of both," she admitted. "I'm always going to distrust anyone who claims to be a scion of the imperial line after so long, and I expect there are several ways around the basic Oath we exchanged."

"What do you want, then?" I asked gruffly, unsure of where this was going.

"I want proof of who you are," she said simply.

"Well, I want a cold beer and a blowjob, but I don't see me getting either of those," I replied without thinking, before wincing at the glare I got from her. "Ah...look, what proof do you want, and who the hell are you? What are you expecting out of this truce?"

"Do you know who we are?" Yen asked.

I shook my head. "No."

"Yes."

I turned to Oracle and gestured her forward from where she'd been hovering behind me, for some reason.

"Okay, Oracle, this is Yen, and..." I asked, gesturing to the other two.

"Tang. Speculatores Cohortes Praetoria," the second elf stated proudly, glaring at me.

"I am Amaat! Speculatores Cohortes Praetoria!" the bird man said, and I nodded to them.

"Well, I'm Jax, as I said, and this is Oracle." Oracle settled gingerly on my shoulder, nodding to them.

"Very well; perhaps your companion would like to explain who we are?" Yen asked.

"I know who you claim to be, and I know who the Speculatores Praetoria were," Oracle said slowly. "If you want us to treat you as Speculatores Praetoria, we want proof, too."

"Okay, look, I'm clearly the only one who doesn't know what the fuck is going on here," I said, rubbing the bridge of my nose. "So, do you have any proof of who you are? And how can we prove who we are?"

"I suggest a second Oath. The Oath of Truce would have failed if we didn't use our identities correctly, but it is...too generalized for something this important. Use these exact words in the Oath: 'I' then your name 'swear by my soul and the empire to speak no lie for the next five minutes. I swear by my soul that every word I utter will be the absolute truth, as best I know it...—and I will swear the same."

"You swear it first," I said, looking from one to another of them, "And you all swear it, not just Yen."

"I, Yen of the Speculatores Cohortes Praetoria, swear by my soul and the empire to speak no lie for the next five minutes. I swear by my soul that every word I utter will be the absolute truth as best I know it," Yen said flatly, without hesitating.

"I, Tang of the Speculatores Cohortes Praetoria..."

Each of them spoke the words, and I waited until the end to say my own.

"I, Jax of the Imperial Line, swear by my soul and the empire to speak no lie for the next five minutes. I swear by my soul that every word I utter will be the absolute truth as best I know it." I repeated after them, my mana dipping drastically before taking a deep breath and meeting each of their gazes.

"I am Jax. My birth name, as far as I know, was Jack Smith, but I chose Jax as the name to call my own. I was acknowledged as a Scion of the Imperial Line by Amon, the Eternal Emperor," I said. A quiver ran through me as the magic of the Oath examined me then relaxed its grip. I could feel it inside me, my own mana prowling through my body, examining my words for truth.

I looked at the three of them, seeing shock clear on their faces, and I gestured to them.

"Come on, then. Your turn."

"I...I am Yen. The name of my birth was Yen'ma Rultahir, and I chose Yen as my common name. I am a scout leader in the Dravith Cohortes Praetoria, and I serve the empire. I acknowledge my Oath and its validity."

There was silence as the other two looked at Yen in shock, and I frowned as I pieced together the meaning behind the ritualistic phrases.

As I did, I realized I felt something. I'd been feeling it all along, but compared to my need to reach Oracle, I'd been ignoring it. I felt something that tied me to Yen. I felt a...pull...a need...then Tang spoke up.

"I am Tang. The name of my birth was Ta'angint Theron, and I chose Tang as my common name. I am a scout in the Dravith Cohortes Praetoria, and I serve the empire. I acknowledge my Oath and its validity."

"I am Amaat. I took my name in battle, and I chose Amaat as my common name. I am a scout in the Dravith Cohortes Praetoria, and I serve the empire. I acknowledge my Oath and its validity."

With each statement, the pull grew like a trio of strings pulled taut and struck inside my soul, making them vibrate. The vibration built gradually, rippling through me, a fourth adding to them as another series of notifications sprang to life, making the world shake around me.

I felt HIM as he...moved forward somehow. My conscious mind was pushed gently aside as Amon moved into primacy.

He opened my eyes, and I felt my lips move; my mana was used as I was wrapped gently in the threads of souls.

"I am all that remains of Amon, the Eternal Emperor, and I formally claim my host Jax as Scion of the Imperial Line. I acknowledge your Oaths, and I accept them in the spirit offered. I pass them to my Scion; may he be worthy of your devotion."

I blinked as he settled back, releasing his hold on me. The world seemed to shake as I flowed forward, back into full control of my body.

"I—I—" I muttered in shock as the vibrations grew…

All three of the newcomers dropped to one knee on the floor and looked up at me.

"All Hail Jax! Hail Scion of the Empire!" they chorused in unison.

EPILOGUE

Thomas spat blood across the flagstones and gritted his teeth, pushing hard with both arms and coming back to his feet.

The aspirant across from him grinned and gestured for him to step back into the ring. Thomas growled in anger and swept up his gladius again, flipping his shield over and tightly gripping the leather handle sewn into its reverse.

"Still want to play?" Coran shouted out to him, and Thomas nodded, saving his breath. "You're a stubborn fucker, you know that?" the aspirant said, shifting his stance into a ready position again as the sergeant called the round to resume.

"Yeah, well, blame my brother. He hits harder than you," Thomas replied, dropping his shield and throwing the sand he'd concealed in that hand forward, blinding his opponent.

Coran backed up quickly, blinking and trying to see, only to have Thomas's sword smash down on his forearm, making him drop his own weapon.

"Oh, you cheating bastard!" Coran cursed him, shaking his hand and trying to get the feeling back.

Thomas grabbed his shield and yanked him forwards, his gladius coming to a rest over Coran's clavicle. "Maybe, but I won, didn't I?" he asked, stepping back. He picked up a water skin and poured it over Coran's face, giving him good-natured abuse as he washed the sand away from his training partner's eyes.

"Thomas!" came the shout from his left, and both men straightened reflexively, their hard-taught and now instinctual response to the voice of their master, Sir Edvard Tunnik, Paladin of Nimon and Lord of the Third Legion.

"Sir!" Thomas responded, ramrod straight as he stood at attention.

"I saw the end of that fight, boy; what did you do?" Edvard asked, and Thomas swallowed hard before replying.

"I cheated, sir! I threw sand in Aspirant Soldier Coran's eyes when he wasn't expecting it."

"Cheated? Did someone make up a fucking rulebook for war when I wasn't looking?" Edvard's response came. The tall man stepped up close to the pair standing in the ring.

"No, sir," Thomas responded, and Edvard nodded.

"Damn right, son. I don't give a shit how you win, just that you do it." The paladin turned and shouted out to the rest of the training cadre, bringing a momentary halt to the afternoon session as the baking summer sun reflected off his black and gold armor.

"Fall in and assemble on this pit!"

Everyone dropped whatever they were doing and sprinted inward in response to the order, sergeants and corporals quickly surrounded by the aspirant soldiers of Nimon's Legion.

"Since this boy arrived, he's fought easily half of you and beaten most. Does anyone dispute his rise from Slave-Aspirant to Aspirant Soldier?"

Thomas's heart sped up. To move from a Slave-Aspirant to an actual Aspirant Soldier was a huge thing. It meant he'd been accepted; he'd gain the right to move around the barracks freely. His slave collar would be removed! He could pick his specializations!

"I dispute!" A voice rose from his left, and Thomas locked eyes on Frankin, a huge half-ogre recruit from the prisons, the same as he'd been.

"I dispute!" came the inevitable shout from Frankin's bootlicker, Grey Rat. In short order, a dozen other voices rose. The obvious approval that Edvard had shown Thomas since lifting him from the rabble had fostered simmering resentment, and now it was coming to the fore.

"Well, Thomas?" Edvard asked, and Thomas let an evil grin curl his lips.

"I claim the right to face my disputers!" Thomas growled; the words had been beaten into him since he'd joined. The Legion of Nimon trained its aspirants well, and the ritual aspects of service combined with the hard training, good food, and Spartan methods to create a force that excelled. He'd been waiting for this day to come; that it had come so quickly had only angered others even more.

The ritual of challenge usually only had two or three aspirants stepping forward to take out disagreements on each other; Thomas had thirteen opponents moving forward.

"That's what I wanted to hear, boy!" Edvard grinned and stepped back, clearing the ring.

"I claim the right to stand beside my Battle-Brother," came a voice from Thomas's right. He glanced over, shocked at seeing Coran still standing beside him.

"Granted," Edvard replied, and he nodded to a corporal who stood next to the iron bell.

"This day, Thomas, Slave-Aspirant, fights to advance his soul. He fights for the right to stand as a full Aspirant Soldier in the service of Nimon, hoping to one day earn his place as a legionnaire of the Third Legion. His Battle-Brother, Coran Steelswitch, claims his right to stand with him as he faces thirteen disputers. This bout will be decided before the eyes of the Death God."

The bell rang three times, its iron celebration filling the air, and everyone who gathered felt the attention of a god settle on them. The air grew heavy and oppressive, colors seemed to dim, and the sun vanished behind a veil of dullness. The aspirants shivered, many feeling the touch of Nimon for the first time.

Thomas looked over at Edvard, watching the man shiver in ecstasy at the presence of his dark god before they locked eyes. Edvard gave him a nod of approval, and the final, fourth clang of the bell filled the air, before being drowned out in the growls of bloodlust that rose from the thirteen men and women surrounding Thomas and Coran.

The pair moved fast, shifting to stand back-to-back, Thomas grabbing the large, square shield up from the floor and gripping the worn leather bands.

"Thanks, Coran," he muttered to his friend and got a grunt in reply.

Thomas had worked his ass off to get this chance. He might never be free again. He'd accepted that when he'd sworn his Oath to Nimon, but at least he wasn't being beaten and tortured daily anymore...well, no more than anyone else.

He'd resigned himself to Nimon's service, knowing the only way he'd ever be free to walk the world again would be if he could reach the rank of Legionnaire Specialist and become a Stalker, or by becoming a legionnaire and serving his full term of thirty years.

The only way he could do either of those things was by kicking everyone else's ass here.

A scream from his left was all Thomas needed to hear as they all started in on him, the first running and smashing his sword down into the middle of Thomas's shield, only to have it shrugged off. A wooden gladius took the eager beaver in the chin, lifting him off his feet to collapse moaning on the floor, two teeth lighter.

Thomas didn't wait for the idiot to fall. He knew enough to know two things; the fool was out of the fight, and the real fighters would be coming as soon as he was distracted. He ducked, a second's breeze marking the passage of an arrow that missed as it flew overhead. Its thick, cloth-wrapped tip would leave a nasty bruise if it hit, and he didn't need the pain.

Lashing his sword out to deflect the next sword, Thomas straightened then kicked its wielder in the balls hard enough to lift him from his feet. The catman let out a high-pitched yowl of pain as he collapsed.

Thomas grinned, twisting to find his next opponent. He *lived* for this shit.

THE END OF BOOK TWO

BANE

UnderVerse Omnibus Two

20th September 2022

(Combining books 3&4 of the UnderVerse)

The city of Himnel is a cesspit of slavery, violence, and back-stabbing, in the midst of a full on industrial revolution, barely kept on the rails by drugs and magic. Jax has found himself in the middle of it.

Jax has made enemies on all sides, but he's found allies as well. They're the kind that you can stand with your back against, even if some of them might help themselves to your wallet when you do.

Robbing the city blind might seem like a tall order, but he doesn't care about the odds, and when all you've got is a hammer, everything looks like a nail.

Add to that, the Sunken City is out there, infested, overrun and crumbling, but it's also full of loot, and Jax damn well needs to get his act together, so once he's robbed the city, why not stop off there for a little 'recreational looting'?

If it's not claimed, it's available, after all…

Get ready for the second Omnibus of the UnderVerse, and the Rise of the Titan!

UNDERVERSE OMNIBUS THREE

8th November 2022

(Combining books 5&6 of the UnderVerse)

Jax might not have started the war, but he'll damn well finish it. But can he and his allies make it through unscathed?

When Jax entered the UnderVerse, it was with the plan of finding his brother, holing up somewhere and maybe, just maybe, trying to take over the world. He's making progress in all of those goals, but maybe not in the ways he wanted.

The God of Death has personally intervened to send his Dark Legion against Jax and his people, with the aim of grinding the upstart Empire usurper into dust. Jax has refugees by the hundreds, Legionnaires of the Empire by the score and best of all, a team that are cheering as he spits in the God of Death's eye.

The sun is setting though, with new enemies appearing and hidden forces being revealed.

The War of the Gods is growing, and when the sun rises again, it'll be in a changed Realm…

Finish the journey of UnderVerse Season One with Omnibus 3!

UnderVerse 7

6^h December 2022

The war between Jax and Nimon is on hold, the borders established, and a form of peace should be descending on the Imperial Territory of Dravith…

But life rarely goes as Jax hopes.

New and old enemies are on the horizon, the land itself is disturbed, and worst of all, the Gods are not all he believed they are…

The Dark Tide Rises…

REVIEWS

Hey! Well, I hope you enjoyed the book? If so, please, please remember to leave a review, its massively important, as not only does it let others know about the book, it also tells Amazon that the book is worth promoting, and makes it more likely that more people will see it.

That in turn will hopefully keep me able to keep writing full time, while listening to crazy German bands screaming in my ears, and frankly, I kinda really like that!

If you want to spread the good word, that'd be amazing, and if you know of anyone that might be interested in stocking my books, I'm happy to reach out and send them samples, but honestly, if you enjoy my madness, that's massive for me.
Thank you.

FACEBOOK AND SOCIAL MEDIA

If you want to reach out, chat or shoot the shit, you can always find me on either my author page here:

www.facebook.com/JezCajiaoAuthor

OR

We've recently set up a new Facebook group to spread the word about cool LitRPG books. It's dedicated to two very simple rules, 1; lets spread the word about new and old brilliant LitRPG books, and 2: Don't be a Dick!

They sound like really simple rules, but you'd be amazed…

Come join us!

https://www.facebook.com/groups/litrpglegion

I'm also on Discord here: **https://discord.gg/u5JYHscCEH**

Or I'm reaching out on other forms of social media atm, I'm just spread a little thin that's all!

You're most likely to find me on Discord, but please, don't be offended when I don't approve friend requests on my personal Facebook pages. I did originally, and several people abused that, sending messages to my family and being generally unpleasant, hence, the *Author* page.

I hope you understand.

PATREON!

Okay then, now for those of you that don't know about Patreon, its essentially a way to support your favorite nutcases, you can sign up for a day or a month or a year, and you get various benefits for it, ranging from my heartfelt thanks, to advance access to the books, to signed books, naming characters and more.

At the time of me writing this, the advanced Patreon readers are getting a sneak peek at Age of Steel, and are voting on the next batch of Character Art as well, so yeah, you get plenty for the support!

There's three wonderful supporters out there that I have to thank personally as well; ASeaInStorm, Leighton, and Nicholas Kauffman, you utter legends you. Thank you all and as promised, the characters are in the works.

www.patreon.com/Jezcajiao

Note: All character details, maps and spell/ability details are on World Anvil:

https://www.worldanvil.com/

This requires an account to access, but a free one is fine, once logged in, search for 'UnderVerse' and the covers should show which is mine.

RECOMMENDATIONS

I'm often asked for personal recommendations, so if this book has whetted your appetite for more LitRPG, please have a look at the following, these are brilliant series by brilliant authors!

Ascend Online by Luke Chmilenko

The Land by Aleron Kong

Challengers Call by Nathan A Thompson

SoulShip also by Nathan

Endless Online by M H Johnson

Silver Fox and the Western Hero, also by M H Johnson

The Good Guys/Bad Guys by Eric Ugland

Condition: Evolution by Kevin Sinclair

Space Seasons by Dawn Chapman

The Wayward Bard by Lars M

LITRPG!

To learn more about LitRPG, talk to other authors including myself, and to just have an awesome time, please join the LitRPG Group

www.facebook.com/groups/LitRPGGroup

FACEBOOK

There's also a few really active Facebook groups I'd recommend you join, as you'll get to hear about great new books, new releases and interact with all your (new) favorite authors! (I may also be there, skulking at the back and enjoying the memes...)

www.facebook.com/groups/LitRPGsociety/

www.facebook.com/groups/LitRPG.books/

www.facebook.com/groups/LitRPGforum/

www.facebook.com/groups/gamelitsociety/

Made in the USA
Monee, IL
22 December 2024